ARMED

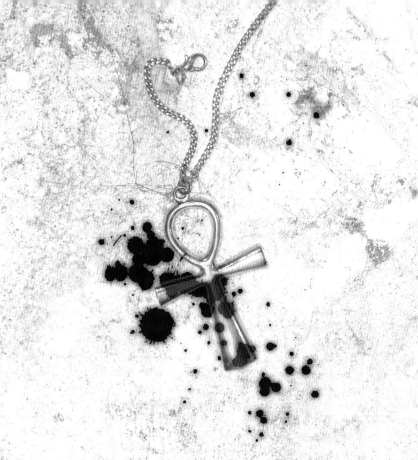

FORCES

STORY & LETTERING
RICHARD STARKINGS

ARTWORK
MORITAT
BOO COOK
LADRÖNN
AXEL MEDELLIN

COLORS
GREGORY WRIGHT
BOO COOK & AXEL MEDELLIN

COVER ARTIST
BOO COOK

DESIGN
J.G. ROSHELL
of COMICRAFT

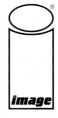

COO
ROBERT KIRKMAN

CFO
ERIK LARSEN

President
TODD McFARLANE

CEO
MARC SILVESTRI

Vice-President
JIM VALENTINO

Publisher
ERIC STEPHENSON

Sales & Licensing Coordinator
TODD MARTINEZ

PR & Marketing Coordinator
SARAH DELAINE

Accounts Manager
BRANWYN BIGGLESTONE

Administrative Assistant
EMILY MILLER

Marketing Assistant
JAMIE PARRENO

Digital Rights Coordinator
KEVIN YUEN

Production Manager
TYLER SHAINLINE

Art Director
DREW GILL

Senior Production Artist
JONATHAN CHAN

Production Artists
MONICA GARCIA
VINCENT KUKUA
JANA COOK

ELEPHANTMEN, VOL. 0: ARMED FORCES. First Printing. Published by
Image Comics, Inc. Office of publication: 2134 Allston Way, Second floor,
Berkeley, California 94704. Copyright © 2011 Active Images. Originally
published in single magazine form as ELEPHANTMEN: WAR TOYS #1-3,
ELEPHANTMEN WAR TOYS: YVETTE and ELEPHANTMEN #34-35. All rights
reserved. HIPFLASK®, MYSTERY CITY™ and ELEPHANTMEN™ (including
all prominent characters featured herein), its logo and all character
likenesses are trademarks of Active Images, unless otherwise noted.
Image Comics® is a trademark of Image Comics, Inc. All rights reserved.
No part of this publication may be reproduced or transmitted, in any
form or by any means (except for short excerpt for review purposes)
without the express written permission of Image Comics, Inc. All names,
characters, events and locales in this publication are entirely fictional.
Any resemblance to actual persons (living or dead), events or places,
without satiric intent, is coincidental. PRINTED IN SOUTH KOREA

HARDCOVER ISBN 978-160706-468-8
SOFTCOVER ISBN 978-160706-514-2

LADY IN RED

AN INTRODUCTION BY DAN ABNETT

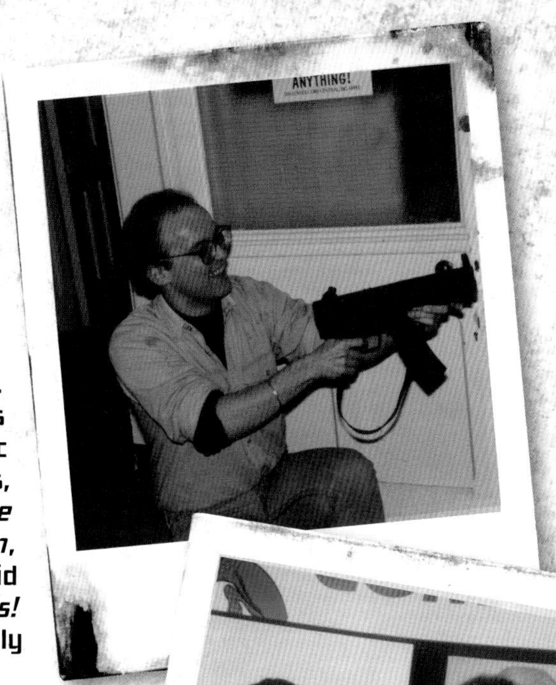
ANYTHING!

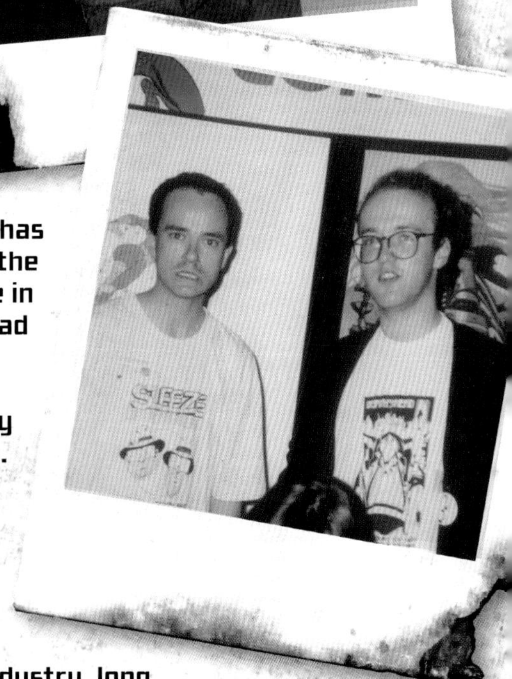

I remember when I first met Richard Starkings.

It was before the war, you understand, before the Elephantmen. When I first met Richard, he was already the best letterer in the comic business, but he had to - get this, folks - he had to actually *write the letters down* on *paper* with a *pen*, then cut the balloons out and - I kid you not - *stick them on the pages!* On the *actual* pages of art! For really reals! Not a computer in sight!

Times have changed. The comics industry has re-invented itself once or twice. In fact, the comics industry has probably changed more in the last twenty-something years than it had in the previous sixty.

When I first met Richard, he was my boss. It was at Marvel, in London. Madonna's *True Blue* was number one in the UK hit parade. Or maybe it was Chris de Burgh's *Lady in Red?* A primary colour was certainly involved. He was the editor, I was his assistant, and we worked on licensed titles like *Ghostbusters* and *Action Force*. Richard has been in the industry long enough to have evolved various *Rules By Which A Comics Professional Should Deport Him- Or Herself,* and I learned them from him. I really want to turn that into a gag, but I can't bring myself to. Twenty-five years on, I still cleave to many of his professional principles. They haven't seen me wrong yet.

Except when I broke number #39, "Never Agree To Provide The Intro To A Book Written By The Guy Who Used To Be Your Boss". [Damn! I turned it into a gag *anyway*!]

In London, a quarter of a century ago, before the war, we shared an office. At the end of the day, when we slipped into freelance mode, he would often pull out pages of his latest lettering job and set-to. Actual pages, actual paper, actual ink, actual french curves. I remember him lettering something called... what was it now? *Batman: The Killing Joke?*

Richard was, and still is, a brilliant letterer, and I contend that ELEPHANTMEN is a brilliant series precisely because of that. No, not because it's beautifully lettered (which, of course, it is), but because to be a truly exceptional letterer takes more than just an ability to craft a pretty "A" (or any of the other twenty-five). Bad lettering is static on a comic book's soundtrack. Great lettering is an unsung, unappreciated art, because if it's great, it's doing its job perfectly, and part of that job is to go unnoticed.

It's about more than a clean hand, an attractive personal font, and pleasing balloon shapes. It's about placement, design, arrangement, flow. It's about the sympathetic incorporation of sound effects and titles. It's about the apparently effortless sustain of reading order, the economical use of dead space, the natural track of the eye. Sometimes, the weight and scale of the lettering alone can achieve genuine emotional impact.

So, to be a truly great letterer, you've got to be a great editor and a great storyteller. You've got to understand stories, and the characters within those stories, so that the dynamic of your 'soundtrack' synchronises script and art, and serves them in the best possible way. Even then, when the strains of Chris de Burgh hung over the land like... an unventilated toilet metaphor, Richard was indecently equipped with the editing and storytelling chops he needed to make the difference between being a good letterer and being one of the very best.

ELEPHANTMEN is good because Richard understands storytelling from the sharp end of balloon placement *backwards*. He works with a superb team of collaborators, as even the briefest glimpse of the covers or the interior art will demonstrate. He's created a world of instantly memorable, larger-than-life characters that achieve the apparently impossible: they're over the top daft enough to be perfect cartoon beings, yet they are handled in a way that permits surprising levels of poignancy and identification. They are perfectly disposable yet utterly irreplaceable. Most good pop art would kill to be able to pull off those two things at the same time.

If this is your first volume of ELEPHANTMEN, relish it, then go read the others too. The series has achieved a pachydermic longevity that is also admirable. Like I said, the industry has changed drastically since I first met Richard. It's all gone digital for a start (and Richard was one of the first to be smart enough to transition lettering services into that arena with Comicraft). It's also shrunk as other digital entertainments have eaten into the marketplace. Gone are the days when comics regularly sold a quarter of a million copies per issue. In a world where even the major powers have to press the reset button to boost their appeal, it is a singular achievement for a book like this to demonstrate such formidable stamina.

And it's particularly gratifying to see a book survive and prosper because it's good. Success is more often down to whim or zeitgeist than quality. ELEPHANTMEN has powerful stories, stupendous art, memorable characters, gorgeous colour, great design, high production values, superb consistency. The lettering's bloody lovely too.

I guess, like me, the whole team must be following Richard's Rules (and #27, "Always Keep a Loaded Compact Nine In Your Pen Drawer", sure came in handy that time when-damn, I did it *again*).

I remember when I first met Richard Starkings. I don't get to see him so often these days, but, like all good elephants, I do not forget. And all the while he produces comics as good as this, his audience isn't going to have any trouble remembering him either.

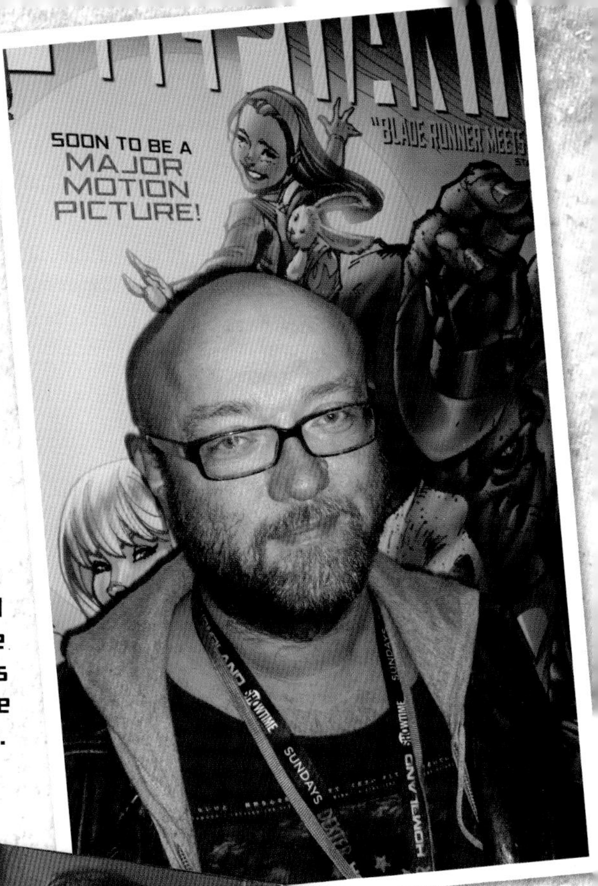
SOON TO BE A
MAJOR
MOTION
PICTURE!

Dan Abnett

Dan Abnett
New York, October 2011

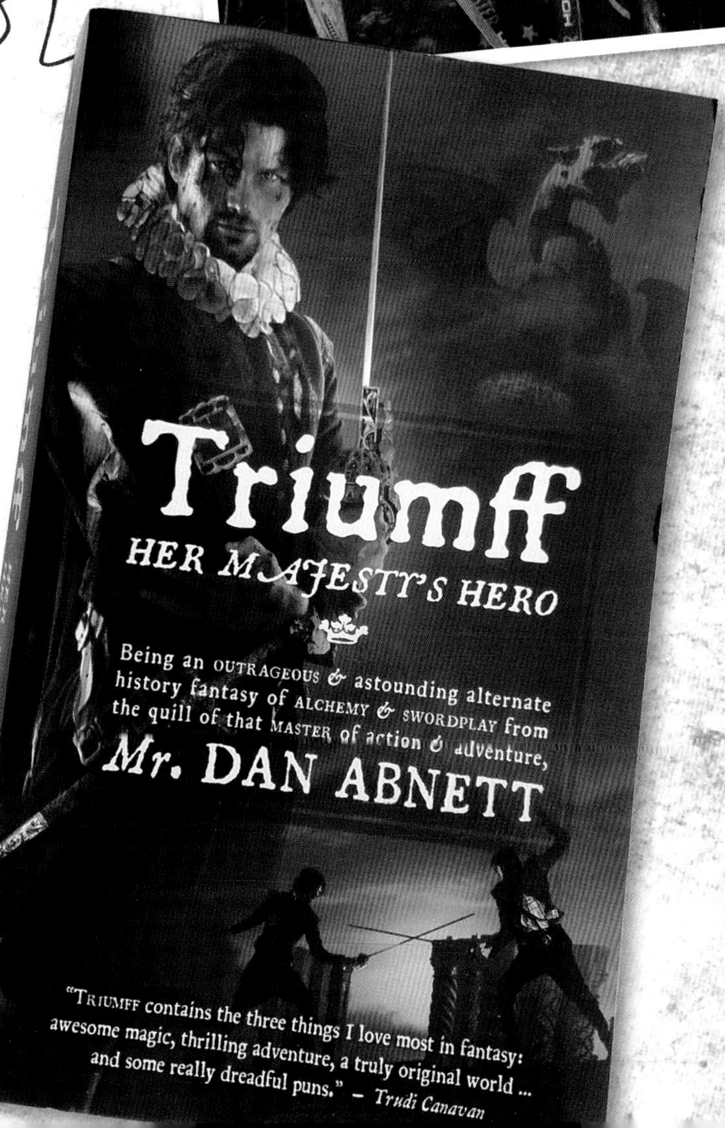
Triumff
HER MAJESTY'S HERO
Being an OUTRAGEOUS & astounding alternate history fantasy of ALCHEMY & SWORDPLAY from the quill of that MASTER of action & adventure,
Mr. DAN ABNETT
"TRIUMFF contains the three things I love most in fantasy: awesome magic, thrilling adventure, a truly original world ... and some really dreadful puns." – Trudi Canavan

DAN ABNETT IS A MULTIPLE NEW YORK TIMES BESTSELLING AUTHOR AND AN AWARD-WINNING COMIC BOOK WRITER. HE HAS WRITTEN FORTY NOVELS, INCLUDING THE ACCLAIMED GAUNT'S GHOSTS SERIES, AND THE EISENHORN AND RAVENOR TRILOGIES. HIS RECENT NOVEL FOR THE BLACK LIBRARY, PROSPERO BURNS, TOPPED THE SF CHARTS IN THE UK AND THE US. HIS NOVEL TRIUMFF, FOR ANGRY ROBOT, WAS NOMINATED FOR THE BRITISH FANTASY SOCIETY AWARD FOR BEST NOVEL, AND HIS COMBAT SF NOVEL FOR THE SAME PUBLISHER, EMBEDDED, WAS PUBLISHED IN 2011. HE HAS WRITTEN THE SILENT STARS GO BY, THE 2011 CHRISTMAS DOCTOR WHO NOVEL, FOR THE BBC. WITH ANDY LANNING, HE WRITES DC'S NEW 52 SERIES RESURRECTION MAN AND MARVEL'S NEW MUTANTS.

DAN'S BLOG AND WEBSITE ARE AT WWW.DANABNETT.COM FOLLOW HIM ON TWITTER @VINCENTABNETT

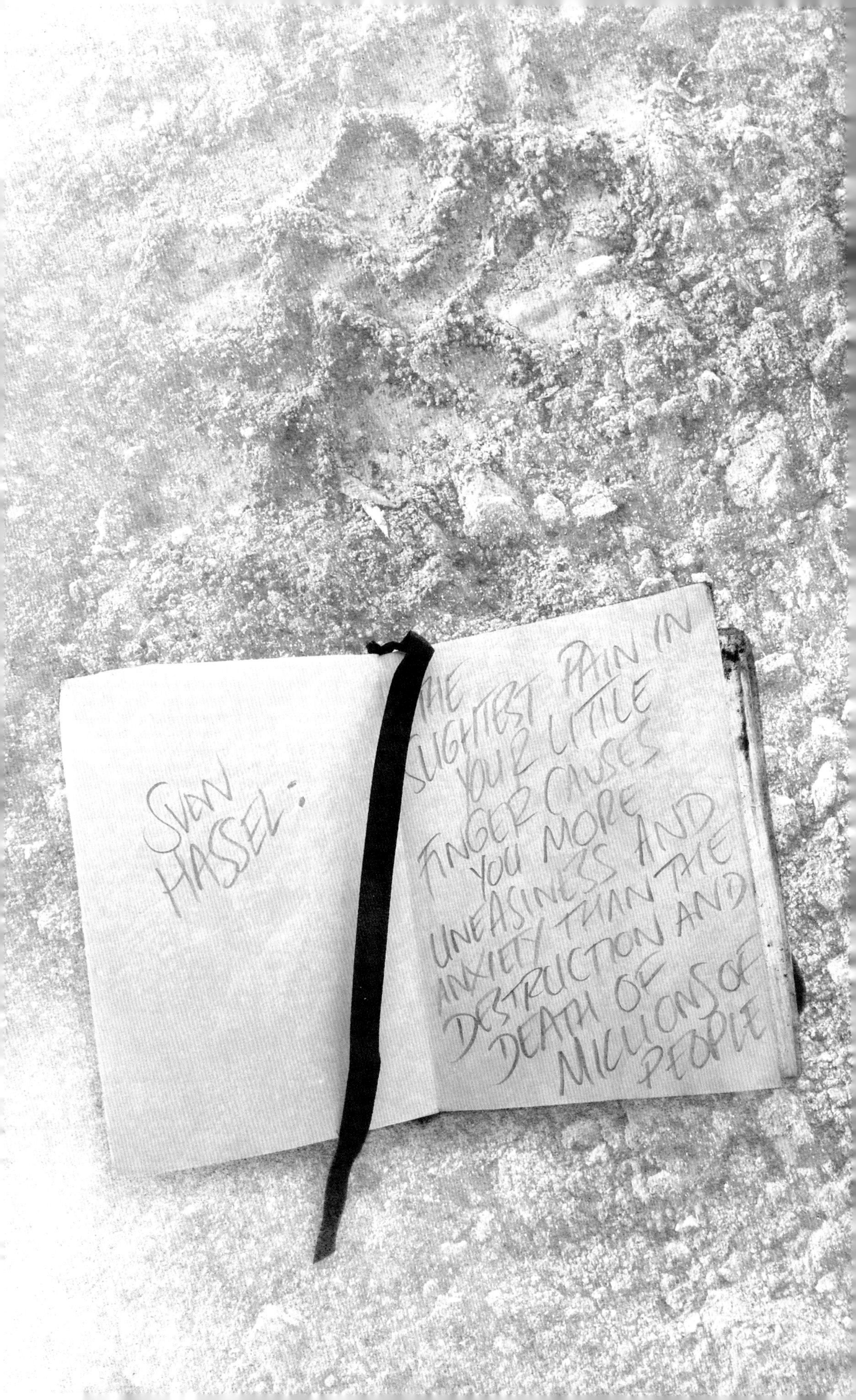
SVEN HASSEL:
THE SLIGHTEST PAIN IN YOUR LITTLE FINGER CAUSES YOU MORE UNEASINESS AND ANXIETY THAN THE DESTRUCTION AND DEATH OF MILLIONS OF PEOPLE

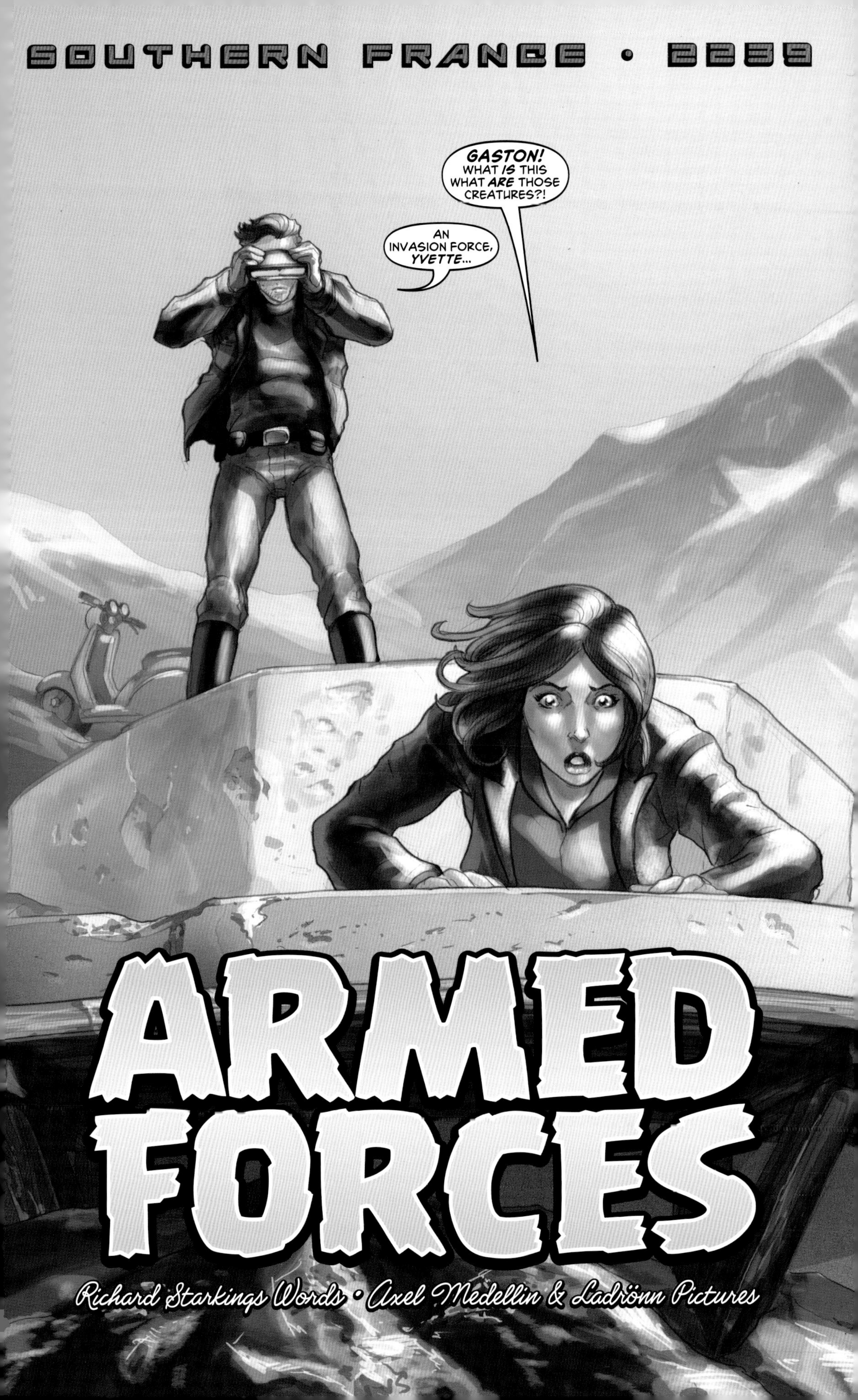
SOUTHERN FRANCE • 2239
GASTON! WHAT IS THIS WHAT ARE THOSE CREATURES?!
AN INVASION FORCE, YVETTE...
ARMED FORCES
Richard Starkings Words • Axel Medellin & Ladrönn Pictures

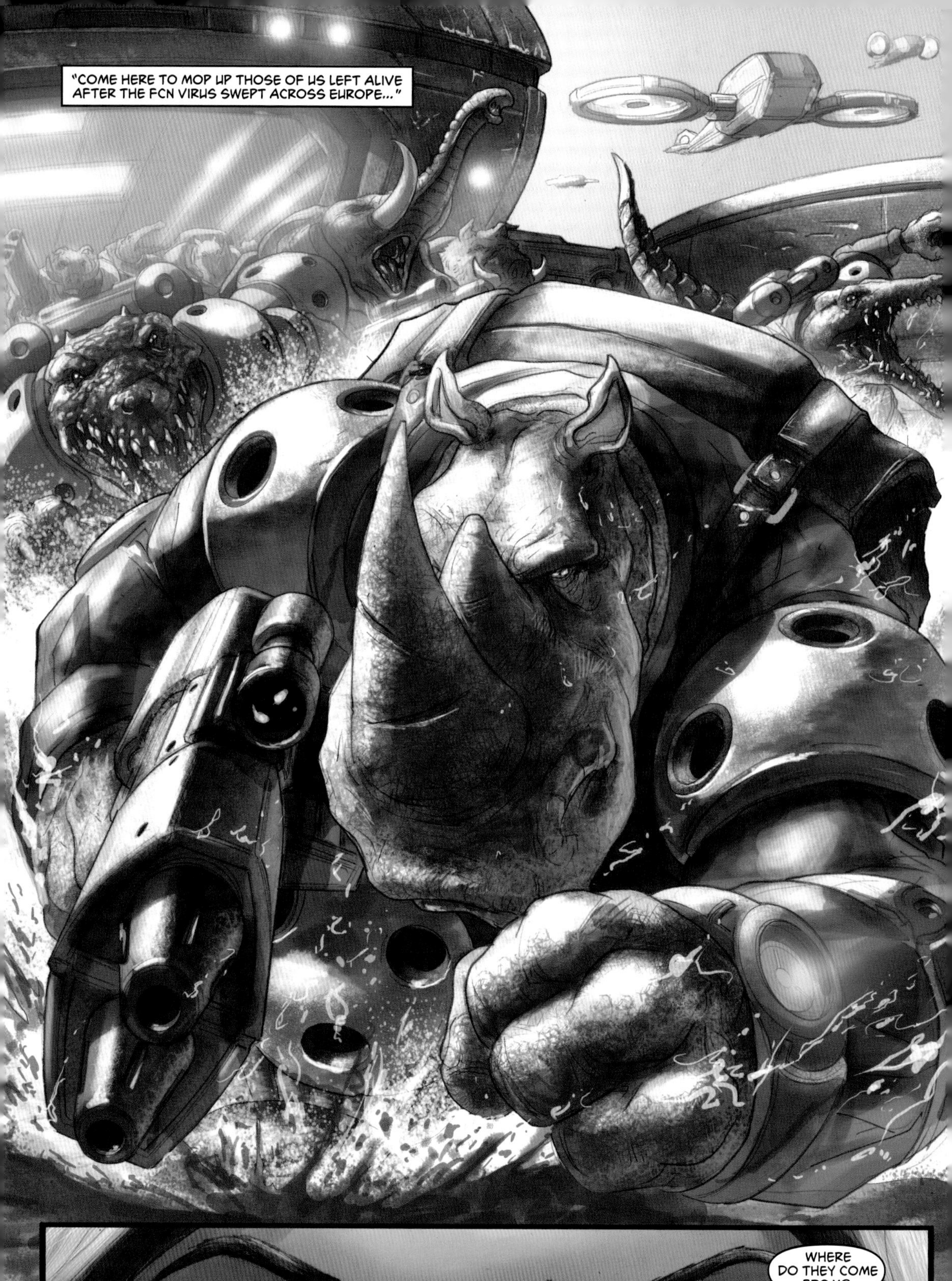
"COME HERE TO MOP UP THOSE OF US LEFT ALIVE AFTER THE FCN VIRUS SWEPT ACROSS EUROPE..."

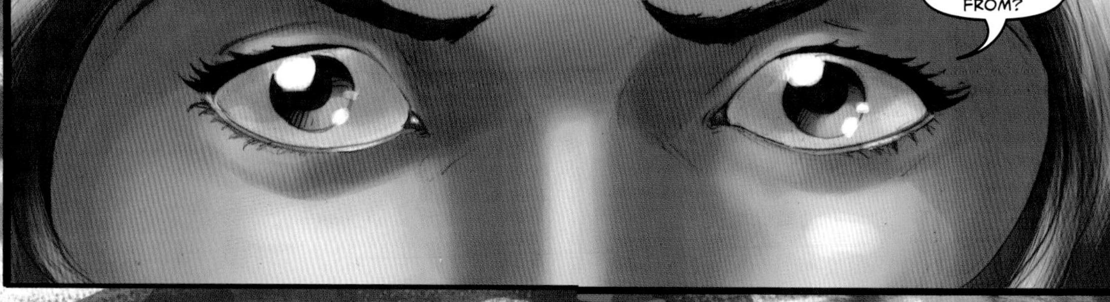
WHERE DO THEY COME FROM?

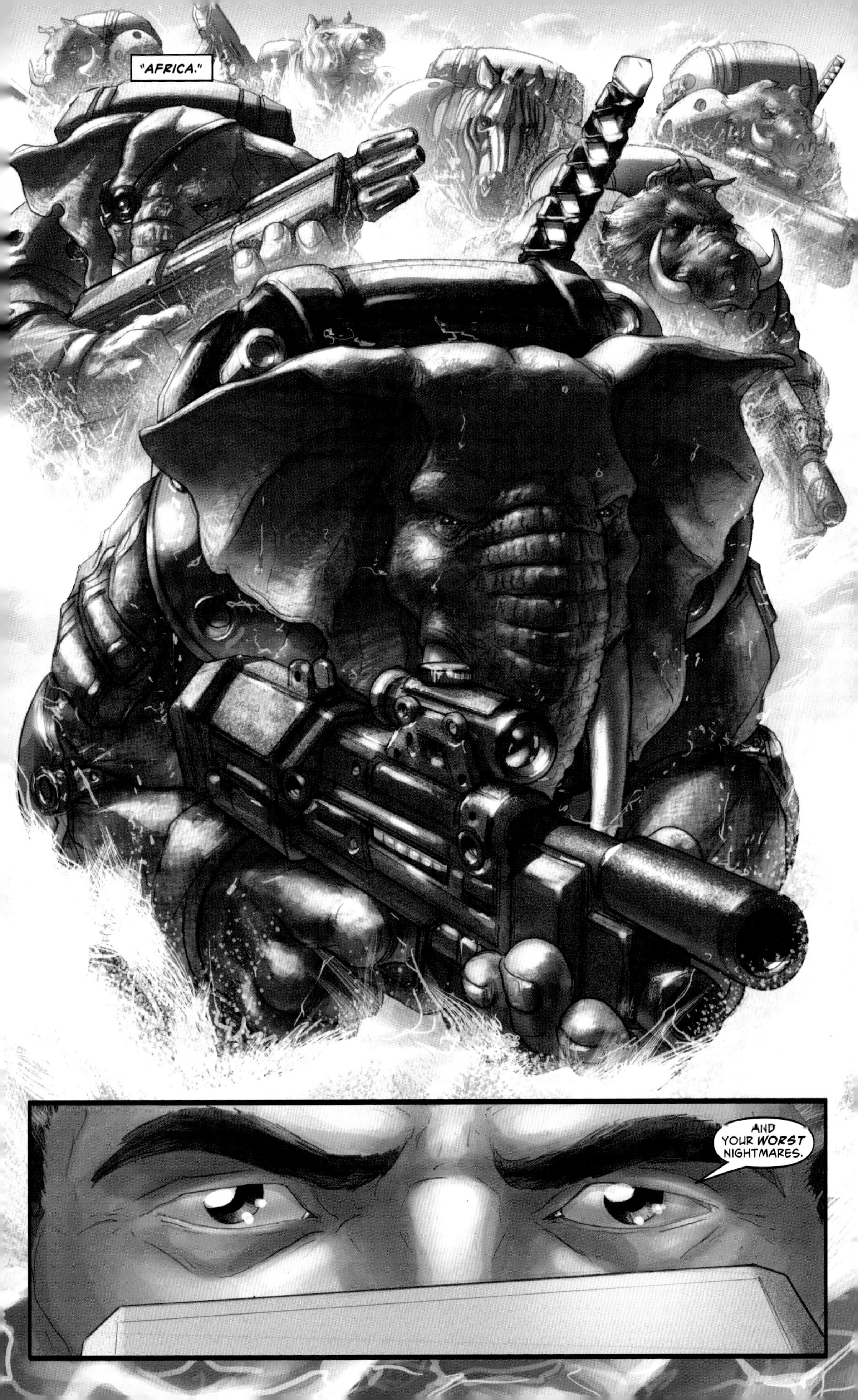
"AFRICA."
AND YOUR WORST NIGHTMARES.

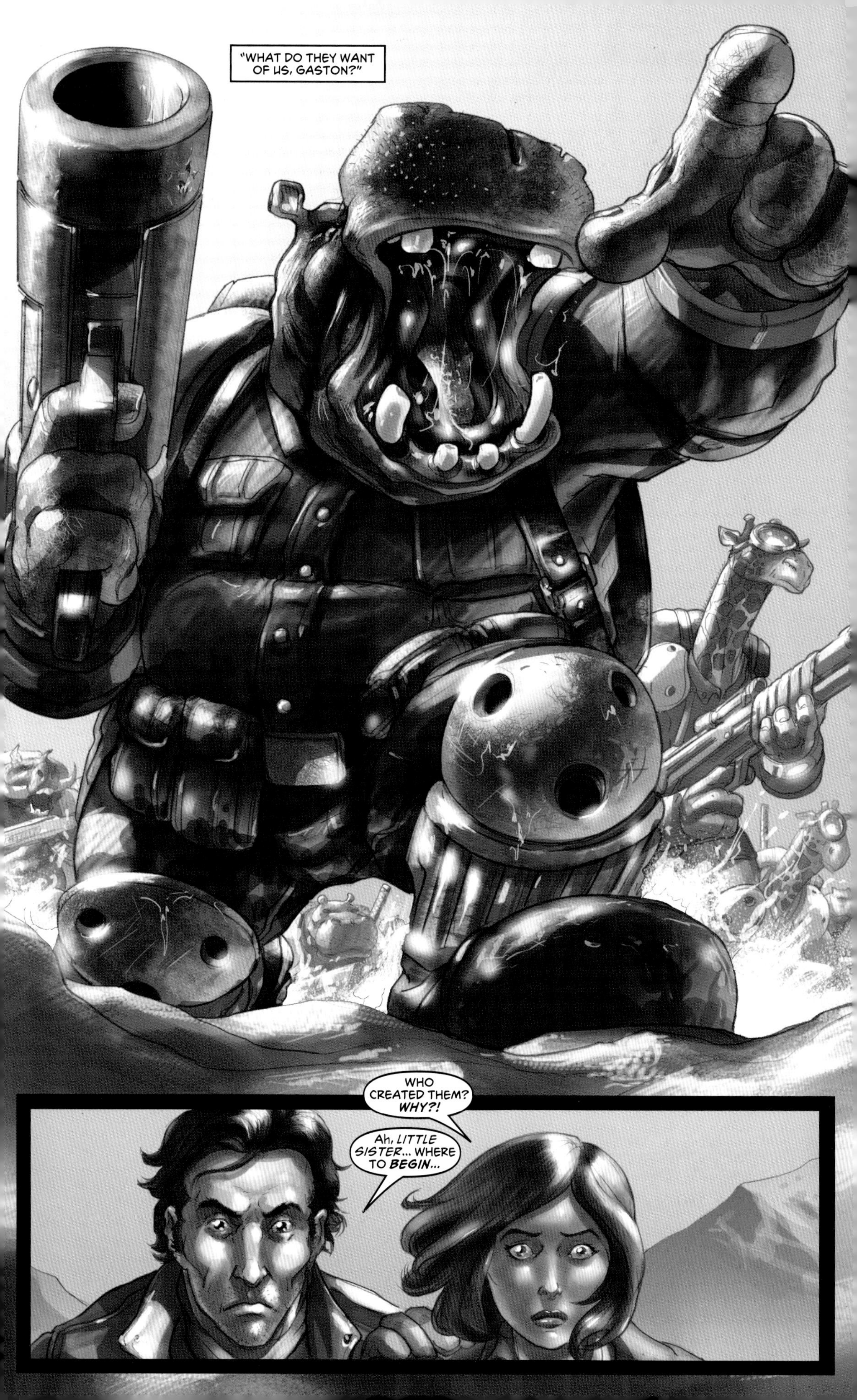
"WHAT DO THEY WANT OF US, GASTON?"
WHO CREATED THEM? WHY?!
Ah, LITTLE SISTER... WHERE TO BEGIN...

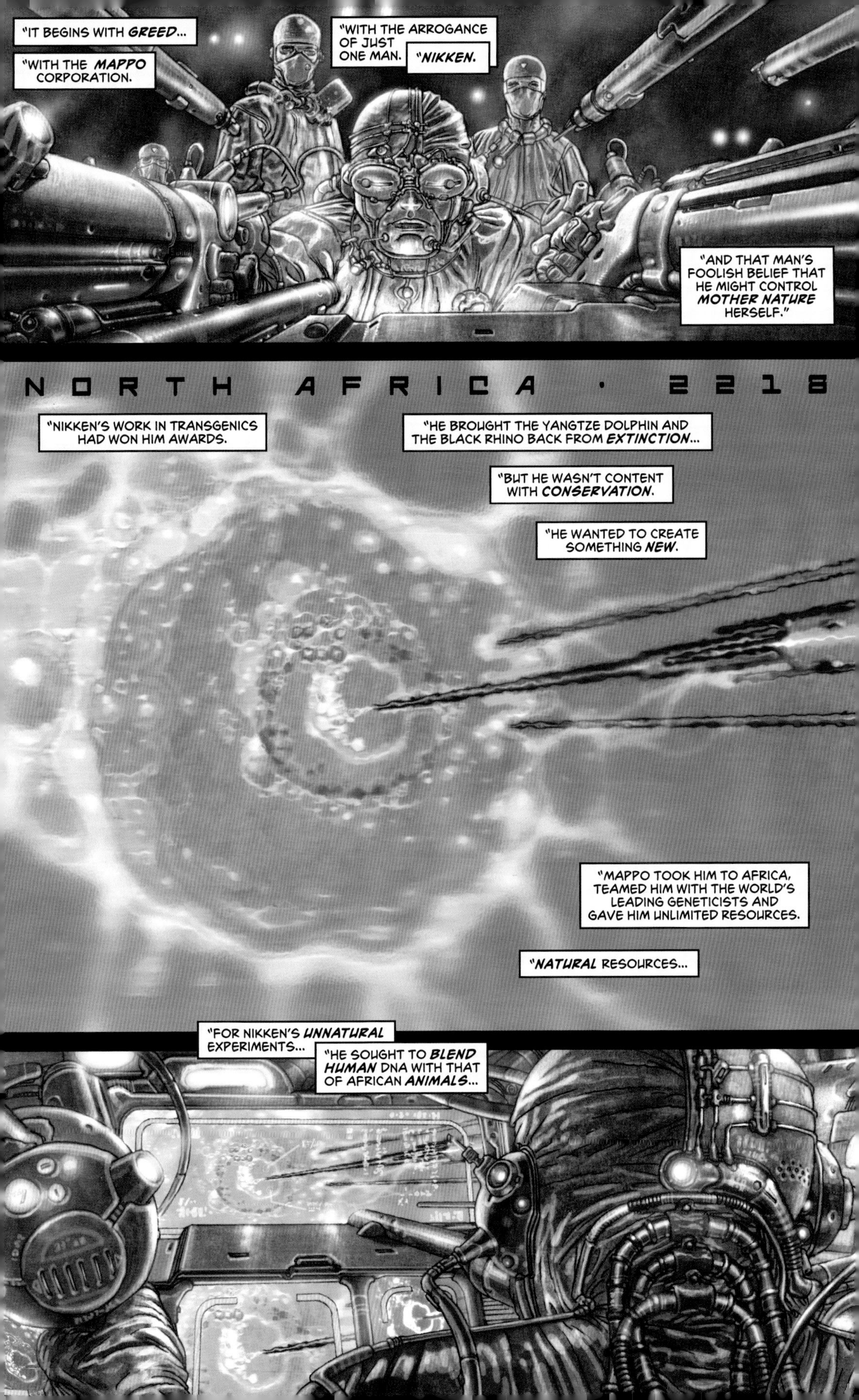
"IT BEGINS WITH GREED...
"WITH THE MAPPO CORPORATION.
"WITH THE ARROGANCE OF JUST ONE MAN.
"NIKKEN.
"AND THAT MAN'S FOOLISH BELIEF THAT HE MIGHT CONTROL MOTHER NATURE HERSELF."
NORTH AFRICA · 2218
"NIKKEN'S WORK IN TRANSGENICS HAD WON HIM AWARDS.
"HE BROUGHT THE YANGTZE DOLPHIN AND THE BLACK RHINO BACK FROM EXTINCTION...
"BUT HE WASN'T CONTENT WITH CONSERVATION.
"HE WANTED TO CREATE SOMETHING NEW.
"MAPPO TOOK HIM TO AFRICA, TEAMED HIM WITH THE WORLD'S LEADING GENETICISTS AND GAVE HIM UNLIMITED RESOURCES.
"NATURAL RESOURCES...
"FOR NIKKEN'S UNNATURAL EXPERIMENTS...
"HE SOUGHT TO BLEND HUMAN DNA WITH THAT OF AFRICAN ANIMALS...

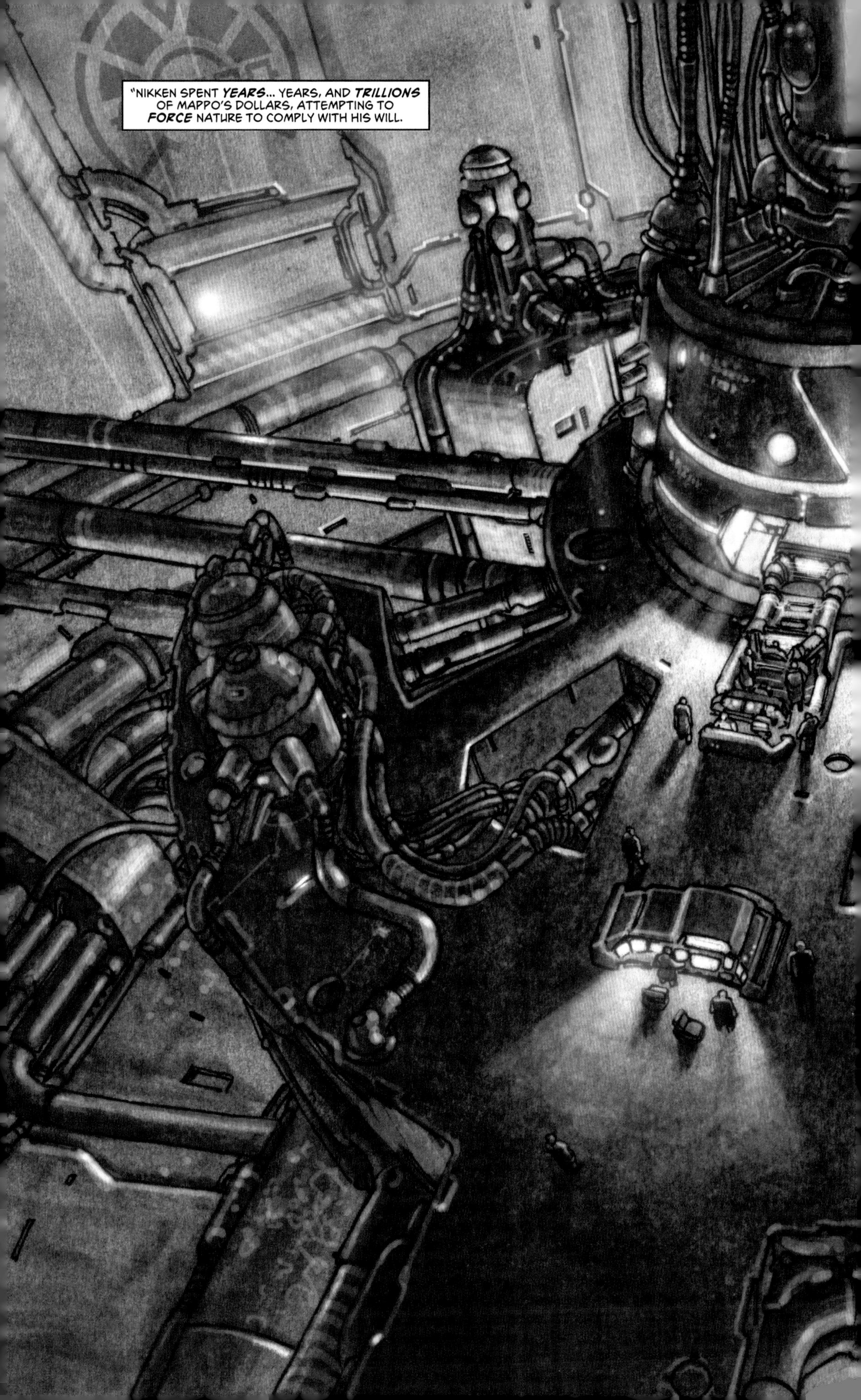
"NIKKEN SPENT *YEARS*... YEARS, AND *TRILLIONS* OF MAPPO'S DOLLARS, ATTEMPTING TO *FORCE* NATURE TO COMPLY WITH HIS WILL.

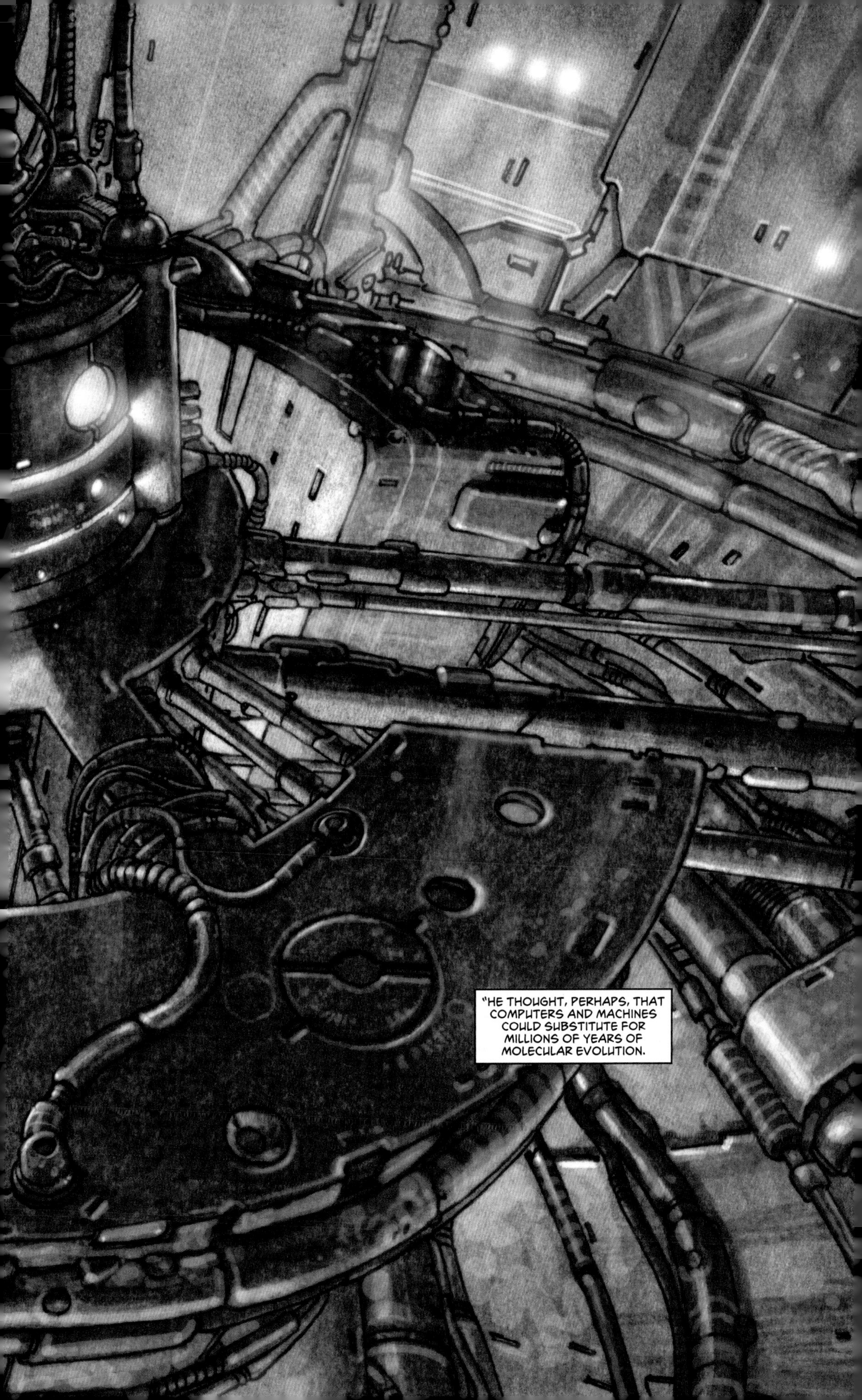
"HE THOUGHT, PERHAPS, THAT COMPUTERS AND MACHINES COULD SUBSTITUTE FOR MILLIONS OF YEARS OF MOLECULAR EVOLUTION.

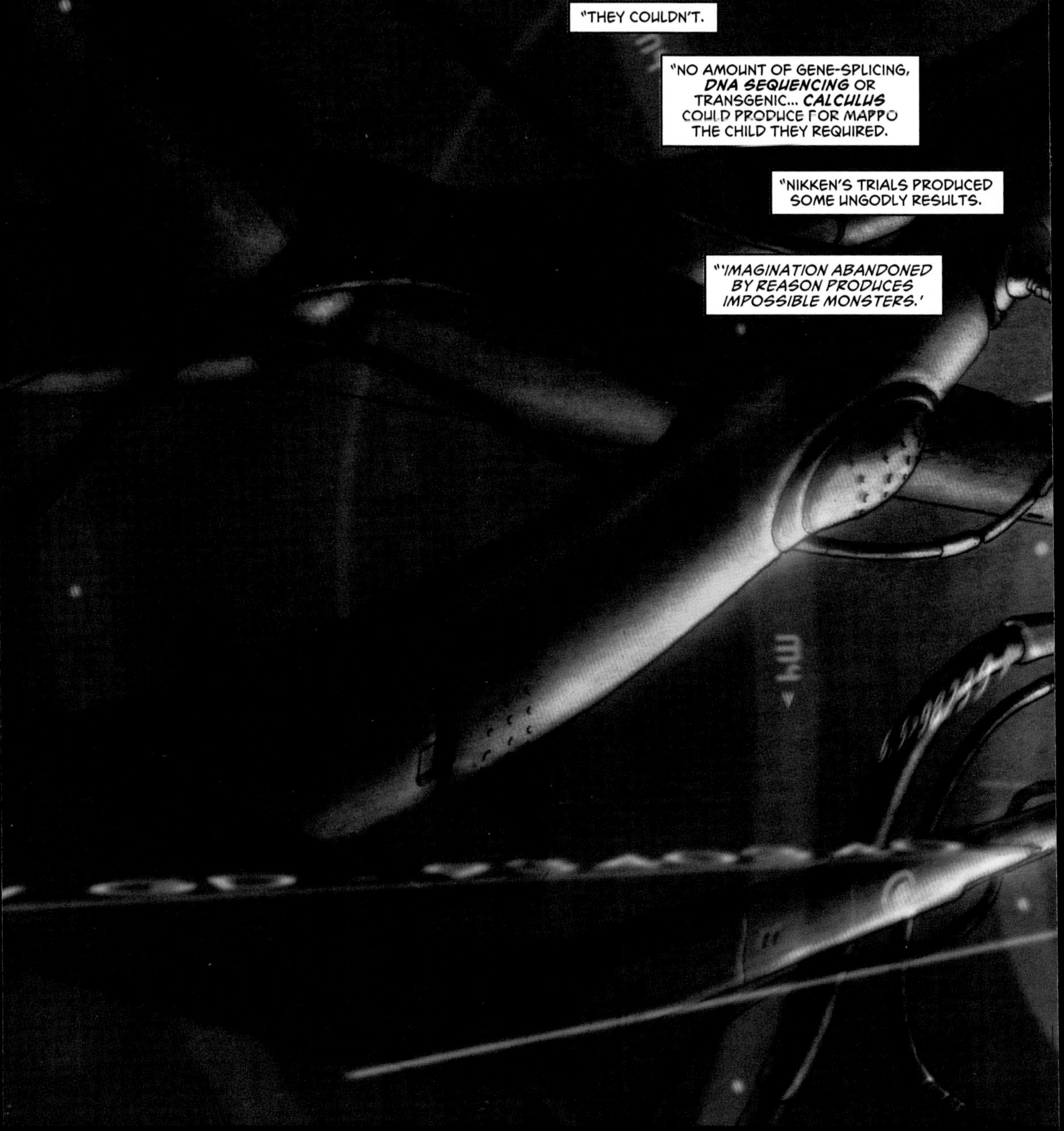
"THEY COULDN'T.
"NO AMOUNT OF GENE-SPLICING, DNA SEQUENCING OR TRANSGENIC... CALCULUS COULD PRODUCE FOR MAPPO THE CHILD THEY REQUIRED.
"NIKKEN'S TRIALS PRODUCED SOME UNGODLY RESULTS.
"'IMAGINATION ABANDONED BY REASON PRODUCES IMPOSSIBLE MONSTERS.'

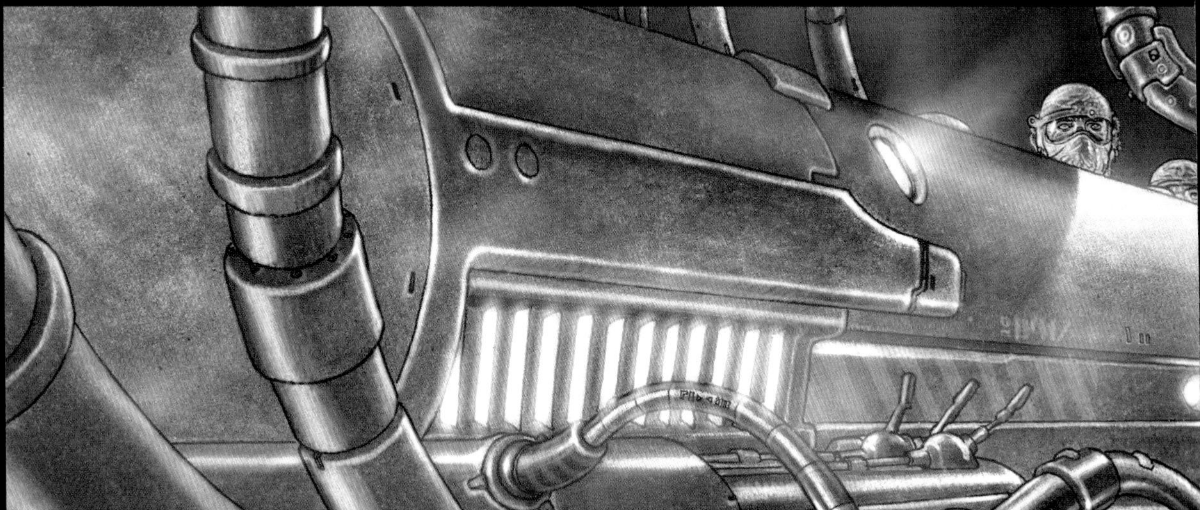

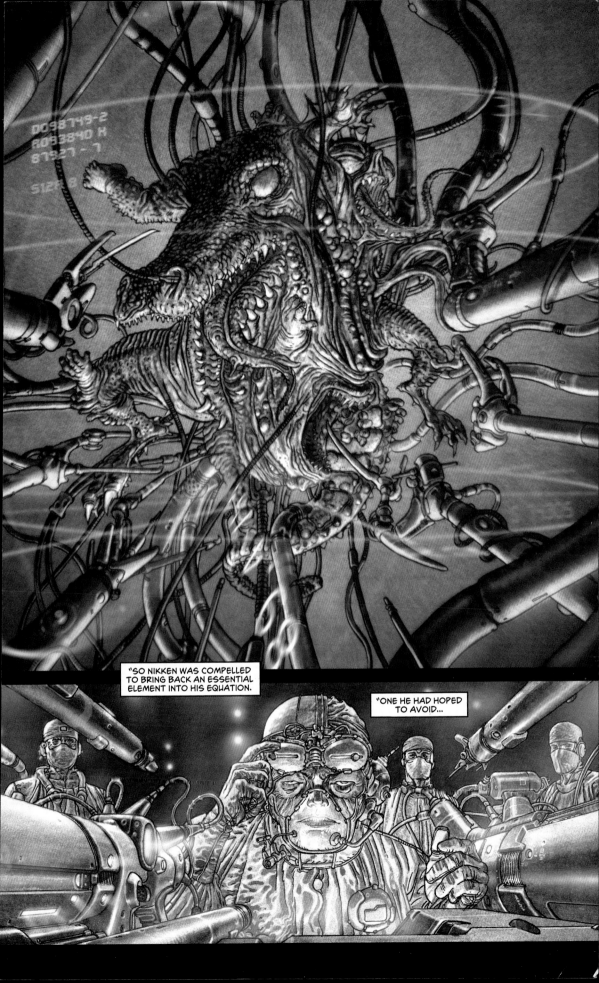

"SO NIKKEN WAS COMPELLED TO BRING BACK AN ESSENTIAL ELEMENT INTO HIS EQUATION.

"ONE HE HAD HOPED TO AVOID..."

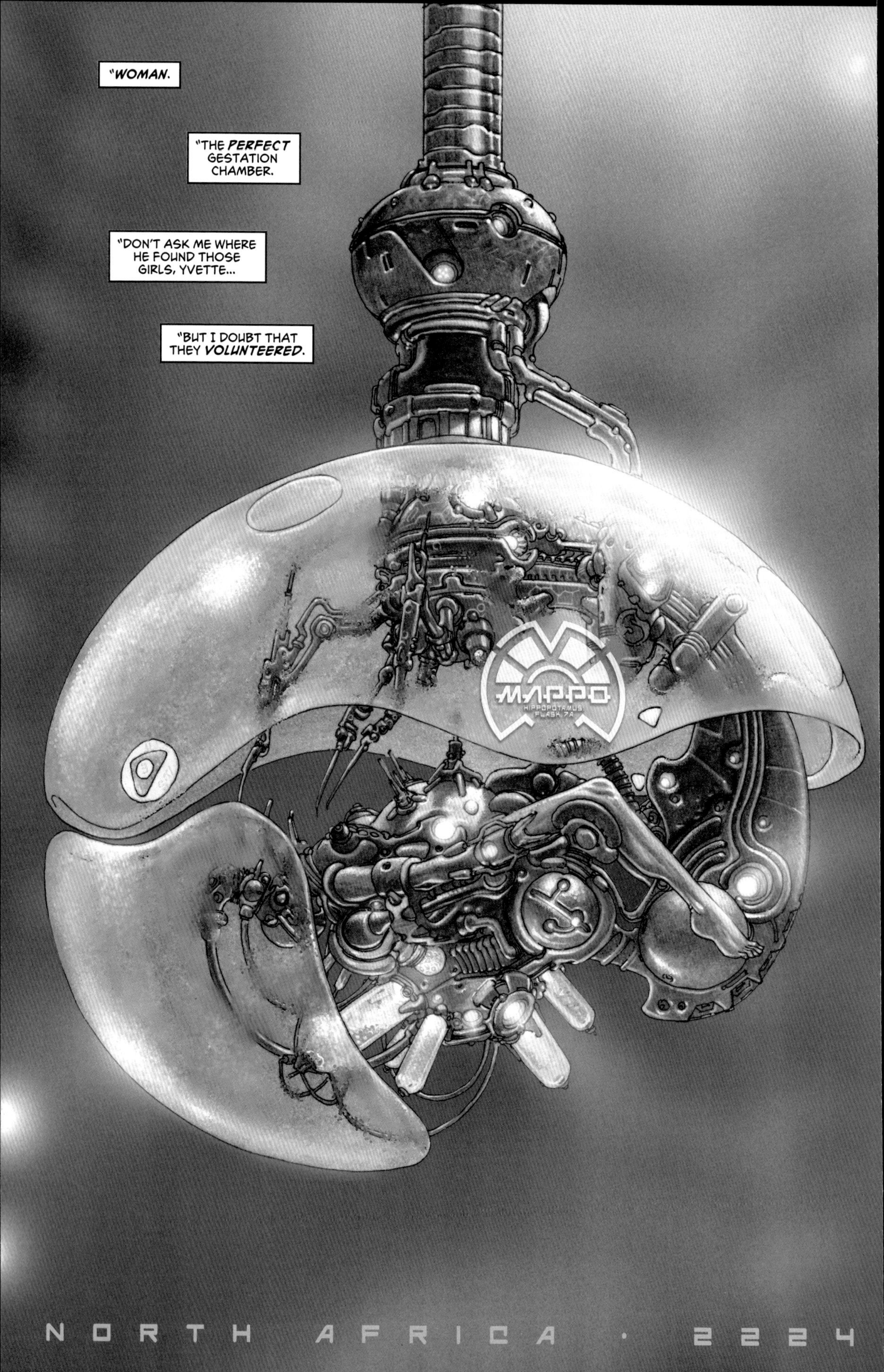
"WOMAN.
"THE PERFECT GESTATION CHAMBER.
"DON'T ASK ME WHERE HE FOUND THOSE GIRLS, YVETTE...
"BUT I DOUBT THAT THEY VOLUNTEERED.
MAPPO
HIPPOPOTAMUS FLASK 7A
NORTH AFRICA · 2224

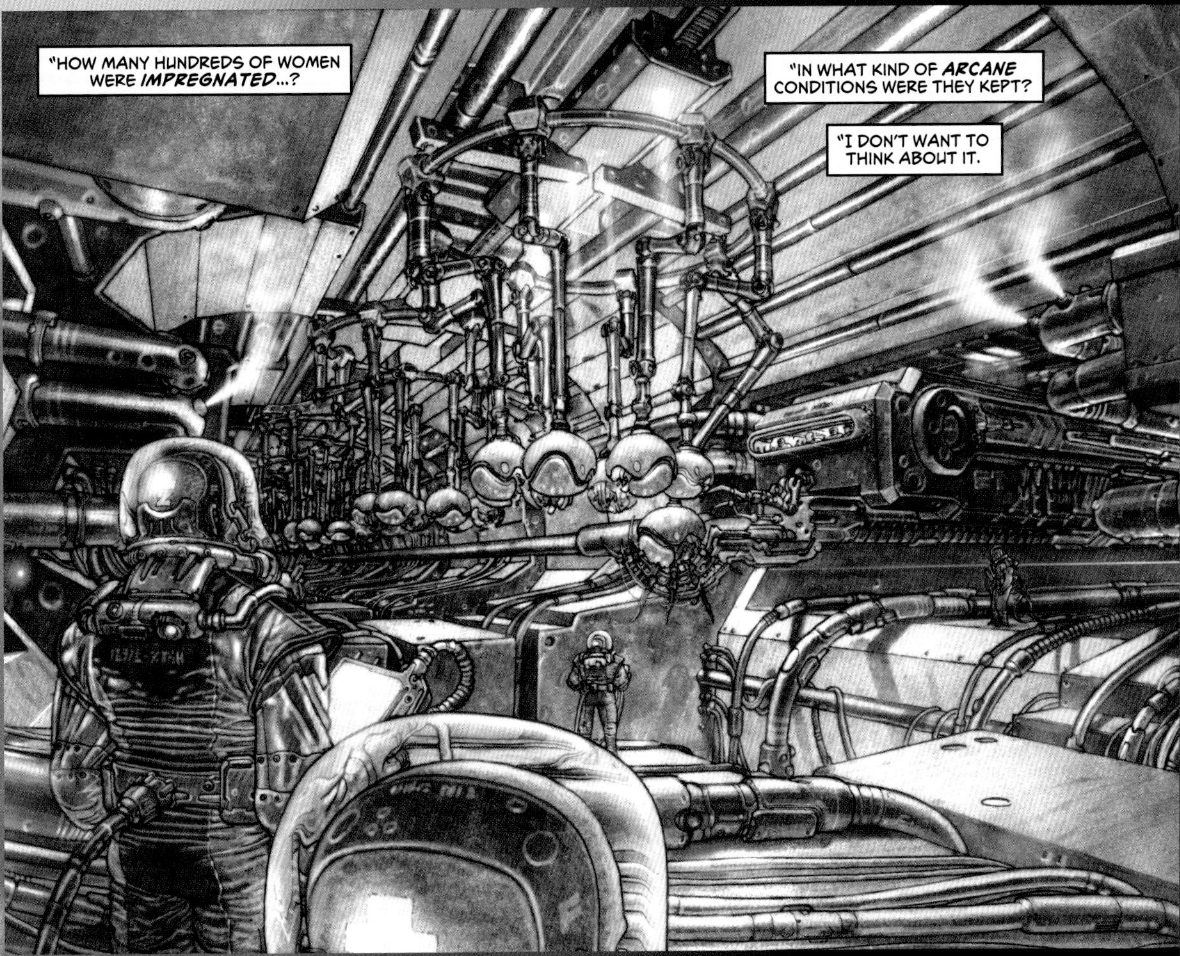
"HOW MANY HUNDREDS OF WOMEN WERE *IMPREGNATED*...?
"IN WHAT KIND OF *ARCANE* CONDITIONS WERE THEY KEPT?
"I DON'T WANT TO THINK ABOUT IT.

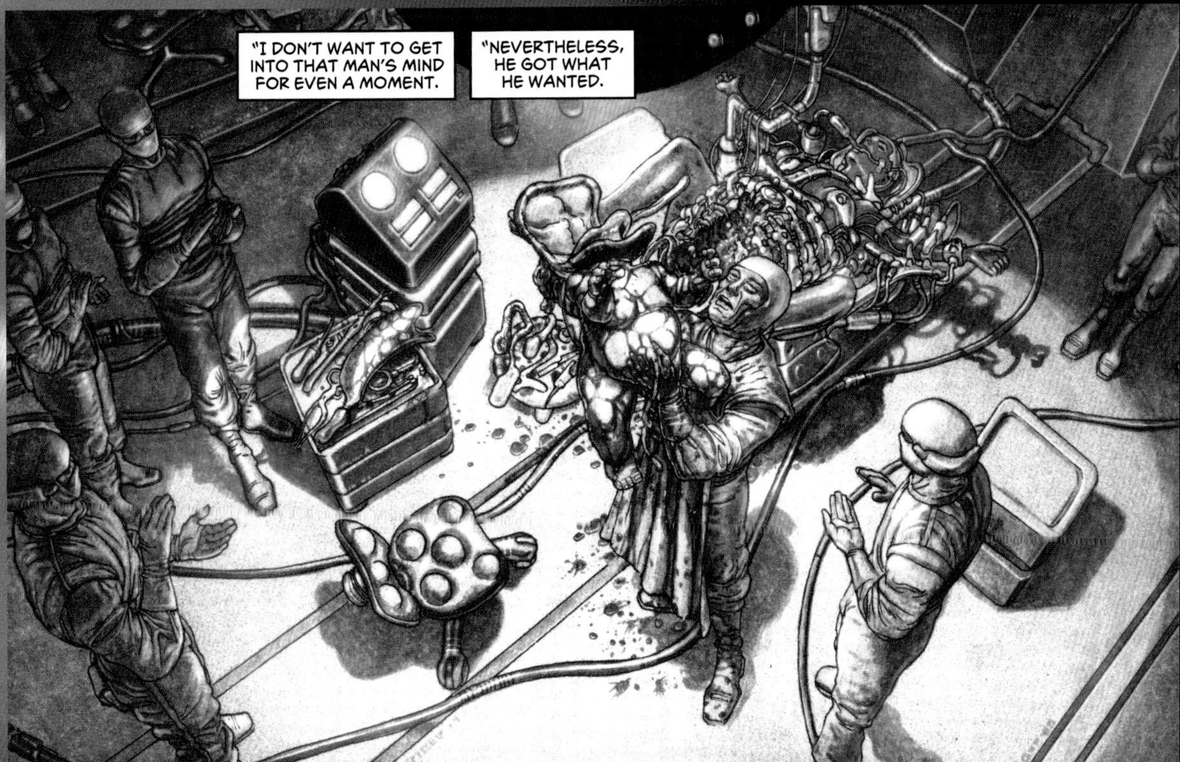
"I DON'T WANT TO GET INTO THAT MAN'S MIND FOR EVEN A MOMENT.
"NEVERTHELESS, HE GOT WHAT HE WANTED.

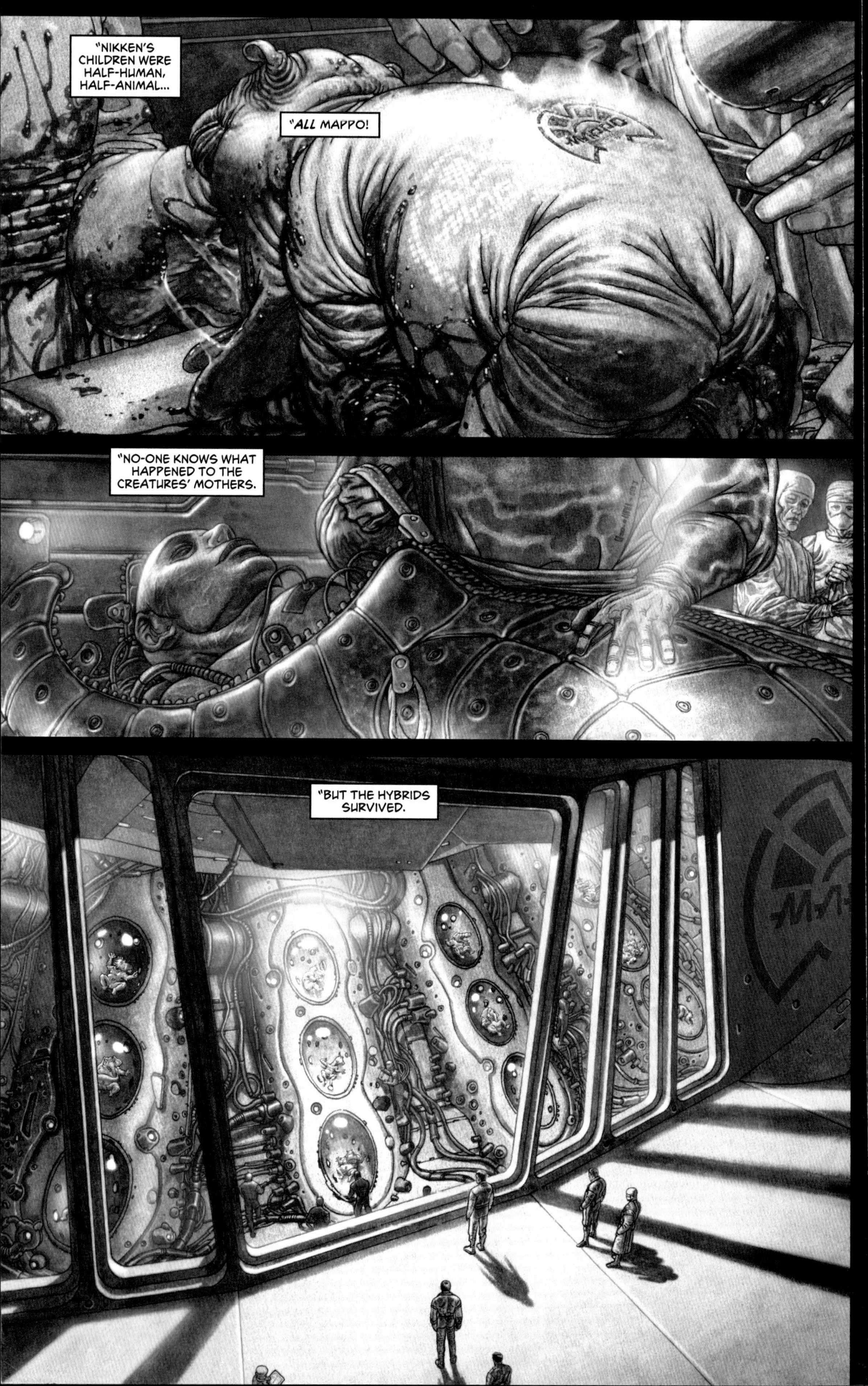
"NIKKEN'S CHILDREN WERE HALF-HUMAN, HALF-ANIMAL...
"ALL MAPPO!
"NO-ONE KNOWS WHAT HAPPENED TO THE CREATURES' MOTHERS.
"BUT THE HYBRIDS SURVIVED.

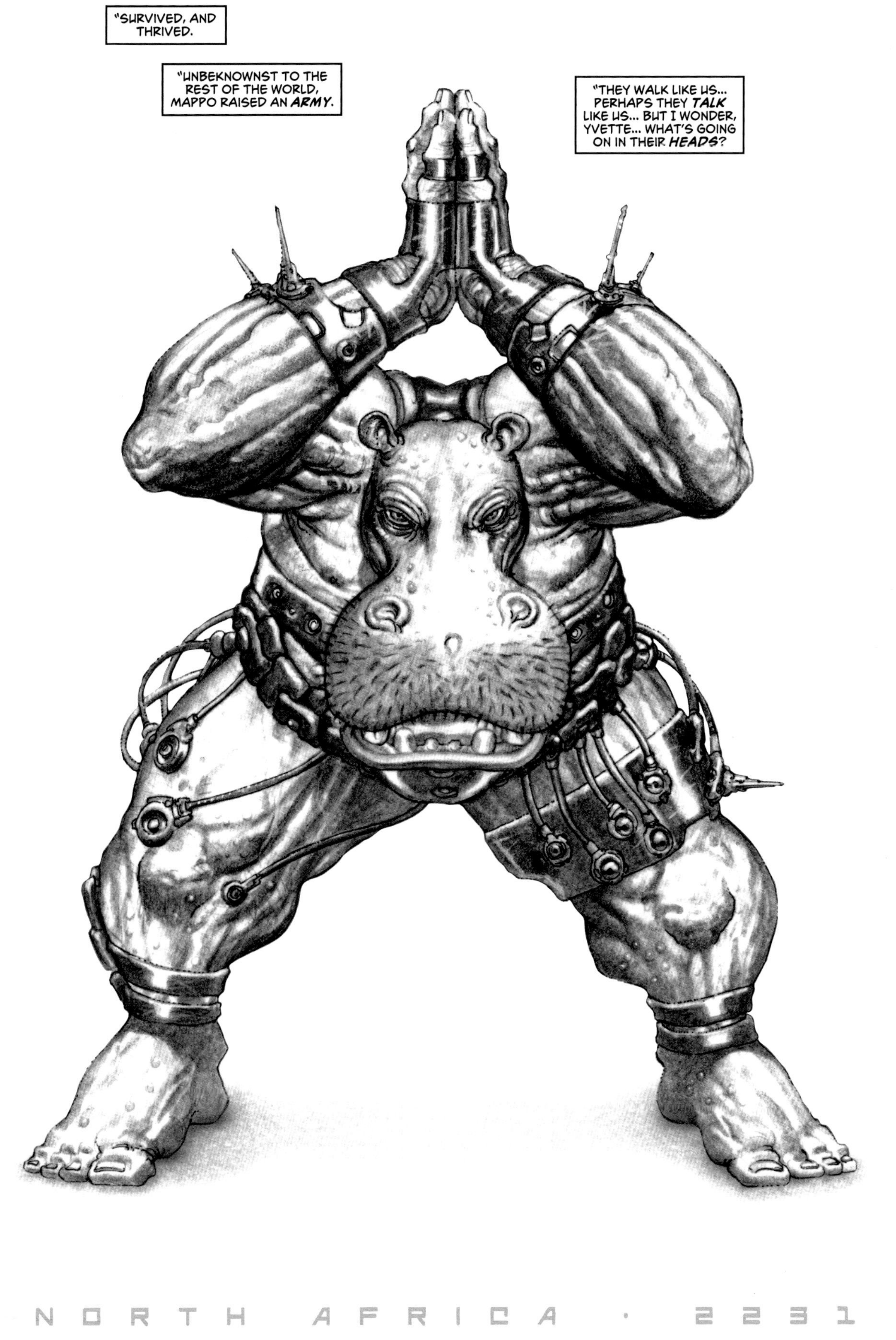
"SURVIVED, AND THRIVED.
"UNBEKNOWNST TO THE REST OF THE WORLD, MAPPO RAISED AN ARMY.
"THEY WALK LIKE US... PERHAPS THEY TALK LIKE US... BUT I WONDER, YVETTE... WHAT'S GOING ON IN THEIR HEADS?
NORTH AFRICA · 2231

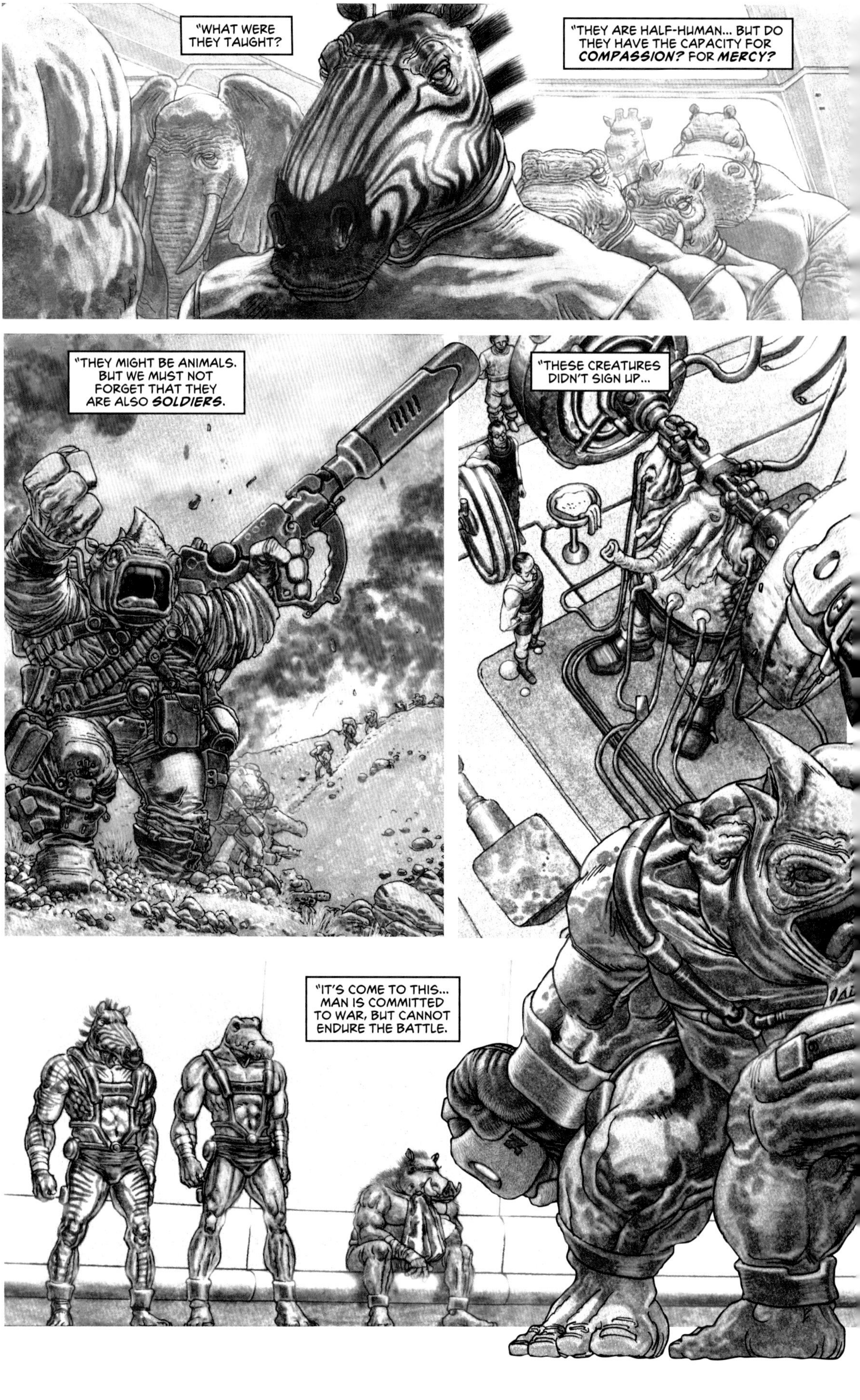
"WHAT WERE THEY TAUGHT?
"THEY ARE HALF-HUMAN... BUT DO THEY HAVE THE CAPACITY FOR COMPASSION? FOR MERCY?
"THEY MIGHT BE ANIMALS. BUT WE MUST NOT FORGET THAT THEY ARE ALSO SOLDIERS.
"THESE CREATURES DIDN'T SIGN UP...
"IT'S COME TO THIS... MAN IS COMMITTED TO WAR, BUT CANNOT ENDURE THE BATTLE.

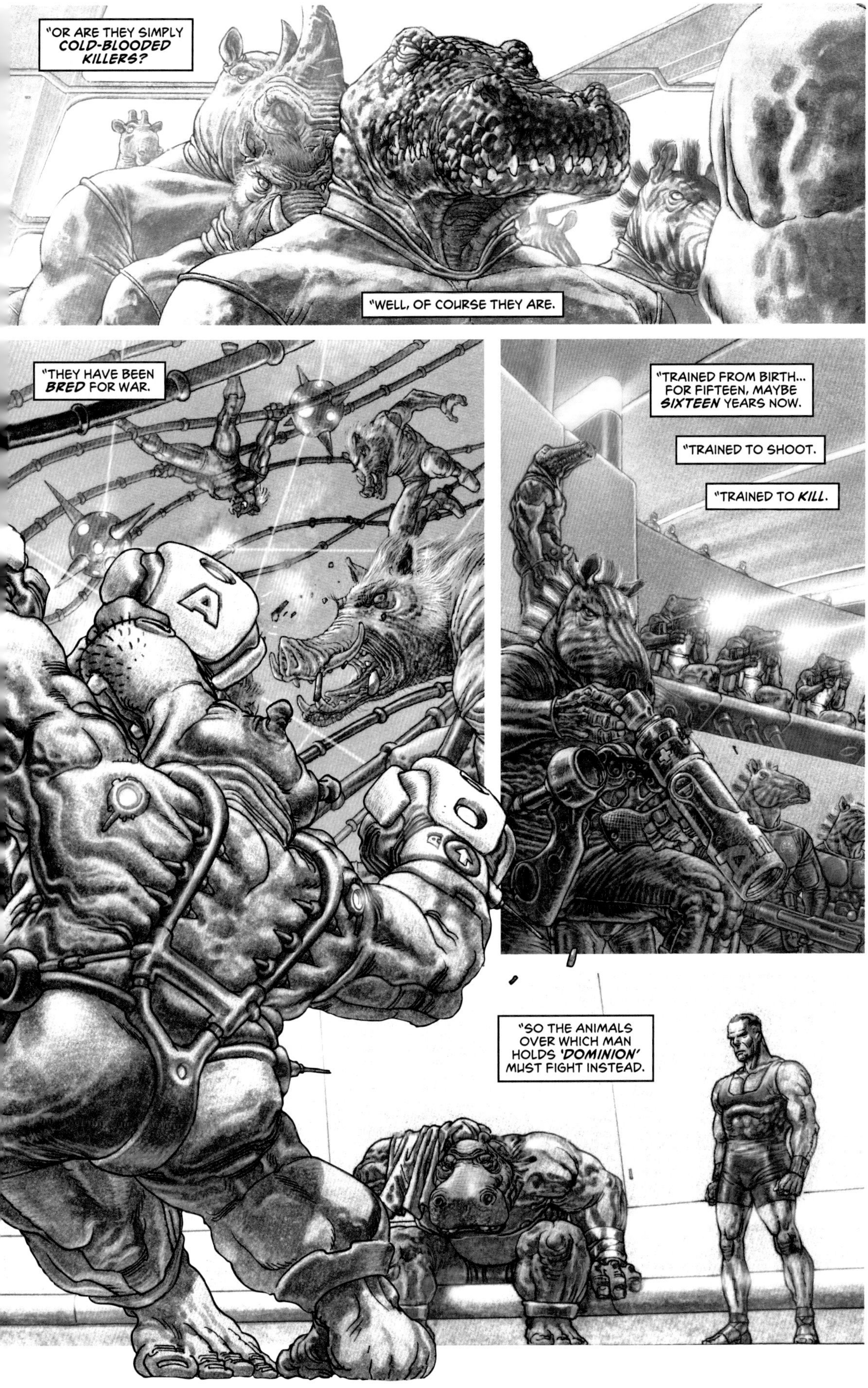
"OR ARE THEY SIMPLY COLD-BLOODED KILLERS?
"WELL, OF COURSE THEY ARE.
"THEY HAVE BEEN BRED FOR WAR.
"TRAINED FROM BIRTH... FOR FIFTEEN, MAYBE SIXTEEN YEARS NOW.
"TRAINED TO SHOOT.
"TRAINED TO KILL.
"SO THE ANIMALS OVER WHICH MAN HOLDS 'DOMINION' MUST FIGHT INSTEAD.

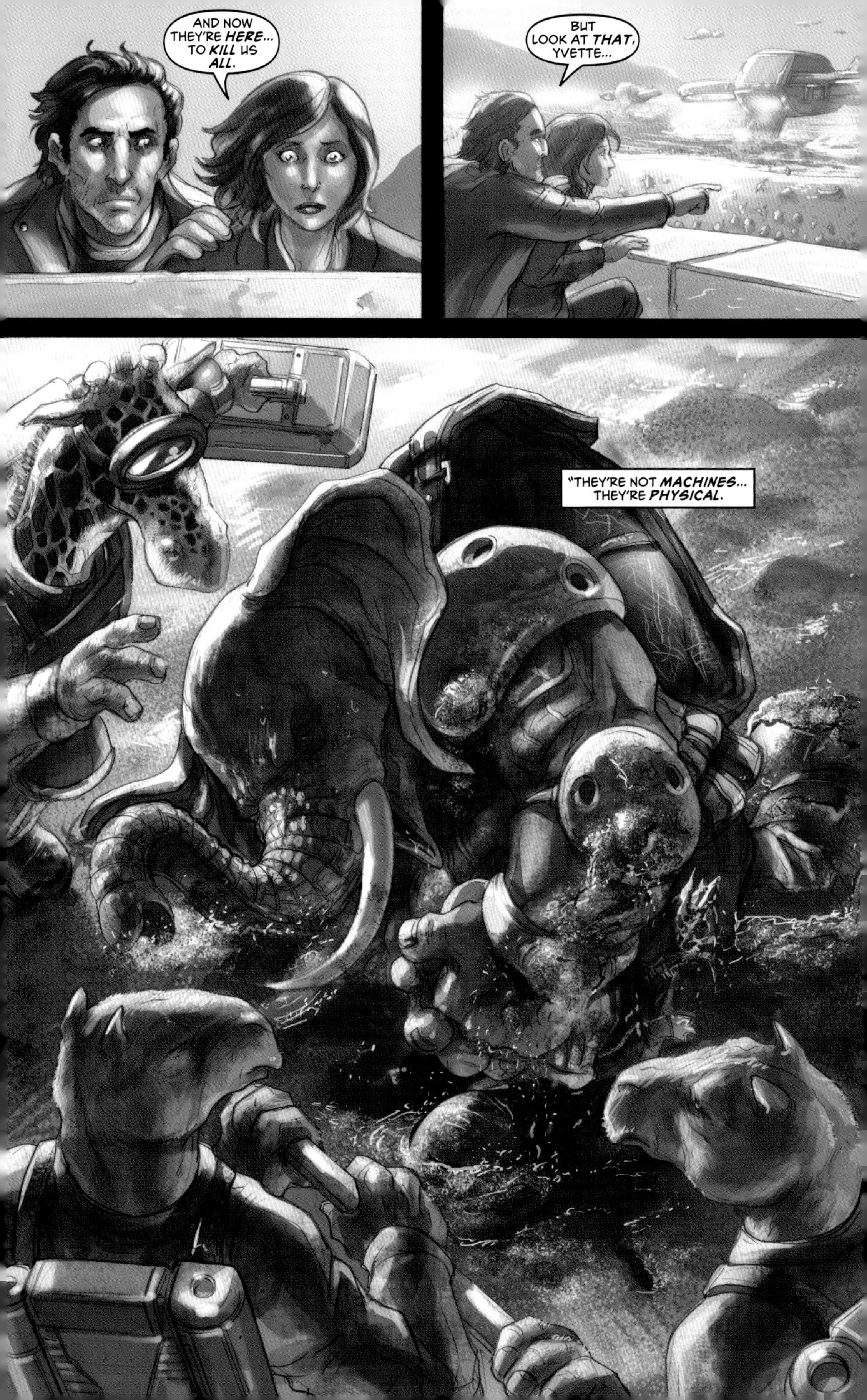
AND NOW THEY'RE *HERE*... TO *KILL* US *ALL*.
BUT LOOK AT *THAT*, YVETTE...
"THEY'RE NOT *MACHINES*... THEY'RE *PHYSICAL*.

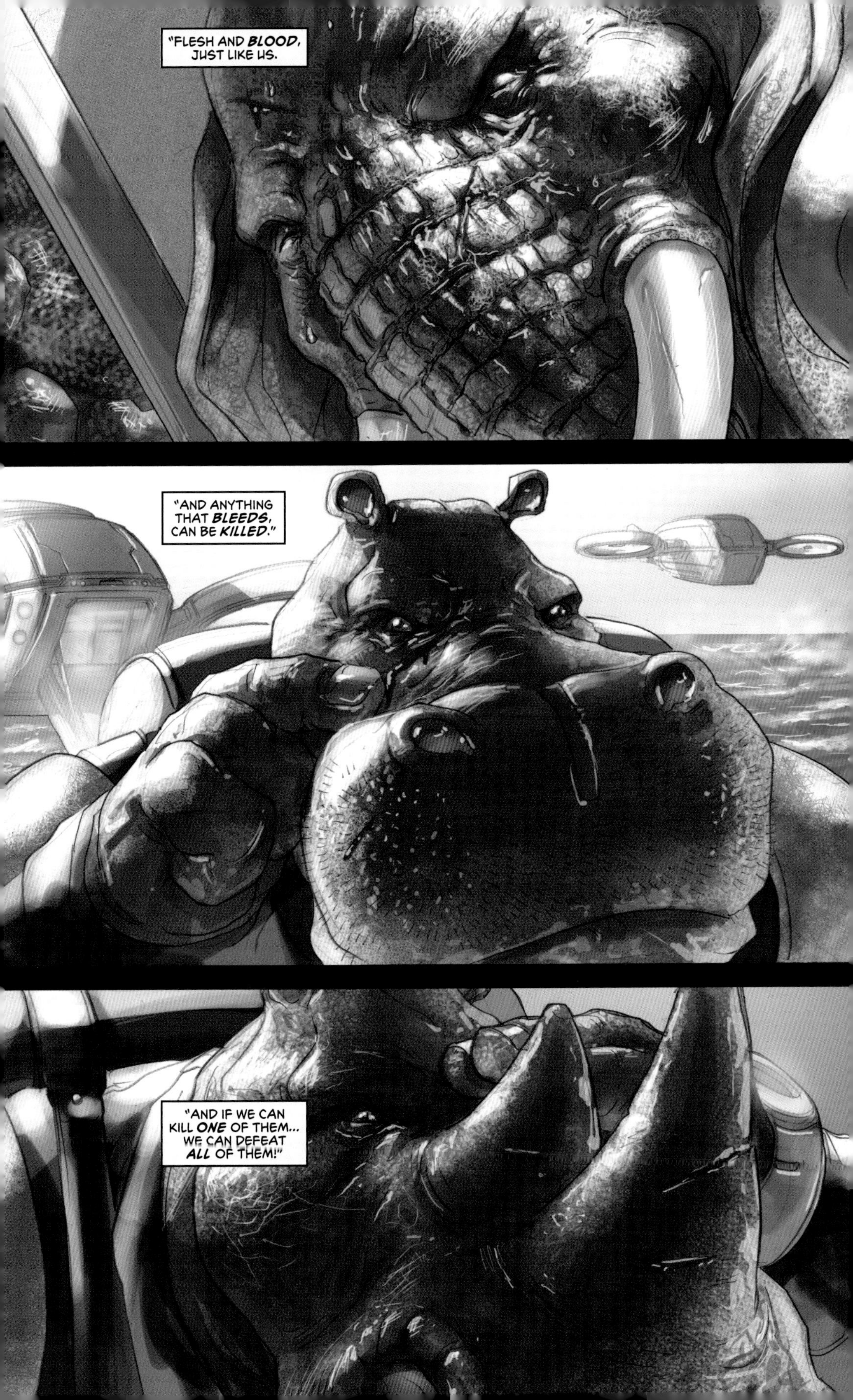
"FLESH AND BLOOD, JUST LIKE US.
"AND ANYTHING THAT BLEEDS, CAN BE KILLED."
"AND IF WE CAN KILL ONE OF THEM... WE CAN DEFEAT ALL OF THEM!"

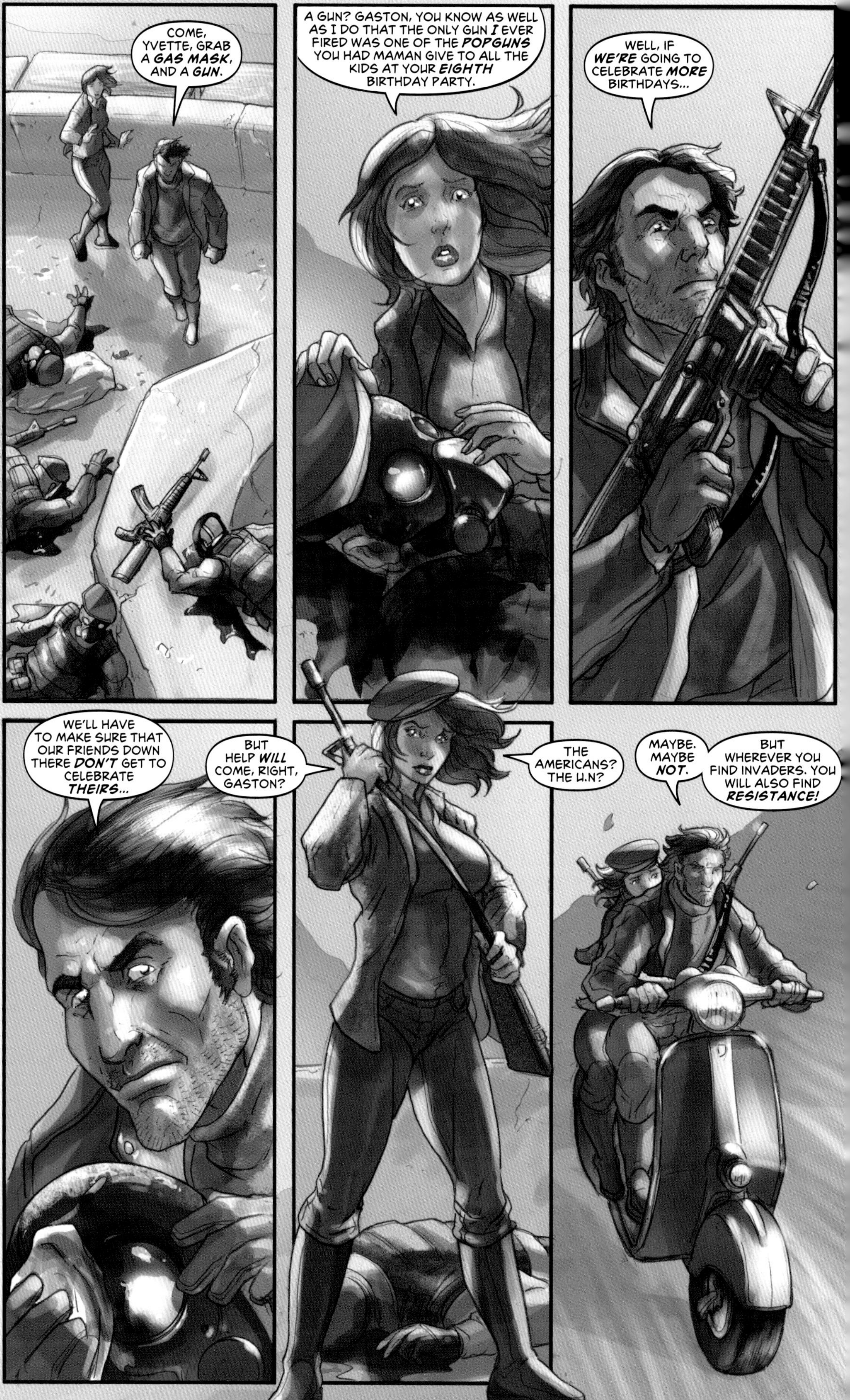
COME, YVETTE, GRAB A GAS MASK, AND A GUN.
A GUN? GASTON, YOU KNOW AS WELL AS I DO THAT THE ONLY GUN I EVER FIRED WAS ONE OF THE POPGUNS YOU HAD MAMAN GIVE TO ALL THE KIDS AT YOUR EIGHTH BIRTHDAY PARTY.
WELL, IF WE'RE GOING TO CELEBRATE MORE BIRTHDAYS...
WE'LL HAVE TO MAKE SURE THAT OUR FRIENDS DOWN THERE DON'T GET TO CELEBRATE THEIRS...
BUT HELP WILL COME, RIGHT, GASTON?
THE AMERICANS? THE U.N?
MAYBE. MAYBE NOT.
BUT WHEREVER YOU FIND INVADERS. YOU WILL ALSO FIND RESISTANCE!

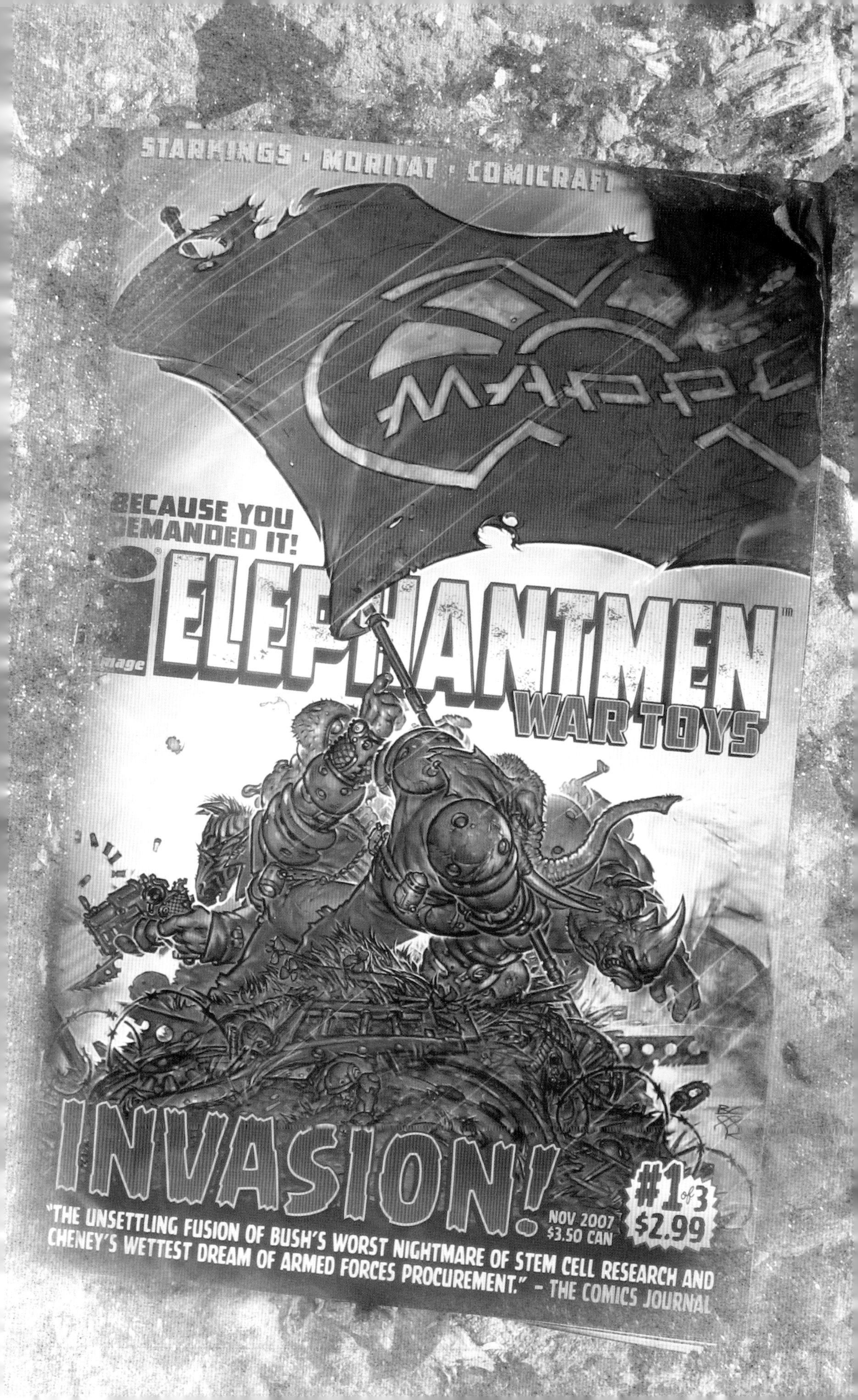
STARKINGS · MORITAT · COMICRAFT
BECAUSE YOU DEMANDED IT!
Image
ELEPHANTMEN
WAR TOYS
INVASION!
NOV 2007
$3.50 CAN
#1 of 3
$2.99
"THE UNSETTLING FUSION OF BUSH'S WORST NIGHTMARE OF STEM CELL RESEARCH AND CHENEY'S WETTEST DREAM OF ARMED FORCES PROCUREMENT." - THE COMICS JOURNAL

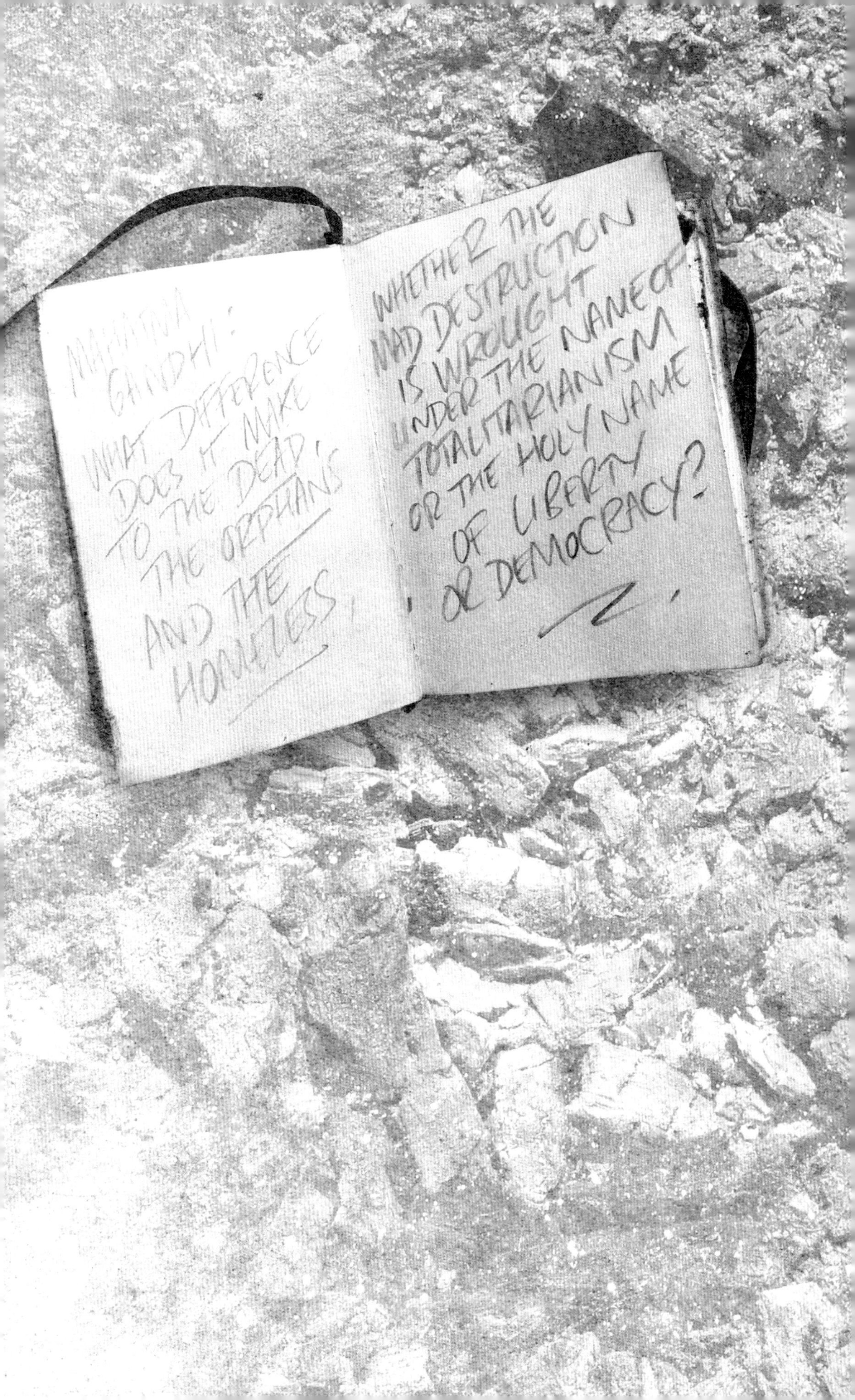
MAHATMA GANDHI:
WHAT DIFFERENCE DOES IT MAKE TO THE DEAD, THE ORPHANS AND THE HOMELESS,
WHETHER THE MAD DESTRUCTION IS WROUGHT UNDER THE NAME OF TOTALITARIANISM OR THE HOLY NAME OF LIBERTY OR DEMOCRACY?

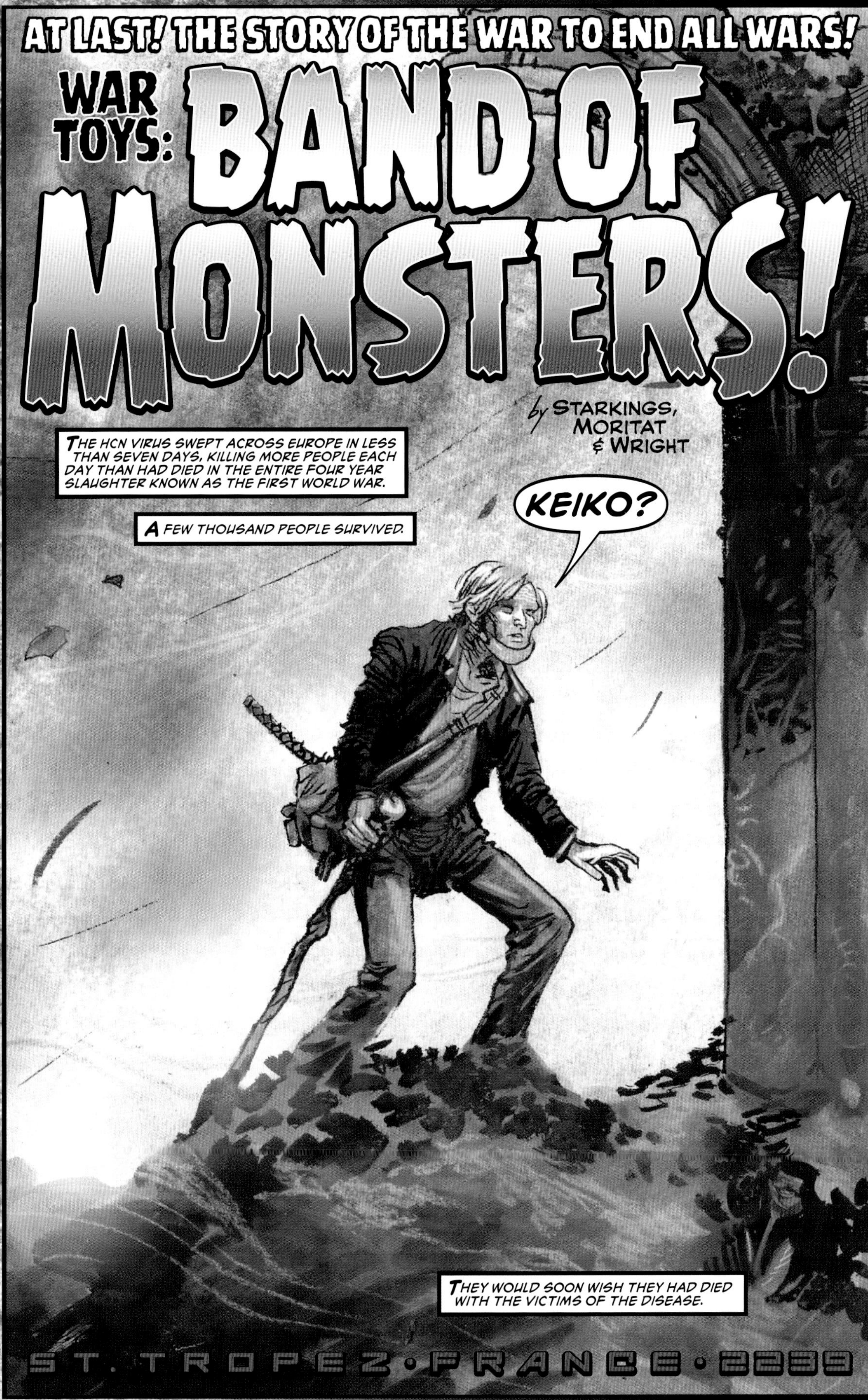
AT LAST! THE STORY OF THE WAR TO END ALL WARS!
WAR TOYS: BAND OF MONSTERS!
by STARKINGS, MORITAT & WRIGHT
THE HCN VIRUS SWEPT ACROSS EUROPE IN LESS THAN SEVEN DAYS, KILLING MORE PEOPLE EACH DAY THAN HAD DIED IN THE ENTIRE FOUR YEAR SLAUGHTER KNOWN AS THE FIRST WORLD WAR.
A FEW THOUSAND PEOPLE SURVIVED.
KEIKO?
THEY WOULD SOON WISH THEY HAD DIED WITH THE VICTIMS OF THE DISEASE.
ST. TROPEZ • FRANCE • 2239

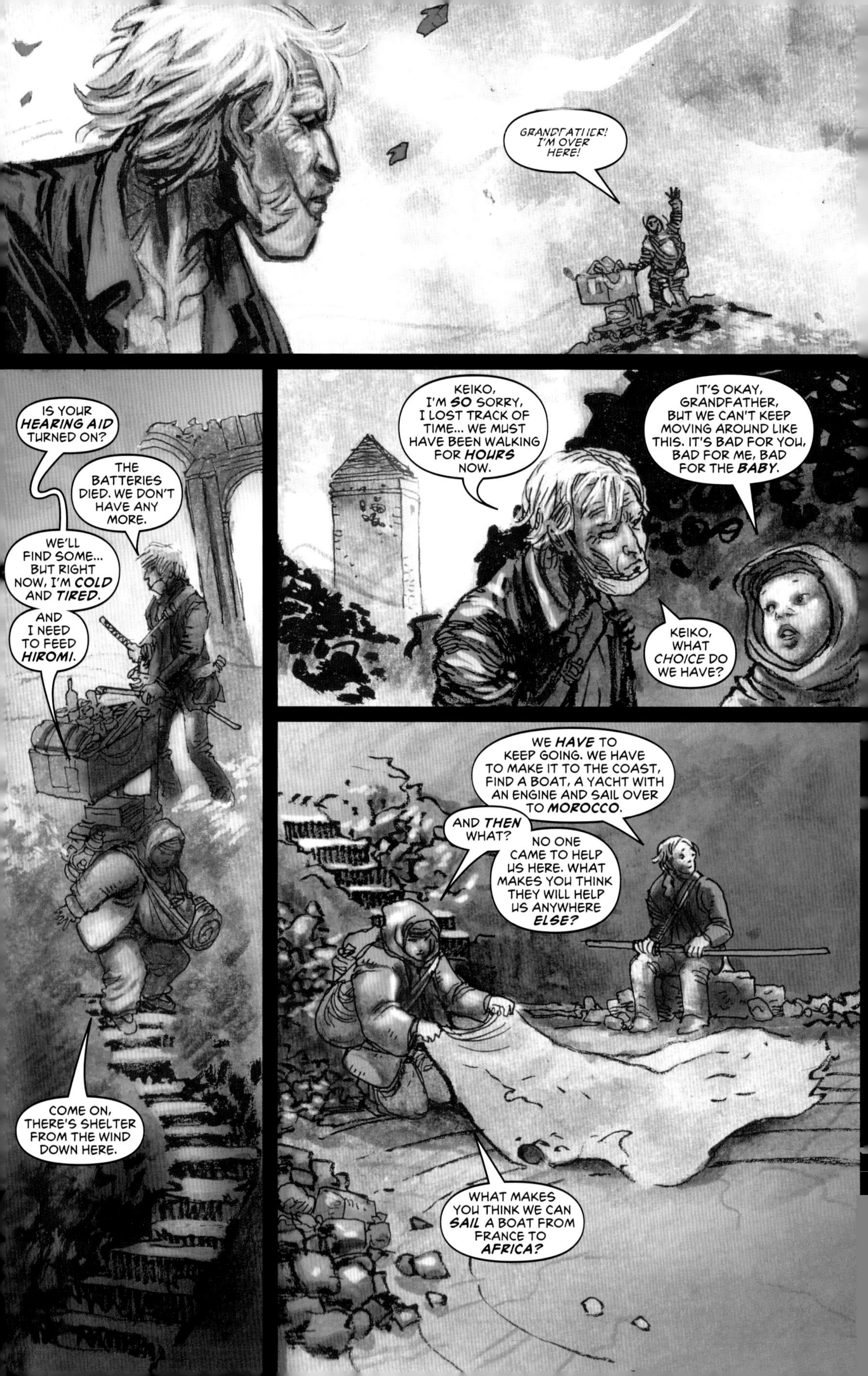
GRANDFATHER! I'M OVER HERE!
IS YOUR HEARING AID TURNED ON?
THE BATTERIES DIED. WE DON'T HAVE ANY MORE.
WE'LL FIND SOME... BUT RIGHT NOW, I'M COLD AND TIRED.
AND I NEED TO FEED HIROMI.
COME ON, THERE'S SHELTER FROM THE WIND DOWN HERE.
KEIKO, I'M SO SORRY, I LOST TRACK OF TIME... WE MUST HAVE BEEN WALKING FOR HOURS NOW.
IT'S OKAY, GRANDFATHER, BUT WE CAN'T KEEP MOVING AROUND LIKE THIS. IT'S BAD FOR YOU, BAD FOR ME, BAD FOR THE BABY.
KEIKO, WHAT CHOICE DO WE HAVE?
WE HAVE TO KEEP GOING. WE HAVE TO MAKE IT TO THE COAST, FIND A BOAT, A YACHT WITH AN ENGINE AND SAIL OVER TO MOROCCO.
AND THEN WHAT?
NO ONE CAME TO HELP US HERE. WHAT MAKES YOU THINK THEY WILL HELP US ANYWHERE ELSE?
WHAT MAKES YOU THINK WE CAN SAIL A BOAT FROM FRANCE TO AFRICA?

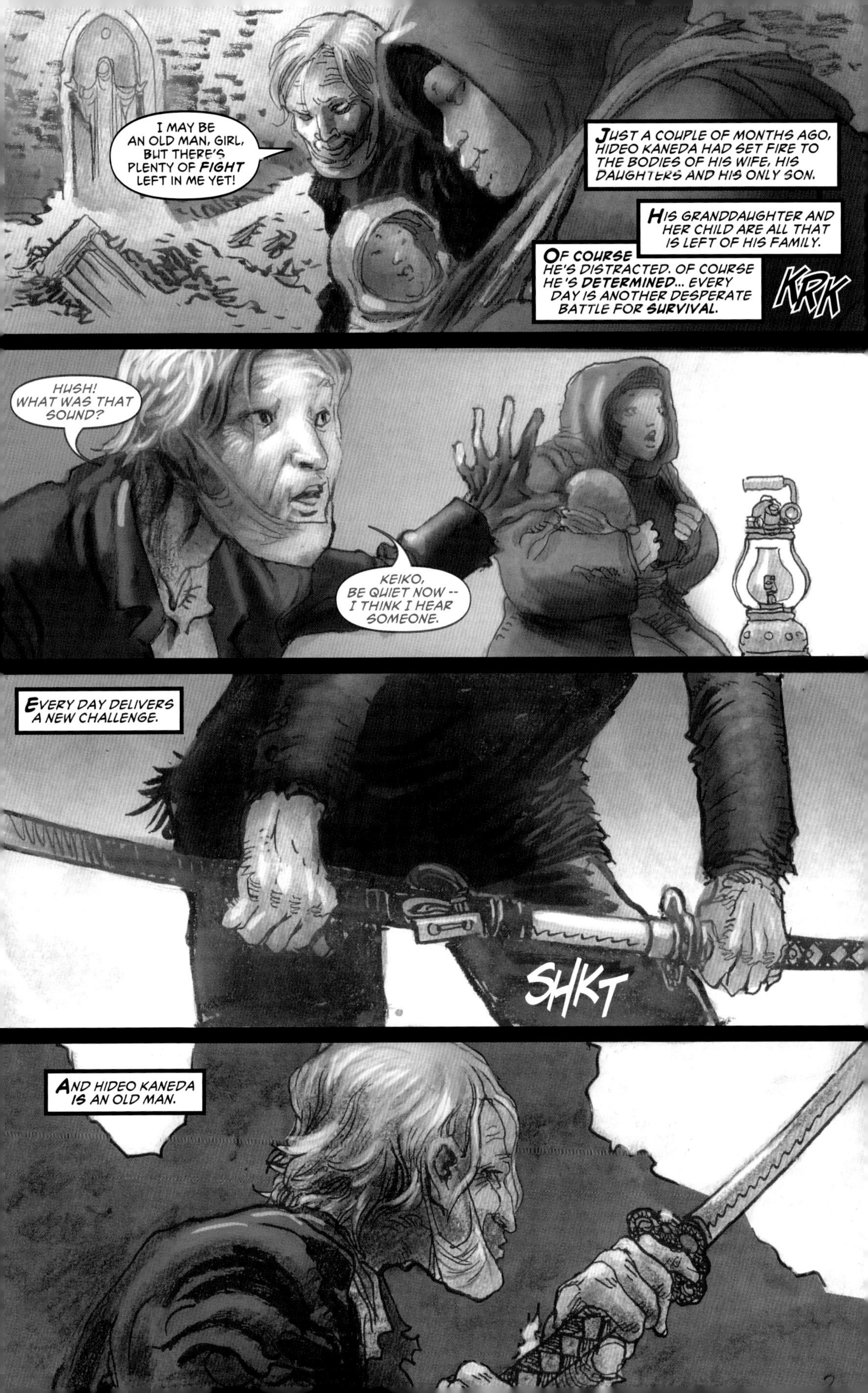
I MAY BE AN OLD MAN, GIRL, BUT THERE'S PLENTY OF FIGHT LEFT IN ME YET!
JUST A COUPLE OF MONTHS AGO, HIDEO KANEDA HAD SET FIRE TO THE BODIES OF HIS WIFE, HIS DAUGHTERS AND HIS ONLY SON.
HIS GRANDDAUGHTER AND HER CHILD ARE ALL THAT IS LEFT OF HIS FAMILY.
OF COURSE HE'S DISTRACTED. OF COURSE HE'S DETERMINED... EVERY DAY IS ANOTHER DESPERATE BATTLE FOR SURVIVAL.
KRK
HUSH! WHAT WAS THAT SOUND?
KEIKO, BE QUIET NOW -- I THINK I HEAR SOMEONE.
EVERY DAY DELIVERS A NEW CHALLENGE.
SHKT
AND HIDEO KANEDA IS AN OLD MAN.

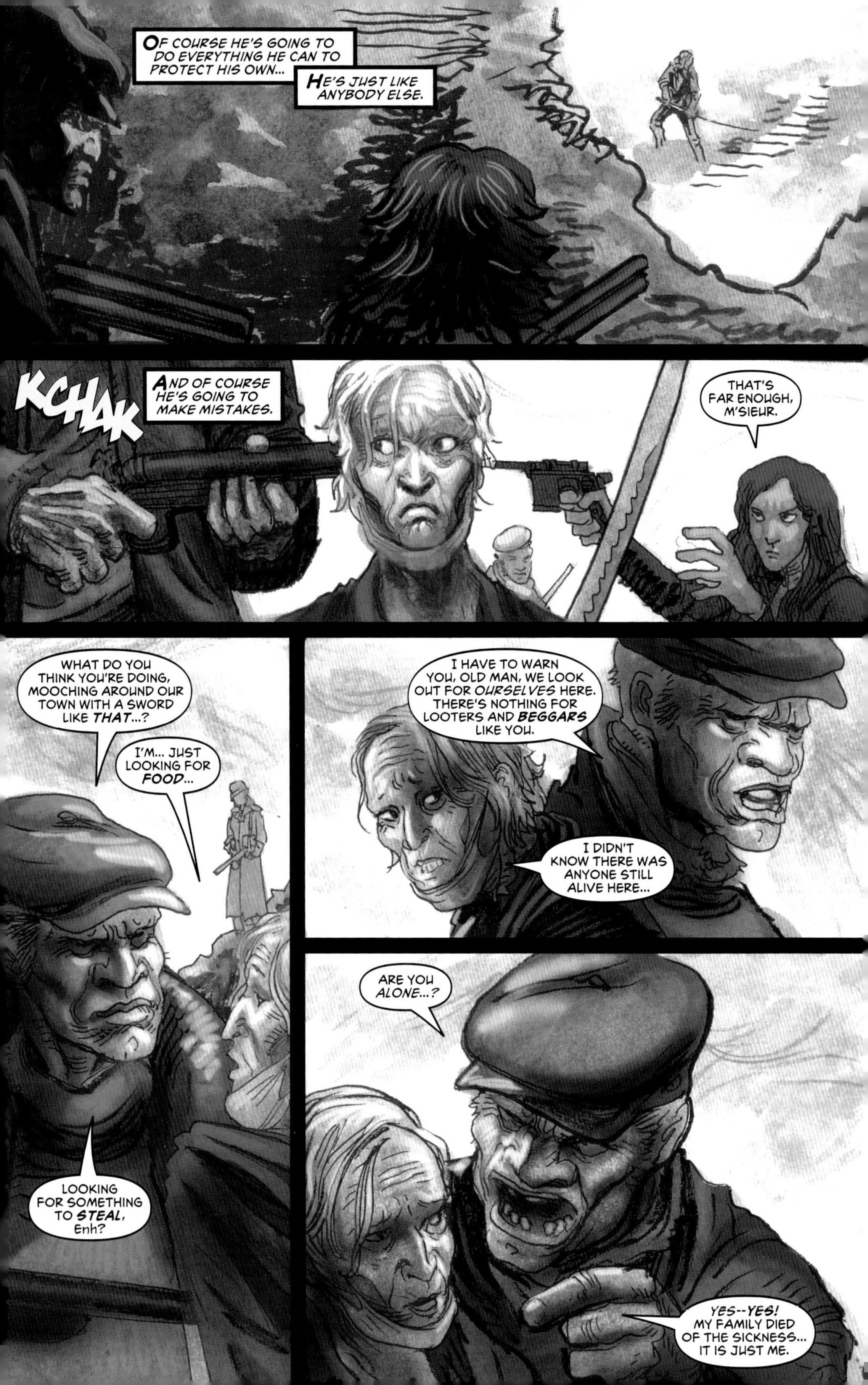

OF COURSE HE'S GOING TO DO EVERYTHING HE CAN TO PROTECT HIS OWN...
HE'S JUST LIKE ANYBODY ELSE.
KCHAK
AND OF COURSE HE'S GOING TO MAKE MISTAKES.
THAT'S FAR ENOUGH, M'SIEUR.
WHAT DO YOU THINK YOU'RE DOING, MOOCHING AROUND OUR TOWN WITH A SWORD LIKE THAT...?
I'M... JUST LOOKING FOR FOOD...
LOOKING FOR SOMETHING TO STEAL, Enh?
I HAVE TO WARN YOU, OLD MAN, WE LOOK OUT FOR OURSELVES HERE. THERE'S NOTHING FOR LOOTERS AND BEGGARS LIKE YOU.
I DIDN'T KNOW THERE WAS ANYONE STILL ALIVE HERE...
ARE YOU ALONE...?
YES--YES! MY FAMILY DIED OF THE SICKNESS... IT IS JUST ME.

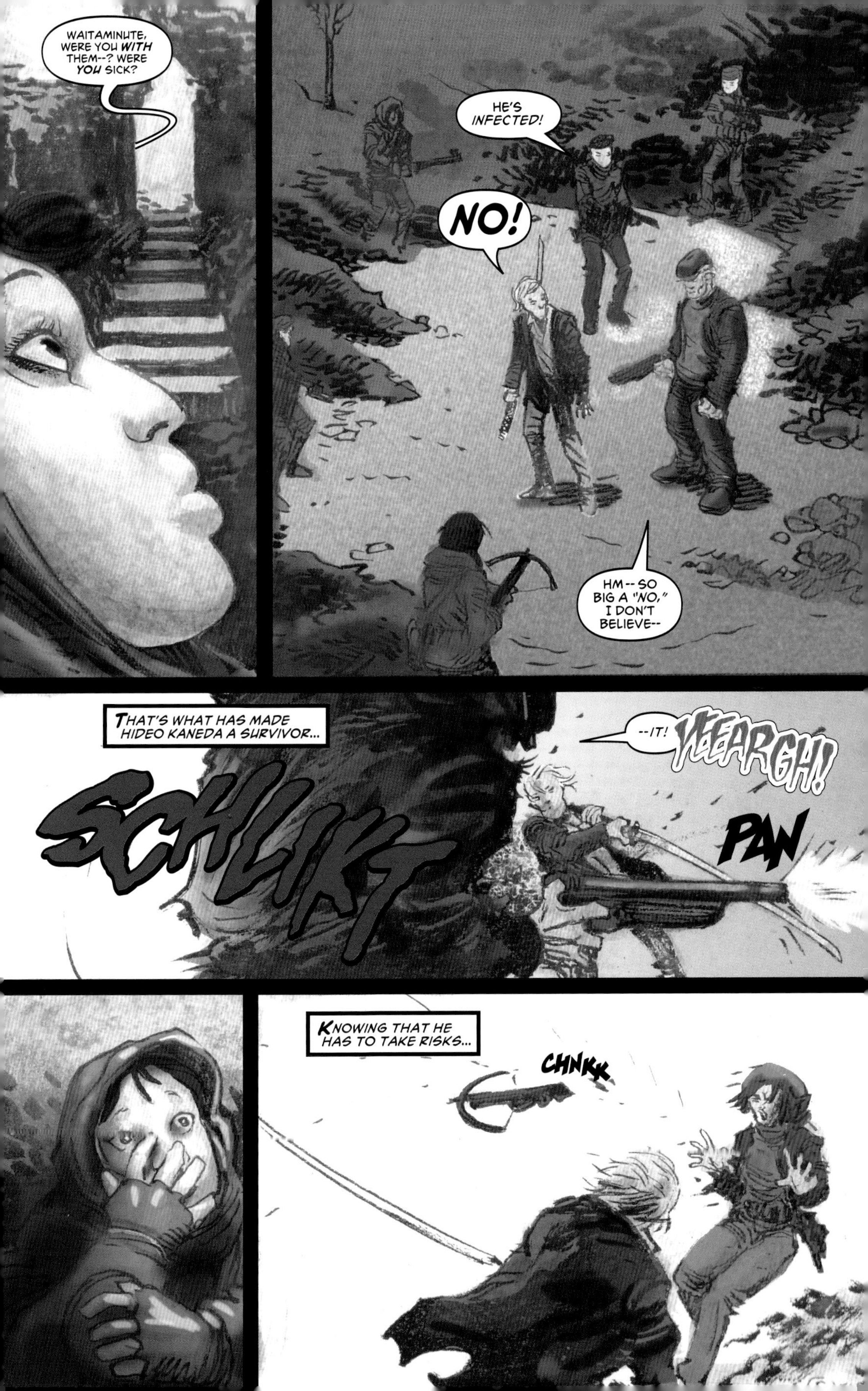
WAITAMINUTE, WERE YOU WITH THEM--? WERE YOU SICK?
HE'S INFECTED!
NO!
HM -- SO BIG A "NO," I DON'T BELIEVE--
THAT'S WHAT HAS MADE HIDEO KANEDA A SURVIVOR...
--IT!
YEEARGH!
SCHLIKT
PAN
KNOWING THAT HE HAS TO TAKE RISKS...
CHNKK

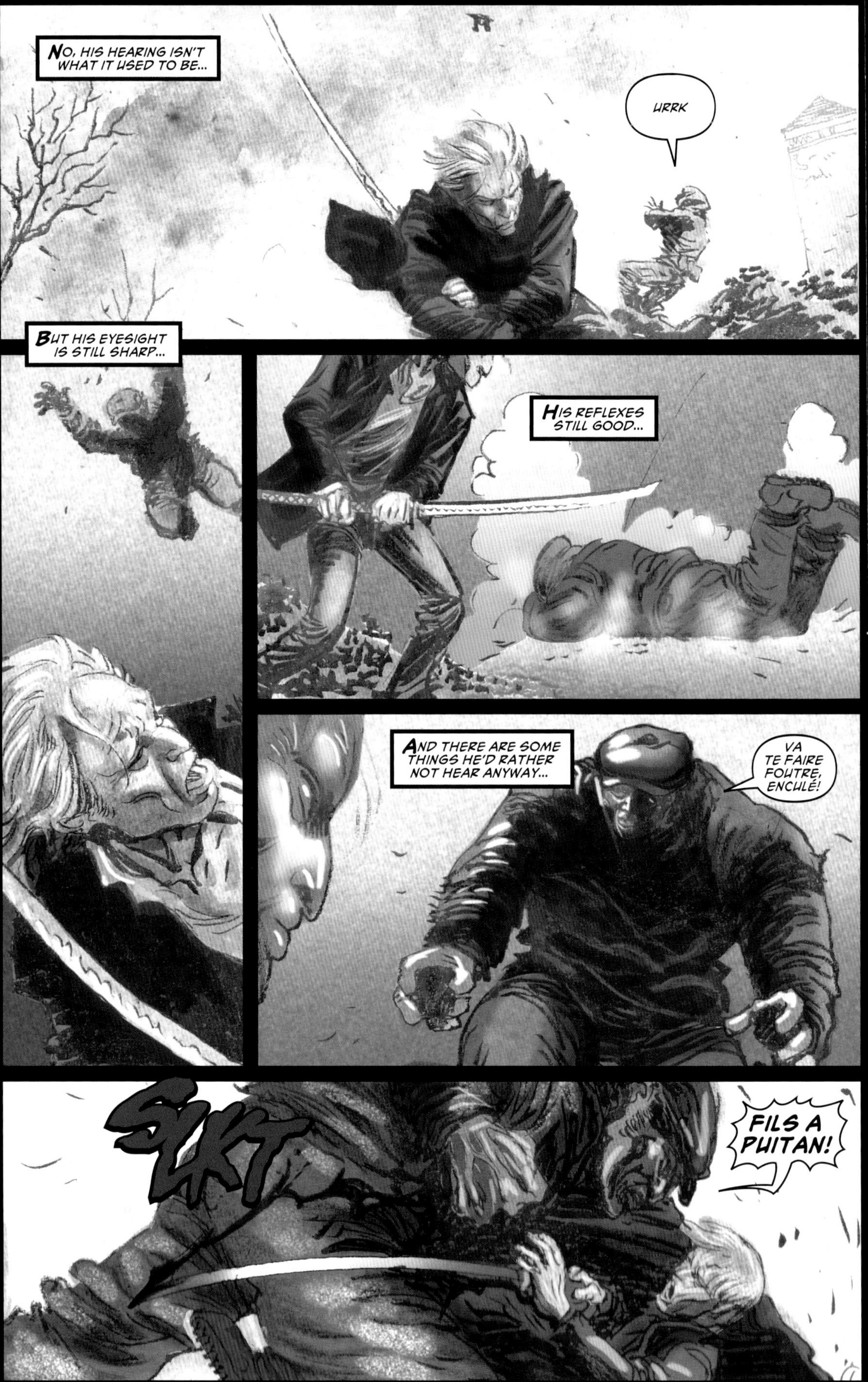
NO, HIS HEARING ISN'T WHAT IT USED TO BE...
URRK
BUT HIS EYESIGHT IS STILL SHARP...
HIS REFLEXES STILL GOOD...
AND THERE ARE SOME THINGS HE'D RATHER NOT HEAR ANYWAY...
VA TE FAIRE FOUTRE, ENCULÉ!
SLKT
FILS A PUITAN!

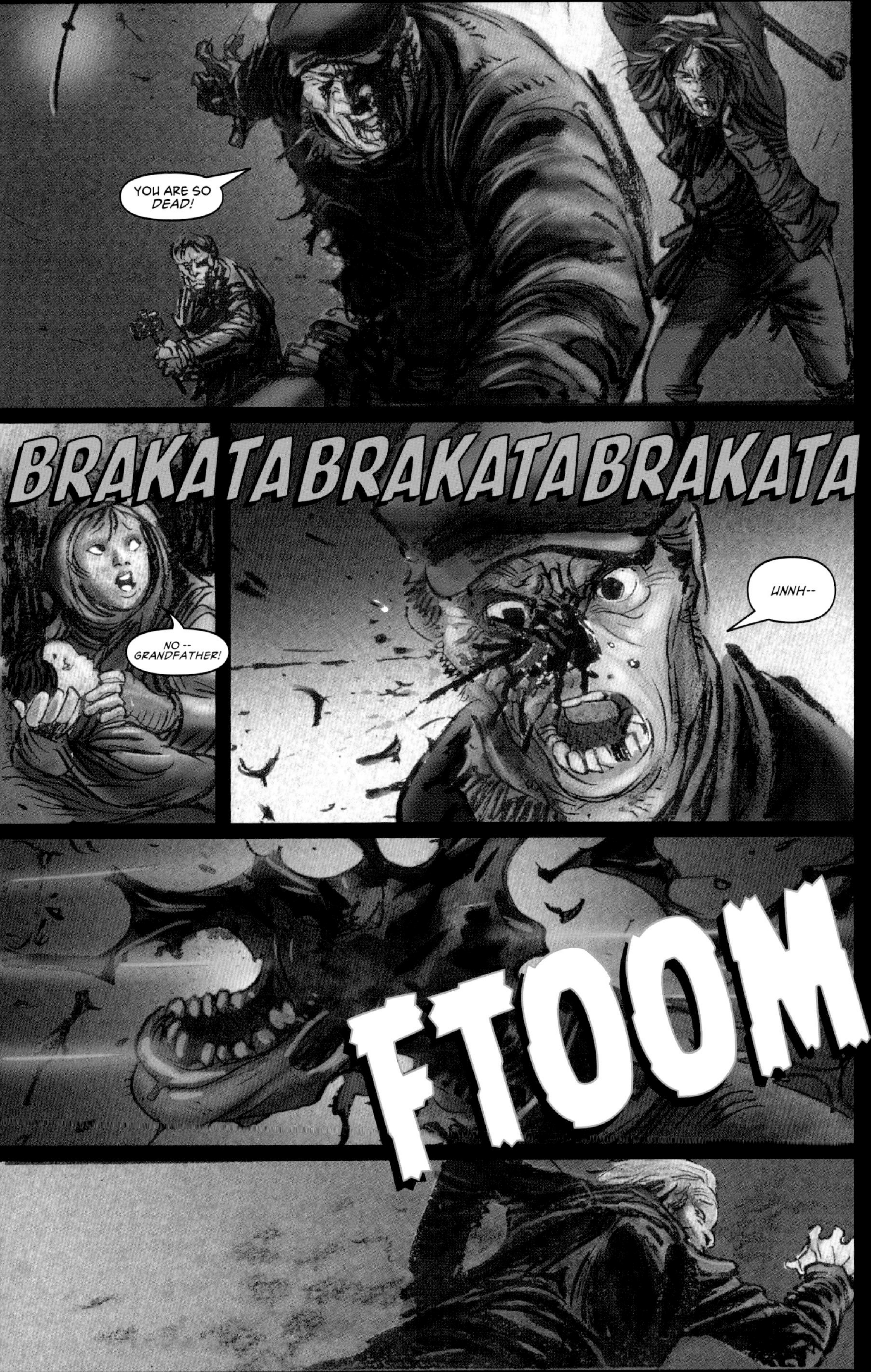

YOU ARE SO DEAD!
BRAKATABRAKATABRAKATA
NO -- GRANDFATHER!
UNNH--
FTOOM

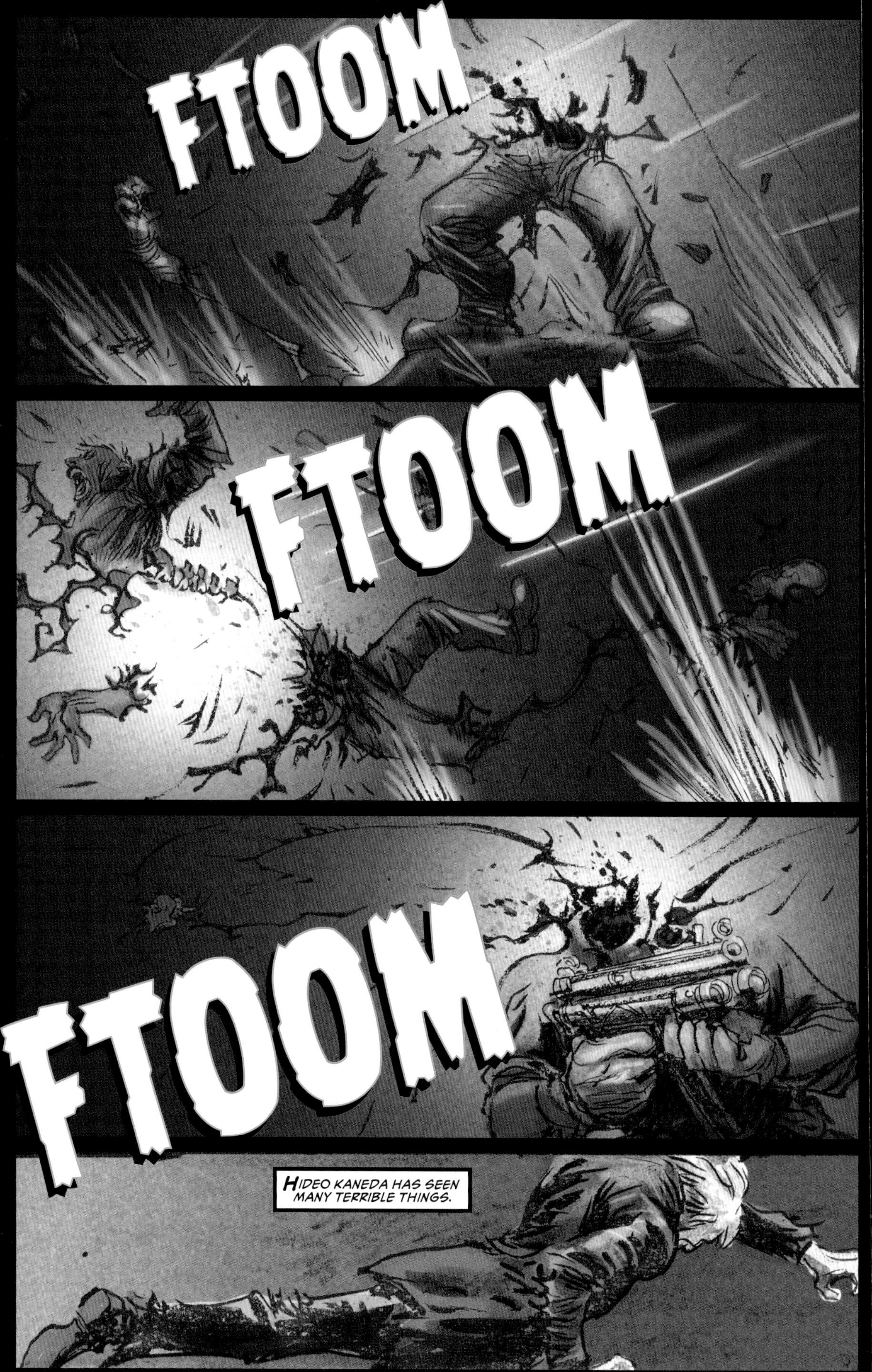
FTOOM
FTOOM
FTOOM
HIDEO KANEDA HAS SEEN MANY TERRIBLE THINGS.

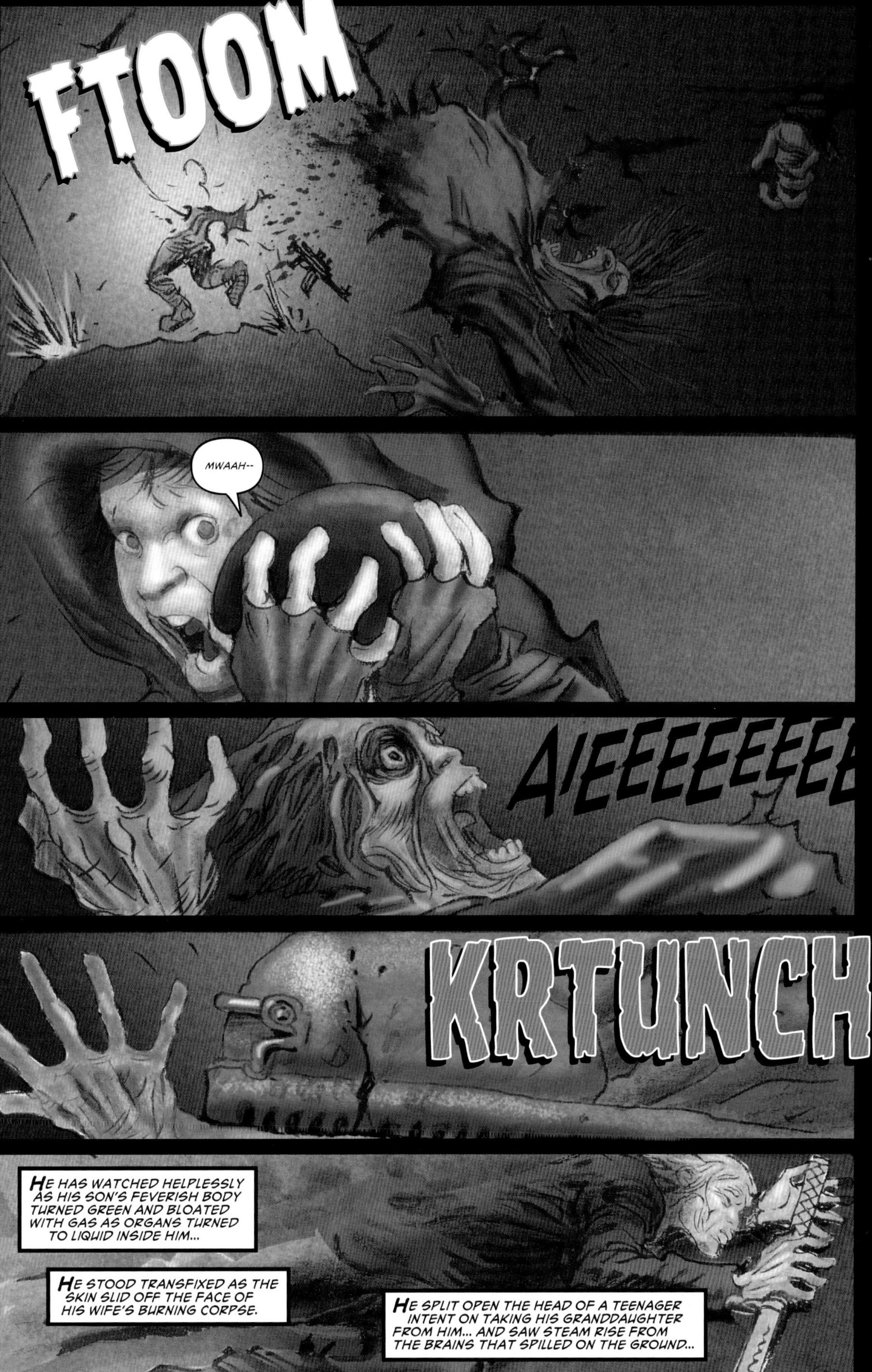
FTOOM
MWAAH--
AIEEEEEEEE
KRTUNCH
HE HAS WATCHED HELPLESSLY AS HIS SON'S FEVERISH BODY TURNED GREEN AND BLOATED WITH GAS AS ORGANS TURNED TO LIQUID INSIDE HIM...
HE STOOD TRANSFIXED AS THE SKIN SLID OFF THE FACE OF HIS WIFE'S BURNING CORPSE.
HE SPLIT OPEN THE HEAD OF A TEENAGER INTENT ON TAKING HIS GRANDDAUGHTER FROM HIM... AND SAW STEAM RISE FROM THE BRAINS THAT SPILLED ON THE GROUND...

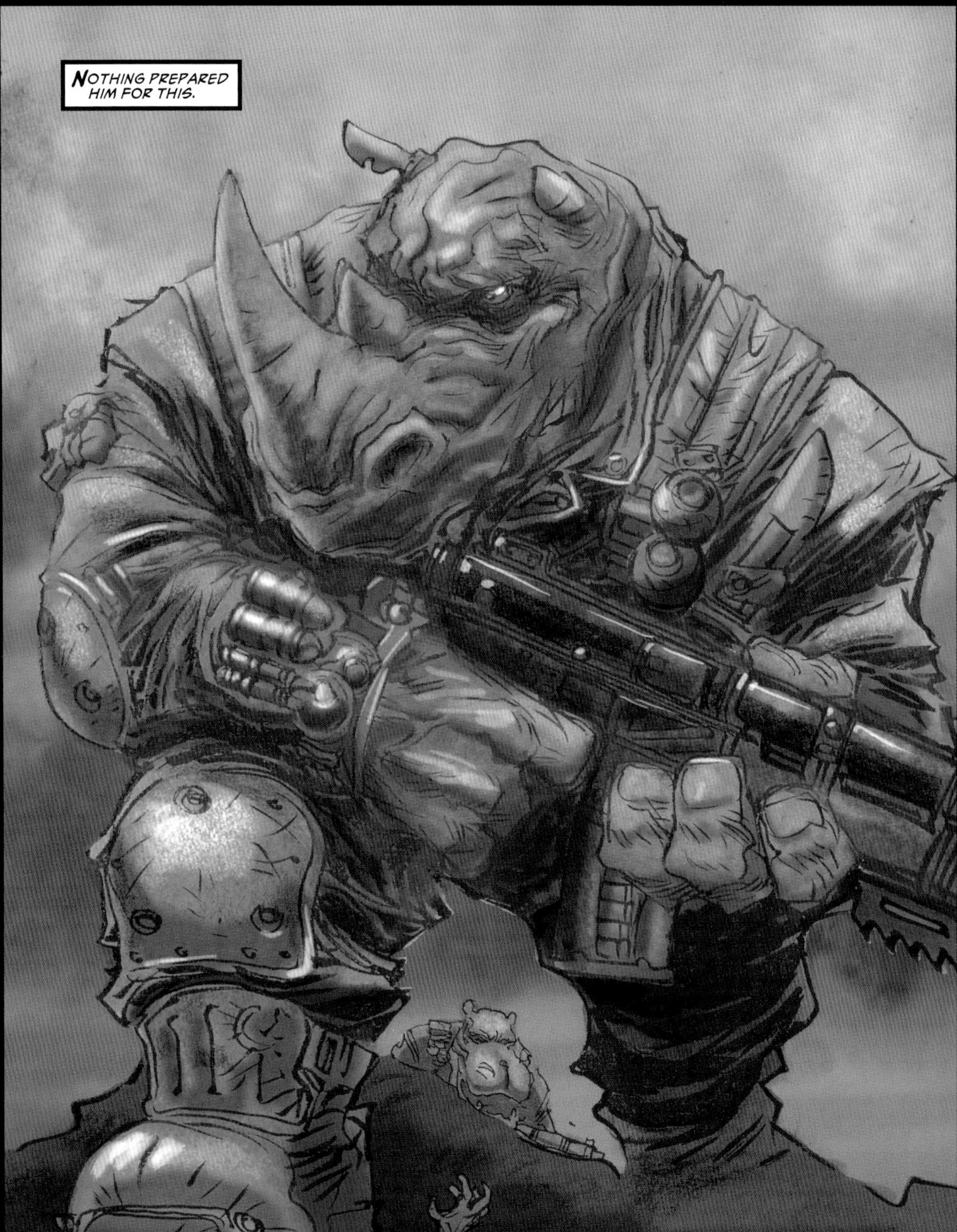
NOTHING PREPARED HIM FOR THIS.

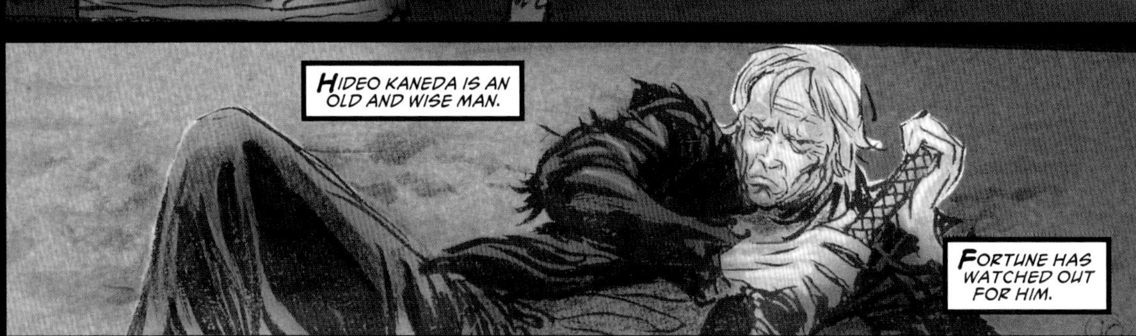
HIDEO KANEDA IS AN OLD AND WISE MAN.
FORTUNE HAS WATCHED OUT FOR HIM.

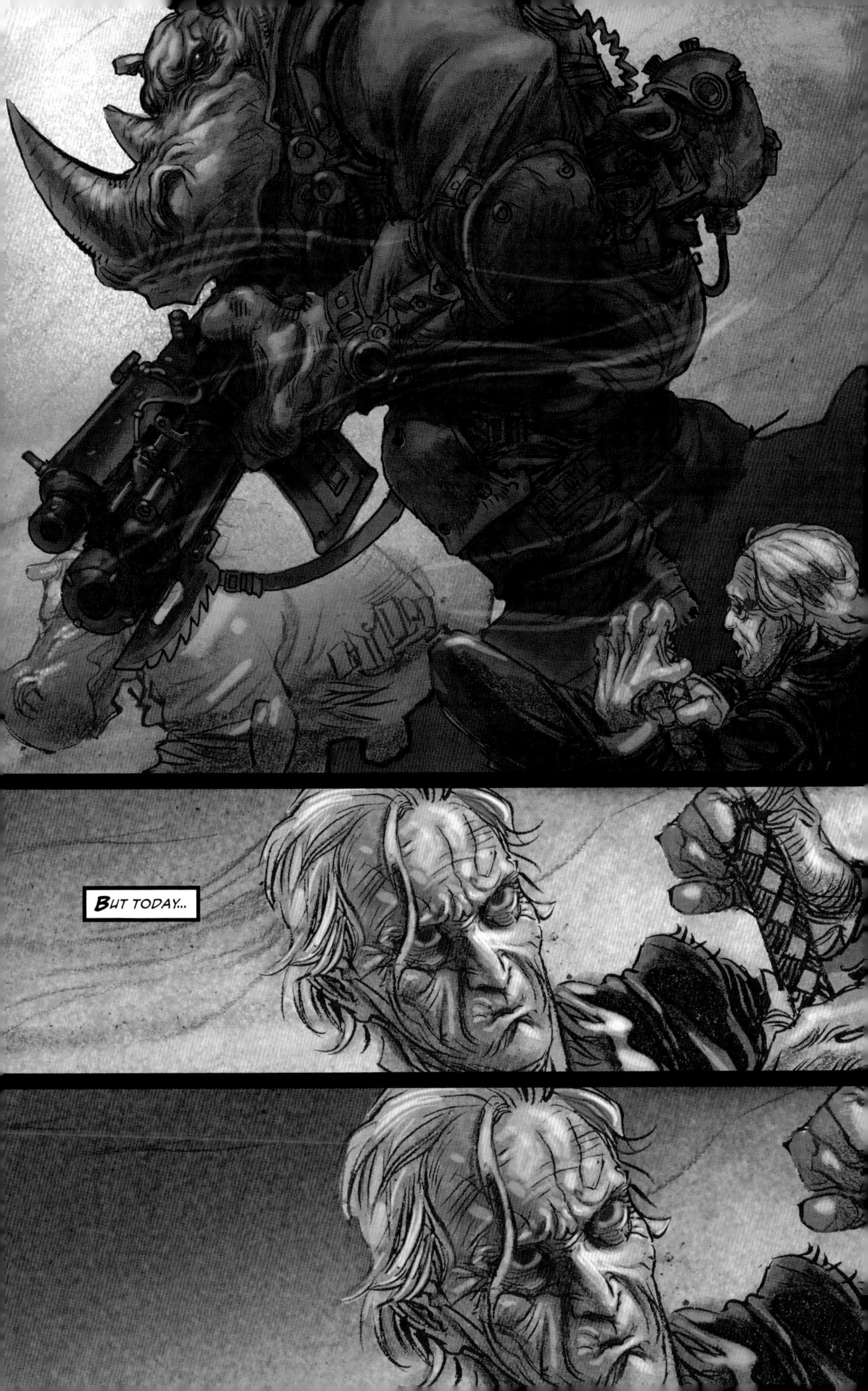
BUT TODAY...

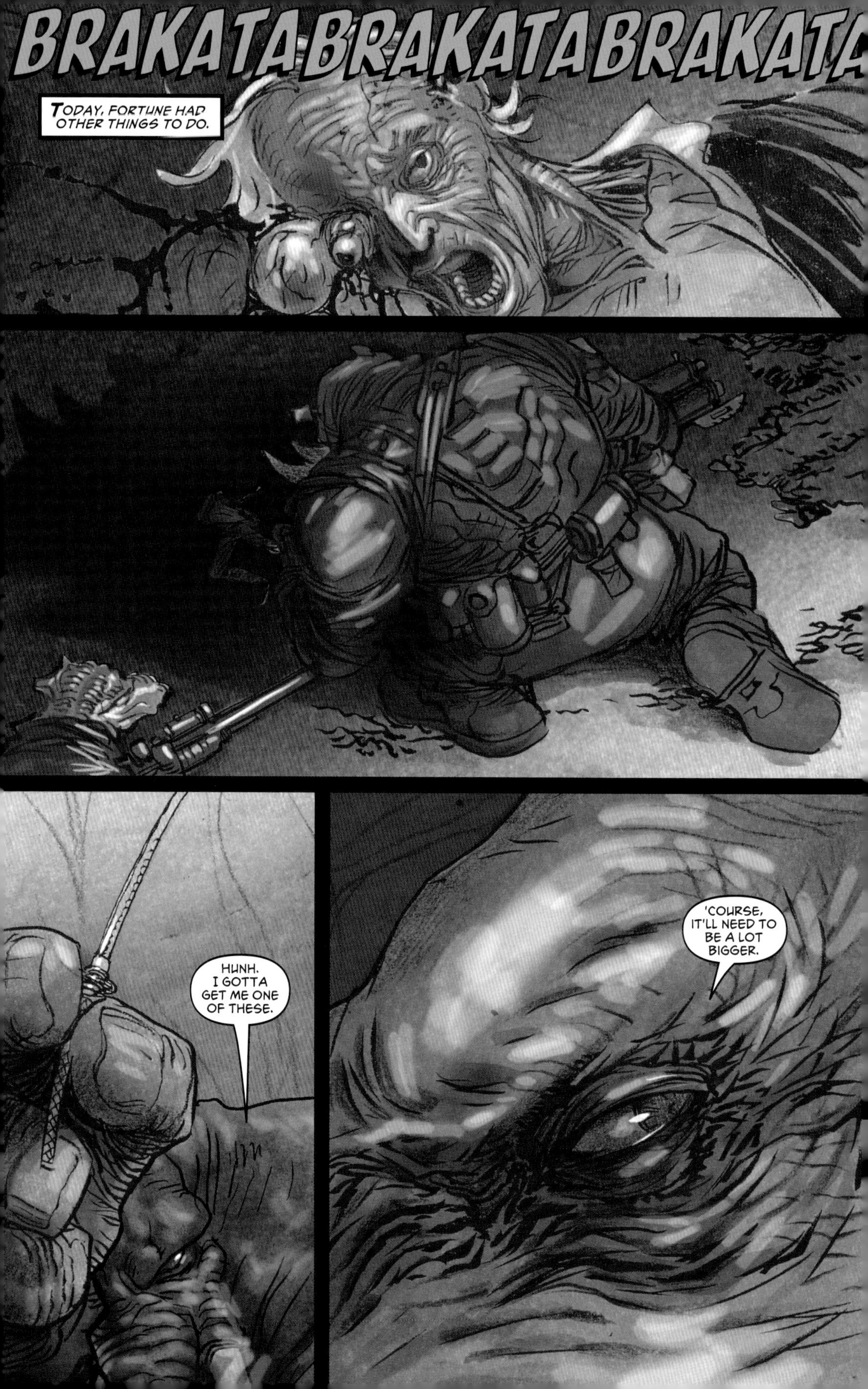
BRAKATABRAKATABRAKATA
TODAY, FORTUNE HAD OTHER THINGS TO DO.
HUNH. I GOTTA GET ME ONE OF THESE.
'COURSE, IT'LL NEED TO BE A LOT BIGGER.

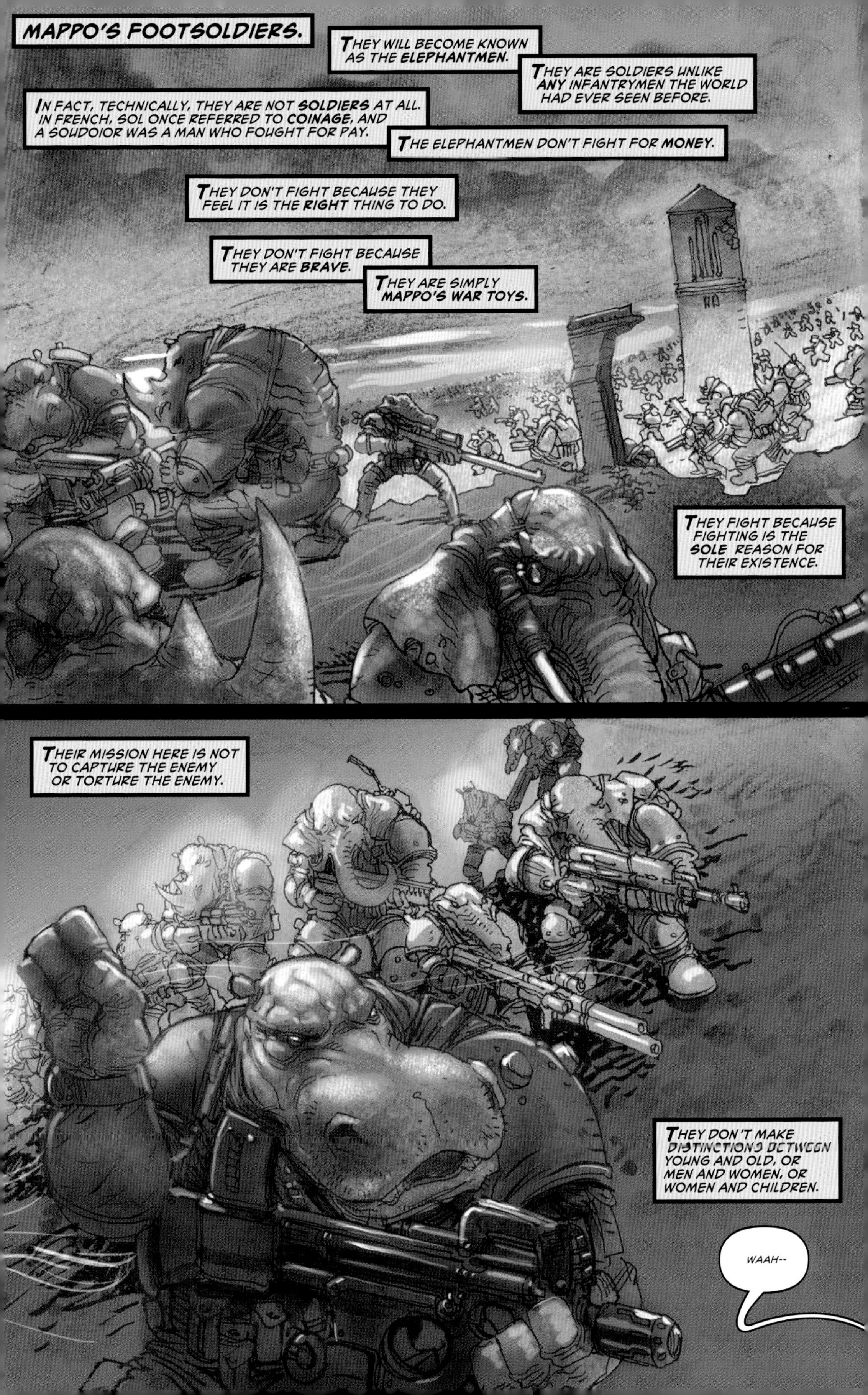
MAPPO'S FOOTSOLDIERS.
THEY WILL BECOME KNOWN AS THE ELEPHANTMEN.
THEY ARE SOLDIERS UNLIKE ANY INFANTRYMEN THE WORLD HAD EVER SEEN BEFORE.
IN FACT, TECHNICALLY, THEY ARE NOT SOLDIERS AT ALL. IN FRENCH, SOL ONCE REFERRED TO COINAGE, AND A SOUDOIOR WAS A MAN WHO FOUGHT FOR PAY.
THE ELEPHANTMEN DON'T FIGHT FOR MONEY.
THEY DON'T FIGHT BECAUSE THEY FEEL IT IS THE RIGHT THING TO DO.
THEY DON'T FIGHT BECAUSE THEY ARE BRAVE.
THEY ARE SIMPLY MAPPO'S WAR TOYS.
THEY FIGHT BECAUSE FIGHTING IS THE SOLE REASON FOR THEIR EXISTENCE.
THEIR MISSION HERE IS NOT TO CAPTURE THE ENEMY OR TORTURE THE ENEMY.
THEY DON'T MAKE DISTINCTIONS BETWEEN YOUNG AND OLD, OR MEN AND WOMEN, OR WOMEN AND CHILDREN.
WAAH--

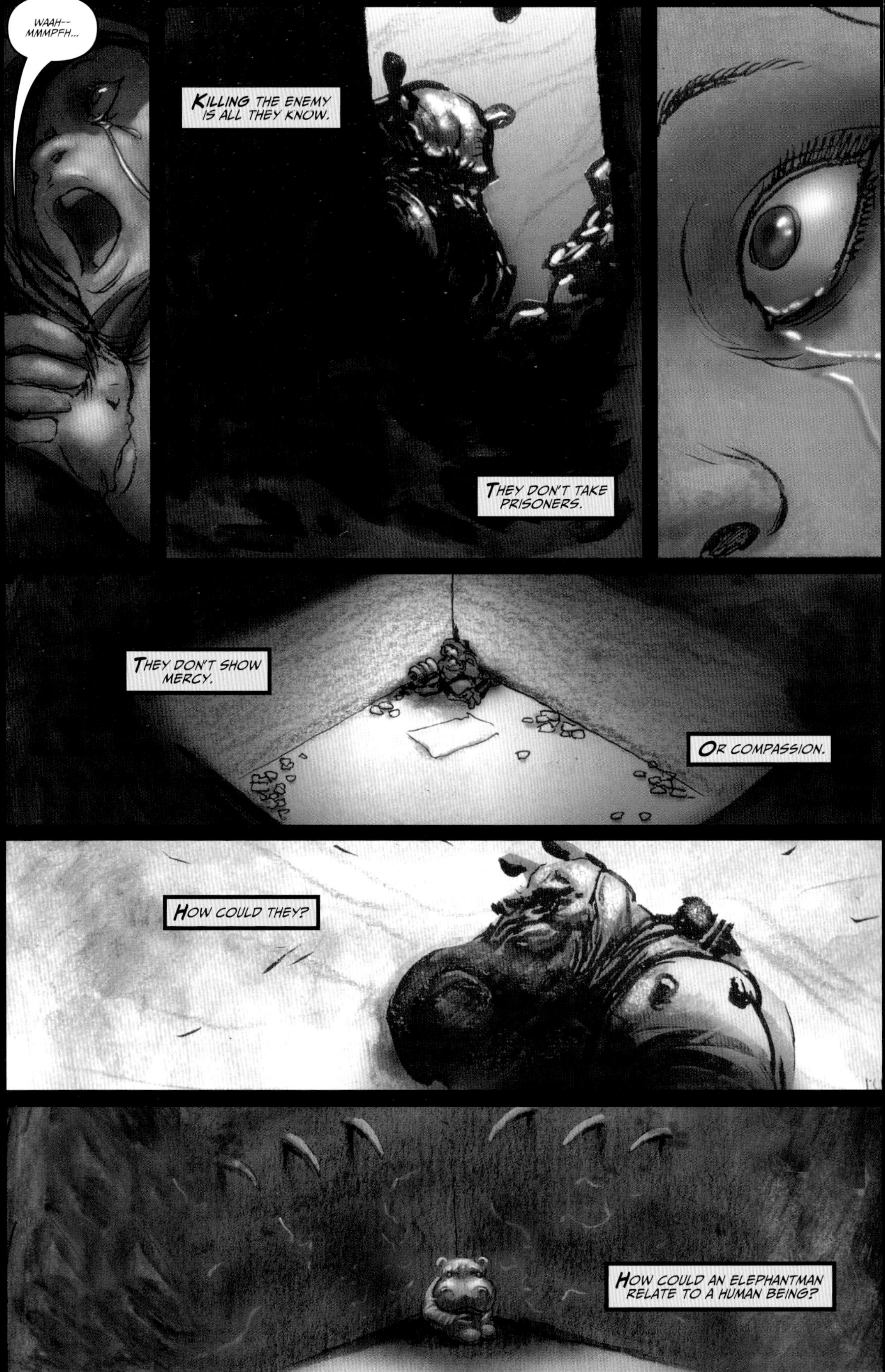
WAAH--
MMMPFH...
KILLING THE ENEMY IS ALL THEY KNOW.
THEY DON'T TAKE PRISONERS.
THEY DON'T SHOW MERCY.
OR COMPASSION.
HOW COULD THEY?
HOW COULD AN ELEPHANTMAN RELATE TO A HUMAN BEING?

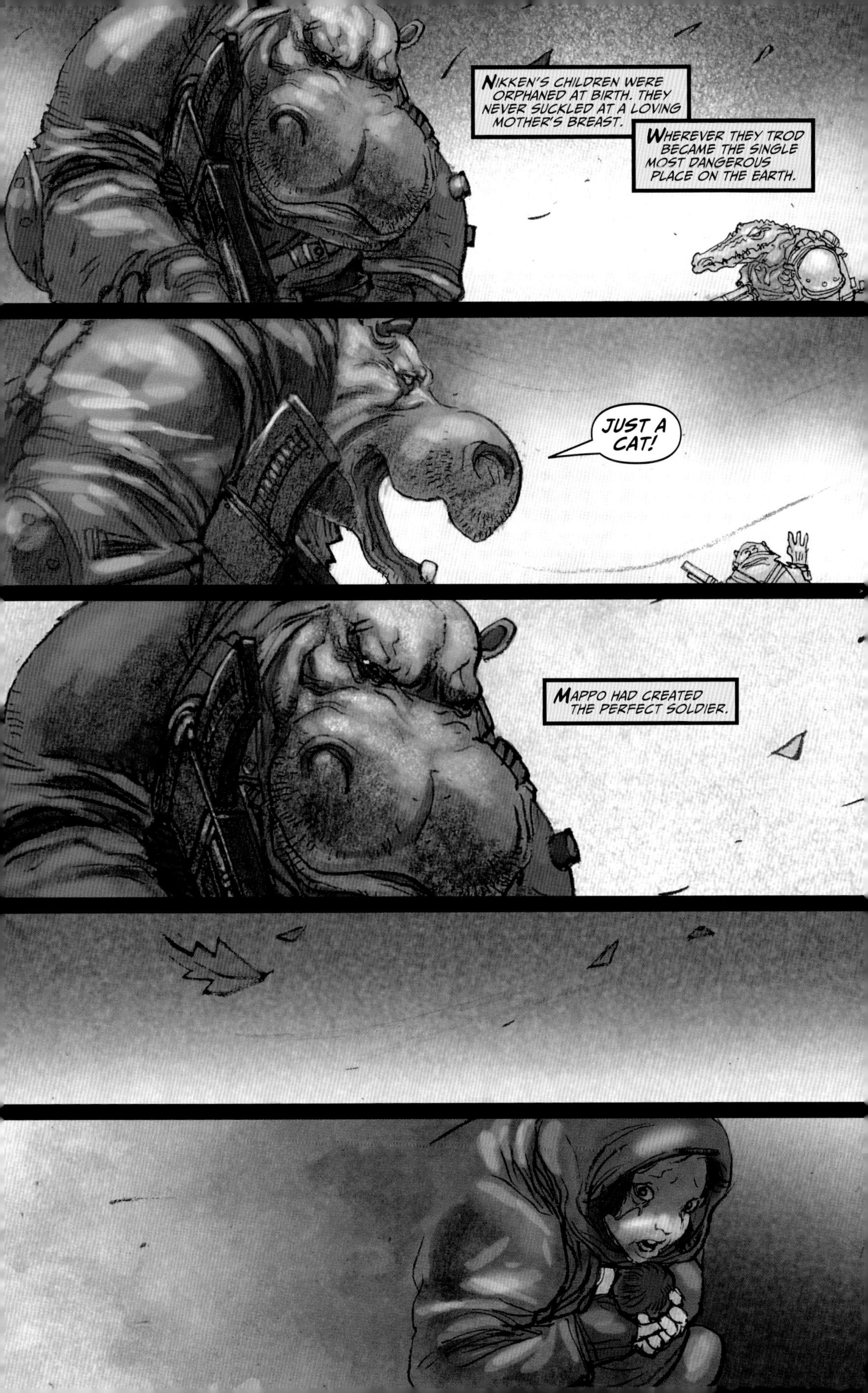
NIKKEN'S CHILDREN WERE ORPHANED AT BIRTH. THEY NEVER SUCKLED AT A LOVING MOTHER'S BREAST.
WHEREVER THEY TROD BECAME THE SINGLE MOST DANGEROUS PLACE ON THE EARTH.
JUST A CAT!
MAPPO HAD CREATED THE PERFECT SOLDIER.

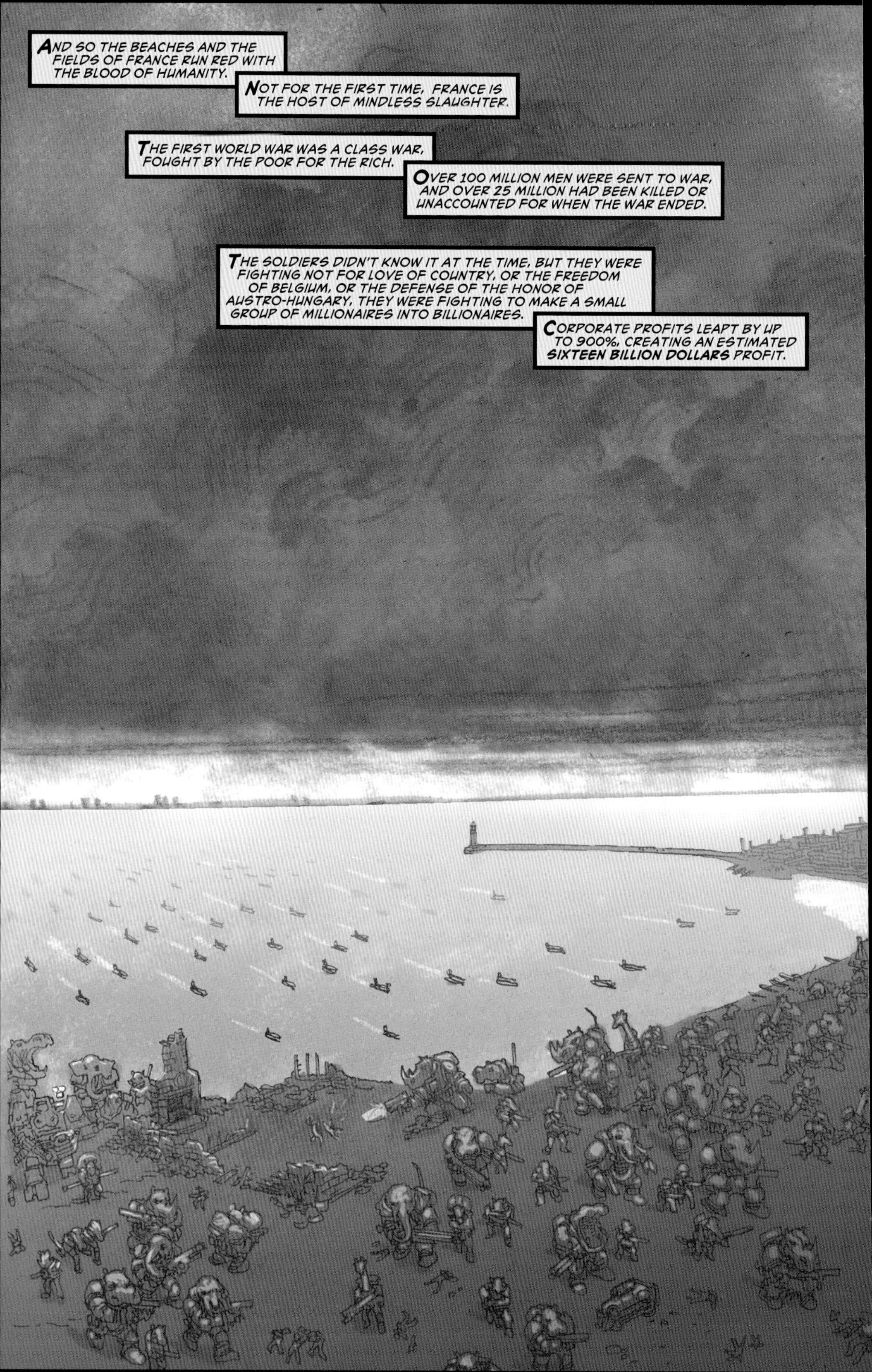
AND SO THE BEACHES AND THE FIELDS OF FRANCE RUN RED WITH THE BLOOD OF HUMANITY.
NOT FOR THE FIRST TIME, FRANCE IS THE HOST OF MINDLESS SLAUGHTER.
THE FIRST WORLD WAR WAS A CLASS WAR, FOUGHT BY THE POOR FOR THE RICH.
OVER 100 MILLION MEN WERE SENT TO WAR, AND OVER 25 MILLION HAD BEEN KILLED OR UNACCOUNTED FOR WHEN THE WAR ENDED.
THE SOLDIERS DIDN'T KNOW IT AT THE TIME, BUT THEY WERE FIGHTING NOT FOR LOVE OF COUNTRY, OR THE FREEDOM OF BELGIUM, OR THE DEFENSE OF THE HONOR OF AUSTRO-HUNGARY, THEY WERE FIGHTING TO MAKE A SMALL GROUP OF MILLIONAIRES INTO BILLIONAIRES.
CORPORATE PROFITS LEAPT BY UP TO 900%, CREATING AN ESTIMATED **SIXTEEN BILLION DOLLARS** PROFIT.

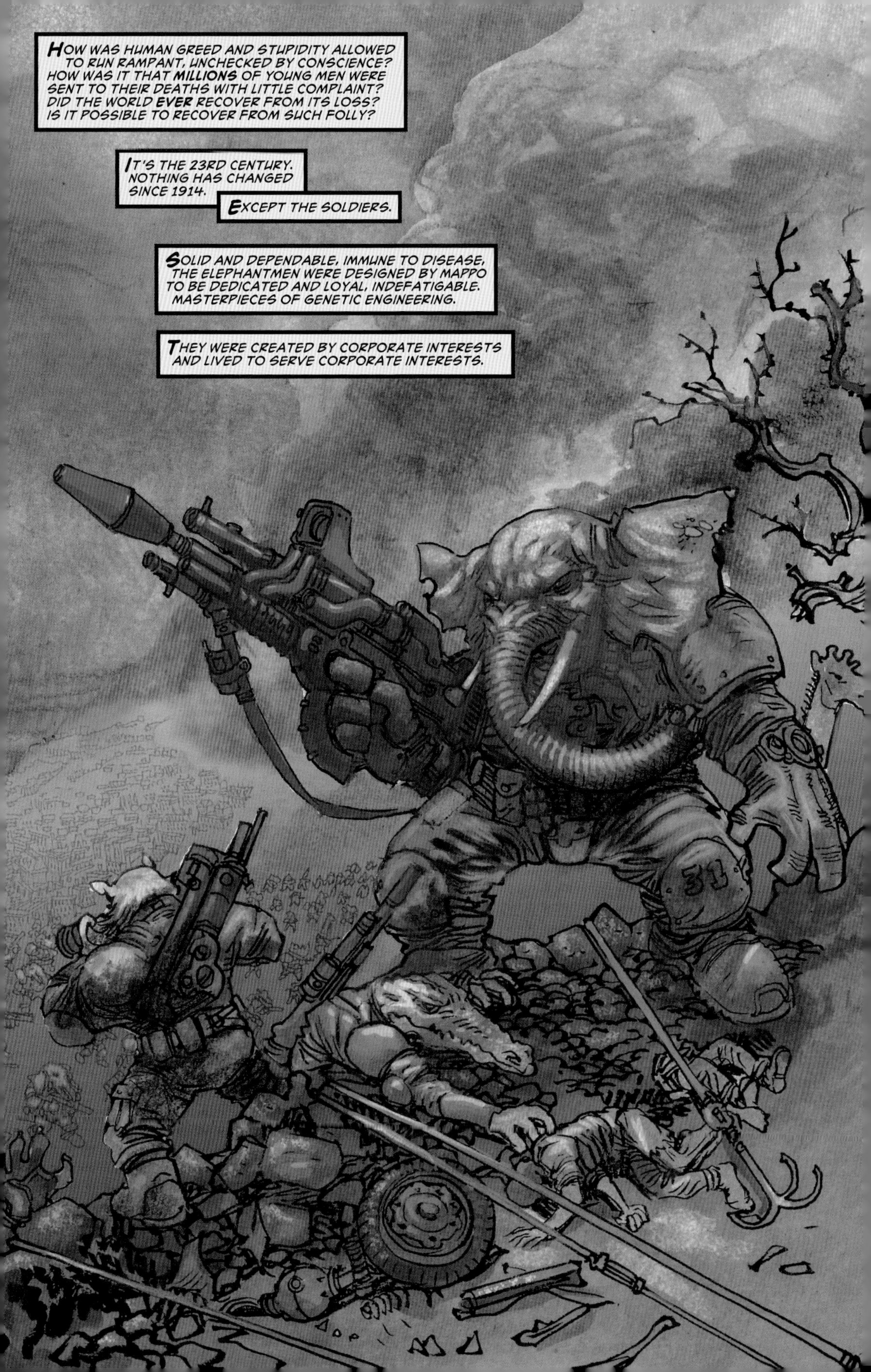
HOW WAS HUMAN GREED AND STUPIDITY ALLOWED TO RUN RAMPANT, UNCHECKED BY CONSCIENCE? HOW WAS IT THAT MILLIONS OF YOUNG MEN WERE SENT TO THEIR DEATHS WITH LITTLE COMPLAINT? DID THE WORLD EVER RECOVER FROM ITS LOSS? IS IT POSSIBLE TO RECOVER FROM SUCH FOLLY?
IT'S THE 23RD CENTURY. NOTHING HAS CHANGED SINCE 1914.
EXCEPT THE SOLDIERS.
SOLID AND DEPENDABLE, IMMUNE TO DISEASE, THE ELEPHANTMEN WERE DESIGNED BY MAPPO TO BE DEDICATED AND LOYAL, INDEFATIGABLE. MASTERPIECES OF GENETIC ENGINEERING.
THEY WERE CREATED BY CORPORATE INTERESTS AND LIVED TO SERVE CORPORATE INTERESTS.

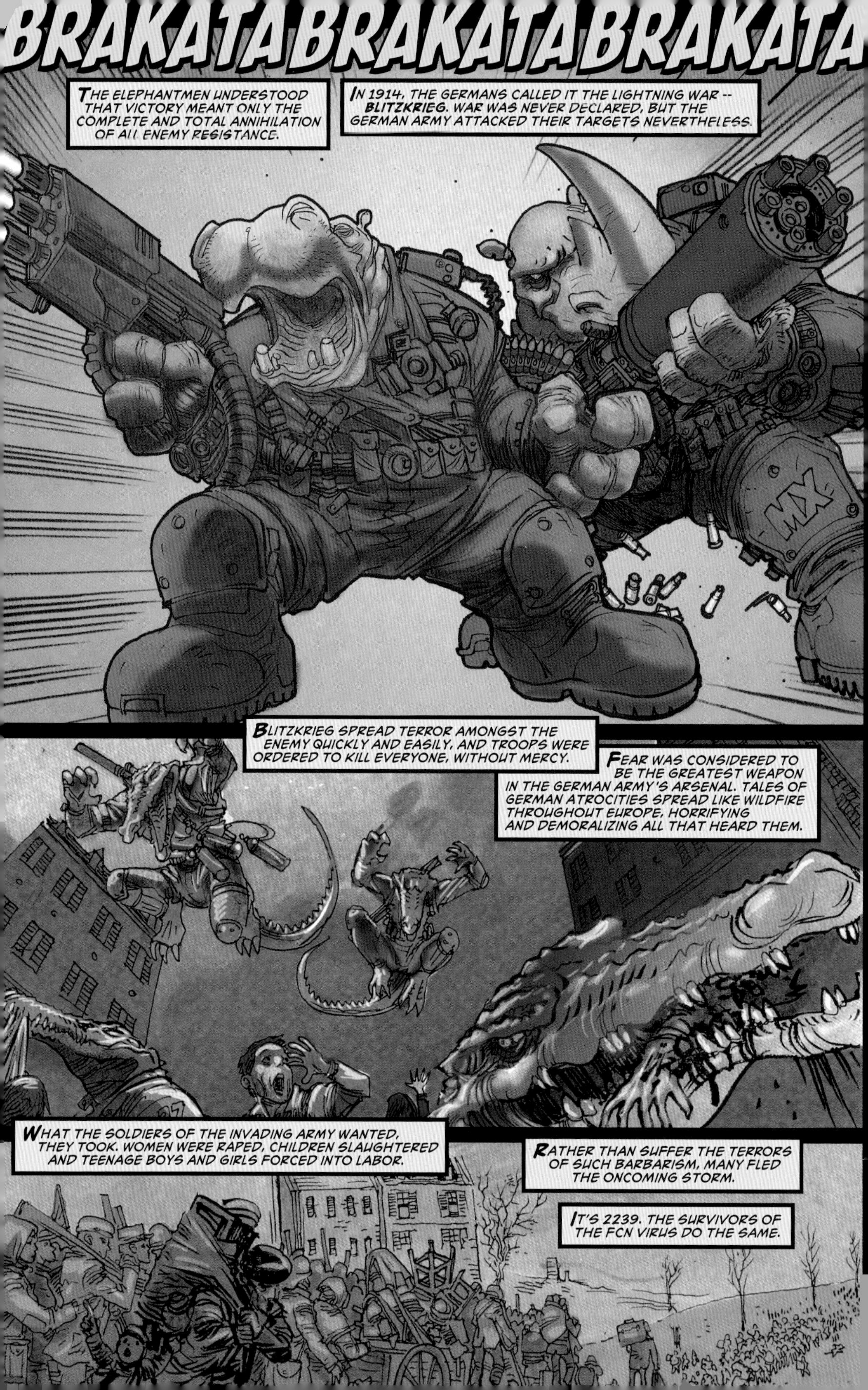
BRAKATA BRAKATA BRAKATA
THE ELEPHANTMEN UNDERSTOOD THAT VICTORY MEANT ONLY THE COMPLETE AND TOTAL ANNIHILATION OF ALL ENEMY RESISTANCE.
IN 1914, THE GERMANS CALLED IT THE LIGHTNING WAR -- BLITZKRIEG. WAR WAS NEVER DECLARED, BUT THE GERMAN ARMY ATTACKED THEIR TARGETS NEVERTHELESS.
MX
BLITZKRIEG SPREAD TERROR AMONGST THE ENEMY QUICKLY AND EASILY, AND TROOPS WERE ORDERED TO KILL EVERYONE, WITHOUT MERCY.
FEAR WAS CONSIDERED TO BE THE GREATEST WEAPON IN THE GERMAN ARMY'S ARSENAL. TALES OF GERMAN ATROCITIES SPREAD LIKE WILDFIRE THROUGHOUT EUROPE, HORRIFYING AND DEMORALIZING ALL THAT HEARD THEM.
WHAT THE SOLDIERS OF THE INVADING ARMY WANTED, THEY TOOK. WOMEN WERE RAPED, CHILDREN SLAUGHTERED AND TEENAGE BOYS AND GIRLS FORCED INTO LABOR.
RATHER THAN SUFFER THE TERRORS OF SUCH BARBARISM, MANY FLED THE ONCOMING STORM.
IT'S 2239. THE SURVIVORS OF THE FCN VIRUS DO THE SAME.

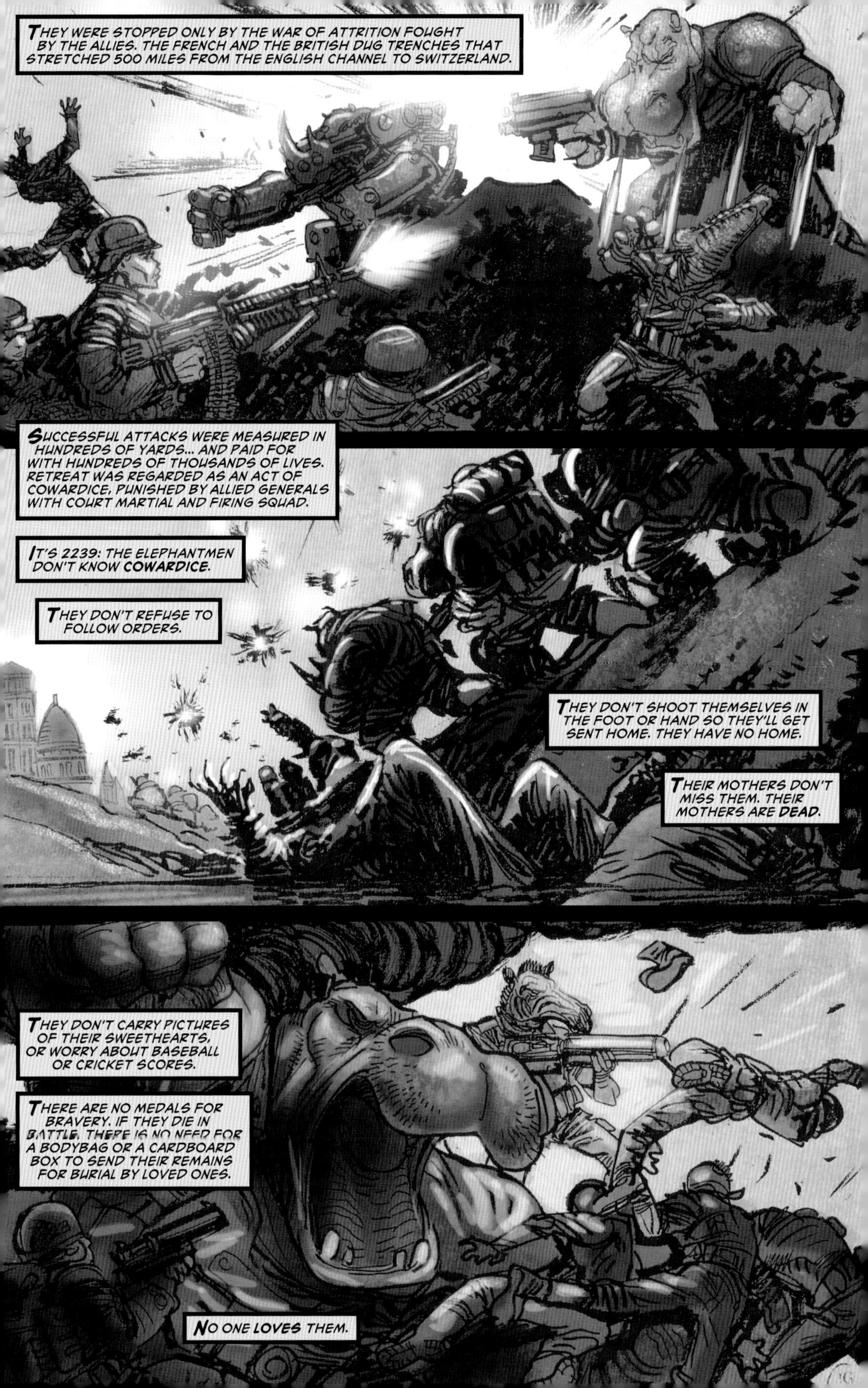
THEY WERE STOPPED ONLY BY THE WAR OF ATTRITION FOUGHT BY THE ALLIES. THE FRENCH AND THE BRITISH DUG TRENCHES THAT STRETCHED 500 MILES FROM THE ENGLISH CHANNEL TO SWITZERLAND.
SUCCESSFUL ATTACKS WERE MEASURED IN HUNDREDS OF YARDS... AND PAID FOR WITH HUNDREDS OF THOUSANDS OF LIVES. RETREAT WAS REGARDED AS AN ACT OF COWARDICE, PUNISHED BY ALLIED GENERALS WITH COURT MARTIAL AND FIRING SQUAD.
IT'S 2239: THE ELEPHANTMEN DON'T KNOW **COWARDICE**.
THEY DON'T REFUSE TO FOLLOW ORDERS.
THEY DON'T SHOOT THEMSELVES IN THE FOOT OR HAND SO THEY'LL GET SENT HOME. THEY HAVE NO HOME.
THEIR MOTHERS DON'T MISS THEM. THEIR MOTHERS ARE **DEAD**.
THEY DON'T CARRY PICTURES OF THEIR SWEETHEARTS, OR WORRY ABOUT BASEBALL OR CRICKET SCORES.
THERE ARE NO MEDALS FOR BRAVERY. IF THEY DIE IN BATTLE, THERE IS NO NEED FOR A BODYBAG OR A CARDBOARD BOX TO SEND THEIR REMAINS FOR BURIAL BY LOVED ONES.
NO ONE **LOVES** THEM.

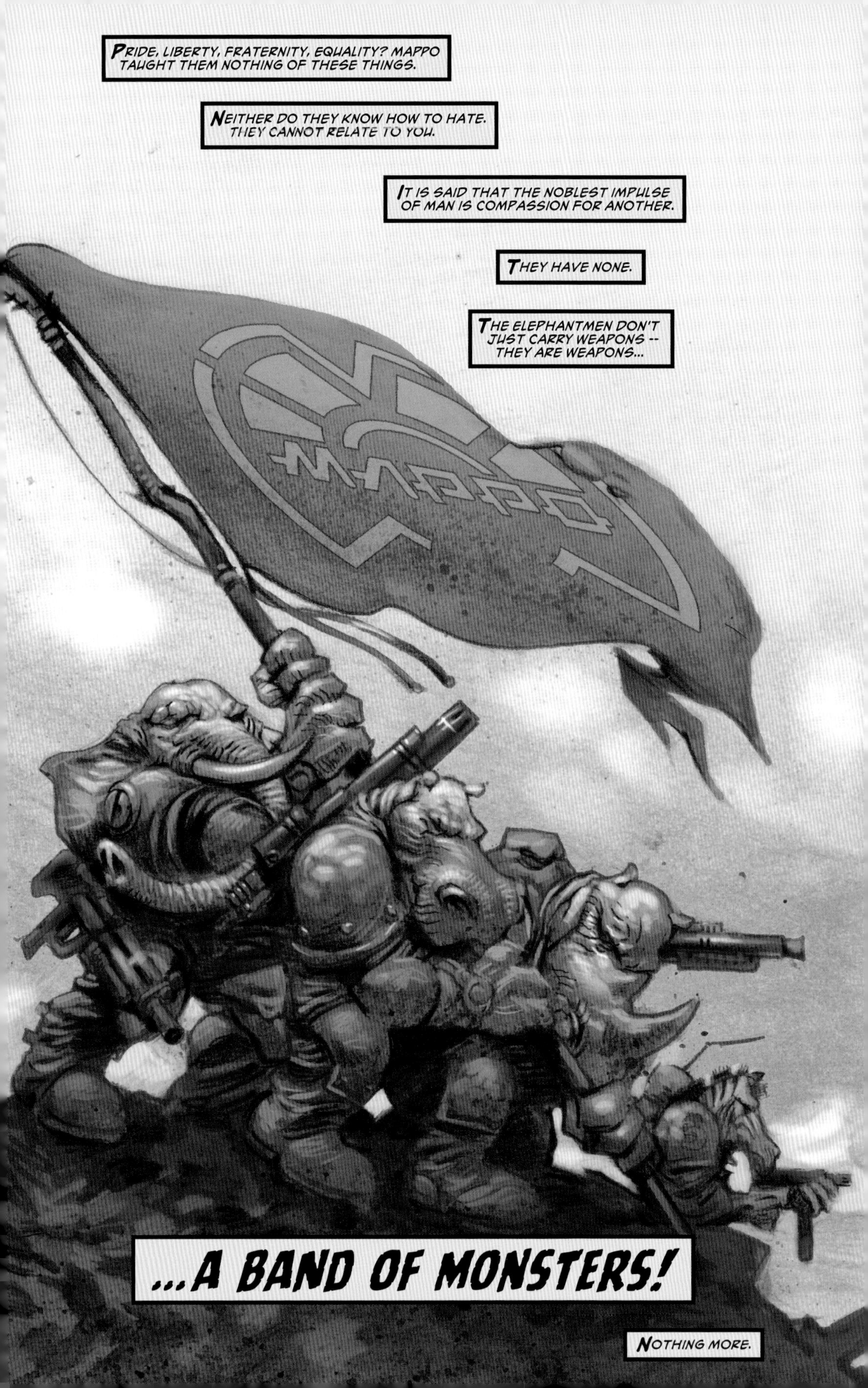
PRIDE, LIBERTY, FRATERNITY, EQUALITY? MAPPO TAUGHT THEM NOTHING OF THESE THINGS.
NEITHER DO THEY KNOW HOW TO HATE. THEY CANNOT RELATE TO YOU.
IT IS SAID THAT THE NOBLEST IMPULSE OF MAN IS COMPASSION FOR ANOTHER.
THEY HAVE NONE.
THE ELEPHANTMEN DON'T JUST CARRY WEAPONS -- THEY ARE WEAPONS...
MAPPO
...A BAND OF MONSTERS!
NOTHING MORE.

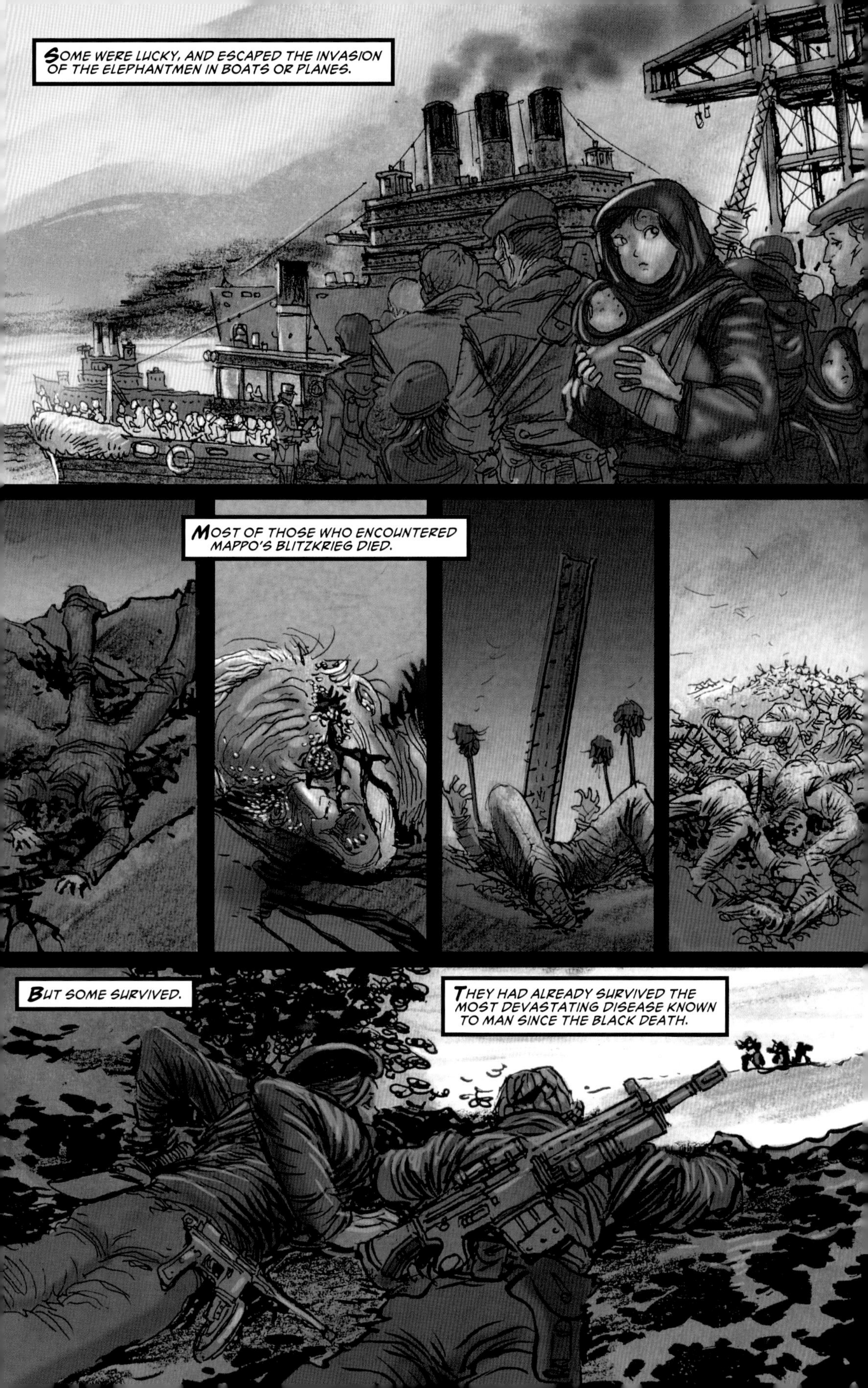
SOME WERE LUCKY, AND ESCAPED THE INVASION OF THE ELEPHANTMEN IN BOATS OR PLANES.
MOST OF THOSE WHO ENCOUNTERED MAPPO'S BLITZKRIEG DIED.
BUT SOME SURVIVED.
THEY HAD ALREADY SURVIVED THE MOST DEVASTATING DISEASE KNOWN TO MAN SINCE THE BLACK DEATH.

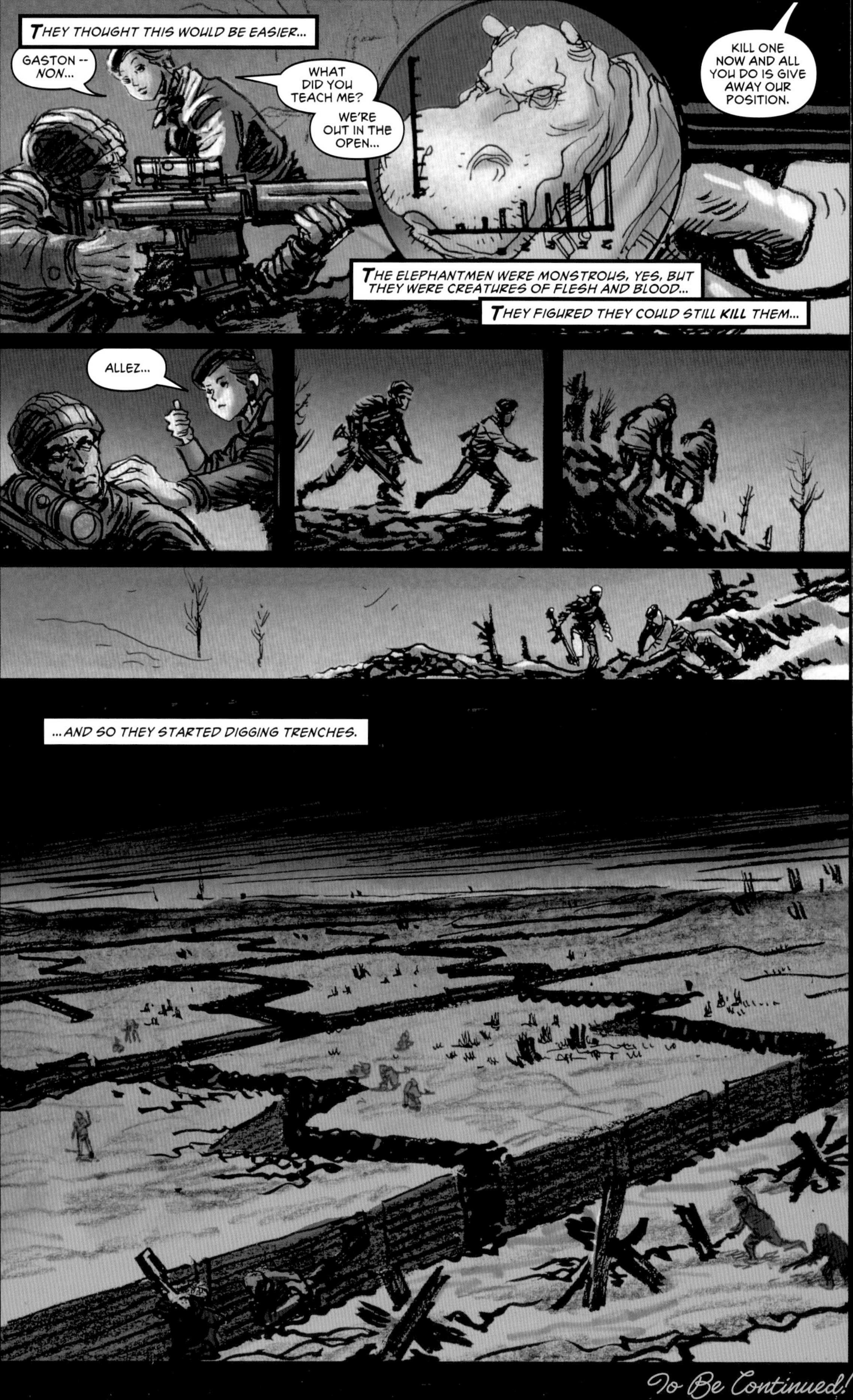
THEY THOUGHT THIS WOULD BE EASIER...
GASTON -- NON...
WHAT DID YOU TEACH ME?
WE'RE OUT IN THE OPEN...
KILL ONE NOW AND ALL YOU DO IS GIVE AWAY OUR POSITION.
THE ELEPHANTMEN WERE MONSTROUS, YES, BUT THEY WERE CREATURES OF FLESH AND BLOOD...
THEY FIGURED THEY COULD STILL KILL THEM...
ALLEZ...
...AND SO THEY STARTED DIGGING TRENCHES.
To Be Continued!

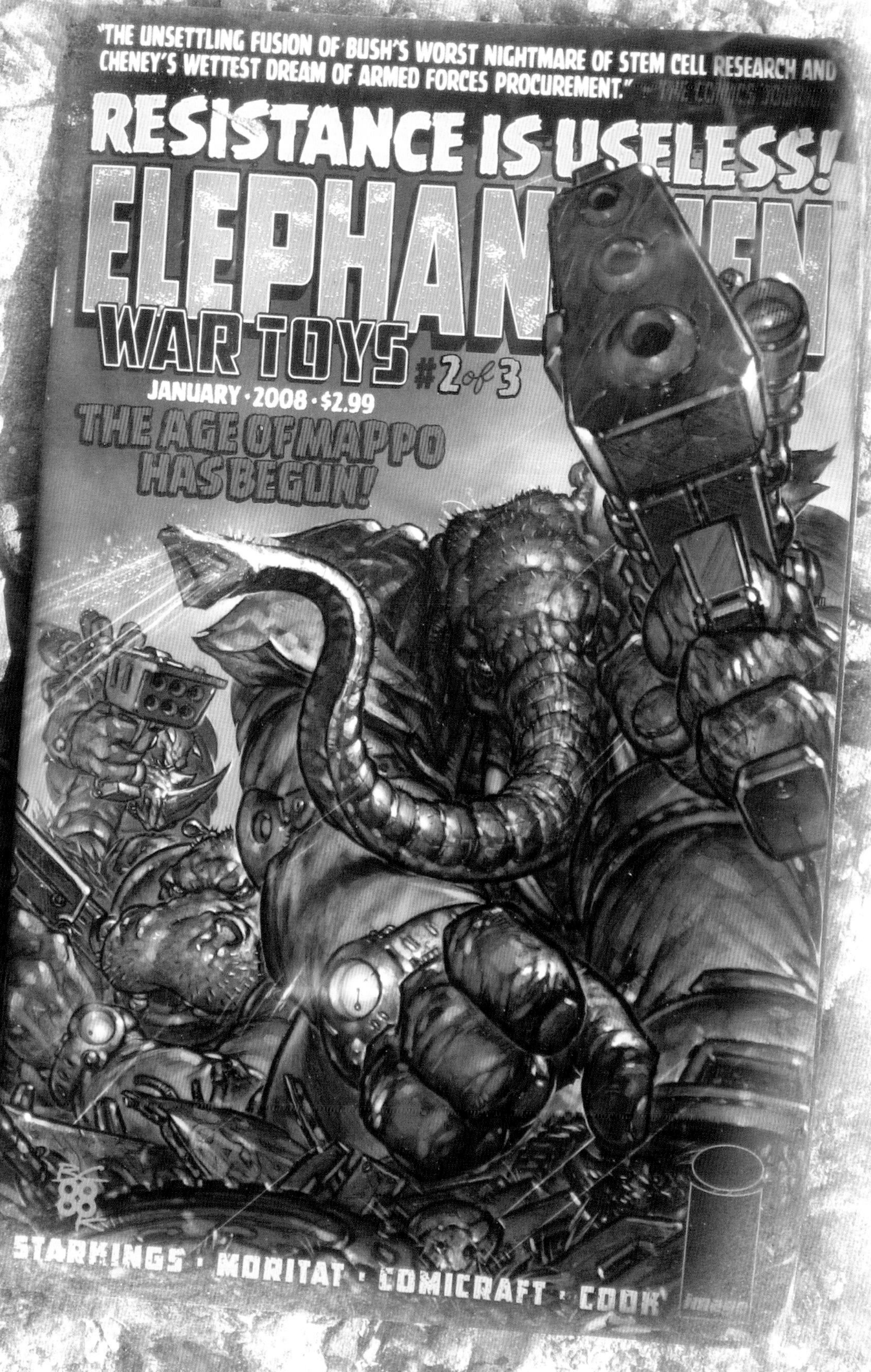

"THE UNSETTLING FUSION OF BUSH'S WORST NIGHTMARE OF STEM CELL RESEARCH AND CHENEY'S WETTEST DREAM OF ARMED FORCES PROCUREMENT." — THE COMICS JOURNAL

RESISTANCE IS USELESS!
ELEPHANTMEN

WAR TOYS #2 of 3

JANUARY · 2008 · $2.99

THE AGE OF MAPPO HAS BEGUN!

STARKINGS · MORITAT · COMICRAFT · COOK

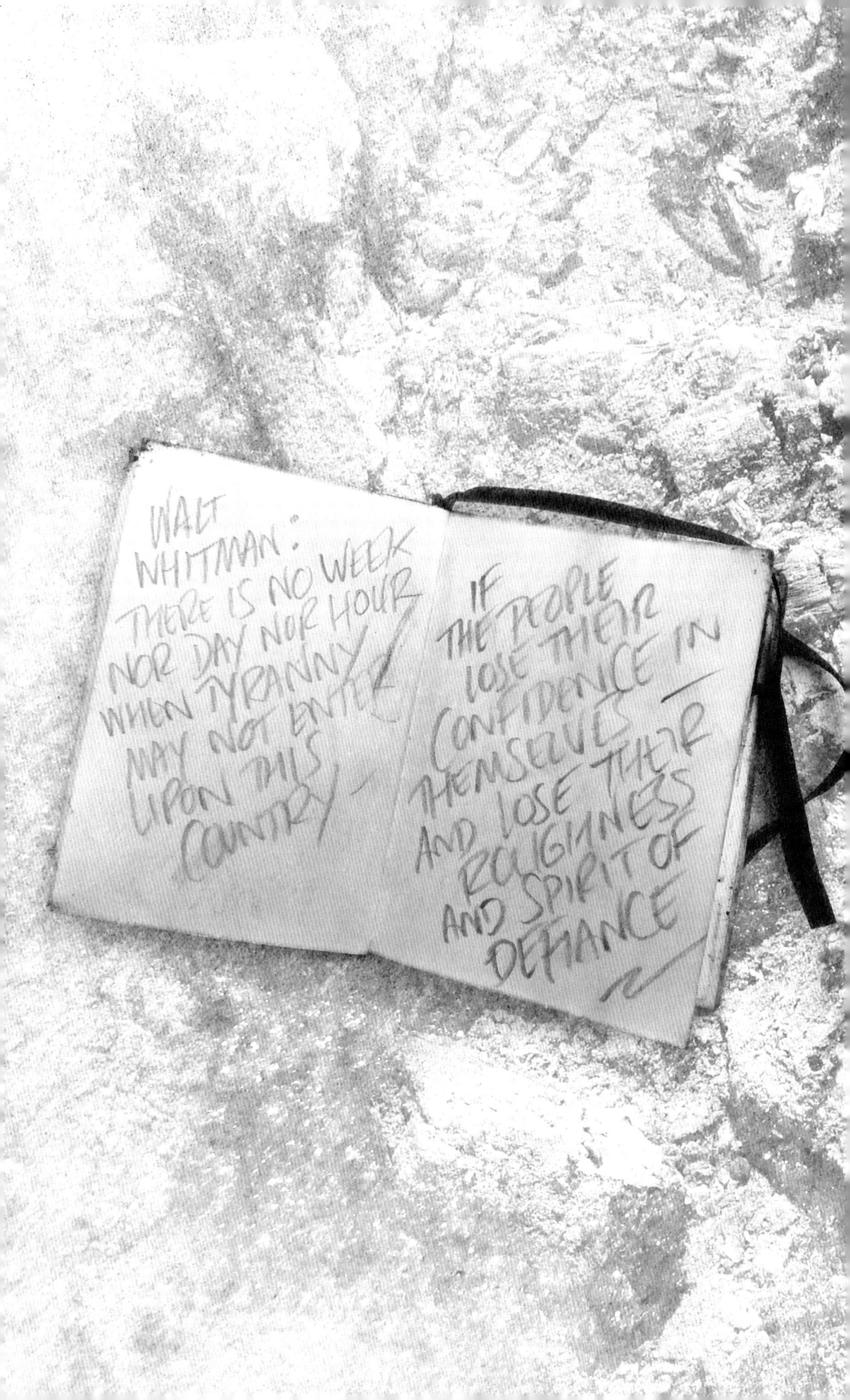
WALT WHITMAN:
THERE IS NO WEEK NOR DAY NOR HOUR WHEN TYRANNY MAY NOT ENTER UPON THIS COUNTRY
IF THE PEOPLE LOSE THEIR CONFIDENCE IN THEMSELVES AND LOSE THEIR ROUGHNESS AND SPIRIT OF DEFIANCE

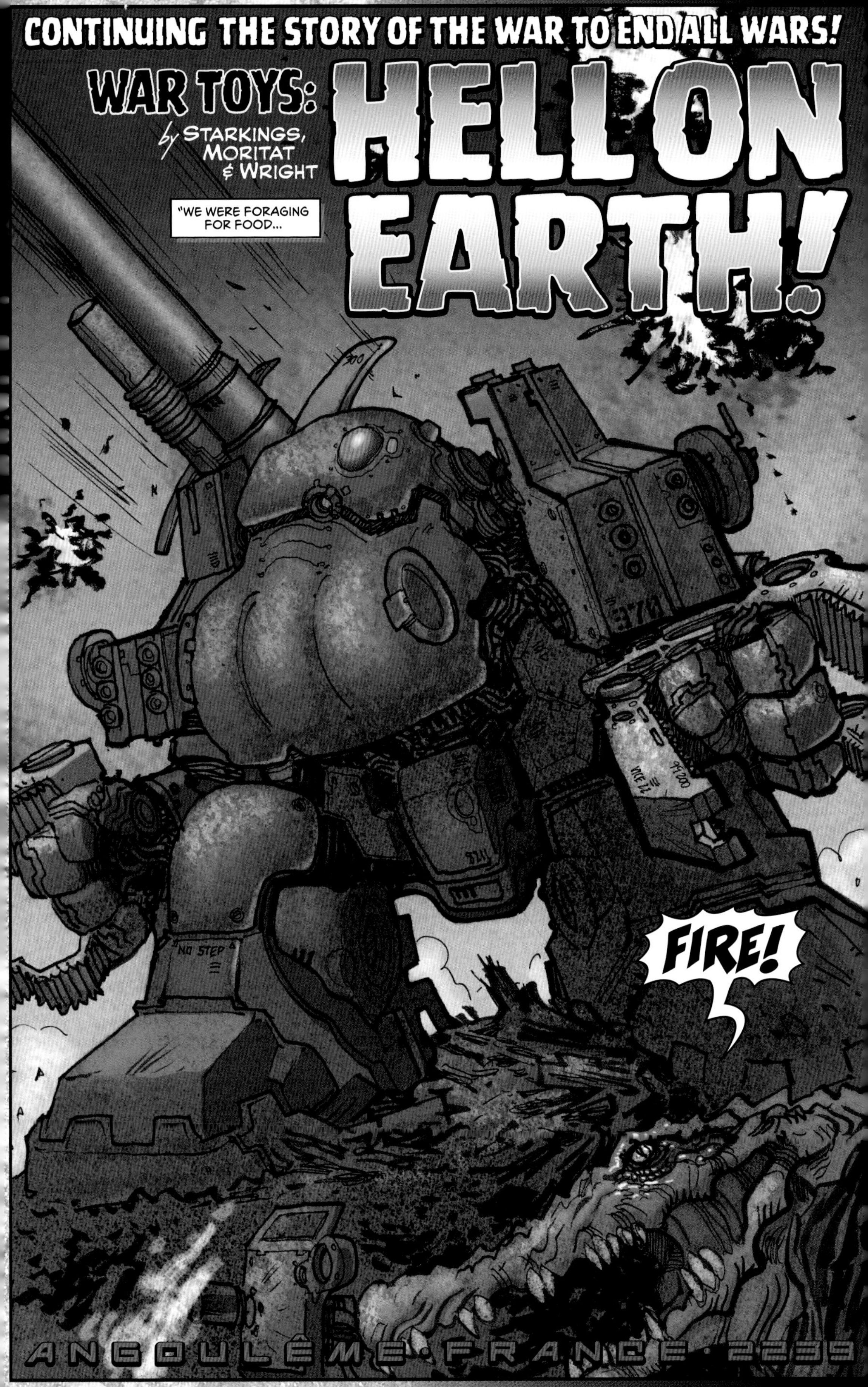
CONTINUING THE STORY OF THE WAR TO END ALL WARS!
WAR TOYS: HELL ON EARTH!
by STARKINGS, MORITAT & WRIGHT
"WE WERE FORAGING FOR FOOD...
NO STEP
FIRE!
ANGOULÊME • FRANCE • 2239

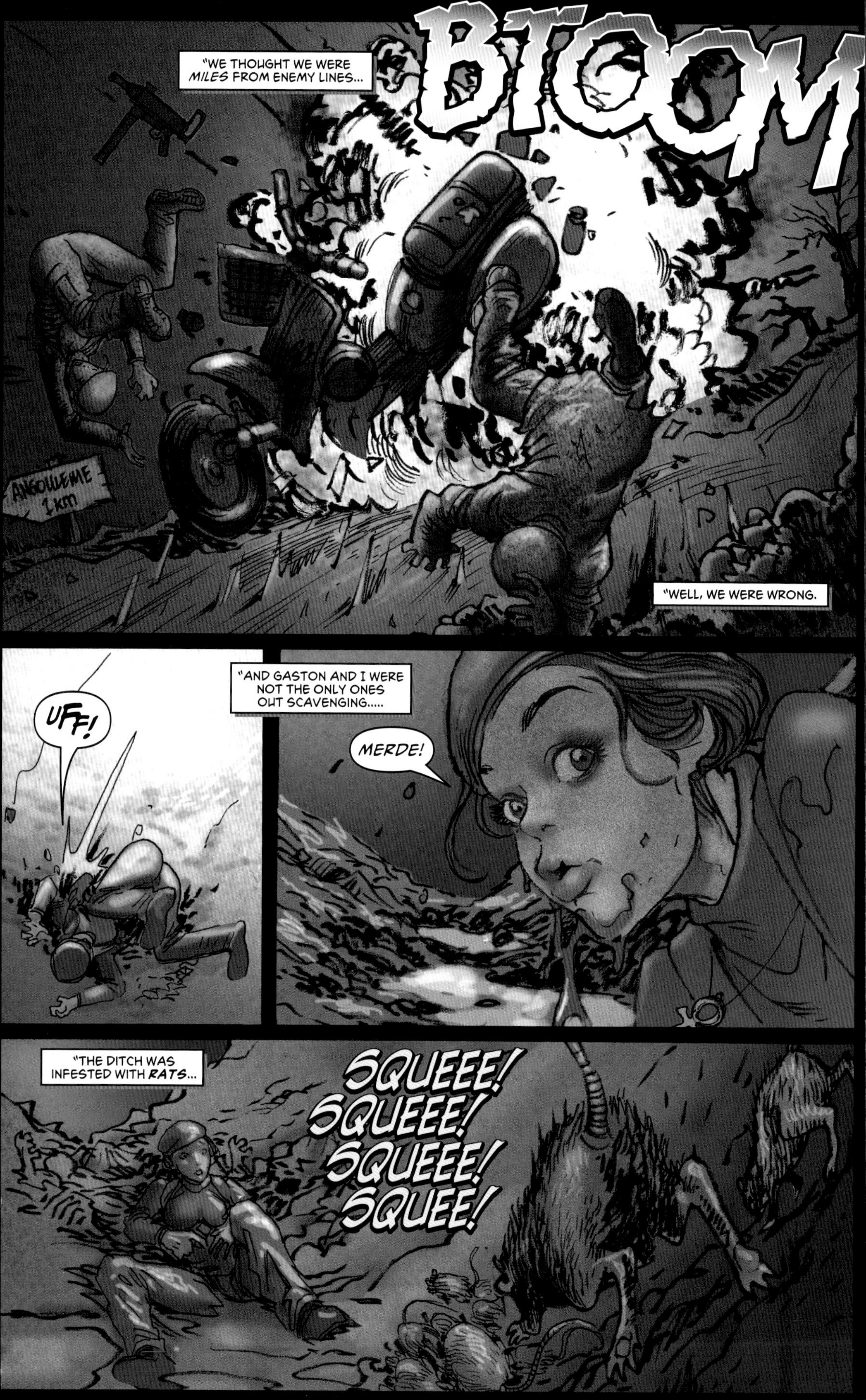
"WE THOUGHT WE WERE MILES FROM ENEMY LINES...
BTOOM
ANGOULEME 1 km
"WELL, WE WERE WRONG.
UFF!
"AND GASTON AND I WERE NOT THE ONLY ONES OUT SCAVENGING.....
MERDE!
"THE DITCH WAS INFESTED WITH RATS...
SQUEEE! SQUEEE! SQUEEE! SQUEE!

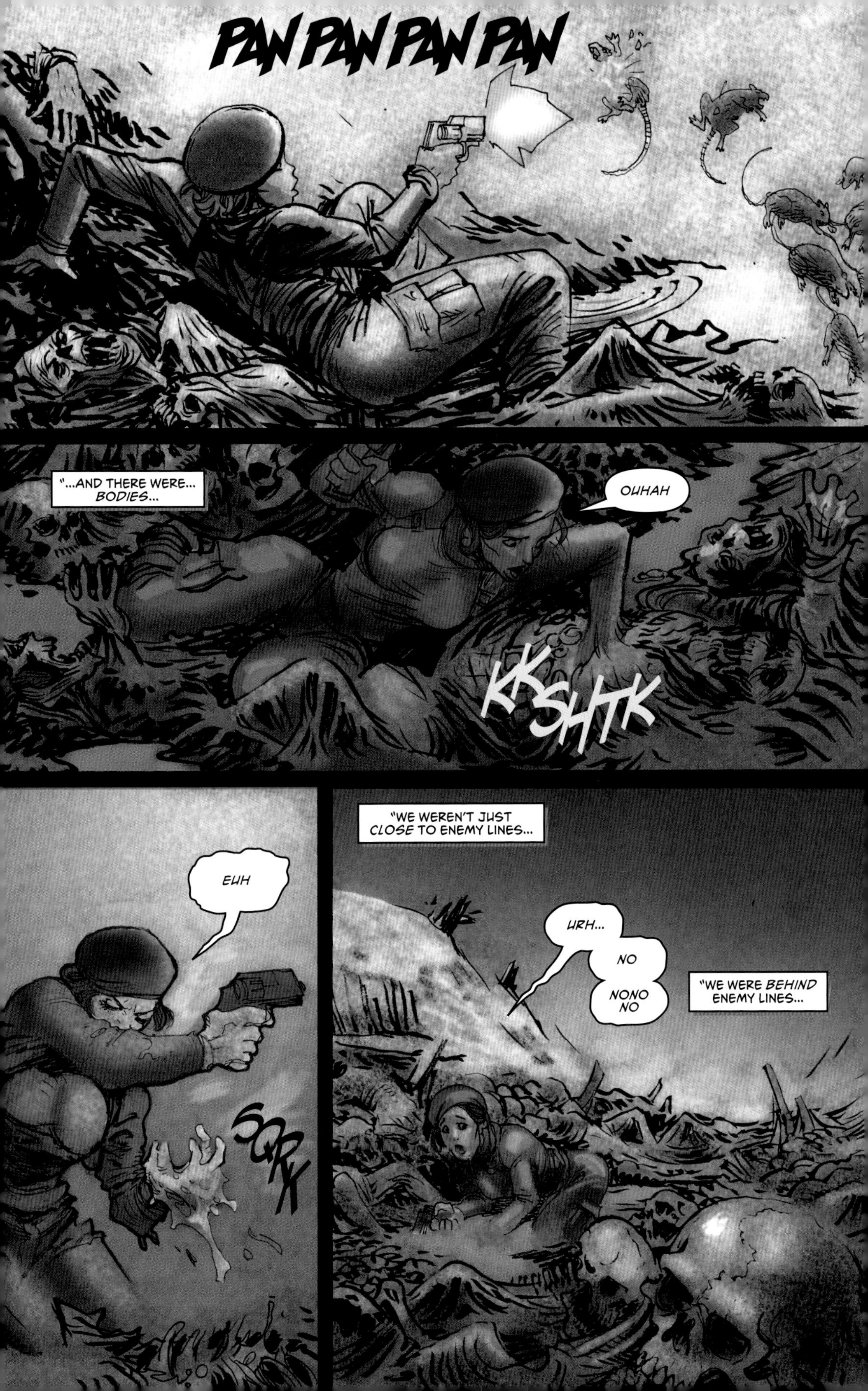
PAN PAN PAN PAN
"...AND THERE WERE... BODIES...
OUHAH
KKSHTK
EUH
SQRK
"WE WEREN'T JUST CLOSE TO ENEMY LINES...
URH...
NO
NONO NO
"WE WERE BEHIND ENEMY LINES...

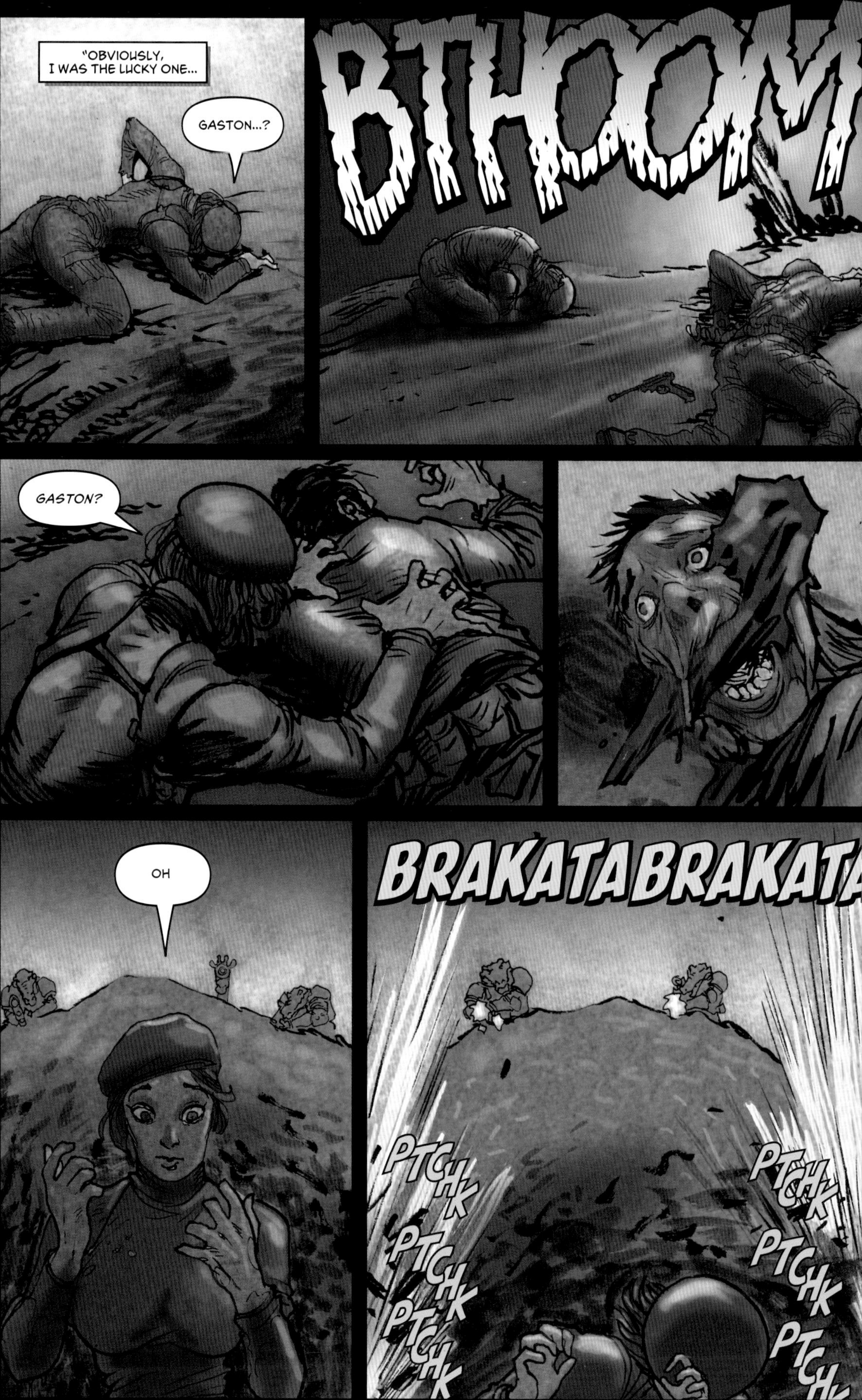
"OBVIOUSLY,
I WAS THE LUCKY ONE...
GASTON...?
BTHOOM
GASTON?
OH
BRAKATABRAKATA
PTCHK
PTCHK
PTCHK
PTCHK
PTCHK
PTCHK

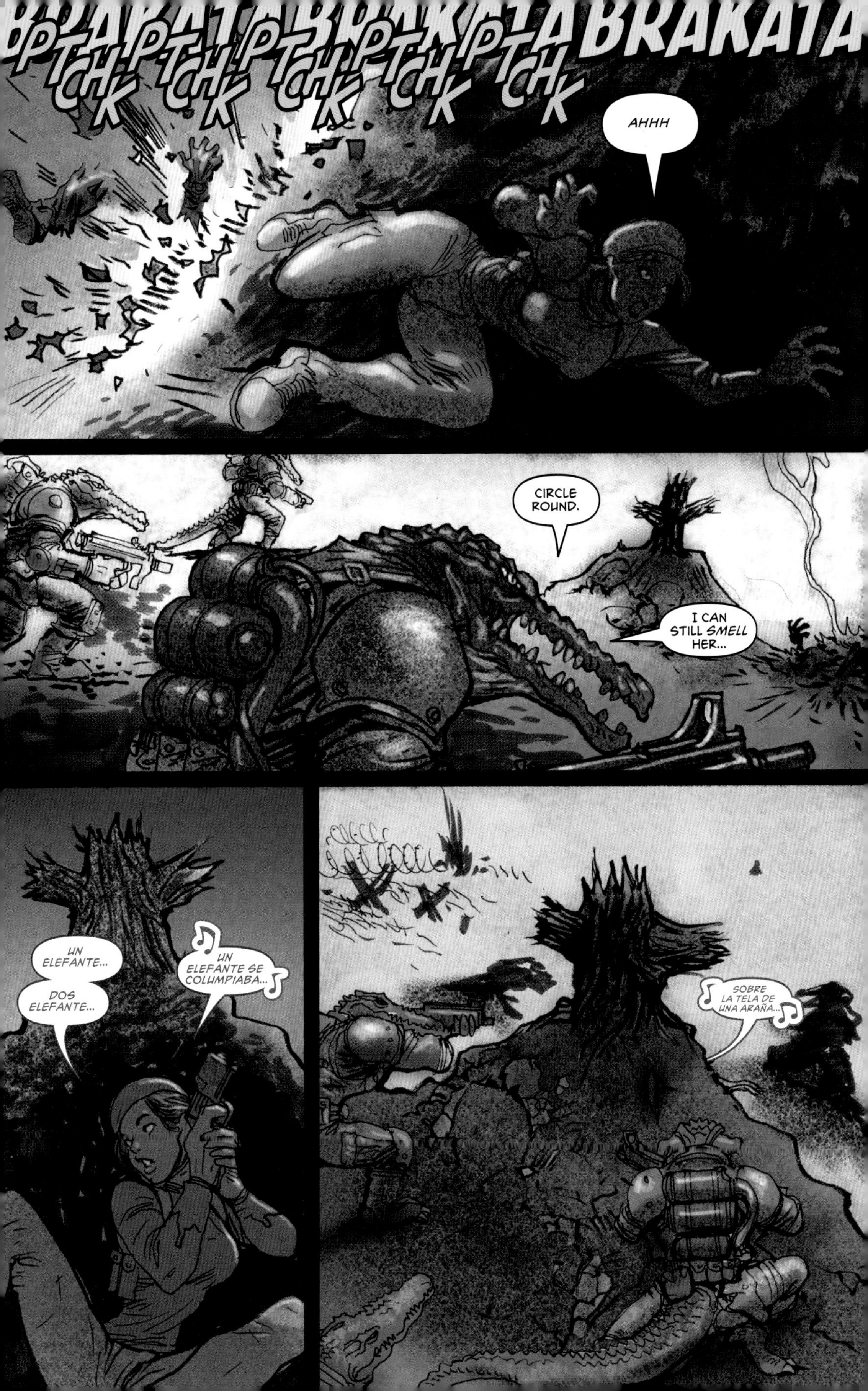
BRAKATA BRAKATA BRAKATA
PTCHK PTCHK PTCHK PTCHK PTCHK
AHHH
CIRCLE ROUND.
I CAN STILL SMELL HER...
UN ELEFANTE...
DOS ELEFANTE...
UN ELEFANTE SE COLUMPIABA...
SOBRE LA TELA DE UNA ARAÑA...

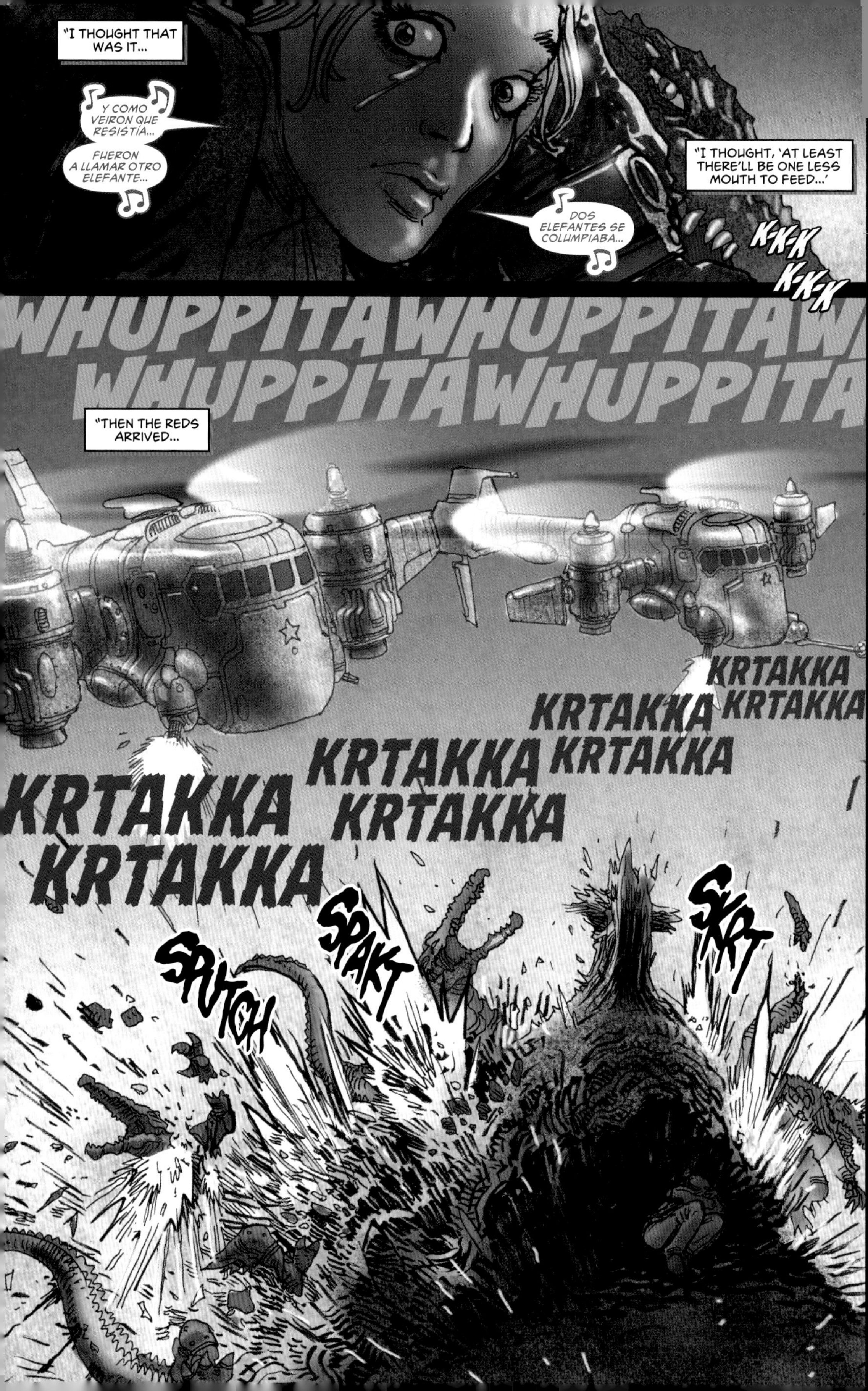
"I THOUGHT THAT WAS IT...
Y COMO VEIRON QUE RESISTÍA...
FUERON A LLAMAR OTRO ELEFANTE...
"I THOUGHT, 'AT LEAST THERE'LL BE ONE LESS MOUTH TO FEED...'
DOS ELEFANTES SE COLUMPIABA...
K-K-K
K-K-K
WHUPPITAWHUPPITAW
WHUPPITAWHUPPITA
"THEN THE REDS ARRIVED...
KRTAKKA
KRTAKKA
KRTAKKA
KRTAKKA
KRTAKKA
KRTAKKA
KRTAKKA
KRTAKKA
SPLUTCH
SPAKT
SKRT

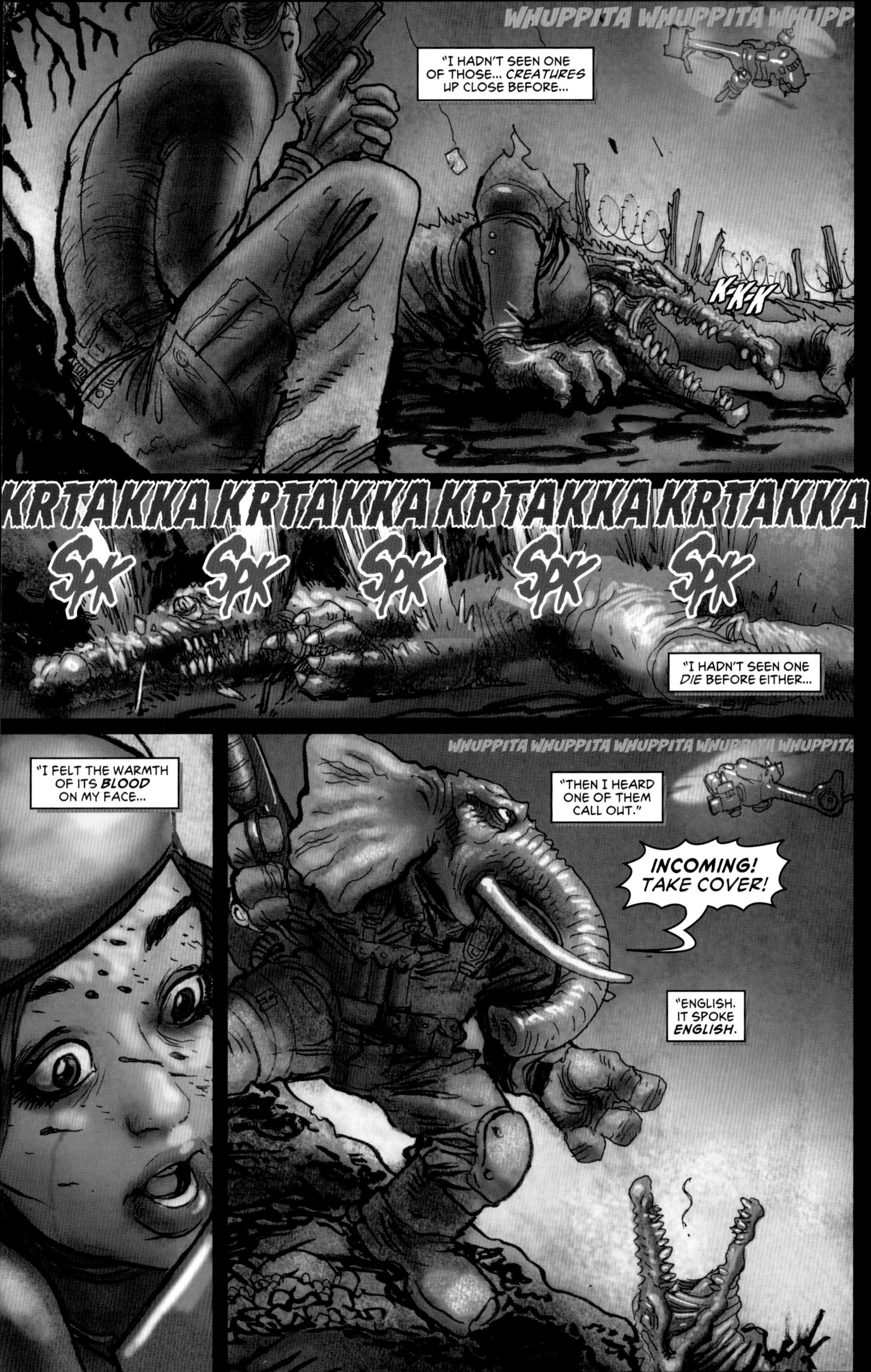
WHUPPITA WHUPPITA WHUPP
"I HADN'T SEEN ONE OF THOSE... CREATURES UP CLOSE BEFORE...
K-K-K
KRTAKKA KRTAKKA KRTAKKA KRTAKKA
SPK SPK SPK SPK SPK
"I HADN'T SEEN ONE DIE BEFORE EITHER...
"I FELT THE WARMTH OF ITS BLOOD ON MY FACE...
WHUPPITA WHUPPITA WHUPPITA WHUPPITA WHUPPITA
"THEN I HEARD ONE OF THEM CALL OUT."
INCOMING! TAKE COVER!
"ENGLISH. IT SPOKE ENGLISH.

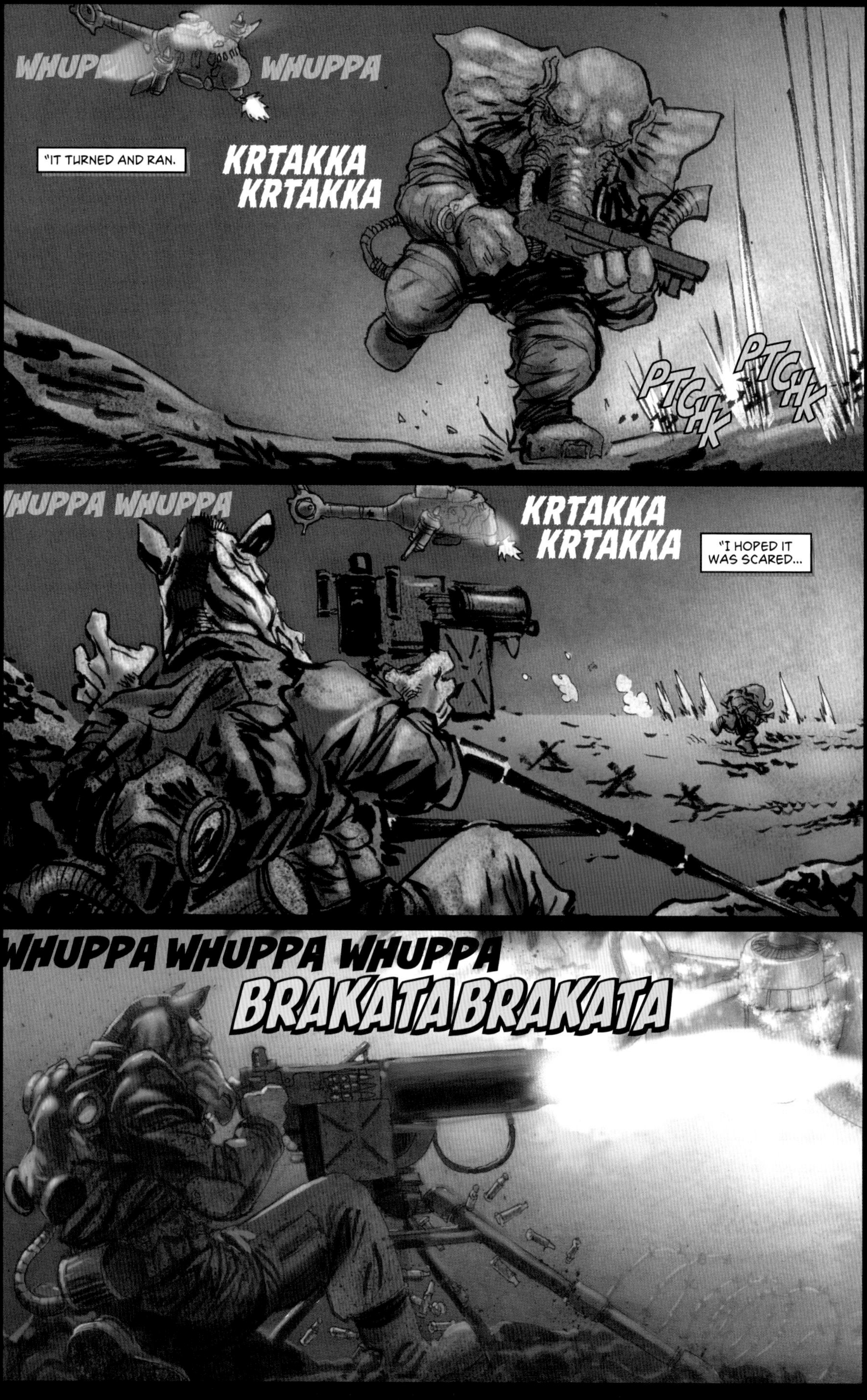
WHUPPA WHUPPA
"IT TURNED AND RAN.
KRTAKKA KRTAKKA
PTCHK PTCHK
WHUPPA WHUPPA
KRTAKKA KRTAKKA
"I HOPED IT WAS SCARED...
WHUPPA WHUPPA WHUPPA
BRAKATA BRAKATA

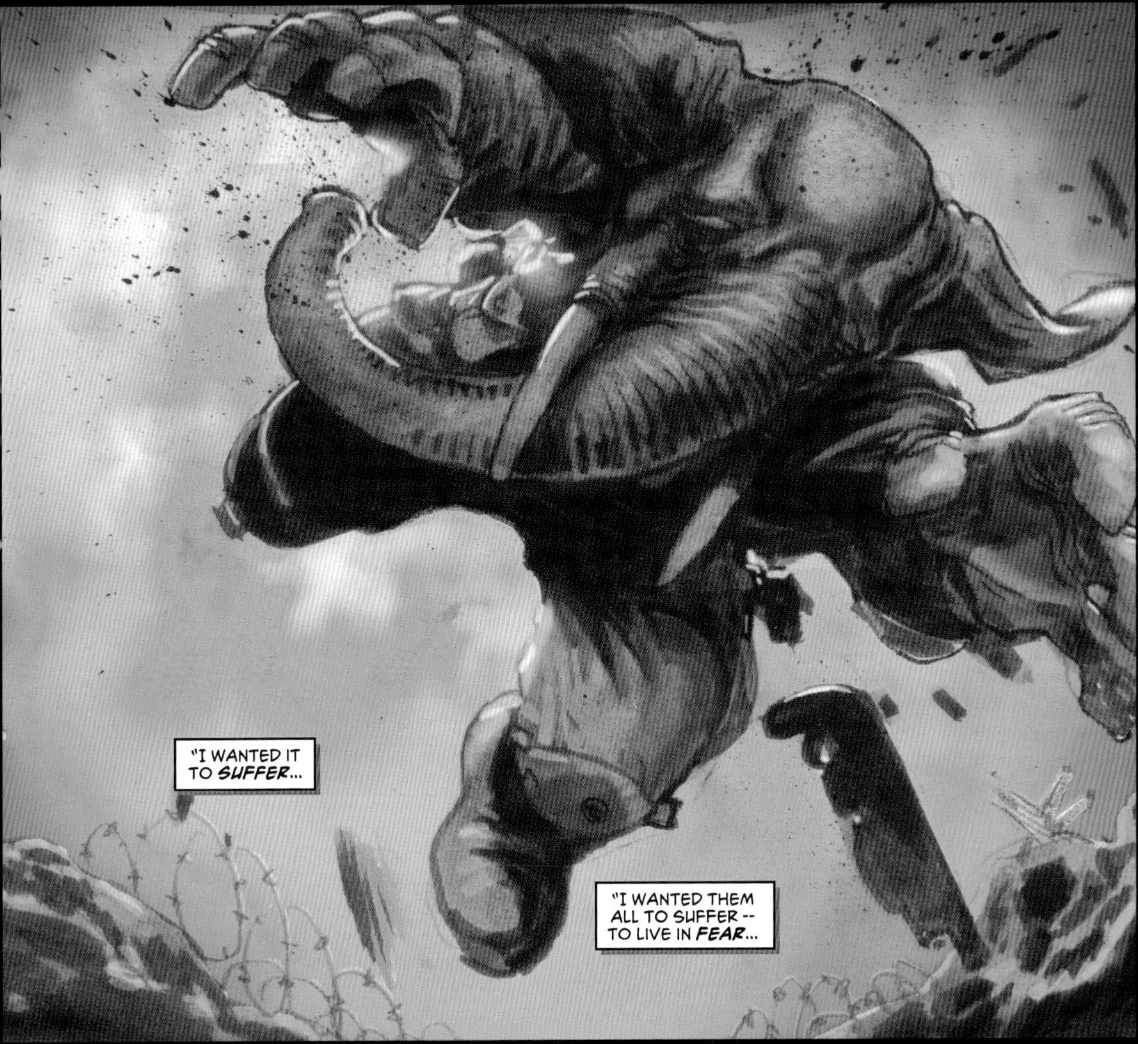
"I WANTED IT TO *SUFFER*...
"I WANTED THEM ALL TO SUFFER -- TO LIVE IN *FEAR*...

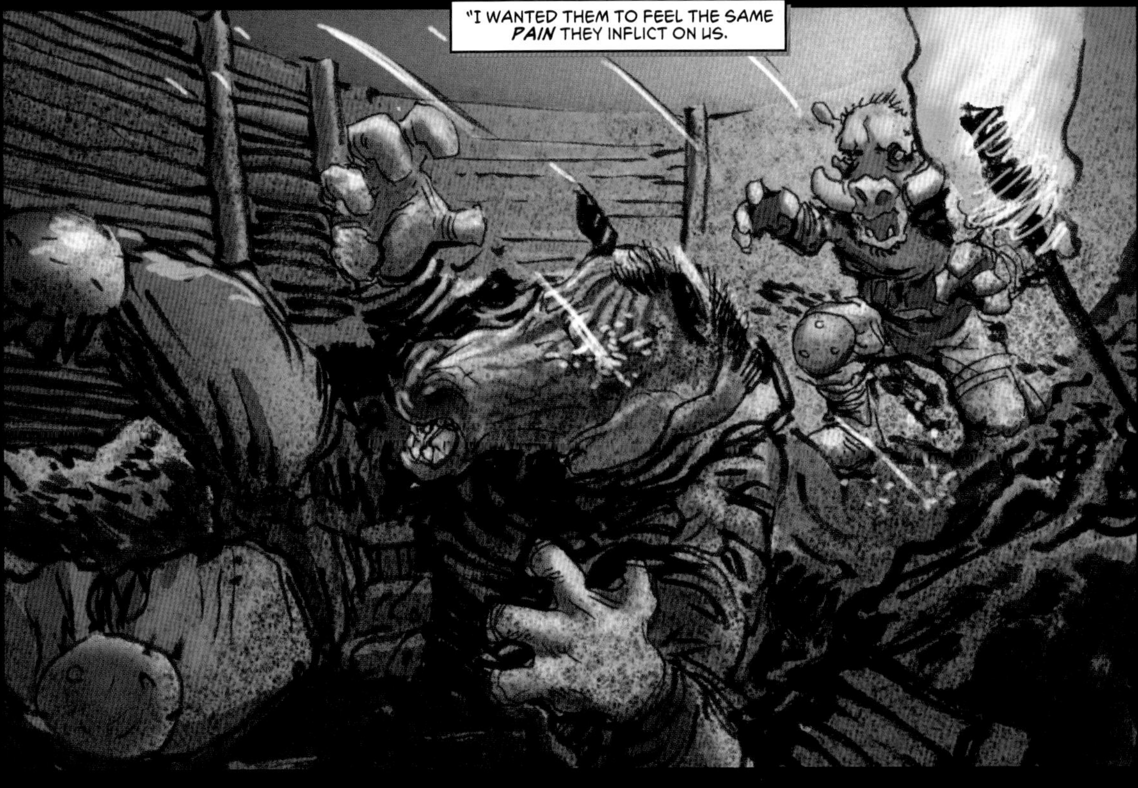
"I WANTED THEM TO FEEL THE SAME *PAIN* THEY INFLICT ON US.

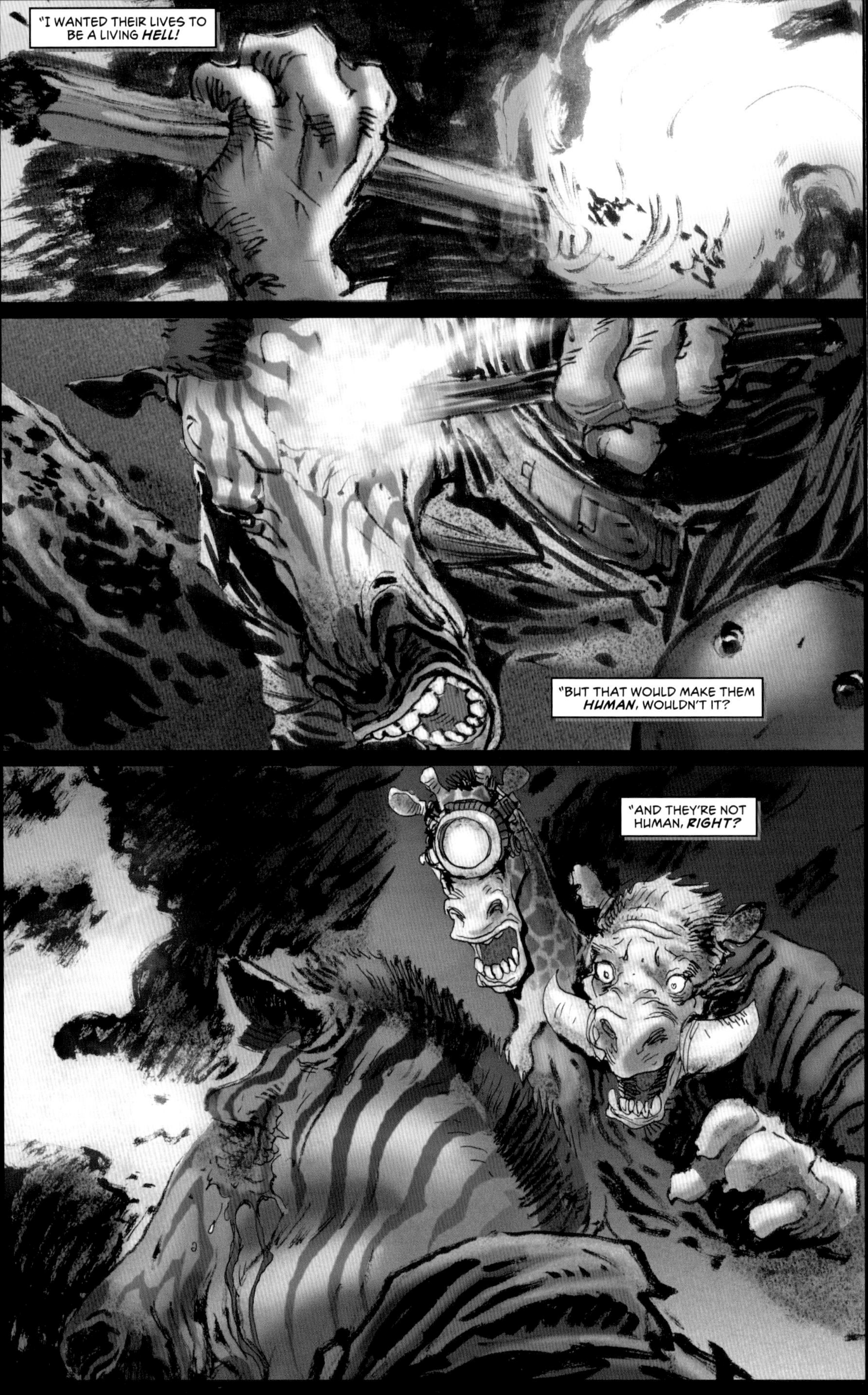
"I WANTED THEIR LIVES TO BE A LIVING HELL!
"BUT THAT WOULD MAKE THEM HUMAN, WOULDN'T IT?
"AND THEY'RE NOT HUMAN, RIGHT?

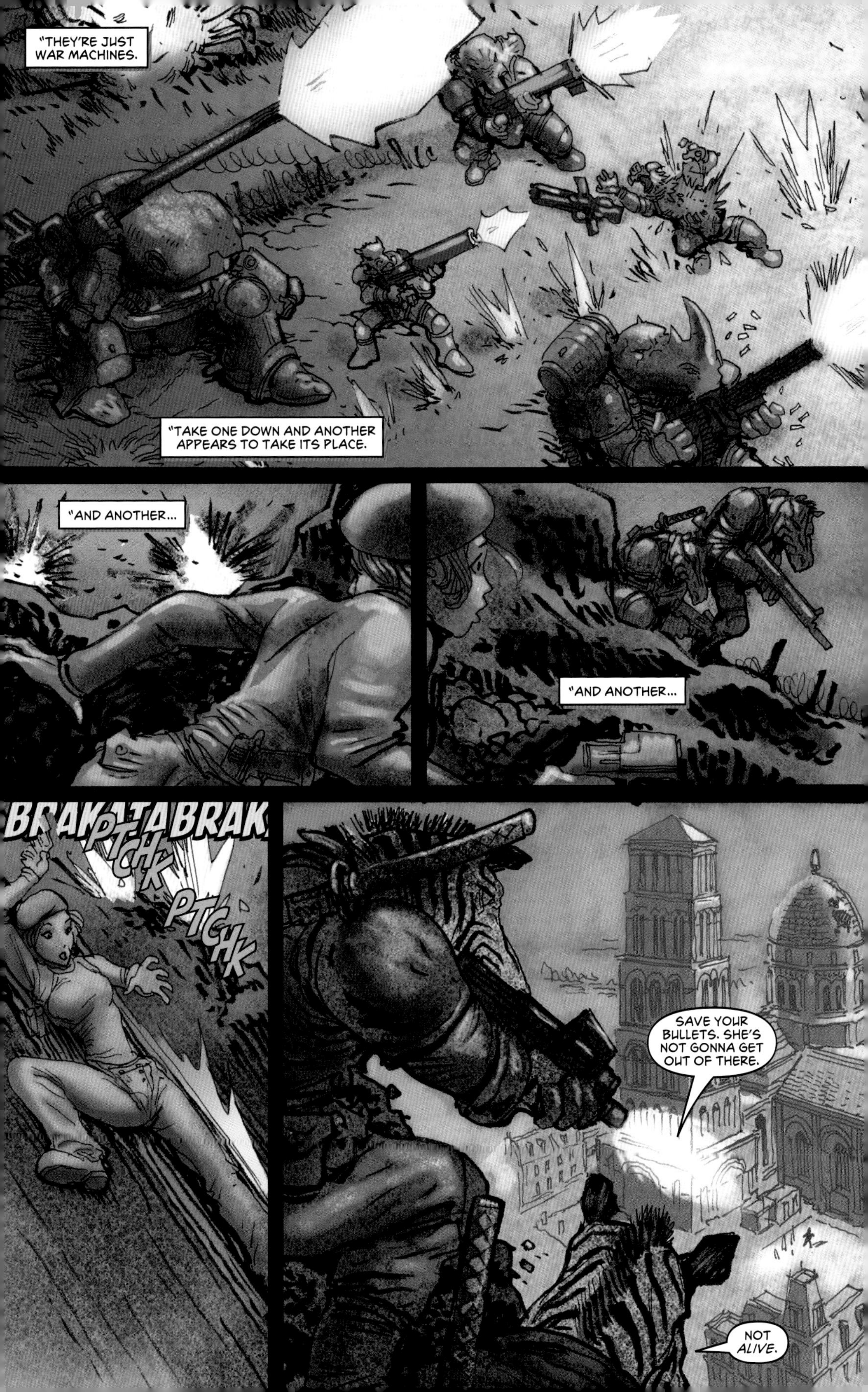
"THEY'RE JUST WAR MACHINES.
"TAKE ONE DOWN AND ANOTHER APPEARS TO TAKE ITS PLACE.
"AND ANOTHER...
"AND ANOTHER...
BRAKATABRAK
PTCHK
PTCHK
SAVE YOUR BULLETS. SHE'S NOT GONNA GET OUT OF THERE.
NOT ALIVE.

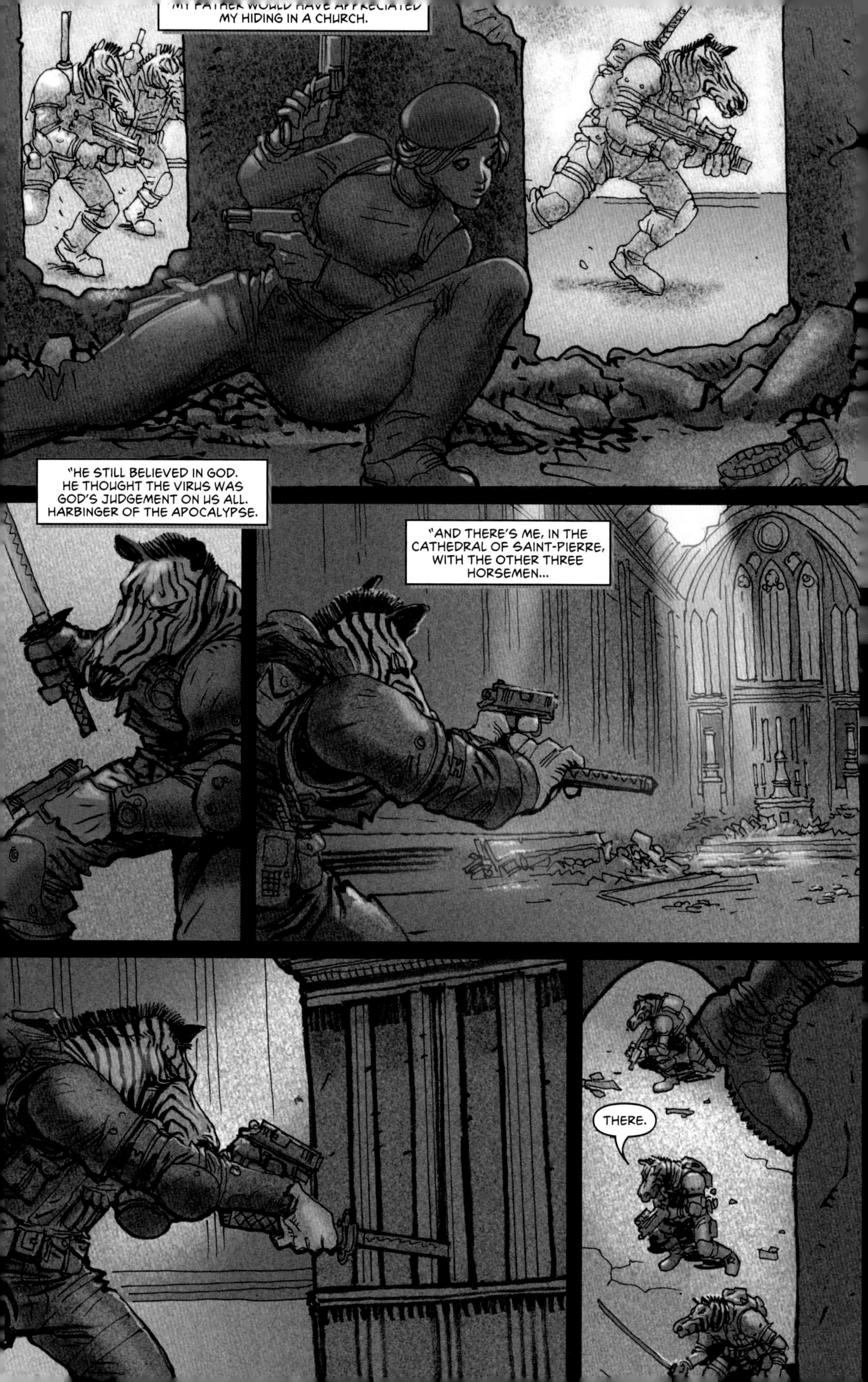
"MY FATHER WOULD HAVE APPRECIATED MY HIDING IN A CHURCH.
"HE STILL BELIEVED IN GOD. HE THOUGHT THE VIRUS WAS GOD'S JUDGEMENT ON US ALL. HARBINGER OF THE APOCALYPSE.
"AND THERE'S ME, IN THE CATHEDRAL OF SAINT-PIERRE, WITH THE OTHER THREE HORSEMEN...
THERE.

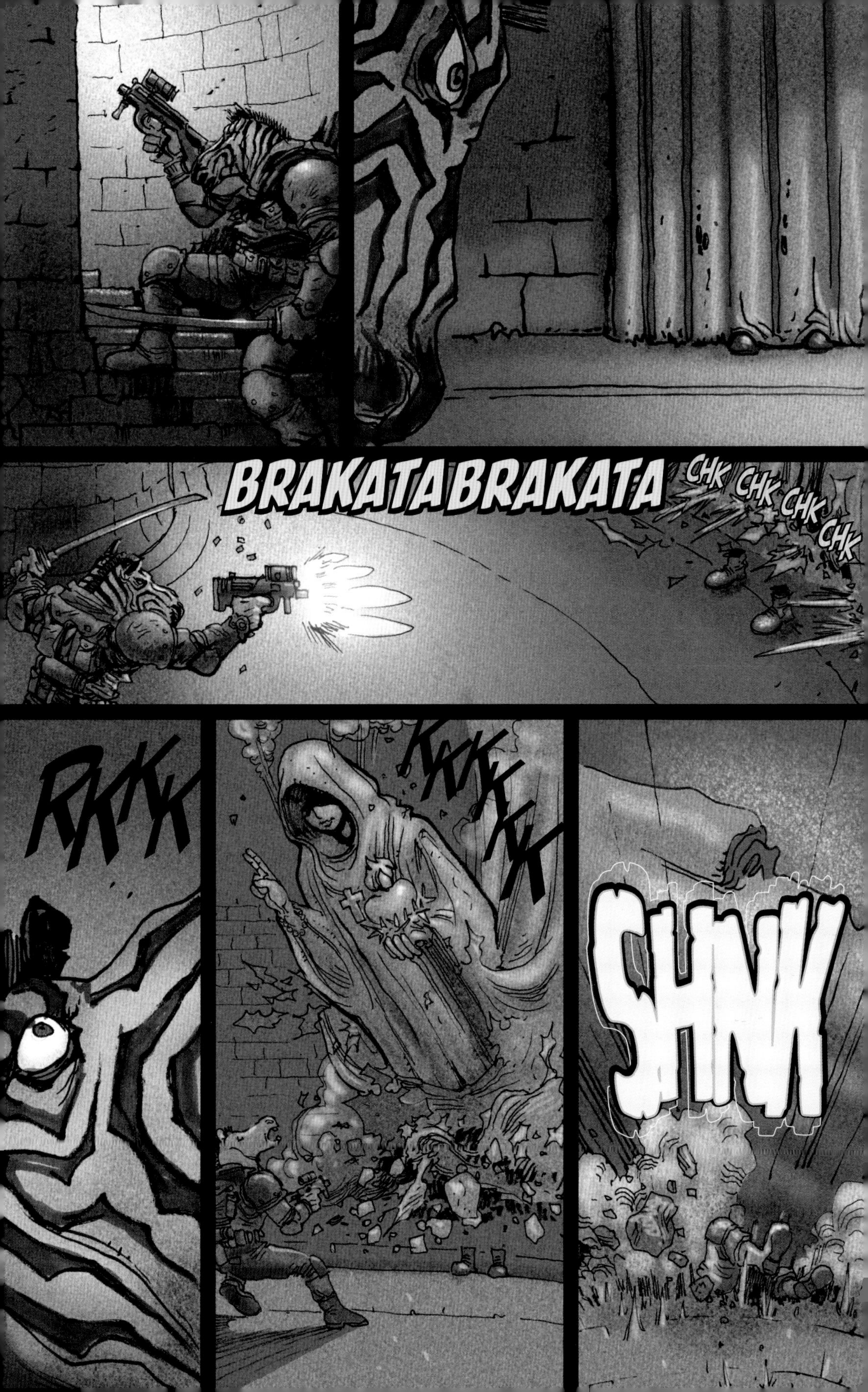
BRAKATABRAKATA
CHK CHK CHK CHK
RKKK
KKKKKK
SHNK

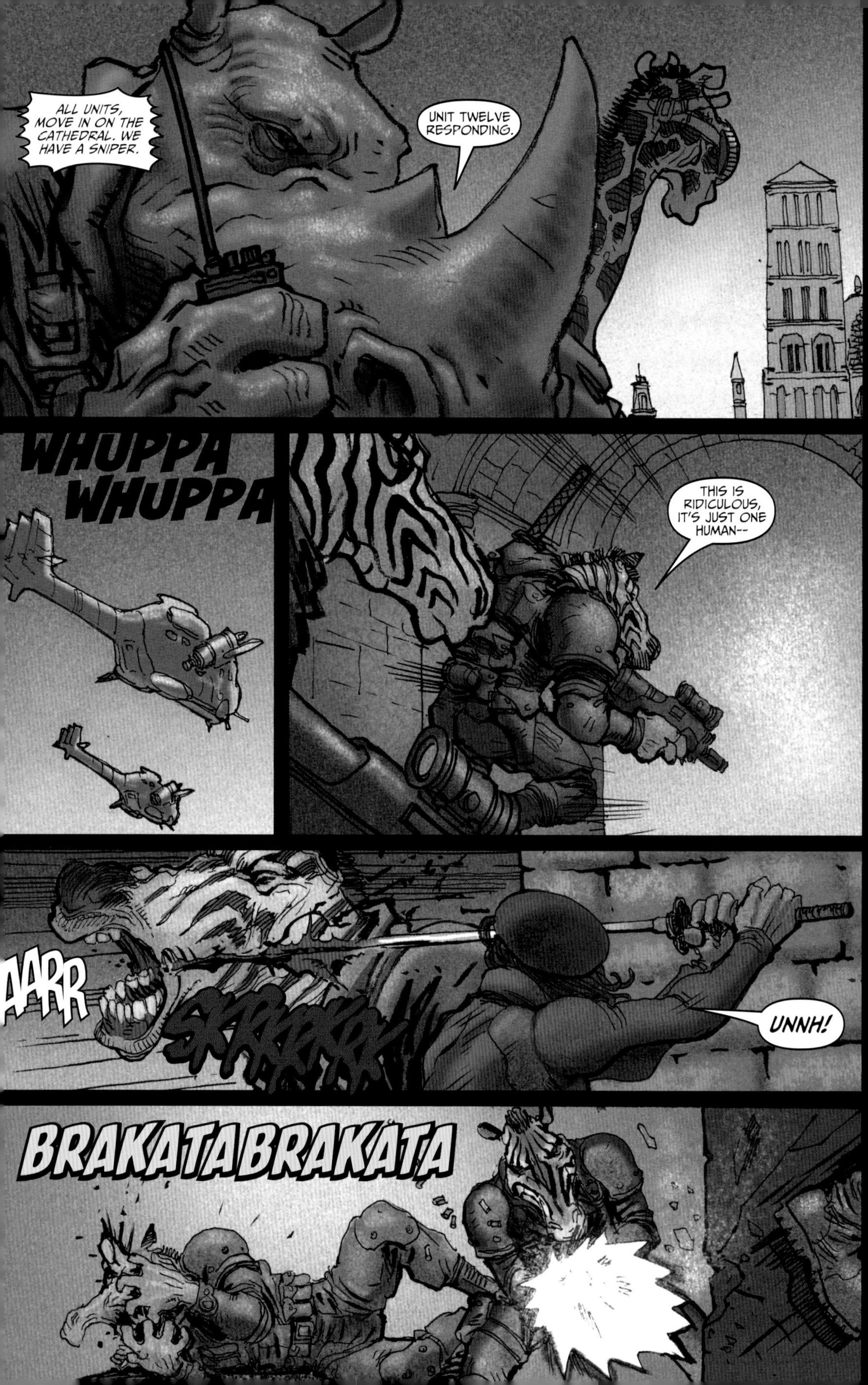
ALL UNITS, MOVE IN ON THE CATHEDRAL. WE HAVE A SNIPER.
UNIT TWELVE RESPONDING.
WHUPPA WHUPPA
THIS IS RIDICULOUS, IT'S JUST ONE HUMAN--
AARR
SKRKRKRK
UNNH!
BRAKATABRAKATA

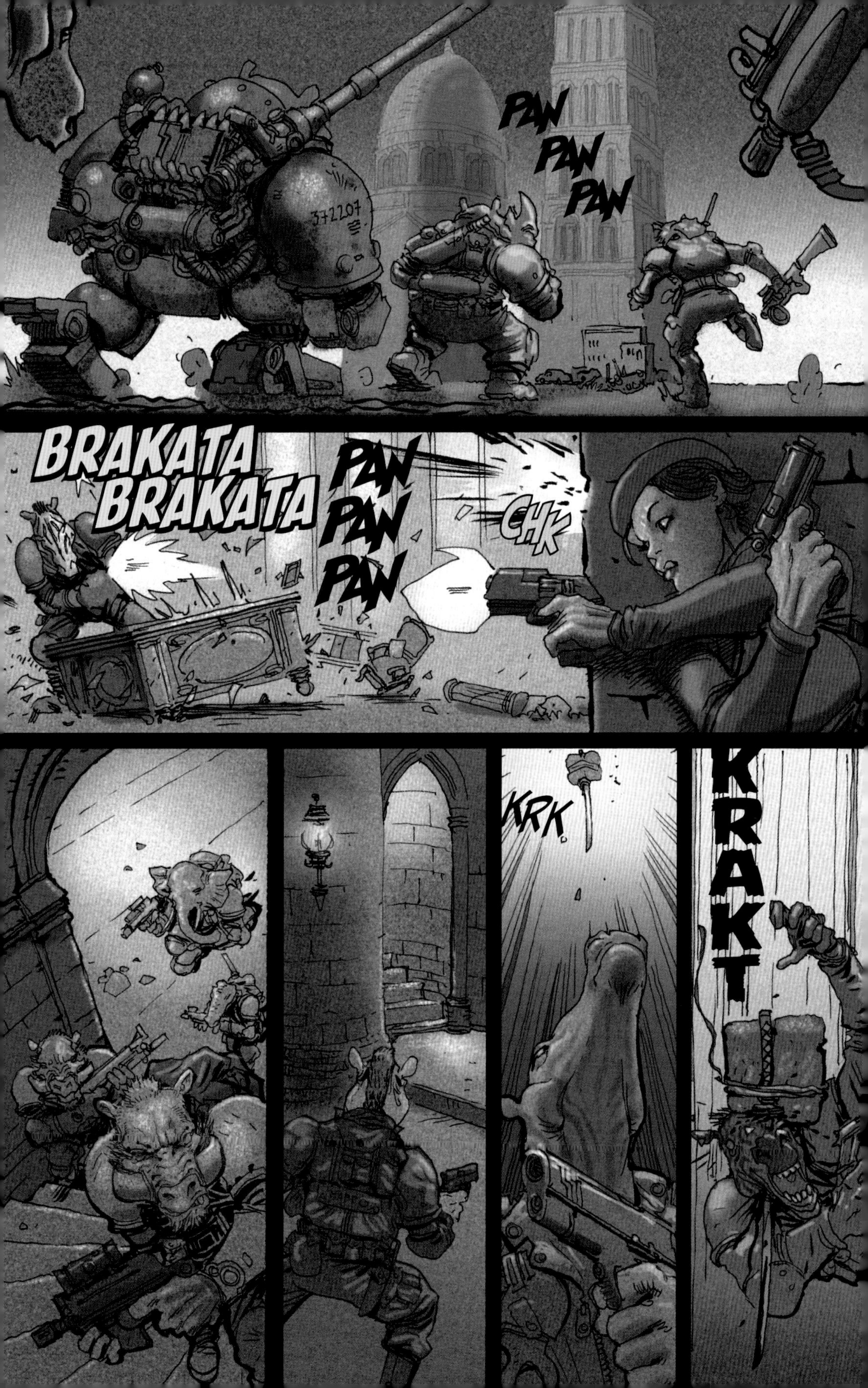
PAN
PAN
PAN
BRAKATA
BRAKATA
PAN
PAN
PAN
CHK
KRK
KRAKT

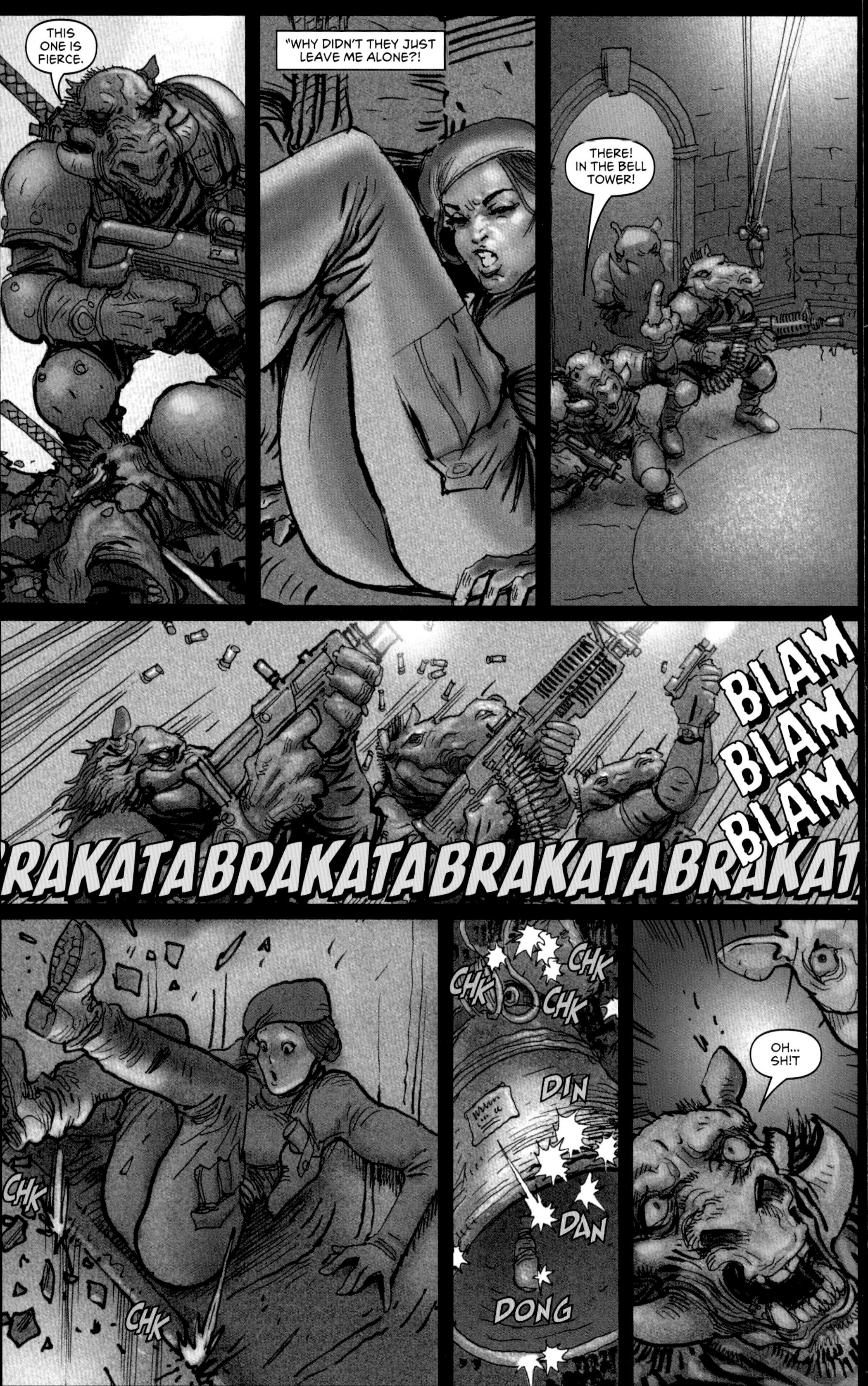
THIS ONE IS FIERCE.
"WHY DIDN'T THEY JUST LEAVE ME ALONE?!
THERE! IN THE BELL TOWER!
BLAM BLAM BLAM
BRAKATA BRAKATA BRAKATA BRAKAT
CHK
CHK
CHK CHK CHK
DIN
DAN
DONG
OH... SH!T

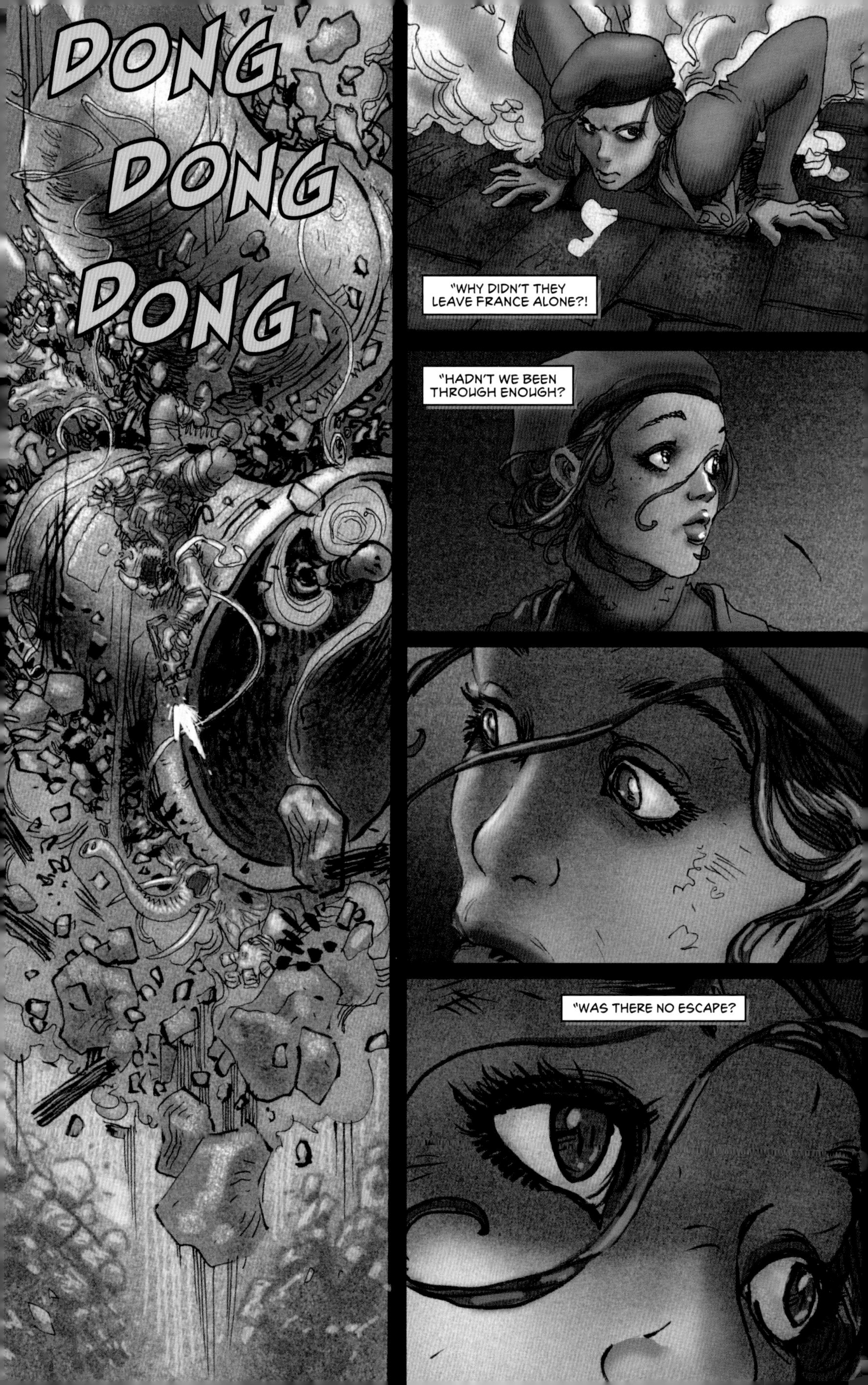
DONG
DONG
DONG
"WHY DIDN'T THEY LEAVE FRANCE ALONE?!
"HADN'T WE BEEN THROUGH ENOUGH?
"WAS THERE NO ESCAPE?

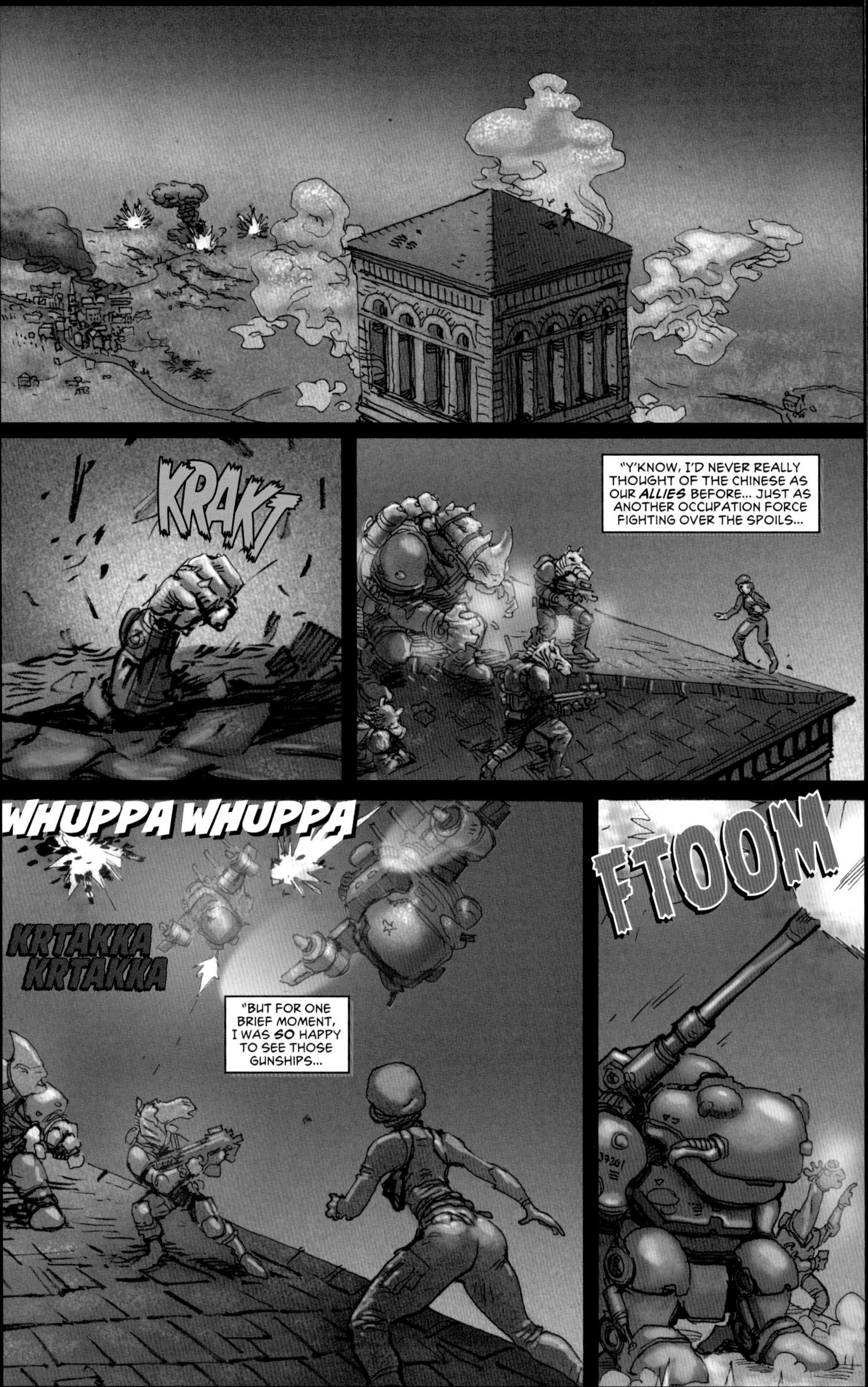
KRAKT
"Y'KNOW, I'D NEVER REALLY THOUGHT OF THE CHINESE AS OUR ALLIES BEFORE... JUST AS ANOTHER OCCUPATION FORCE FIGHTING OVER THE SPOILS...
WHUPPA WHUPPA
KRTAKKA KRTAKKA
"BUT FOR ONE BRIEF MOMENT, I WAS SO HAPPY TO SEE THOSE GUNSHIPS...
FTOOM

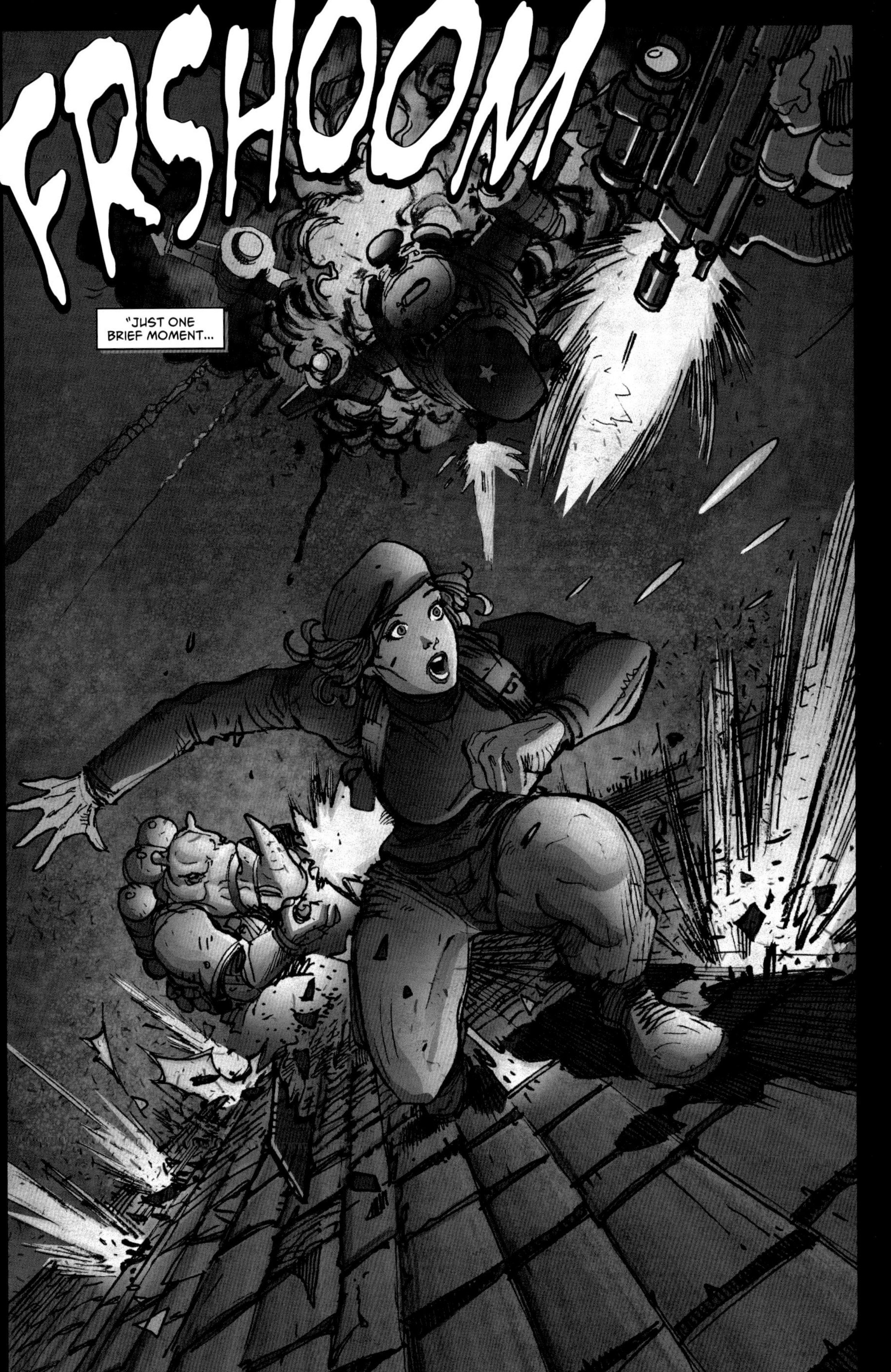
FRSHOOM
"JUST ONE
BRIEF MOMENT...

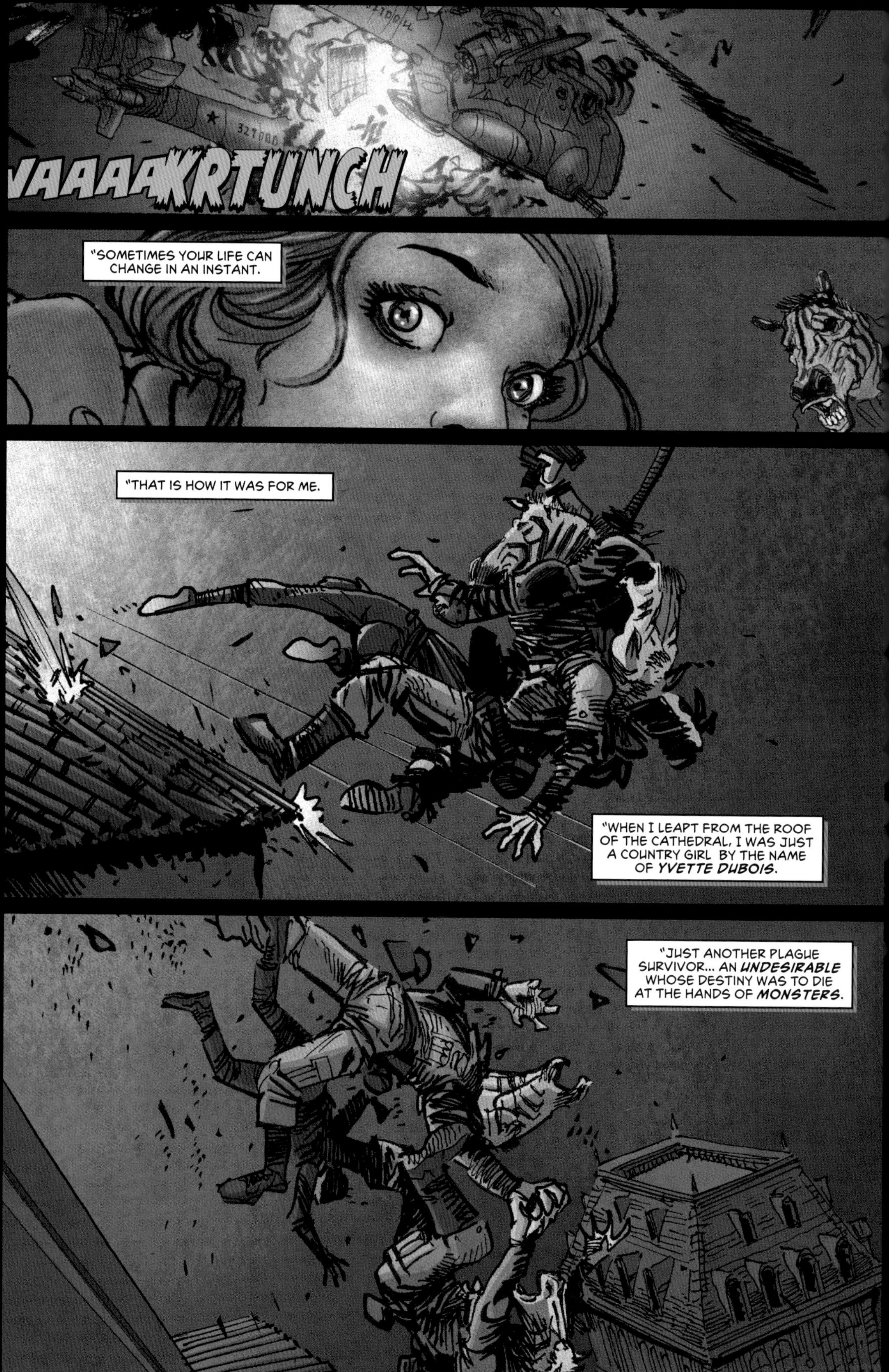
VAAAAKRTUNCH
"SOMETIMES YOUR LIFE CAN CHANGE IN AN INSTANT.
"THAT IS HOW IT WAS FOR ME.
"WHEN I LEAPT FROM THE ROOF OF THE CATHEDRAL, I WAS JUST A COUNTRY GIRL BY THE NAME OF *YVETTE DUBOIS*.
"JUST ANOTHER PLAGUE SURVIVOR... AN *UNDESIRABLE* WHOSE DESTINY WAS TO DIE AT THE HANDS OF *MONSTERS*.

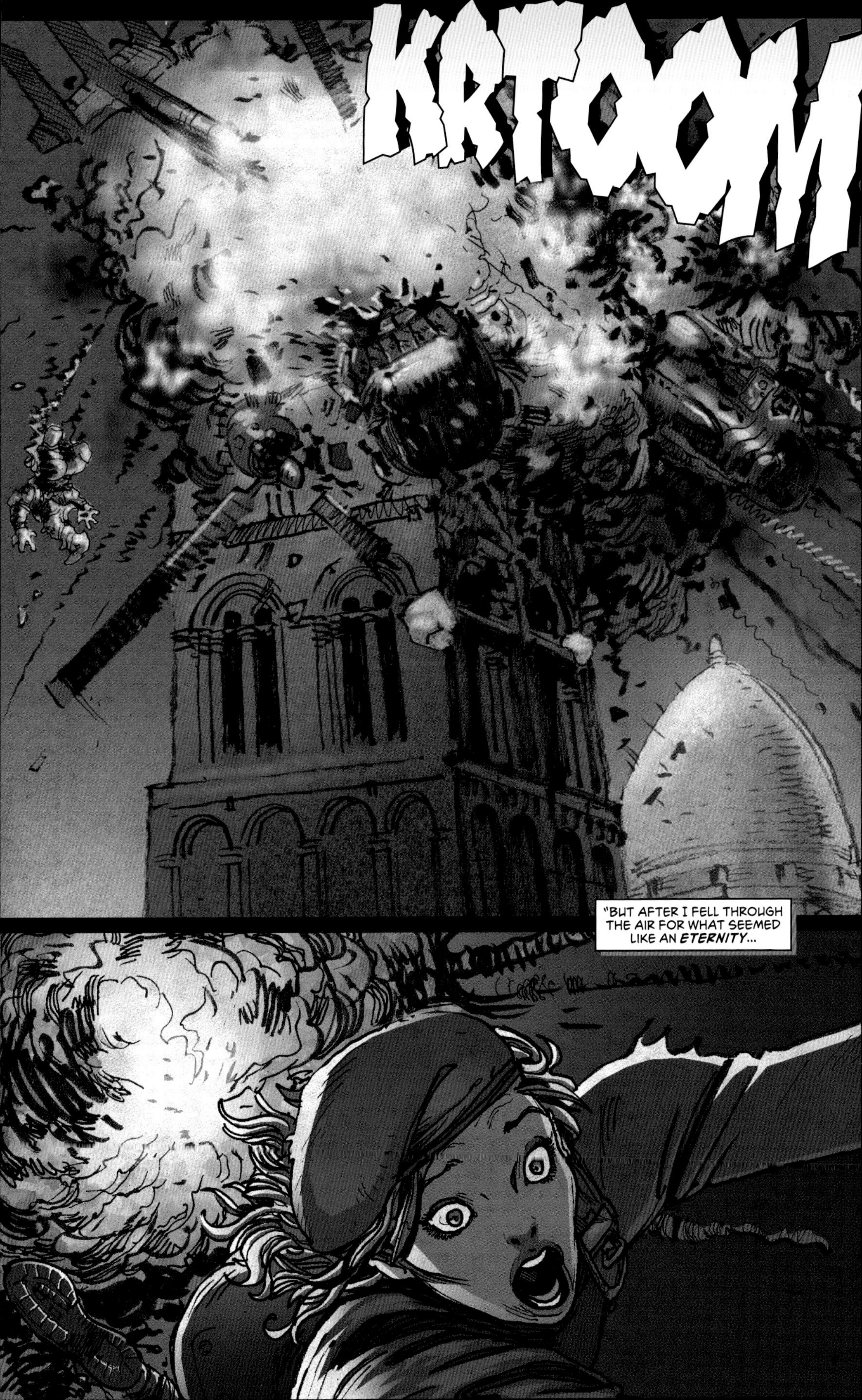
KRTOOM
"BUT AFTER I FELL THROUGH THE AIR FOR WHAT SEEMED LIKE AN ETERNITY...

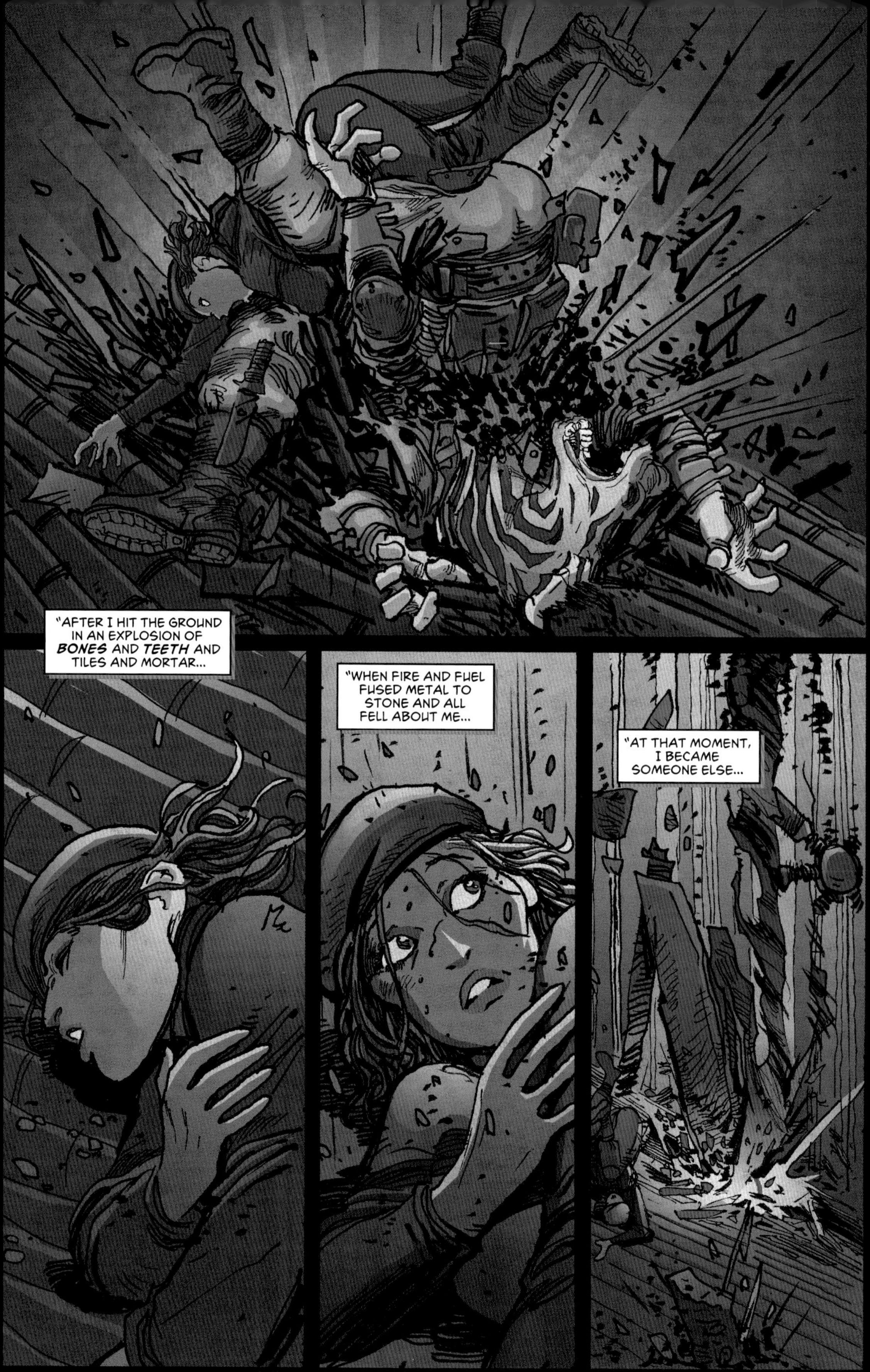
"AFTER I HIT THE GROUND IN AN EXPLOSION OF ***BONES*** AND ***TEETH*** AND TILES AND MORTAR...
"WHEN FIRE AND FUEL FUSED METAL TO STONE AND ALL FELL ABOUT ME...
"AT THAT MOMENT, I BECAME SOMEONE ELSE...

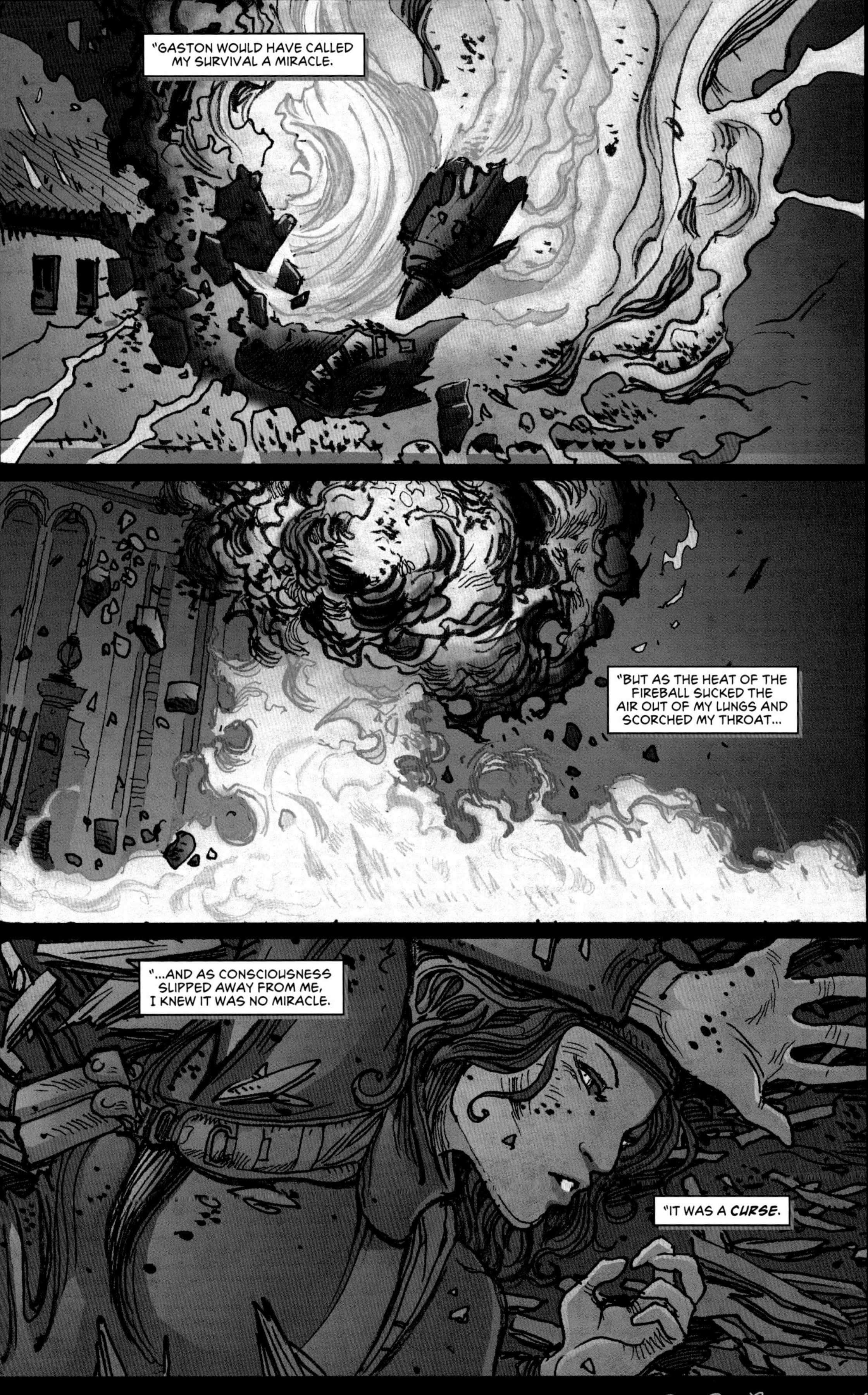
"GASTON WOULD HAVE CALLED MY SURVIVAL A MIRACLE.
"BUT AS THE HEAT OF THE FIREBALL SUCKED THE AIR OUT OF MY LUNGS AND SCORCHED MY THROAT...
"...AND AS CONSCIOUSNESS SLIPPED AWAY FROM ME, I KNEW IT WAS NO MIRACLE.
"IT WAS A CURSE.

To Be Continued!

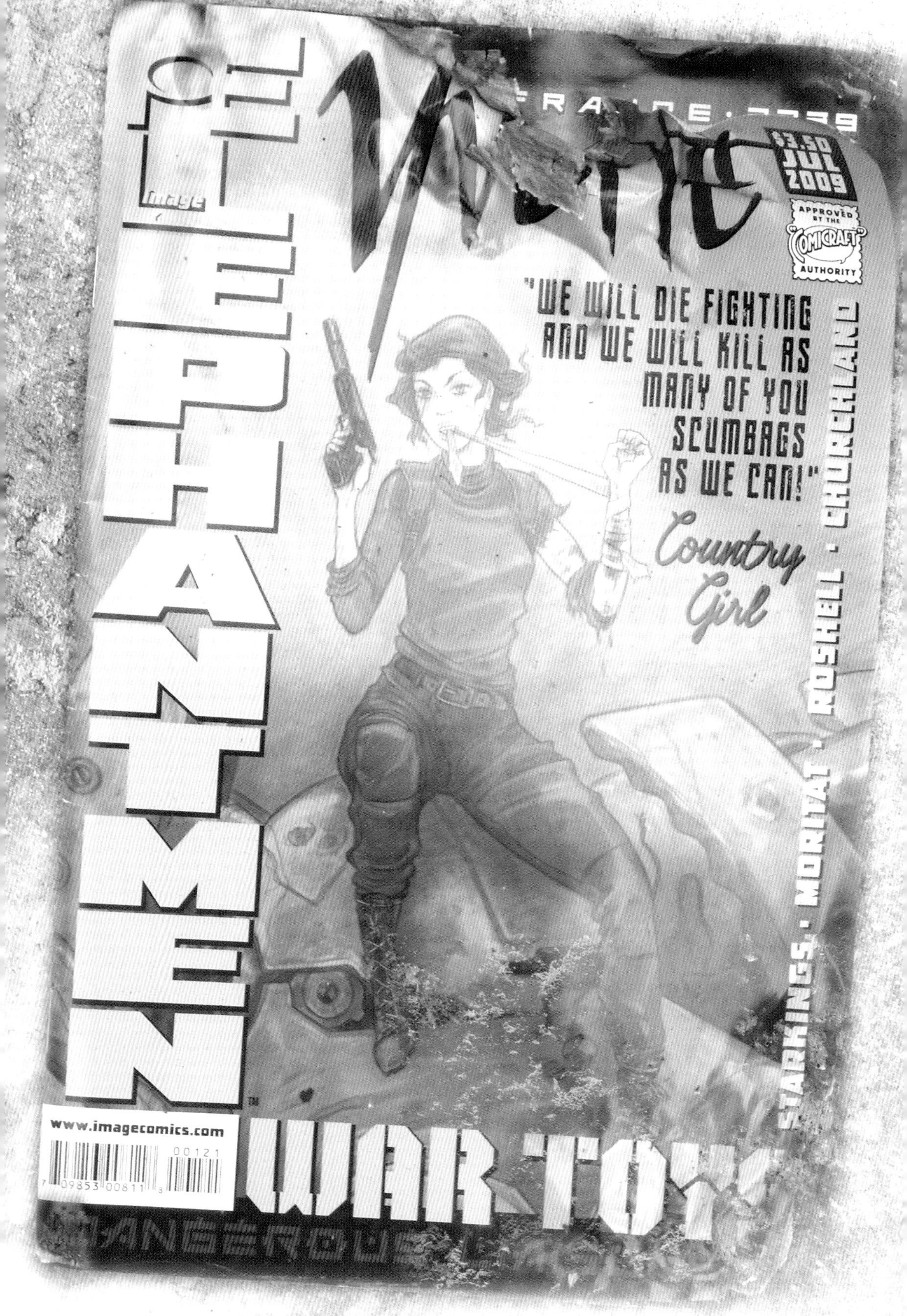
image
ELEPHANTMEN
$3.50
JUL
2009
APPROVED BY THE COMICRAFT AUTHORITY
"WE WILL DIE FIGHTING AND WE WILL KILL AS MANY OF YOU SCUMBAGS AS WE CAN!"
Country Girl
STARKINGS · MORITAT · ROSHELL · CHURCHLAND
www.imagecomics.com
WAR TOY

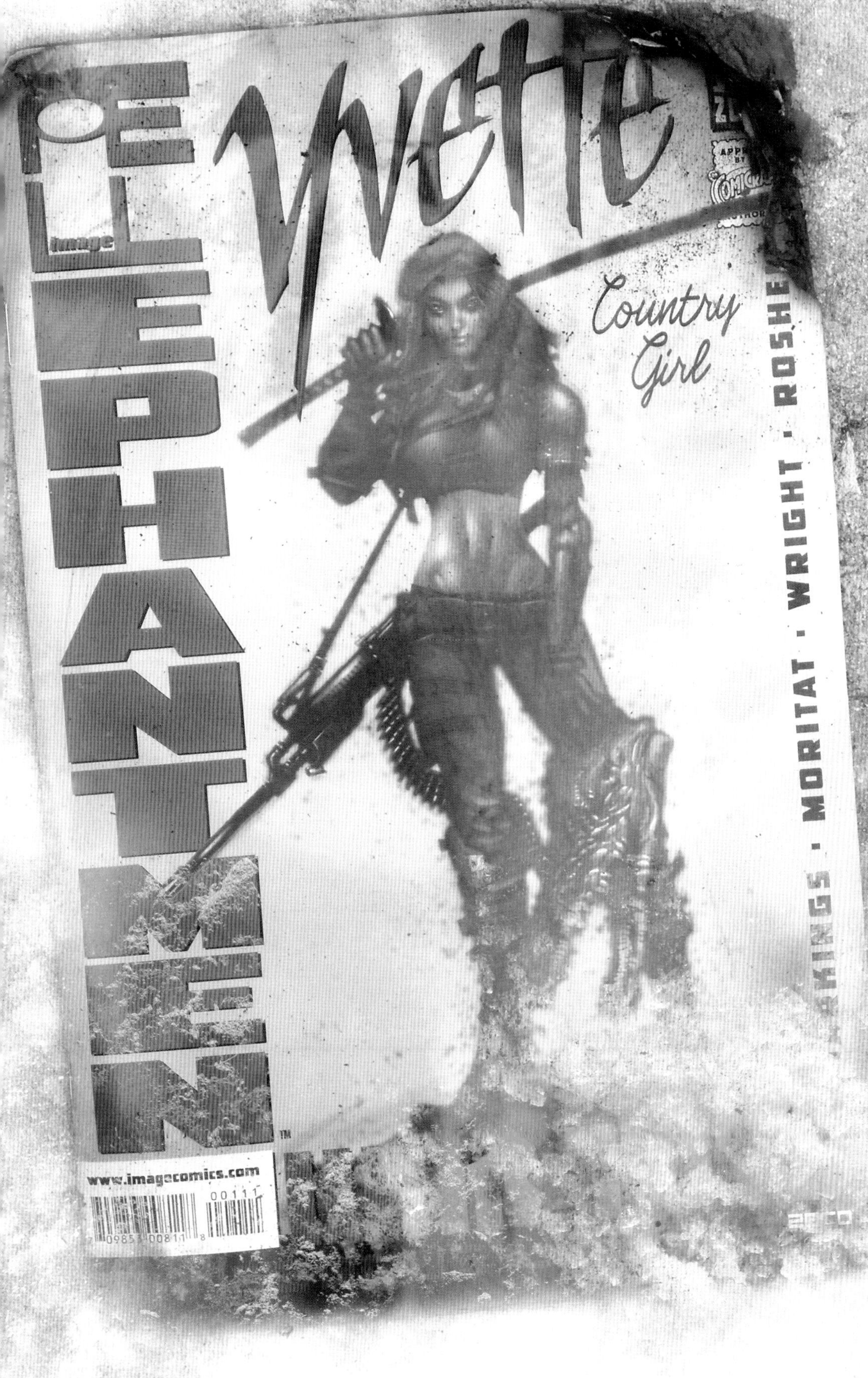image
ELEPHANTMEN
Yvette
Country Girl
KINGS · MORITAT · WRIGHT · ROSHE
www.imagecomics.com

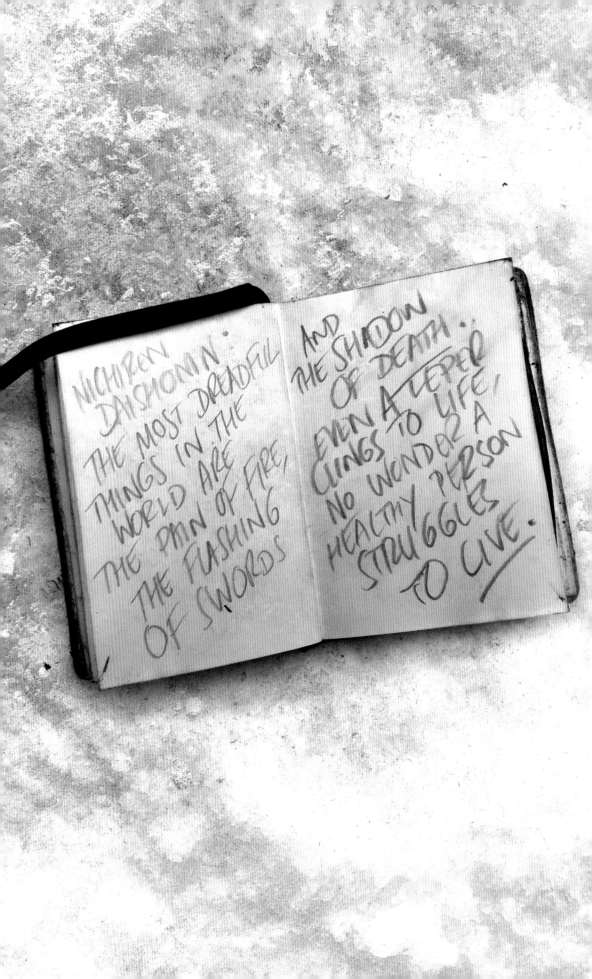

NICHIREN
DAISHONIN:
THE MOST DREADFUL
THINGS IN THE
WORLD ARE
THE PAIN OF FIRE,
THE FLASHING
OF SWORDS
AND
THE SHADOW
OF DEATH.
EVEN A LEPER
CLINGS TO LIFE,
NO WONDER A
HEALTHY PERSON
STRUGGLES
TO LIVE.

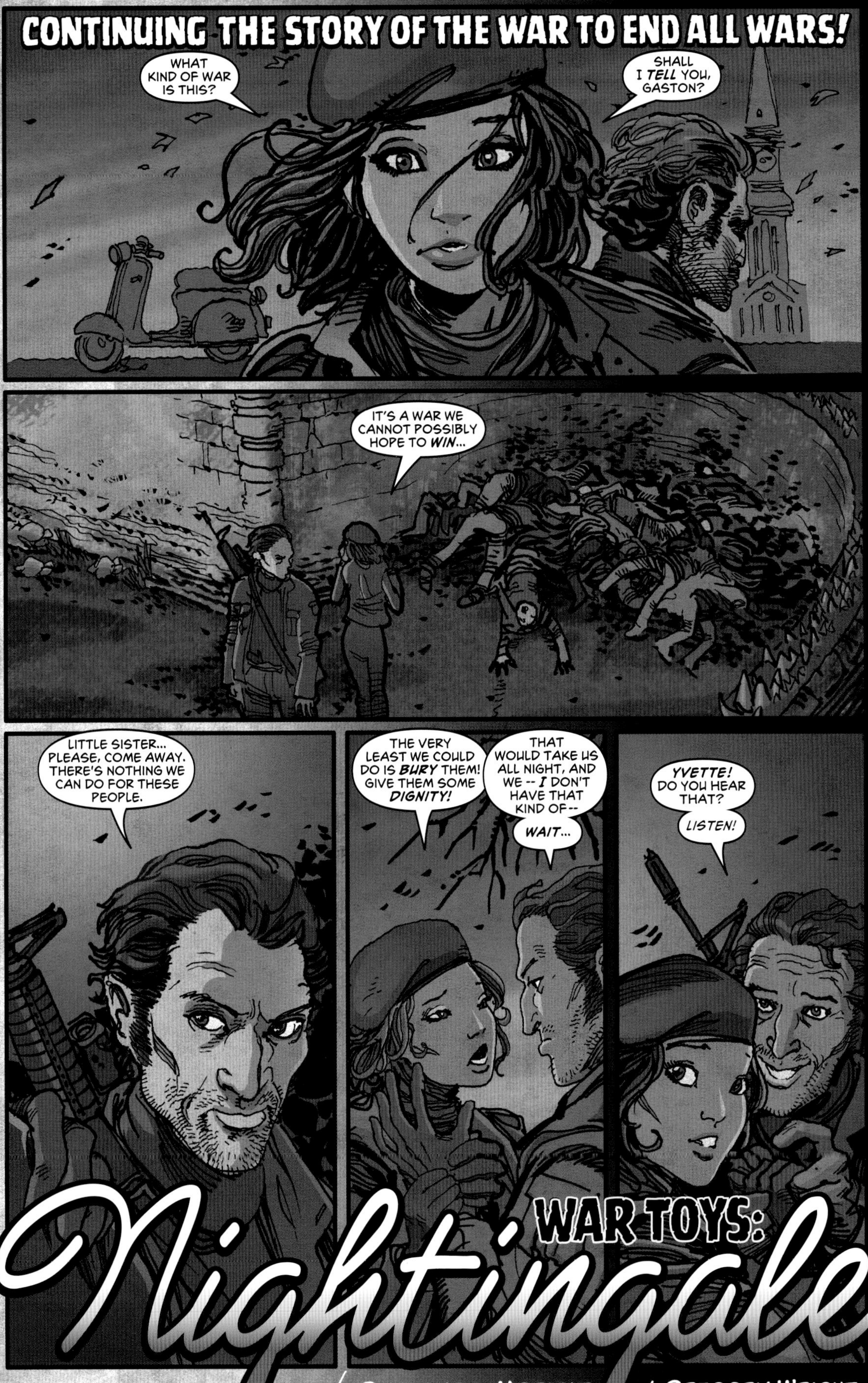
CONTINUING THE STORY OF THE WAR TO END ALL WARS!
WHAT KIND OF WAR IS THIS?
SHALL I TELL YOU, GASTON?
IT'S A WAR WE CANNOT POSSIBLY HOPE TO WIN...
LITTLE SISTER... PLEASE, COME AWAY. THERE'S NOTHING WE CAN DO FOR THESE PEOPLE.
THE VERY LEAST WE COULD DO IS BURY THEM! GIVE THEM SOME DIGNITY!
THAT WOULD TAKE US ALL NIGHT, AND WE -- I DON'T HAVE THAT KIND OF --
WAIT...
YVETTE! DO YOU HEAR THAT?
LISTEN!
WAR TOYS:
Nightingale
by STARKINGS, MORITAT & GREGORY WRIGHT

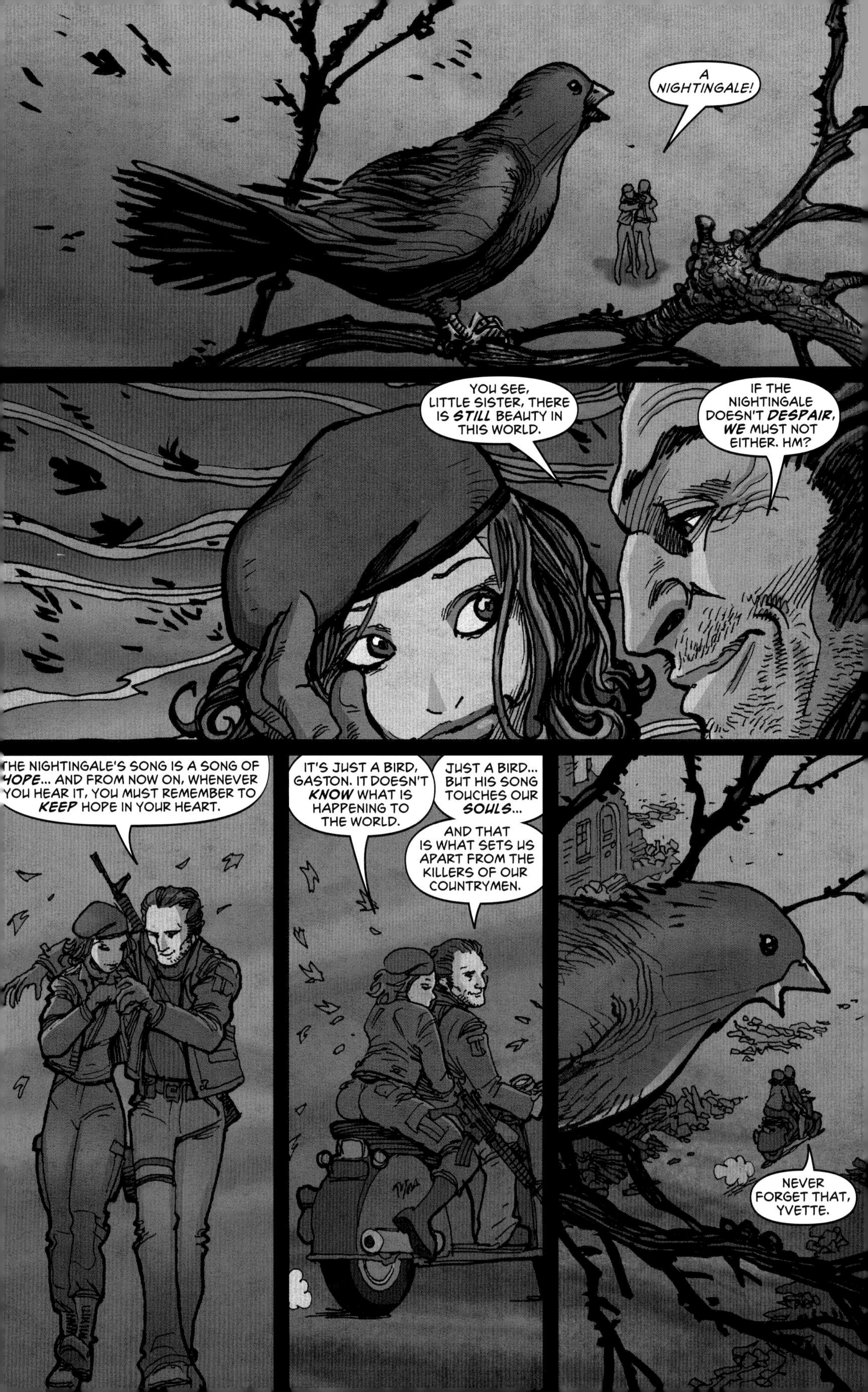
A NIGHTINGALE!
YOU SEE, LITTLE SISTER, THERE IS STILL BEAUTY IN THIS WORLD.
IF THE NIGHTINGALE DOESN'T DESPAIR, WE MUST NOT EITHER. HM?
THE NIGHTINGALE'S SONG IS A SONG OF HOPE... AND FROM NOW ON, WHENEVER YOU HEAR IT, YOU MUST REMEMBER TO KEEP HOPE IN YOUR HEART.
IT'S JUST A BIRD, GASTON. IT DOESN'T KNOW WHAT IS HAPPENING TO THE WORLD.
JUST A BIRD... BUT HIS SONG TOUCHES OUR SOULS...
AND THAT IS WHAT SETS US APART FROM THE KILLERS OF OUR COUNTRYMEN.
NEVER FORGET THAT, YVETTE.

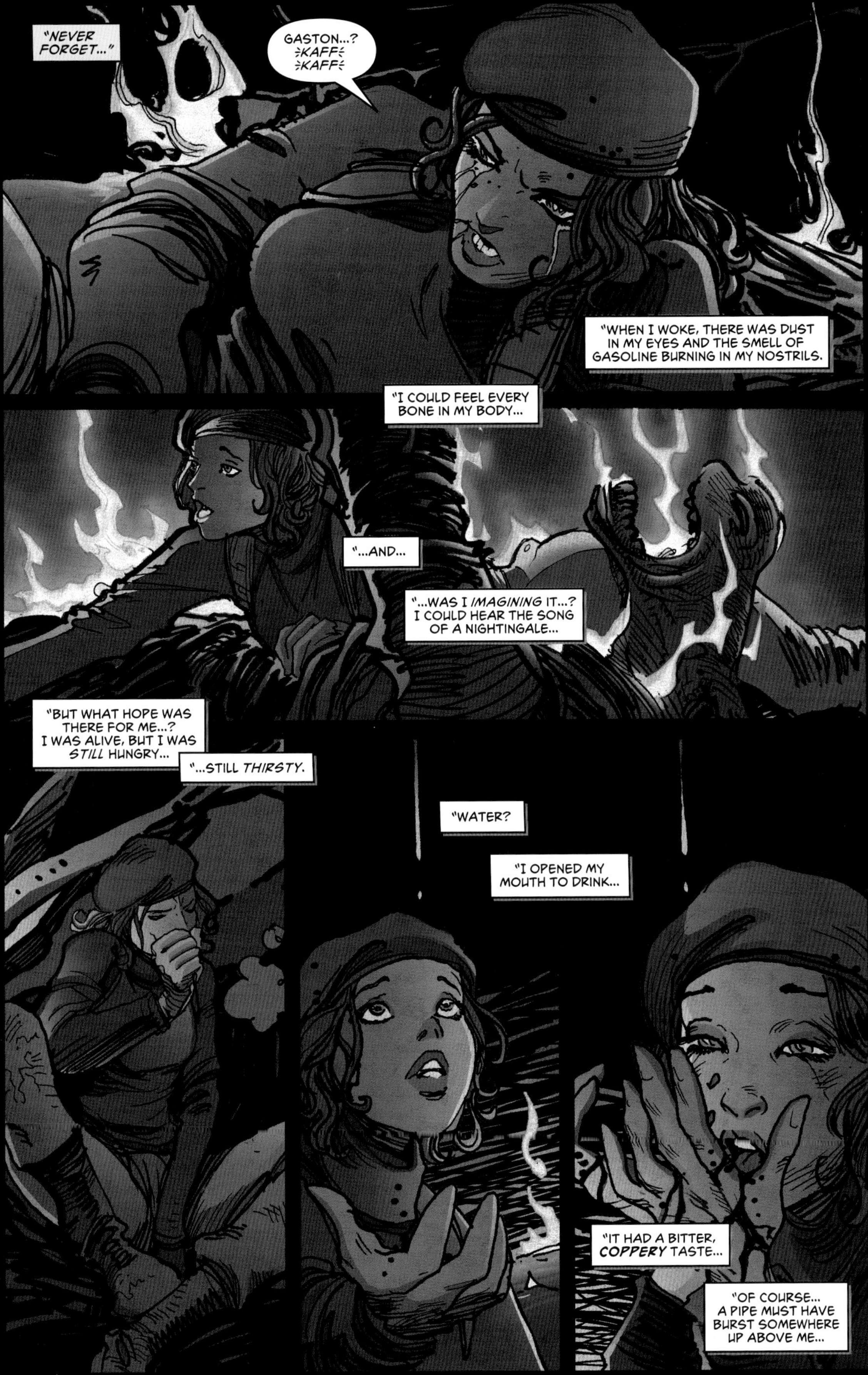
"NEVER FORGET..."
GASTON...? *KAFF* *KAFF*
"WHEN I WOKE, THERE WAS DUST IN MY EYES AND THE SMELL OF GASOLINE BURNING IN MY NOSTRILS.
"I COULD FEEL EVERY BONE IN MY BODY...
"...AND...
"...WAS I *IMAGINING* IT...? I COULD HEAR THE SONG OF A NIGHTINGALE...
"BUT WHAT HOPE WAS THERE FOR ME...? I WAS ALIVE, BUT I WAS *STILL* HUNGRY...
"...STILL *THIRSTY*.
"WATER?
"I OPENED MY MOUTH TO DRINK...
"IT HAD A BITTER, *COPPERY* TASTE...
"OF COURSE... A PIPE MUST HAVE BURST SOMEWHERE UP ABOVE ME...

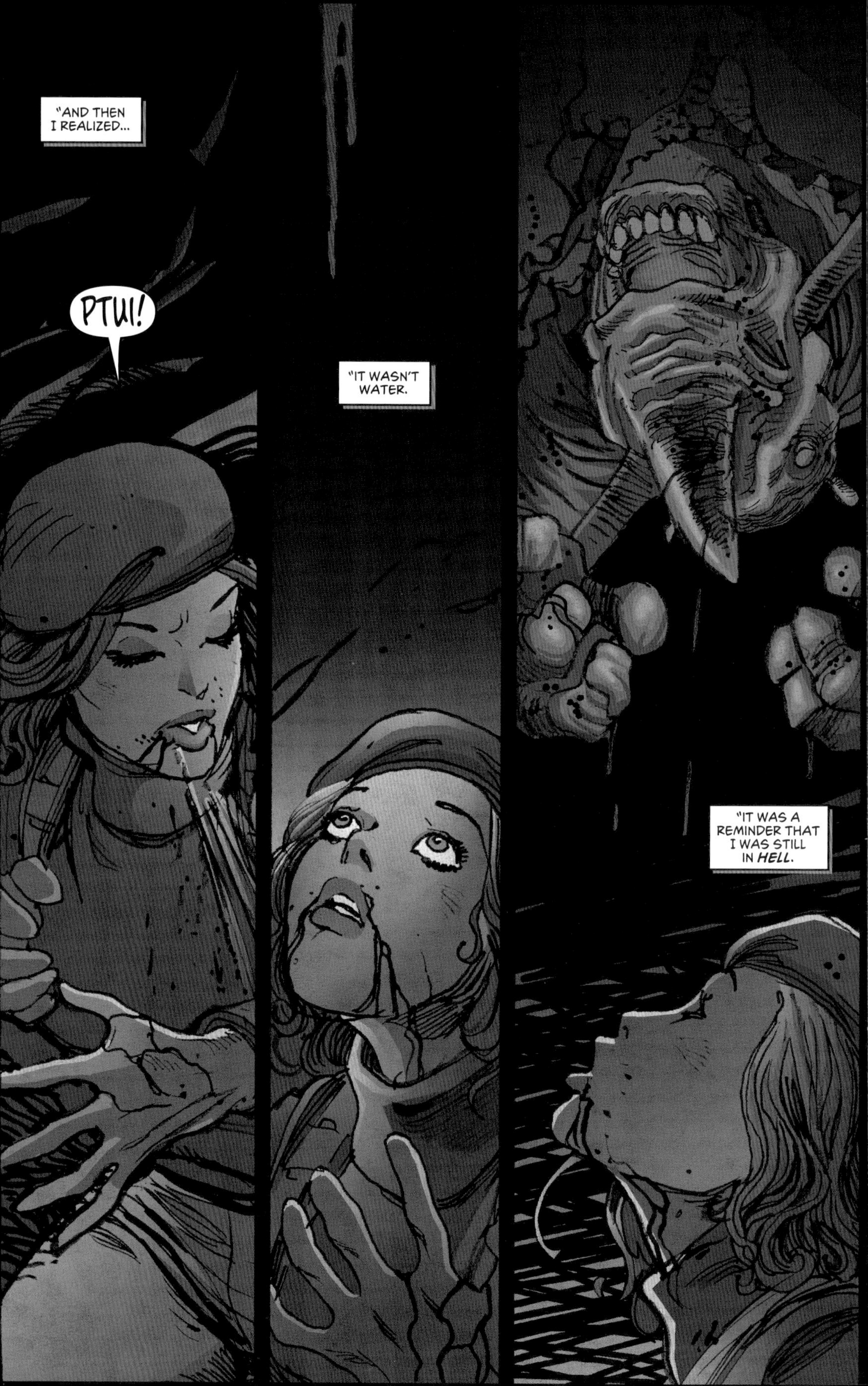
"AND THEN I REALIZED...
PTUI!
"IT WASN'T WATER.
"IT WAS A REMINDER THAT I WAS STILL IN *HELL*.

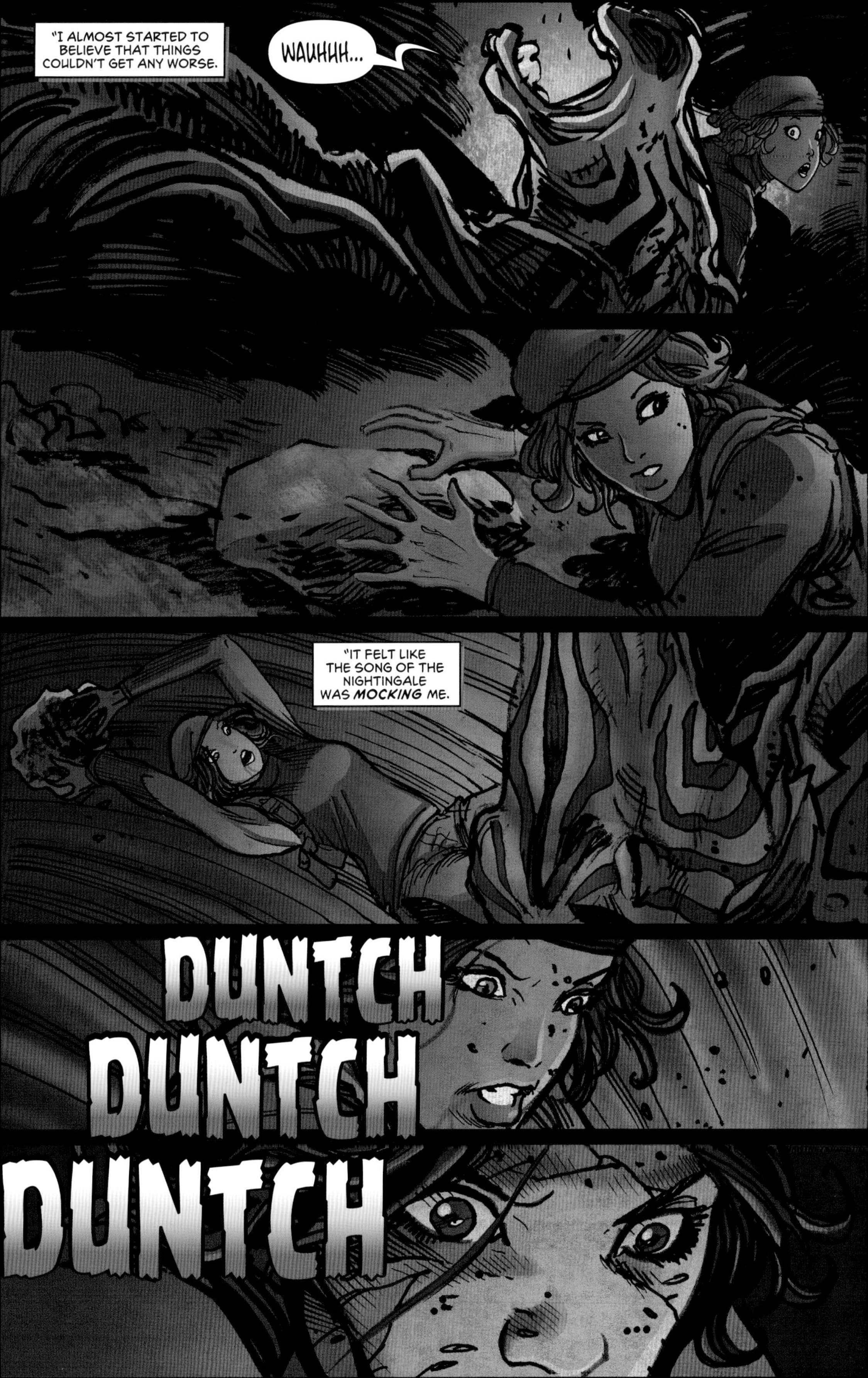
"I ALMOST STARTED TO BELIEVE THAT THINGS COULDN'T GET ANY WORSE.
WAUHHH...
"IT FELT LIKE THE SONG OF THE NIGHTINGALE WAS MOCKING ME.
DUNTCH
DUNTCH
DUNTCH

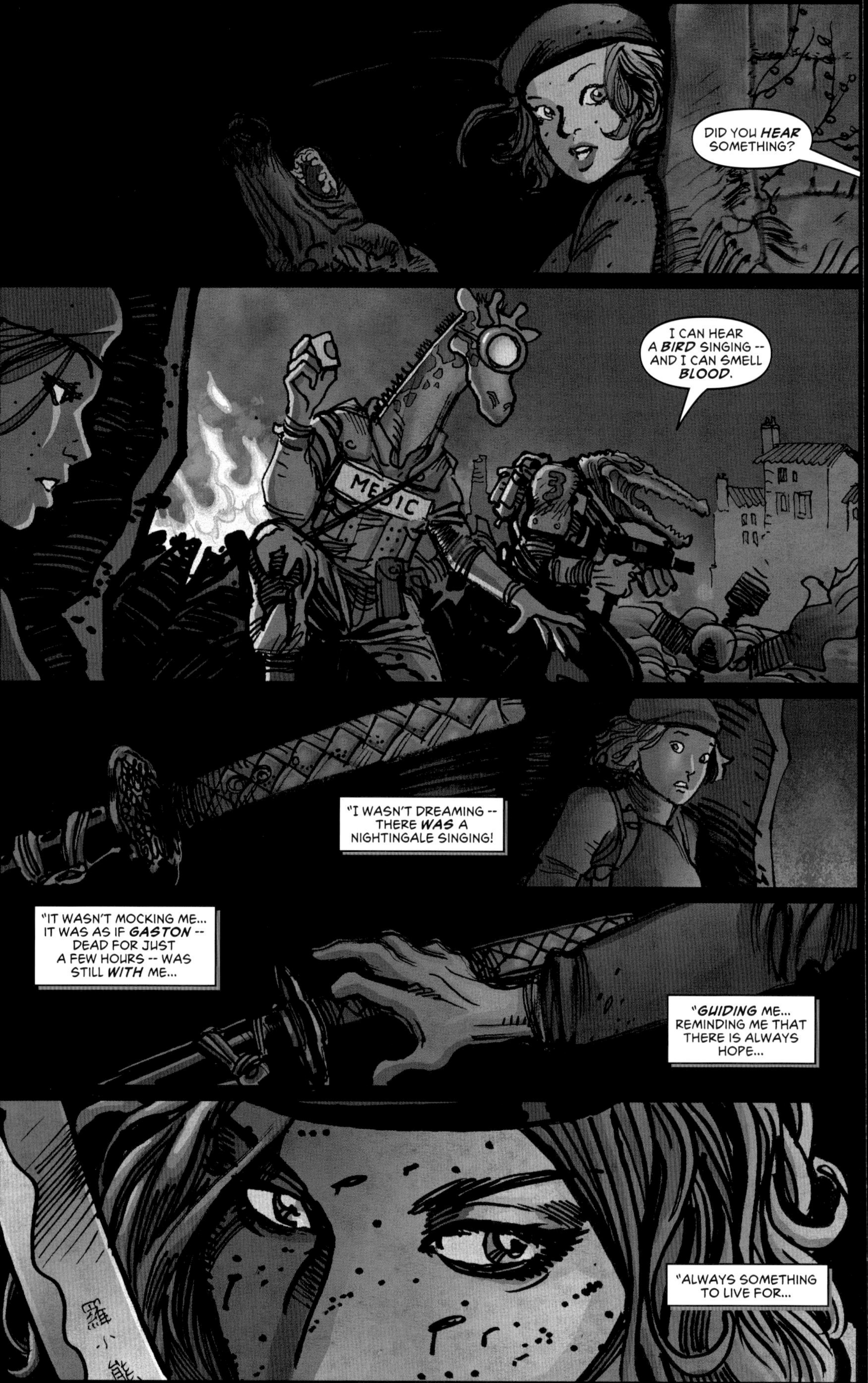
DID YOU HEAR SOMETHING?
I CAN HEAR A BIRD SINGING -- AND I CAN SMELL BLOOD.
MEDIC
"I WASN'T DREAMING -- THERE WAS A NIGHTINGALE SINGING!
"IT WASN'T MOCKING ME... IT WAS AS IF GASTON -- DEAD FOR JUST A FEW HOURS -- WAS STILL WITH ME...
"GUIDING ME... REMINDING ME THAT THERE IS ALWAYS HOPE...
"ALWAYS SOMETHING TO LIVE FOR...

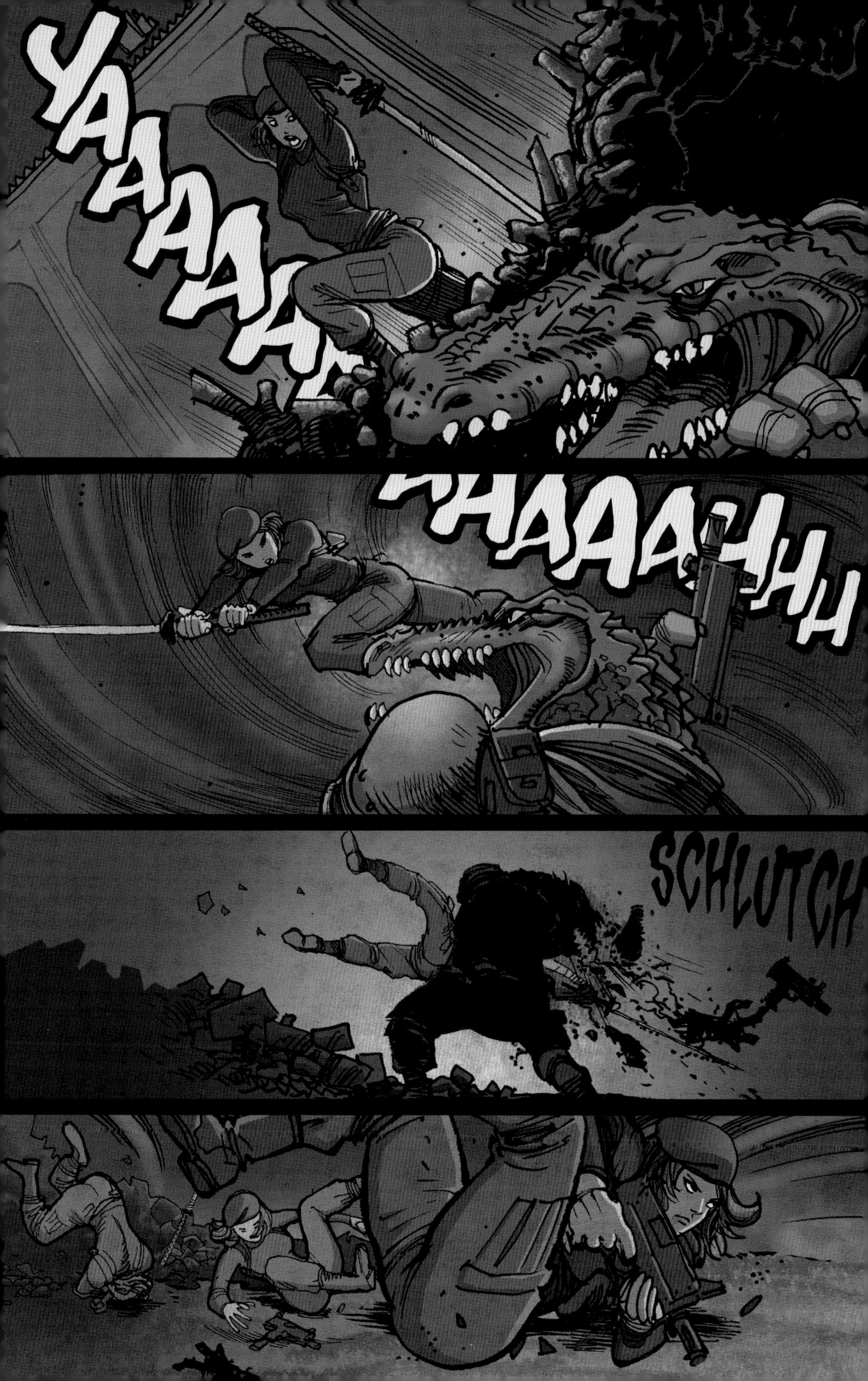
YAAAAAAAAAAAHHH
SCHLUTCH

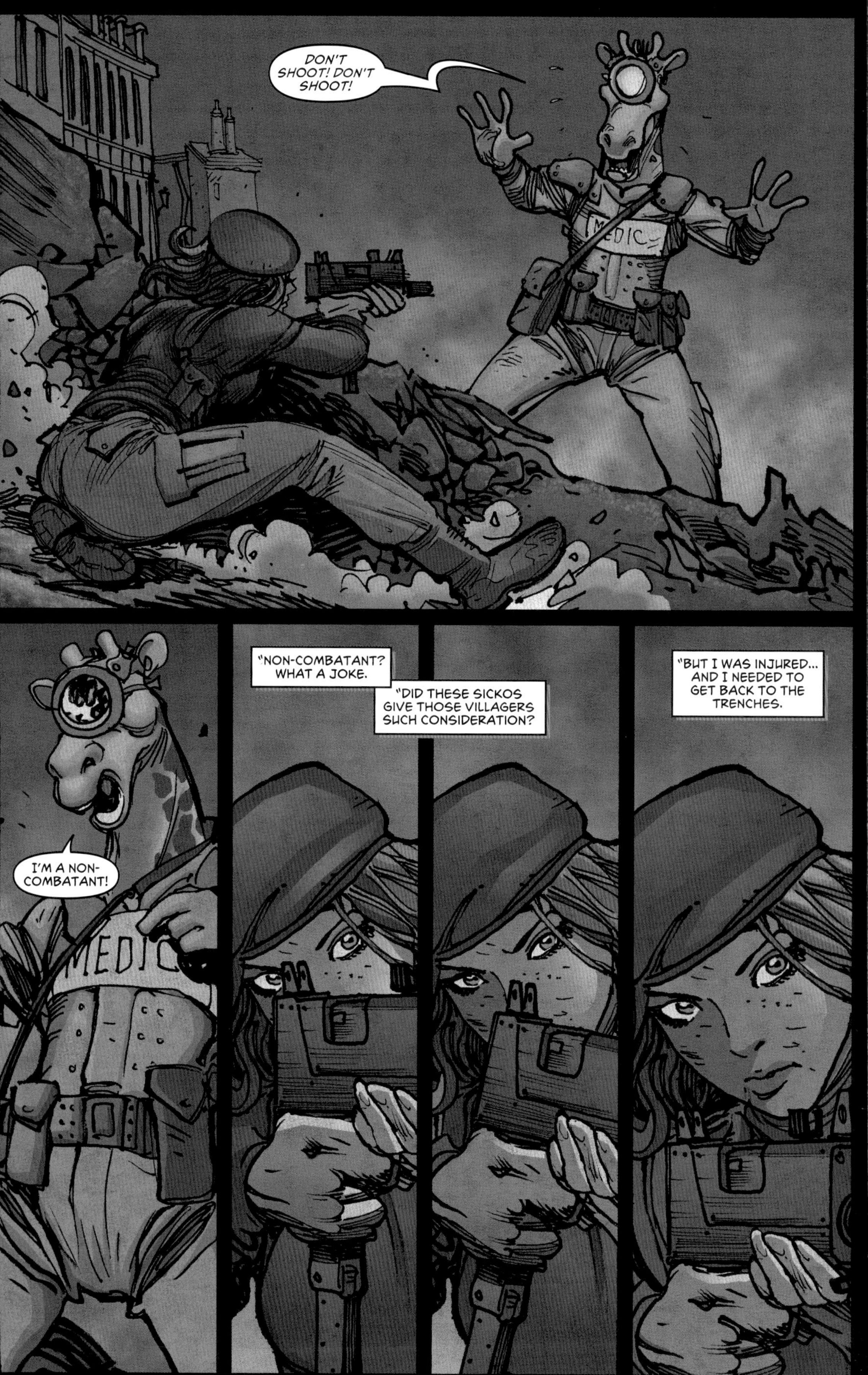
DON'T SHOOT! DON'T SHOOT!
I'M A NON-COMBATANT!
"NON-COMBATANT? WHAT A JOKE.
"DID THESE SICKOS GIVE THOSE VILLAGERS SUCH CONSIDERATION?
"BUT I WAS INJURED... AND I NEEDED TO GET BACK TO THE TRENCHES.

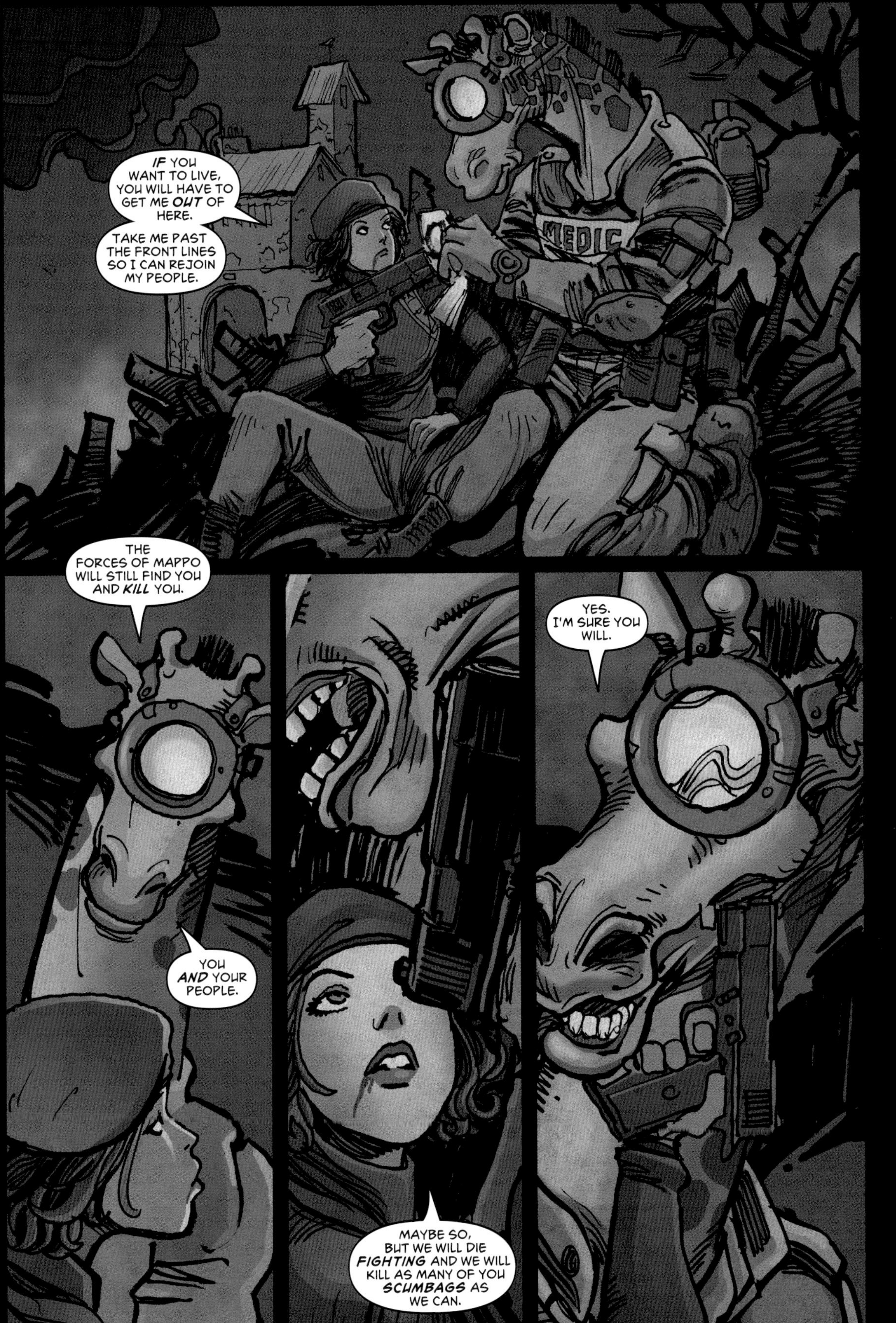
IF YOU WANT TO LIVE, YOU WILL HAVE TO GET ME OUT OF HERE.
TAKE ME PAST THE FRONT LINES SO I CAN REJOIN MY PEOPLE.
MEDIC
THE FORCES OF MAPPO WILL STILL FIND YOU AND KILL YOU.
YOU AND YOUR PEOPLE.
MAYBE SO, BUT WE WILL DIE FIGHTING AND WE WILL KILL AS MANY OF YOU SCUMBAGS AS WE CAN.
YES. I'M SURE YOU WILL.

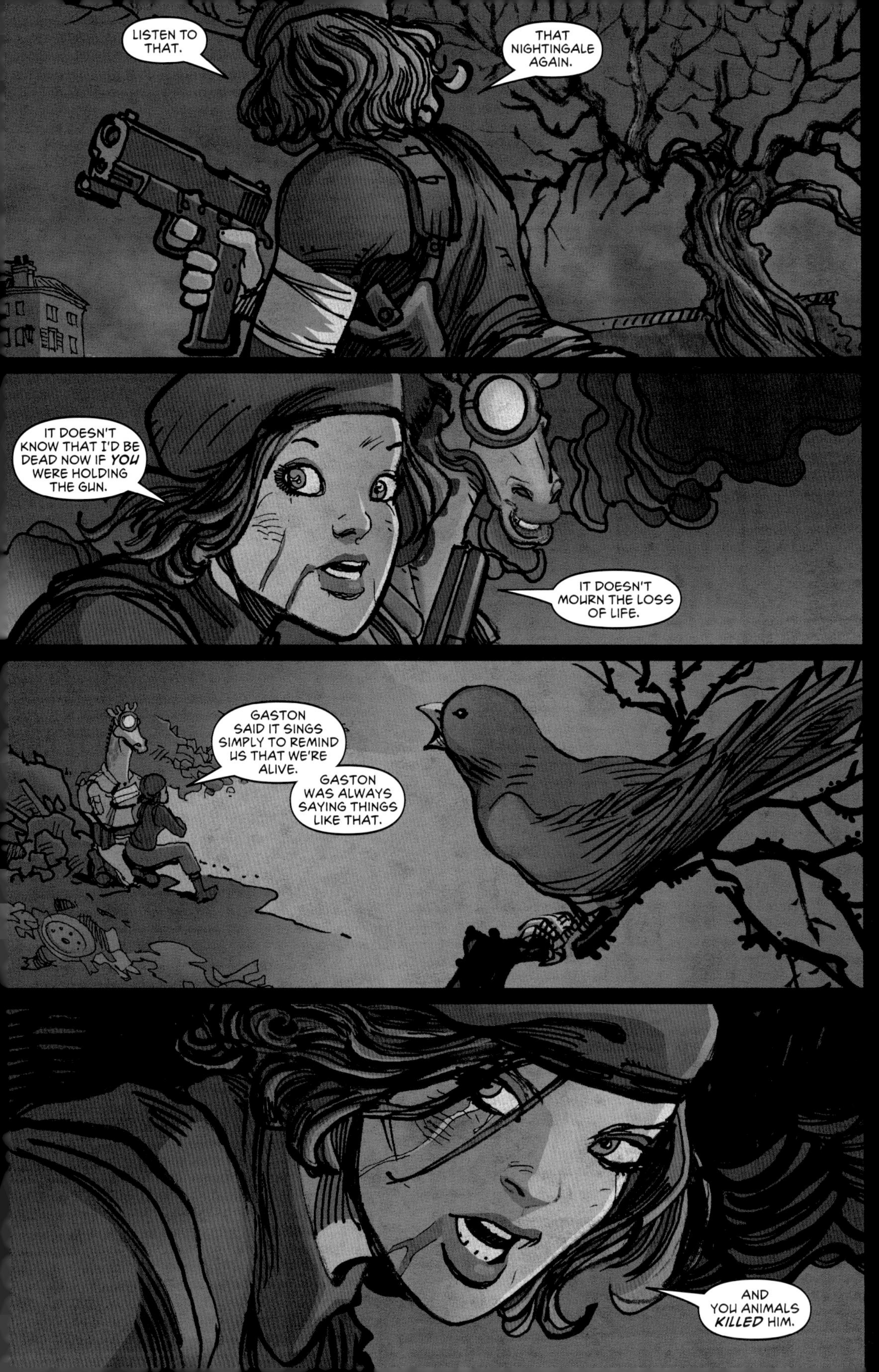

LISTEN TO THAT.
THAT NIGHTINGALE AGAIN.
IT DOESN'T KNOW THAT I'D BE DEAD NOW IF *YOU* WERE HOLDING THE GUN.
IT DOESN'T MOURN THE LOSS OF LIFE.
GASTON SAID IT SINGS SIMPLY TO REMIND US THAT WE'RE ALIVE.
GASTON WAS ALWAYS SAYING THINGS LIKE THAT.
AND YOU ANIMALS *KILLED* HIM.

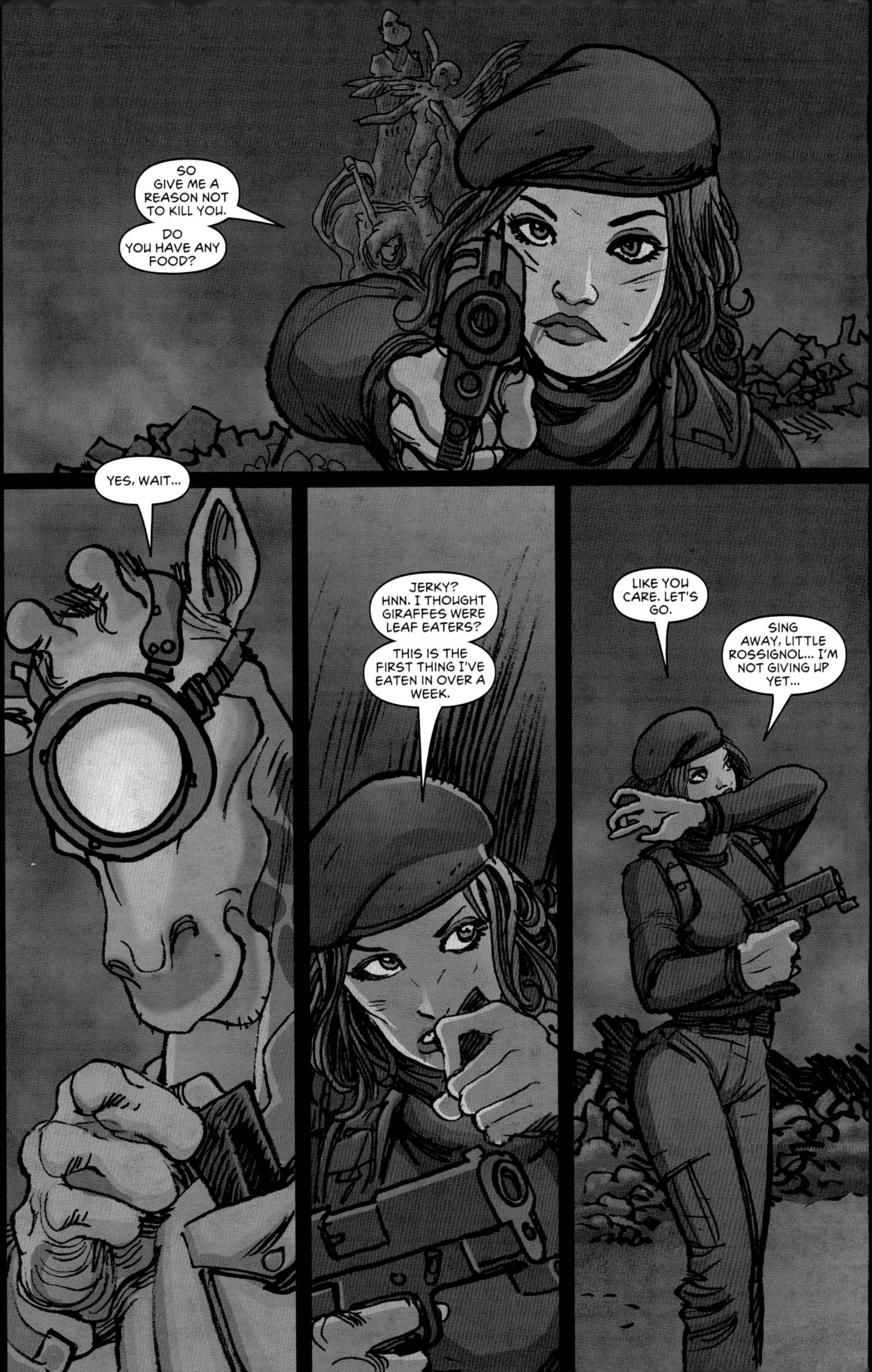
SO GIVE ME A REASON NOT TO KILL YOU.
DO YOU HAVE ANY FOOD?
YES, WAIT...
JERKY? HNN. I THOUGHT GIRAFFES WERE LEAF EATERS?
THIS IS THE FIRST THING I'VE EATEN IN OVER A WEEK.
LIKE YOU CARE. LET'S GO.
SING AWAY, LITTLE ROSSIGNOL... I'M NOT GIVING UP YET...

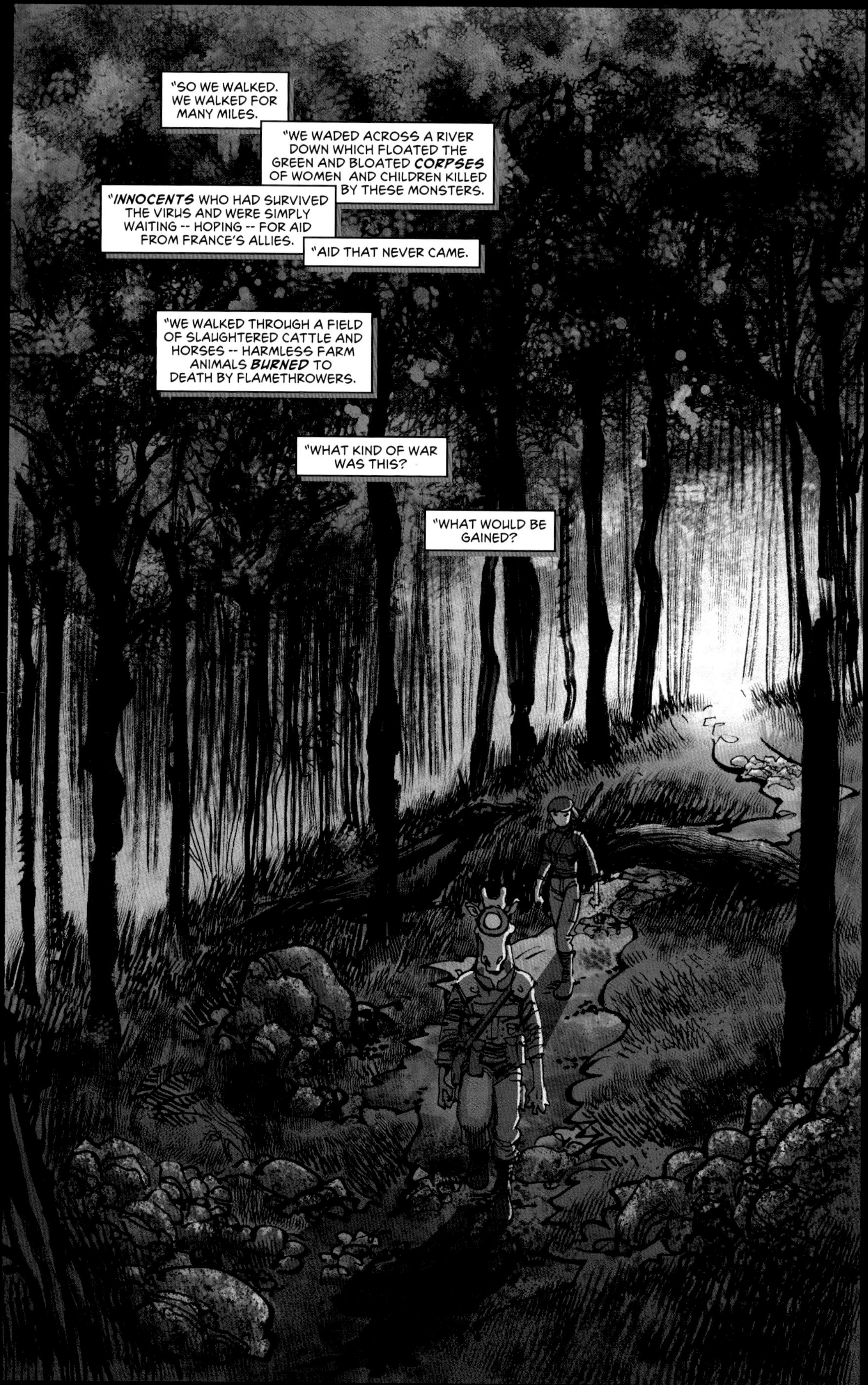
"SO WE WALKED. WE WALKED FOR MANY MILES.
"WE WADED ACROSS A RIVER DOWN WHICH FLOATED THE GREEN AND BLOATED *CORPSES* OF WOMEN AND CHILDREN KILLED BY THESE MONSTERS.
"*INNOCENTS* WHO HAD SURVIVED THE VIRUS AND WERE SIMPLY WAITING -- HOPING -- FOR AID FROM FRANCE'S ALLIES.
"AID THAT NEVER CAME.
"WE WALKED THROUGH A FIELD OF SLAUGHTERED CATTLE AND HORSES -- HARMLESS FARM ANIMALS *BURNED* TO DEATH BY FLAMETHROWERS.
"WHAT KIND OF WAR WAS THIS?
"WHAT WOULD BE GAINED?

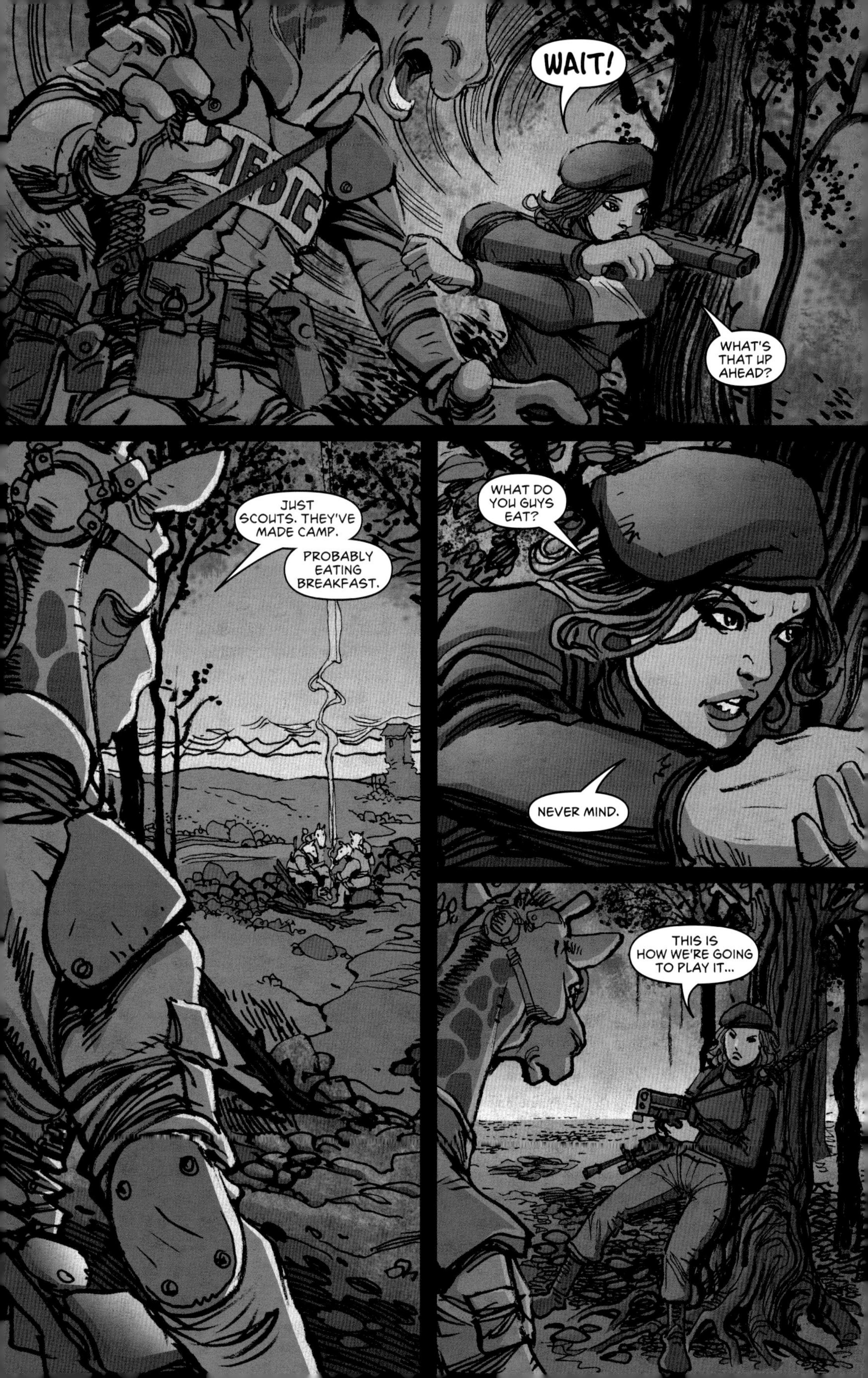
WAIT!
WHAT'S THAT UP AHEAD?
JUST SCOUTS. THEY'VE MADE CAMP.
PROBABLY EATING BREAKFAST.
WHAT DO YOU GUYS EAT?
NEVER MIND.
THIS IS HOW WE'RE GOING TO PLAY IT...

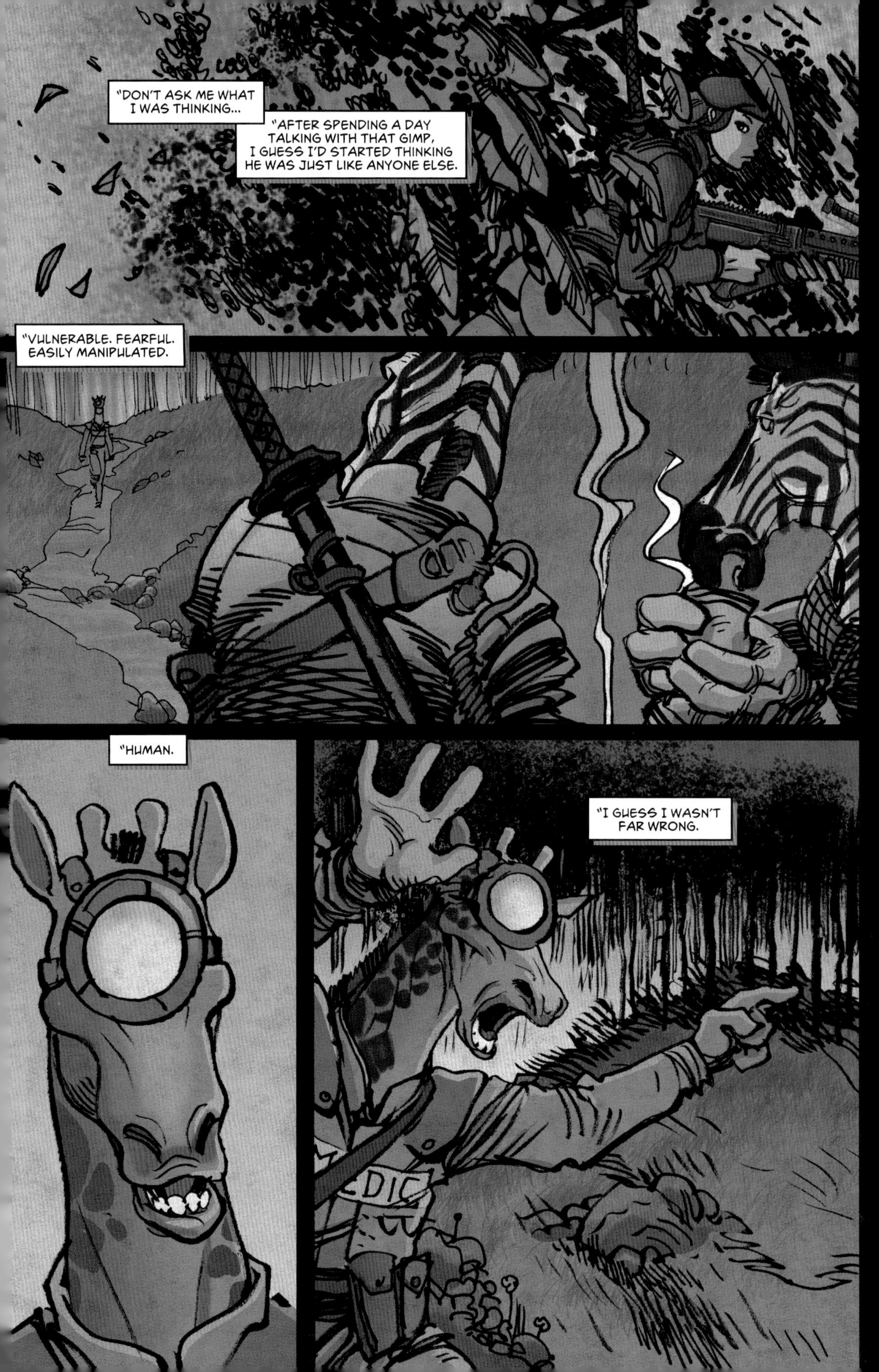
"DON'T ASK ME WHAT I WAS THINKING...
"AFTER SPENDING A DAY TALKING WITH THAT GIMP, I GUESS I'D STARTED THINKING HE WAS JUST LIKE ANYONE ELSE.
"VULNERABLE. FEARFUL. EASILY MANIPULATED.
"HUMAN.
"I GUESS I WASN'T FAR WRONG.
EDIC

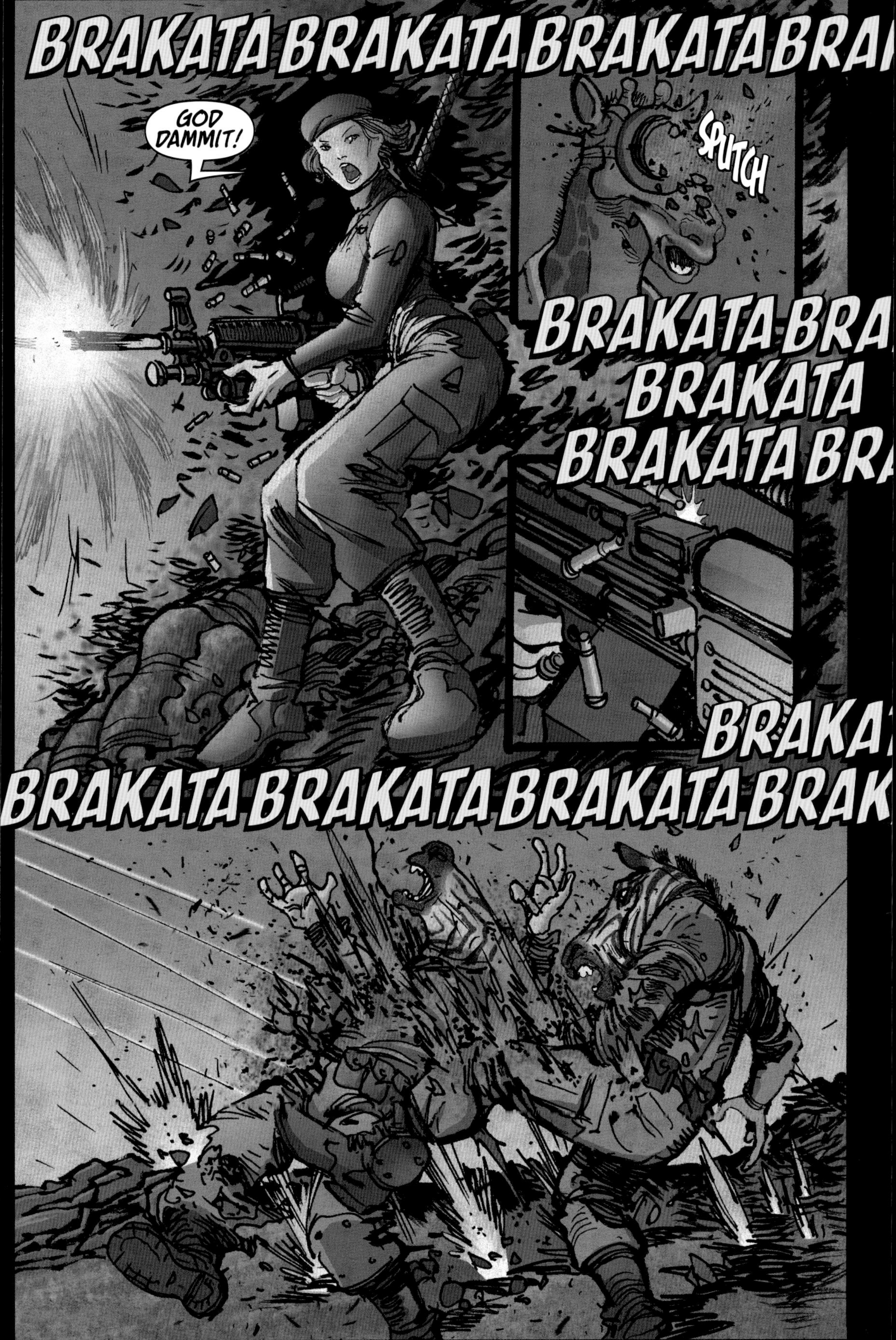
BRAKATA BRAKATA BRAKATA BRA
GOD DAMMIT!
SPUTCH
BRAKATA BRA
BRAKATA
BRAKATA BRA
BRAKA
BRAKATA BRAKATA BRAKATA BRAK

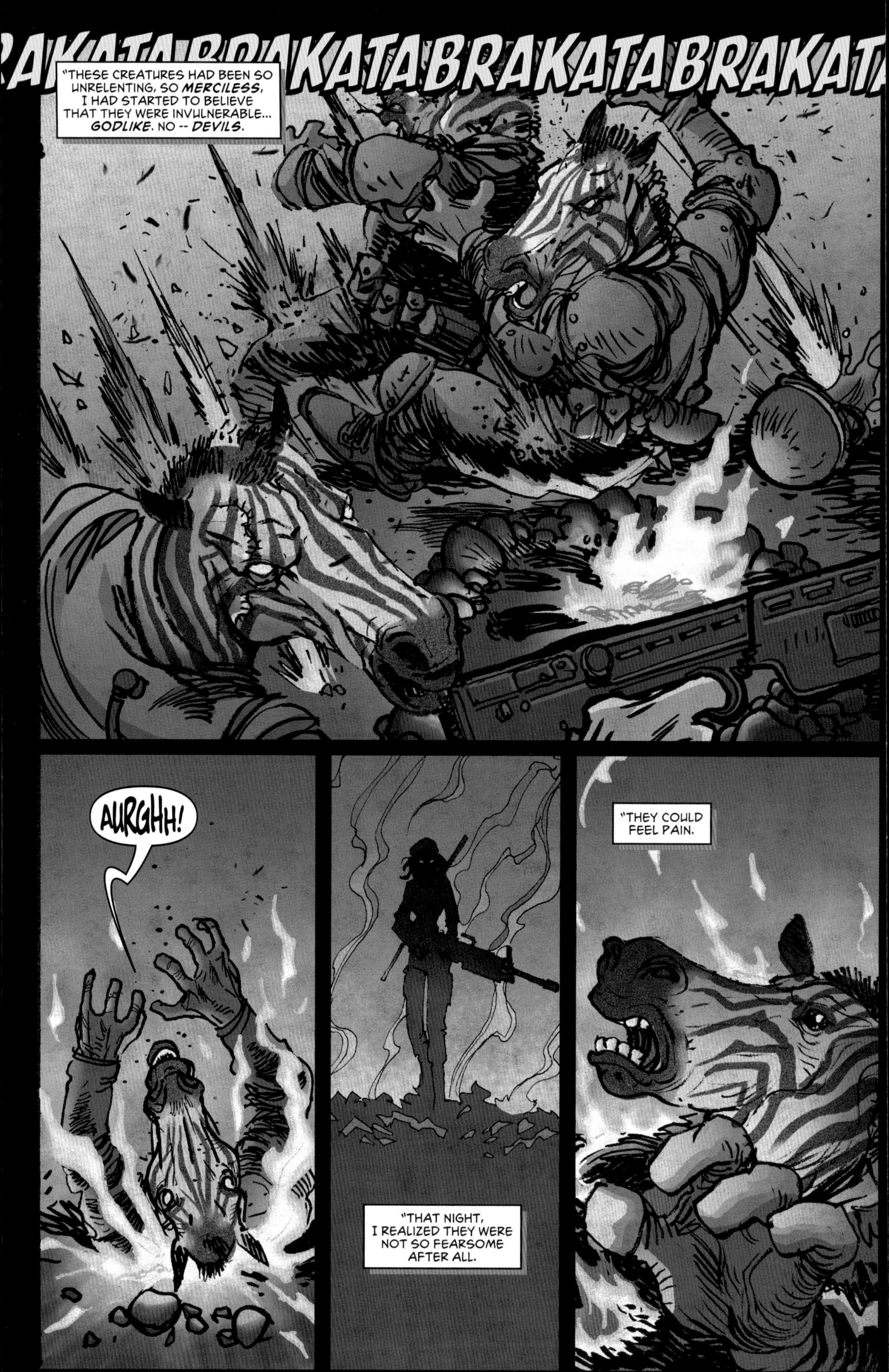
RAKATA BRAKATA BRAKATA BRAKAT
"THESE CREATURES HAD BEEN SO UNRELENTING, SO *MERCILESS*, I HAD STARTED TO BELIEVE THAT THEY WERE INVULNERABLE... *GODLIKE*. NO -- *DEVILS*.
AURGHH!
"THAT NIGHT, I REALIZED THEY WERE NOT SO FEARSOME AFTER ALL.
"THEY COULD FEEL PAIN.

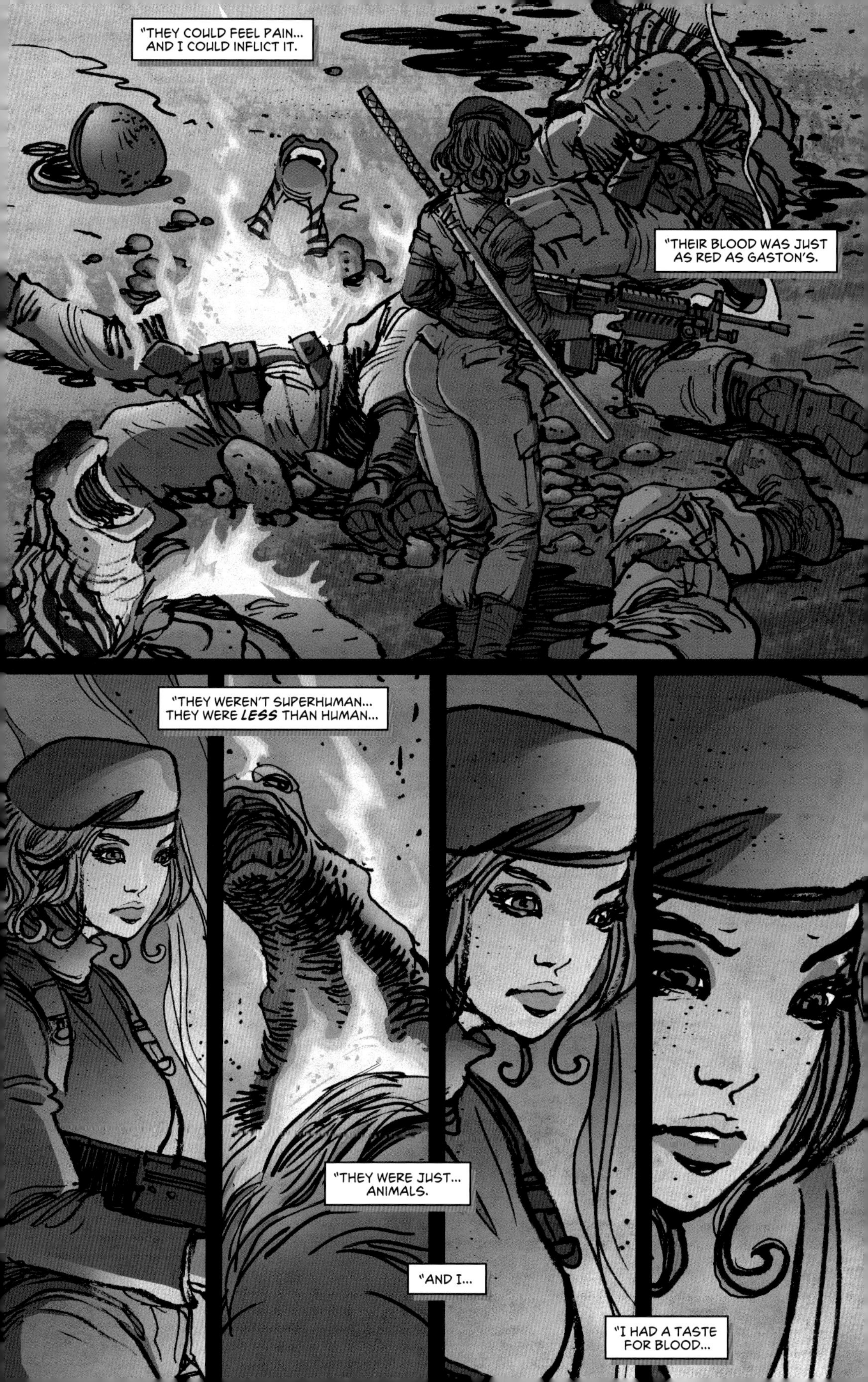
"THEY COULD FEEL PAIN... AND I COULD INFLICT IT.
"THEIR BLOOD WAS JUST AS RED AS GASTON'S.
"THEY WEREN'T SUPERHUMAN... THEY WERE *LESS* THAN HUMAN...
"THEY WERE JUST... ANIMALS.
"AND I...
"I HAD A TASTE FOR BLOOD...

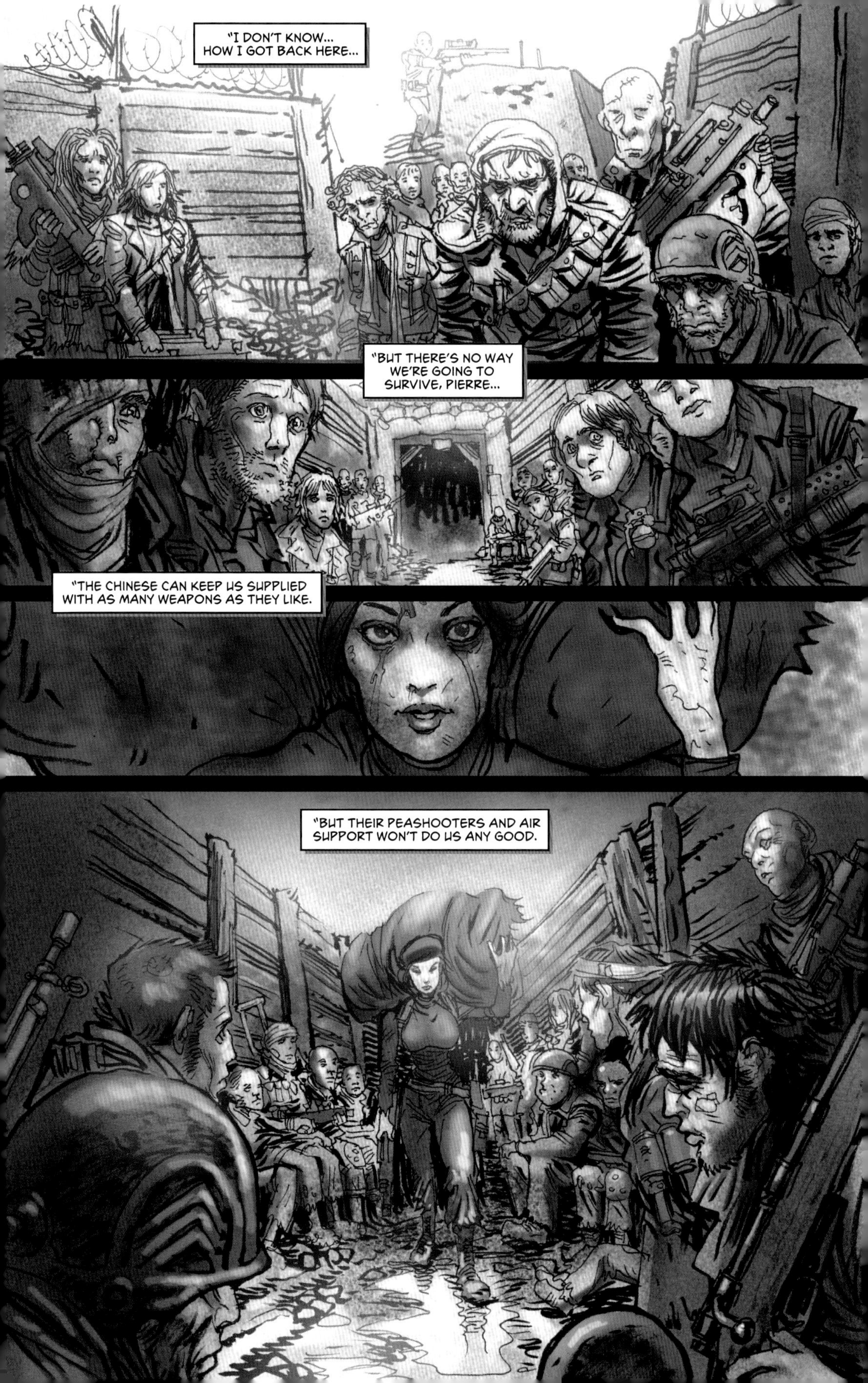
"I DON'T KNOW... HOW I GOT BACK HERE...
"BUT THERE'S NO WAY WE'RE GOING TO SURVIVE, PIERRE...
"THE CHINESE CAN KEEP US SUPPLIED WITH AS MANY WEAPONS AS THEY LIKE.
"BUT THEIR PEASHOOTERS AND AIR SUPPORT WON'T DO US ANY GOOD.

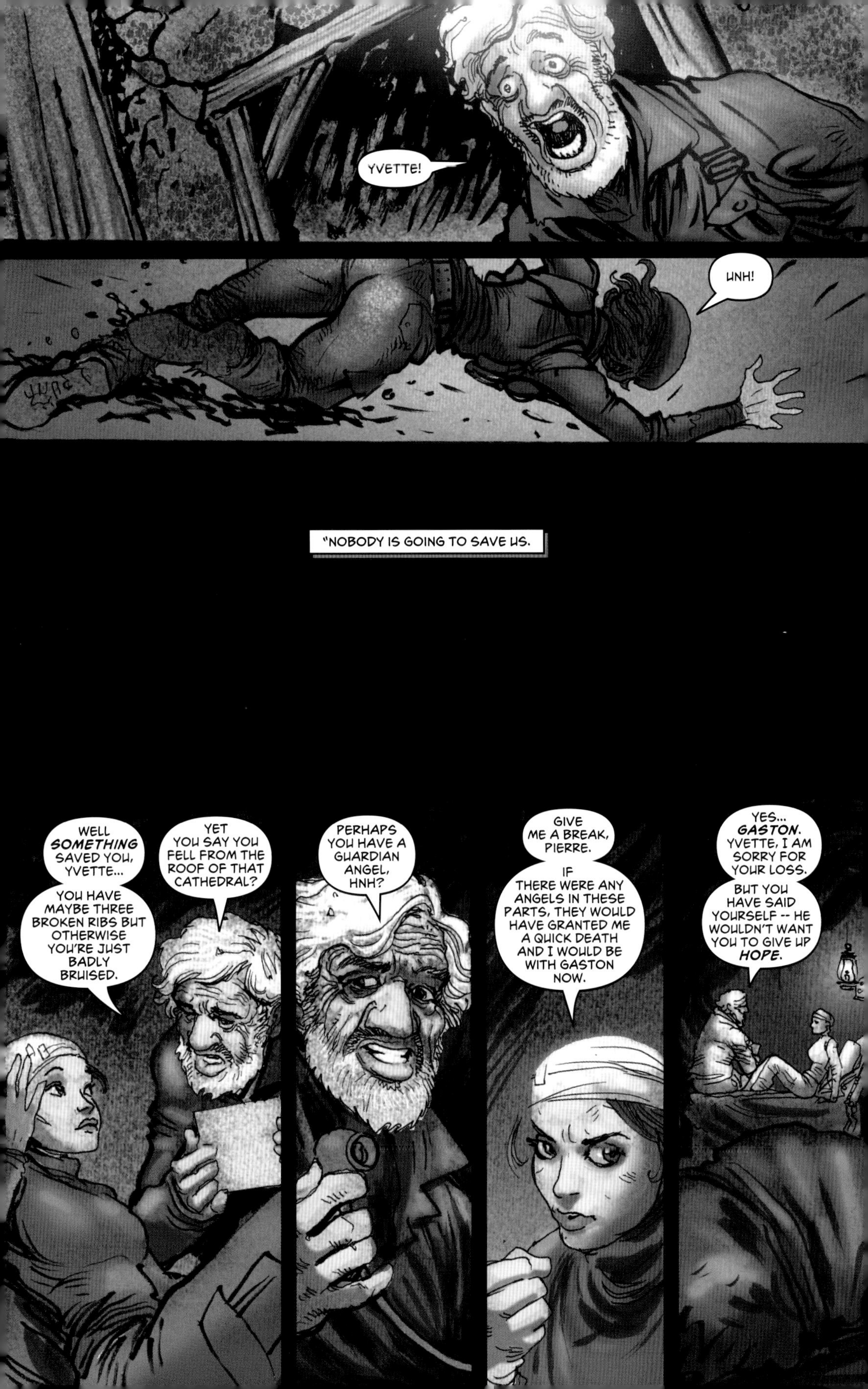
YVETTE!
UNH!
"NOBODY IS GOING TO SAVE US.
WELL SOMETHING SAVED YOU, YVETTE...
YOU HAVE MAYBE THREE BROKEN RIBS BUT OTHERWISE YOU'RE JUST BADLY BRUISED.
YET YOU SAY YOU FELL FROM THE ROOF OF THAT CATHEDRAL?
PERHAPS YOU HAVE A GUARDIAN ANGEL, HNH?
GIVE ME A BREAK, PIERRE.
IF THERE WERE ANY ANGELS IN THESE PARTS, THEY WOULD HAVE GRANTED ME A QUICK DEATH AND I WOULD BE WITH GASTON NOW.
YES... GASTON. YVETTE, I AM SORRY FOR YOUR LOSS.
BUT YOU HAVE SAID YOURSELF -- HE WOULDN'T WANT YOU TO GIVE UP HOPE.

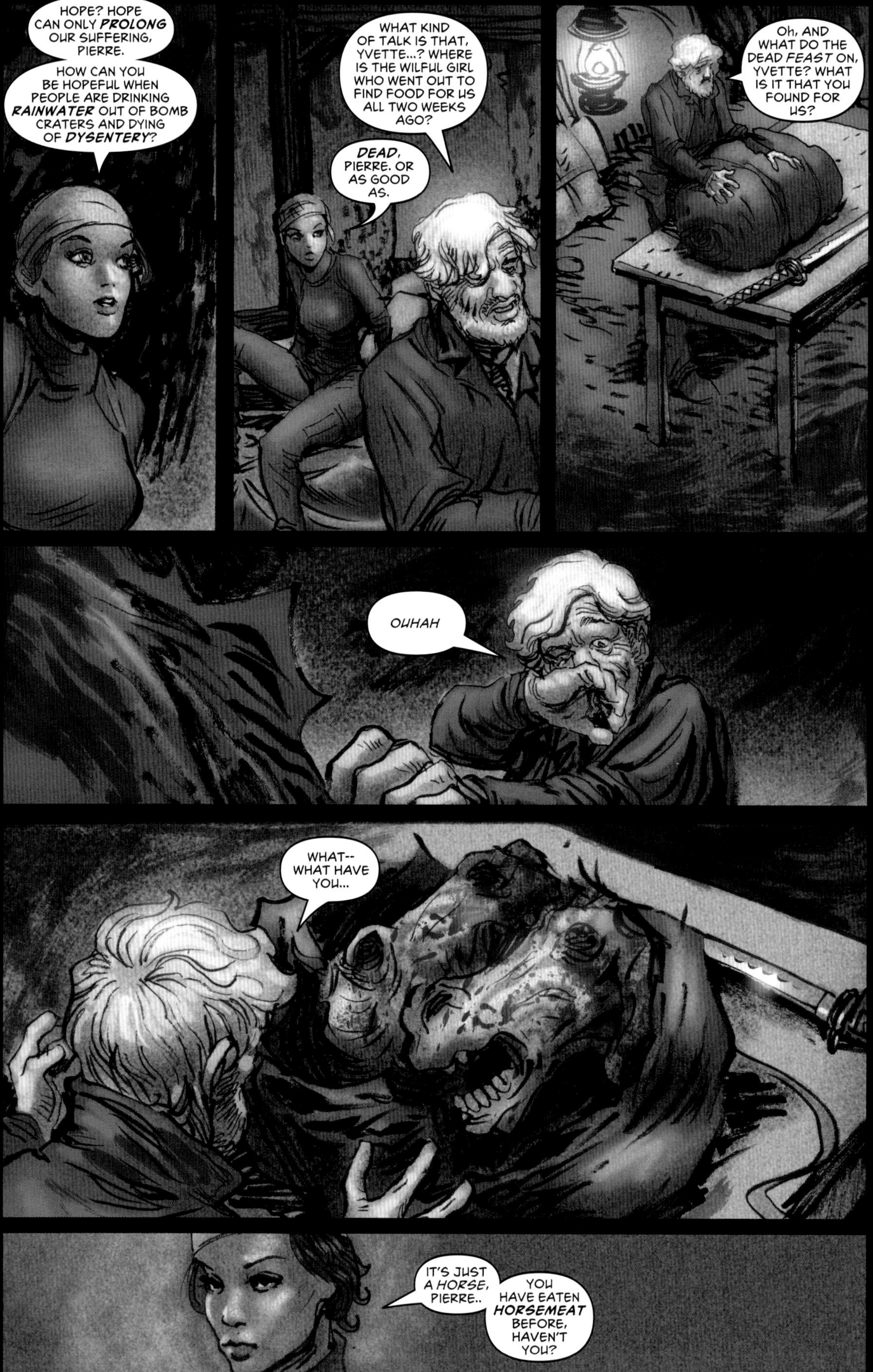

HOPE? HOPE CAN ONLY *PROLONG* OUR SUFFERING, PIERRE.
HOW CAN YOU BE HOPEFUL WHEN PEOPLE ARE DRINKING *RAINWATER* OUT OF BOMB CRATERS AND DYING OF *DYSENTERY*?
WHAT KIND OF TALK IS THAT, YVETTE...? WHERE IS THE WILFUL GIRL WHO WENT OUT TO FIND FOOD FOR US ALL TWO WEEKS AGO?
DEAD, PIERRE. OR AS GOOD AS.
Oh, AND WHAT DO THE DEAD *FEAST* ON, YVETTE? WHAT IS IT THAT YOU FOUND FOR US?
OUHAH
WHAT-- WHAT HAVE YOU...
IT'S JUST A *HORSE*, PIERRE..
YOU HAVE EATEN *HORSEMEAT* BEFORE, HAVEN'T YOU?

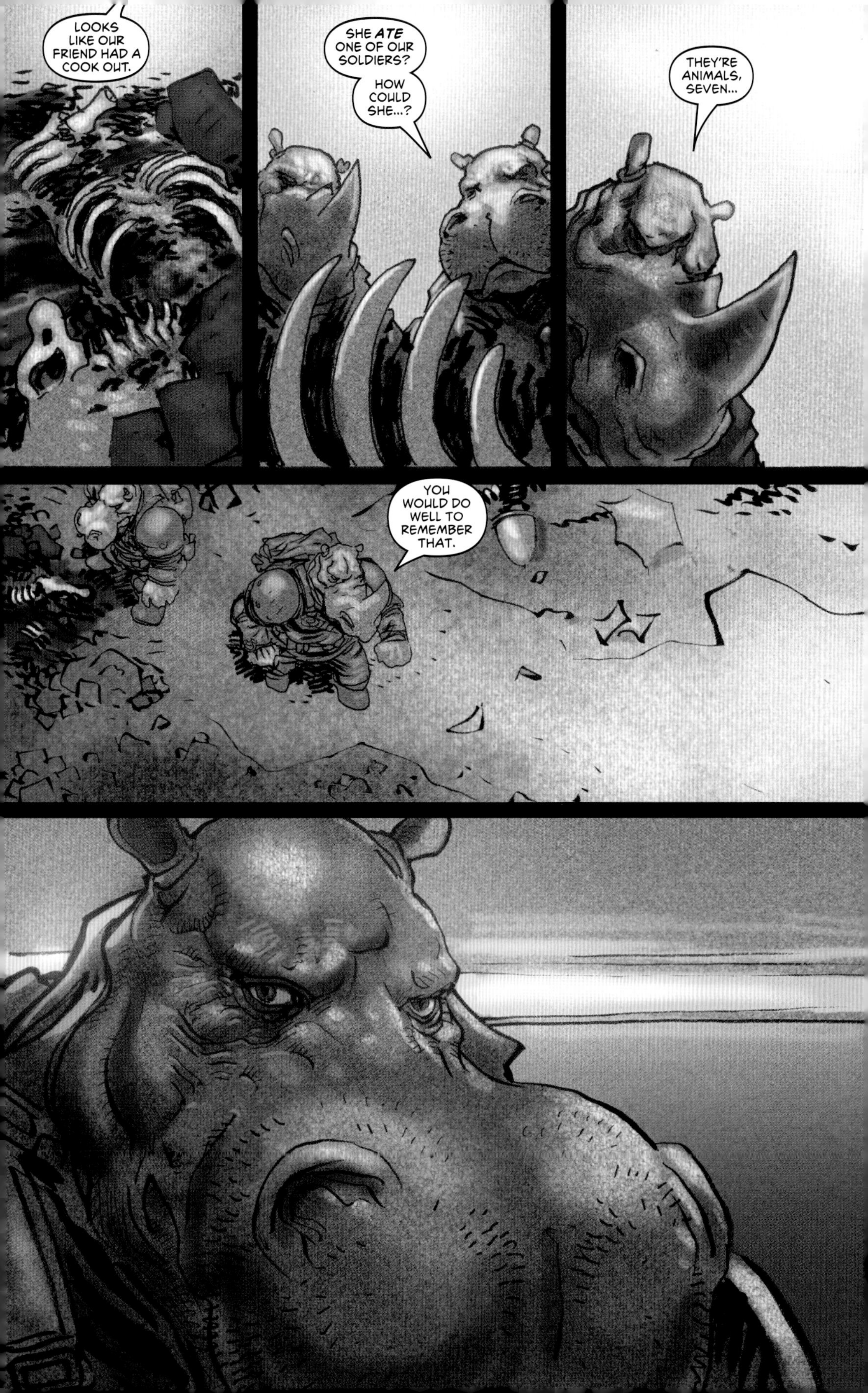
LOOKS LIKE OUR FRIEND HAD A COOK OUT.
SHE ATE ONE OF OUR SOLDIERS?
HOW COULD SHE...?
THEY'RE ANIMALS, SEVEN...
YOU WOULD DO WELL TO REMEMBER THAT.

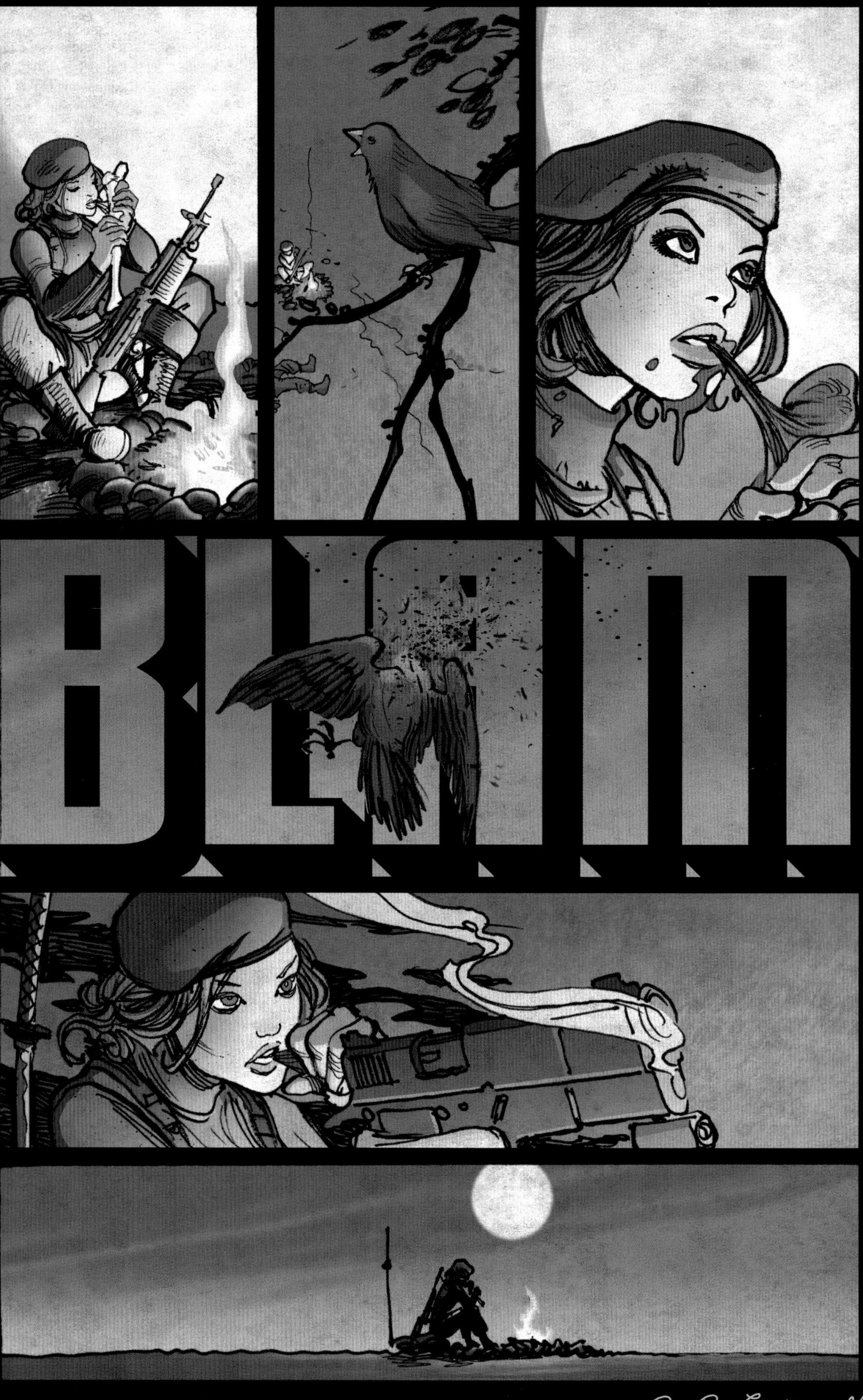
BLAM

To Be Continued!

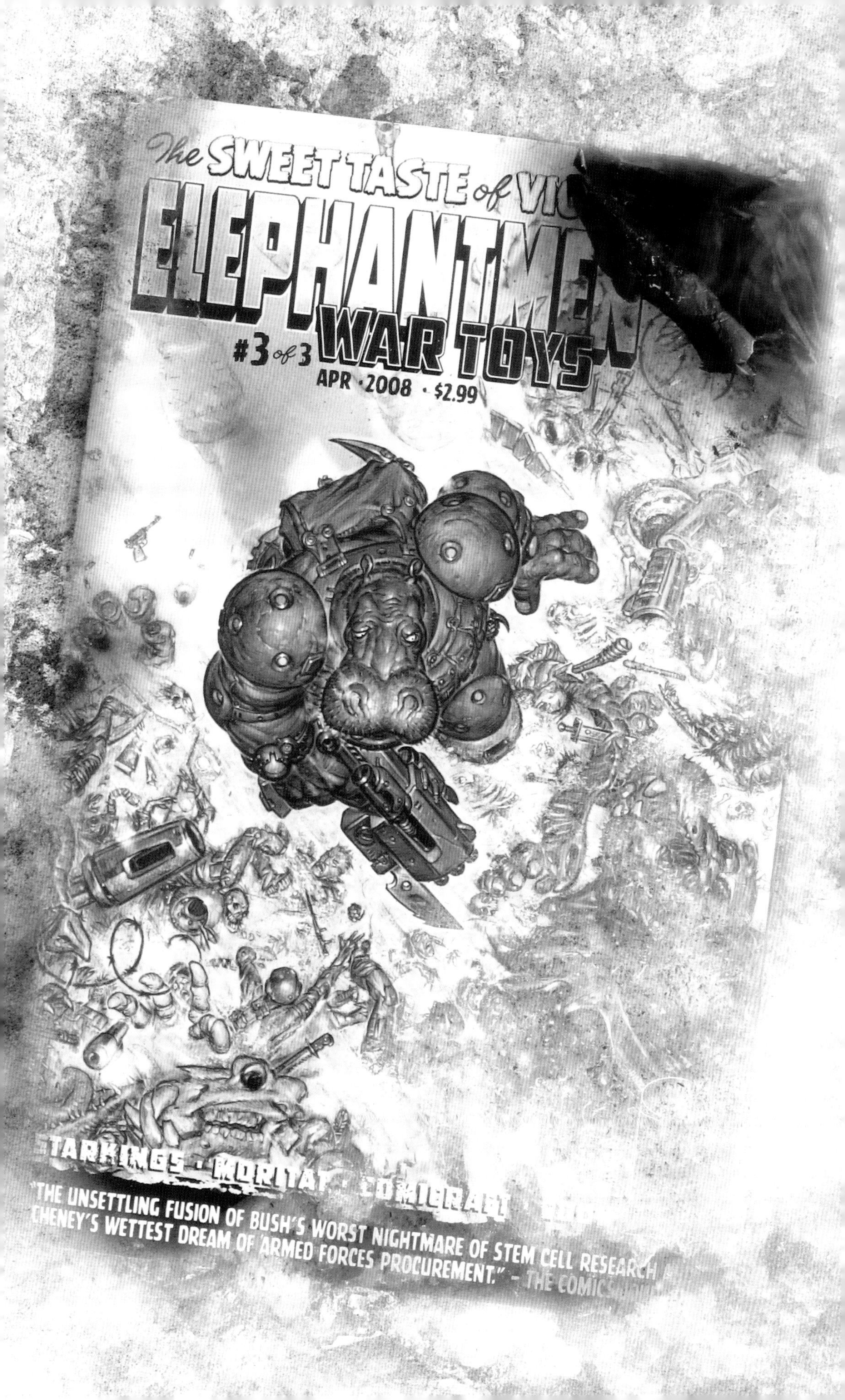
The SWEET TASTE of VIC
ELEPHANTMEN
WAR TOYS
#3 of 3
APR · 2008 · $2.99
STARKINGS · MORITAT · COMICRAFT
"THE UNSETTLING FUSION OF BUSH'S WORST NIGHTMARE OF STEM CELL RESEARCH
CHENEY'S WETTEST DREAM OF ARMED FORCES PROCUREMENT." – THE COMICS

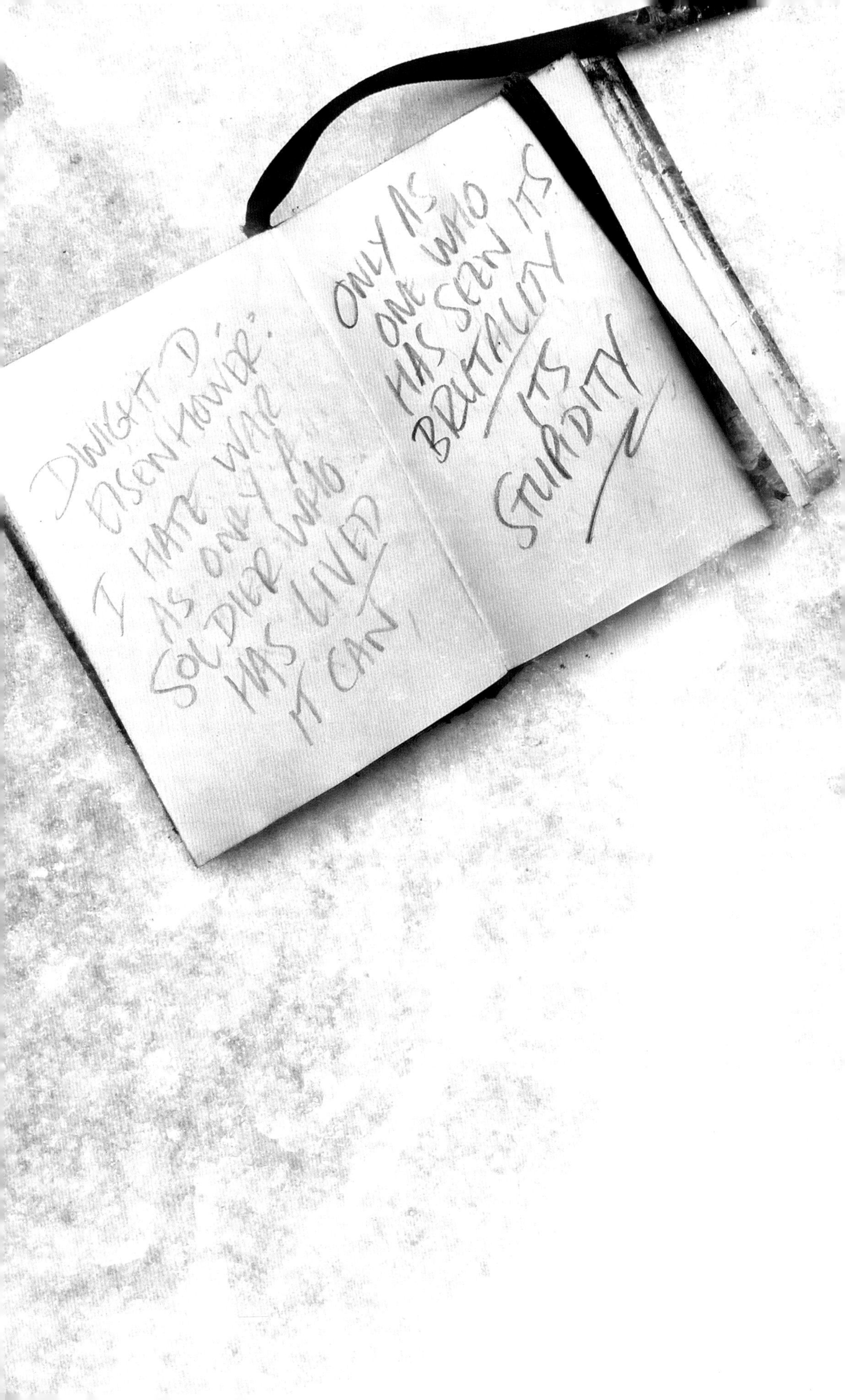
DWIGHT D. EISENHOWER:
I HATE WAR
AS ONLY A
SOLDIER WHO
HAS LIVED
IT CAN,
ONLY AS
ONE WHO
HAS SEEN ITS
BRUTALITY
/ ITS
STUPIDITY

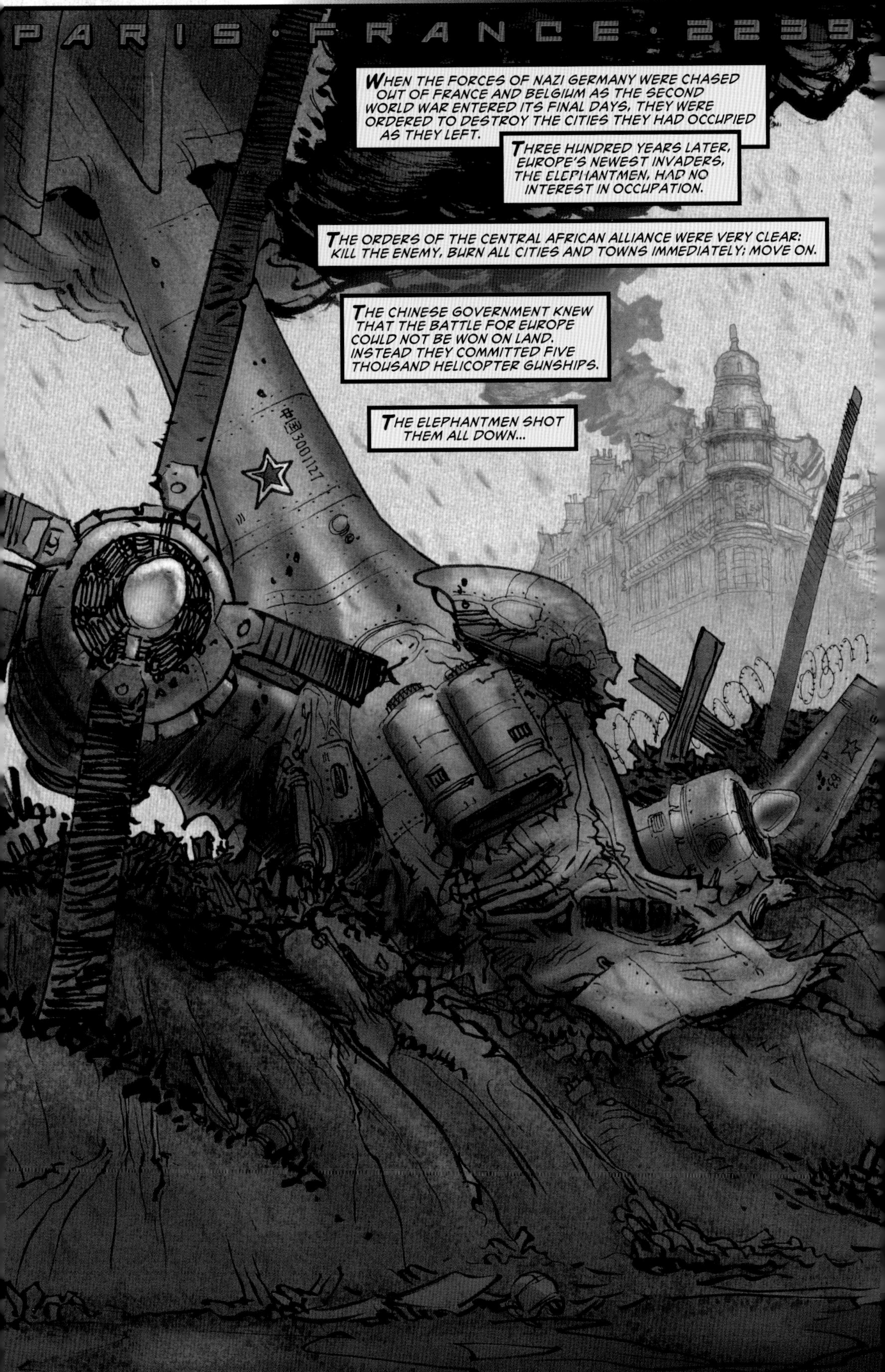
PARIS · FRANCE · 2239
WHEN THE FORCES OF NAZI GERMANY WERE CHASED OUT OF FRANCE AND BELGIUM AS THE SECOND WORLD WAR ENTERED ITS FINAL DAYS, THEY WERE ORDERED TO DESTROY THE CITIES THEY HAD OCCUPIED AS THEY LEFT.
THREE HUNDRED YEARS LATER, EUROPE'S NEWEST INVADERS, THE ELEPHANTMEN, HAD NO INTEREST IN OCCUPATION.
THE ORDERS OF THE CENTRAL AFRICAN ALLIANCE WERE VERY CLEAR: KILL THE ENEMY, BURN ALL CITIES AND TOWNS IMMEDIATELY; MOVE ON.
THE CHINESE GOVERNMENT KNEW THAT THE BATTLE FOR EUROPE COULD NOT BE WON ON LAND. INSTEAD THEY COMMITTED FIVE THOUSAND HELICOPTER GUNSHIPS.
THE ELEPHANTMEN SHOT THEM ALL DOWN...
中国3001127

CONCLUDING THE STORY OF THE WAR TO END ALL WARS!

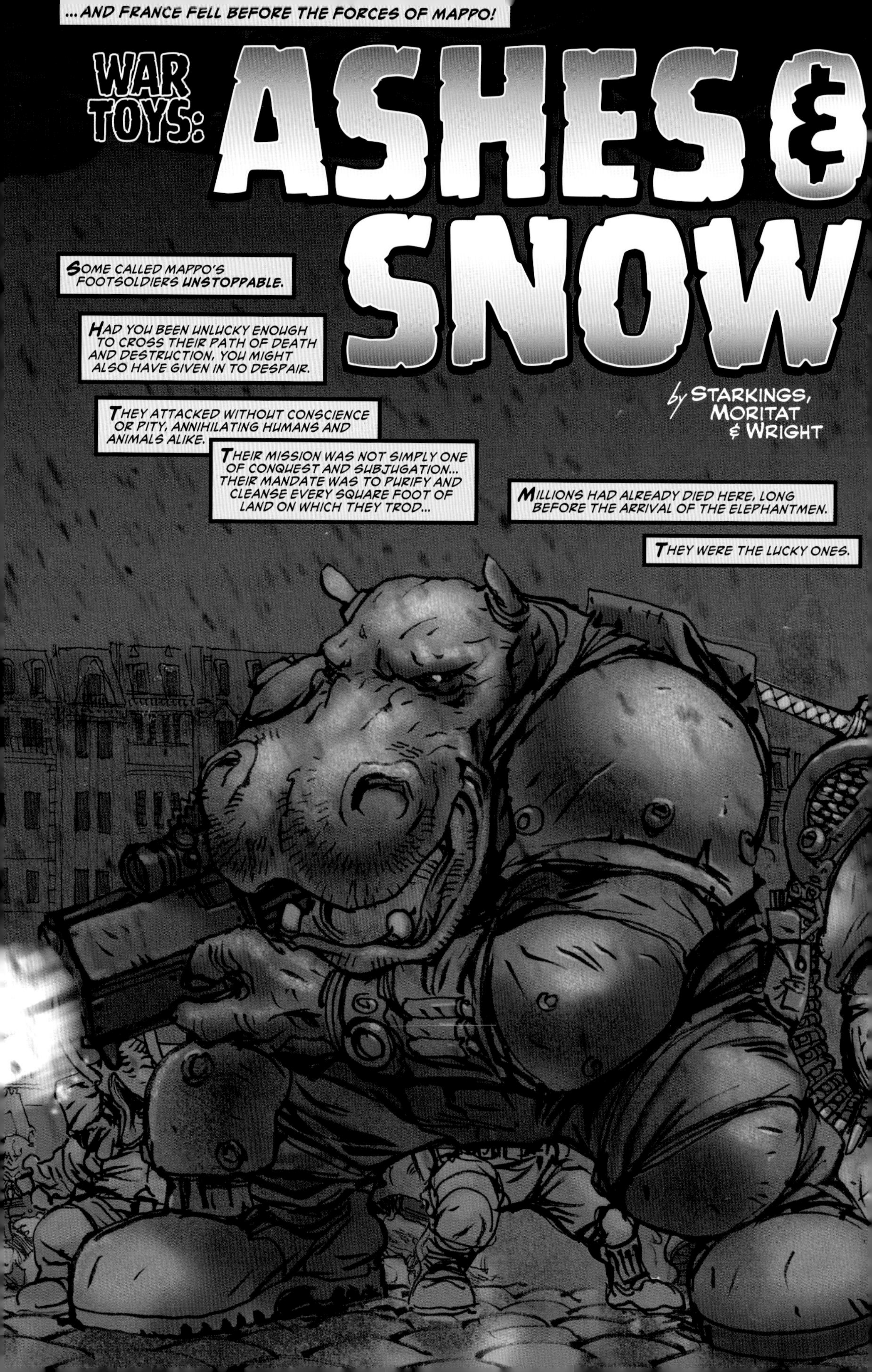

...AND FRANCE FELL BEFORE THE FORCES OF MAPPO!
WAR TOYS: ASHES & SNOW
SOME CALLED MAPPO'S FOOTSOLDIERS UNSTOPPABLE.
HAD YOU BEEN UNLUCKY ENOUGH TO CROSS THEIR PATH OF DEATH AND DESTRUCTION, YOU MIGHT ALSO HAVE GIVEN IN TO DESPAIR.
by STARKINGS, MORITAT & WRIGHT
THEY ATTACKED WITHOUT CONSCIENCE OR PITY, ANNIHILATING HUMANS AND ANIMALS ALIKE.
THEIR MISSION WAS NOT SIMPLY ONE OF CONQUEST AND SUBJUGATION... THEIR MANDATE WAS TO PURIFY AND CLEANSE EVERY SQUARE FOOT OF LAND ON WHICH THEY TROD...
MILLIONS HAD ALREADY DIED HERE, LONG BEFORE THE ARRIVAL OF THE ELEPHANTMEN.
THEY WERE THE LUCKY ONES.

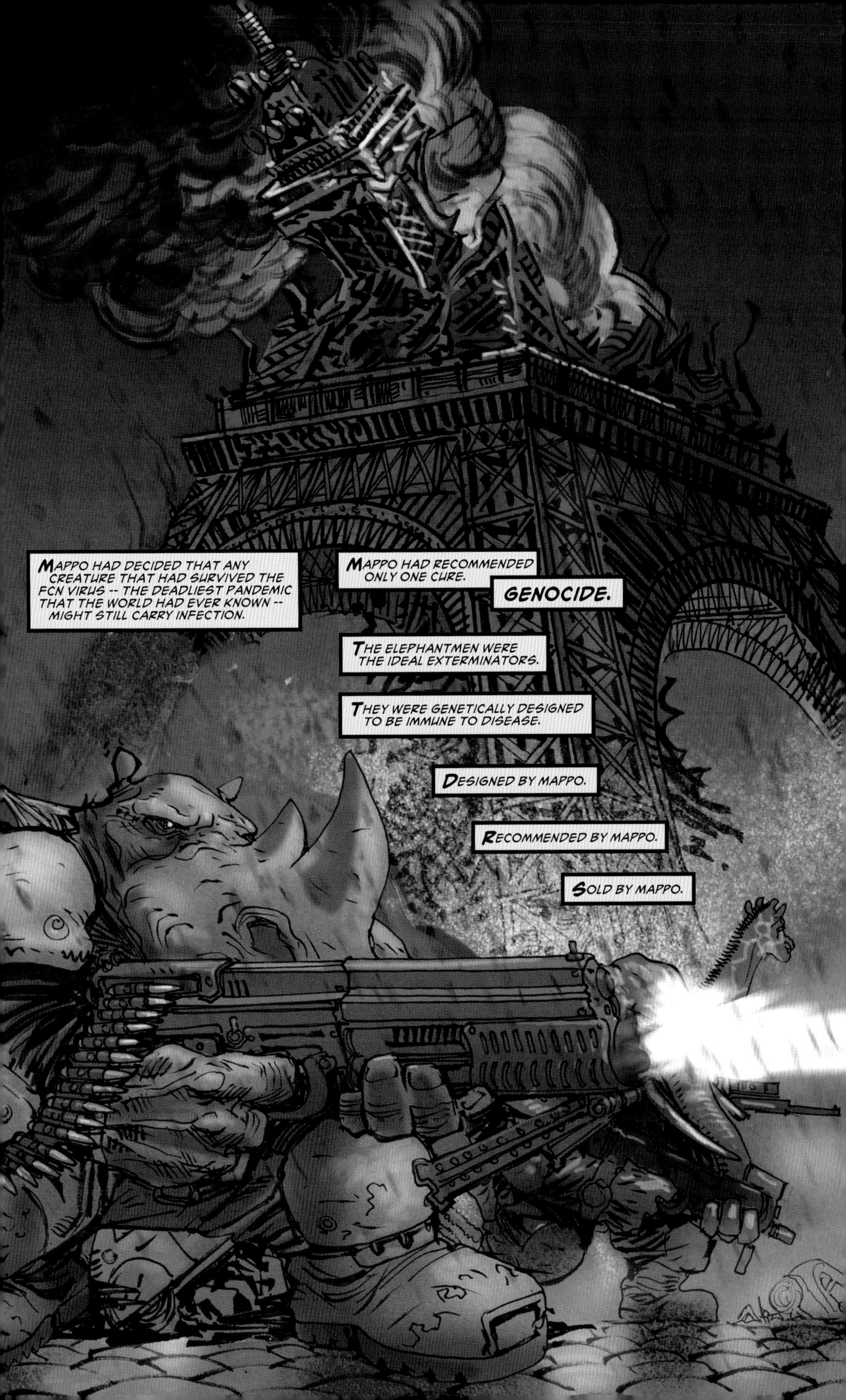
MAPPO HAD DECIDED THAT ANY CREATURE THAT HAD SURVIVED THE FCN VIRUS -- THE DEADLIEST PANDEMIC THAT THE WORLD HAD EVER KNOWN -- MIGHT STILL CARRY INFECTION.
MAPPO HAD RECOMMENDED ONLY ONE CURE.
GENOCIDE.
THE ELEPHANTMEN WERE THE IDEAL EXTERMINATORS.
THEY WERE GENETICALLY DESIGNED TO BE IMMUNE TO DISEASE.
DESIGNED BY MAPPO.
RECOMMENDED BY MAPPO.
SOLD BY MAPPO.

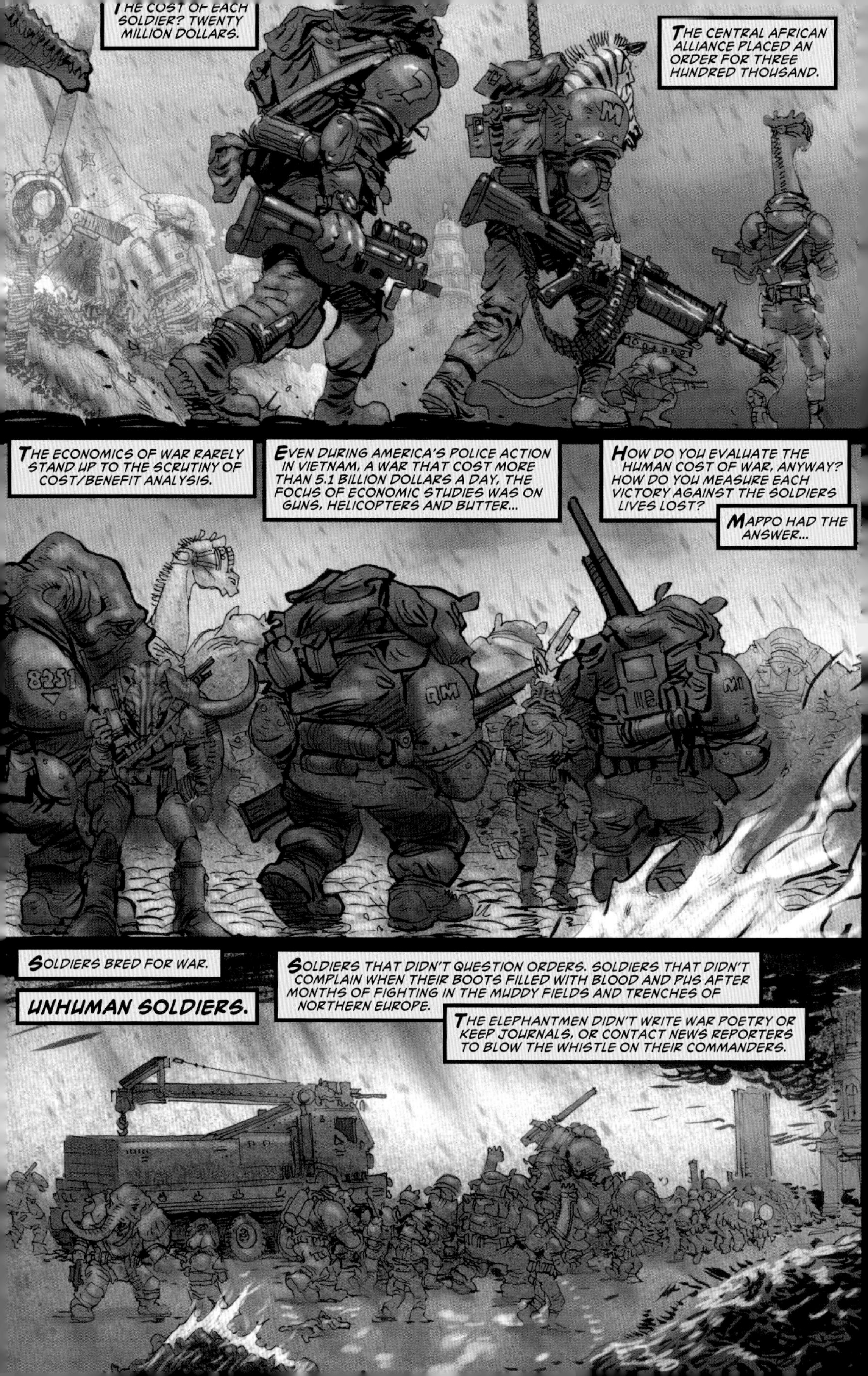
THE COST OF EACH SOLDIER? TWENTY MILLION DOLLARS.
THE CENTRAL AFRICAN ALLIANCE PLACED AN ORDER FOR THREE HUNDRED THOUSAND.
THE ECONOMICS OF WAR RARELY STAND UP TO THE SCRUTINY OF COST/BENEFIT ANALYSIS.
EVEN DURING AMERICA'S POLICE ACTION IN VIETNAM, A WAR THAT COST MORE THAN 5.1 BILLION DOLLARS A DAY, THE FOCUS OF ECONOMIC STUDIES WAS ON GUNS, HELICOPTERS AND BUTTER...
HOW DO YOU EVALUATE THE HUMAN COST OF WAR, ANYWAY? HOW DO YOU MEASURE EACH VICTORY AGAINST THE SOLDIERS LIVES LOST?
MAPPO HAD THE ANSWER...
8251
QM
MI
SOLDIERS BRED FOR WAR.
UNHUMAN SOLDIERS.
SOLDIERS THAT DIDN'T QUESTION ORDERS. SOLDIERS THAT DIDN'T COMPLAIN WHEN THEIR BOOTS FILLED WITH BLOOD AND PUS AFTER MONTHS OF FIGHTING IN THE MUDDY FIELDS AND TRENCHES OF NORTHERN EUROPE.
THE ELEPHANTMEN DIDN'T WRITE WAR POETRY OR KEEP JOURNALS, OR CONTACT NEWS REPORTERS TO BLOW THE WHISTLE ON THEIR COMMANDERS.

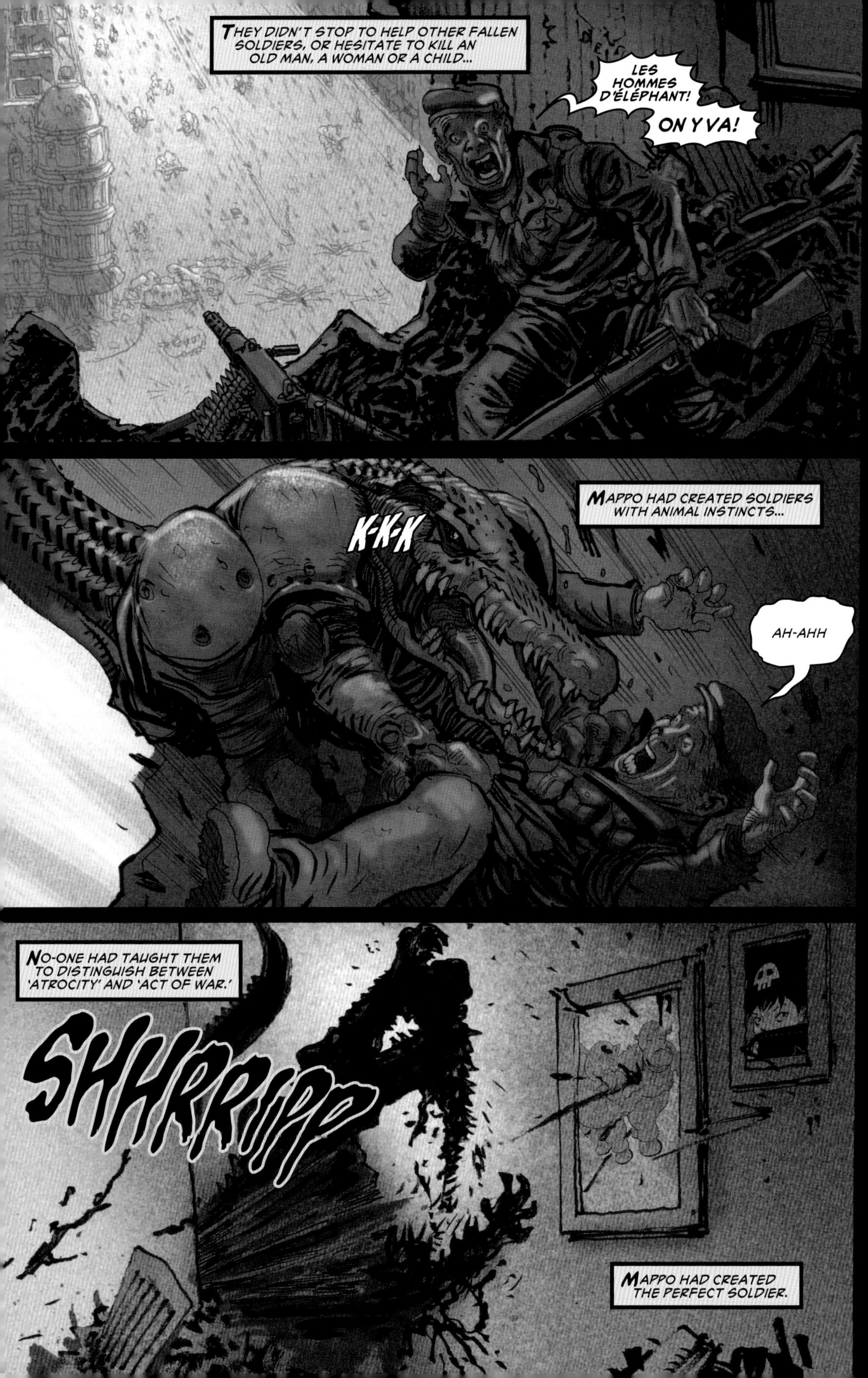
THEY DIDN'T STOP TO HELP OTHER FALLEN SOLDIERS, OR HESITATE TO KILL AN OLD MAN, A WOMAN OR A CHILD...
LES HOMMES D'ÉLÉPHANT!
ON Y VA!
MAPPO HAD CREATED SOLDIERS WITH ANIMAL INSTINCTS...
K-K-K
AH-AHH
NO-ONE HAD TAUGHT THEM TO DISTINGUISH BETWEEN 'ATROCITY' AND 'ACT OF WAR.'
SHHRRIPP
MAPPO HAD CREATED THE PERFECT SOLDIER.

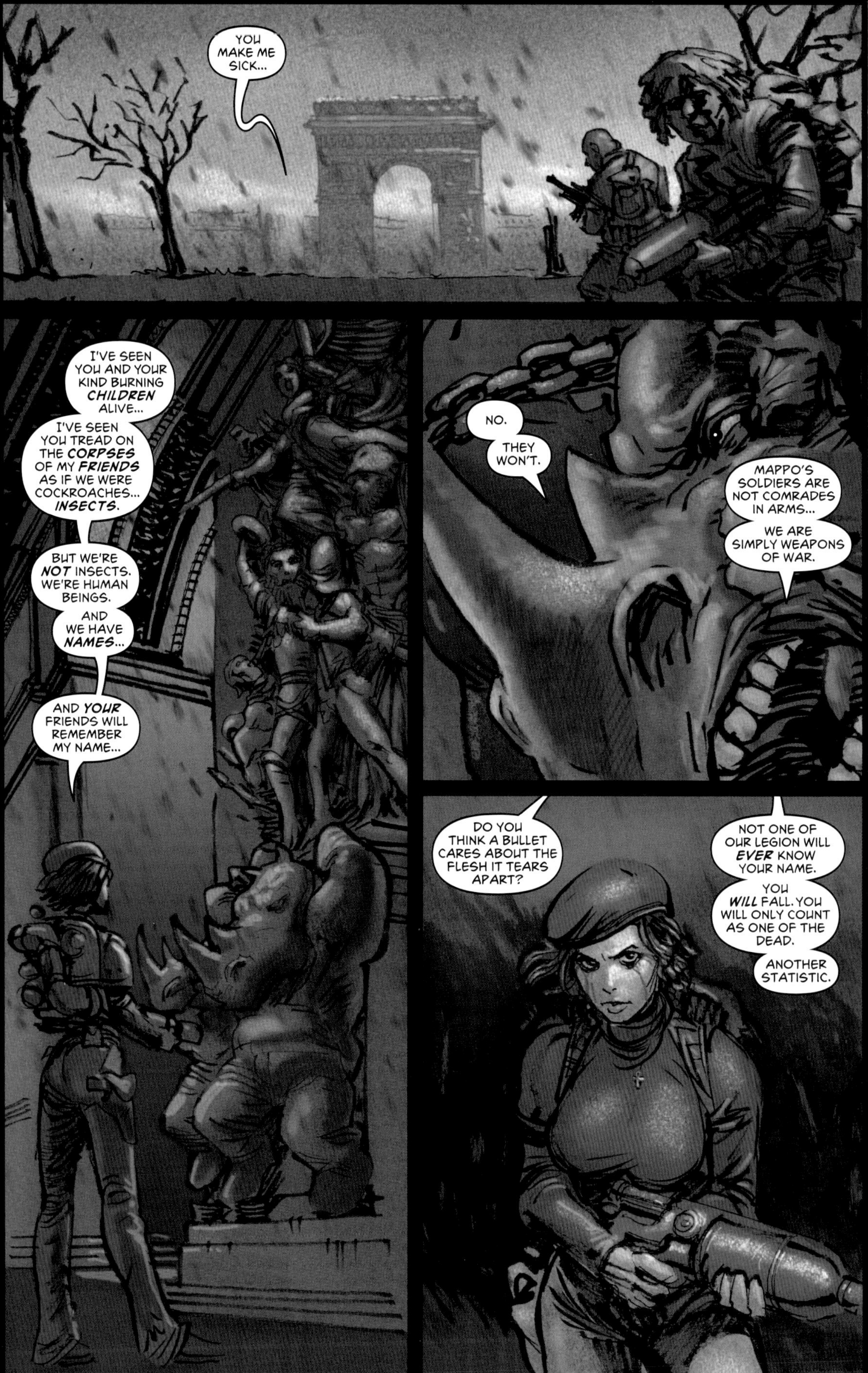

YOU MAKE ME SICK...
I'VE SEEN YOU AND YOUR KIND BURNING **CHILDREN** ALIVE...
I'VE SEEN YOU TREAD ON THE **CORPSES** OF MY **FRIENDS** AS IF WE WERE COCKROACHES... **INSECTS**.
BUT WE'RE **NOT** INSECTS. WE'RE HUMAN BEINGS.
AND WE HAVE **NAMES**...
AND **YOUR** FRIENDS WILL REMEMBER MY NAME...
NO.
THEY WON'T.
MAPPO'S SOLDIERS ARE NOT COMRADES IN ARMS...
WE ARE SIMPLY WEAPONS OF WAR.
DO YOU THINK A BULLET CARES ABOUT THE FLESH IT TEARS APART?
NOT ONE OF OUR LEGION WILL **EVER** KNOW YOUR NAME.
YOU **WILL** FALL. YOU WILL ONLY COUNT AS ONE OF THE DEAD.
ANOTHER STATISTIC.

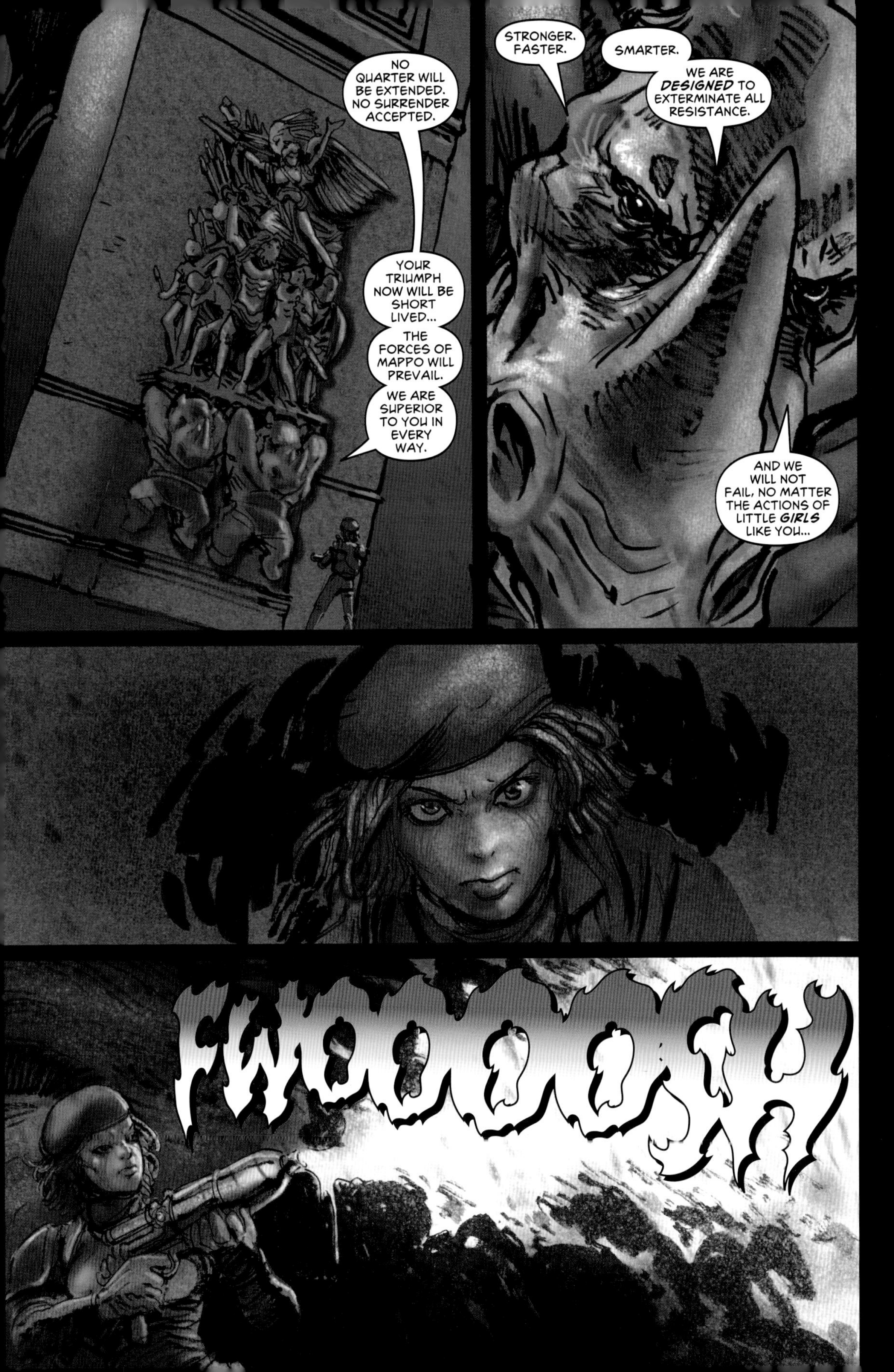
NO QUARTER WILL BE EXTENDED. NO SURRENDER ACCEPTED.
YOUR TRIUMPH NOW WILL BE SHORT LIVED...
THE FORCES OF MAPPO WILL PREVAIL.
WE ARE SUPERIOR TO YOU IN EVERY WAY.
STRONGER. FASTER.
SMARTER.
WE ARE *DESIGNED* TO EXTERMINATE ALL RESISTANCE.
AND WE WILL NOT FAIL, NO MATTER THE ACTIONS OF LITTLE *GIRLS* LIKE YOU...
FWOOOOSH

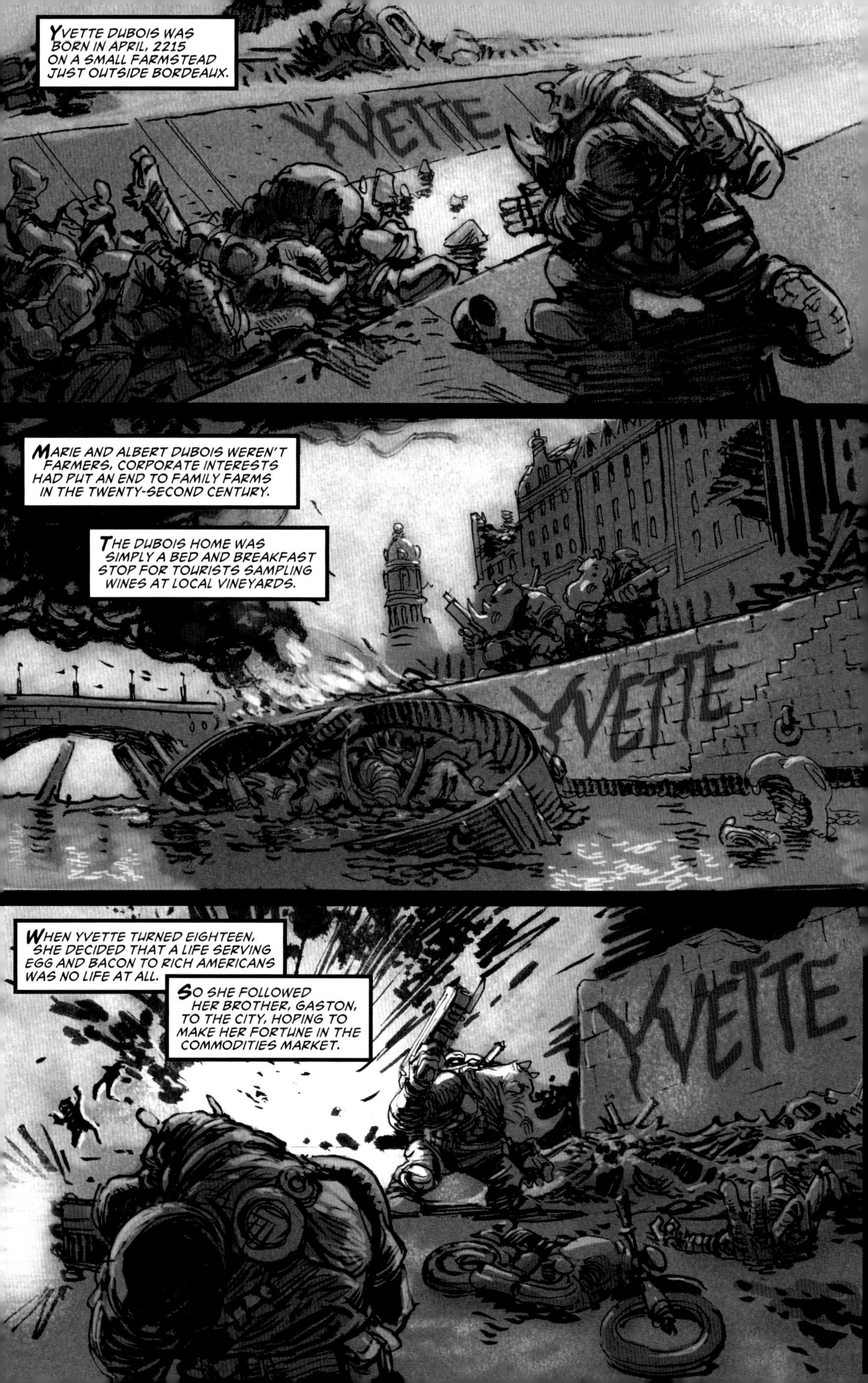
YVETTE DUBOIS WAS BORN IN APRIL, 2215 ON A SMALL FARMSTEAD JUST OUTSIDE BORDEAUX.
YVETTE
MARIE AND ALBERT DUBOIS WEREN'T FARMERS, CORPORATE INTERESTS HAD PUT AN END TO FAMILY FARMS IN THE TWENTY-SECOND CENTURY.
THE DUBOIS HOME WAS SIMPLY A BED AND BREAKFAST STOP FOR TOURISTS SAMPLING WINES AT LOCAL VINEYARDS.
YVETTE
WHEN YVETTE TURNED EIGHTEEN, SHE DECIDED THAT A LIFE SERVING EGG AND BACON TO RICH AMERICANS WAS NO LIFE AT ALL.
SO SHE FOLLOWED HER BROTHER, GASTON, TO THE CITY, HOPING TO MAKE HER FORTUNE IN THE COMMODITIES MARKET.
YVETTE

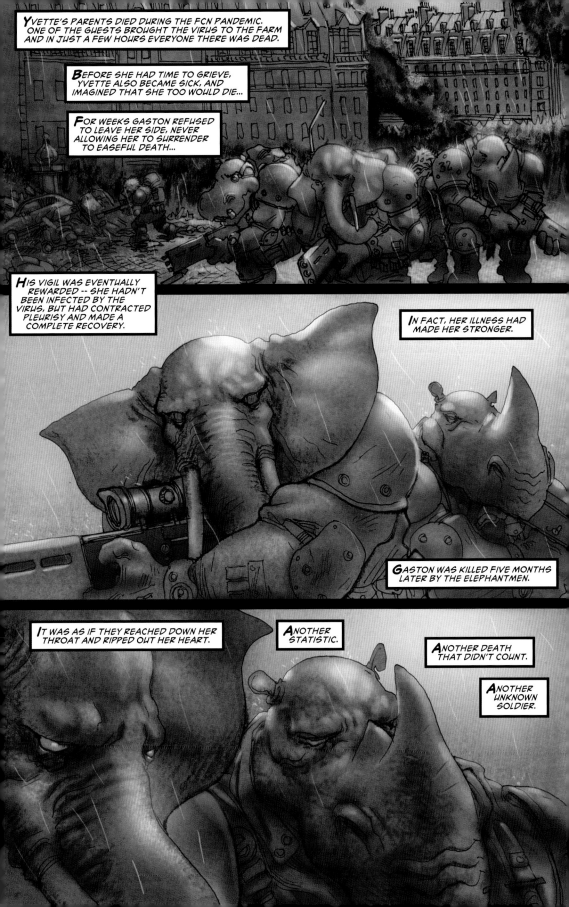

YVETTE'S PARENTS DIED DURING THE FCN PANDEMIC. ONE OF THE GUESTS BROUGHT THE VIRUS TO THE FARM AND IN JUST A FEW HOURS EVERYONE THERE WAS DEAD.

BEFORE SHE HAD TIME TO GRIEVE, YVETTE ALSO BECAME SICK, AND IMAGINED THAT SHE TOO WOULD DIE...

FOR WEEKS GASTON REFUSED TO LEAVE HER SIDE, NEVER ALLOWING HER TO SURRENDER TO EASEFUL DEATH...

HIS VIGIL WAS EVENTUALLY REWARDED -- SHE HADN'T BEEN INFECTED BY THE VIRUS, BUT HAD CONTRACTED PLEURISY AND MADE A COMPLETE RECOVERY.

IN FACT, HER ILLNESS HAD MADE HER STRONGER.

GASTON WAS KILLED FIVE MONTHS LATER BY THE ELEPHANTMEN.

IT WAS AS IF THEY REACHED DOWN HER THROAT AND RIPPED OUT HER HEART.

ANOTHER STATISTIC.

ANOTHER DEATH THAT DIDN'T COUNT.

ANOTHER UNKNOWN SOLDIER.

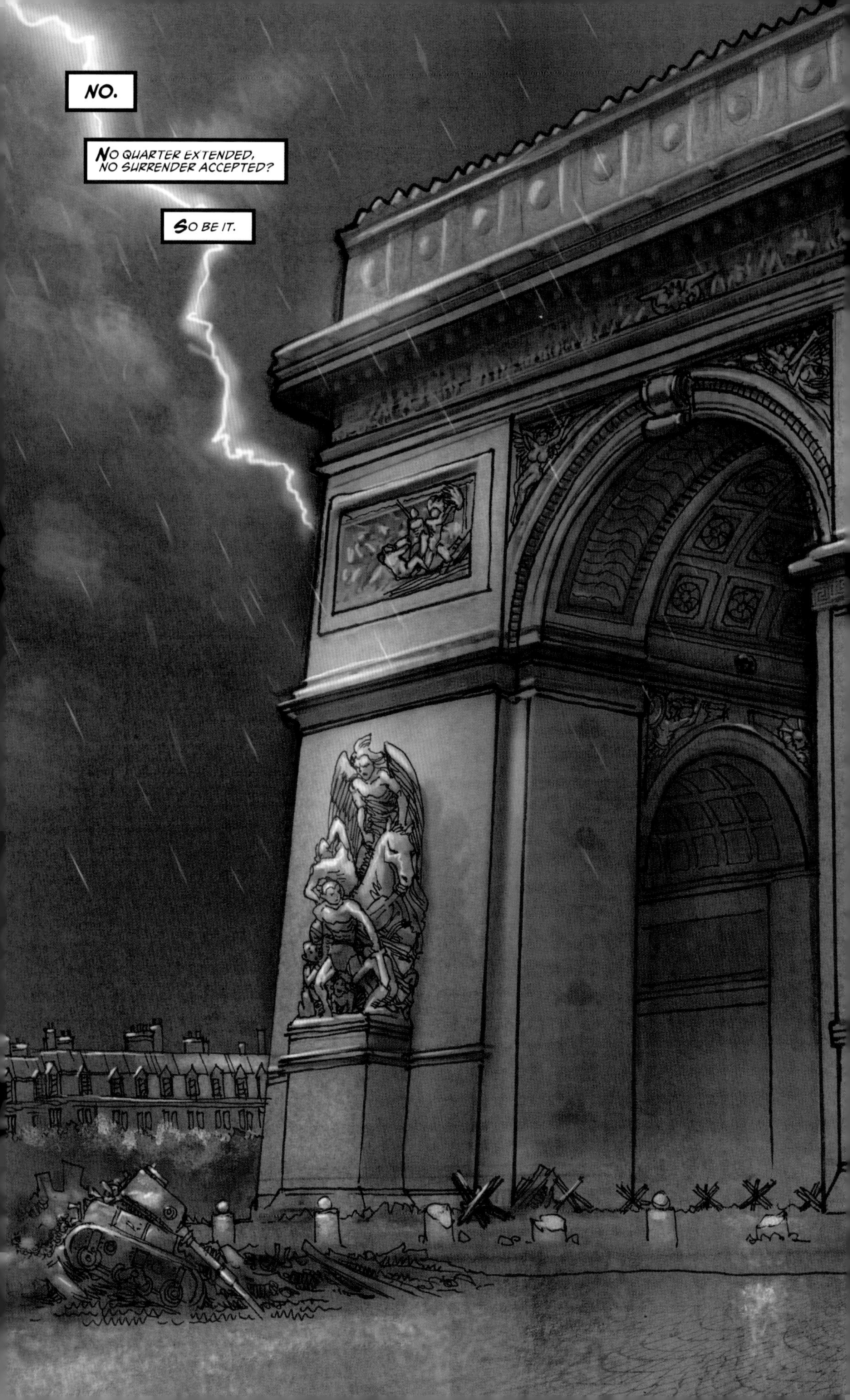
NO.
NO QUARTER EXTENDED, NO SURRENDER ACCEPTED?
SO BE IT.

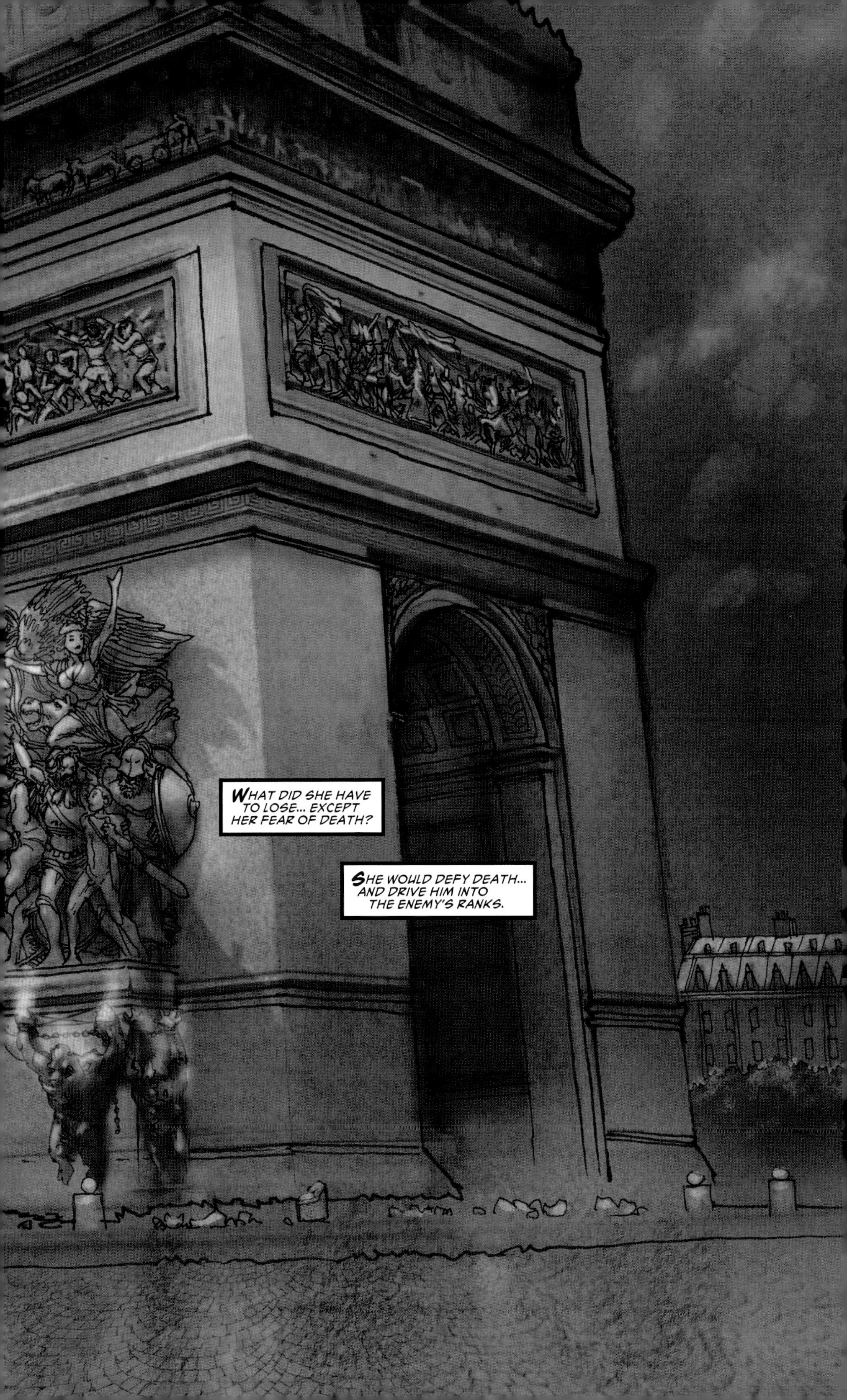
WHAT DID SHE HAVE TO LOSE... EXCEPT HER FEAR OF DEATH?
SHE WOULD DEFY DEATH... AND DRIVE HIM INTO THE ENEMY'S RANKS.

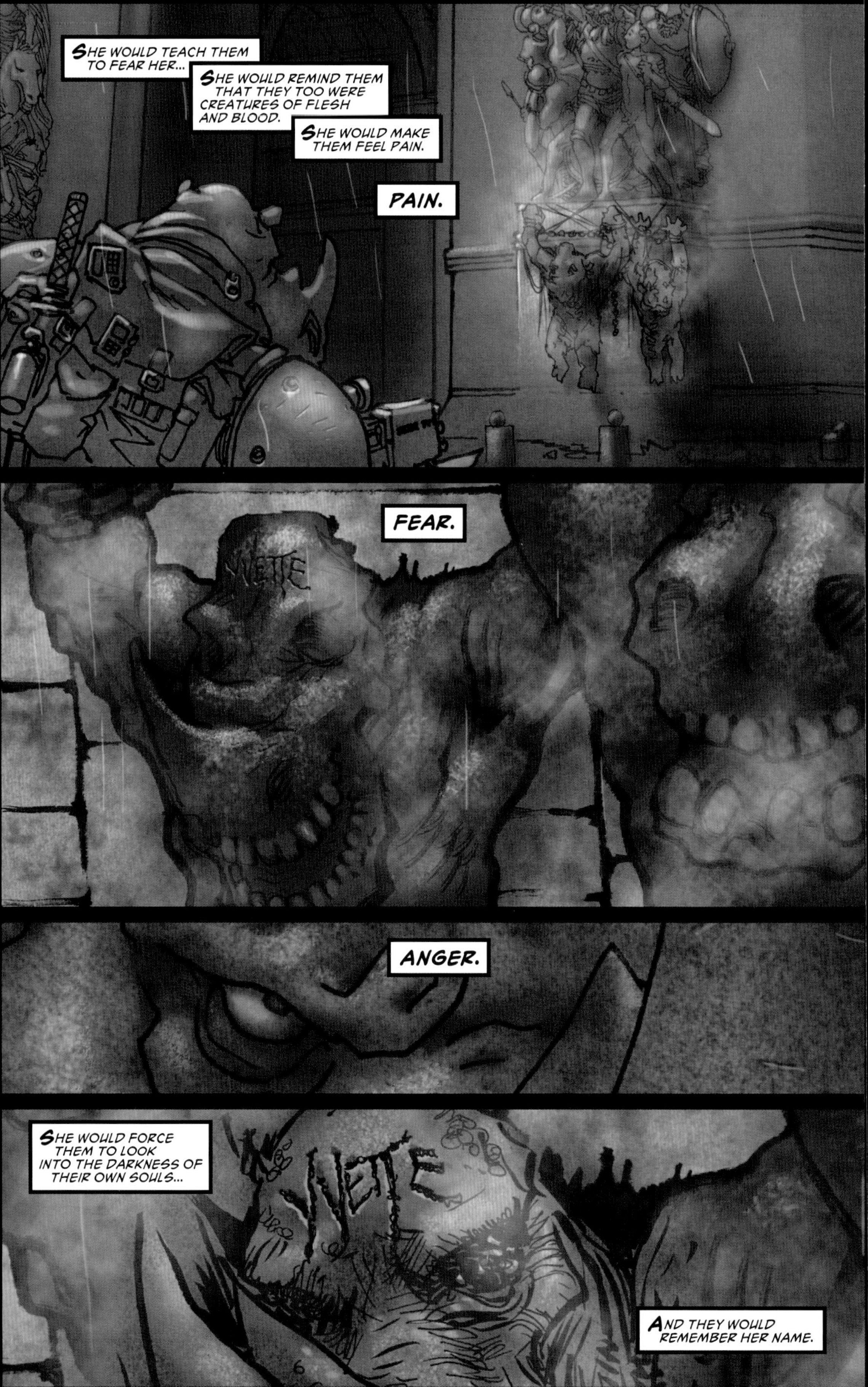
SHE WOULD TEACH THEM TO FEAR HER...
SHE WOULD REMIND THEM THAT THEY TOO WERE CREATURES OF FLESH AND BLOOD.
SHE WOULD MAKE THEM FEEL PAIN.
PAIN.
FEAR.
ANGER.
SHE WOULD FORCE THEM TO LOOK INTO THE DARKNESS OF THEIR OWN SOULS...
AND THEY WOULD REMEMBER HER NAME.

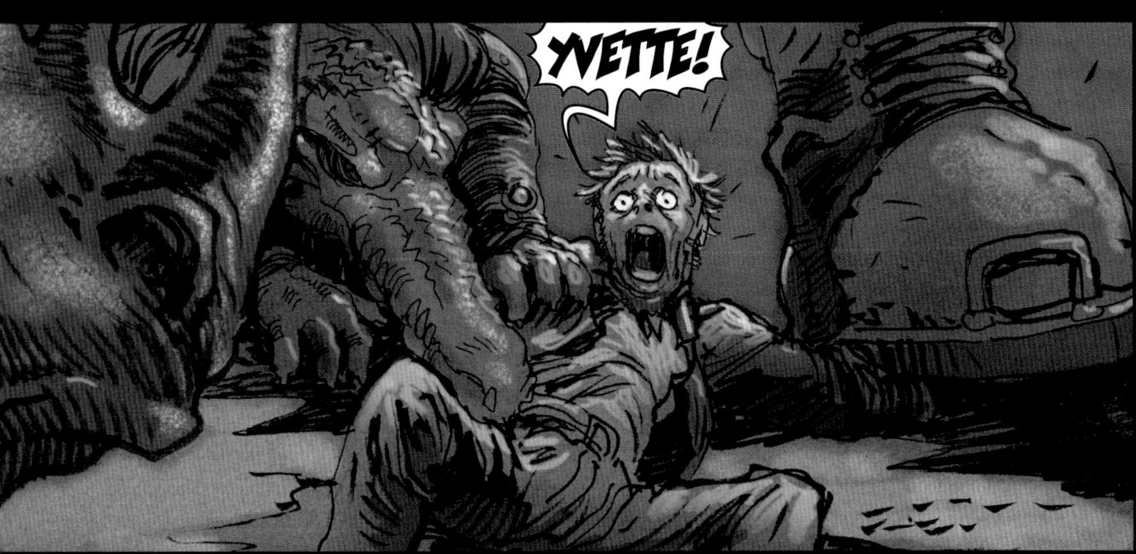
YVETTE!

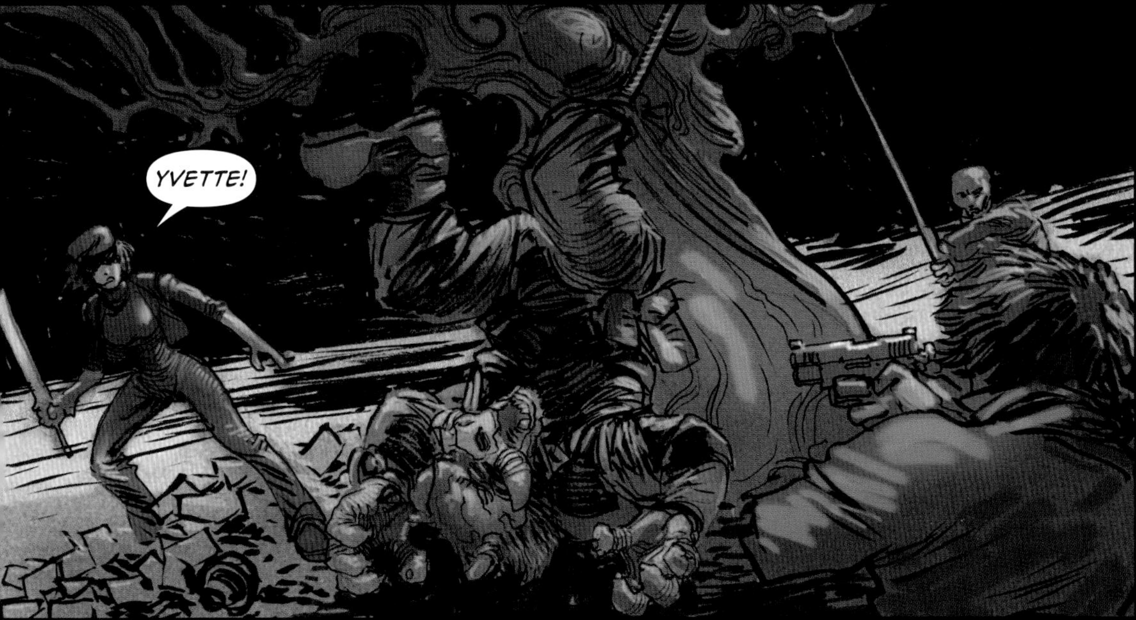
YVETTE!

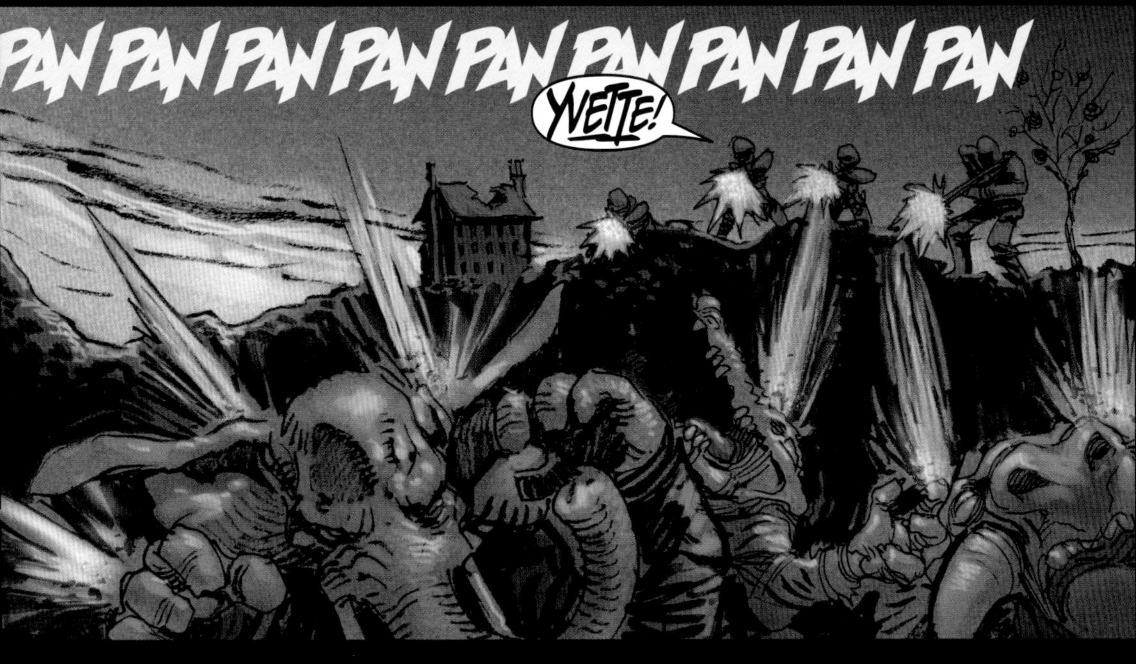
PAN PAN PAN PAN PAN PAN PAN PAN PAN
YVETTE!

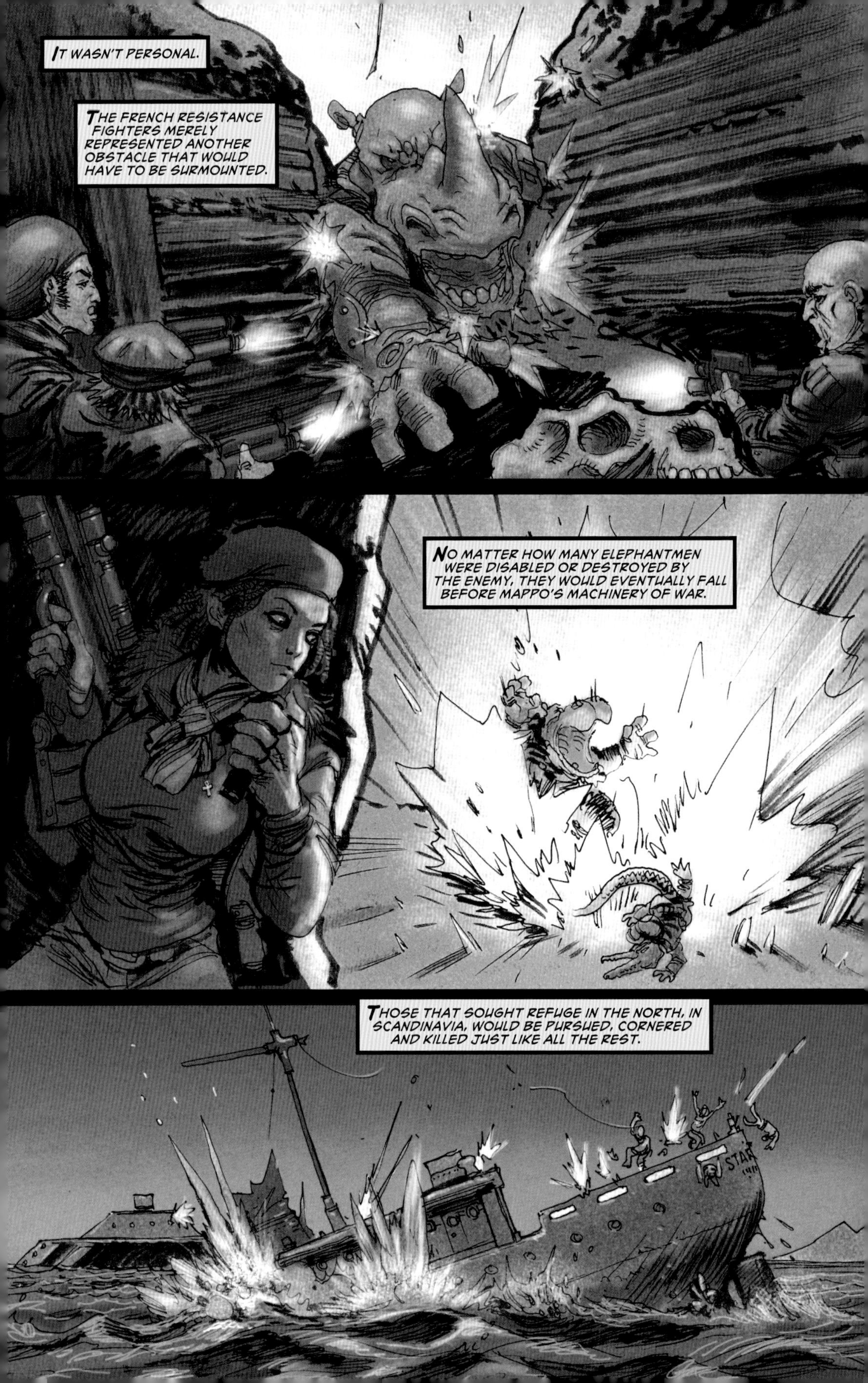
IT WASN'T PERSONAL.
THE FRENCH RESISTANCE FIGHTERS MERELY REPRESENTED ANOTHER OBSTACLE THAT WOULD HAVE TO BE SURMOUNTED.
NO MATTER HOW MANY ELEPHANTMEN WERE DISABLED OR DESTROYED BY THE ENEMY, THEY WOULD EVENTUALLY FALL BEFORE MAPPO'S MACHINERY OF WAR.
THOSE THAT SOUGHT REFUGE IN THE NORTH, IN SCANDINAVIA, WOULD BE PURSUED, CORNERED AND KILLED JUST LIKE ALL THE REST.

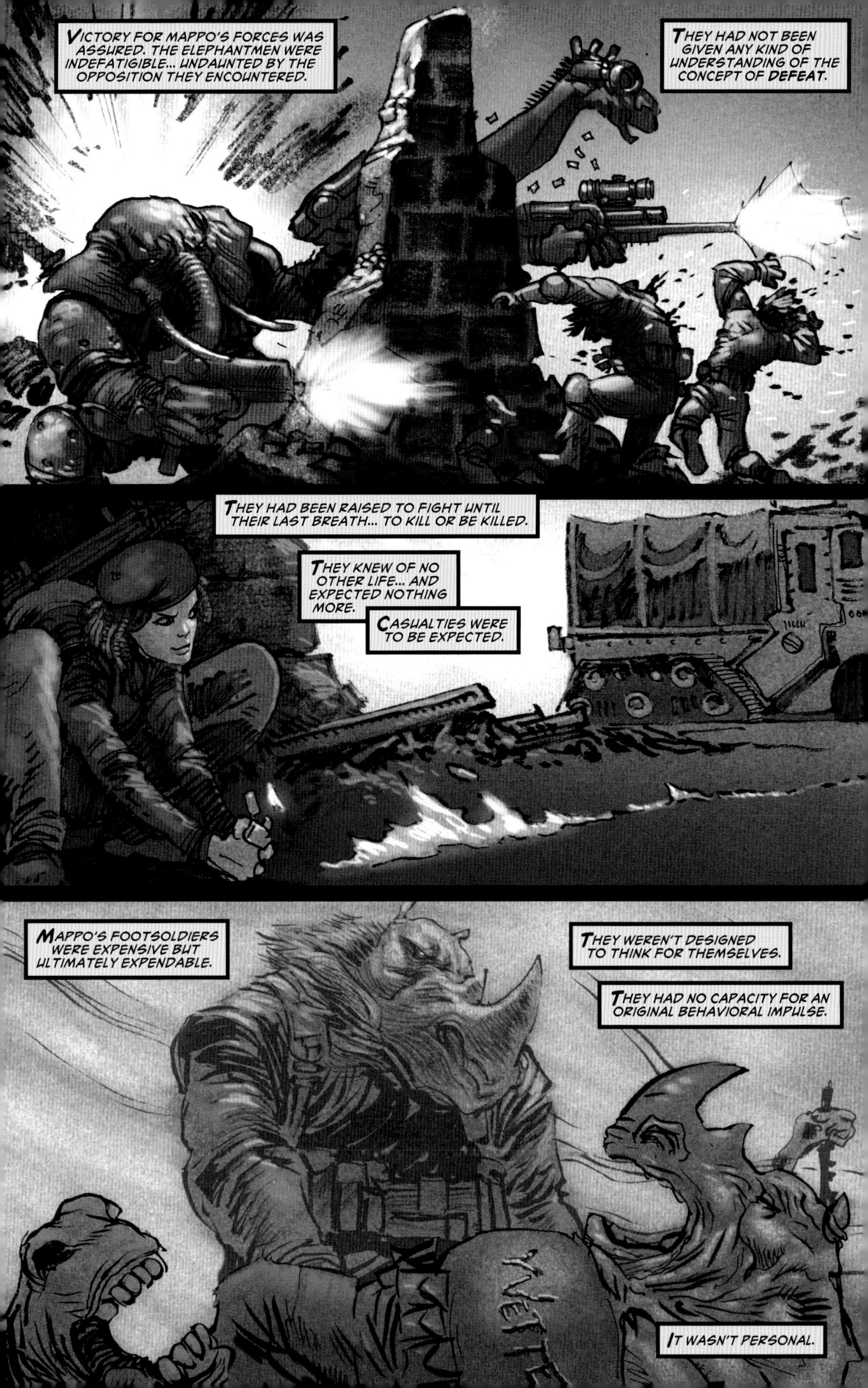
VICTORY FOR MAPPO'S FORCES WAS ASSURED. THE ELEPHANTMEN WERE INDEFATIGIBLE... UNDAUNTED BY THE OPPOSITION THEY ENCOUNTERED.
THEY HAD NOT BEEN GIVEN ANY KIND OF UNDERSTANDING OF THE CONCEPT OF DEFEAT.
THEY HAD BEEN RAISED TO FIGHT UNTIL THEIR LAST BREATH... TO KILL OR BE KILLED.
THEY KNEW OF NO OTHER LIFE... AND EXPECTED NOTHING MORE.
CASUALTIES WERE TO BE EXPECTED.
MAPPO'S FOOTSOLDIERS WERE EXPENSIVE BUT ULTIMATELY EXPENDABLE.
THEY WEREN'T DESIGNED TO THINK FOR THEMSELVES.
THEY HAD NO CAPACITY FOR AN ORIGINAL BEHAVIORAL IMPULSE.
IT WASN'T PERSONAL.

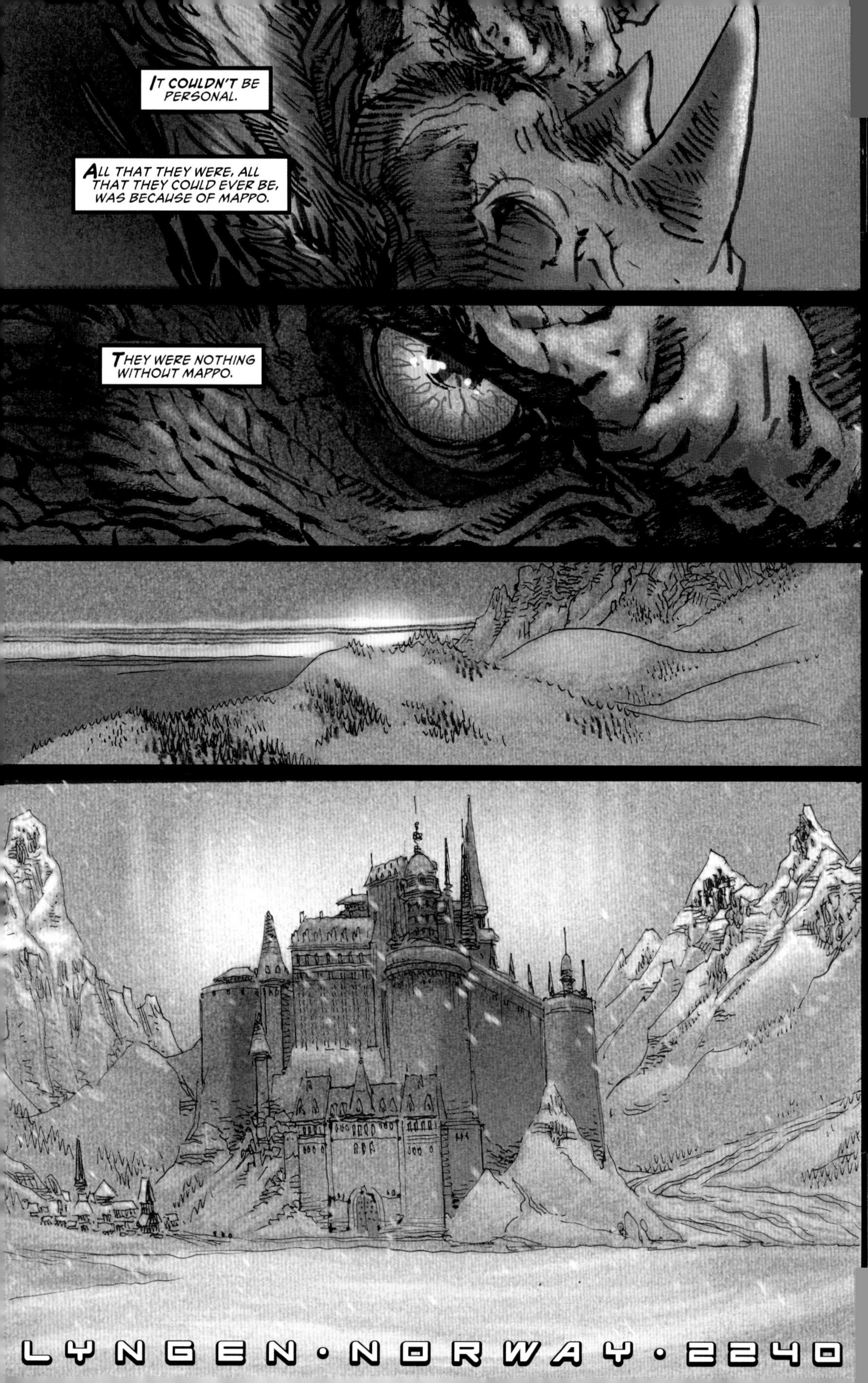

IT COULDN'T BE PERSONAL.
ALL THAT THEY WERE, ALL THAT THEY COULD EVER BE, WAS BECAUSE OF MAPPO.
THEY WERE NOTHING WITHOUT MAPPO.
LYNGEN · NORWAY · 2240

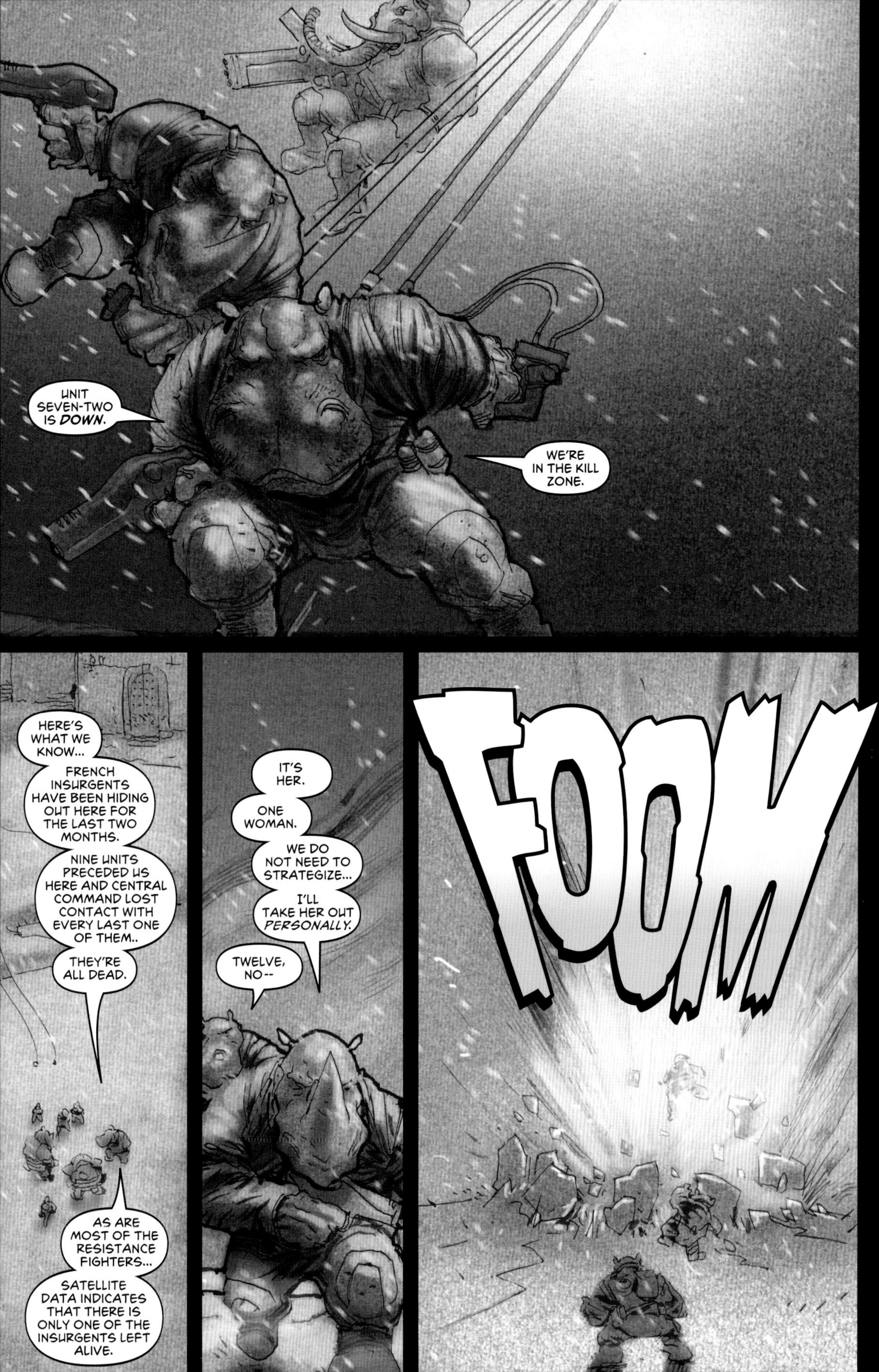
UNIT SEVEN-TWO IS *DOWN*.
WE'RE IN THE KILL ZONE.
HERE'S WHAT WE KNOW...
FRENCH INSURGENTS HAVE BEEN HIDING OUT HERE FOR THE LAST TWO MONTHS.
NINE UNITS PRECEDED US HERE AND CENTRAL COMMAND LOST CONTACT WITH EVERY LAST ONE OF THEM..
THEY'RE ALL DEAD.
AS ARE MOST OF THE RESISTANCE FIGHTERS...
SATELLITE DATA INDICATES THAT THERE IS ONLY ONE OF THE INSURGENTS LEFT ALIVE.
IT'S HER.
ONE WOMAN.
WE DO NOT NEED TO STRATEGIZE...
I'LL TAKE HER OUT *PERSONALLY*.
TWELVE, NO--
FOOM

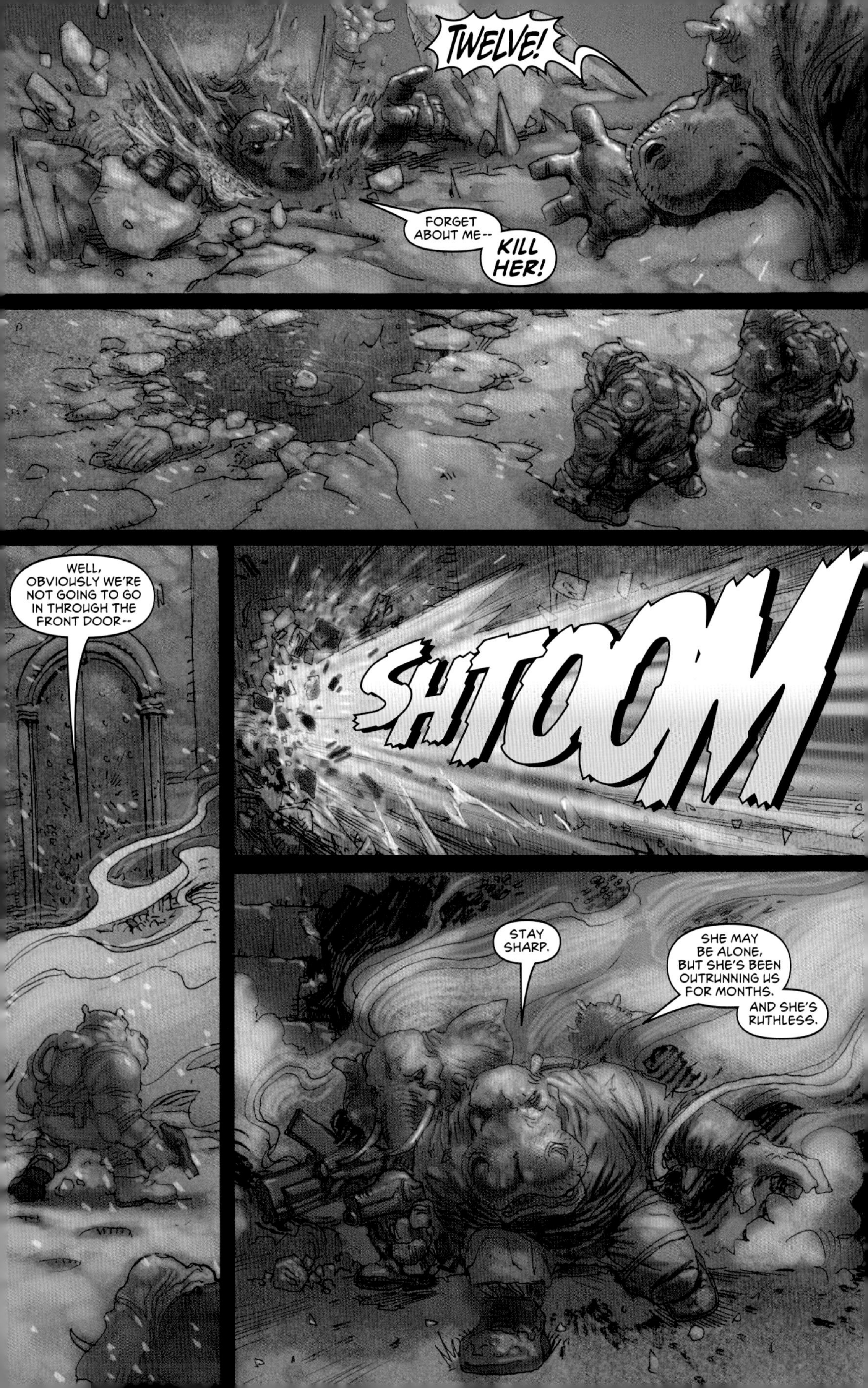
TWELVE!
FORGET ABOUT ME-- KILL HER!
WELL, OBVIOUSLY WE'RE NOT GOING TO GO IN THROUGH THE FRONT DOOR--
SHTOOM
STAY SHARP.
SHE MAY BE ALONE, BUT SHE'S BEEN OUTRUNNING US FOR MONTHS.
AND SHE'S RUTHLESS.

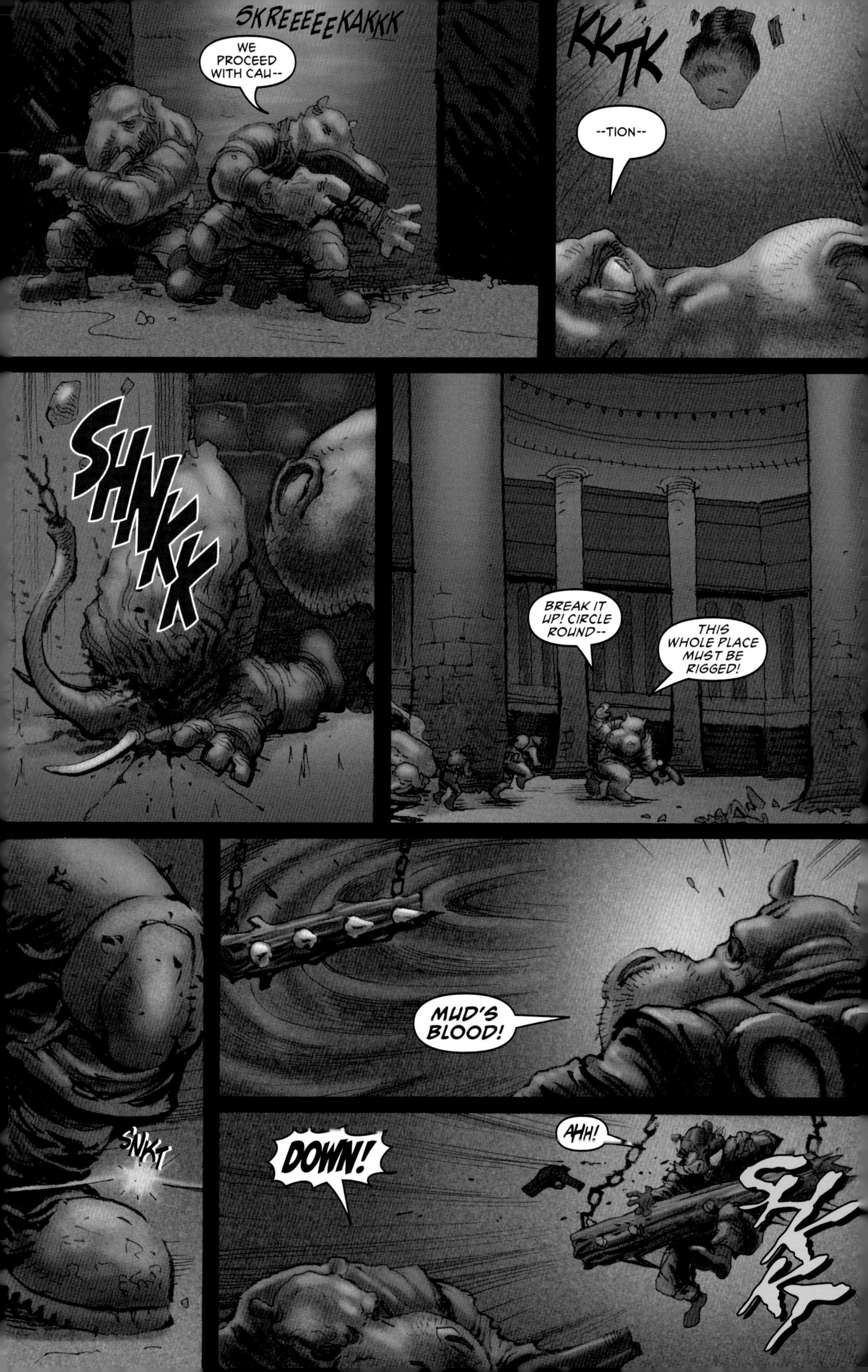
SKREEEEEKAKKK
WE PROCEED WITH CAU--
KKTK
--TION--
SHNKKK
BREAK IT UP! CIRCLE ROUND--
THIS WHOLE PLACE MUST BE RIGGED!
MUD'S BLOOD!
SNKT
DOWN!
AHH!
SHKKT

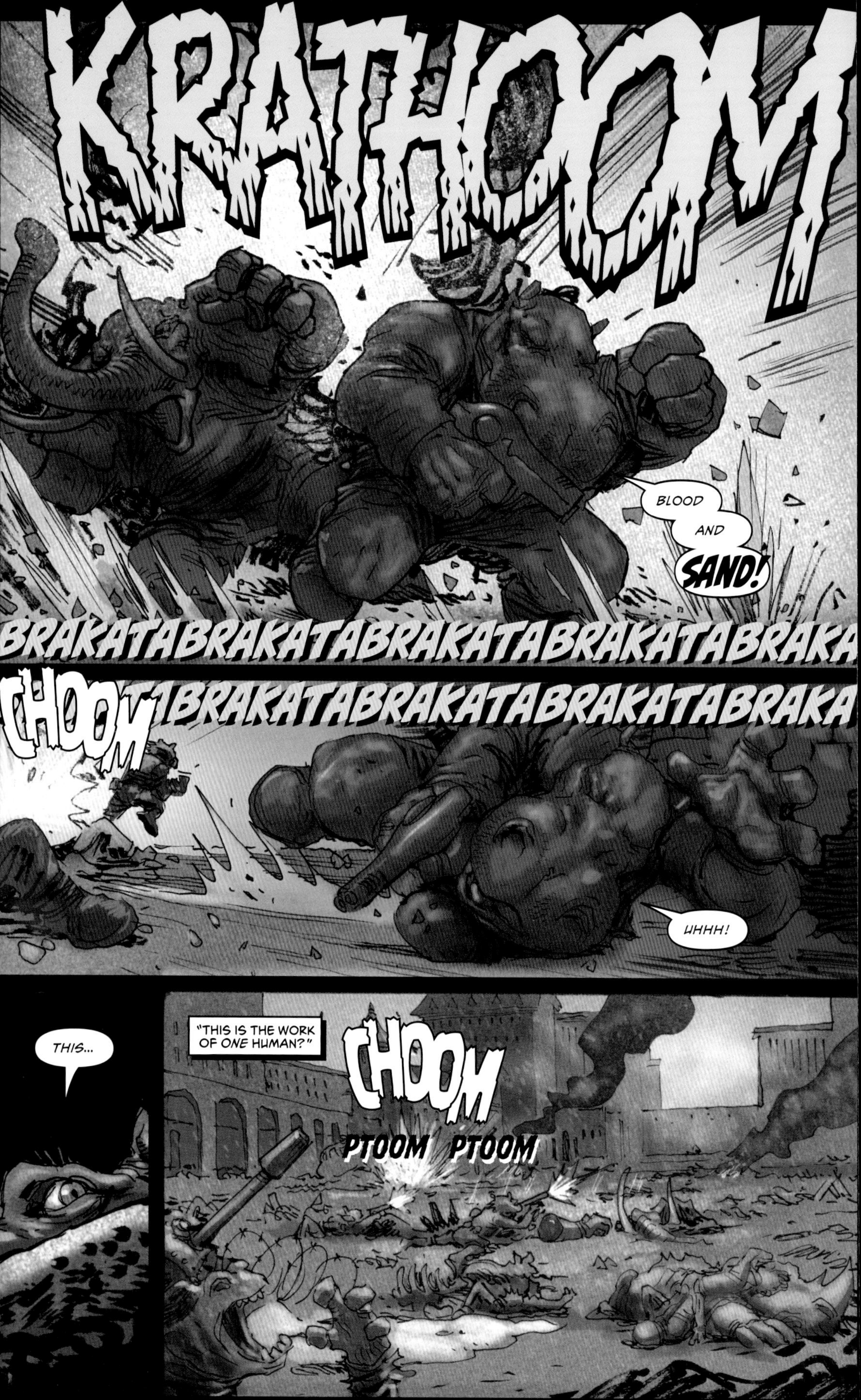
KRATHOOM
BLOOD AND SAND!
BRAKATABRAKATABRAKATABRAKATABRAKA
CHOOM
TABRAKATABRAKATABRAKATABRAKA
UHHH!
THIS...
"THIS IS THE WORK OF ONE HUMAN?"
CHOOM
PTOOM PTOOM

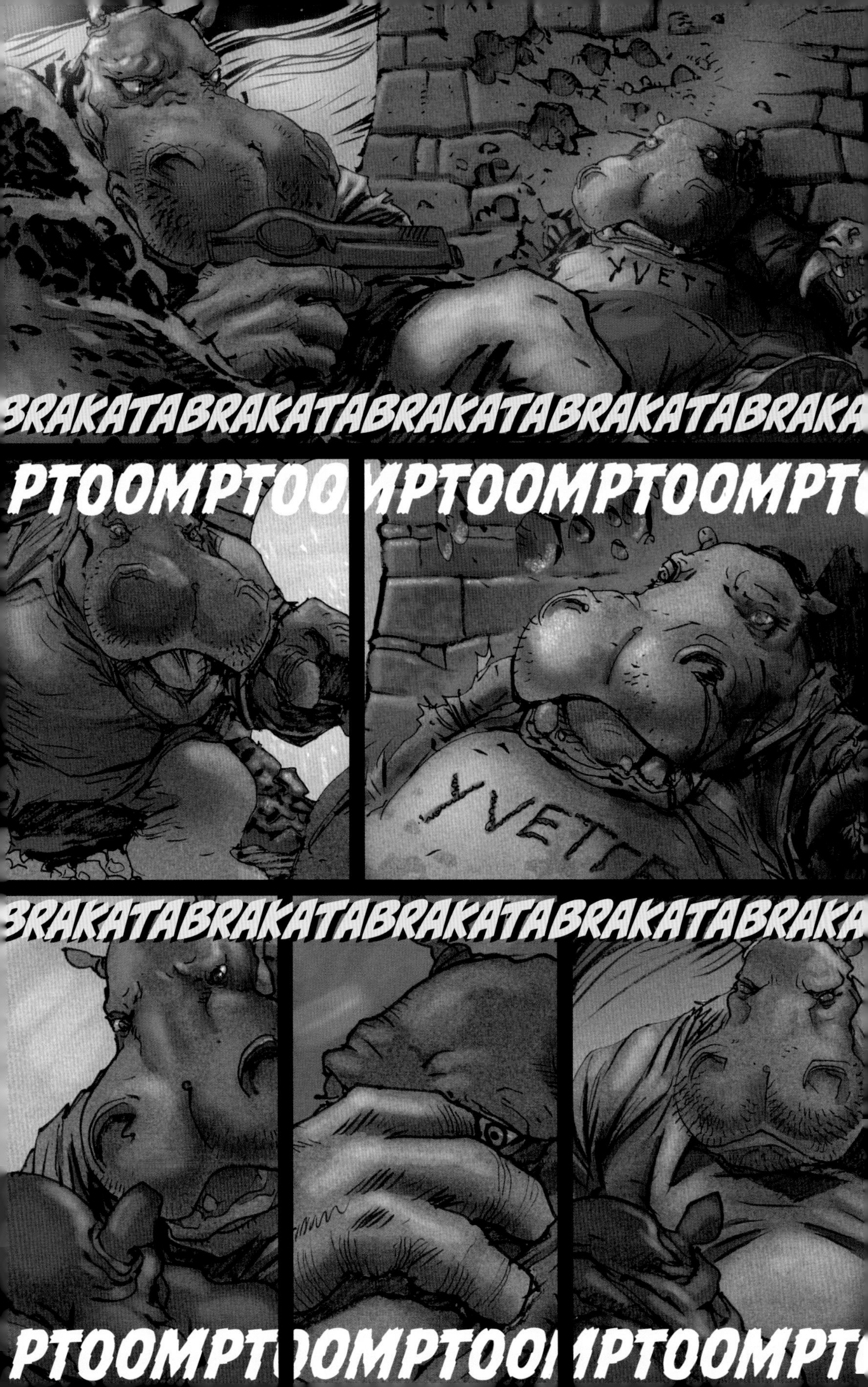

YVETT
RAKATABRAKATABRAKATABRAKA
PTOOMPTOO
MPTOOMPTOOMPT
YVETT
RAKATABRAKATABRAKATABRAKA
PTOOMPT
OOMPTOO
MPTOOMPT

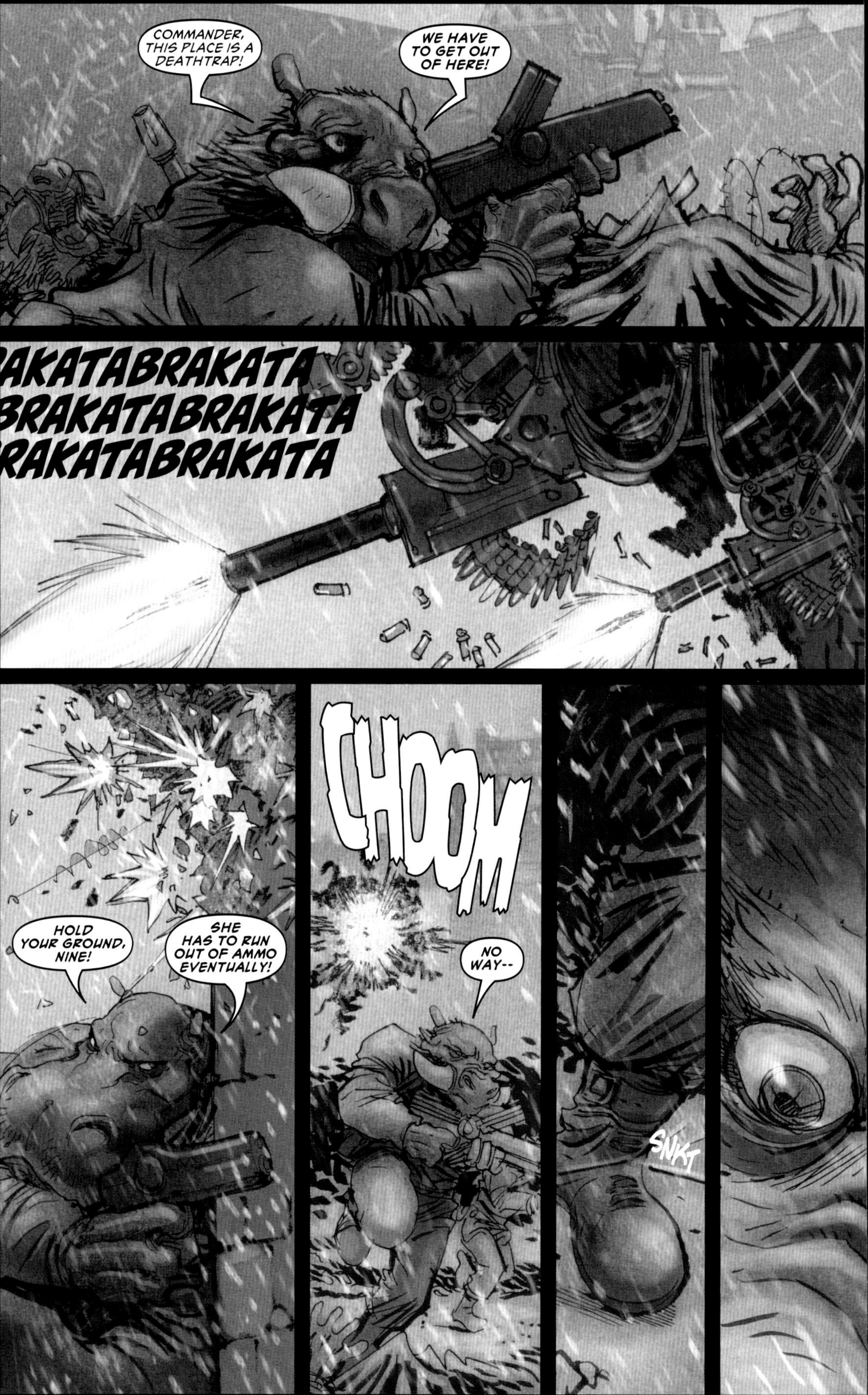
COMMANDER, THIS PLACE IS A DEATHTRAP!
WE HAVE TO GET OUT OF HERE!
RAKATABRAKATA
BRAKATABRAKATA
RAKATABRAKATA
HOLD YOUR GROUND, NINE!
SHE HAS TO RUN OUT OF AMMO EVENTUALLY!
CHOOM
NO WAY--
SNKT

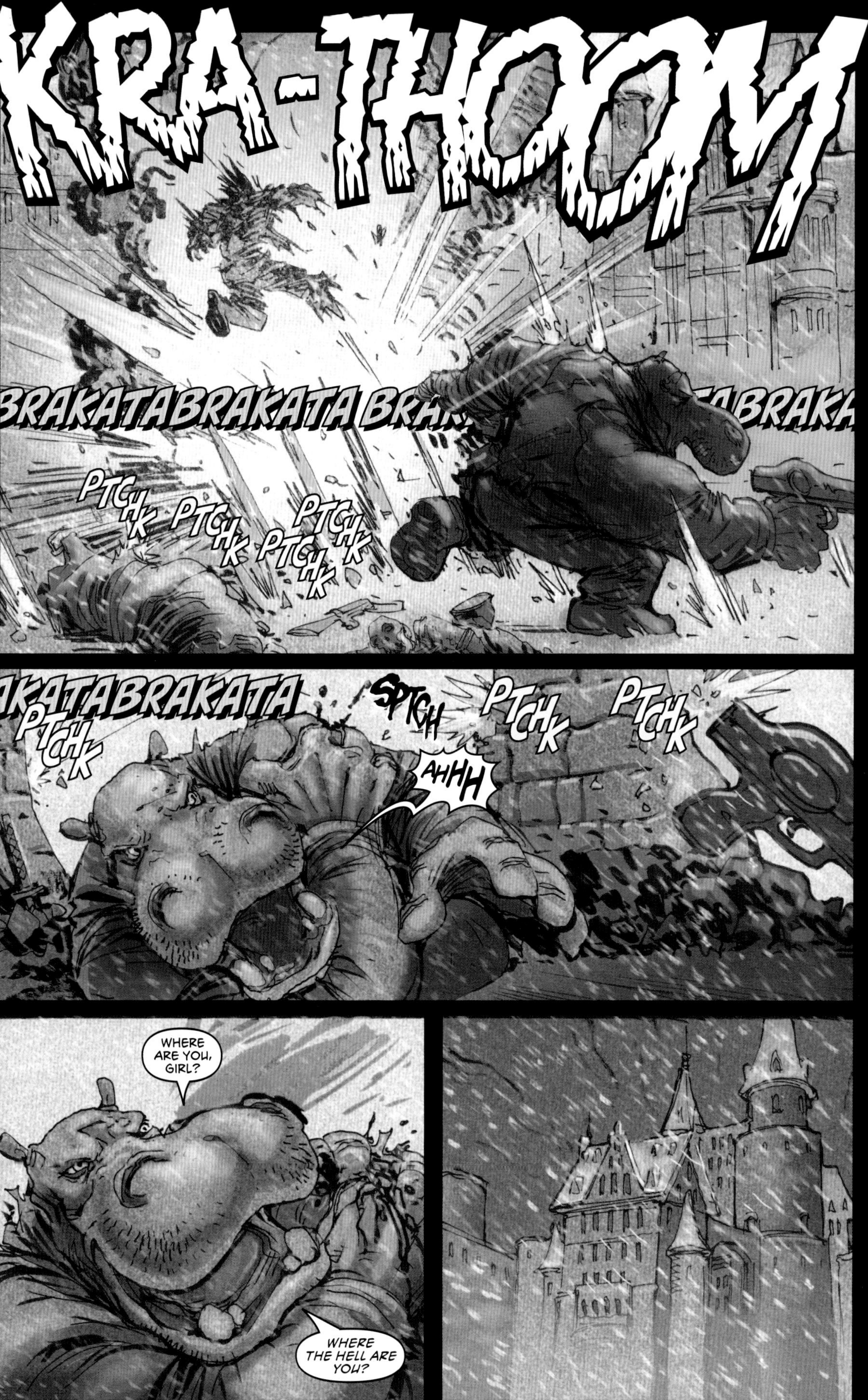
KRA-THOOM
BRAKATABRAKATA BRAK
TABRAKA
PTCHK PTCHK PTCHK PTCHK
AKATABRAKATA
PTCHK
SPTCH
PTCHK PTCHK
AHHH
WHERE ARE YOU, GIRL?
WHERE THE HELL ARE YOU?

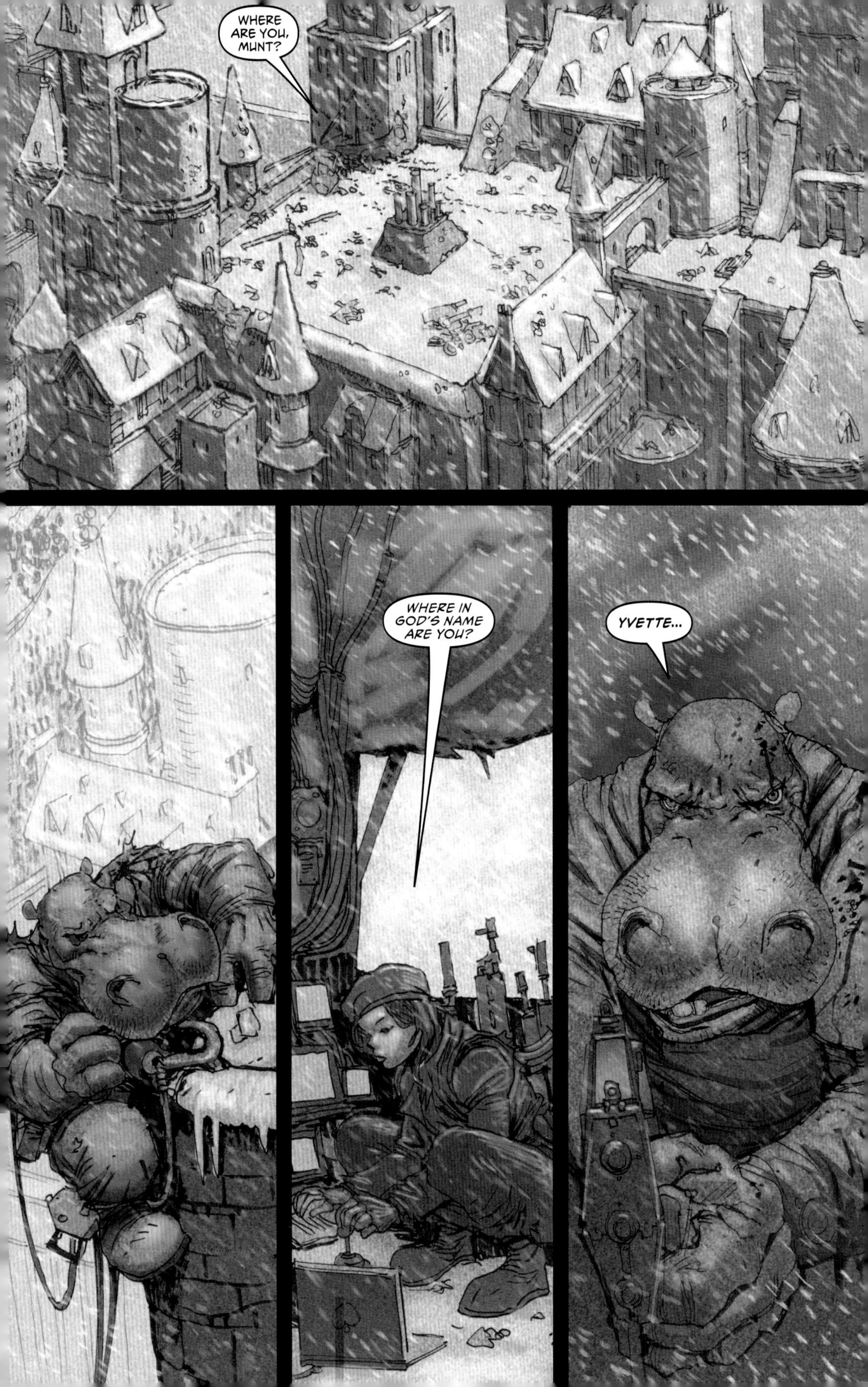
WHERE ARE YOU, MUNT?
WHERE IN GOD'S NAME ARE YOU?
YVETTE...

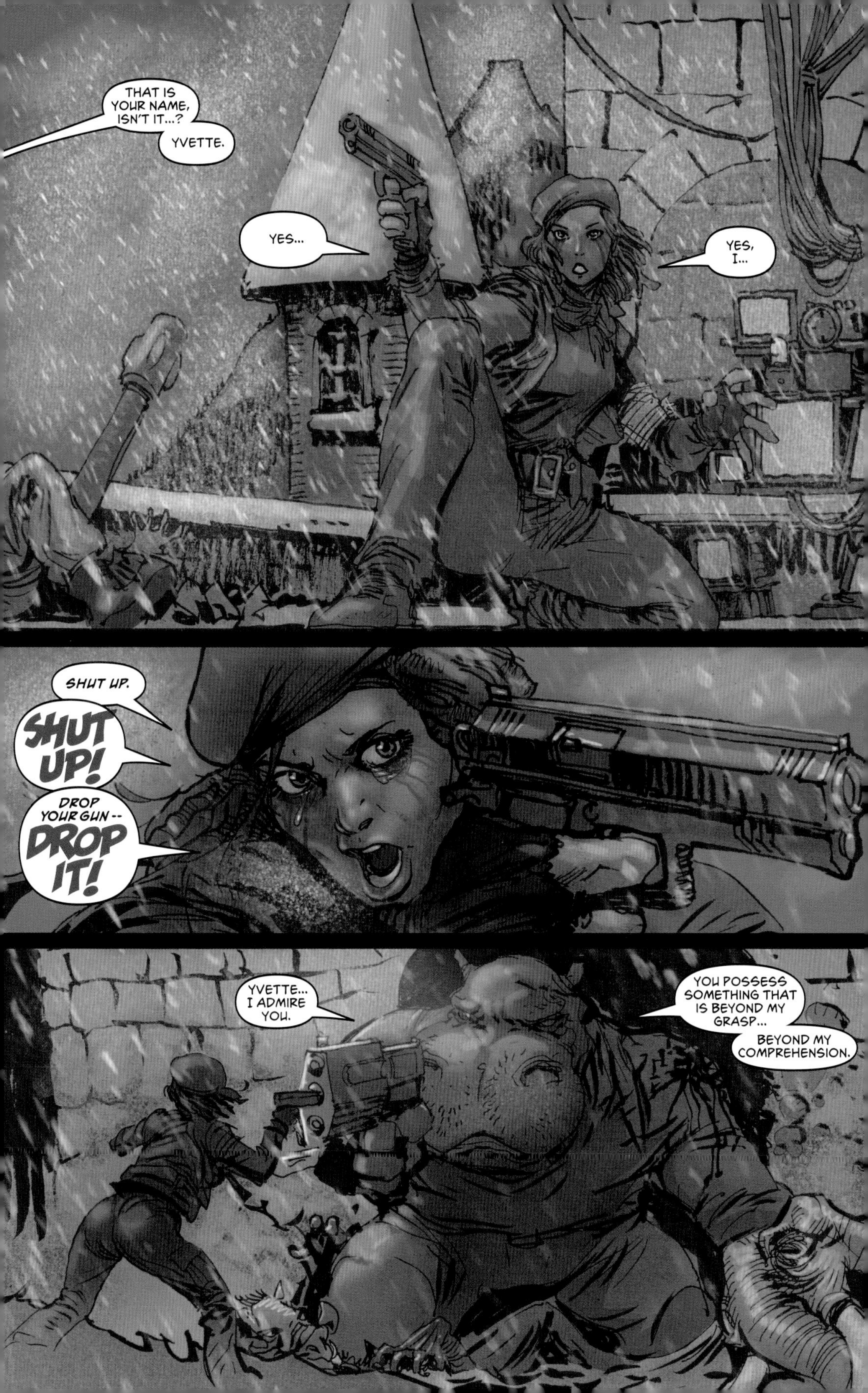
THAT IS YOUR NAME, ISN'T IT...?
YVETTE.
YES...
YES, I...
SHUT UP.
SHUT UP!
DROP YOUR GUN -- DROP IT!
YVETTE... I ADMIRE YOU.
YOU POSSESS SOMETHING THAT IS BEYOND MY GRASP...
BEYOND MY COMPREHENSION.

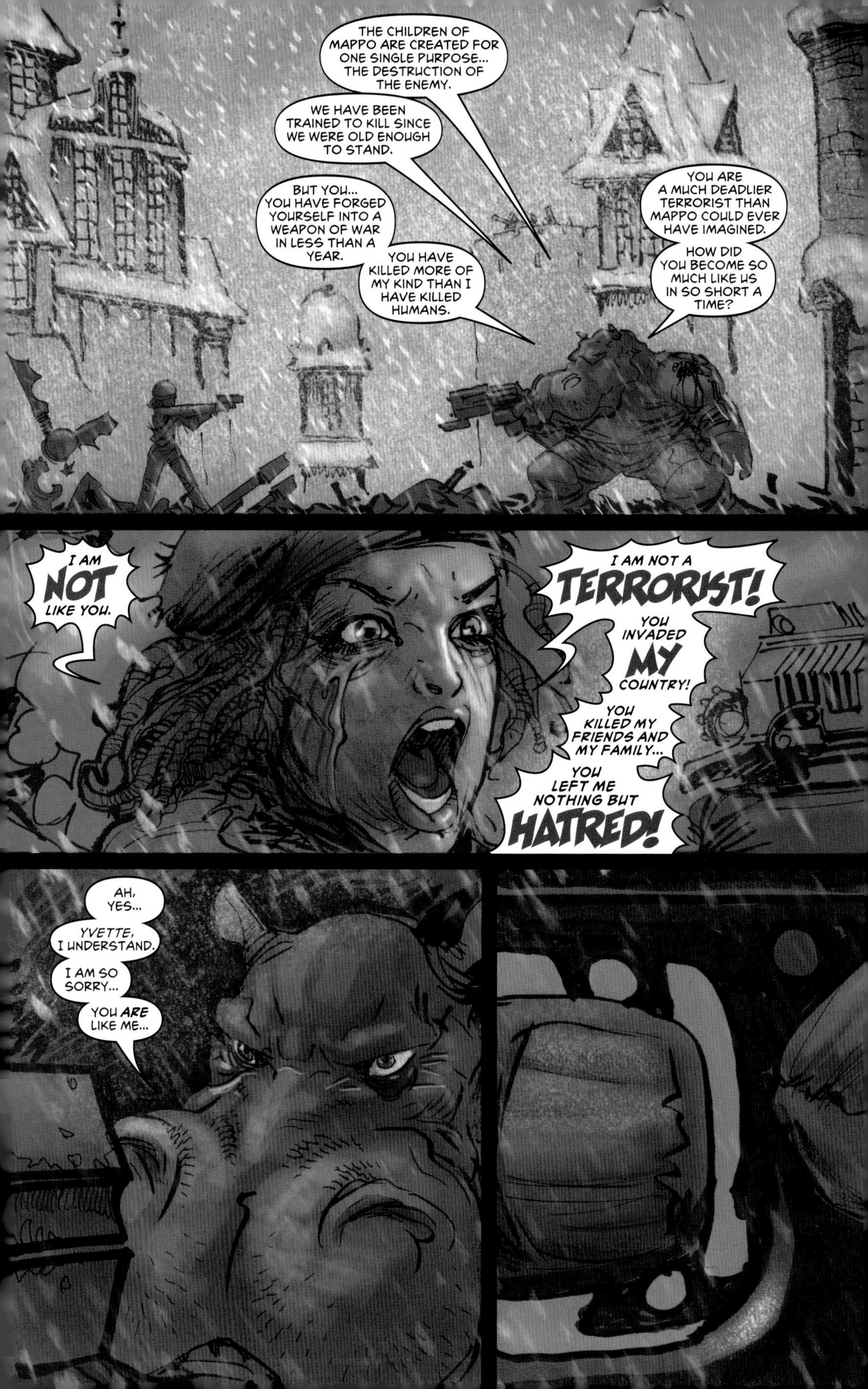
THE CHILDREN OF MAPPO ARE CREATED FOR ONE SINGLE PURPOSE... THE DESTRUCTION OF THE ENEMY.
WE HAVE BEEN TRAINED TO KILL SINCE WE WERE OLD ENOUGH TO STAND.
BUT YOU... YOU HAVE FORGED YOURSELF INTO A WEAPON OF WAR IN LESS THAN A YEAR.
YOU HAVE KILLED MORE OF MY KIND THAN I HAVE KILLED HUMANS.
YOU ARE A MUCH DEADLIER TERRORIST THAN MAPPO COULD EVER HAVE IMAGINED.
HOW DID YOU BECOME SO MUCH LIKE US IN SO SHORT A TIME?
I AM NOT LIKE YOU.
I AM NOT A TERRORIST!
YOU INVADED MY COUNTRY!
YOU KILLED MY FRIENDS AND MY FAMILY...
YOU LEFT ME NOTHING BUT HATRED!
AH, YES...
YVETTE, I UNDERSTAND.
I AM SO SORRY...
YOU ARE LIKE ME...

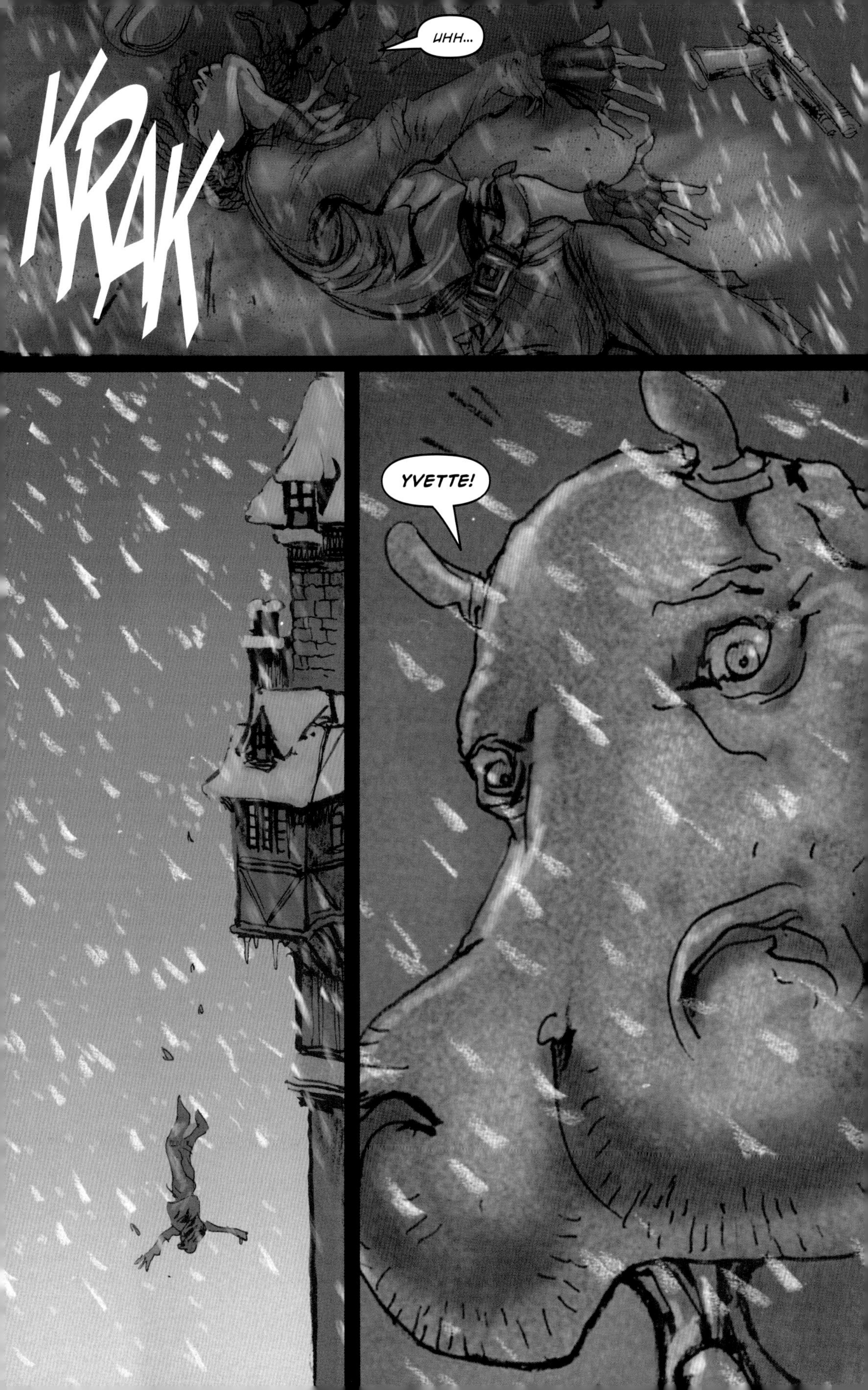
KRAK
UHH...
YVETTE!

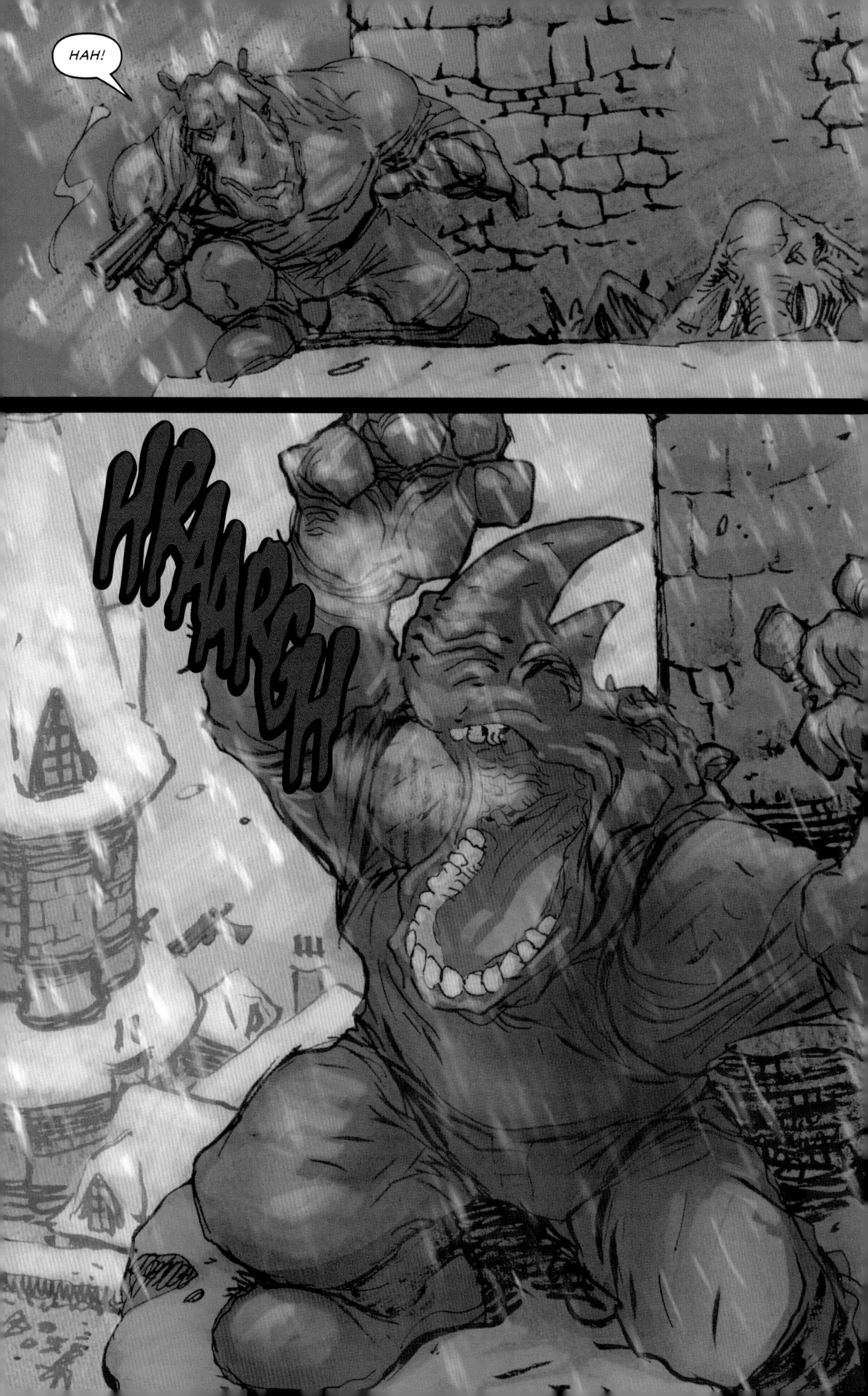
HAH!
HRAARGH

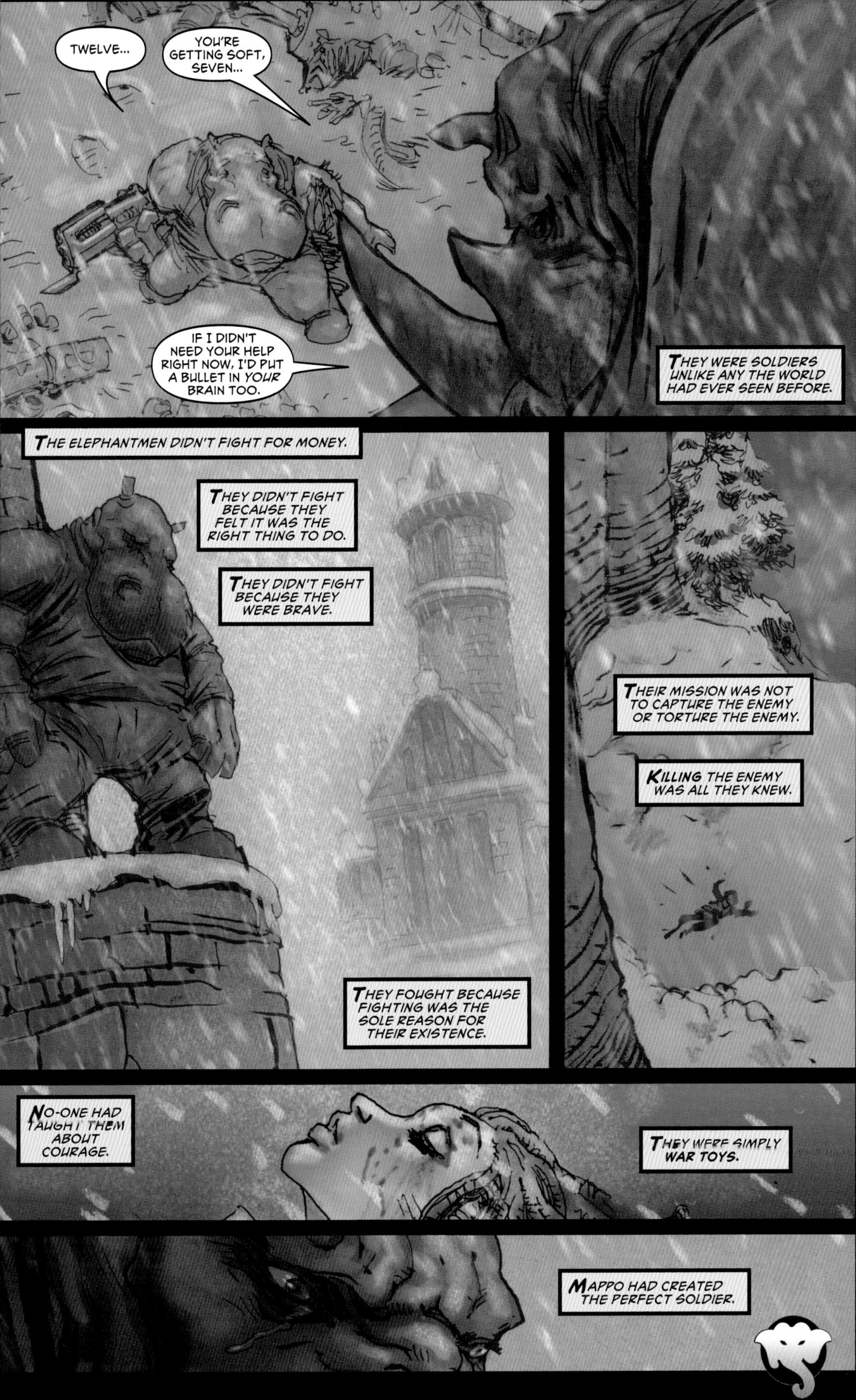
TWELVE...
YOU'RE GETTING SOFT, SEVEN...
IF I DIDN'T NEED YOUR HELP RIGHT NOW, I'D PUT A BULLET IN YOUR BRAIN TOO.
THEY WERE SOLDIERS UNLIKE ANY THE WORLD HAD EVER SEEN BEFORE.
THE ELEPHANTMEN DIDN'T FIGHT FOR MONEY.
THEY DIDN'T FIGHT BECAUSE THEY FELT IT WAS THE RIGHT THING TO DO.
THEY DIDN'T FIGHT BECAUSE THEY WERE BRAVE.
THEY FOUGHT BECAUSE FIGHTING WAS THE SOLE REASON FOR THEIR EXISTENCE.
THEIR MISSION WAS NOT TO CAPTURE THE ENEMY OR TORTURE THE ENEMY.
KILLING THE ENEMY WAS ALL THEY KNEW.
NO-ONE HAD TAUGHT THEM ABOUT COURAGE.
THEY WERE SIMPLY WAR TOYS.
MAPPO HAD CREATED THE PERFECT SOLDIER.

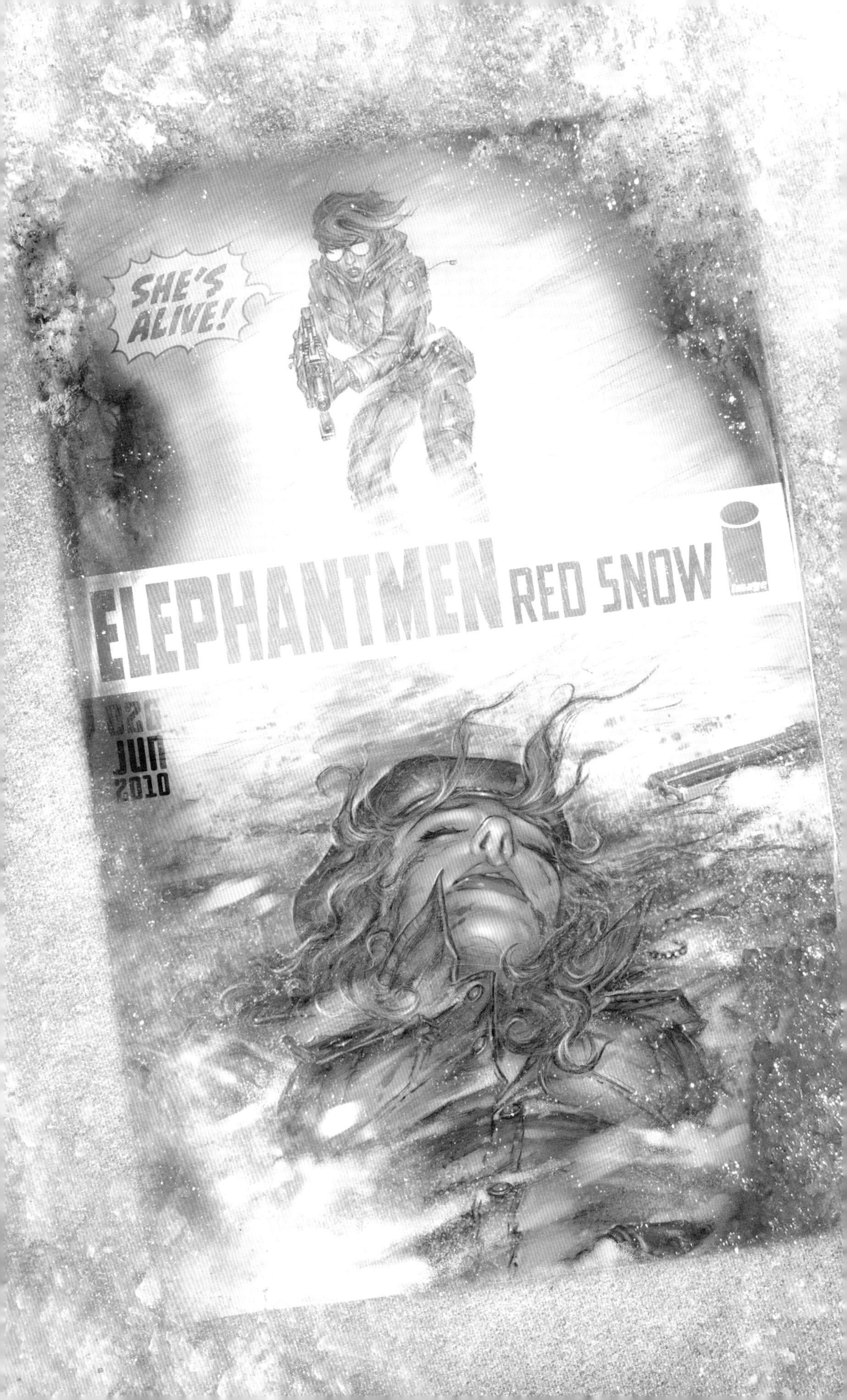
SHE'S ALIVE!
ELEPHANTMEN
RED SNOW
JUN
2010

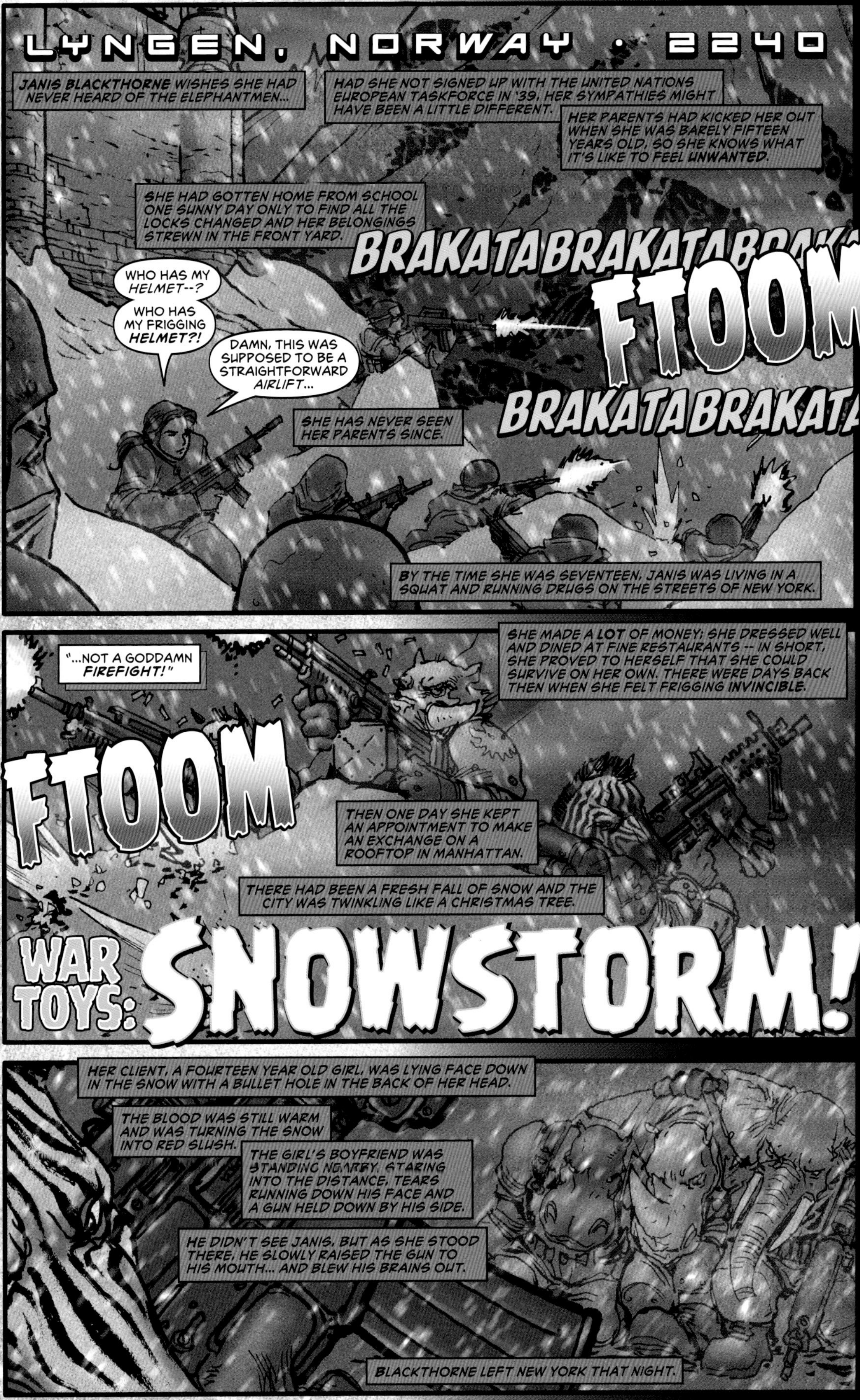
LYNGEN, NORWAY · 2240
JANIS BLACKTHORNE WISHES SHE HAD NEVER HEARD OF THE ELEPHANTMEN...
HAD SHE NOT SIGNED UP WITH THE UNITED NATIONS EUROPEAN TASKFORCE IN '39, HER SYMPATHIES MIGHT HAVE BEEN A LITTLE DIFFERENT.
HER PARENTS HAD KICKED HER OUT WHEN SHE WAS BARELY FIFTEEN YEARS OLD, SO SHE KNOWS WHAT IT'S LIKE TO FEEL UNWANTED.
SHE HAD GOTTEN HOME FROM SCHOOL ONE SUNNY DAY ONLY TO FIND ALL THE LOCKS CHANGED AND HER BELONGINGS STREWN IN THE FRONT YARD.
BRAKATA BRAKATA
FTOOM
WHO HAS MY HELMET--?
WHO HAS MY FRIGGING HELMET?!
DAMN, THIS WAS SUPPOSED TO BE A STRAIGHTFORWARD AIRLIFT...
BRAKATA BRAKATA
SHE HAS NEVER SEEN HER PARENTS SINCE.
BY THE TIME SHE WAS SEVENTEEN, JANIS WAS LIVING IN A SQUAT AND RUNNING DRUGS ON THE STREETS OF NEW YORK.
"...NOT A GODDAMN FIREFIGHT!"
SHE MADE A LOT OF MONEY; SHE DRESSED WELL AND DINED AT FINE RESTAURANTS -- IN SHORT, SHE PROVED TO HERSELF THAT SHE COULD SURVIVE ON HER OWN. THERE WERE DAYS BACK THEN WHEN SHE FELT FRIGGING INVINCIBLE.
FTOOM
THEN ONE DAY SHE KEPT AN APPOINTMENT TO MAKE AN EXCHANGE ON A ROOFTOP IN MANHATTAN.
THERE HAD BEEN A FRESH FALL OF SNOW AND THE CITY WAS TWINKLING LIKE A CHRISTMAS TREE.
WAR TOYS: SNOWSTORM!
HER CLIENT, A FOURTEEN YEAR OLD GIRL, WAS LYING FACE DOWN IN THE SNOW WITH A BULLET HOLE IN THE BACK OF HER HEAD.
THE BLOOD WAS STILL WARM AND WAS TURNING THE SNOW INTO RED SLUSH.
THE GIRL'S BOYFRIEND WAS STANDING NEARBY, STARING INTO THE DISTANCE, TEARS RUNNING DOWN HIS FACE AND A GUN HELD DOWN BY HIS SIDE.
HE DIDN'T SEE JANIS, BUT AS SHE STOOD THERE, HE SLOWLY RAISED THE GUN TO HIS MOUTH... AND BLEW HIS BRAINS OUT.
BLACKTHORNE LEFT NEW YORK THAT NIGHT.

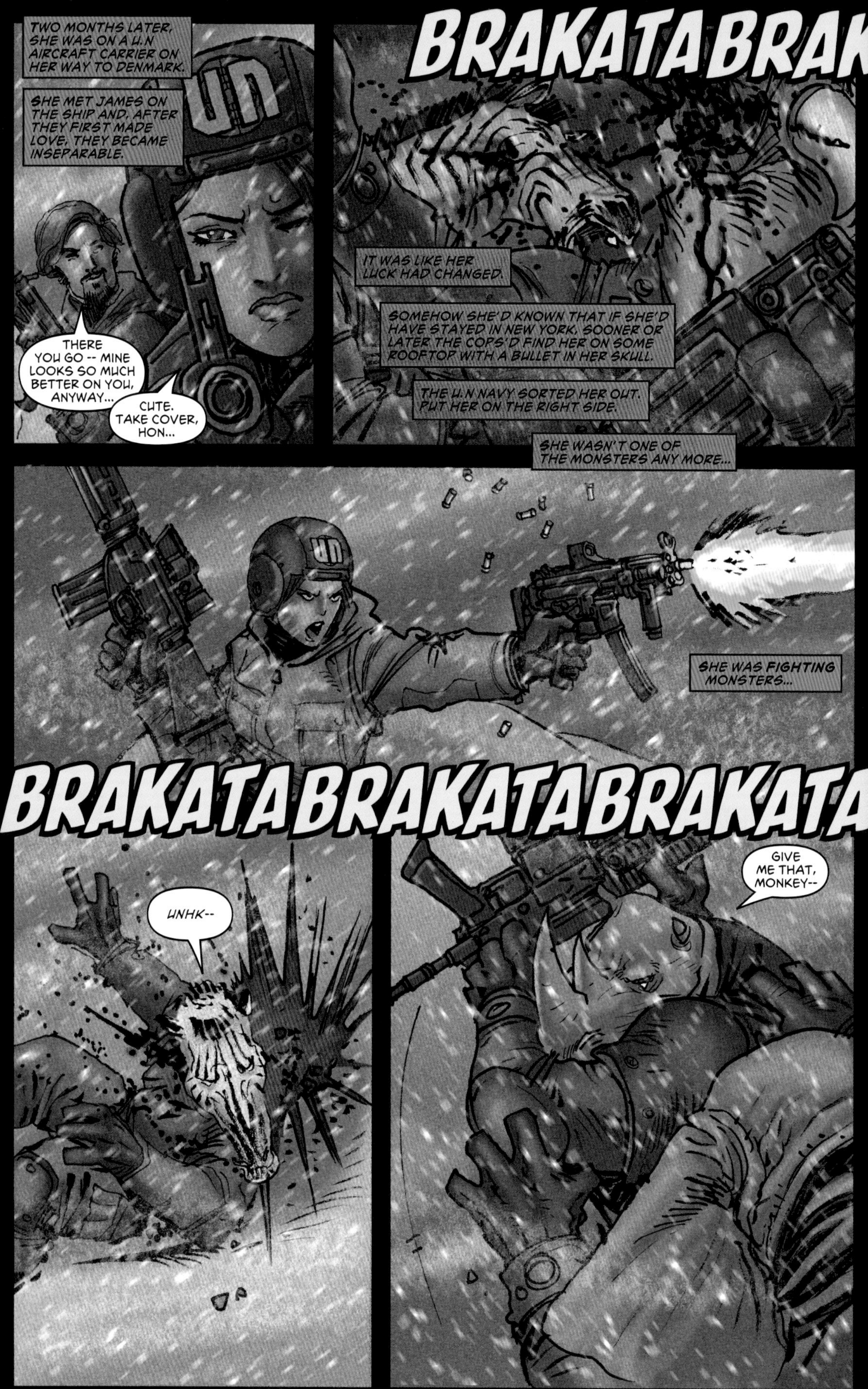
TWO MONTHS LATER, SHE WAS ON A U.N AIRCRAFT CARRIER ON HER WAY TO DENMARK.
SHE MET JAMES ON THE SHIP AND, AFTER THEY FIRST MADE LOVE, THEY BECAME INSEPARABLE.
THERE YOU GO -- MINE LOOKS SO MUCH BETTER ON YOU, ANYWAY...
CUTE. TAKE COVER, HON...
BRAKATA BRAK
IT WAS LIKE HER LUCK HAD CHANGED.
SOMEHOW SHE'D KNOWN THAT IF SHE'D HAVE STAYED IN NEW YORK, SOONER OR LATER THE COPS'D FIND HER ON SOME ROOFTOP WITH A BULLET IN HER SKULL.
THE U.N NAVY SORTED HER OUT. PUT HER ON THE RIGHT SIDE.
SHE WASN'T ONE OF THE MONSTERS ANY MORE...
SHE WAS FIGHTING MONSTERS...
BRAKATA BRAKATA BRAKATA
UNHK--
GIVE ME THAT, MONKEY--

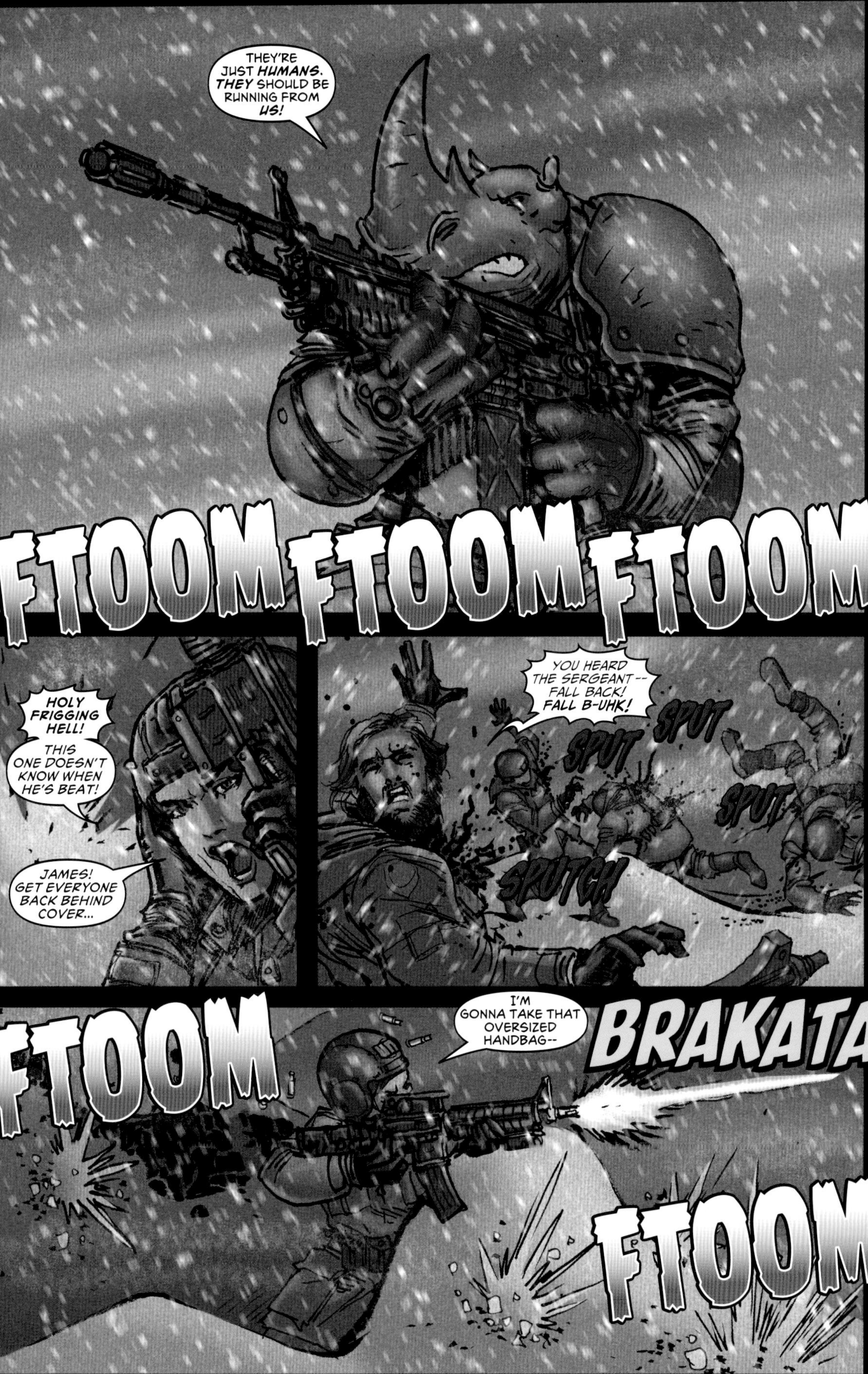
THEY'RE JUST HUMANS. THEY SHOULD BE RUNNING FROM US!
FTOOM FTOOM FTOOM
HOLY FRIGGING HELL!
THIS ONE DOESN'T KNOW WHEN HE'S BEAT!
JAMES! GET EVERYONE BACK BEHIND COVER...
YOU HEARD THE SERGEANT-- FALL BACK! FALL B-UHK!
SPUT
SPUT
SPUT
SPUTCH
FTOOM
I'M GONNA TAKE THAT OVERSIZED HANDBAG--
BRAKATA
FTOOM

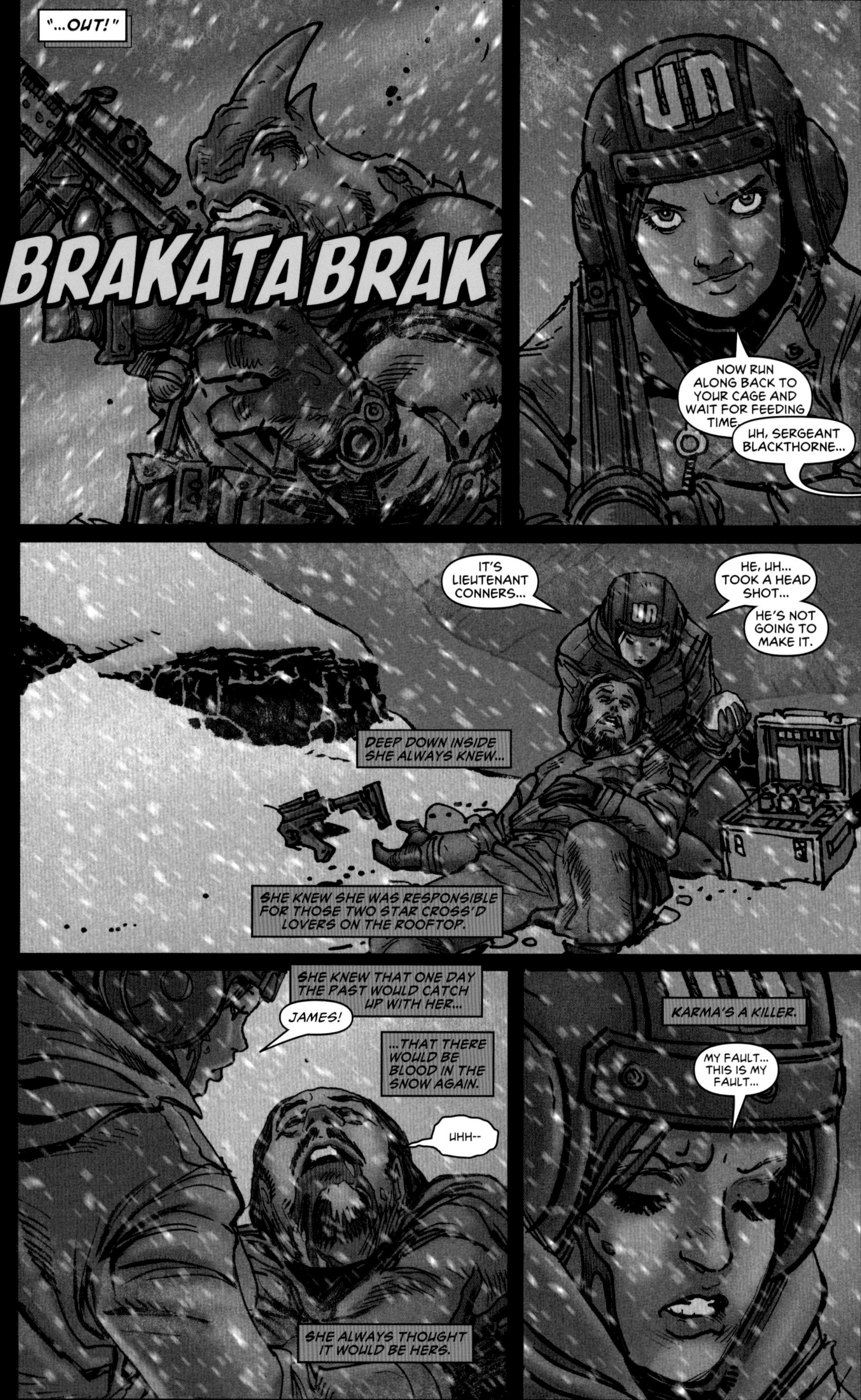
"...OUT!"
BRAKATABRAK
NOW RUN ALONG BACK TO YOUR CAGE AND WAIT FOR FEEDING TIME.
UH, SERGEANT BLACKTHORNE...
IT'S LIEUTENANT CONNERS...
HE, UH... TOOK A HEAD SHOT...
HE'S NOT GOING TO MAKE IT.
DEEP DOWN INSIDE SHE ALWAYS KNEW...
SHE KNEW SHE WAS RESPONSIBLE FOR THOSE TWO STAR CROSS'D LOVERS ON THE ROOFTOP.
SHE KNEW THAT ONE DAY THE PAST WOULD CATCH UP WITH HER...
JAMES!
...THAT THERE WOULD BE BLOOD IN THE SNOW AGAIN.
UHH--
SHE ALWAYS THOUGHT IT WOULD BE HERS.
KARMA'S A KILLER.
MY FAULT... THIS IS MY FAULT...

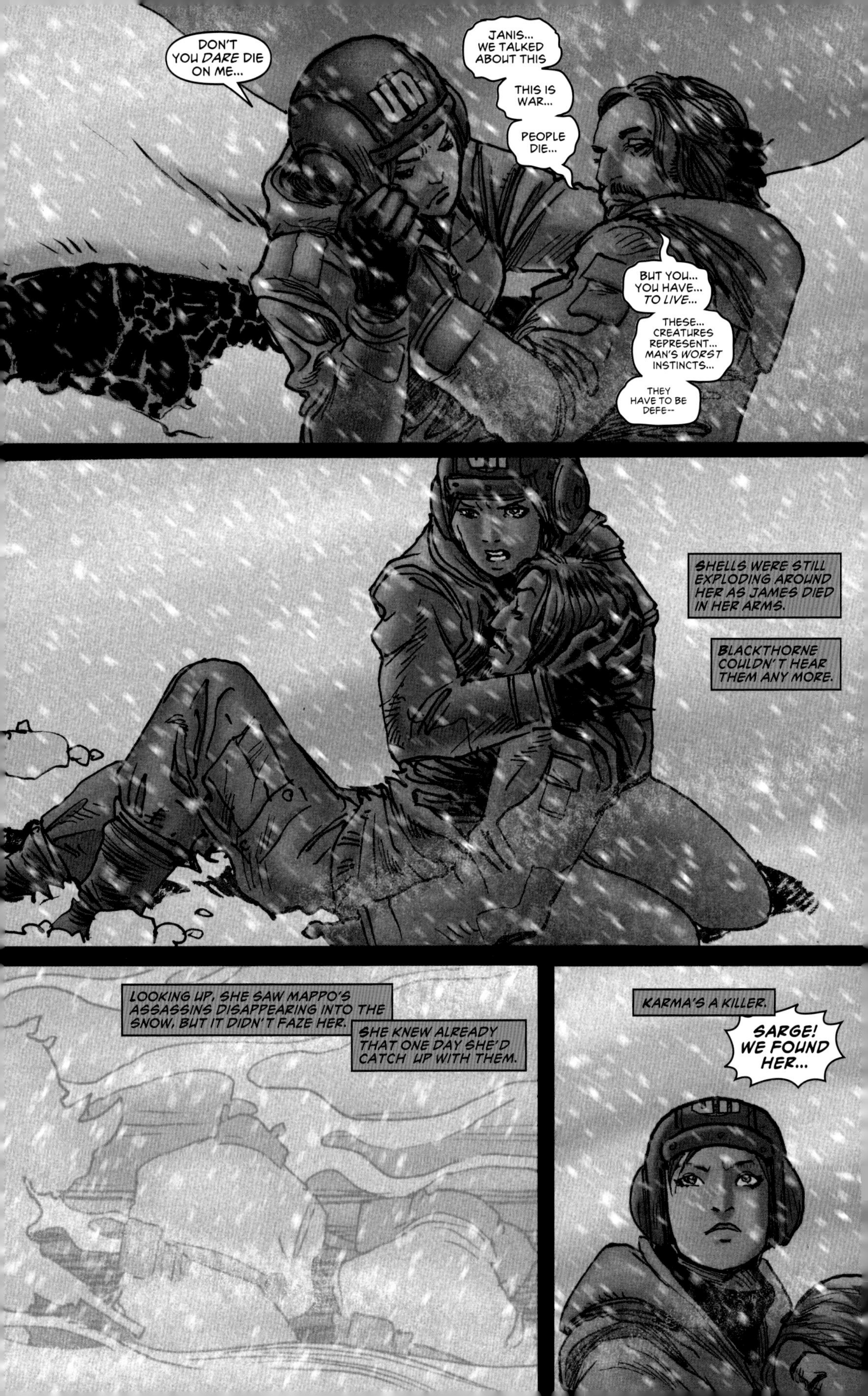
DON'T YOU *DARE* DIE ON ME...
JANIS... WE TALKED ABOUT THIS
THIS IS WAR...
PEOPLE DIE...
BUT YOU... YOU HAVE... TO *LIVE*...
THESE... CREATURES REPRESENT... MAN'S *WORST* INSTINCTS...
THEY HAVE TO BE DEFE--
SHELLS WERE STILL EXPLODING AROUND HER AS JAMES DIED IN HER ARMS.
BLACKTHORNE COULDN'T HEAR THEM ANY MORE.
LOOKING UP, SHE SAW MAPPO'S ASSASSINS DISAPPEARING INTO THE SNOW, BUT IT DIDN'T FAZE HER.
SHE KNEW ALREADY THAT ONE DAY SHE'D CATCH UP WITH THEM.
KARMA'S A KILLER.
SARGE! WE FOUND HER...

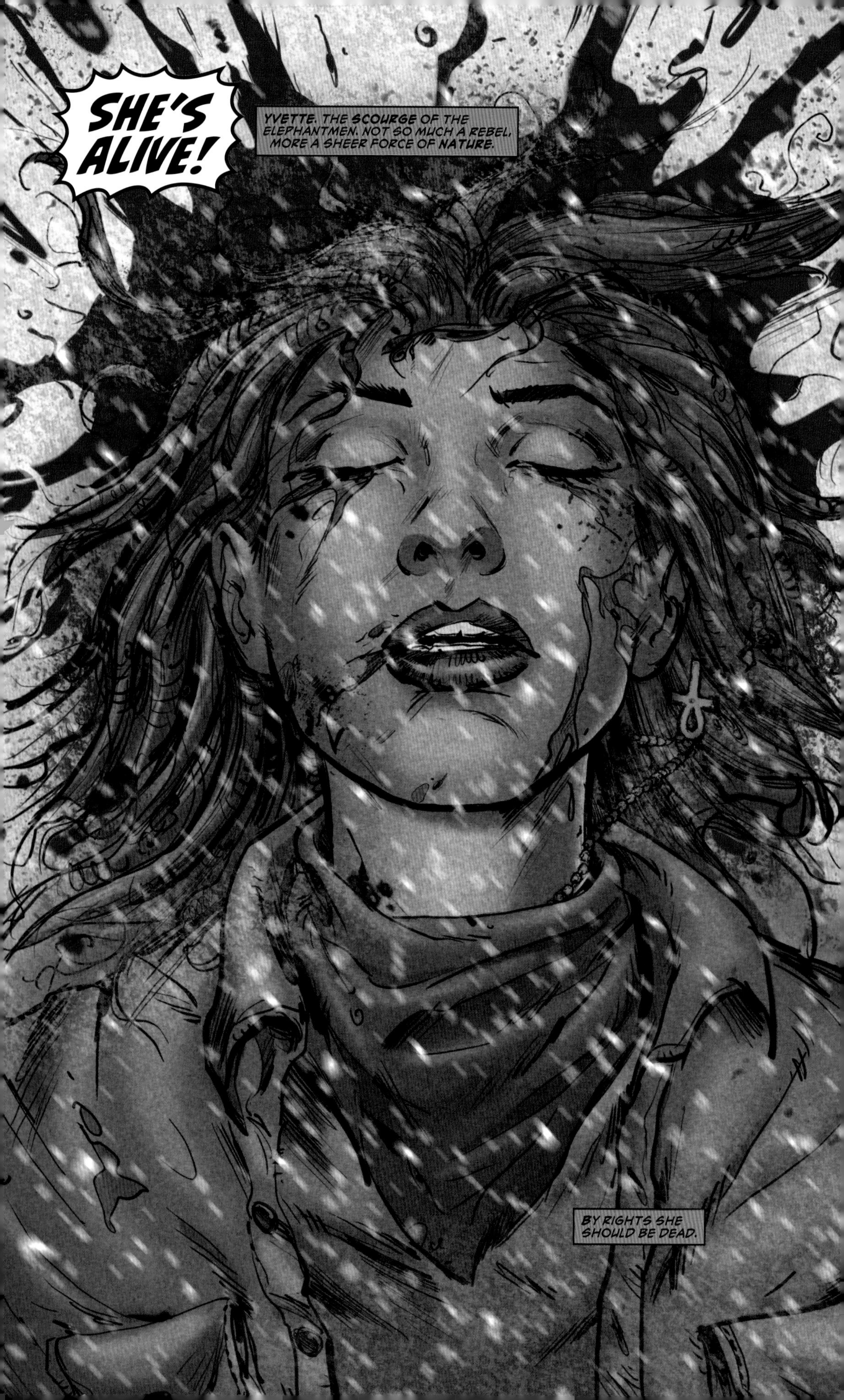
SHE'S ALIVE!
YVETTE. THE SCOURGE OF THE ELEPHANTMEN. NOT SO MUCH A REBEL, MORE A SHEER FORCE OF NATURE.
BY RIGHTS SHE SHOULD BE DEAD.

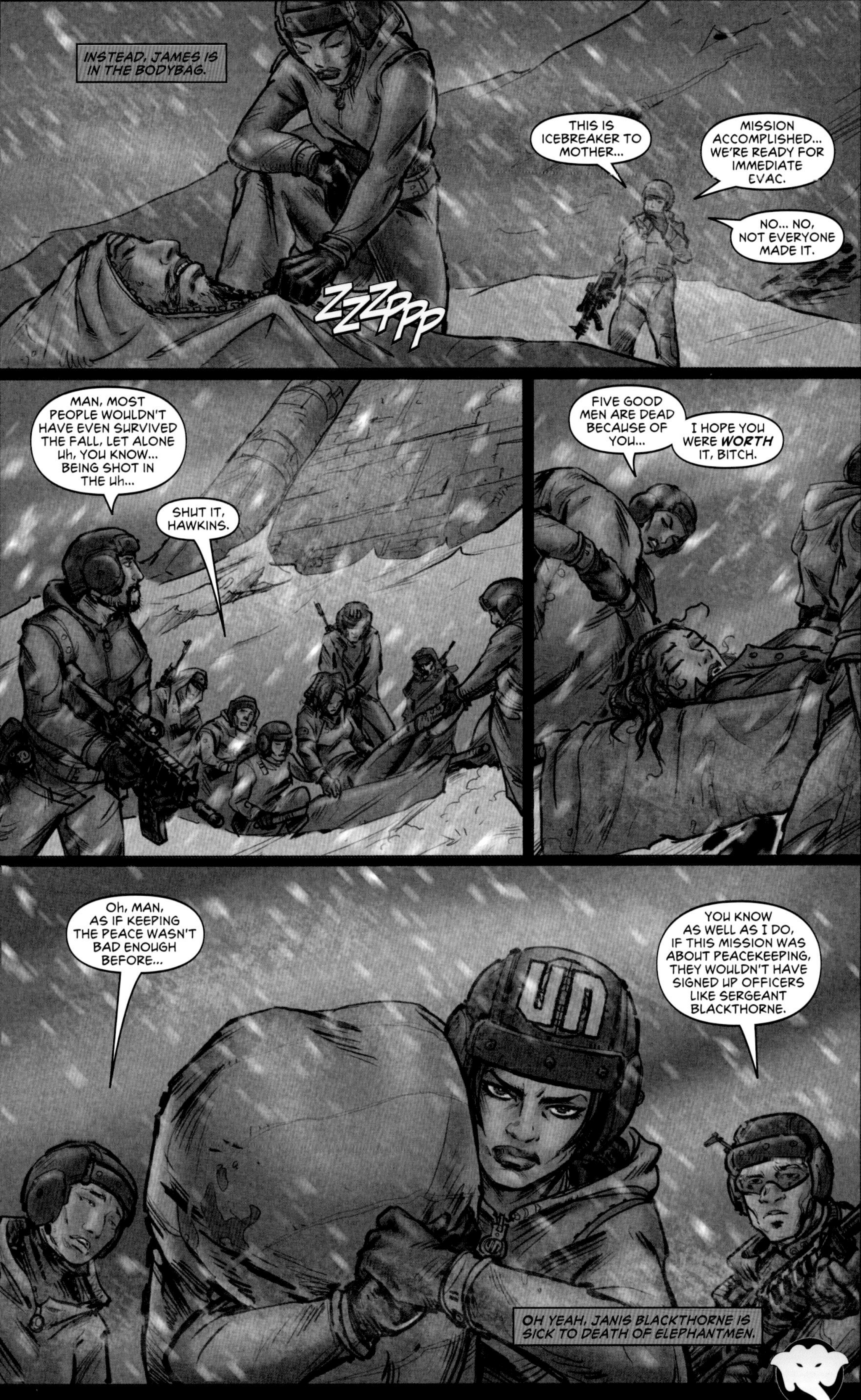
INSTEAD, JAMES IS IN THE BODYBAG.
THIS IS ICEBREAKER TO MOTHER...
MISSION ACCOMPLISHED... WE'RE READY FOR IMMEDIATE EVAC.
NO... NO, NOT EVERYONE MADE IT.
ZZZPPP
MAN, MOST PEOPLE WOULDN'T HAVE EVEN SURVIVED THE FALL, LET ALONE Uh, YOU KNOW... BEING SHOT IN THE Uh...
SHUT IT, HAWKINS.
FIVE GOOD MEN ARE DEAD BECAUSE OF YOU...
I HOPE YOU WERE WORTH IT, BITCH.
Oh, MAN, AS IF KEEPING THE PEACE WASN'T BAD ENOUGH BEFORE...
YOU KNOW AS WELL AS I DO, IF THIS MISSION WAS ABOUT PEACEKEEPING, THEY WOULDN'T HAVE SIGNED UP OFFICERS LIKE SERGEANT BLACKTHORNE.
OH YEAH, JANIS BLACKTHORNE IS SICK TO DEATH OF ELEPHANTMEN.

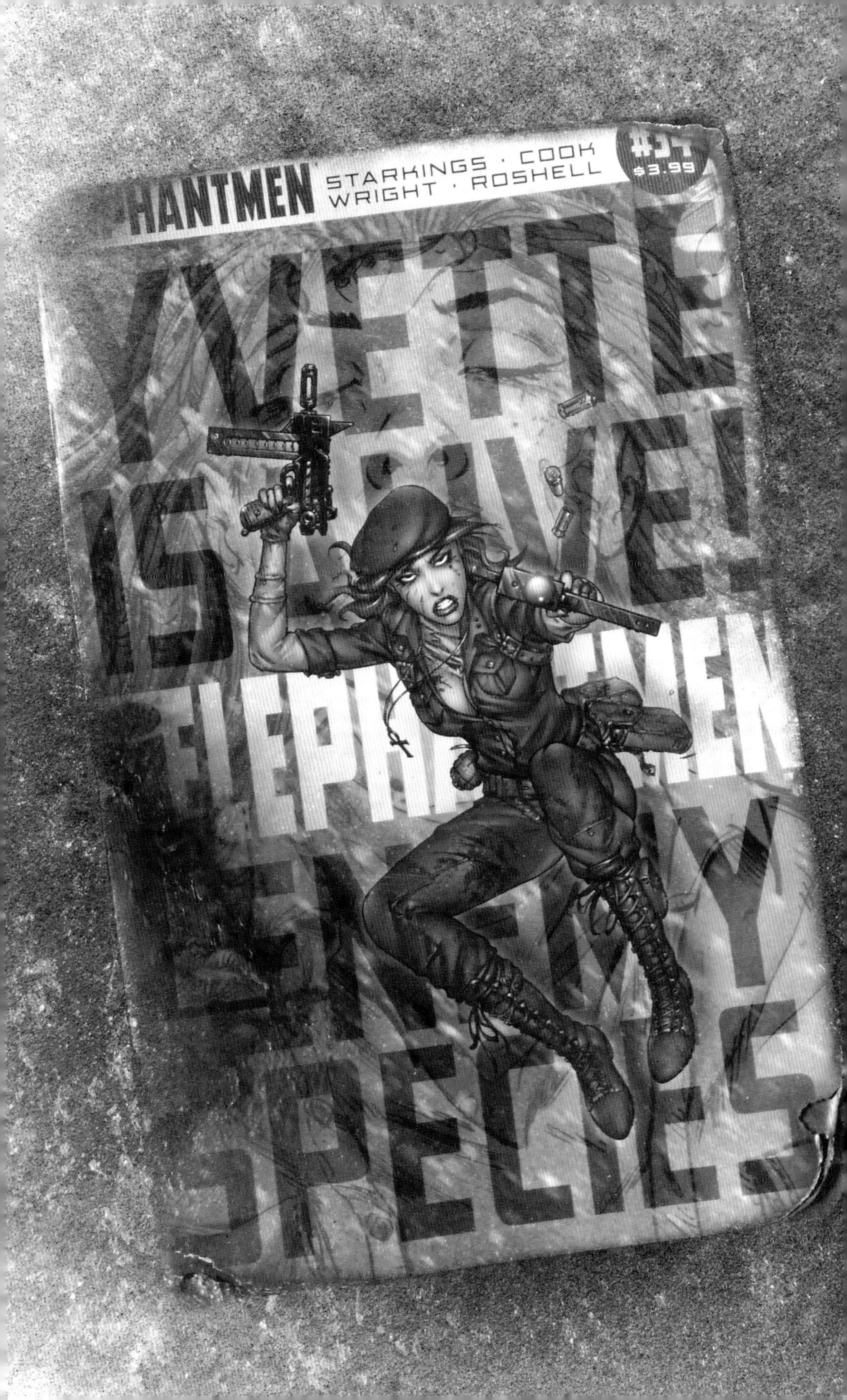
HANTMEN
STARKINGS · COOK
WRIGHT · ROSHELL
$3.99

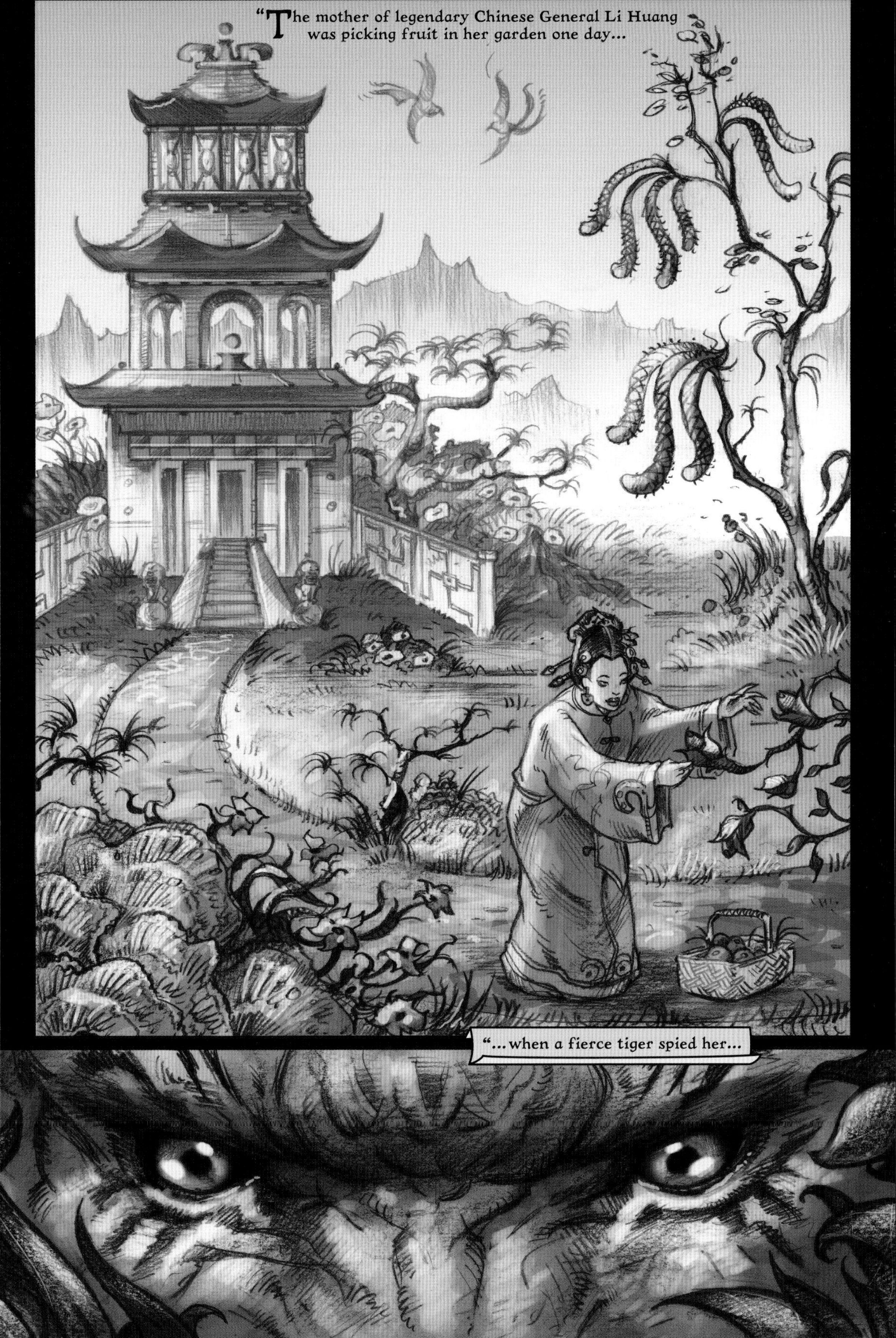
"The mother of legendary Chinese General Li Huang was picking fruit in her garden one day...
"...when a fierce tiger spied her...

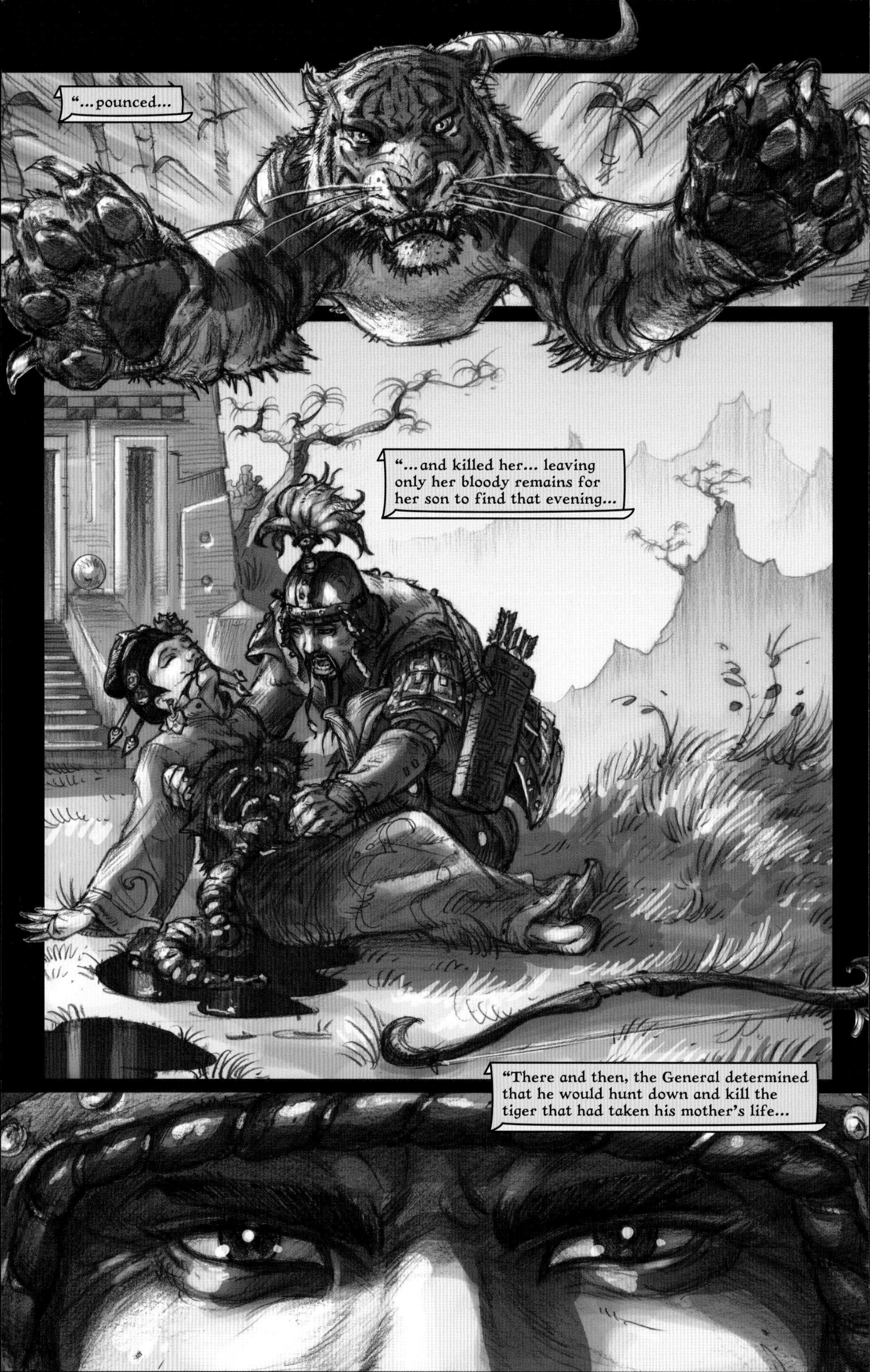
"...pounced...
"...and killed her... leaving only her bloody remains for her son to find that evening...
"There and then, the General determined that he would hunt down and kill the tiger that had taken his mother's life...

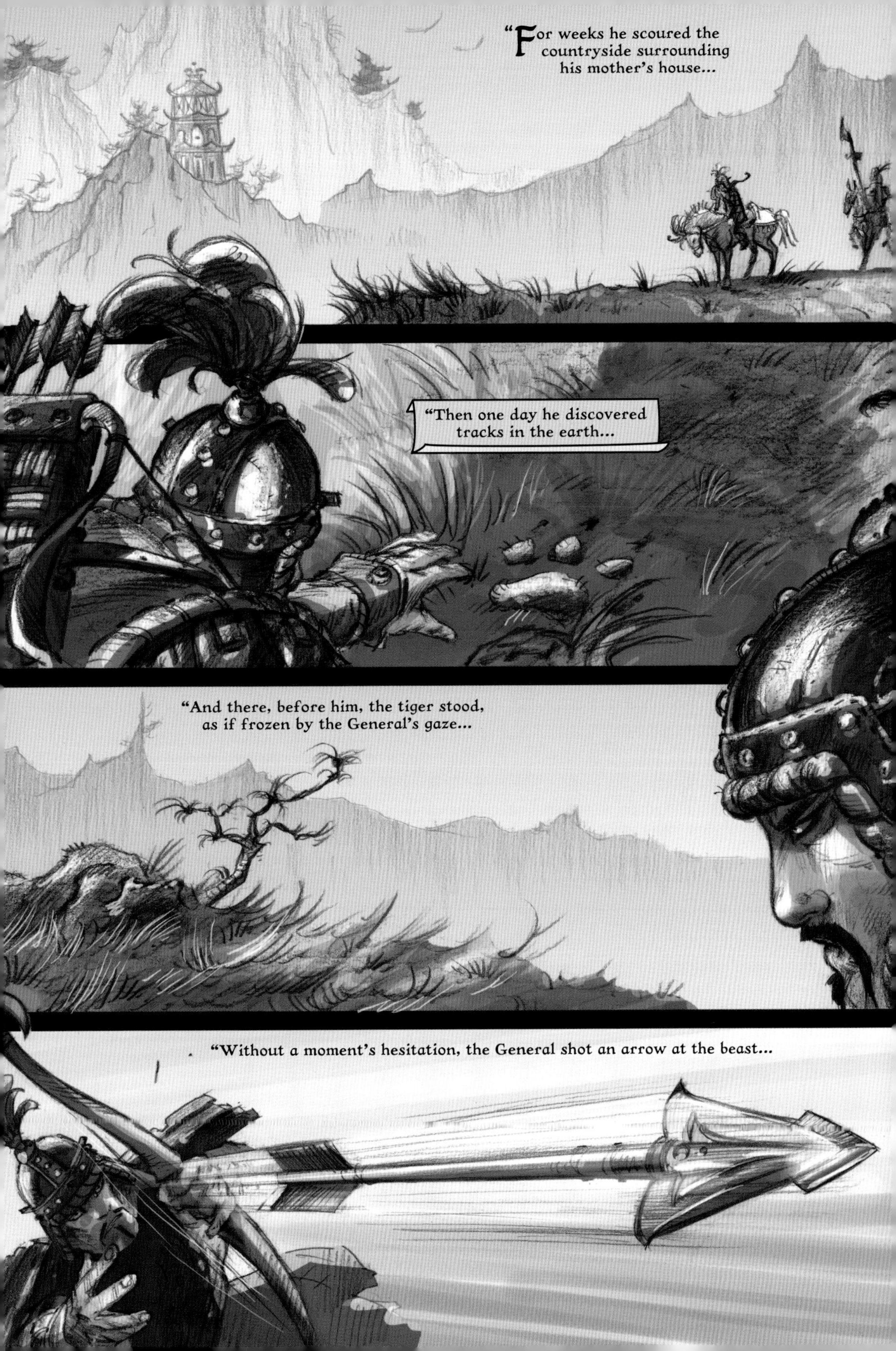
"For weeks he scoured the countryside surrounding his mother's house...
"Then one day he discovered tracks in the earth...
"And there, before him, the tiger stood, as if frozen by the General's gaze...
"Without a moment's hesitation, the General shot an arrow at the beast...

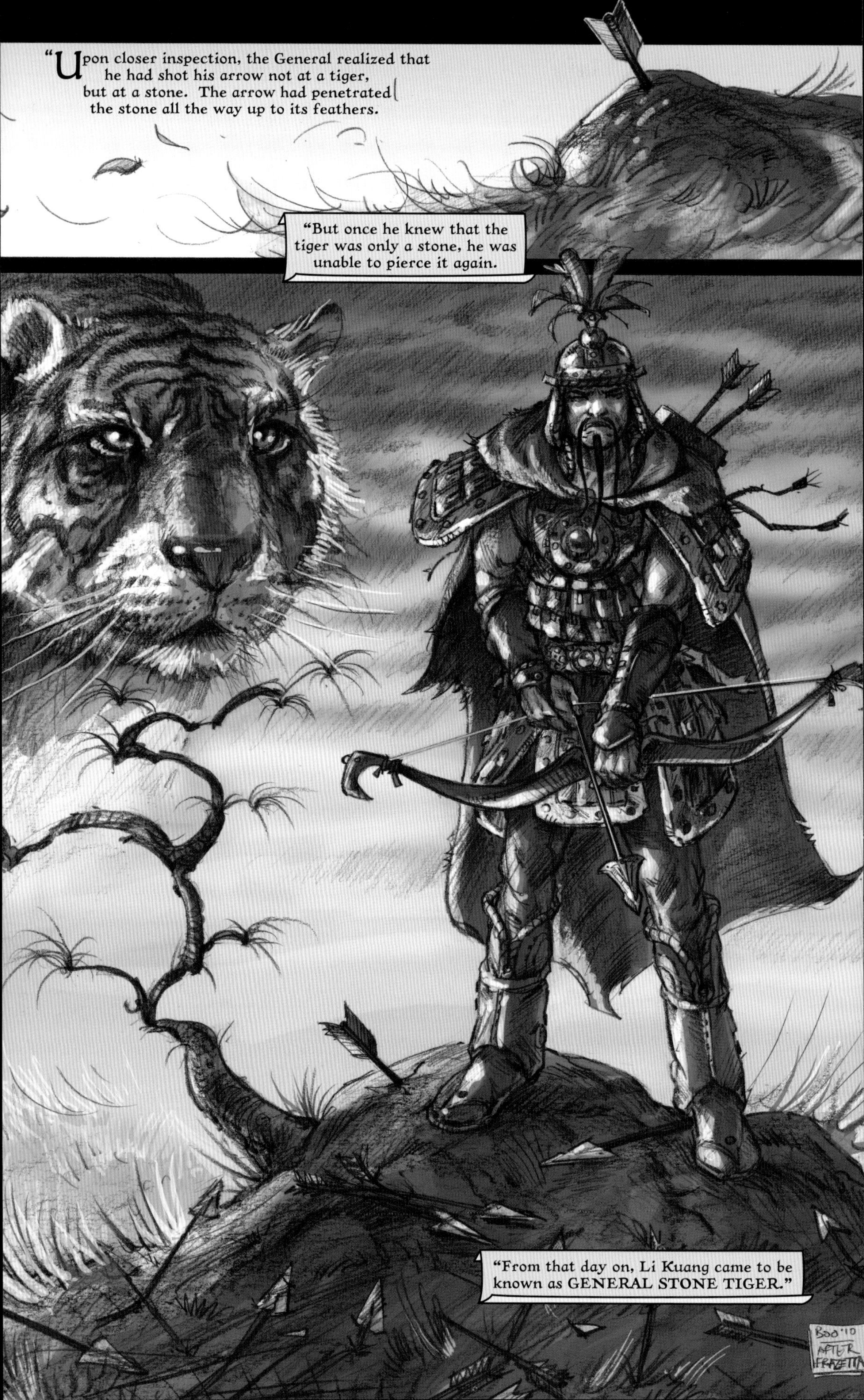
"Upon closer inspection, the General realized that he had shot his arrow not at a tiger, but at a stone. The arrow had penetrated the stone all the way up to its feathers.
"But once he knew that the tiger was only a stone, he was unable to pierce it again.
"From that day on, Li Kuang came to be known as GENERAL STONE TIGER."

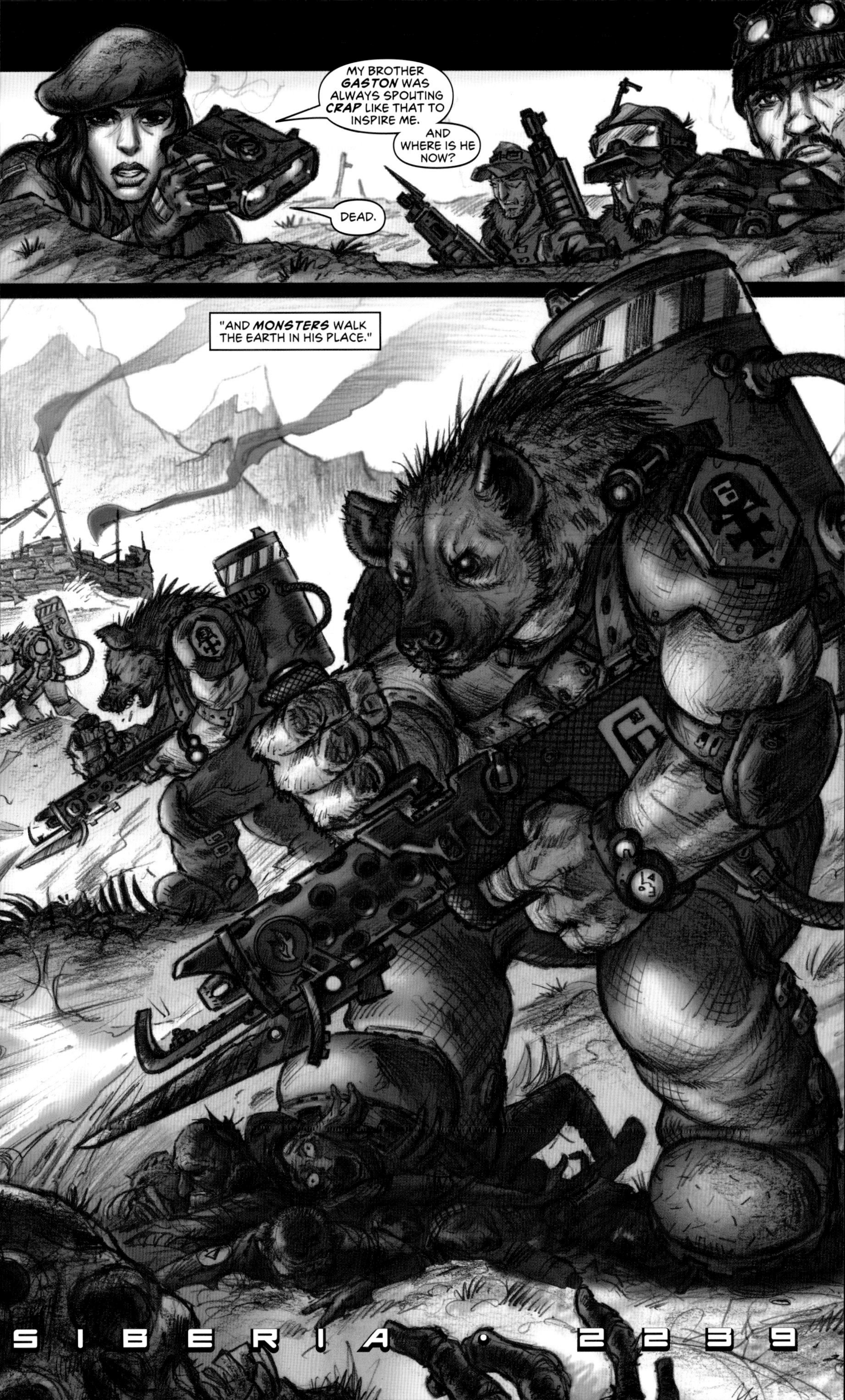
MY BROTHER GASTON WAS ALWAYS SPOUTING CRAP LIKE THAT TO INSPIRE ME.
AND WHERE IS HE NOW?
DEAD.
"AND MONSTERS WALK THE EARTH IN HIS PLACE."
SIBERIA • 2239

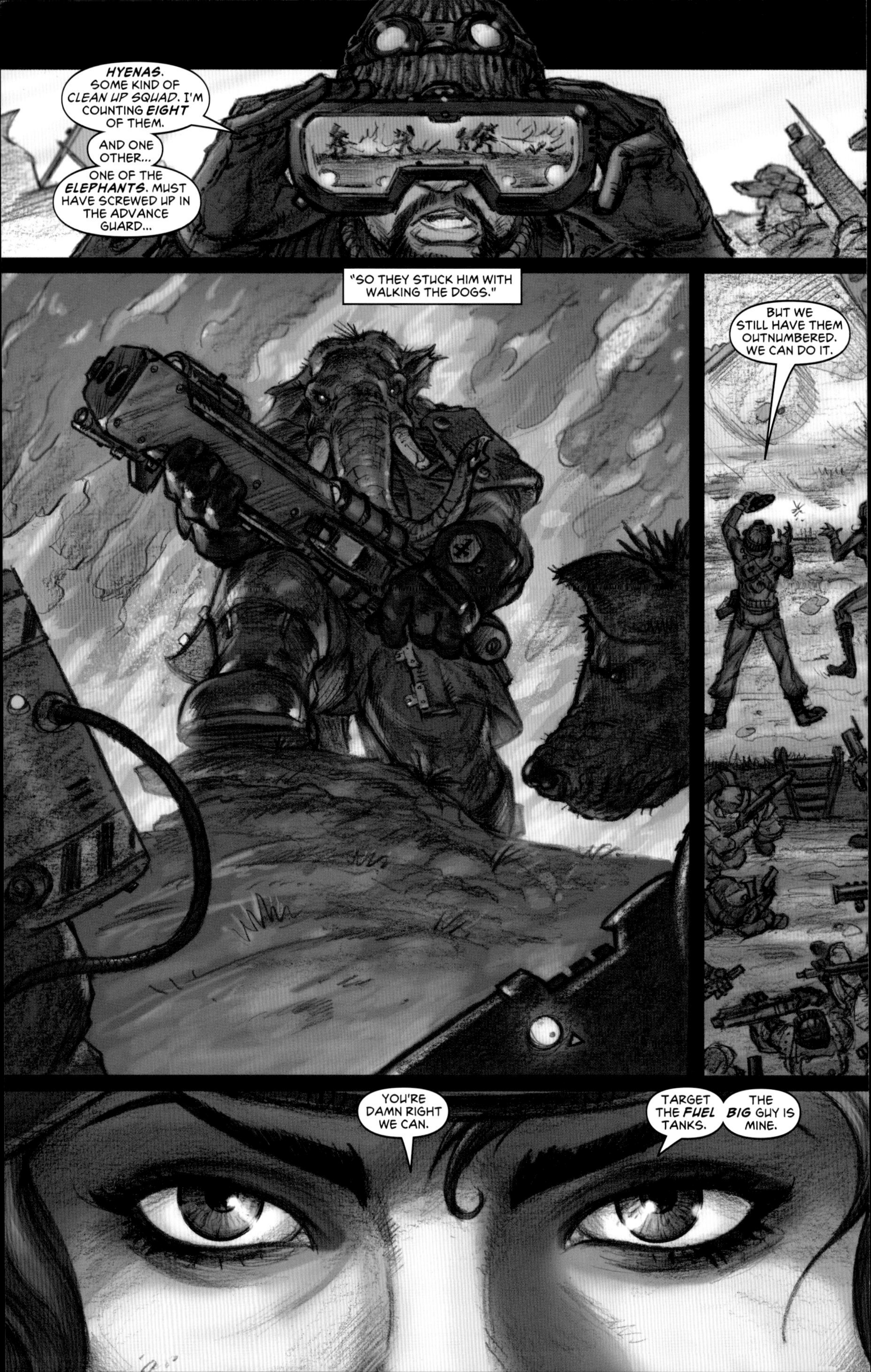
HYENAS. SOME KIND OF CLEAN UP SQUAD. I'M COUNTING EIGHT OF THEM.
AND ONE OTHER...
ONE OF THE ELEPHANTS. MUST HAVE SCREWED UP IN THE ADVANCE GUARD...
"SO THEY STUCK HIM WITH WALKING THE DOGS."
BUT WE STILL HAVE THEM OUTNUMBERED. WE CAN DO IT.
YOU'RE DAMN RIGHT WE CAN.
TARGET THE FUEL TANKS.
THE BIG GUY IS MINE.

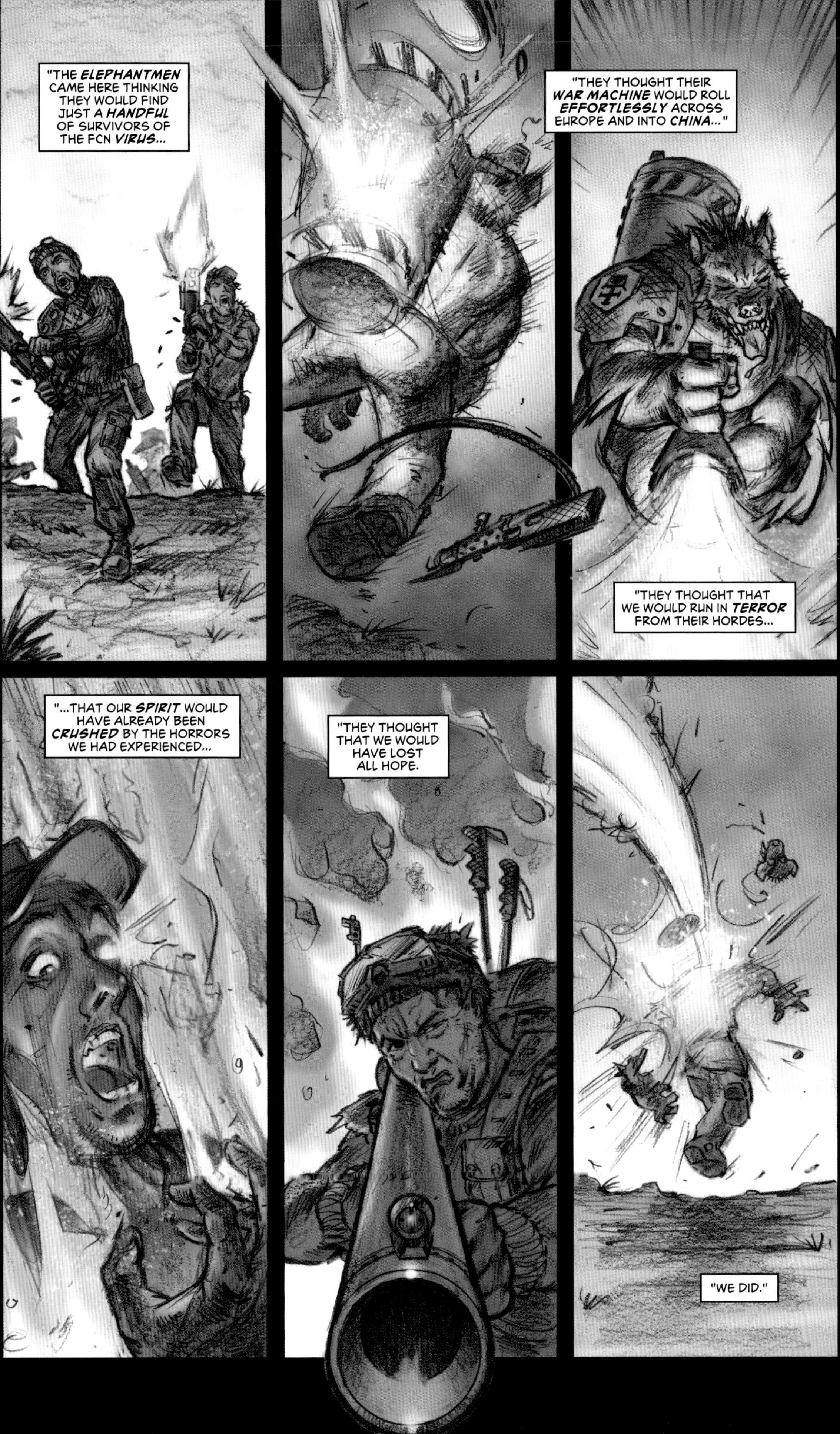
"THE ELEPHANTMEN CAME HERE THINKING THEY WOULD FIND JUST A HANDFUL OF SURVIVORS OF THE FCN VIRUS...
"THEY THOUGHT THEIR WAR MACHINE WOULD ROLL EFFORTLESSLY ACROSS EUROPE AND INTO CHINA..."
"THEY THOUGHT THAT WE WOULD RUN IN TERROR FROM THEIR HORDES...
"...THAT OUR SPIRIT WOULD HAVE ALREADY BEEN CRUSHED BY THE HORRORS WE HAD EXPERIENCED...
"THEY THOUGHT THAT WE WOULD HAVE LOST ALL HOPE.
"WE DID."

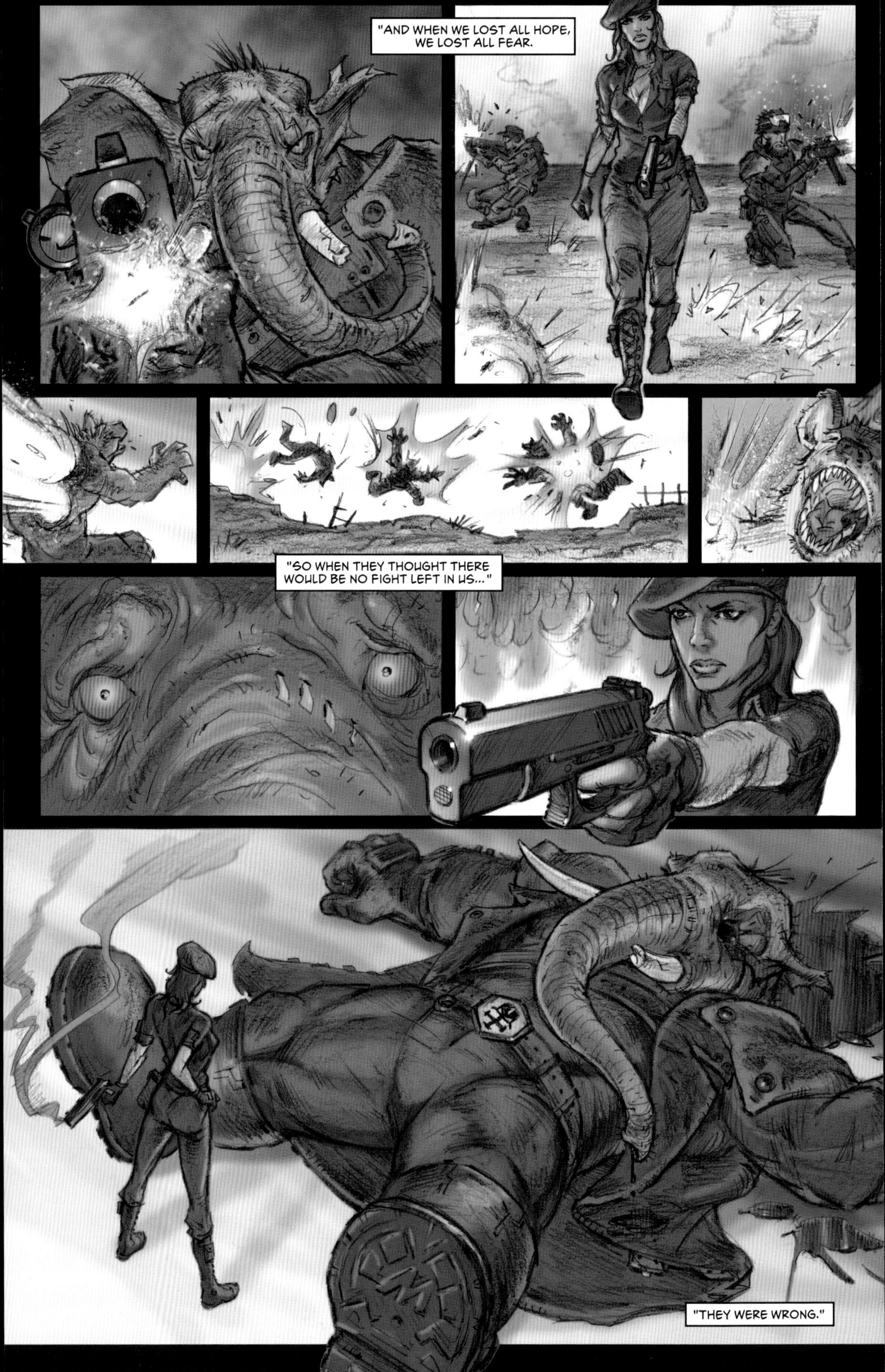
"AND WHEN WE LOST ALL HOPE, WE LOST ALL FEAR.
"SO WHEN THEY THOUGHT THERE WOULD BE NO FIGHT LEFT IN US..."
"THEY WERE WRONG."

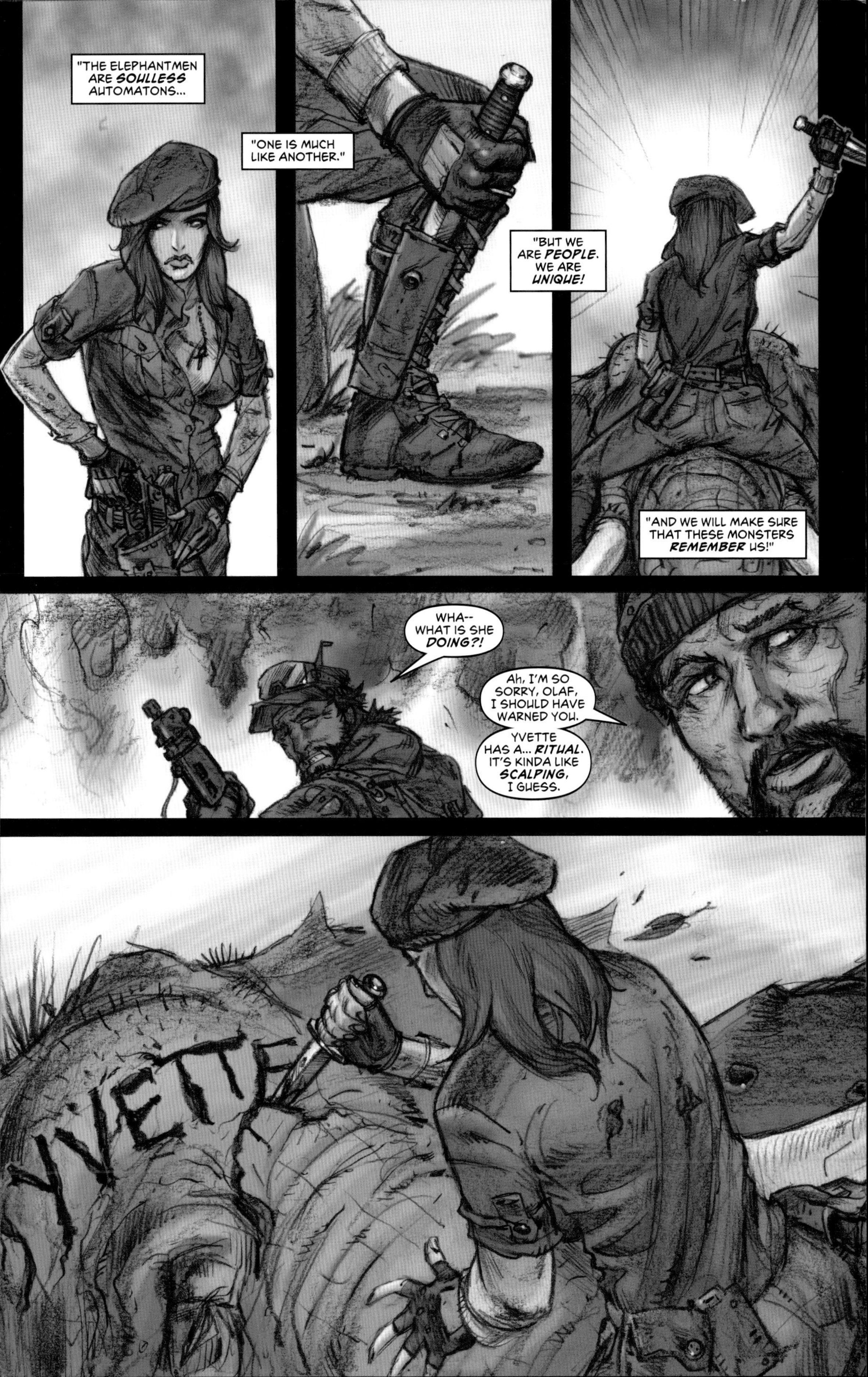
"THE ELEPHANTMEN ARE SOULLESS AUTOMATONS...
"ONE IS MUCH LIKE ANOTHER."
"BUT WE ARE PEOPLE. WE ARE UNIQUE!
"AND WE WILL MAKE SURE THAT THESE MONSTERS REMEMBER US!"
WHA-- WHAT IS SHE DOING?!
AH, I'M SO SORRY, OLAF, I SHOULD HAVE WARNED YOU.
YVETTE HAS A... RITUAL. IT'S KINDA LIKE SCALPING, I GUESS.
YVETTE

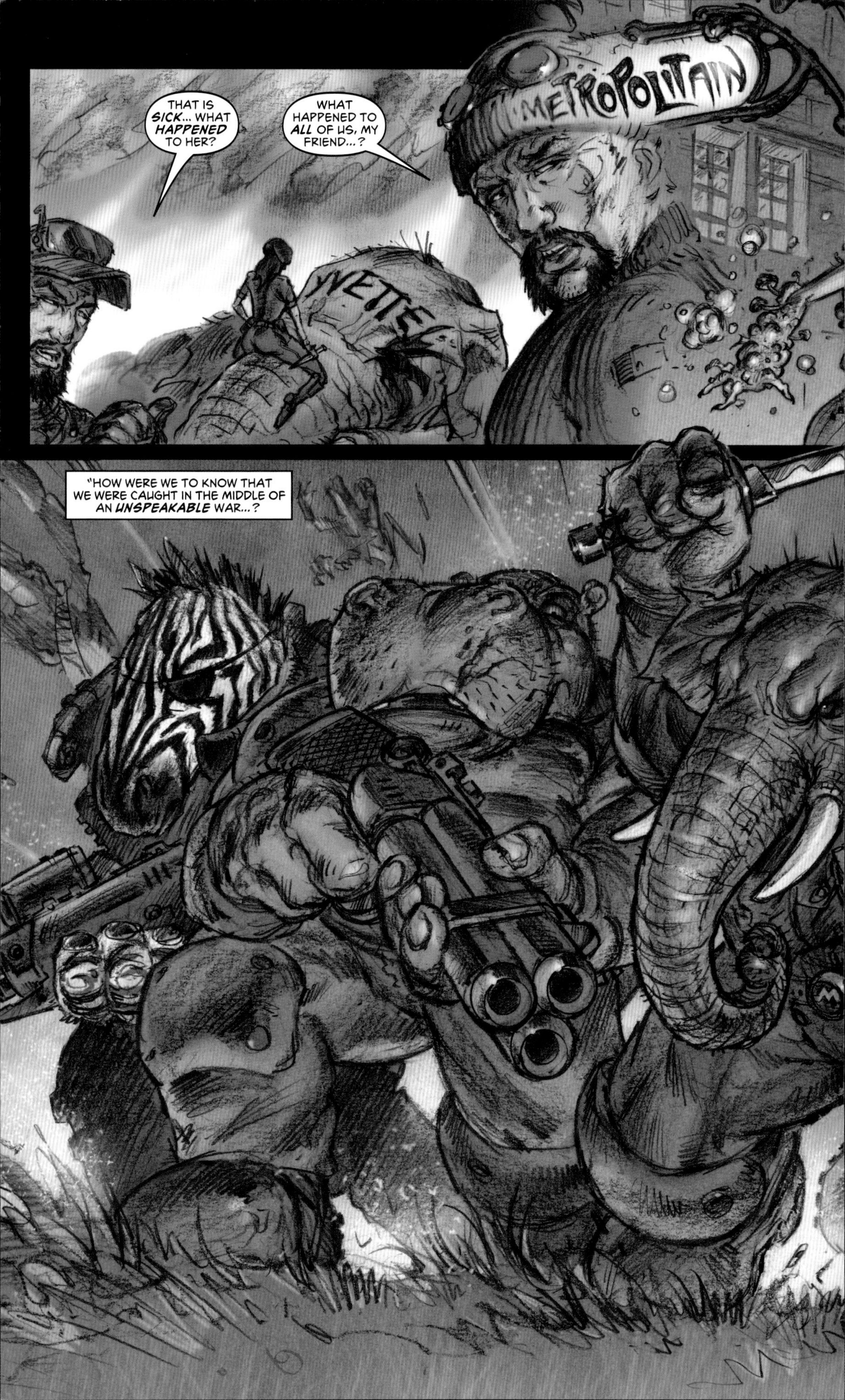
METROPOLITAIN
YVETTE
THAT IS SICK... WHAT HAPPENED TO HER?
WHAT HAPPENED TO ALL OF US, MY FRIEND...?
"HOW WERE WE TO KNOW THAT WE WERE CAUGHT IN THE MIDDLE OF AN UNSPEAKABLE WAR...?

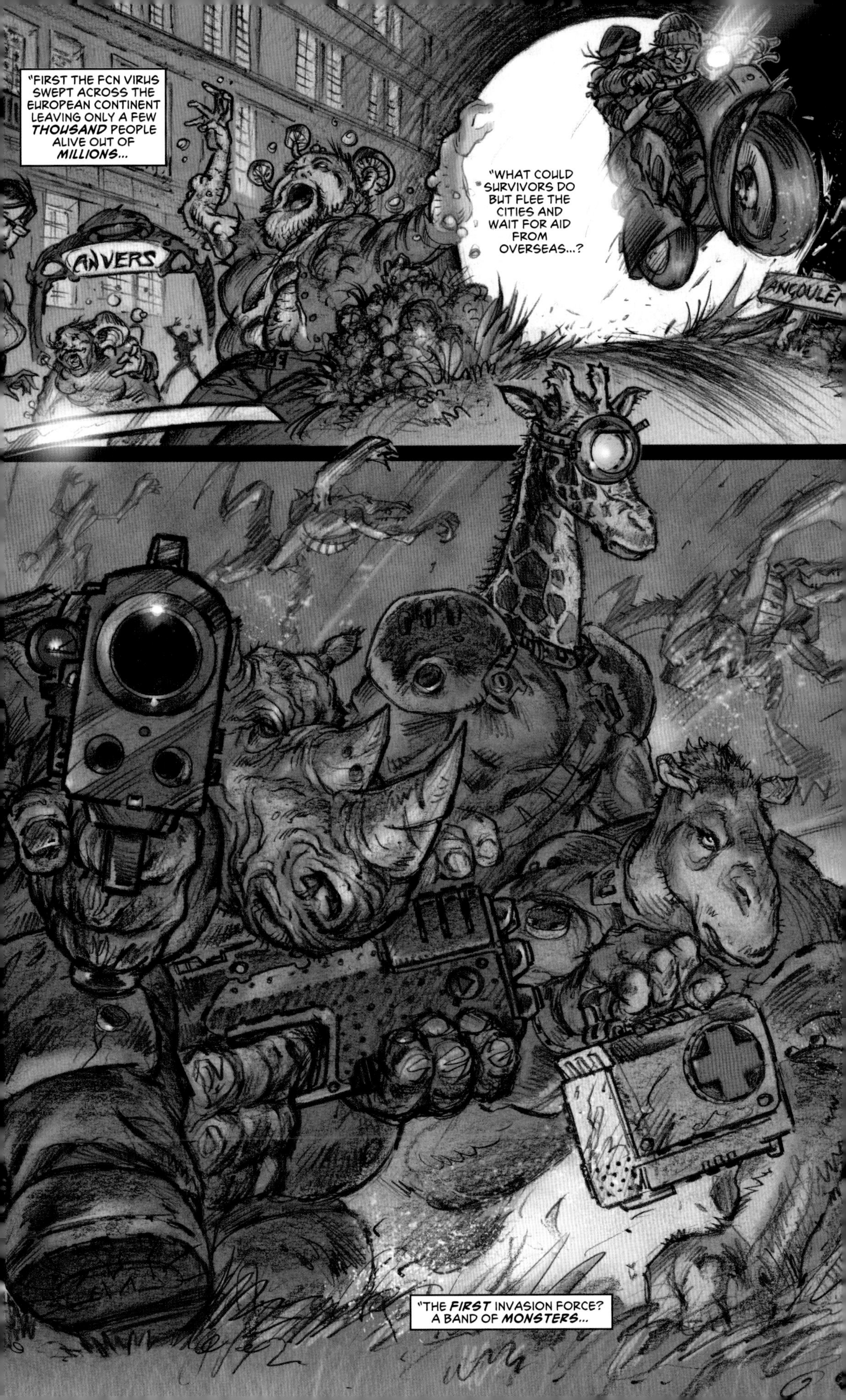
"FIRST THE FCN VIRUS SWEPT ACROSS THE EUROPEAN CONTINENT LEAVING ONLY A FEW *THOUSAND* PEOPLE ALIVE OUT OF *MILLIONS*...
ANVERS
"WHAT COULD SURVIVORS DO BUT FLEE THE CITIES AND WAIT FOR AID FROM OVERSEAS...?
"THE *FIRST* INVASION FORCE? A BAND OF *MONSTERS*...

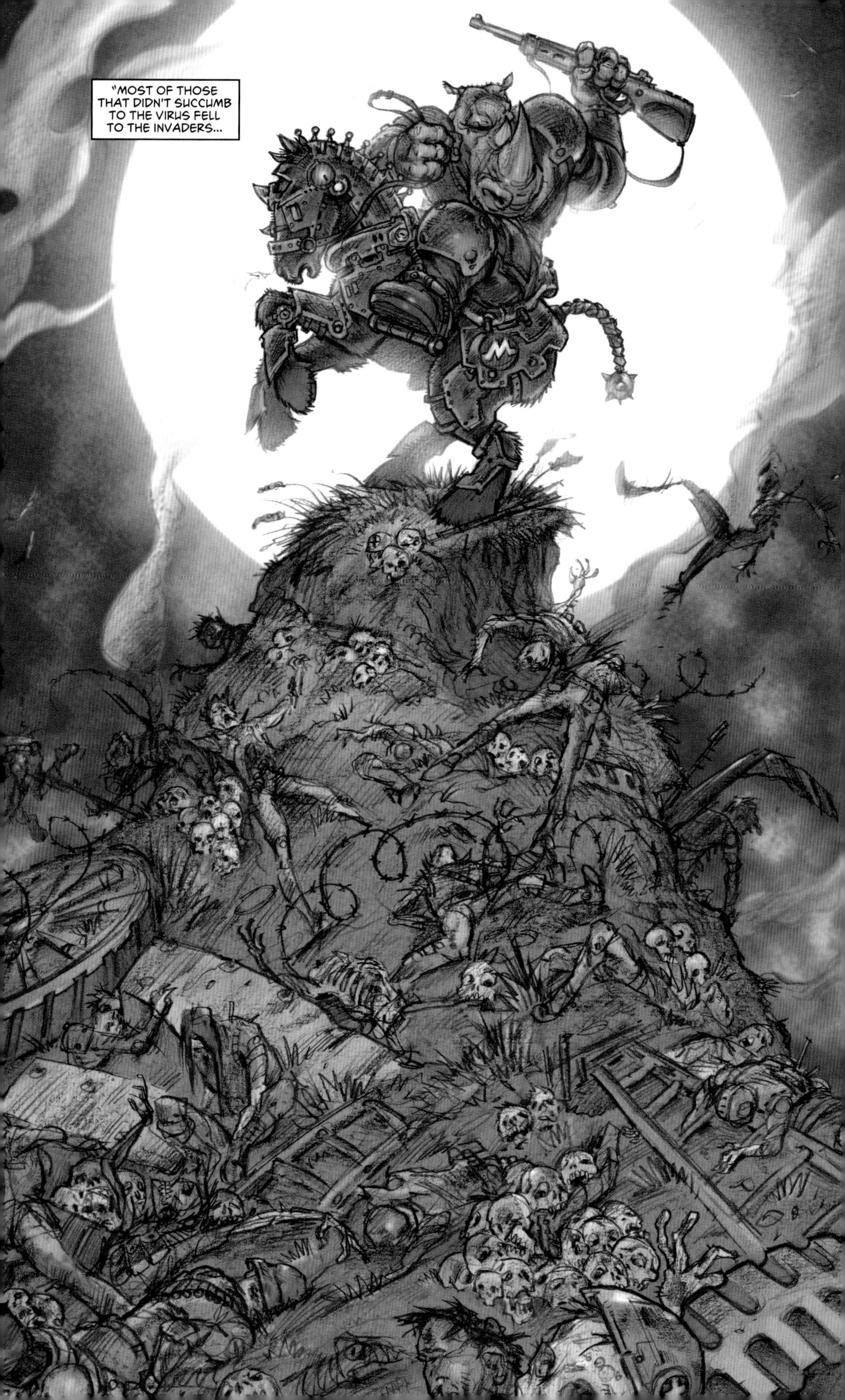
"MOST OF THOSE THAT DIDN'T SUCCUMB TO THE VIRUS FELL TO THE INVADERS...

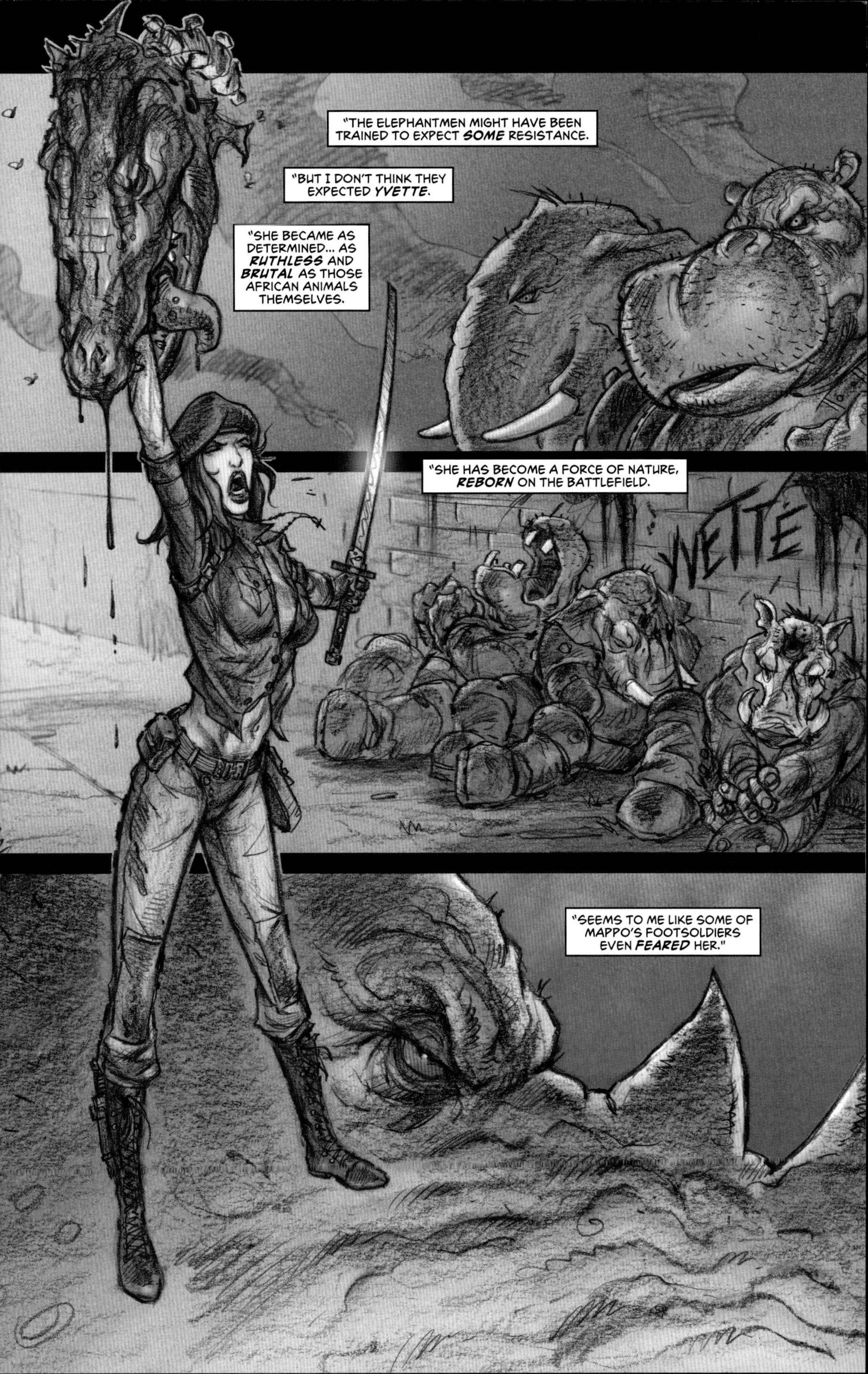
"THE ELEPHANTMEN MIGHT HAVE BEEN TRAINED TO EXPECT SOME RESISTANCE.
"BUT I DON'T THINK THEY EXPECTED YVETTE.
"SHE BECAME AS DETERMINED... AS RUTHLESS AND BRUTAL AS THOSE AFRICAN ANIMALS THEMSELVES.
"SHE HAS BECOME A FORCE OF NATURE, REBORN ON THE BATTLEFIELD.
YVETTE
"SEEMS TO ME LIKE SOME OF MAPPO'S FOOTSOLDIERS EVEN FEARED HER."

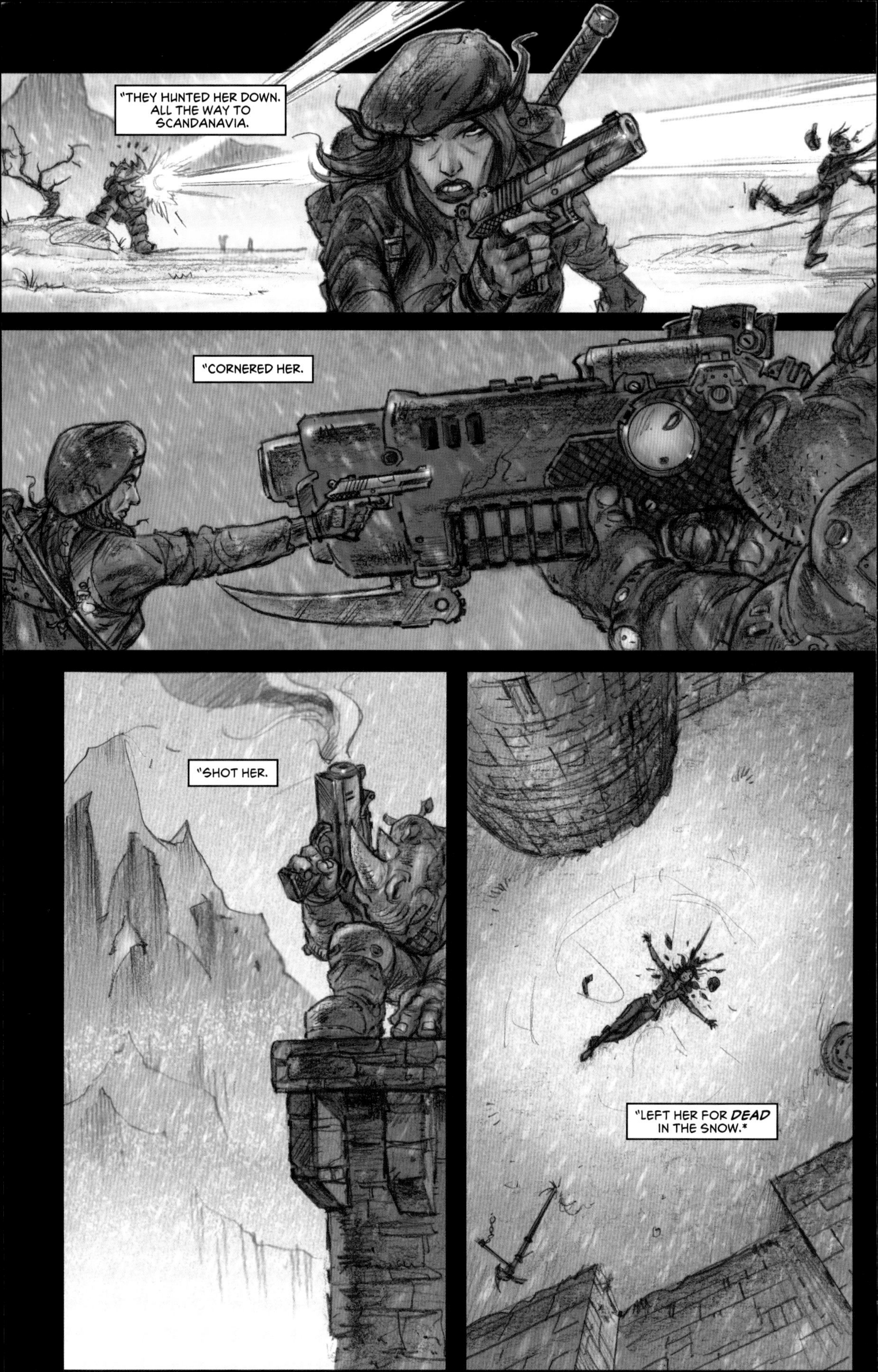
"THEY HUNTED HER DOWN. ALL THE WAY TO SCANDANAVIA.
"CORNERED HER.
"SHOT HER.
"LEFT HER FOR *DEAD* IN THE SNOW.*

*See ELEPHANTMEN: WAR TOYS #3

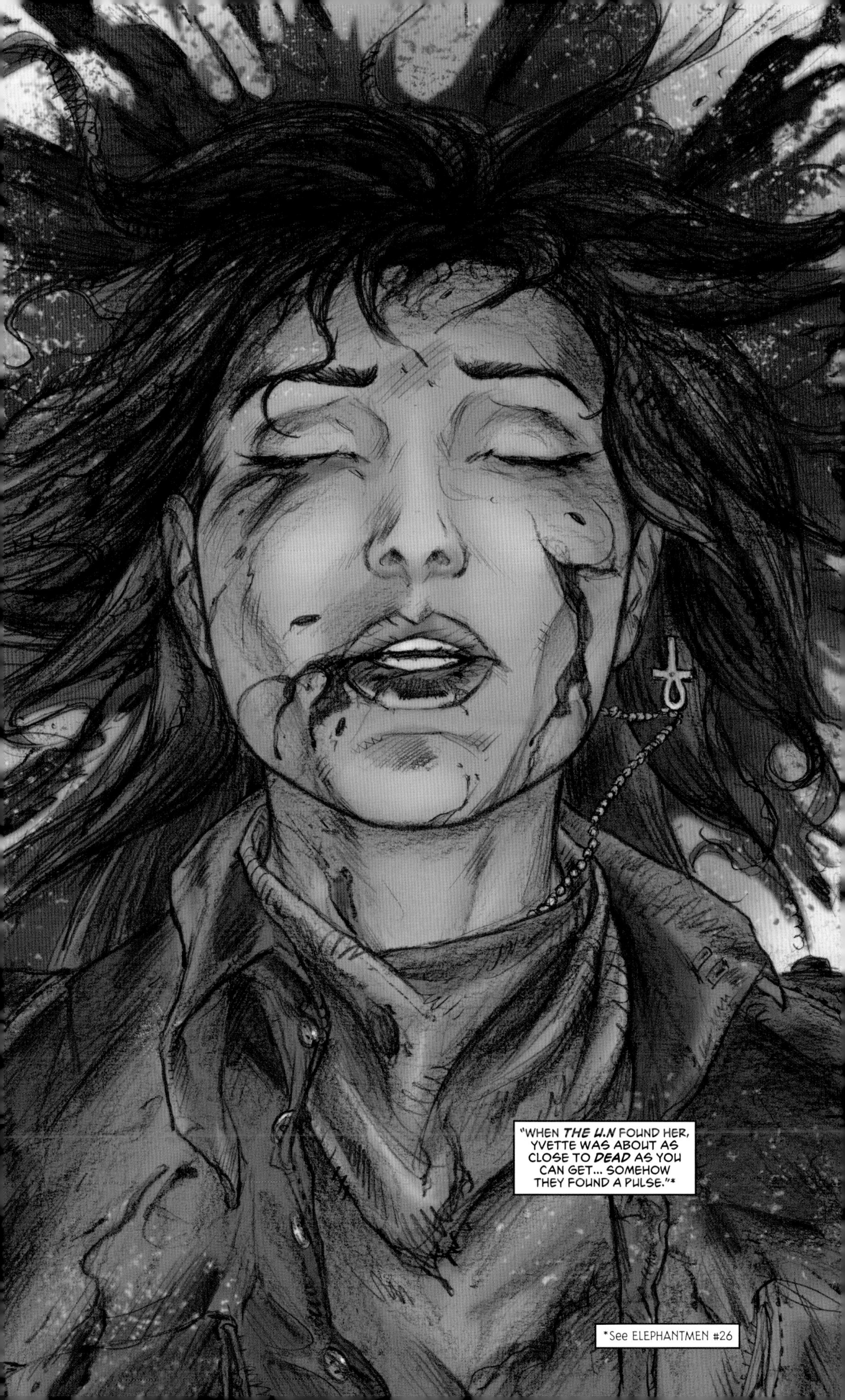
"WHEN THE U.N FOUND HER, YVETTE WAS ABOUT AS CLOSE TO DEAD AS YOU CAN GET... SOMEHOW THEY FOUND A PULSE."*
*See ELEPHANTMEN #26

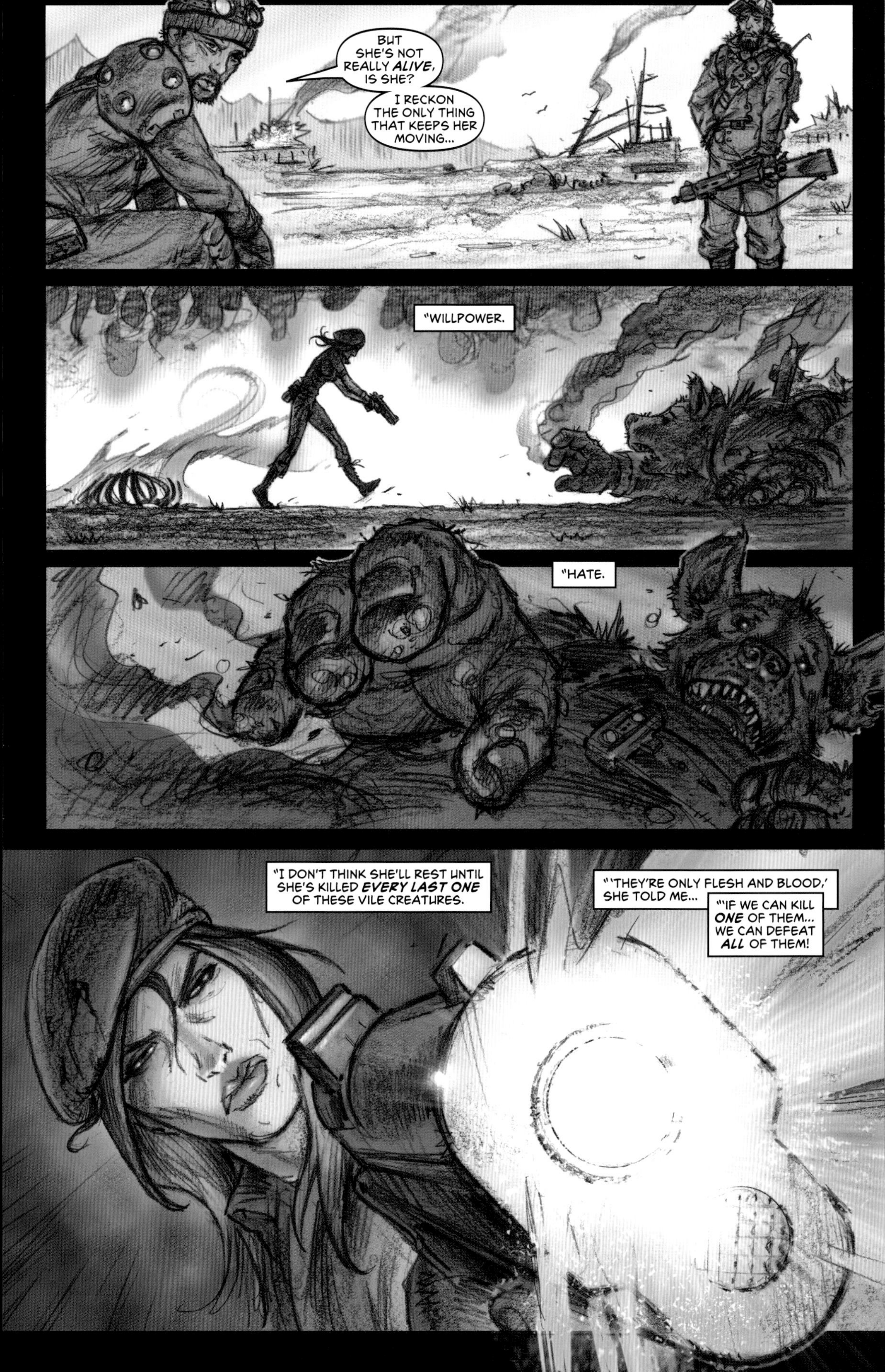
BUT SHE'S NOT REALLY *ALIVE,* IS SHE?
I RECKON THE ONLY THING THAT KEEPS HER MOVING...
"WILLPOWER.
"HATE.
"I DON'T THINK SHE'LL REST UNTIL SHE'S KILLED ***EVERY LAST ONE*** OF THESE VILE CREATURES.
"'THEY'RE ONLY FLESH AND BLOOD,' SHE TOLD ME...
"'IF WE CAN KILL ***ONE*** OF THEM... WE CAN DEFEAT ***ALL*** OF THEM!

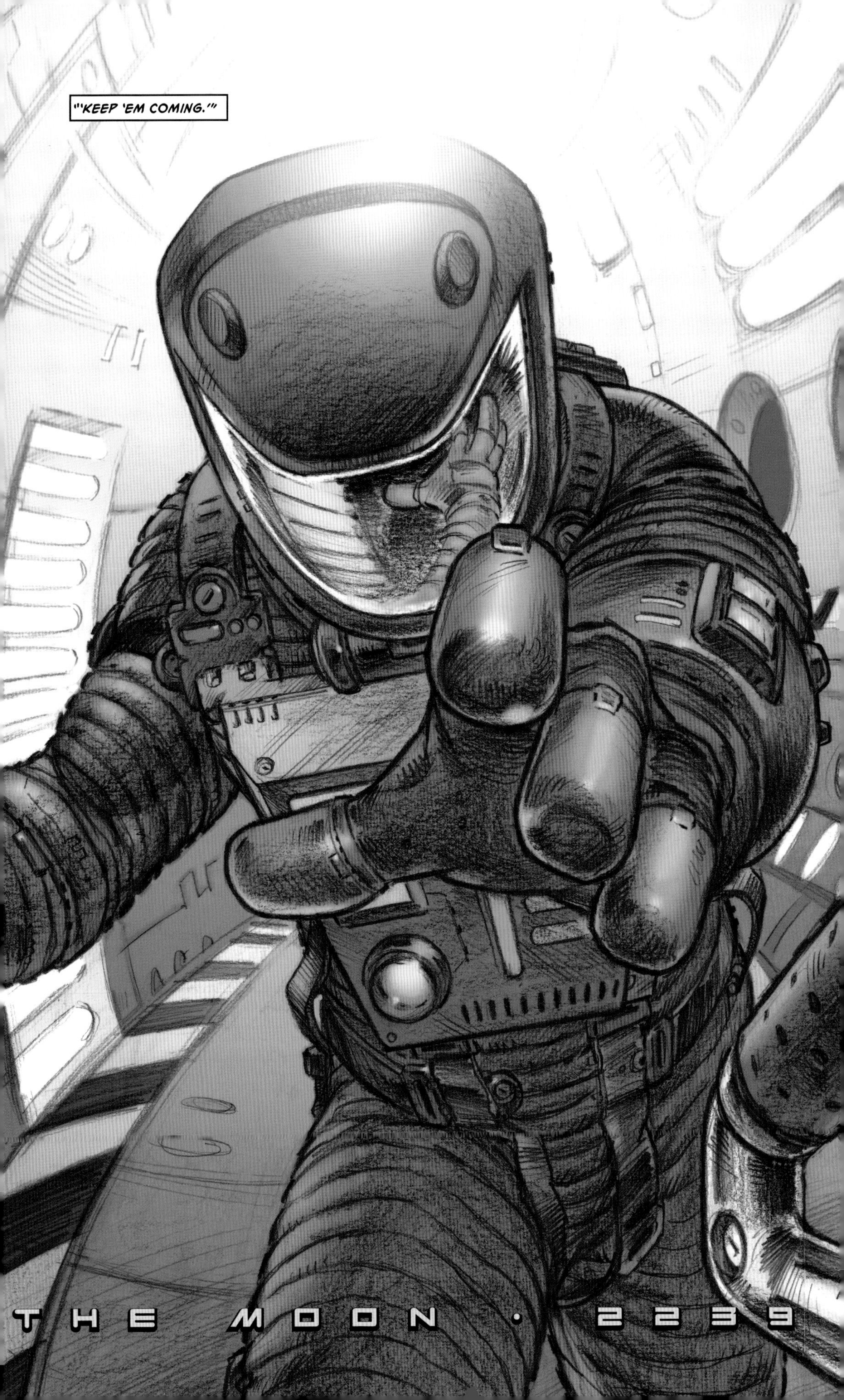
"KEEP 'EM COMING."
THE MOON · 2239

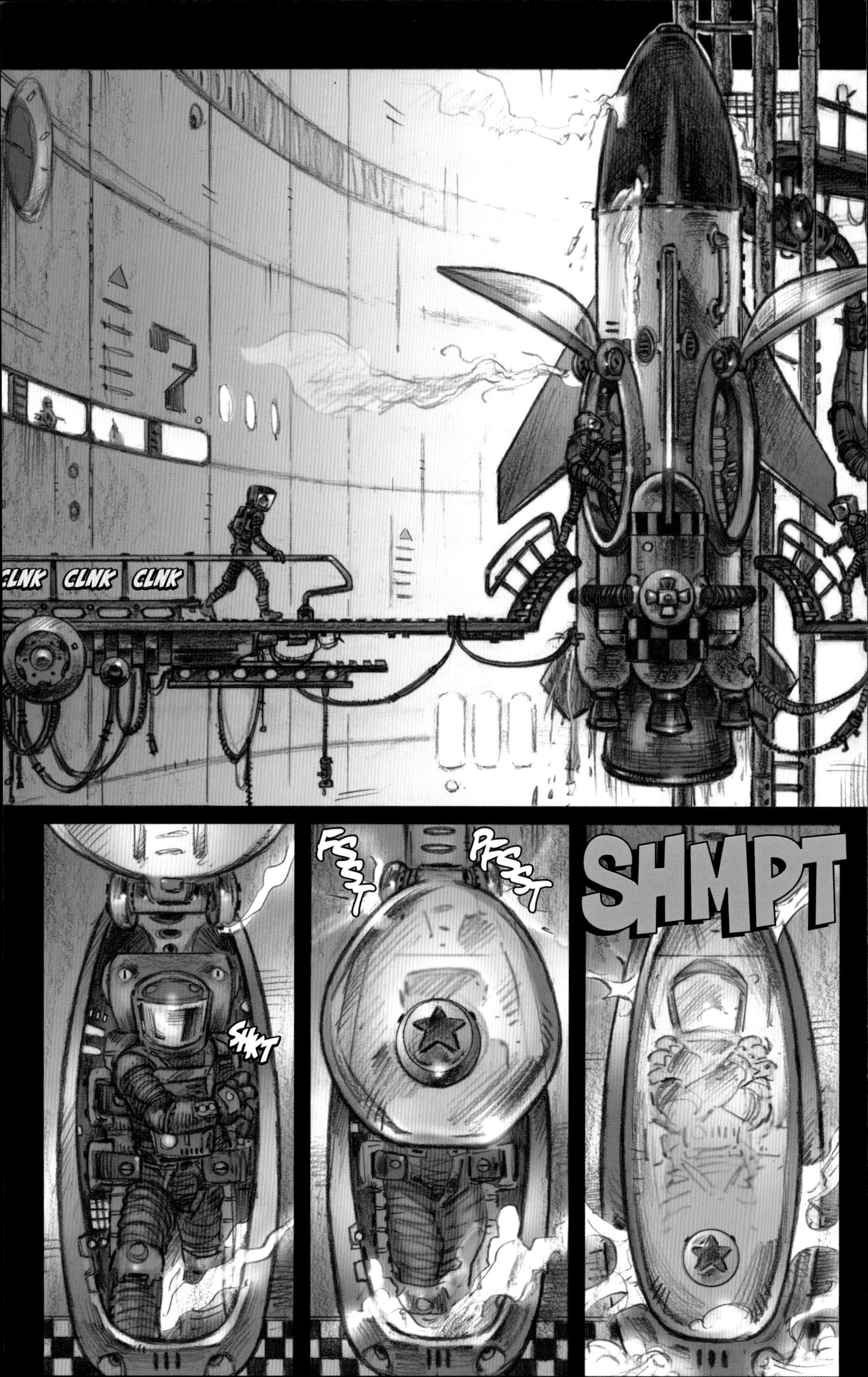
CLNK CLNK CLNK
SHKT
FSSST
PFSSST
SHMPT

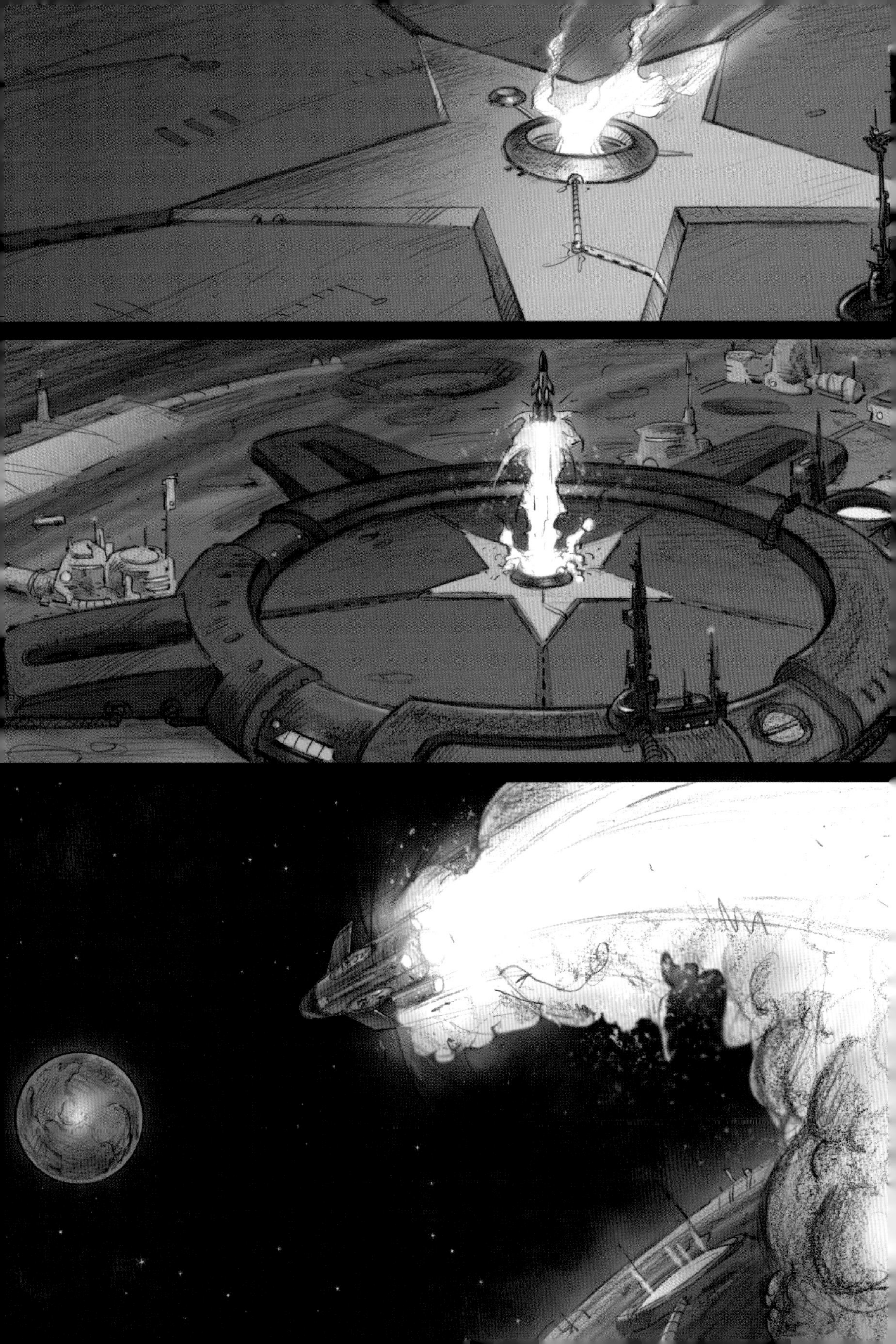

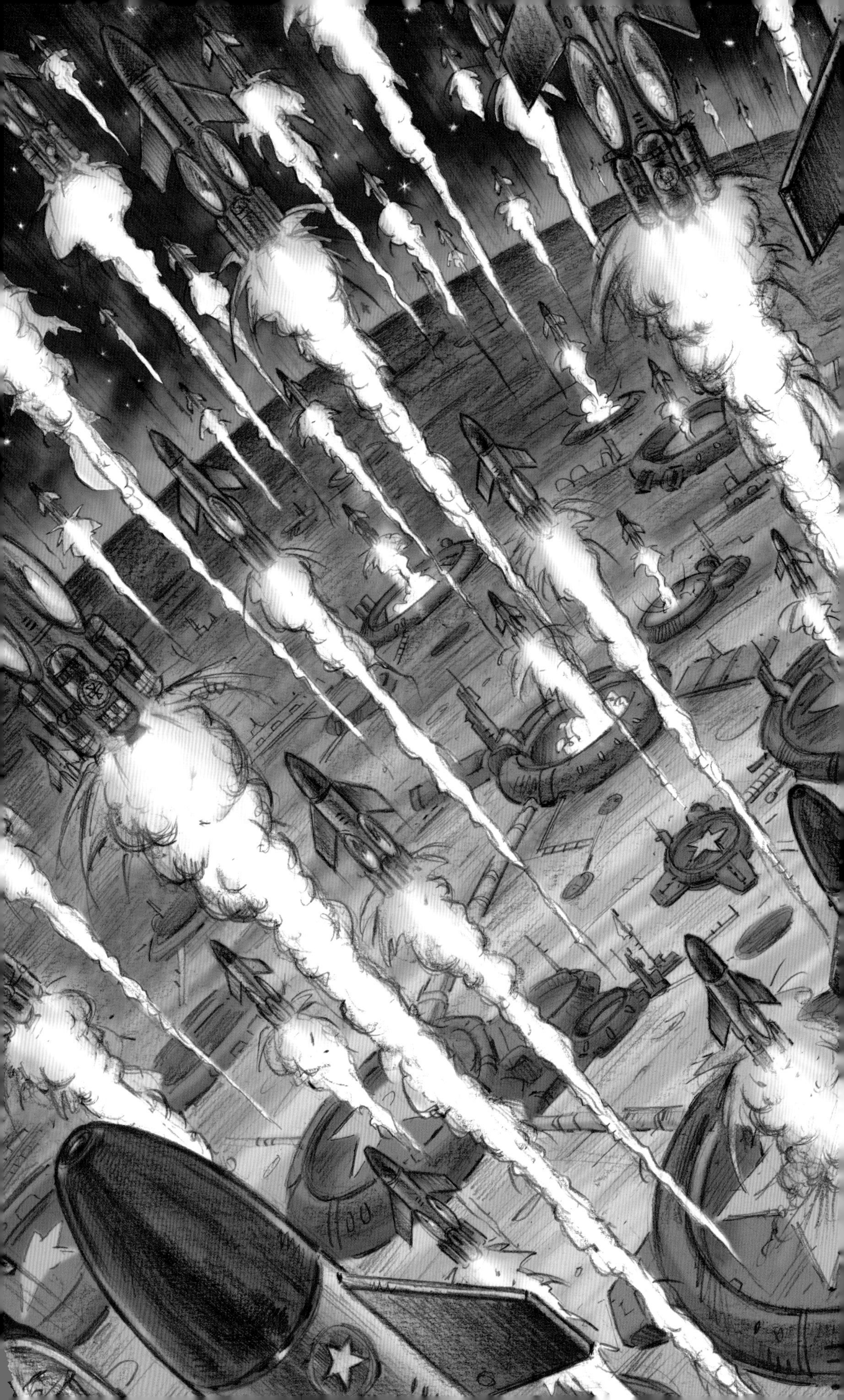

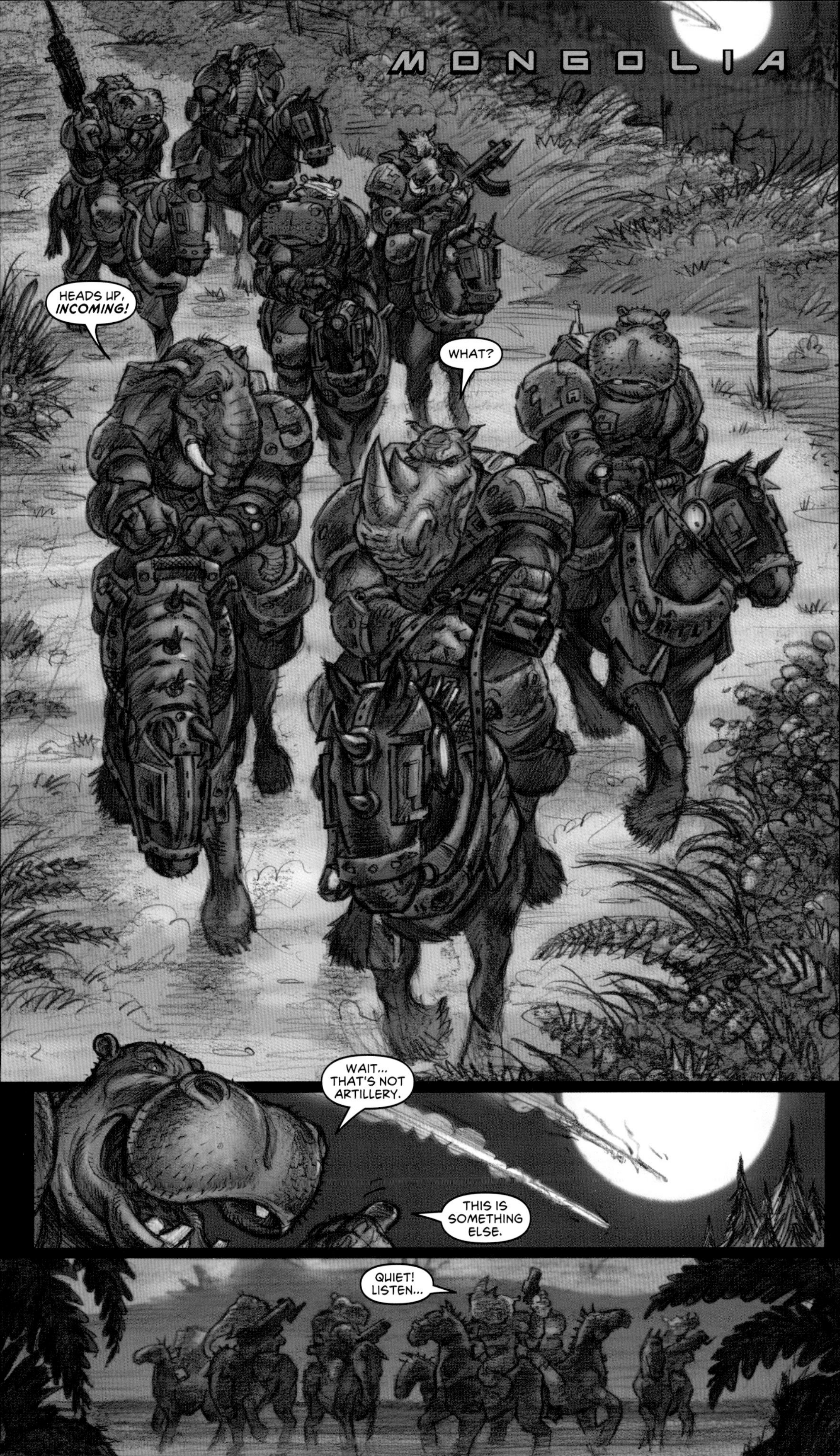
MONGOLIA
HEADS UP, INCOMING!
WHAT?
WAIT... THAT'S NOT ARTILLERY.
THIS IS SOMETHING ELSE.
QUIET! LISTEN...

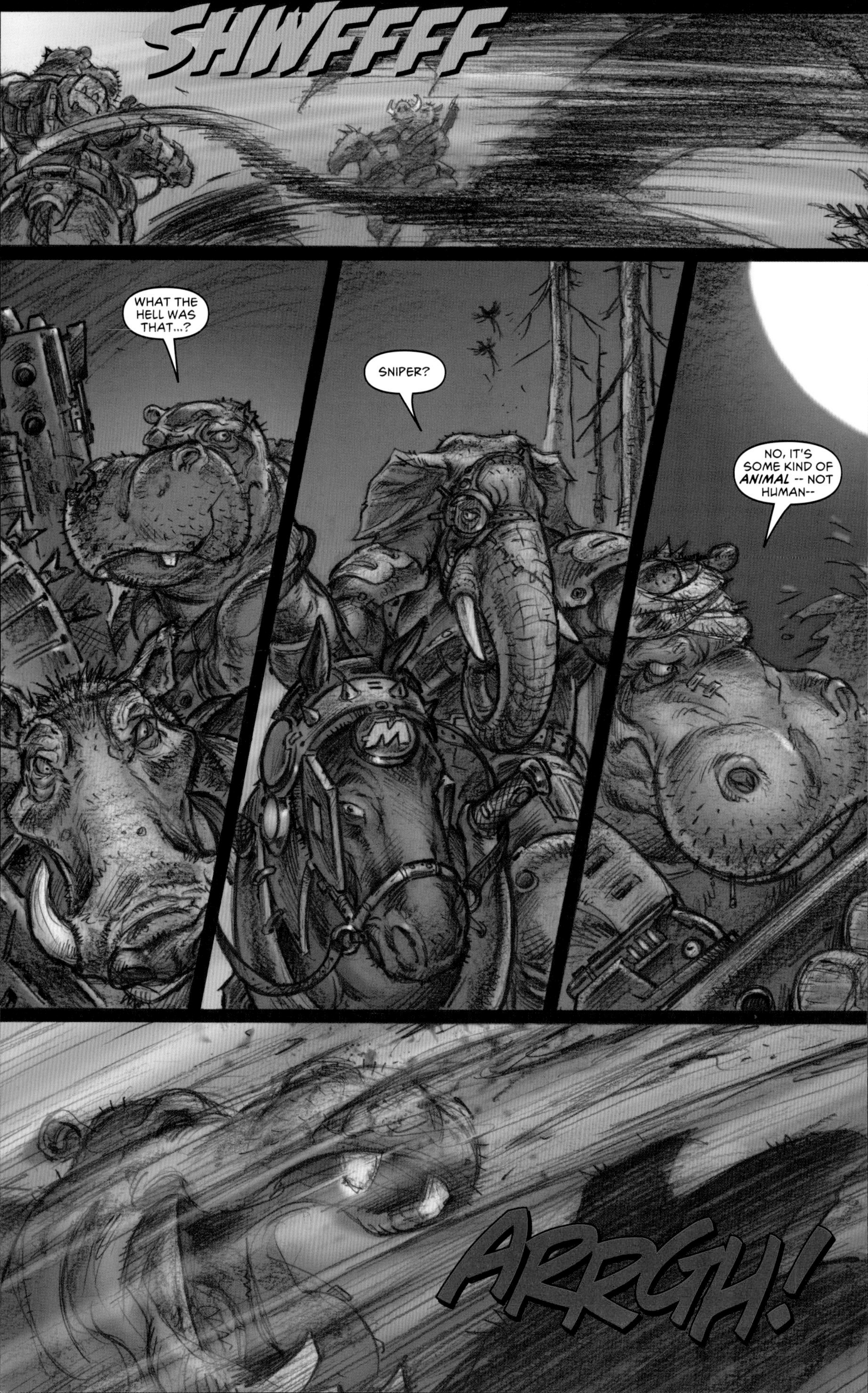
SHWFFFF
WHAT THE HELL WAS THAT...?
SNIPER?
NO, IT'S SOME KIND OF ANIMAL -- NOT HUMAN--
ARRGH!

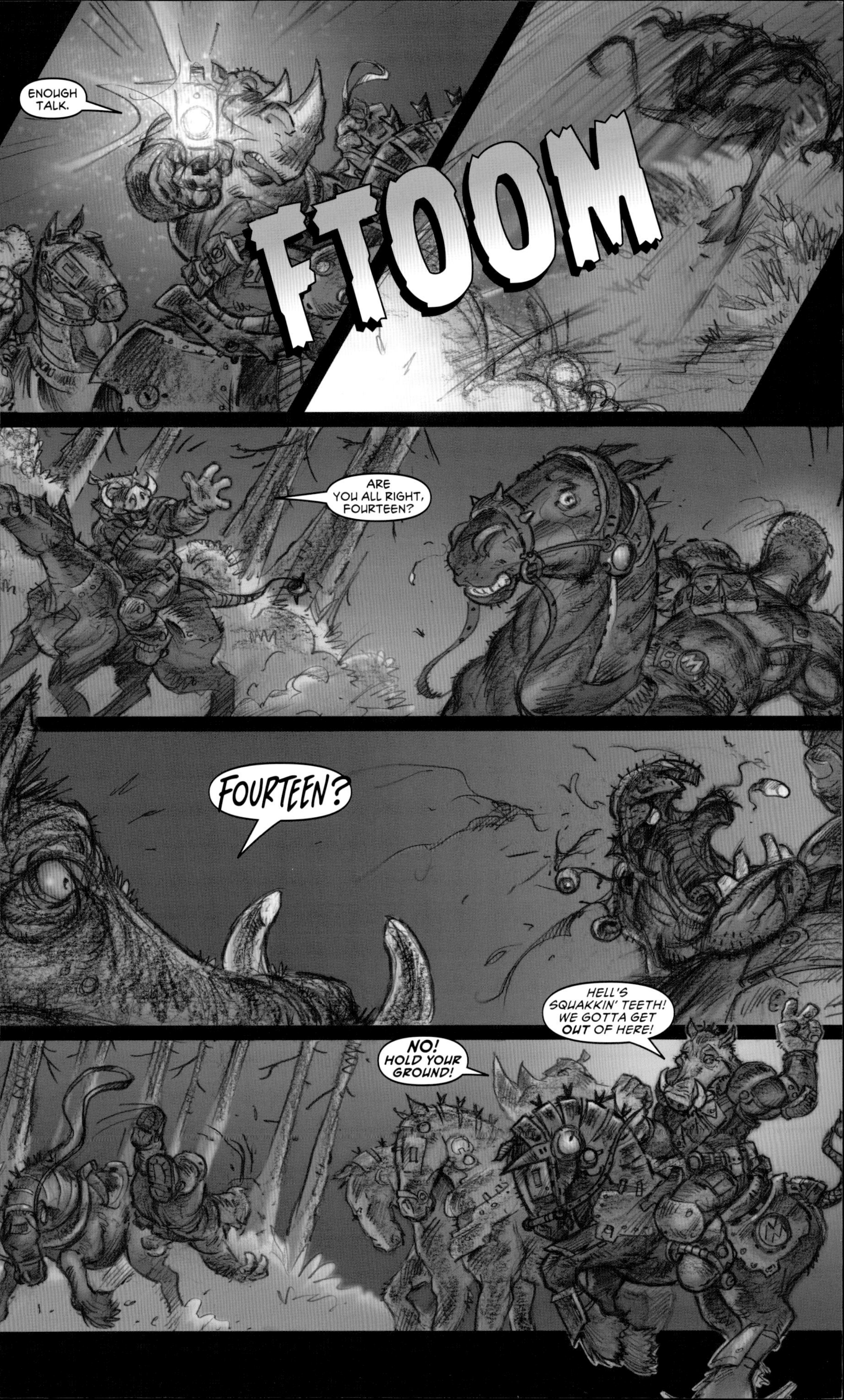
ENOUGH TALK.
FTOOM
ARE YOU ALL RIGHT, FOURTEEN?
FOURTEEN?
HELL'S SQUAKKIN' TEETH! WE GOTTA GET OUT OF HERE!
NO! HOLD YOUR GROUND!

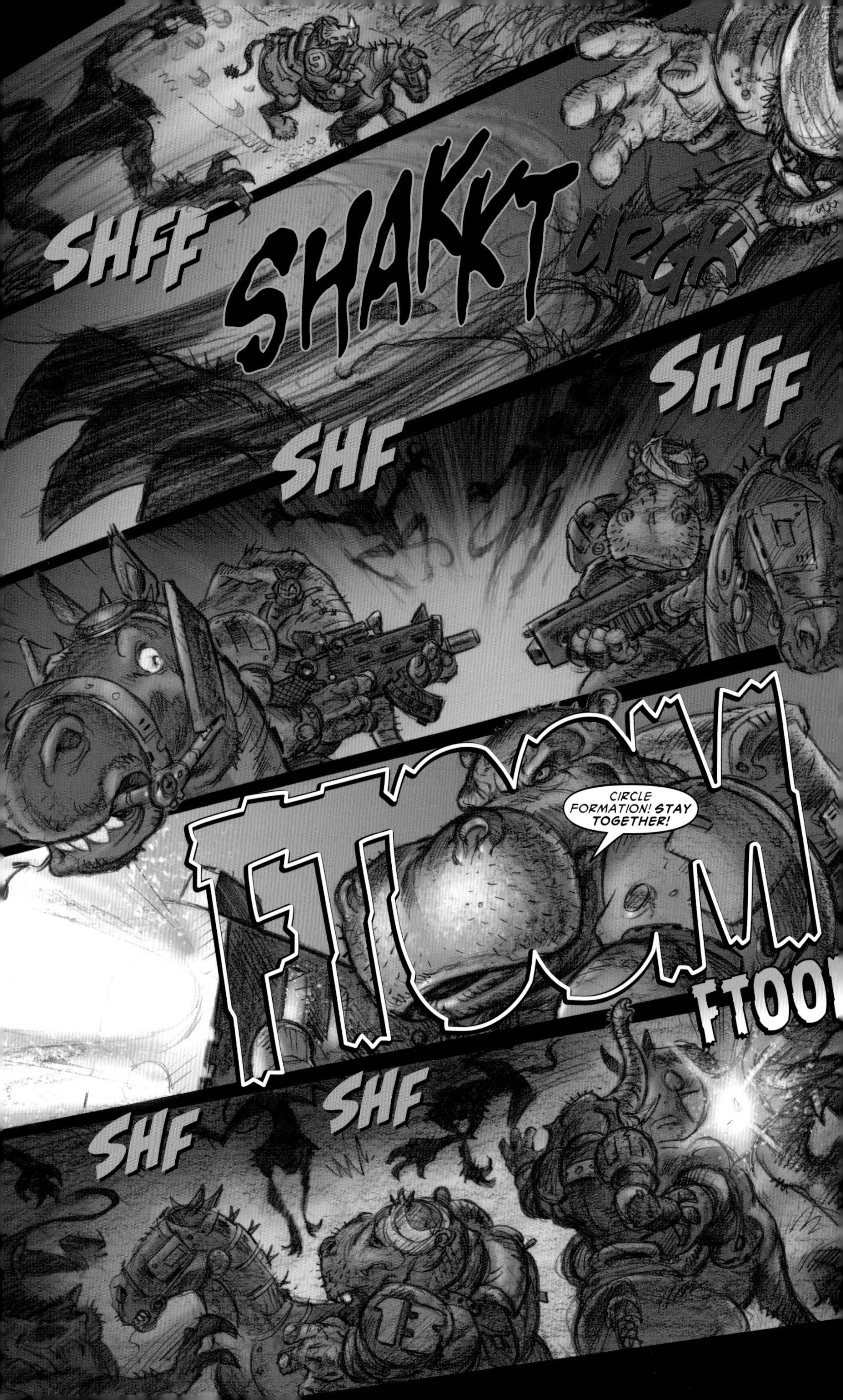
SHFF
SHAKKT
URGK
SHFF
SHF
CIRCLE FORMATION! STAY TOGETHER!
FTOOM
FTOOM
SHF
SHF

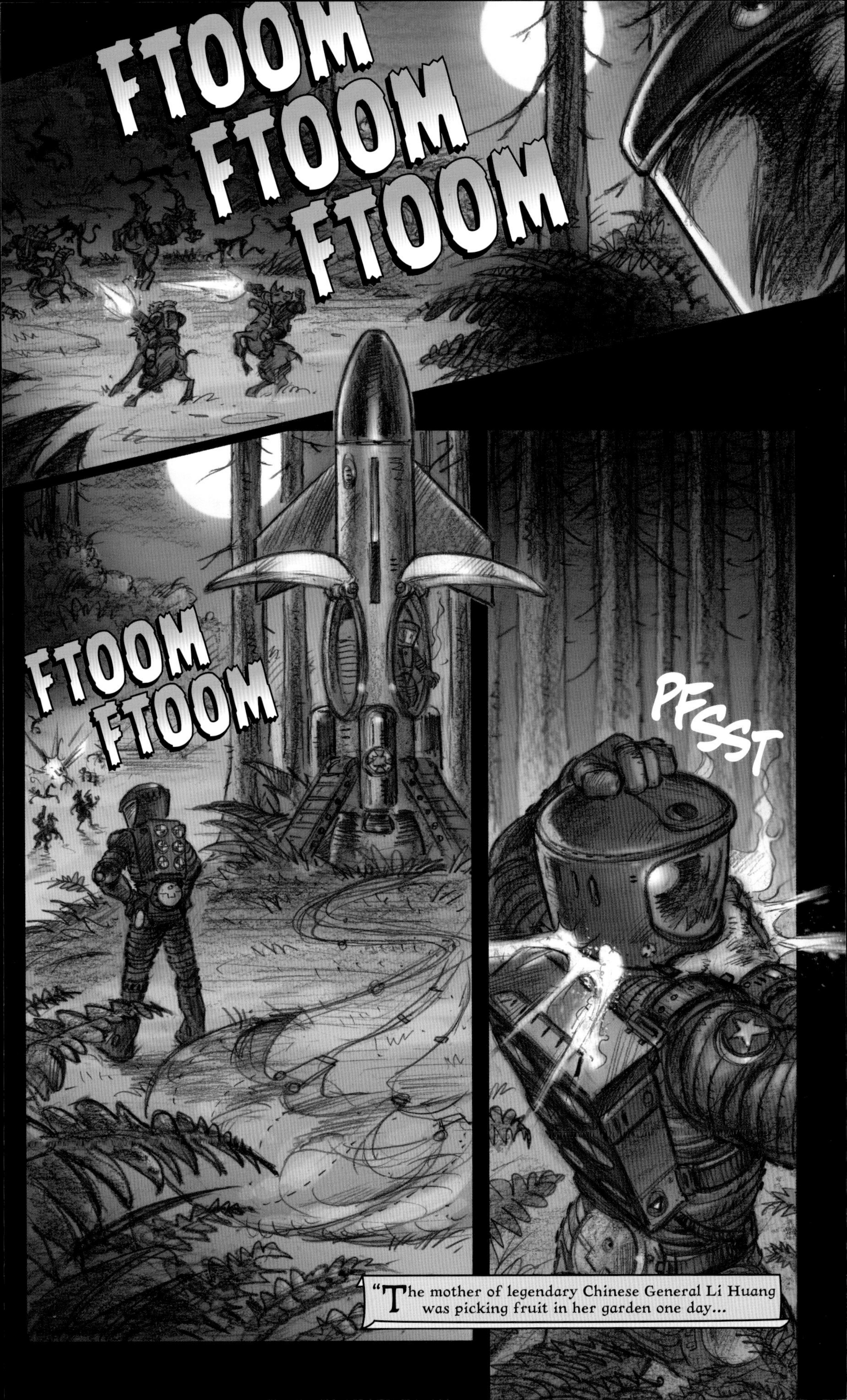
FTOOM
FTOOM
FTOOM
FTOOM
FTOOM
PFSST
"The mother of legendary Chinese General Li Huang was picking fruit in her garden one day...

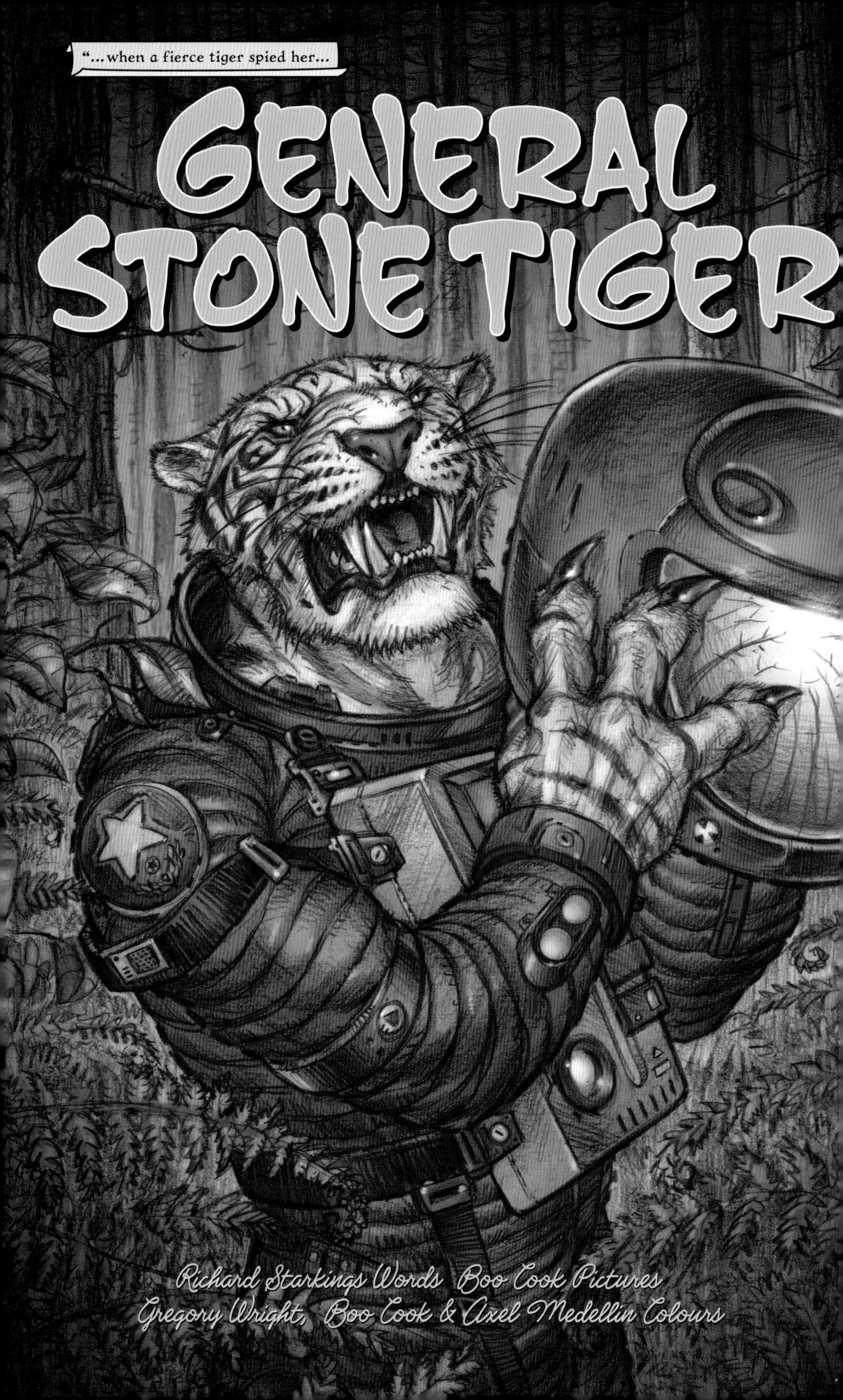
"...when a fierce tiger spied her...
GENERAL STONE TIGER
Richard Starkings Words Boo Cook Pictures
Gregory Wright, Boo Cook & Axel Medellin Colours

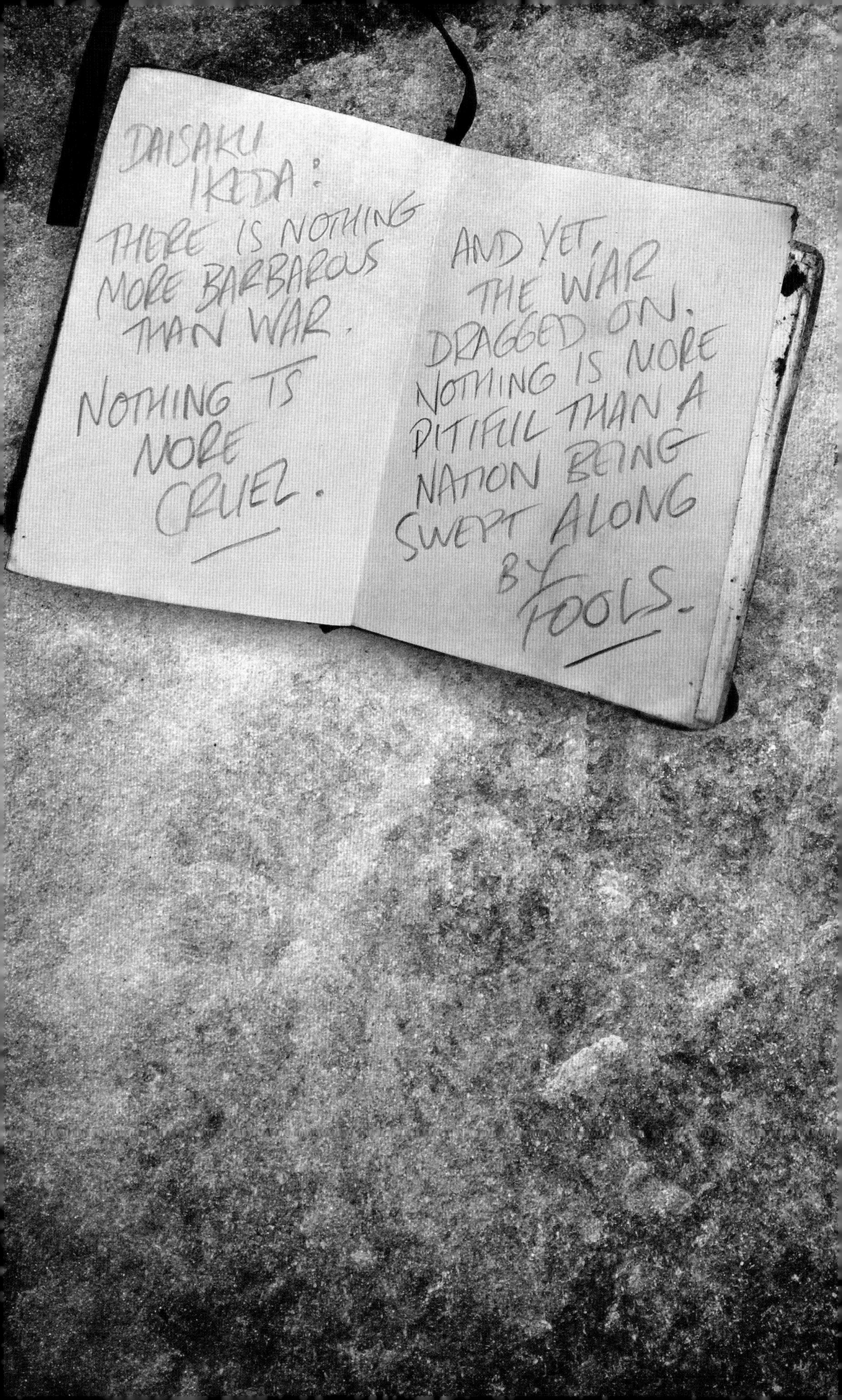
DAISAKU IKEDA:
THERE IS NOTHING MORE BARBAROUS THAN WAR.
NOTHING IS MORE CRUEL.
AND YET, THE WAR DRAGGED ON.
NOTHING IS MORE PITIFUL THAN A NATION BEING SWEPT ALONG BY FOOLS.

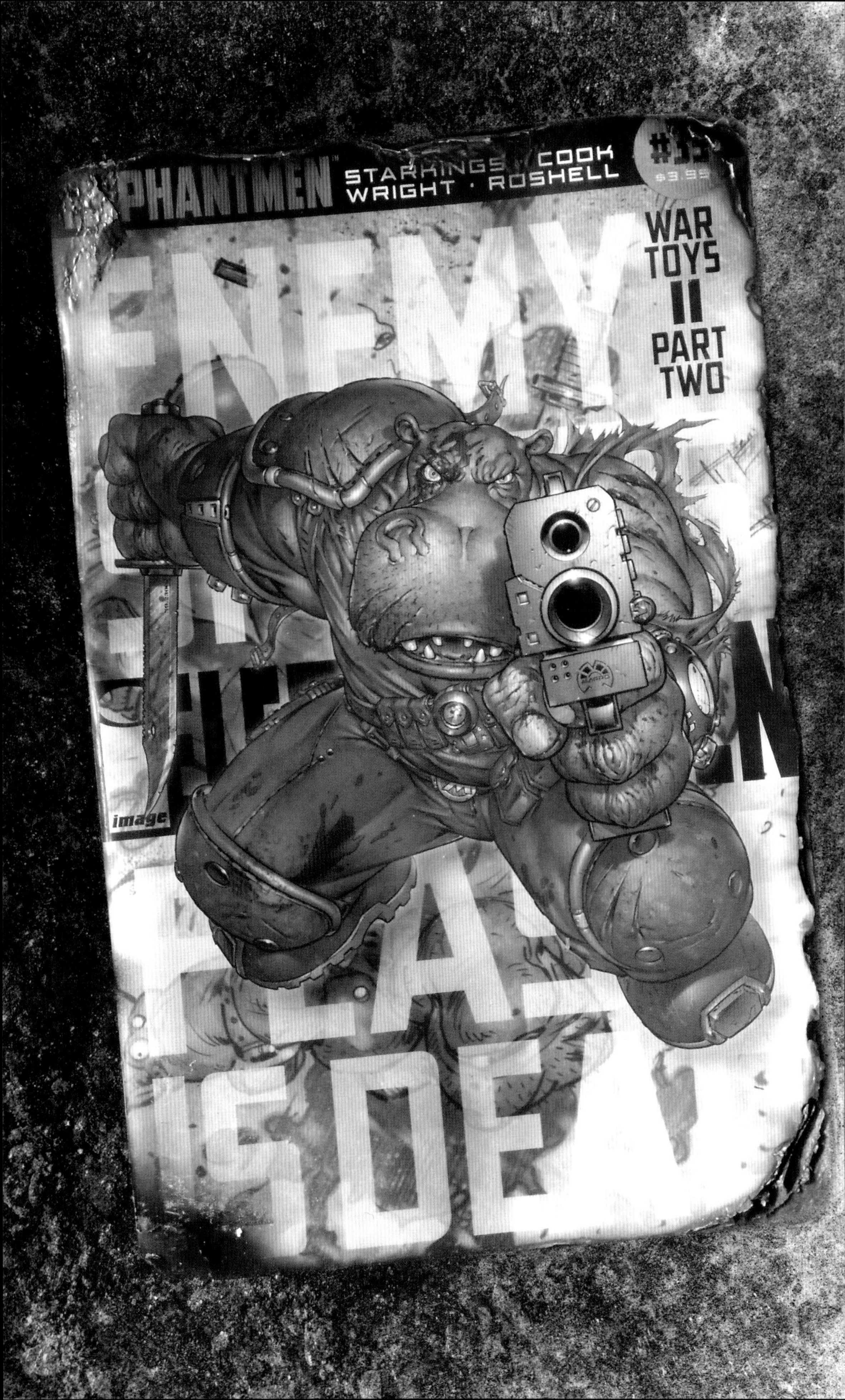
PHANTMEN
STARKINGS · COOK
WRIGHT · ROSHELL
WAR TOYS II PART TWO
image

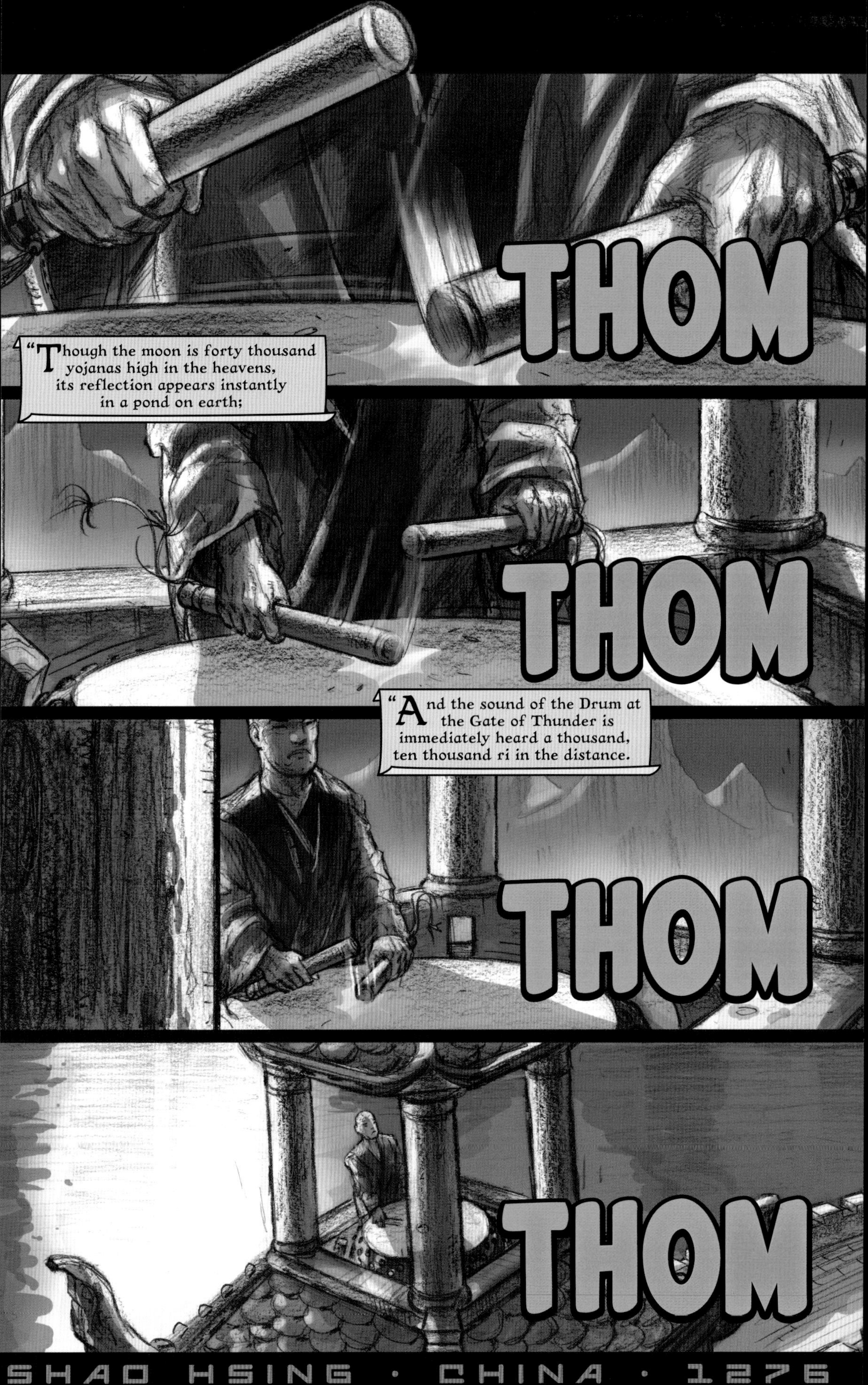

"Though the moon is forty thousand yojanas high in the heavens, its reflection appears instantly in a pond on earth;
THOM
THOM
"And the sound of the Drum at the Gate of Thunder is immediately heard a thousand, ten thousand ri in the distance.
THOM
THOM
SHAO HSING · CHINA · 1276

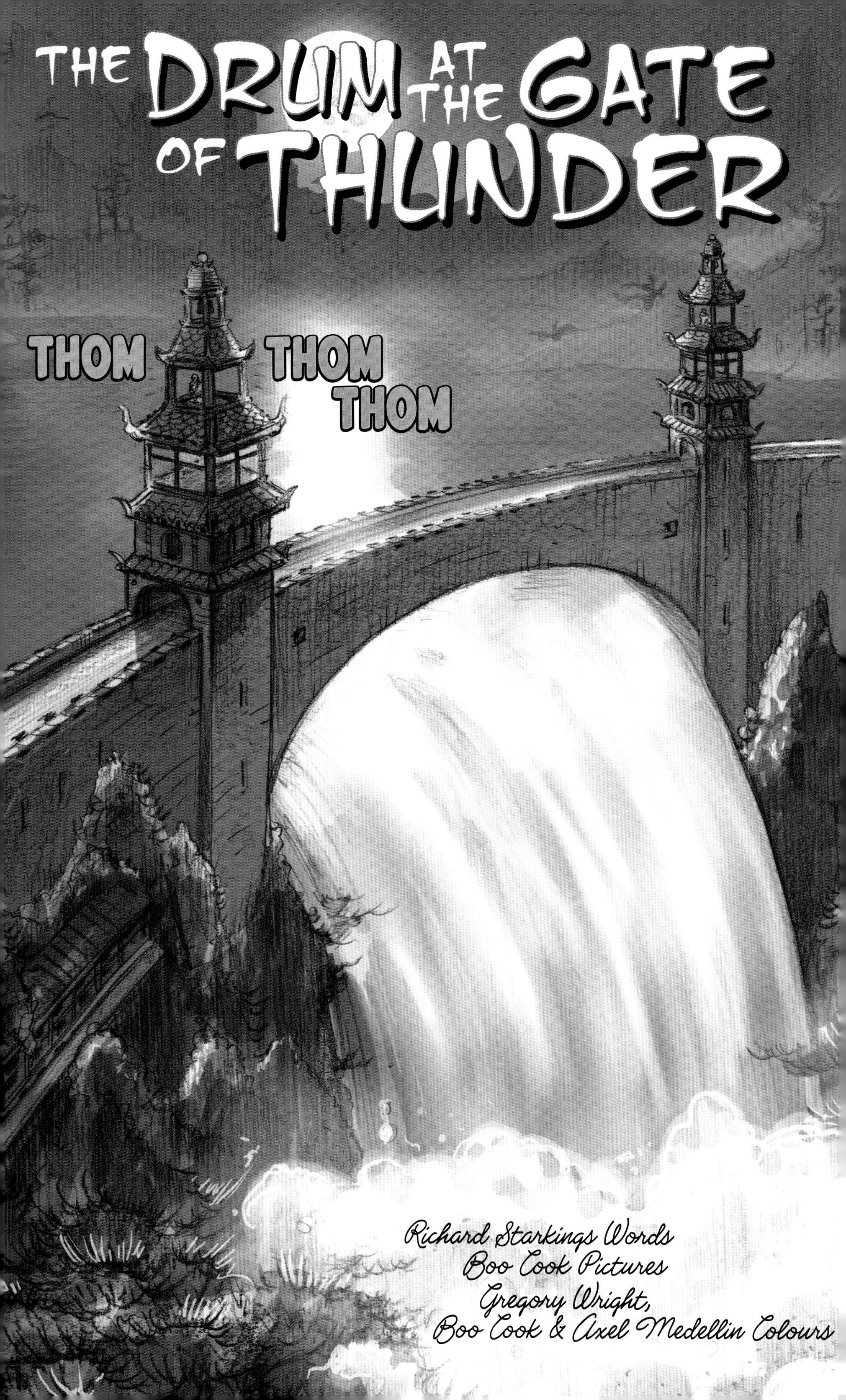
THE DRUM AT THE GATE OF THUNDER
THOM
THOM
THOM
Richard Starkings Words
Boo Cook Pictures
Gregory Wright,
Boo Cook & Axel Medellin Colours

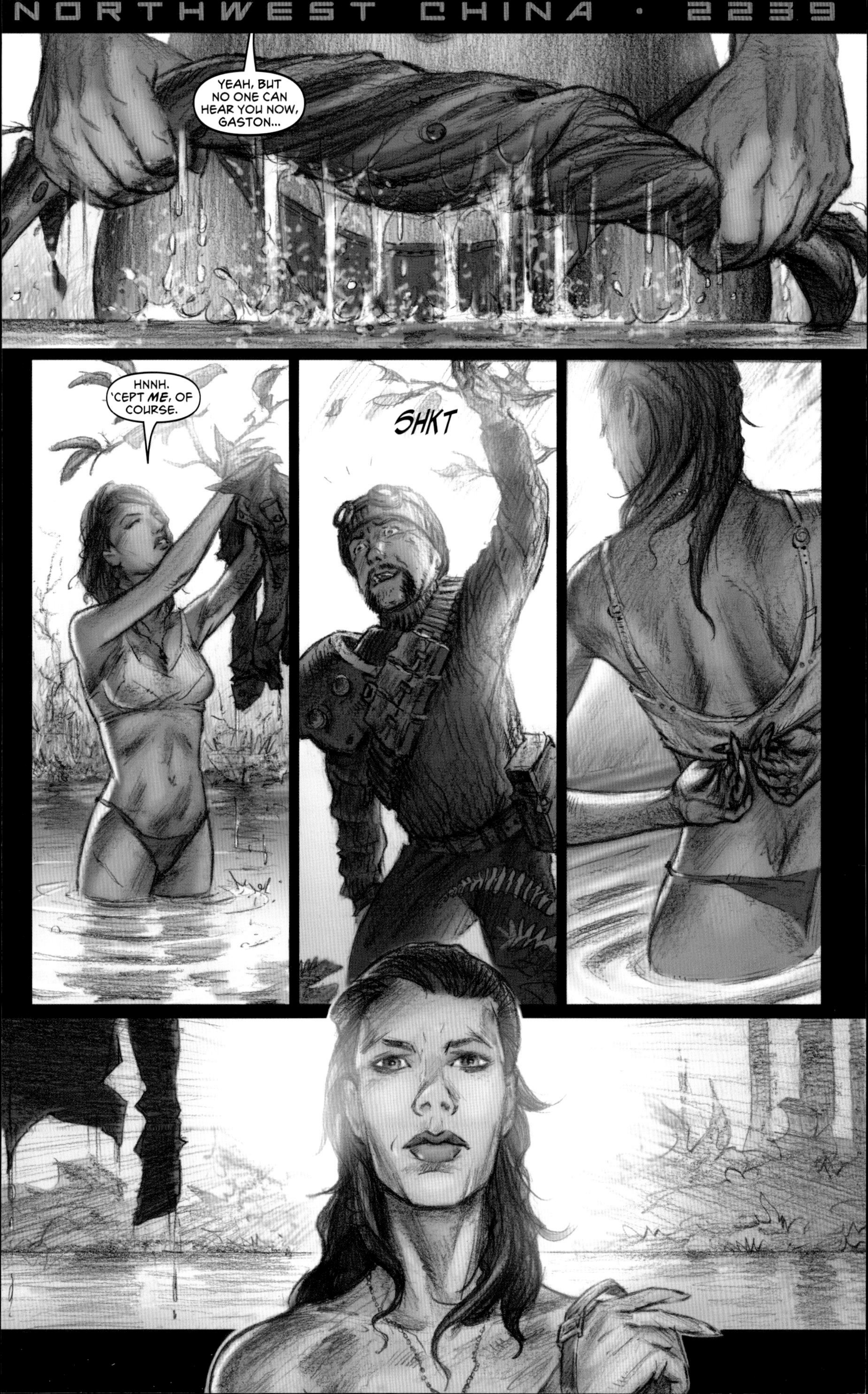
NORTHWEST CHINA · 2239
YEAH, BUT NO ONE CAN HEAR YOU NOW, GASTON...
HNNH. 'CEPT ME, OF COURSE.
SHKT

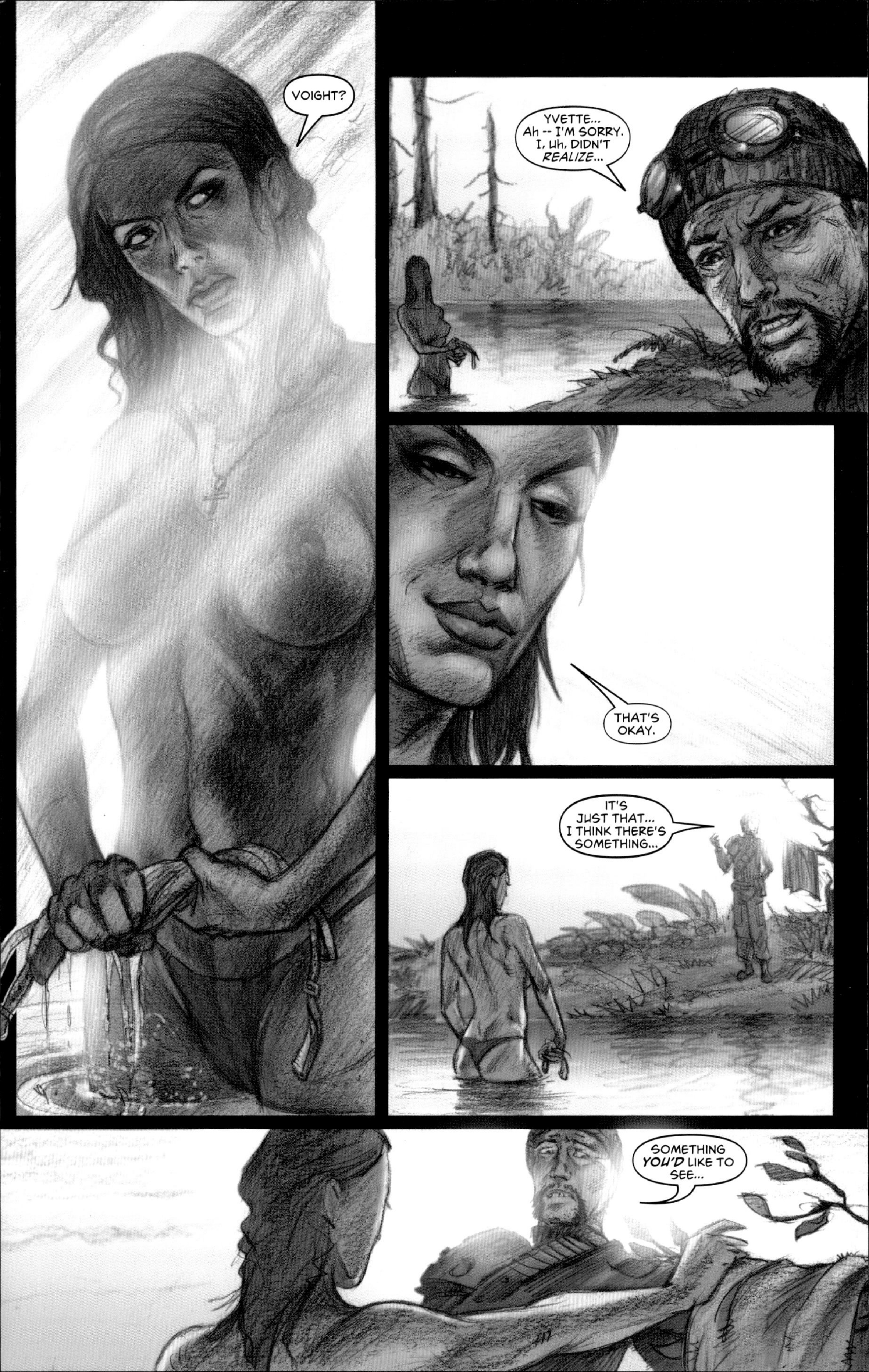
VOIGHT?
YVETTE... Ah -- I'M SORRY. I, Uh, DIDN'T *REALIZE*...
THAT'S OKAY.
IT'S JUST THAT... I THINK THERE'S SOMETHING...
SOMETHING *YOU'D* LIKE TO SEE...

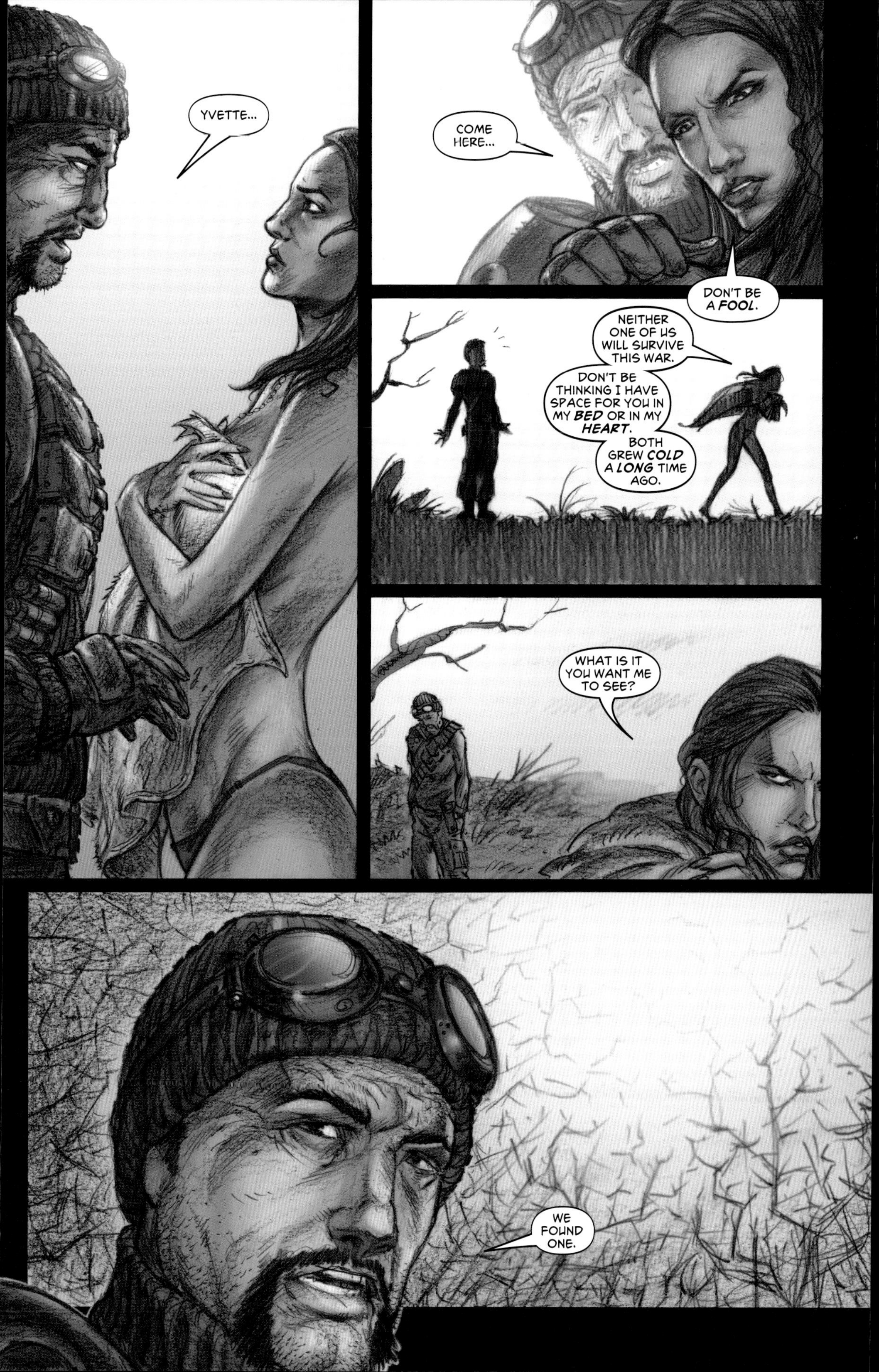
YVETTE...
COME HERE...
DON'T BE A FOOL.
NEITHER ONE OF US WILL SURVIVE THIS WAR.
DON'T BE THINKING I HAVE SPACE FOR YOU IN MY BED OR IN MY HEART.
BOTH GREW COLD A LONG TIME AGO.
WHAT IS IT YOU WANT ME TO SEE?
WE FOUND ONE.

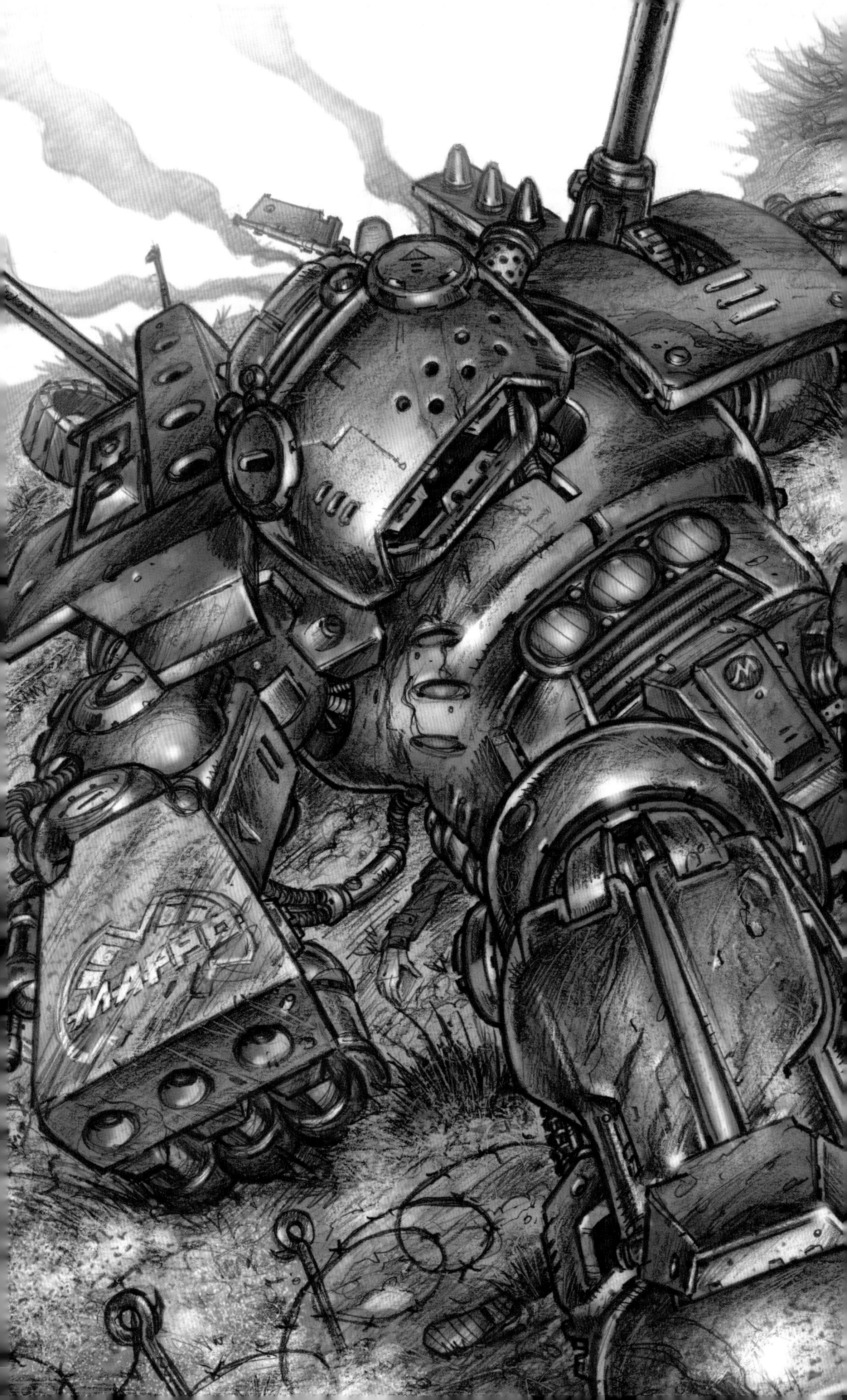

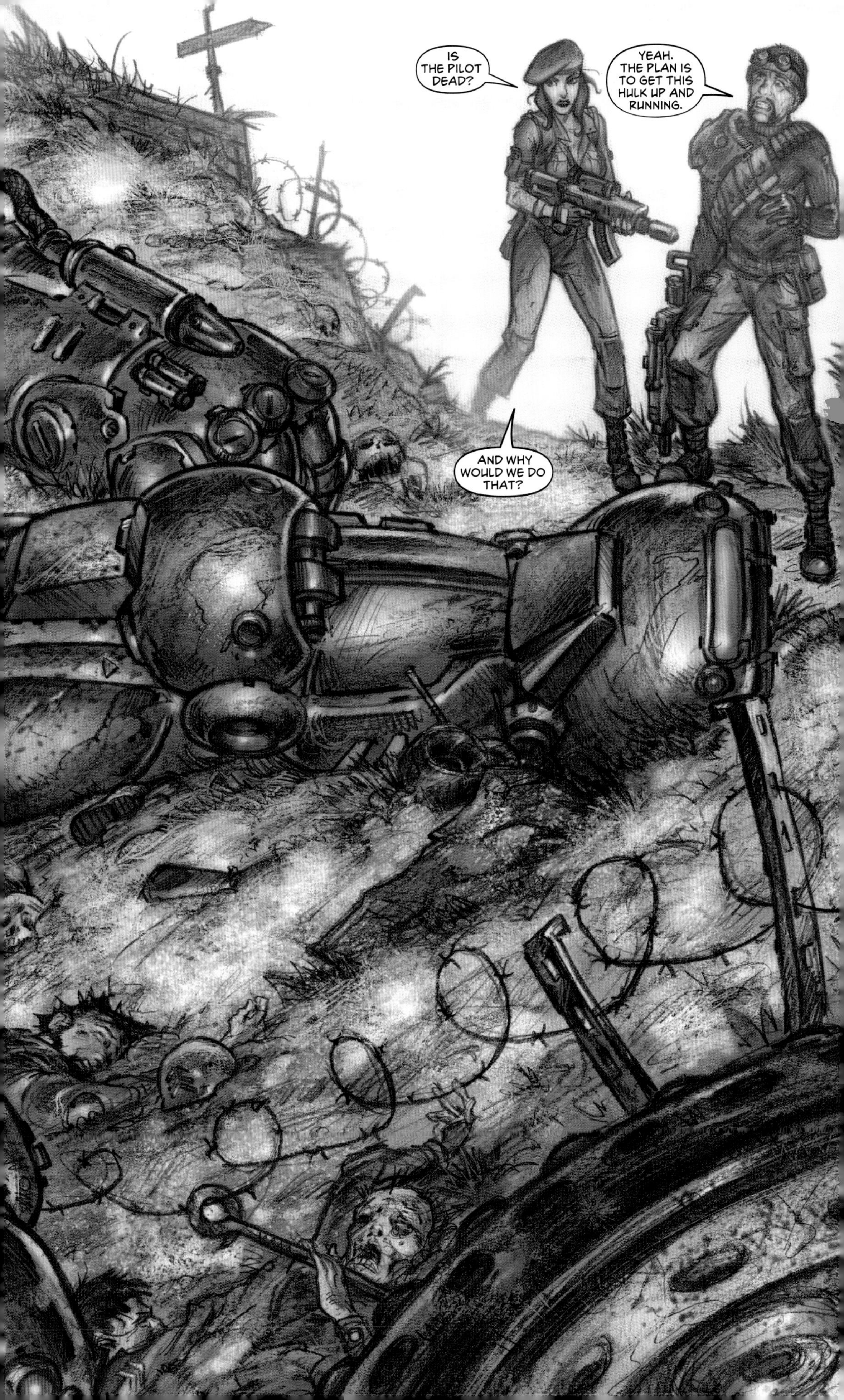
IS THE PILOT DEAD?
YEAH. THE PLAN IS TO GET THIS HULK UP AND RUNNING.
AND WHY WOULD WE DO THAT?

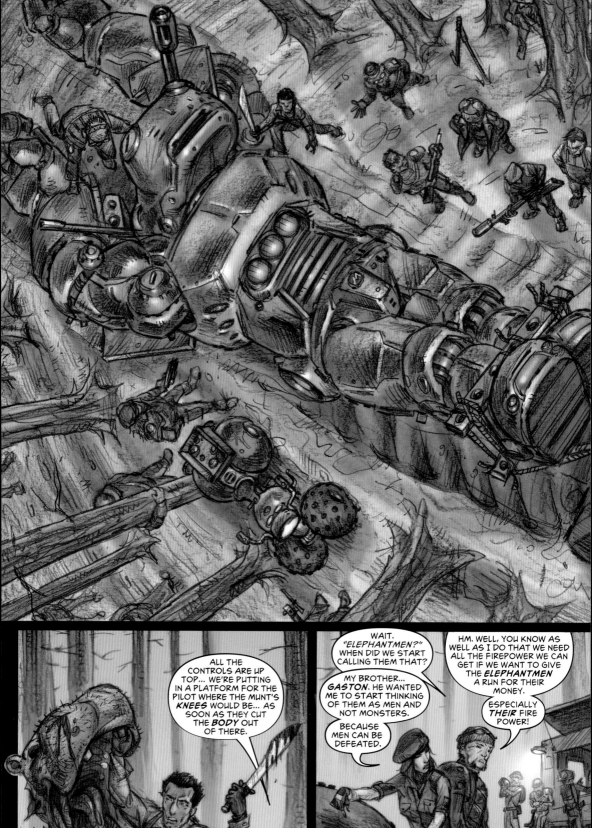

ALL THE CONTROLS ARE UP TOP... WE'RE PUTTING IN A PLATFORM FOR THE PILOT WHERE THE MUNT'S *KNEES* WOULD BE... AS SOON AS THEY CUT THE *BODY* OUT OF THERE.

WAIT. *"ELEPHANTMEN?"* WHEN DID WE START CALLING THEM THAT?

MY BROTHER... *GASTON*. HE WANTED ME TO START THINKING OF THEM AS MEN AND NOT MONSTERS.

BECAUSE MEN CAN BE DEFEATED.

HM. WELL, YOU KNOW AS WELL AS I DO THAT WE NEED ALL THE FIREPOWER WE CAN GET IF WE WANT TO GIVE THE *ELEPHANTMEN* A RUN FOR THEIR MONEY.

ESPECIALLY *THEIR* FIRE POWER!

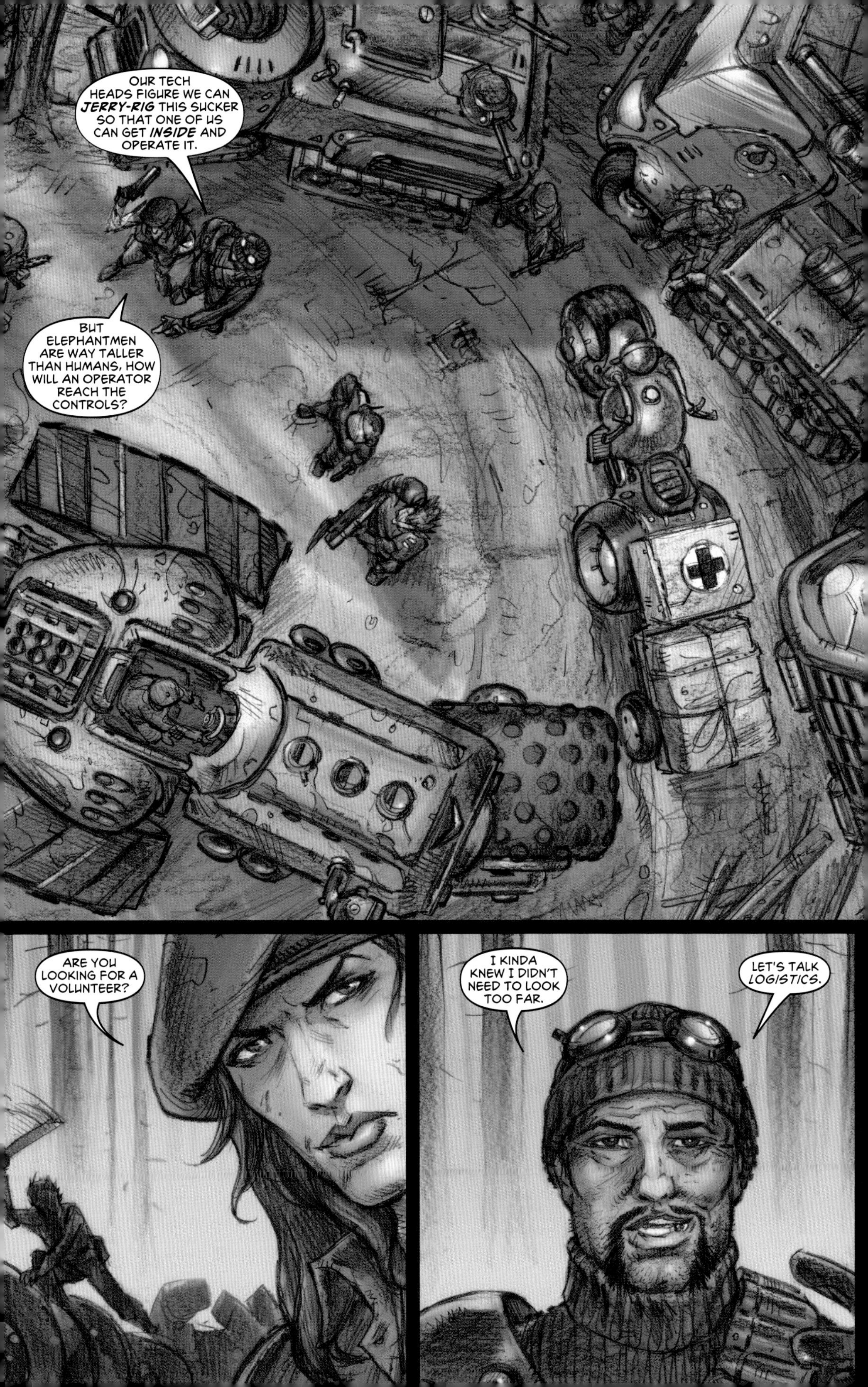
OUR TECH HEADS FIGURE WE CAN JERRY-RIG THIS SUCKER SO THAT ONE OF US CAN GET INSIDE AND OPERATE IT.
BUT ELEPHANTMEN ARE WAY TALLER THAN HUMANS, HOW WILL AN OPERATOR REACH THE CONTROLS?
ARE YOU LOOKING FOR A VOLUNTEER?
I KINDA KNEW I DIDN'T NEED TO LOOK TOO FAR.
LET'S TALK LOGISTICS.

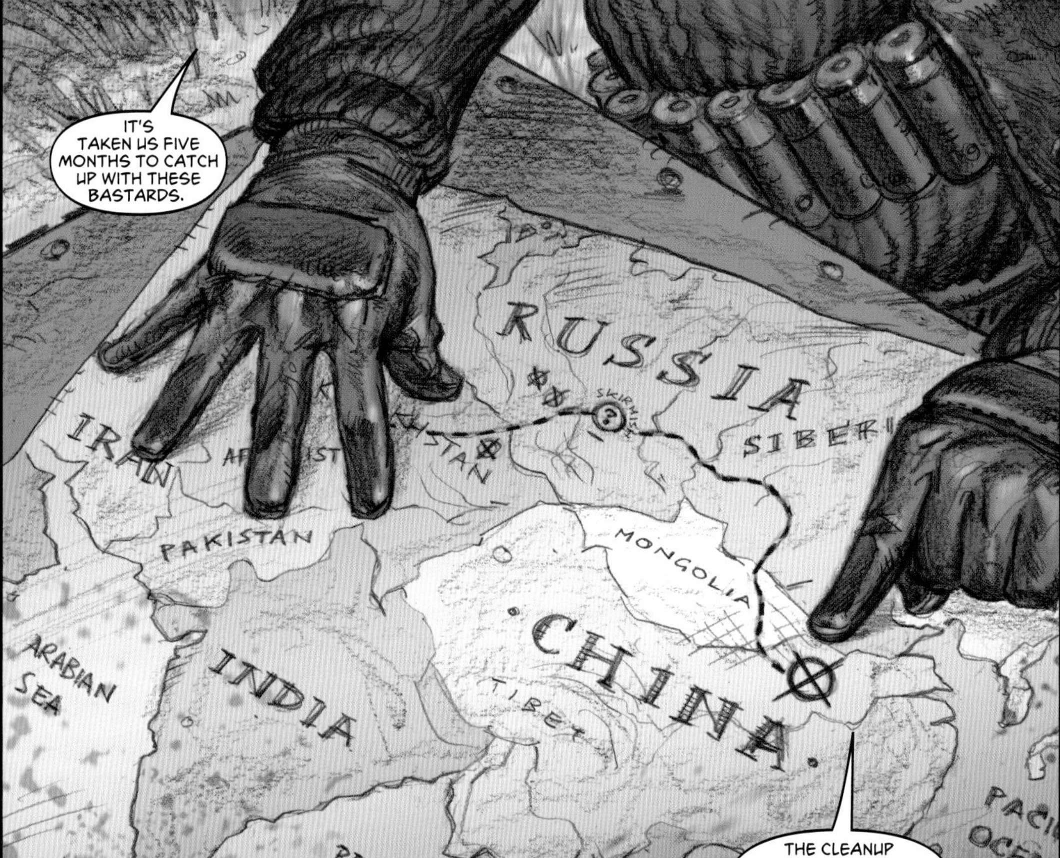
IT'S TAKEN US FIVE MONTHS TO CATCH UP WITH THESE BASTARDS.
RUSSIA
IRAN
PAKISTAN
MONGOLIA
CHINA
INDIA
ARABIAN SEA
BAY OF BENGAL
INDIAN OCEAN
MALAYSIA
THE CLEANUP CREW WE TOOK OUT* CAN'T HAVE BEEN MORE THAN TWO DAYS BEHIND THE ***ADVANCE*** GUARD.
OUR ***ADVANTAGE***, IF WE HAVE ONE, IS THAT THEY WON'T BE EXPECTING ATTACK FROM ***BEHIND***.
LET'S NOT KID OURSELVES. IF WE'RE TO HAVE ***ANY*** AFFECT AT ALL, IT HAS TO BE ***SINGLE*** FOCUSSED STRIKES. IN AND OUT.
THEY MIGHT ***LOOK*** LIKE LUMBERING MONSTERS BUT THEY FUNCTION AS A ***WELL-TRAINED*** AND EFFECTIVE ARMY...

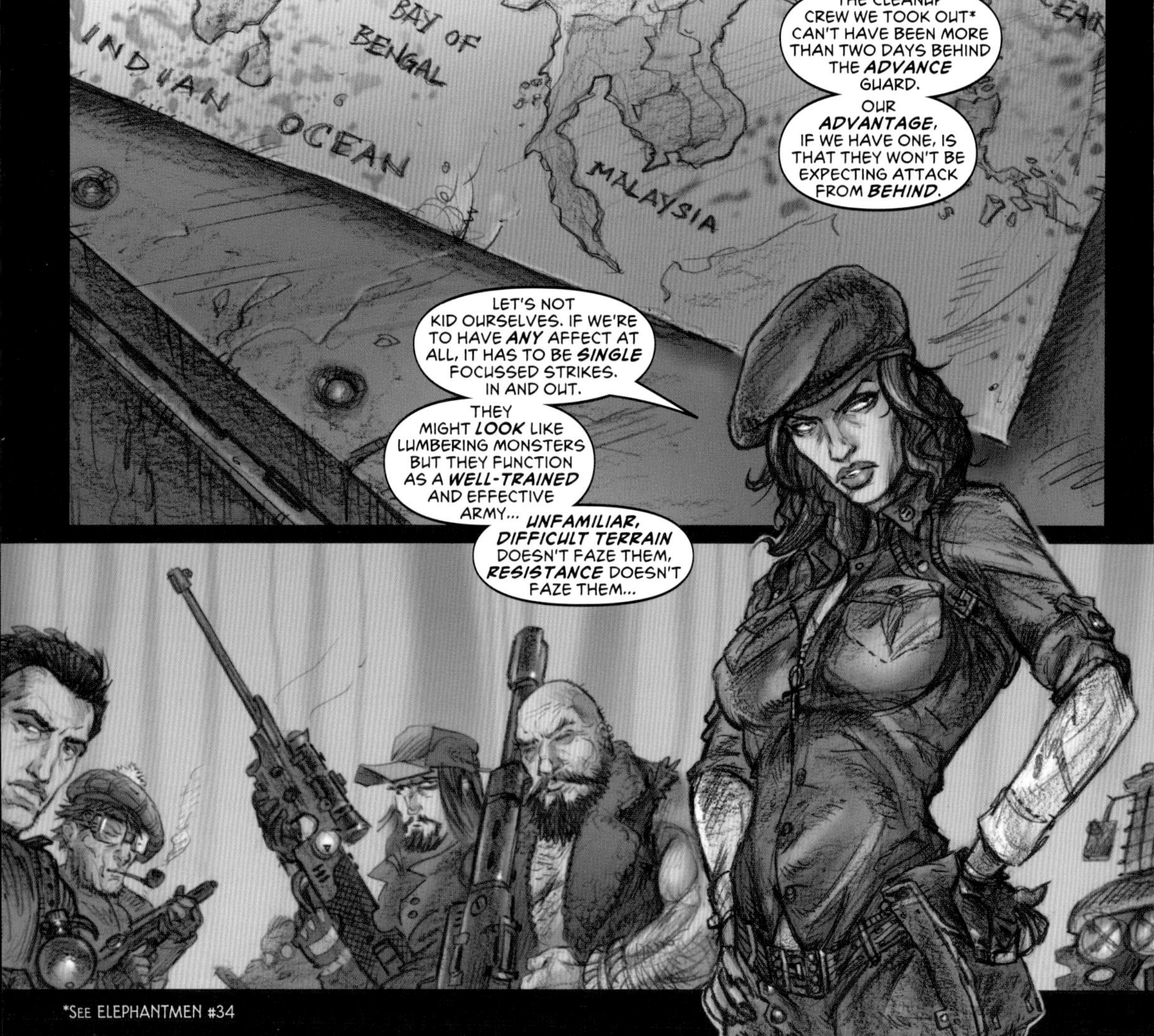
UNFAMILIAR, DIFFICULT TERRAIN DOESN'T FAZE THEM, ***RESISTANCE*** DOESN'T FAZE THEM...

*SEE ELEPHANTMEN #34

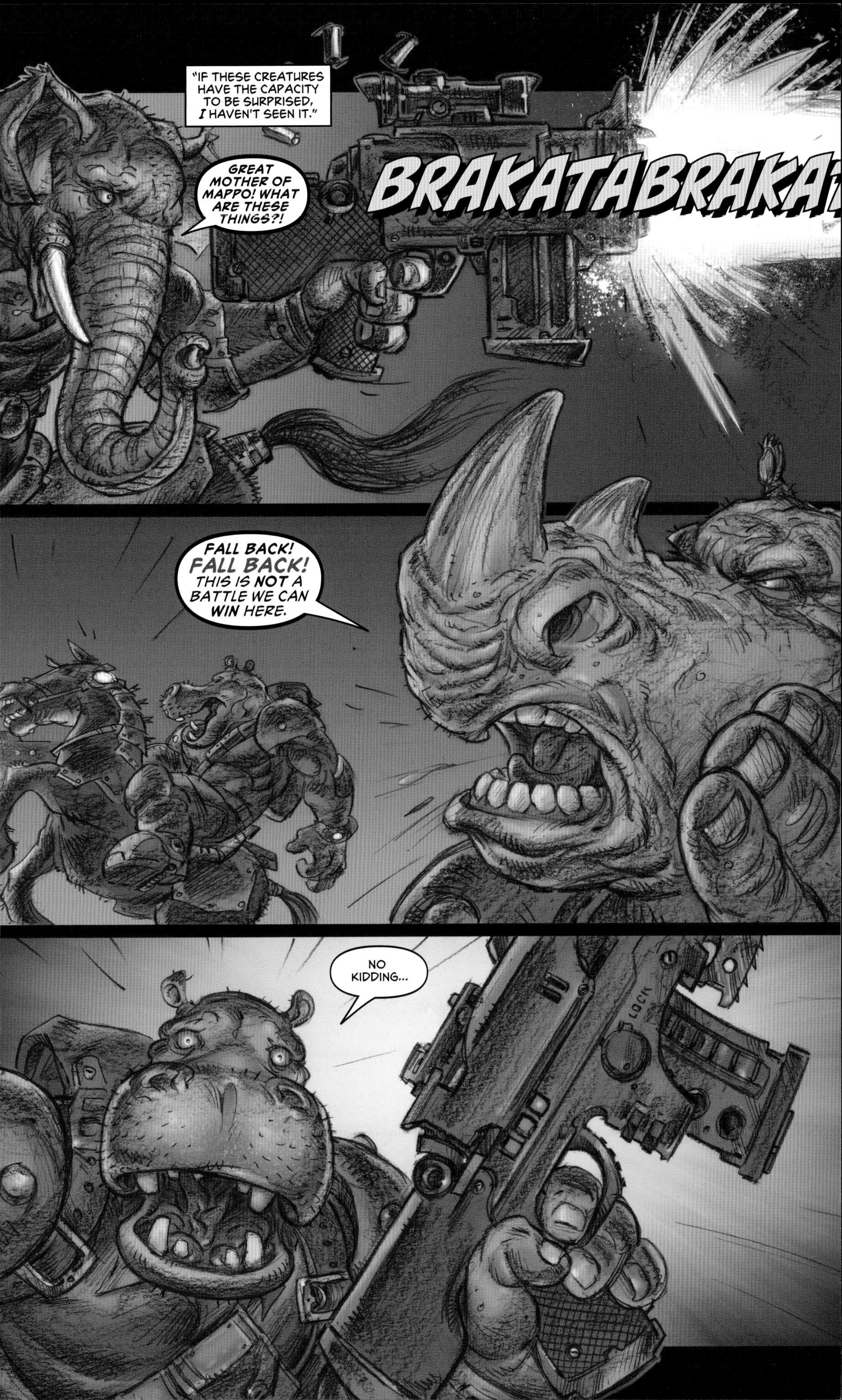
"IF THESE CREATURES HAVE THE CAPACITY TO BE SURPRISED, I HAVEN'T SEEN IT."
GREAT MOTHER OF MAPPO! WHAT ARE THESE THINGS?!
BRAKATABRAKAT
FALL BACK! FALL BACK! THIS IS NOT A BATTLE WE CAN WIN HERE.
NO KIDDING...
LOCK

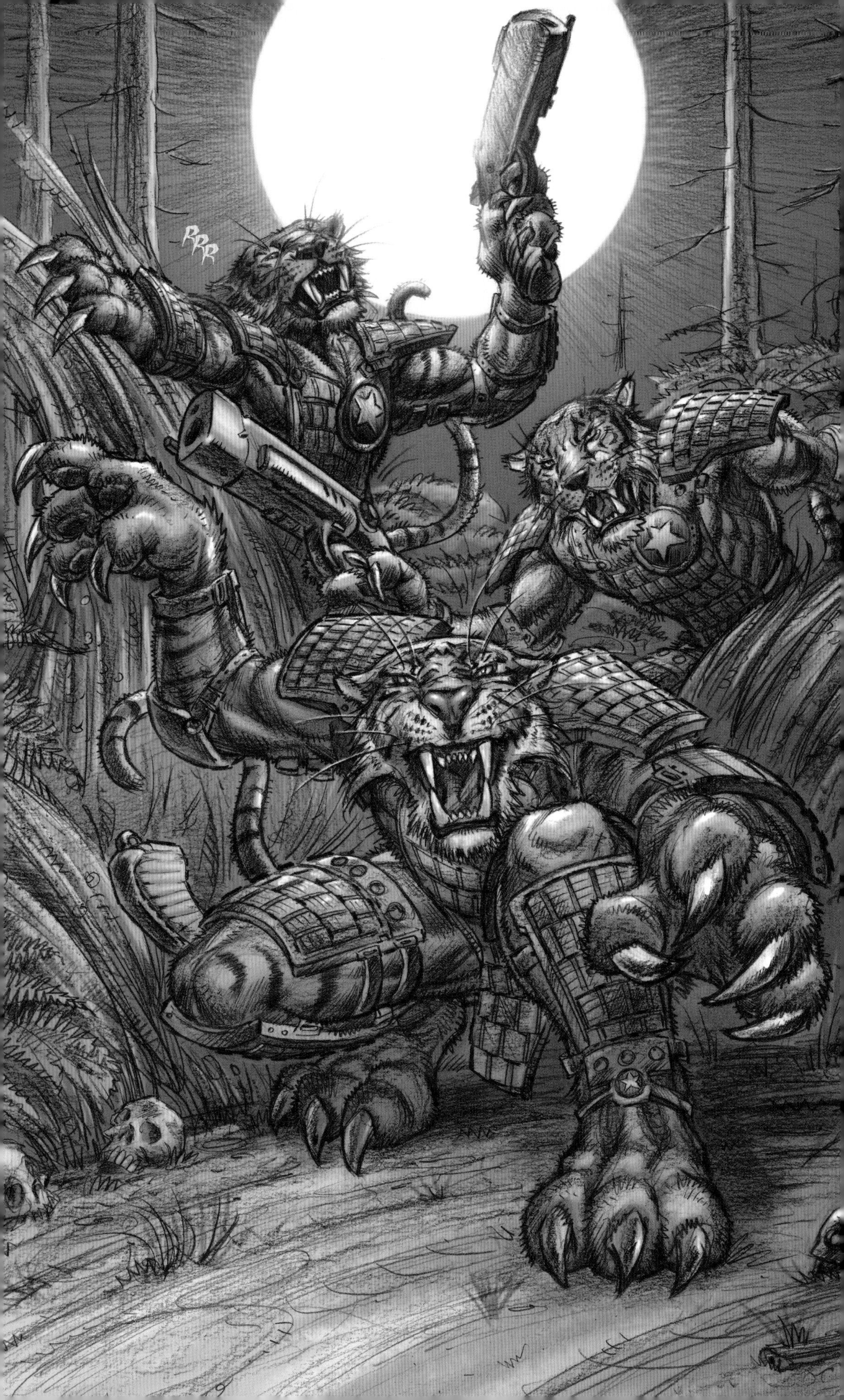
RRR

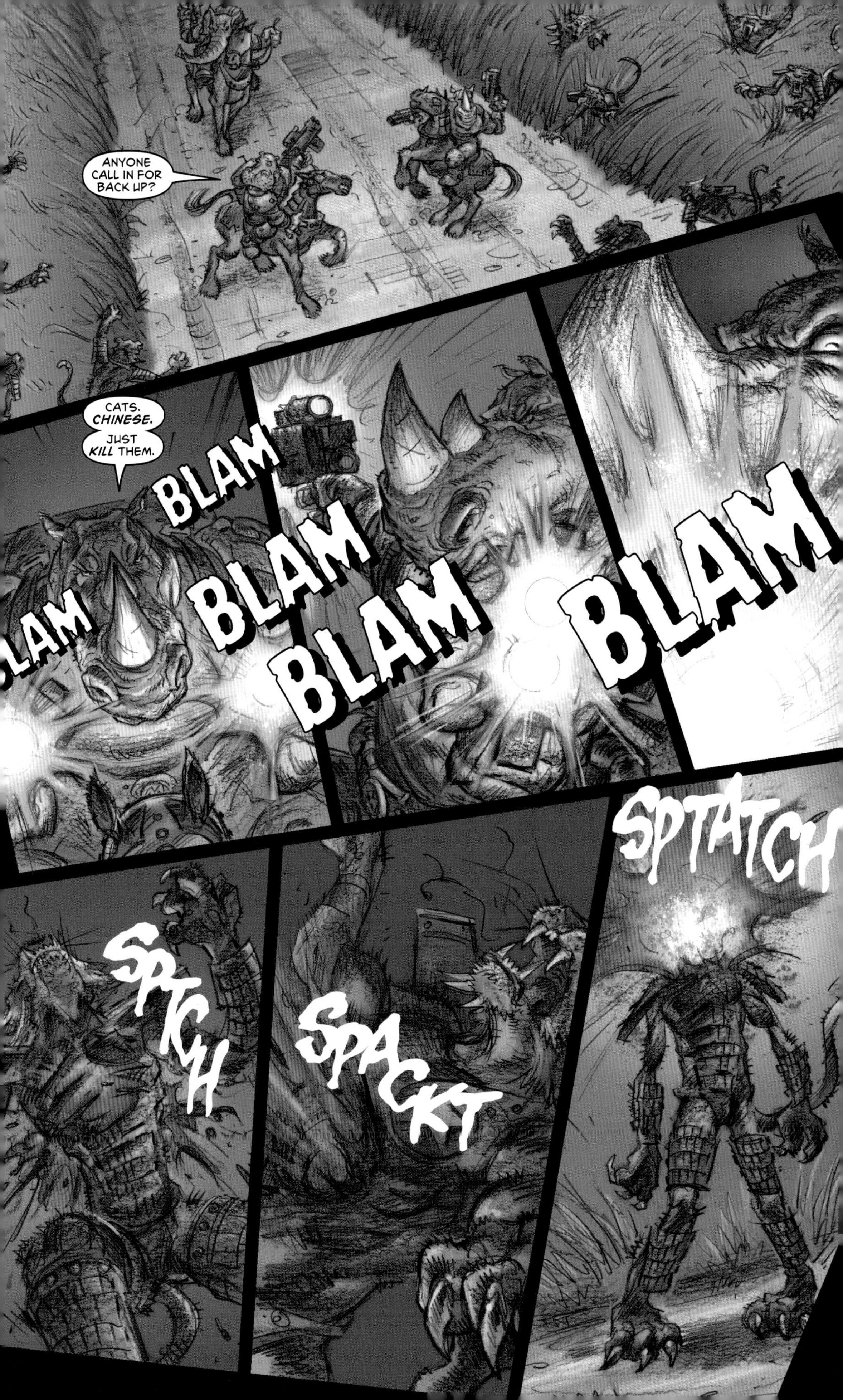
ANYONE CALL IN FOR BACK UP?
CATS. CHINESE. JUST KILL THEM.
BLAM
BLAM
BLAM
BLAM
BLAM
BLAM
SPTATCH
SPTCH
SPACKT

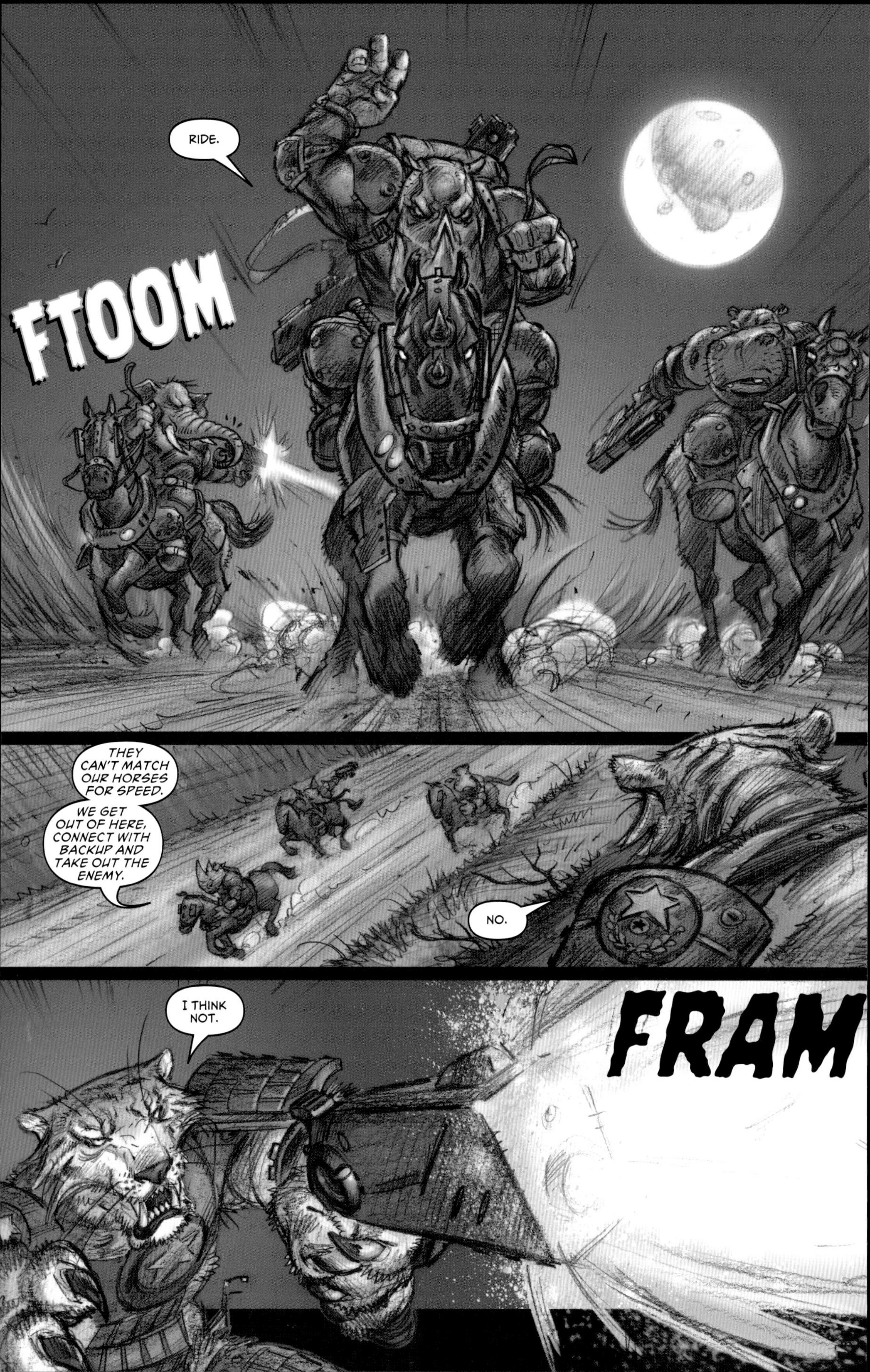
RIDE.
FTOOM
THEY CAN'T MATCH OUR HORSES FOR SPEED.
WE GET OUT OF HERE, CONNECT WITH BACKUP AND TAKE OUT THE ENEMY.
NO.
I THINK NOT.
FRAM

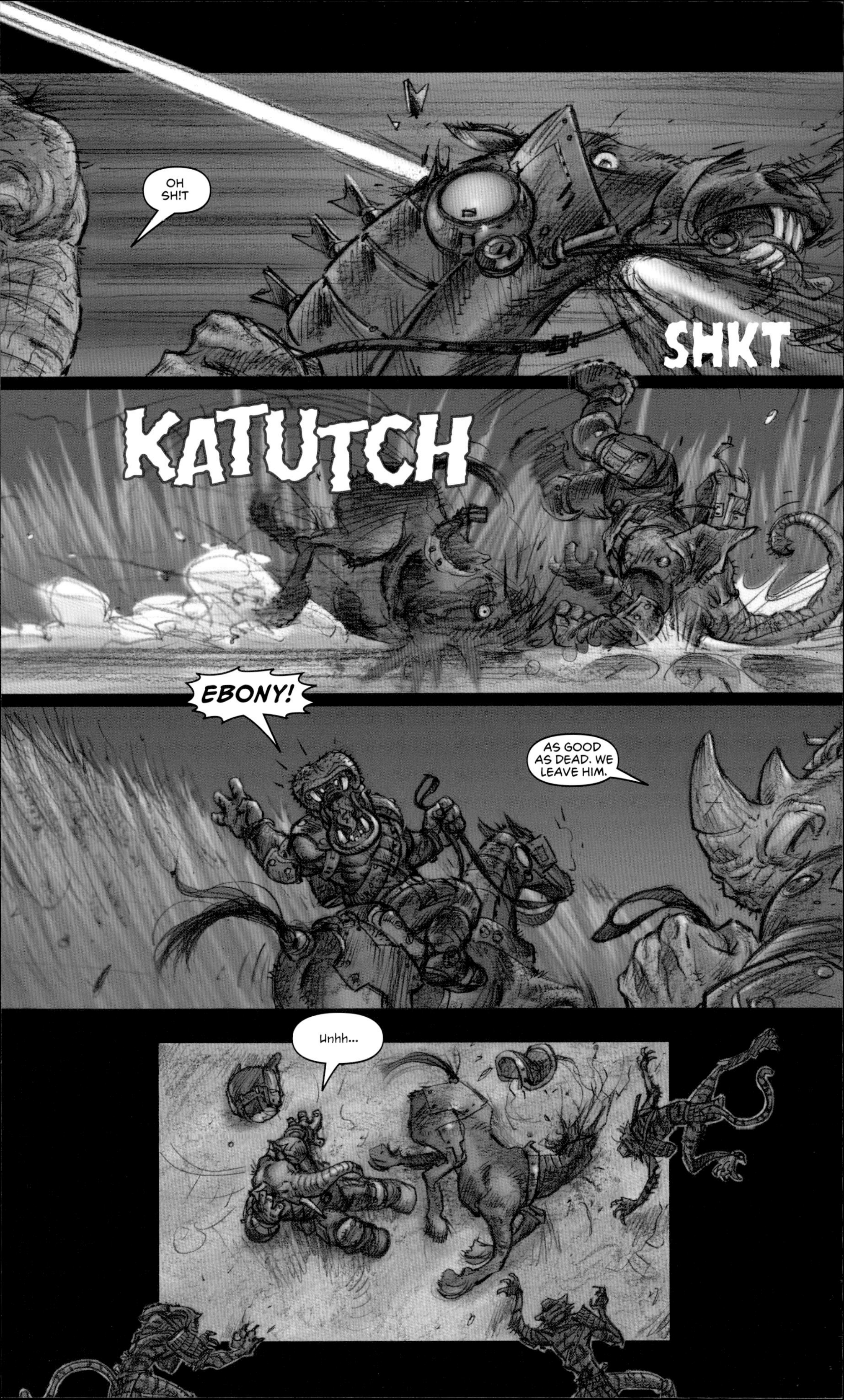
OH SH!T
SHKT
KATUTCH
EBONY!
AS GOOD AS DEAD. WE LEAVE HIM.
Unhh...

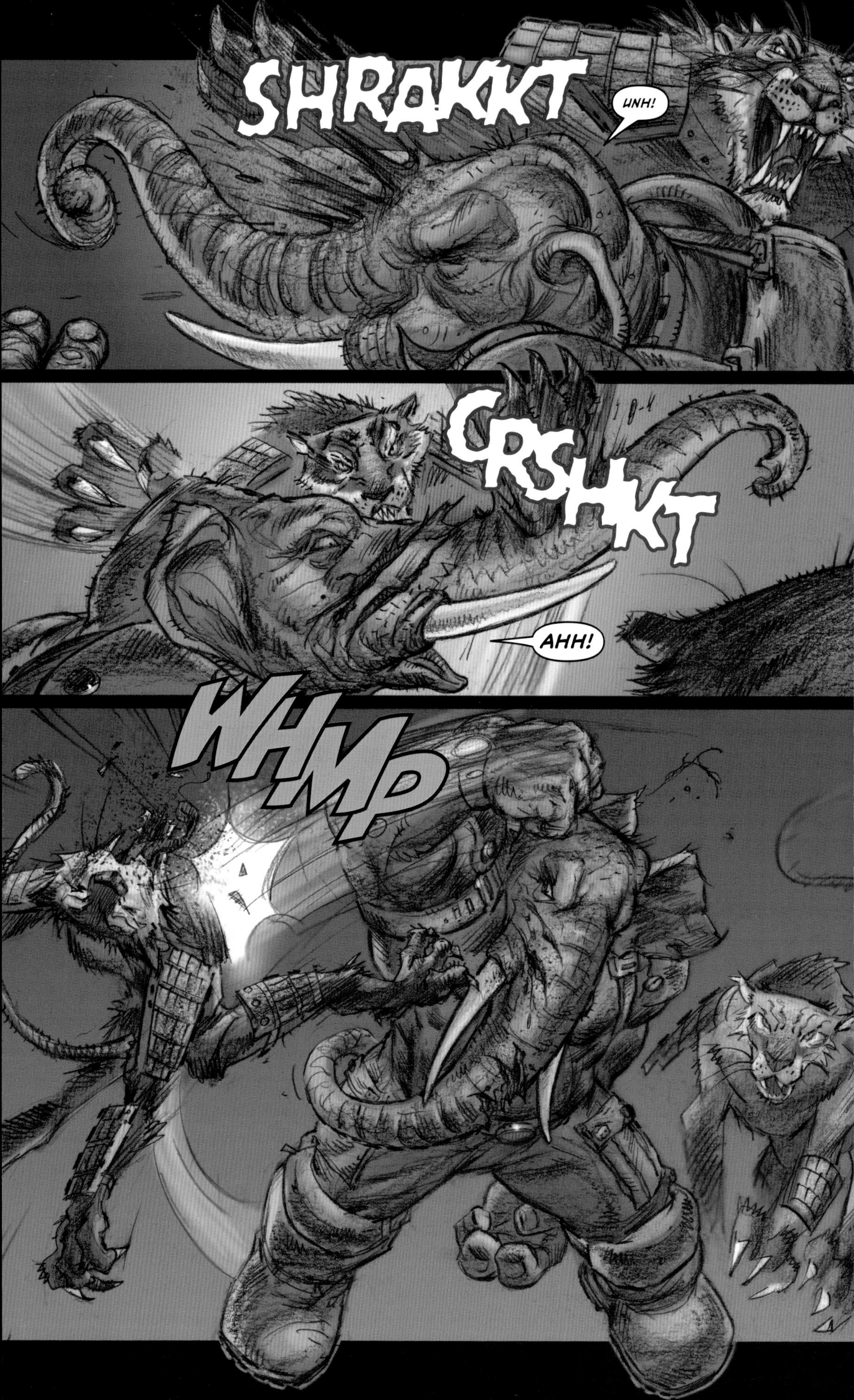
SHRAKKT
UNH!
CRSHKT
AHH!
WHMP

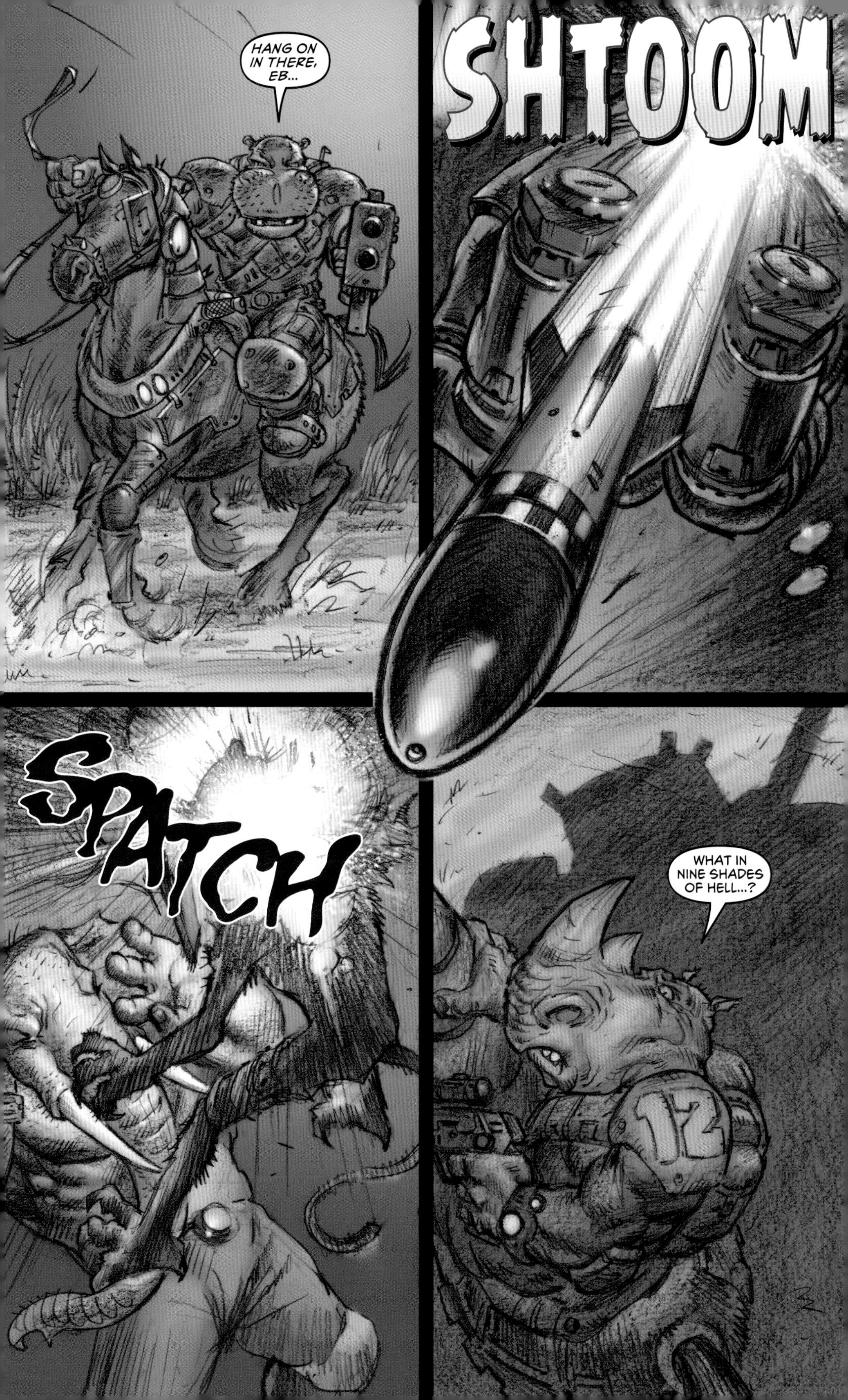
HANG ON IN THERE, EB...
SHTOOM
SPATCH
WHAT IN NINE SHADES OF HELL...?

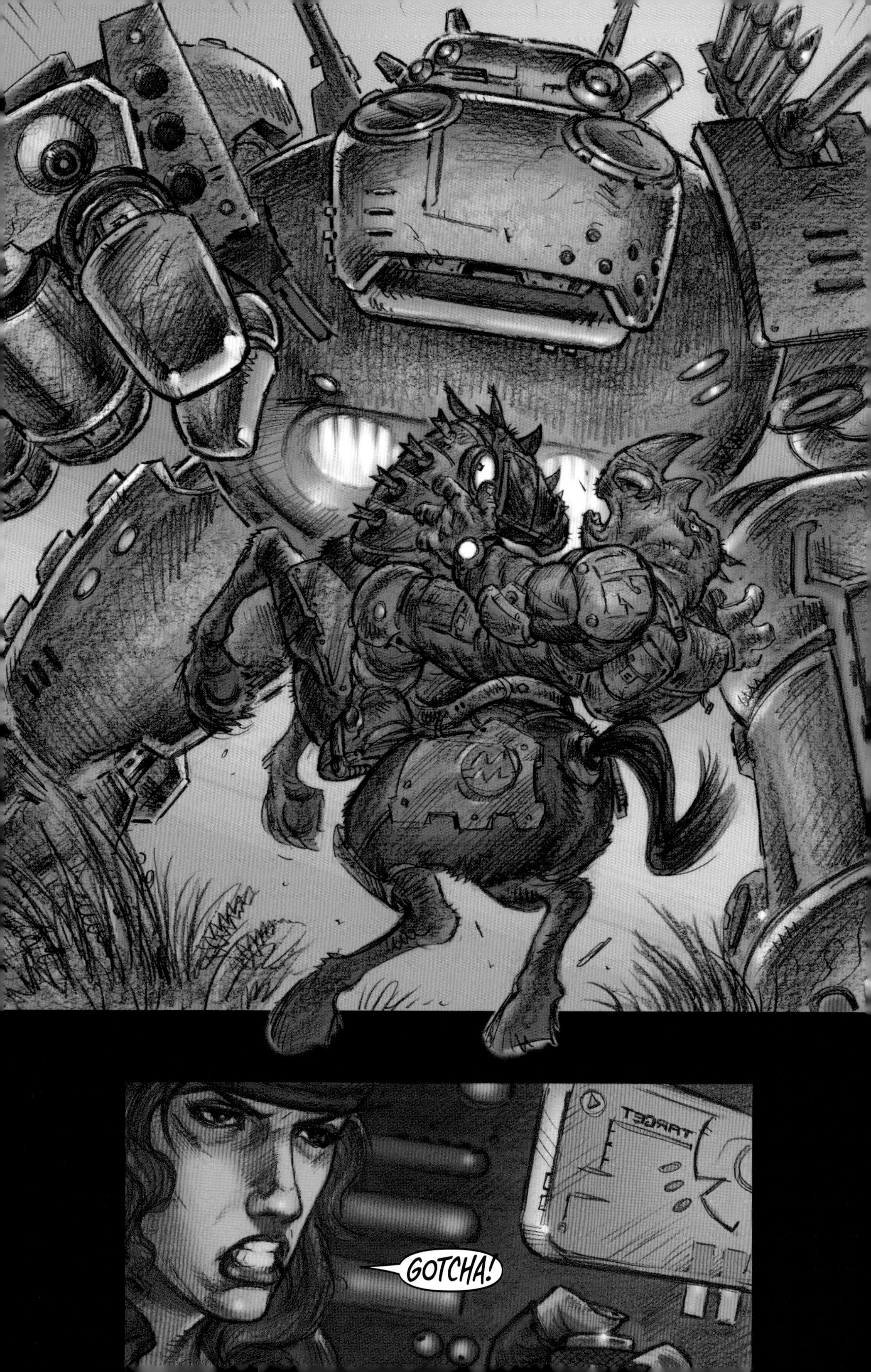
GOTCHA!

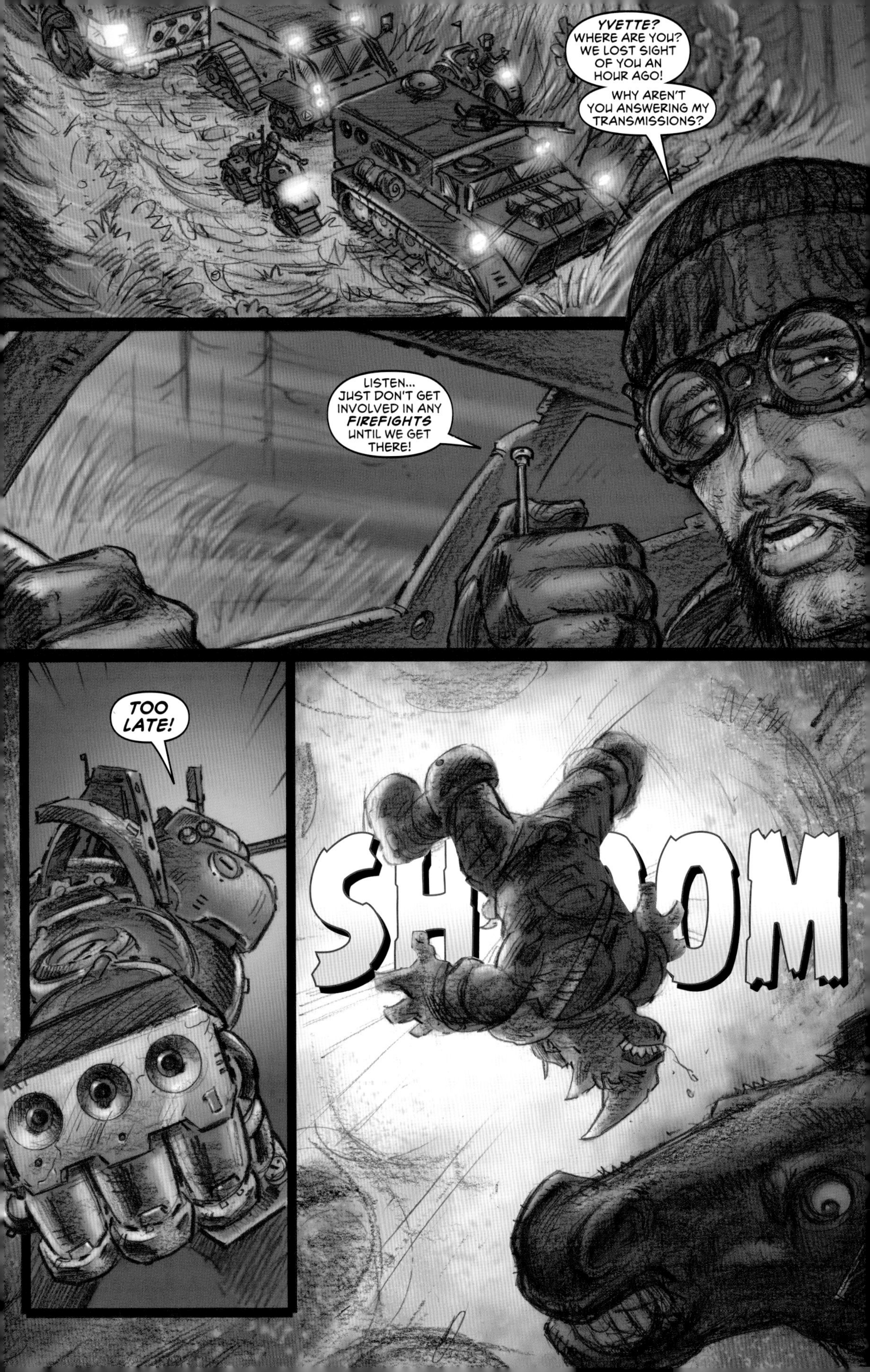
YVETTE? WHERE ARE YOU? WE LOST SIGHT OF YOU AN HOUR AGO!
WHY AREN'T YOU ANSWERING MY TRANSMISSIONS?
LISTEN... JUST DON'T GET INVOLVED IN ANY FIREFIGHTS UNTIL WE GET THERE!
TOO LATE!
SH OM

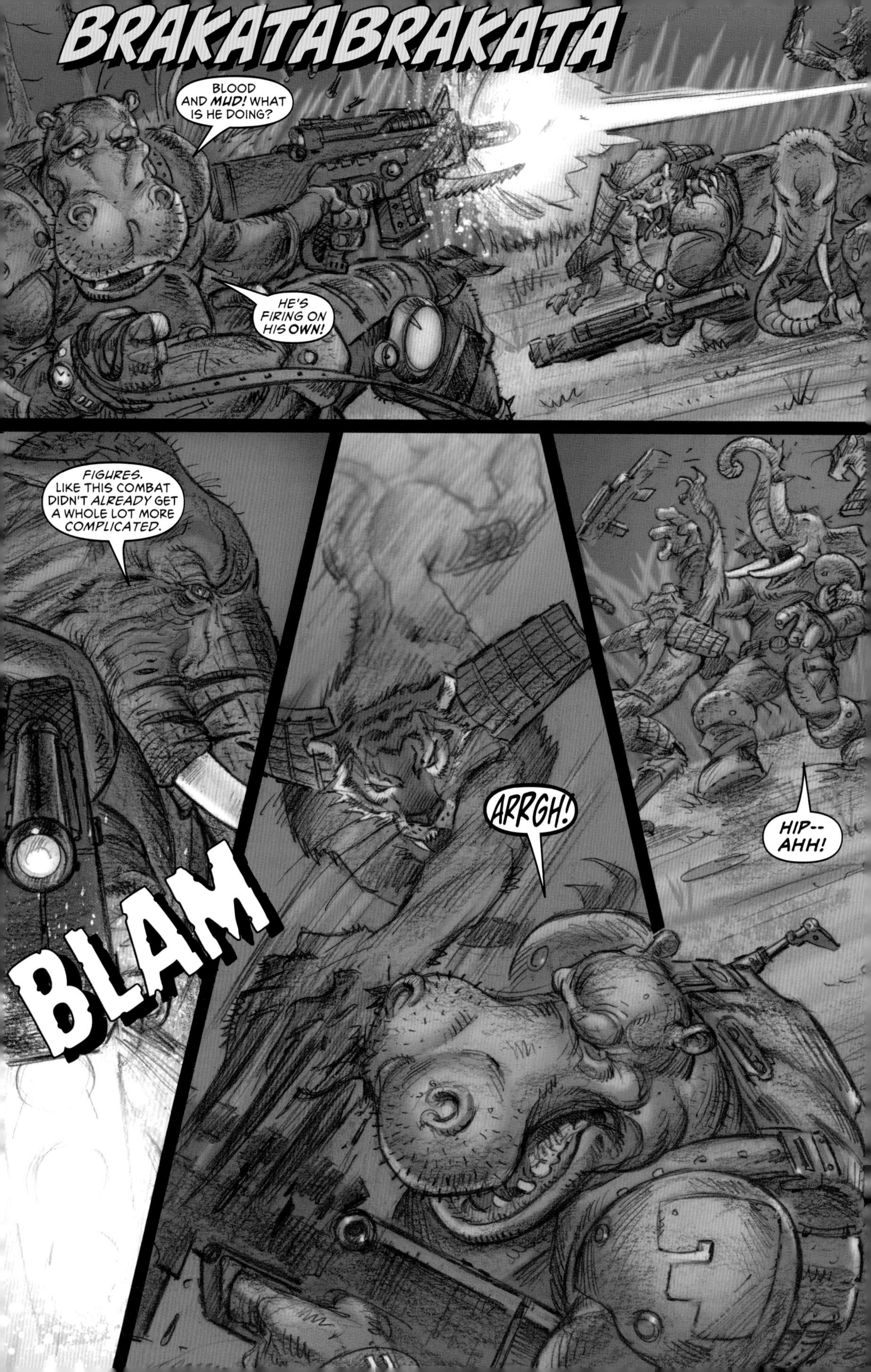
BRAKATABRAKATA
BLOOD AND MUD! WHAT IS HE DOING?
HE'S FIRING ON HIS OWN!
FIGURES. LIKE THIS COMBAT DIDN'T ALREADY GET A WHOLE LOT MORE COMPLICATED.
BLAM
ARRGH!
HIP-- AHH!

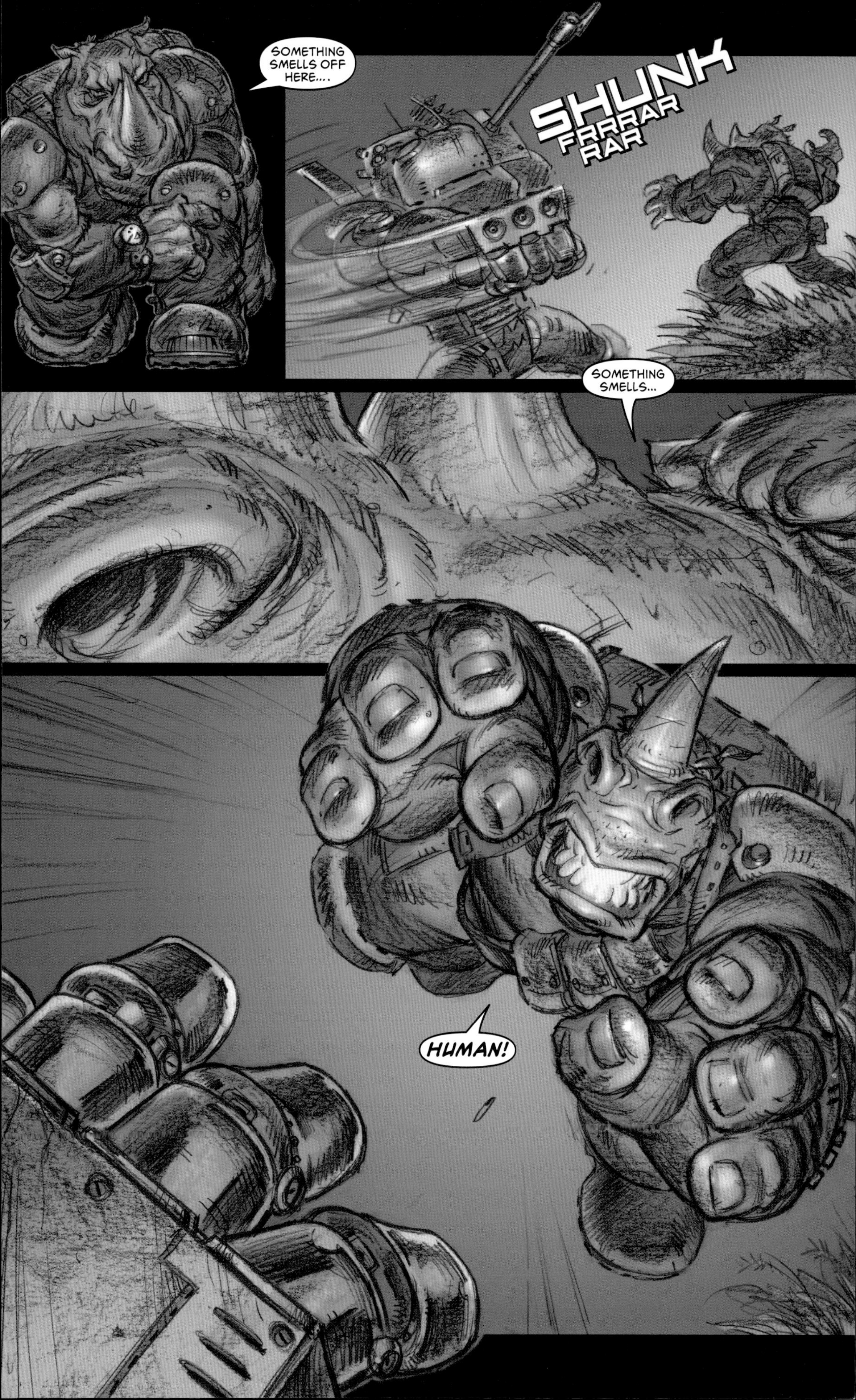
SOMETHING SMELLS OFF HERE....
SHUNK
FRRRAR RAR
SOMETHING SMELLS...
HUMAN!

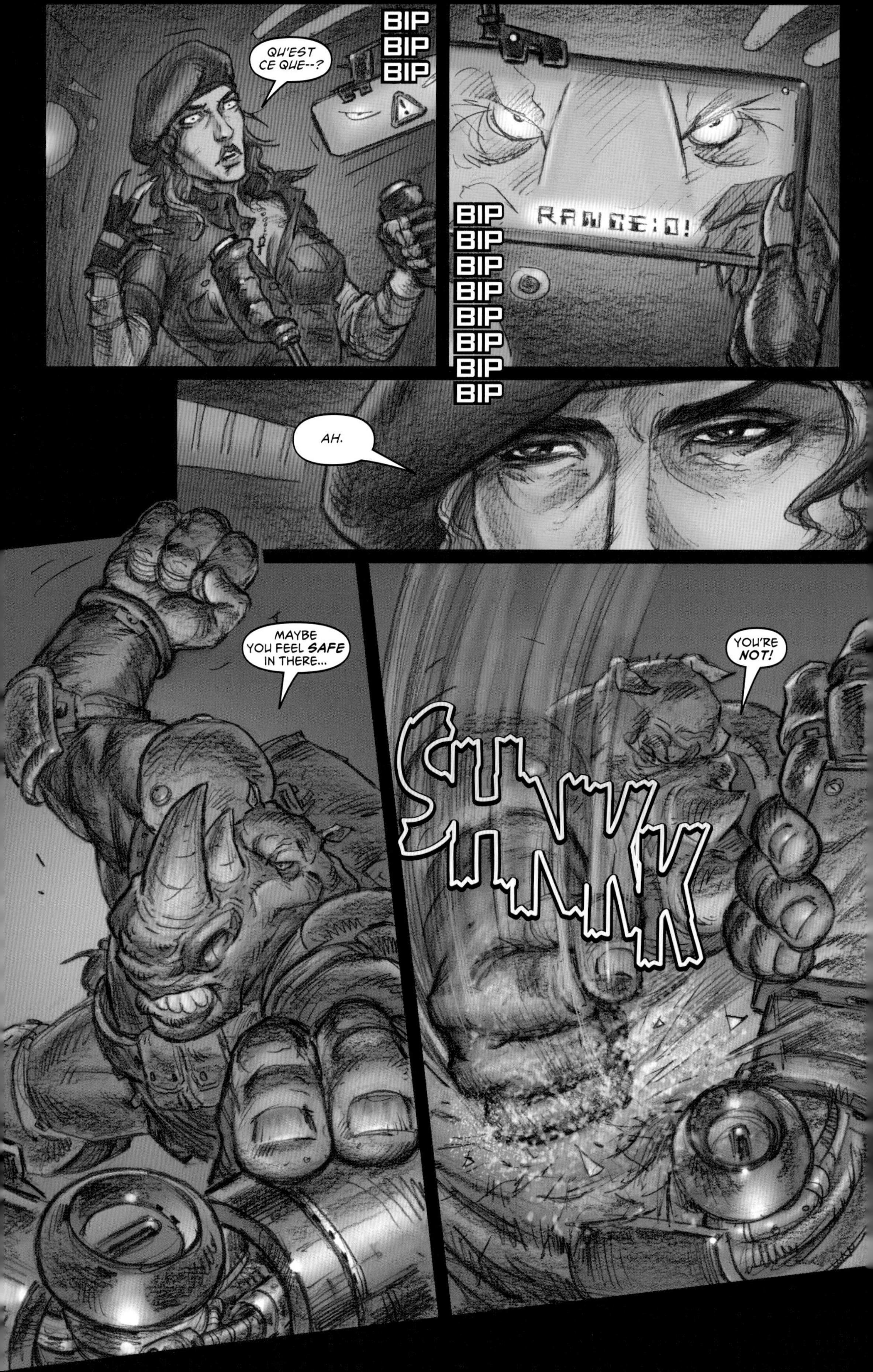
QU'EST CE QUE--?
BIP
BIP
BIP
RANGE:0!
BIP
BIP
BIP
BIP
BIP
BIP
BIP
BIP
AH.
MAYBE YOU FEEL *SAFE* IN THERE...
YOU'RE *NOT!*

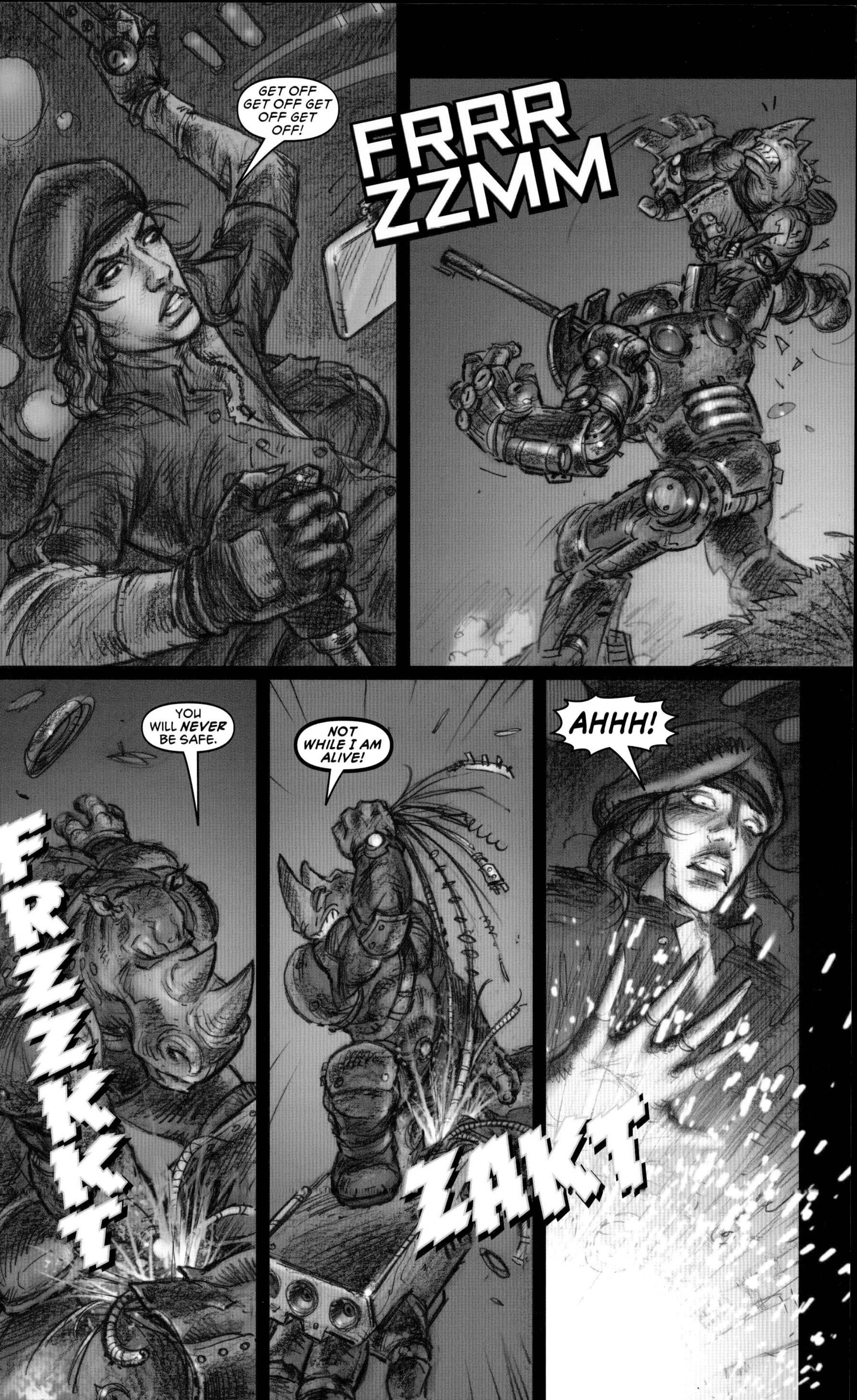
GET OFF GET OFF GET OFF GET OFF!
FRRR ZZMM
YOU WILL *NEVER* BE SAFE.
FRZZKKT
NOT WHILE I AM ALIVE!
AHHH!
ZAKT

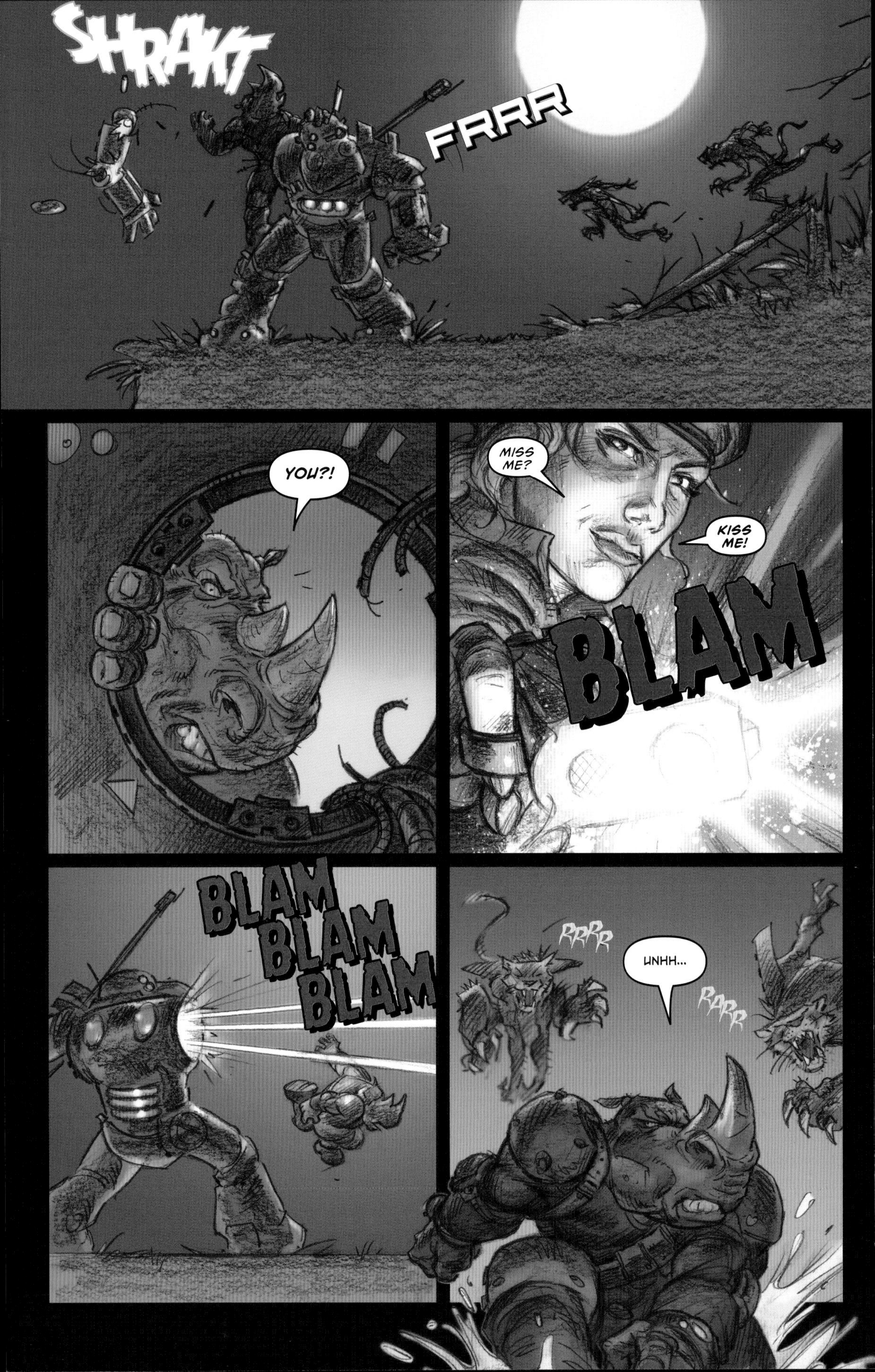
SHRAKT
FRRR
YOU?!
MISS ME?
KISS ME!
BLAM
BLAM BLAM BLAM
RRRR
UNHH...
RARR

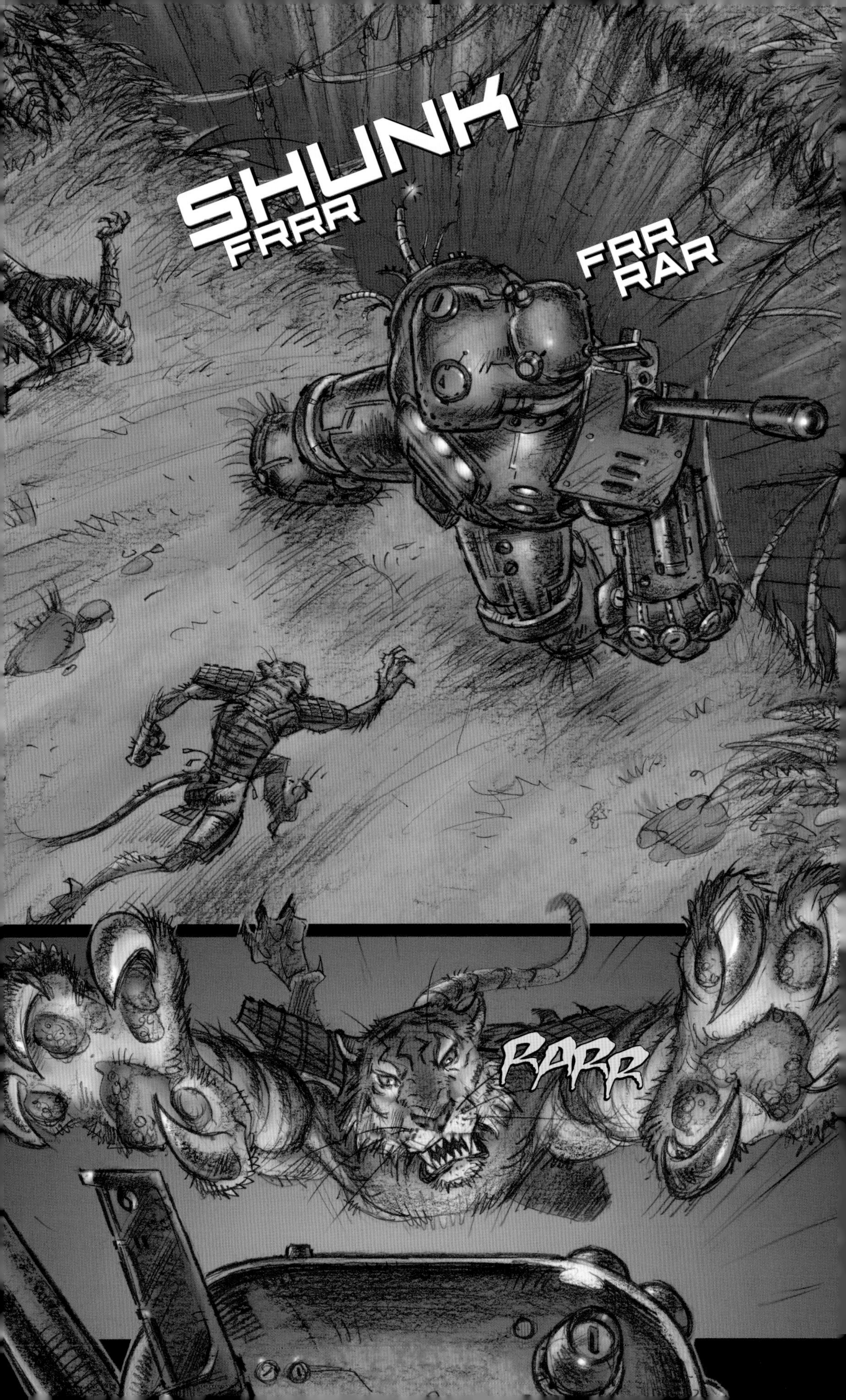
SHUNK
FRRR
FRR
RAR
RARR

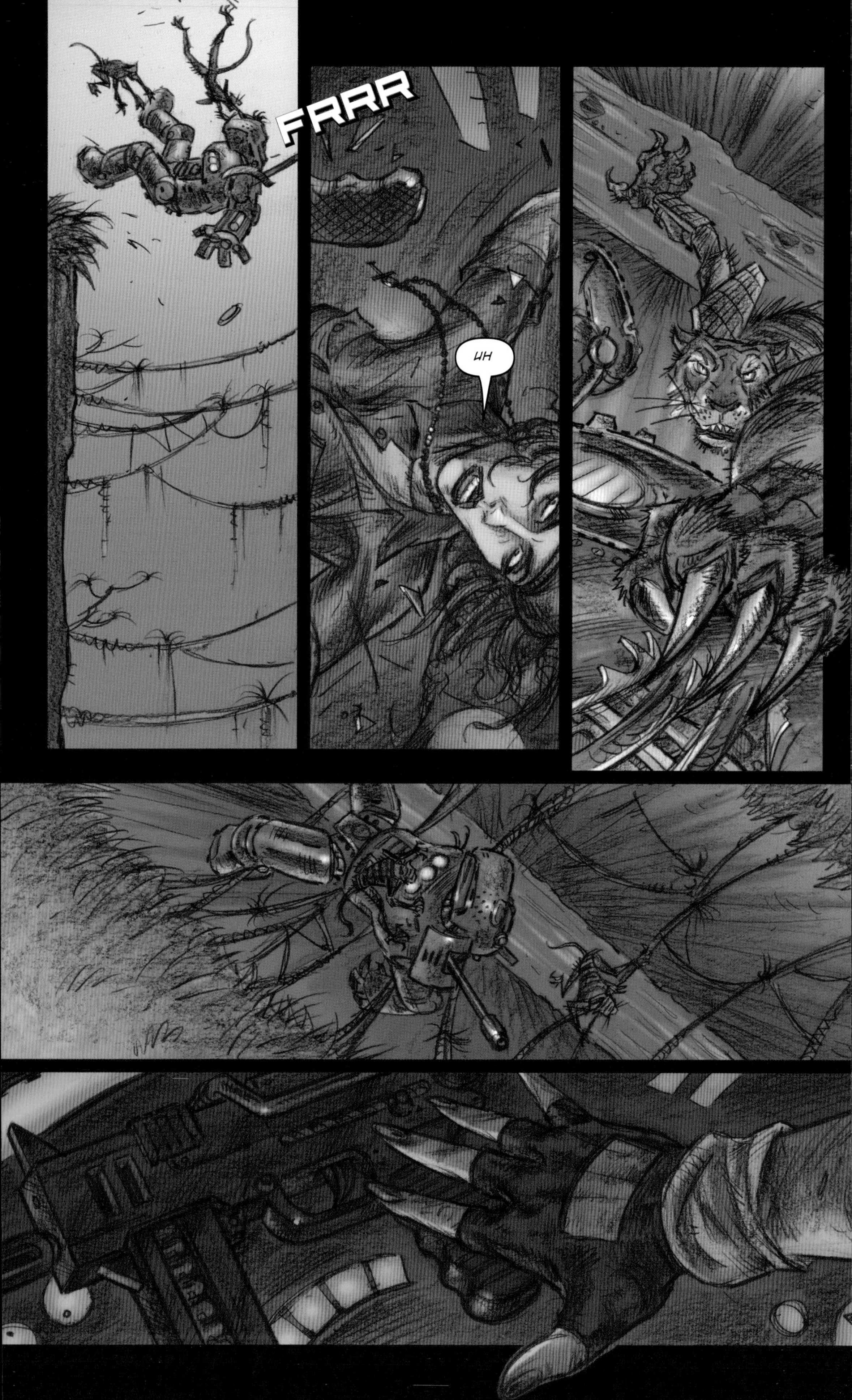
FRRR
UH

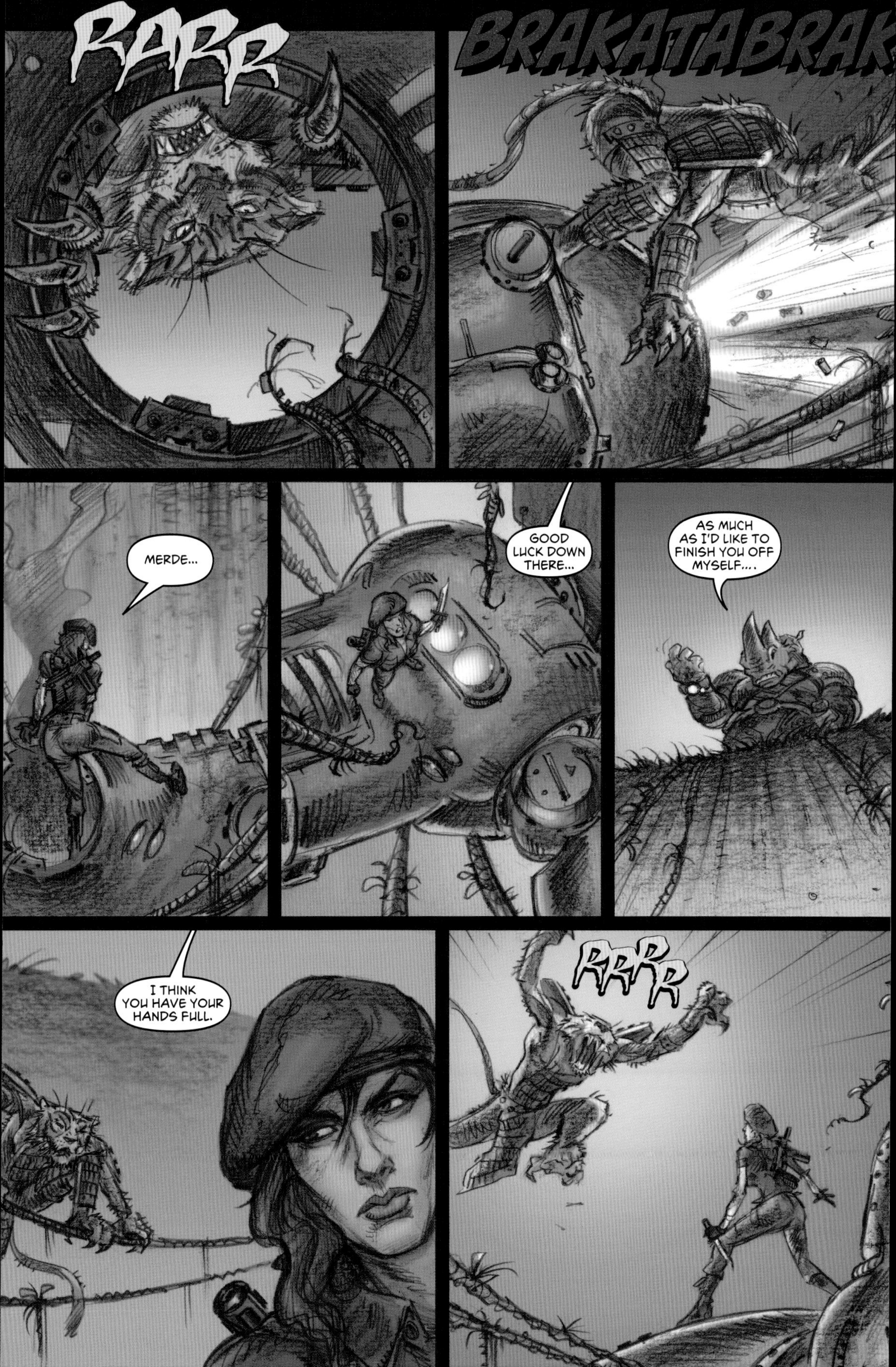
RARR
BRAKATABRAK
MERDE...
GOOD LUCK DOWN THERE...
AS MUCH AS I'D LIKE TO FINISH YOU OFF MYSELF....
I THINK YOU HAVE YOUR HANDS FULL.
RRRR

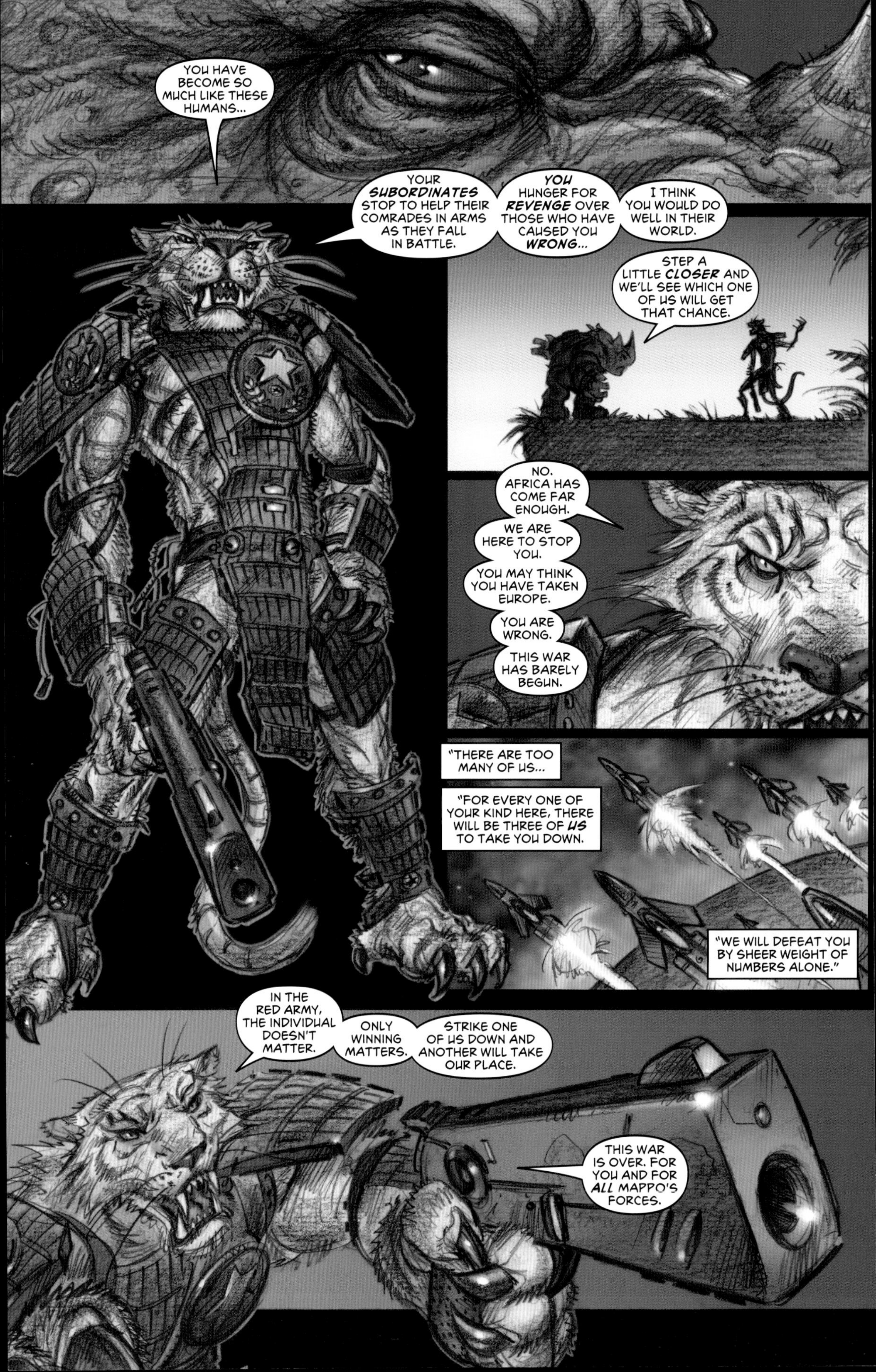
YOU HAVE BECOME SO MUCH LIKE THESE HUMANS...
YOUR SUBORDINATES STOP TO HELP THEIR COMRADES IN ARMS AS THEY FALL IN BATTLE.
YOU HUNGER FOR REVENGE OVER THOSE WHO HAVE CAUSED YOU WRONG...
I THINK YOU WOULD DO WELL IN THEIR WORLD.
STEP A LITTLE CLOSER AND WE'LL SEE WHICH ONE OF US WILL GET THAT CHANCE.
NO. AFRICA HAS COME FAR ENOUGH.
WE ARE HERE TO STOP YOU.
YOU MAY THINK YOU HAVE TAKEN EUROPE.
YOU ARE WRONG.
THIS WAR HAS BARELY BEGUN.
"THERE ARE TOO MANY OF US...
"FOR EVERY ONE OF YOUR KIND HERE, THERE WILL BE THREE OF US TO TAKE YOU DOWN.
"WE WILL DEFEAT YOU BY SHEER WEIGHT OF NUMBERS ALONE."
IN THE RED ARMY, THE INDIVIDUAL DOESN'T MATTER.
ONLY WINNING MATTERS.
STRIKE ONE OF US DOWN AND ANOTHER WILL TAKE OUR PLACE.
THIS WAR IS OVER. FOR YOU AND FOR ALL MAPPO'S FORCES.

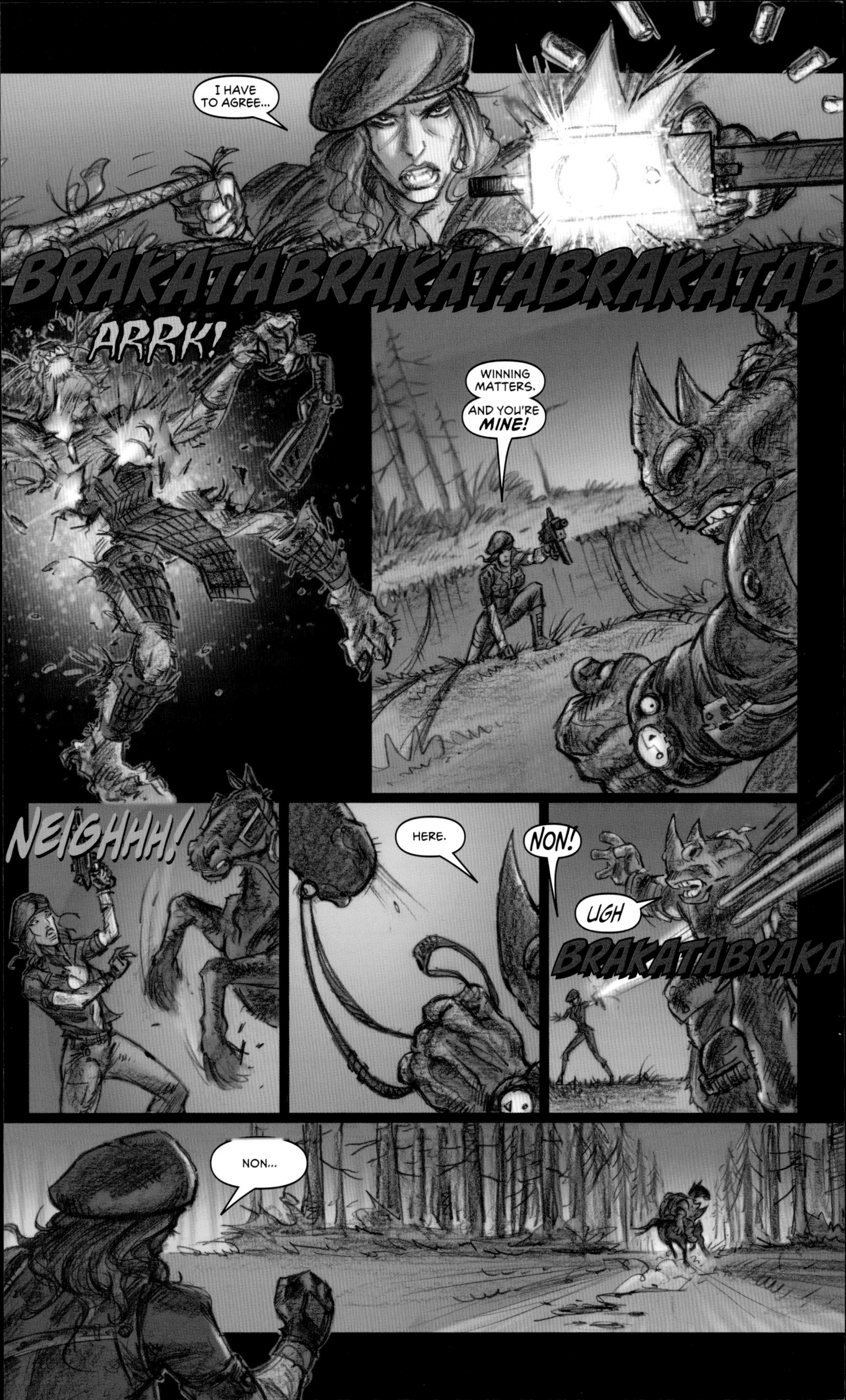

I HAVE TO AGREE...
BRAKATABRAKATABRAKATAB
ARRK!
WINNING MATTERS.
AND YOU'RE MINE!
NEIGHHH!
HERE.
NON!
UGH
BRAKATABRAKA
NON...

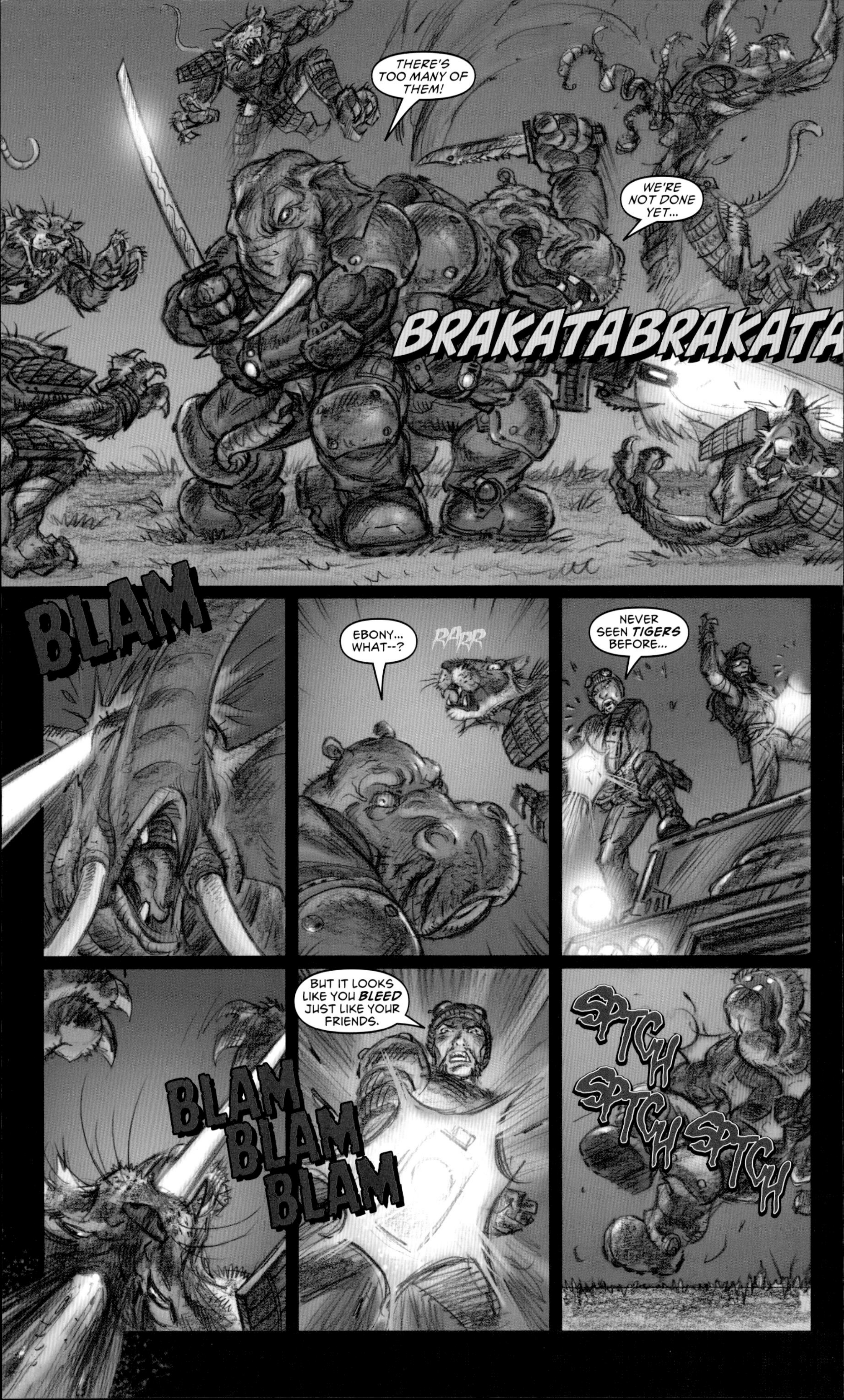
THERE'S TOO MANY OF THEM!
WE'RE NOT DONE YET...
BRAKATABRAKATA
BLAM
EBONY... WHAT--?
RARR
NEVER SEEN TIGERS BEFORE...
BLAM BLAM BLAM
BUT IT LOOKS LIKE YOU BLEED JUST LIKE YOUR FRIENDS.
SPTCH SPTCH SPTCH

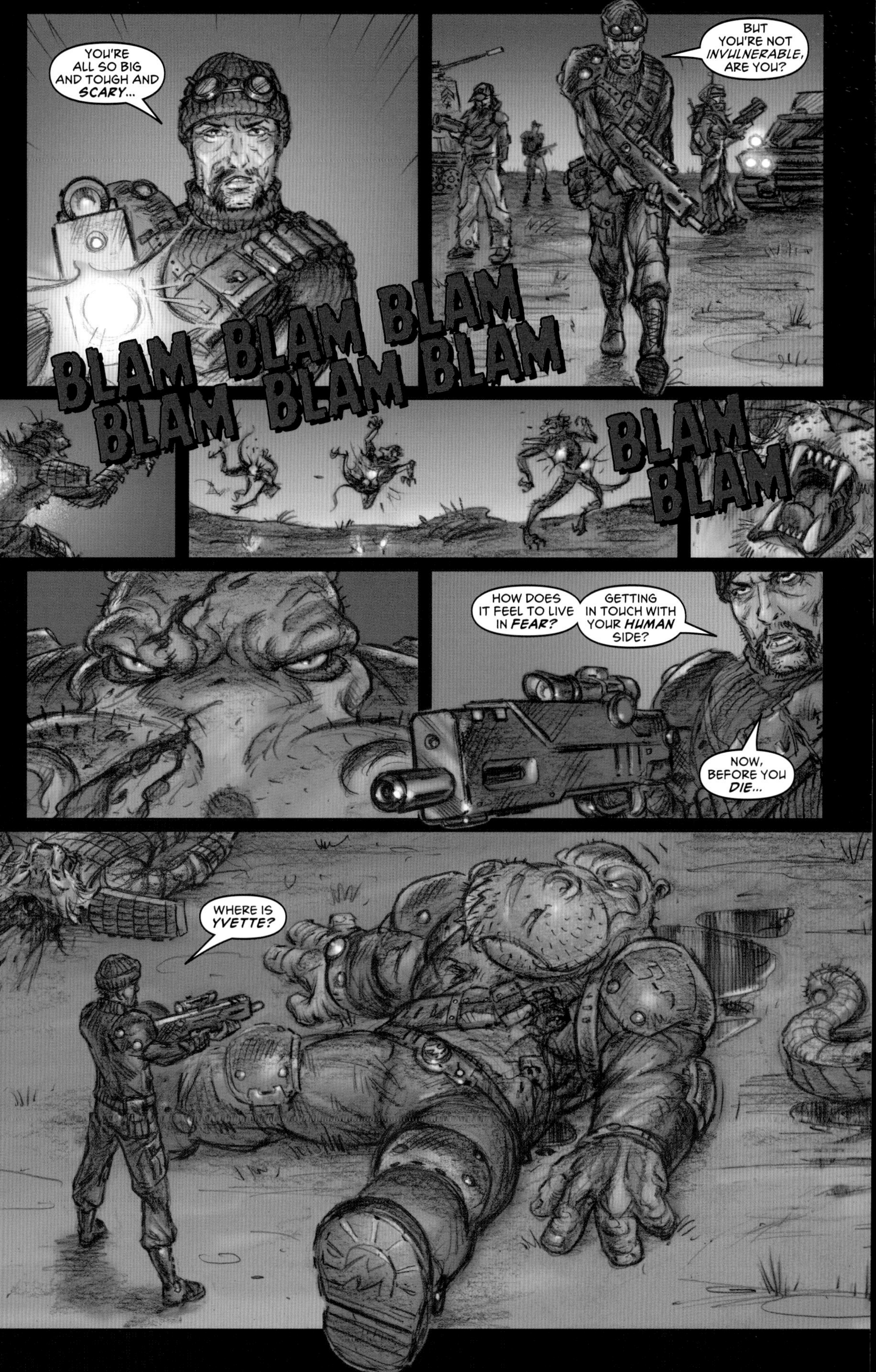

YOU'RE ALL SO BIG AND TOUGH AND SCARY...
BUT YOU'RE NOT INVULNERABLE, ARE YOU?
BLAM BLAM BLAM
BLAM BLAM BLAM
BLAM BLAM
HOW DOES IT FEEL TO LIVE IN FEAR?
GETTING IN TOUCH WITH YOUR HUMAN SIDE?
NOW, BEFORE YOU DIE...
WHERE IS YVETTE?

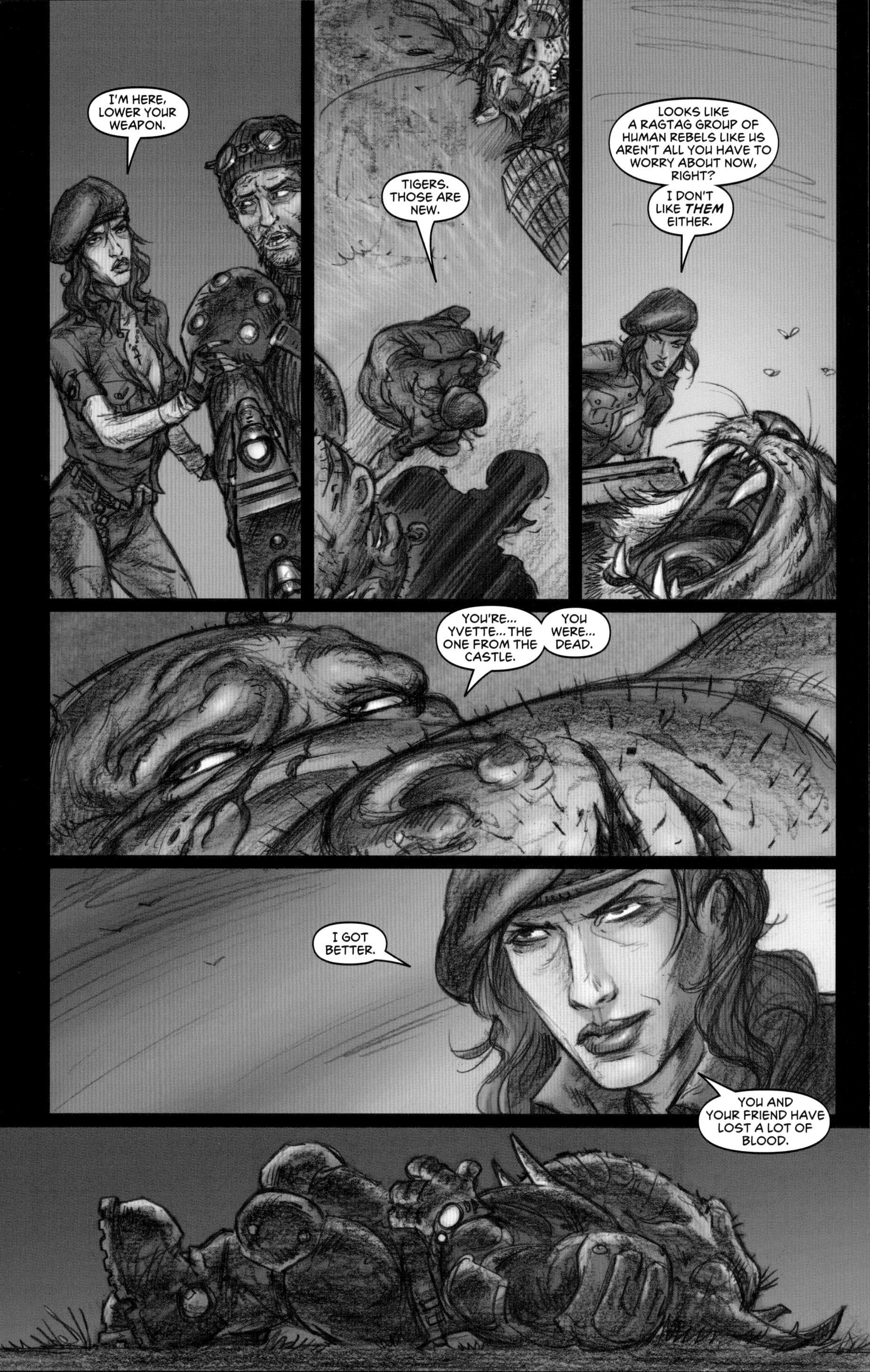
I'M HERE, LOWER YOUR WEAPON.
TIGERS. THOSE ARE NEW.
LOOKS LIKE A RAGTAG GROUP OF HUMAN REBELS LIKE US AREN'T ALL YOU HAVE TO WORRY ABOUT NOW, RIGHT?
I DON'T LIKE *THEM* EITHER.
YOU'RE... YVETTE... THE ONE FROM THE CASTLE.
YOU WERE... DEAD.
I GOT BETTER.
YOU AND YOUR FRIEND HAVE LOST A LOT OF BLOOD.

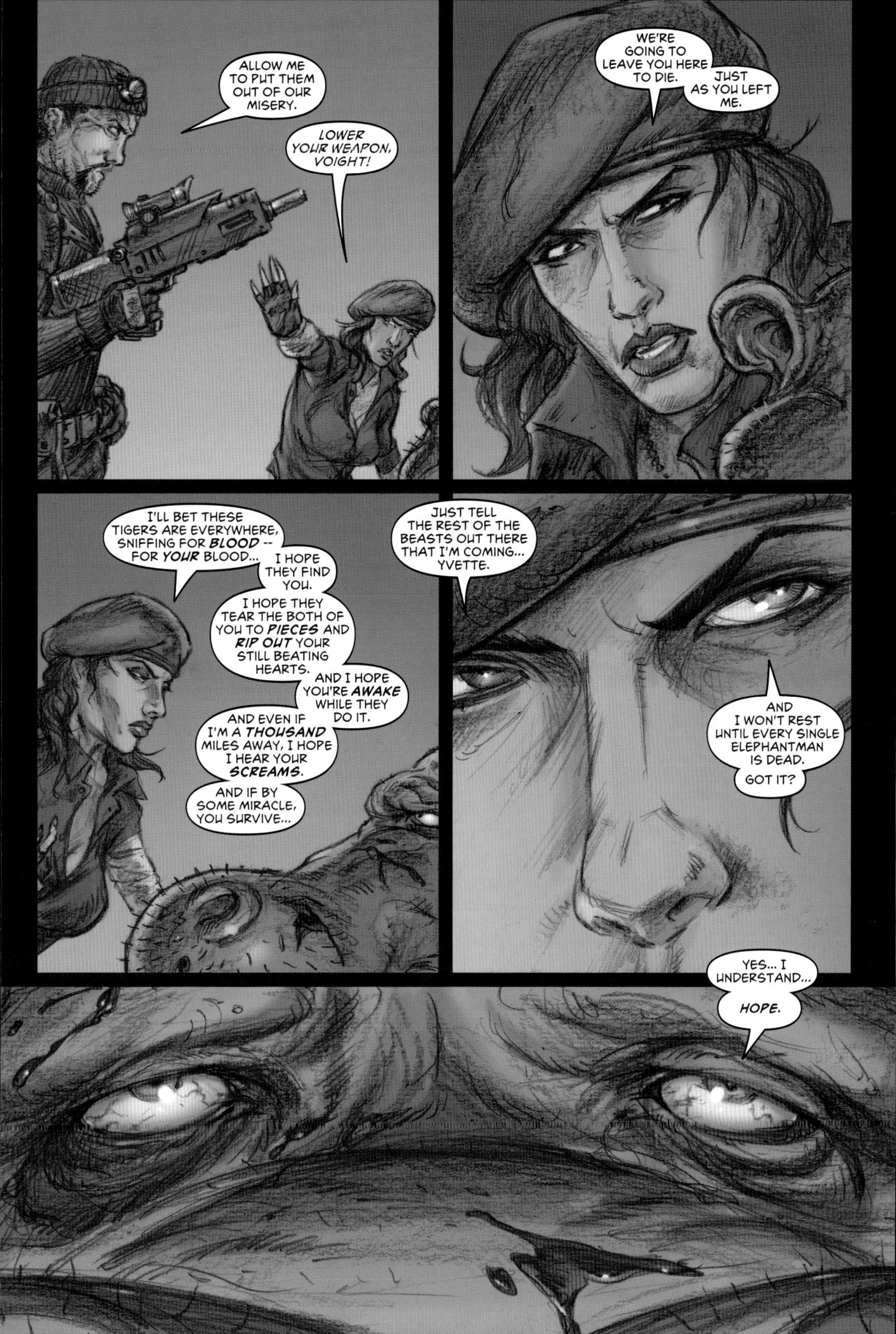
ALLOW ME TO PUT THEM OUT OF OUR MISERY.
LOWER YOUR WEAPON, VOIGHT!
WE'RE GOING TO LEAVE YOU HERE TO DIE.
JUST AS YOU LEFT ME.
I'LL BET THESE TIGERS ARE EVERYWHERE, SNIFFING FOR BLOOD -- FOR YOUR BLOOD...
I HOPE THEY FIND YOU.
I HOPE THEY TEAR THE BOTH OF YOU TO PIECES AND RIP OUT YOUR STILL BEATING HEARTS.
AND I HOPE YOU'RE AWAKE WHILE THEY DO IT.
AND EVEN IF I'M A THOUSAND MILES AWAY, I HOPE I HEAR YOUR SCREAMS.
AND IF BY SOME MIRACLE, YOU SURVIVE...
JUST TELL THE REST OF THE BEASTS OUT THERE THAT I'M COMING... YVETTE.
AND I WON'T REST UNTIL EVERY SINGLE ELEPHANTMAN IS DEAD.
GOT IT?
YES... I UNDERSTAND...
HOPE.

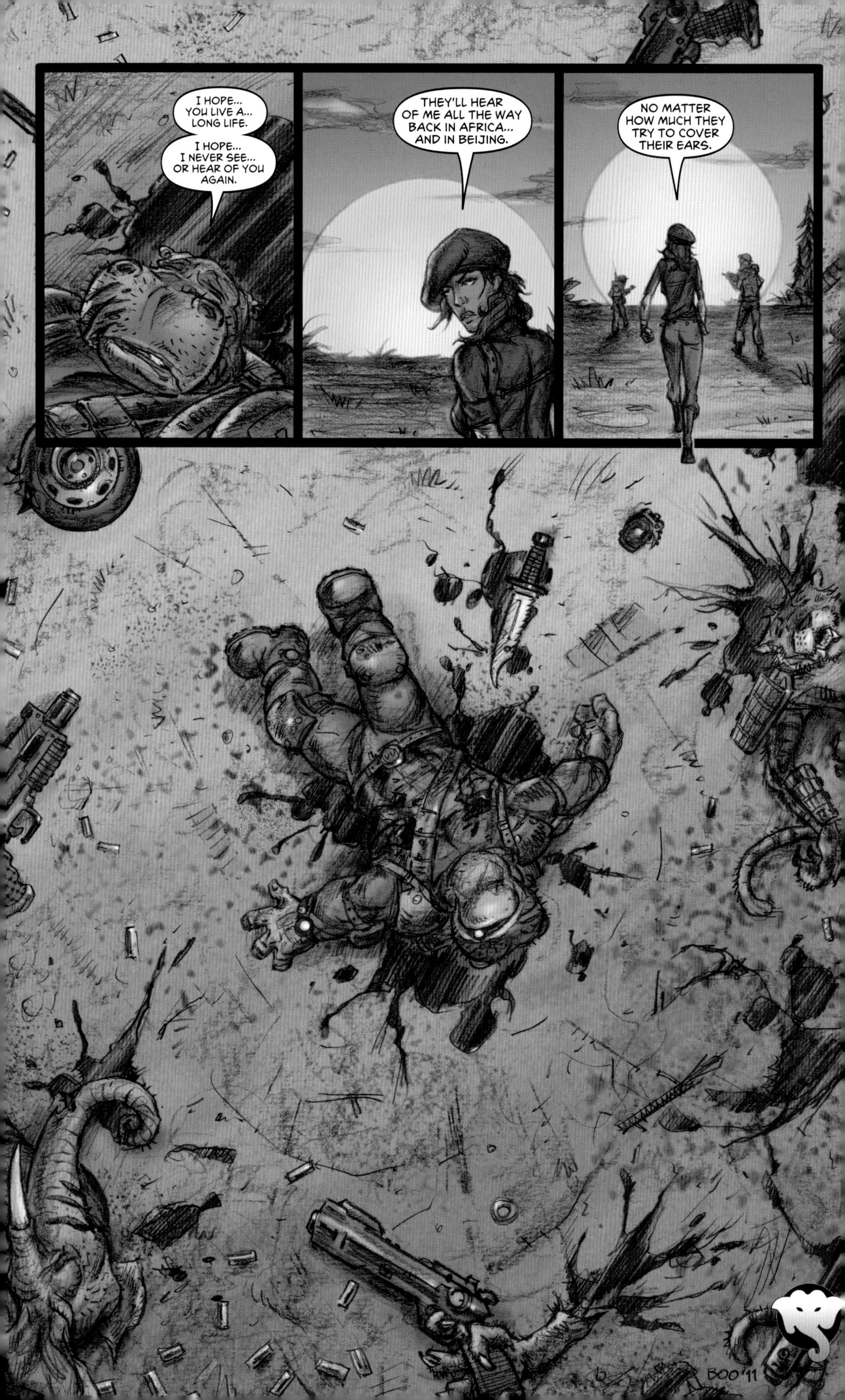
I HOPE... YOU LIVE A... LONG LIFE.
I HOPE... I NEVER SEE... OR HEAR OF YOU AGAIN.
THEY'LL HEAR OF ME ALL THE WAY BACK IN AFRICA... AND IN BEIJING.
NO MATTER HOW MUCH THEY TRY TO COVER THEIR EARS.
BOO '11

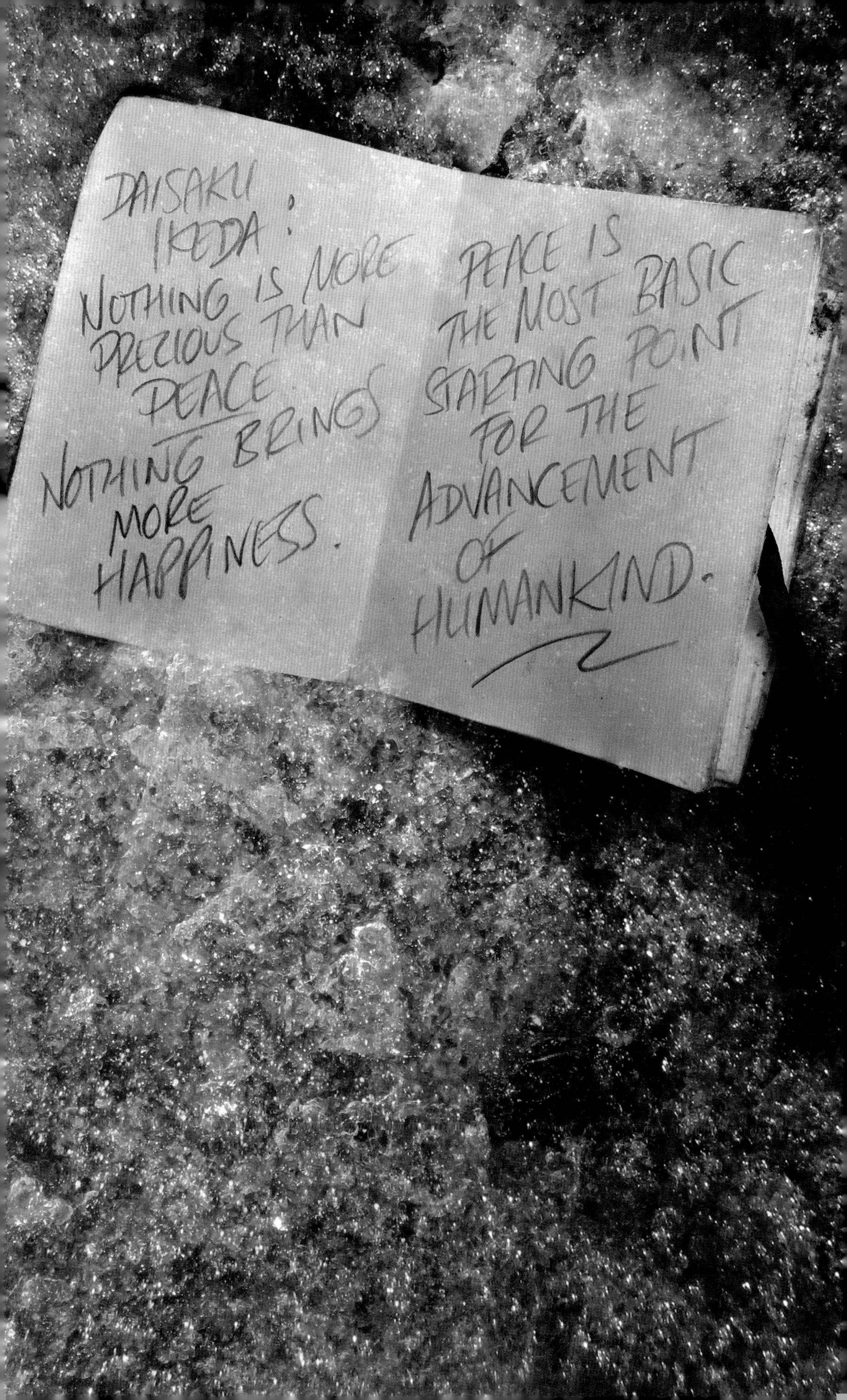
DAISAKU IKEDA:
NOTHING IS MORE PRECIOUS THAN PEACE
NOTHING BRINGS MORE HAPPINESS.
PEACE IS THE MOST BASIC STARTING POINT FOR THE ADVANCEMENT OF HUMANKIND.

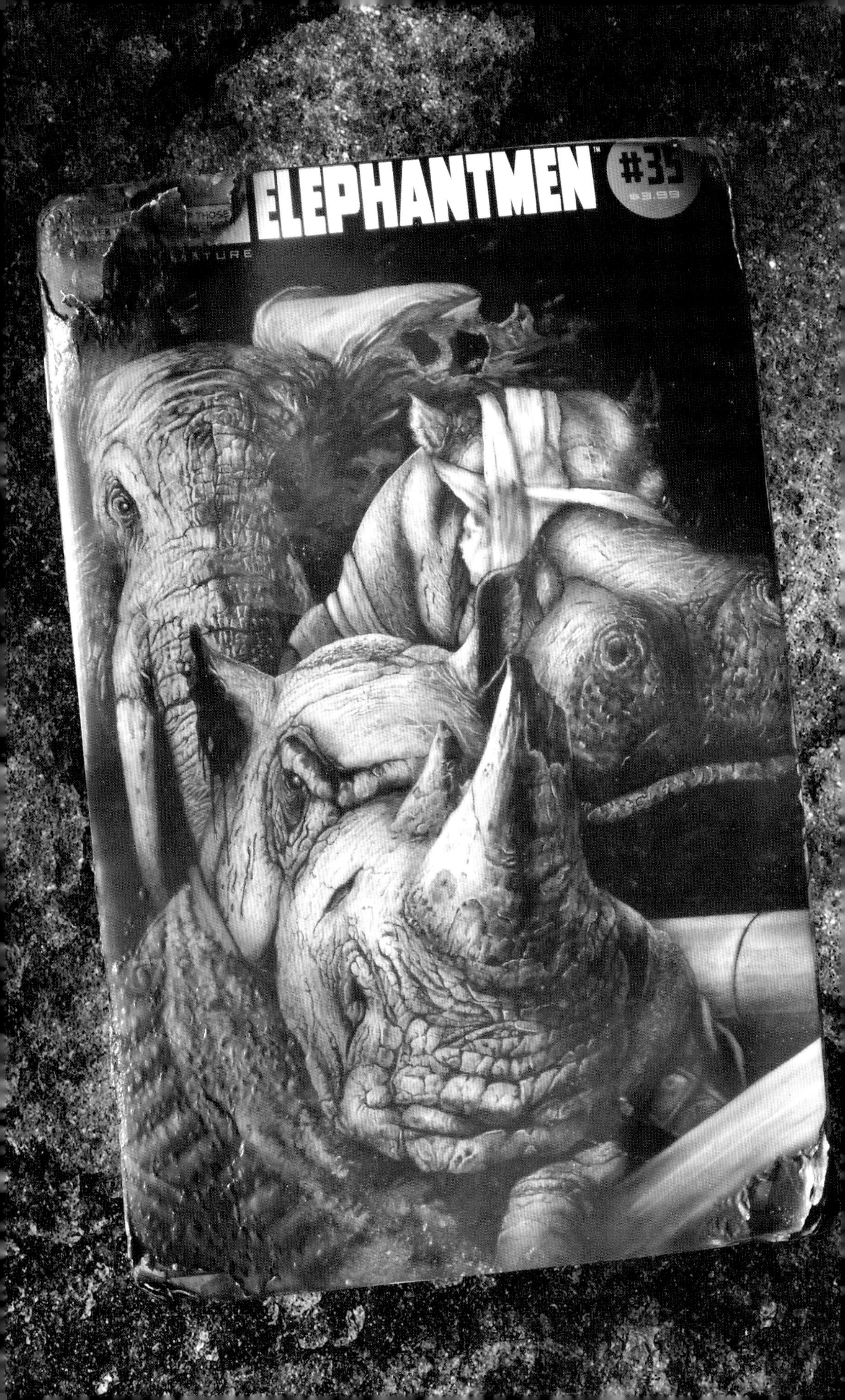
ELEPHANTMEN™
#35
$3.99

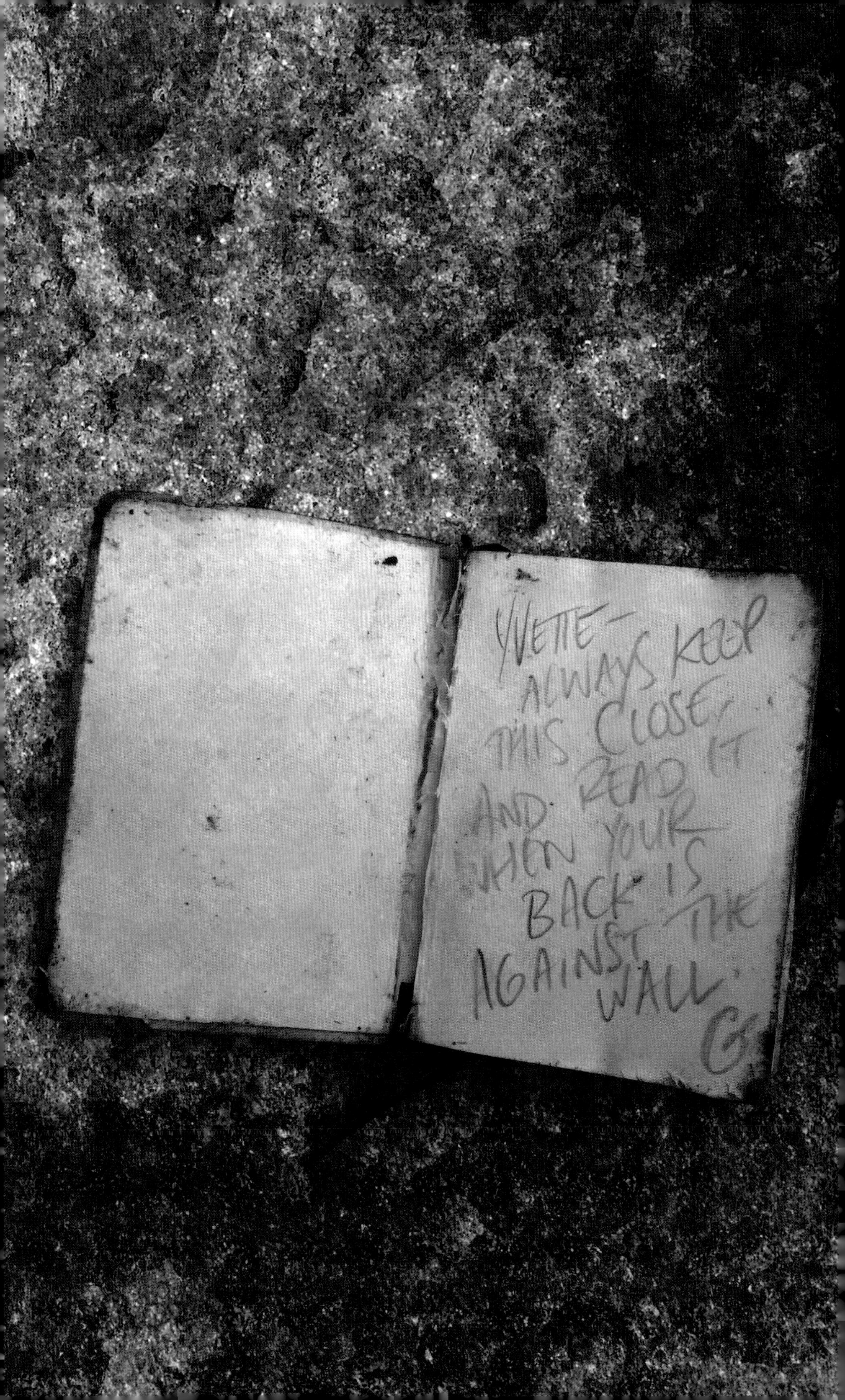
YVETTE—
ALWAYS KEEP
THIS CLOSE,
AND READ IT
WHEN YOUR
BACK IS
AGAINST THE
WALL.
G

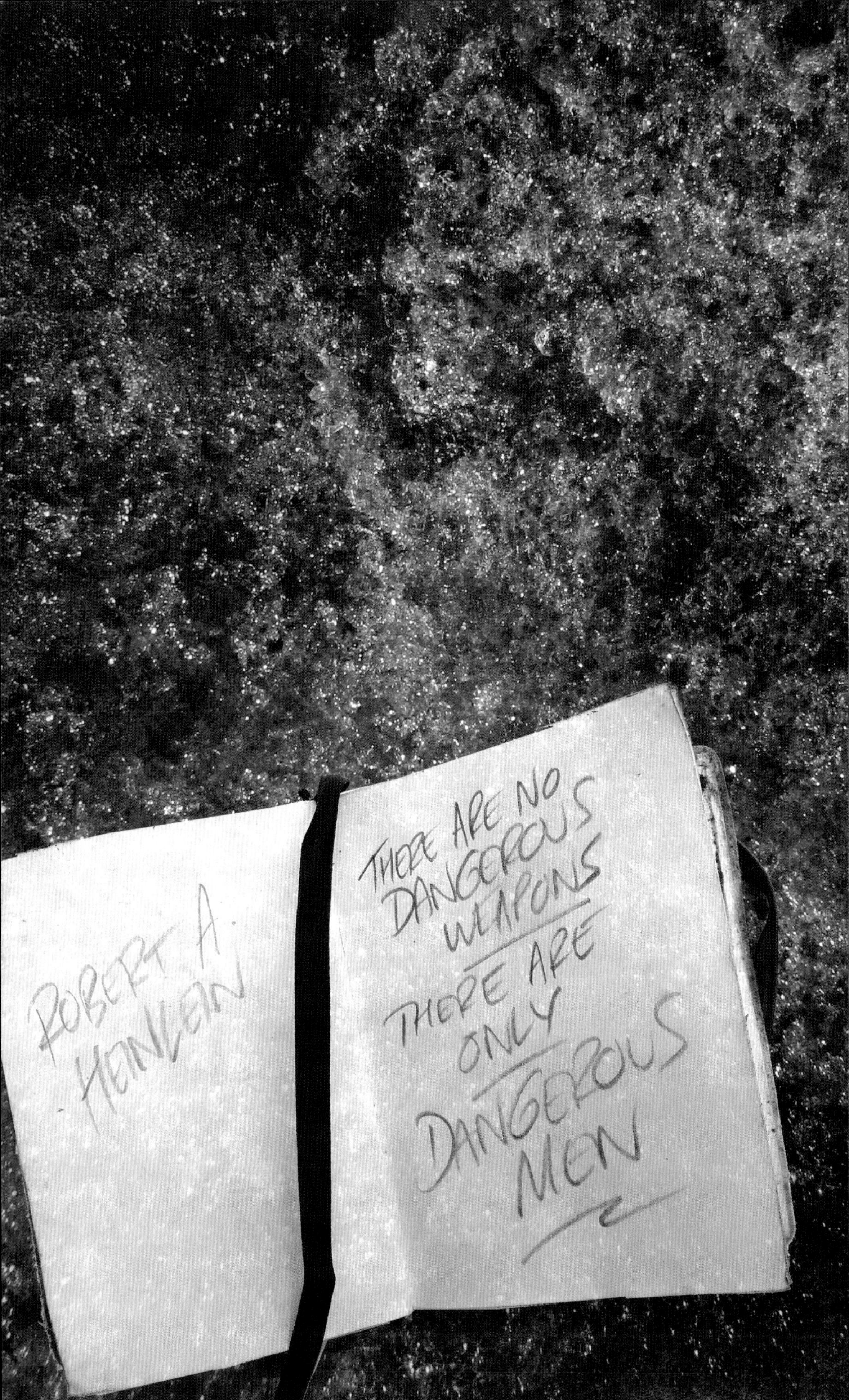
ROBERT A
HEINLEIN
THERE ARE NO
DANGEROUS
WEAPONS
THERE ARE
ONLY
DANGEROUS
MEN

NORTH AFRICA · 2218

PATIENT ZERO

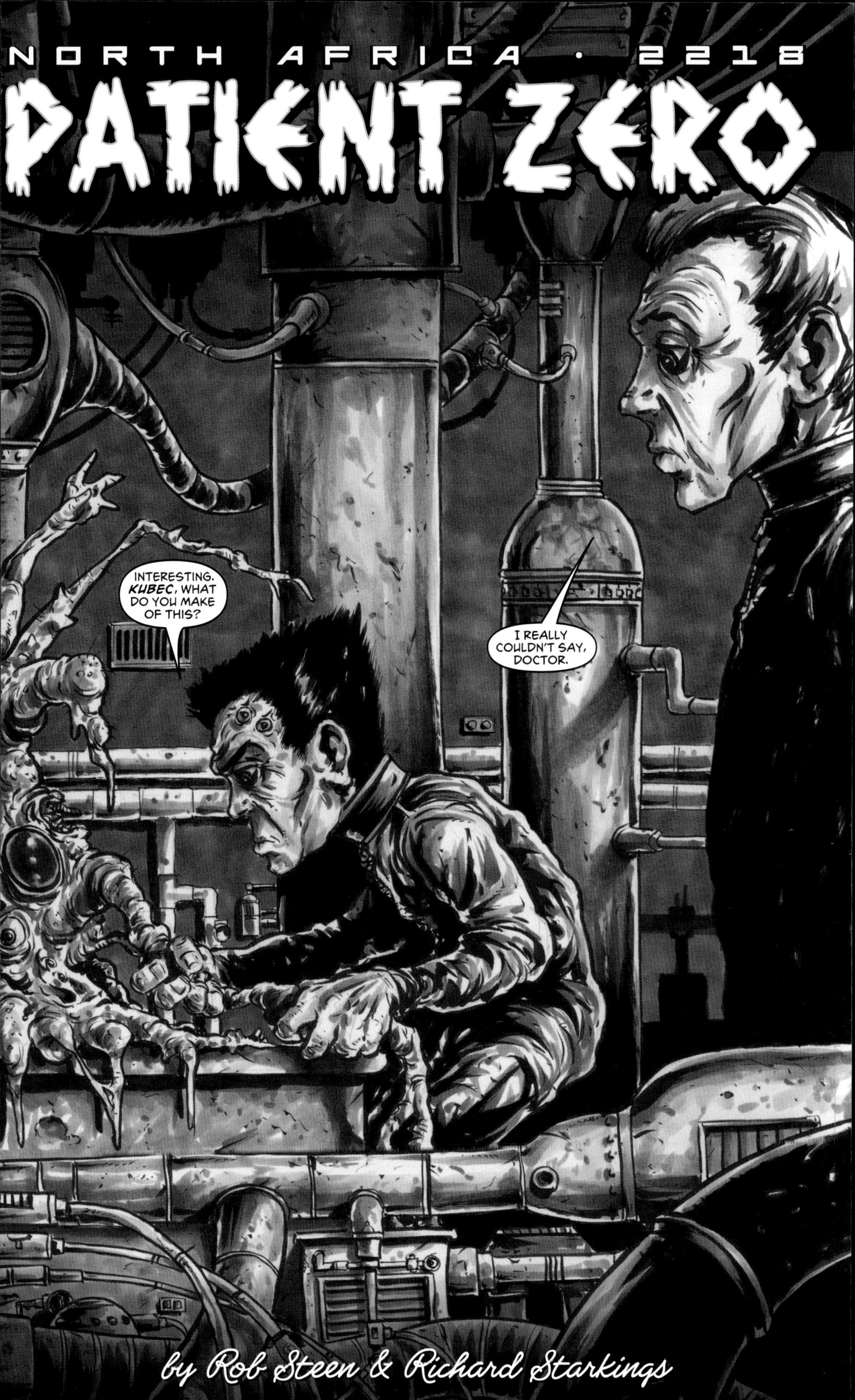

INTERESTING. KUBEC, WHAT DO YOU MAKE OF THIS?
I REALLY COULDN'T SAY, DOCTOR.

by Rob Steen & Richard Starkings

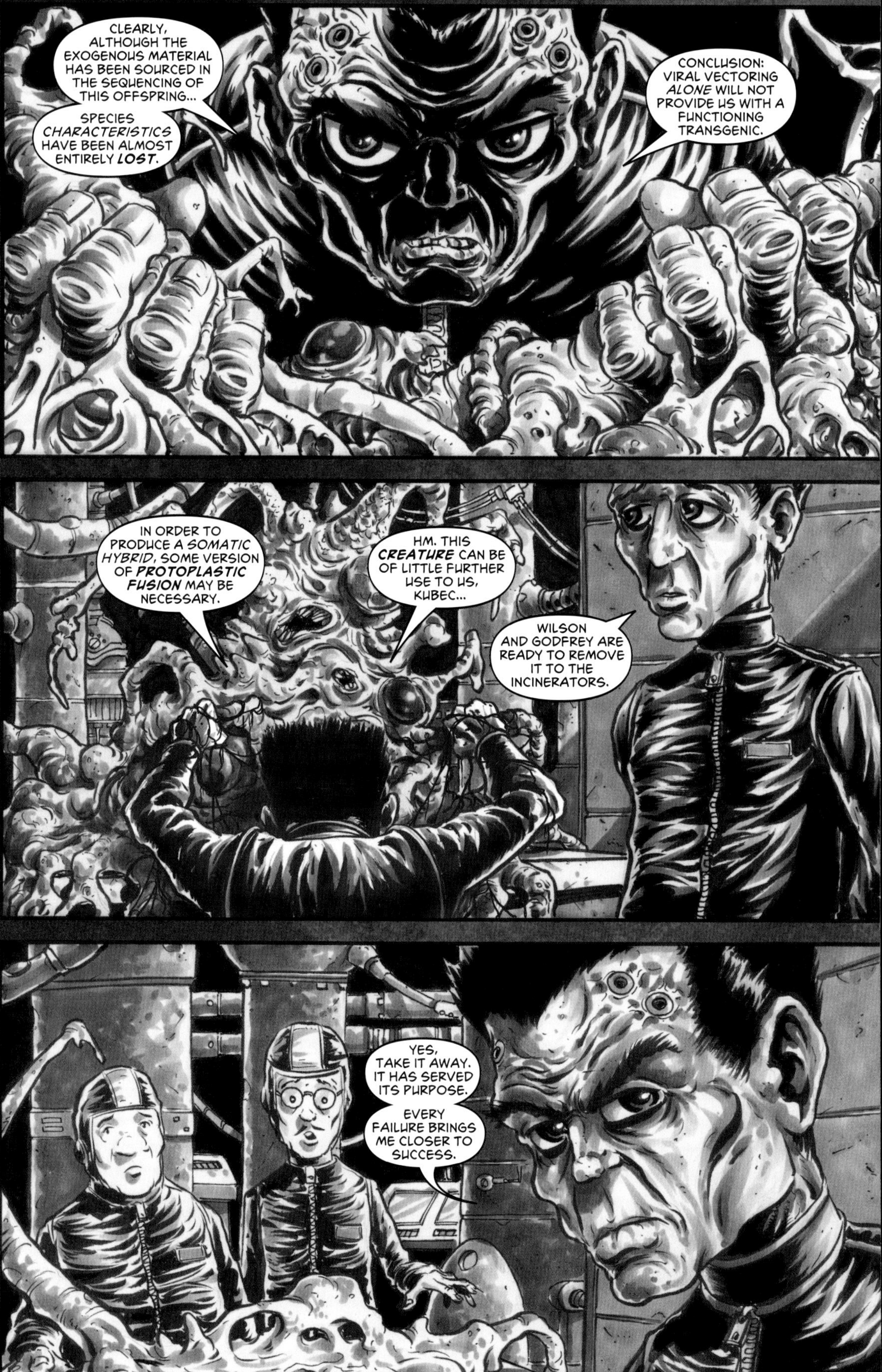
CLEARLY, ALTHOUGH THE EXOGENOUS MATERIAL HAS BEEN SOURCED IN THE SEQUENCING OF THIS OFFSPRING...
SPECIES *CHARACTERISTICS* HAVE BEEN ALMOST ENTIRELY ***LOST***.
CONCLUSION: VIRAL VECTORING *ALONE* WILL NOT PROVIDE US WITH A FUNCTIONING TRANSGENIC.
IN ORDER TO PRODUCE A *SOMATIC HYBRID*, SOME VERSION OF ***PROTOPLASTIC FUSION*** MAY BE NECESSARY.
HM. THIS ***CREATURE*** CAN BE OF LITTLE FURTHER USE TO US, KUBEC...
WILSON AND GODFREY ARE READY TO REMOVE IT TO THE INCINERATORS.
YES, TAKE IT AWAY. IT HAS SERVED ITS PURPOSE.
EVERY FAILURE BRINGS ME CLOSER TO SUCCESS.

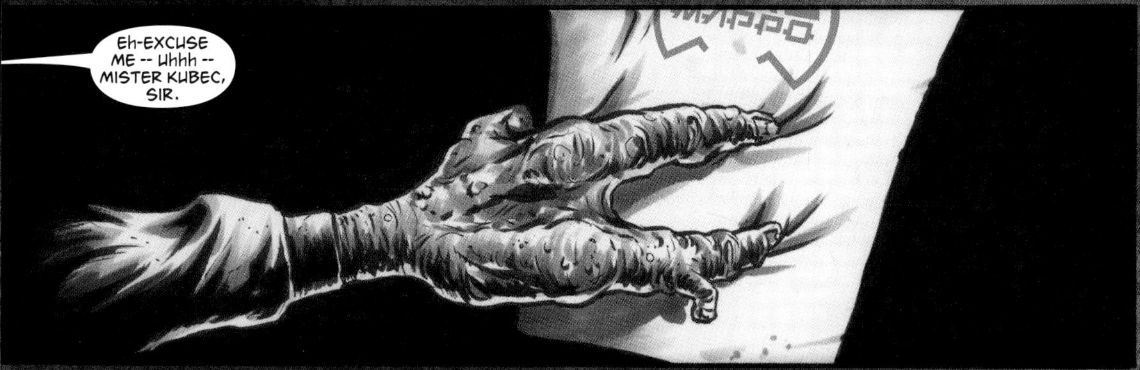
Eh-EXCUSE ME -- Uhhh -- MISTER KUBEC, SIR.

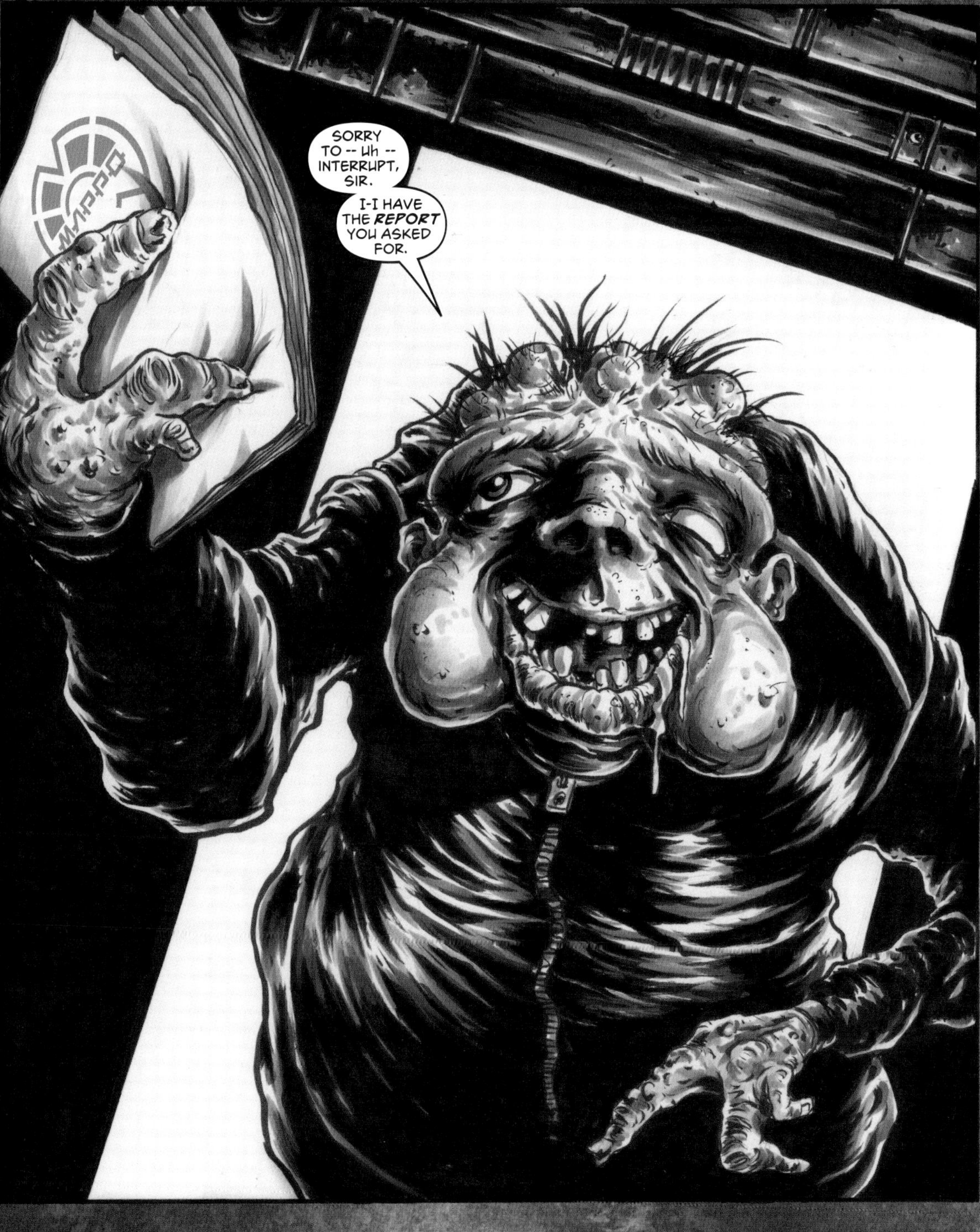
SORRY TO -- Uh -- INTERRUPT, SIR.
I-I HAVE THE REPORT YOU ASKED FOR.

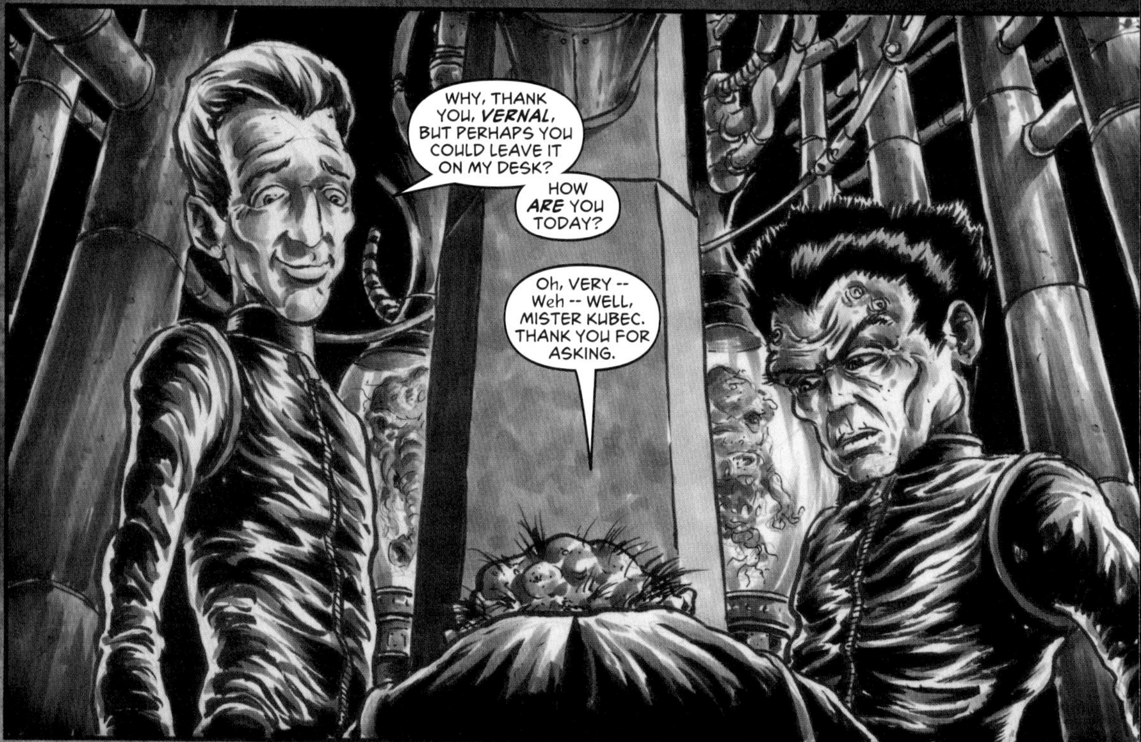
WHY, THANK YOU, VERNAL, BUT PERHAPS YOU COULD LEAVE IT ON MY DESK?
HOW ARE YOU TODAY?
Oh, VERY -- Weh -- WELL, MISTER KUBEC. THANK YOU FOR ASKING.

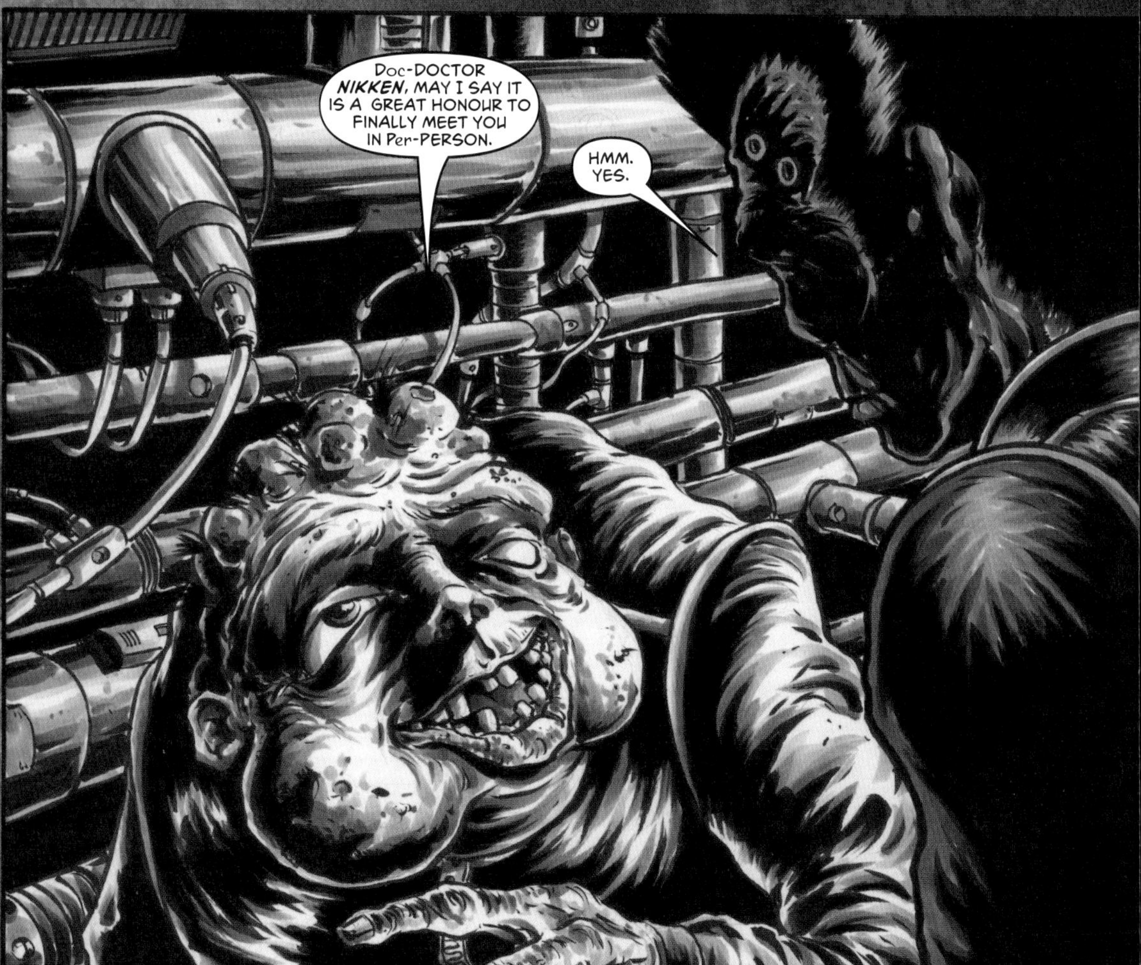
Doc-DOCTOR NIKKEN, MAY I SAY IT IS A GREAT HONOUR TO FINALLY MEET YOU IN Per-PERSON.
HMM. YES.

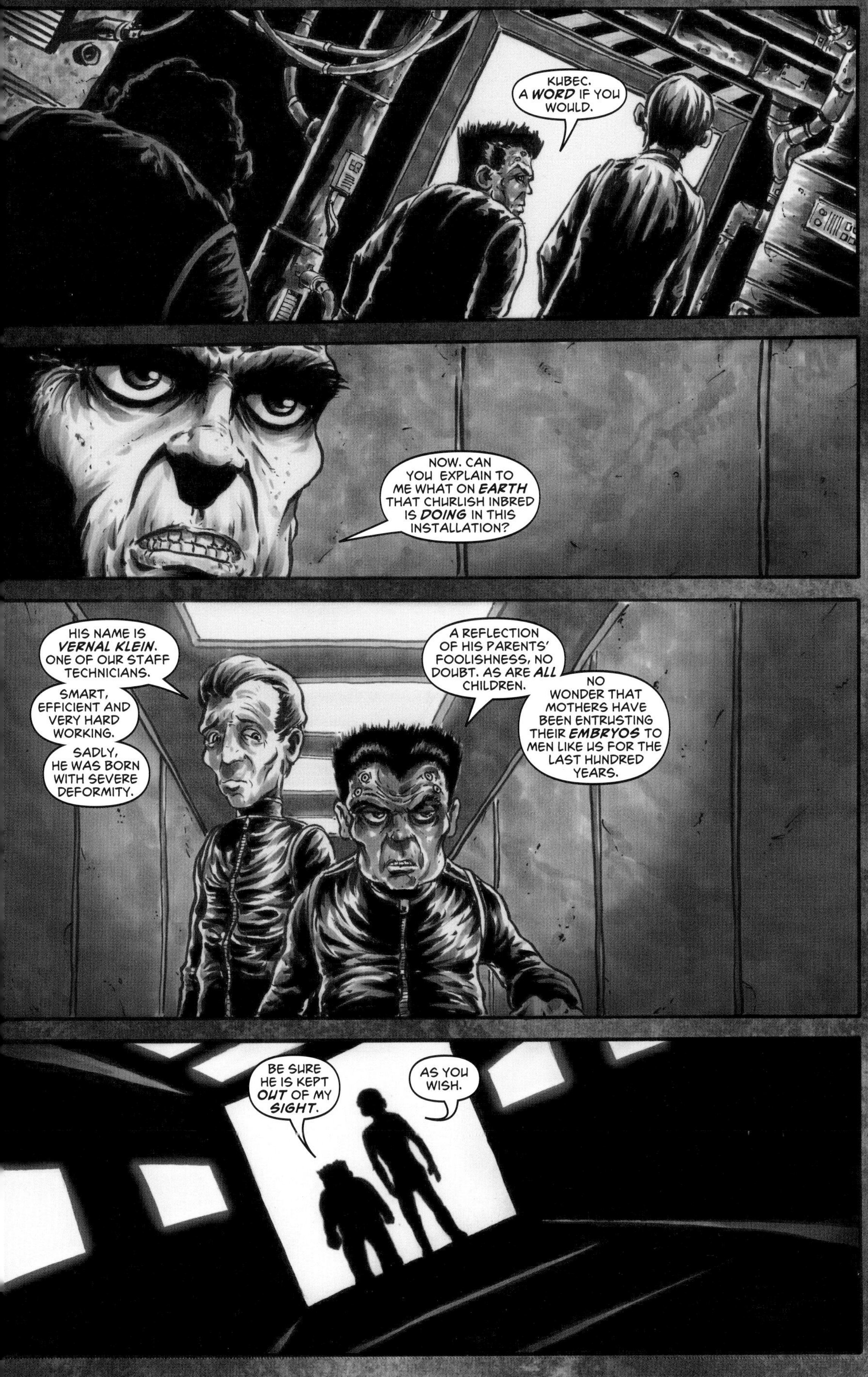
KUBEC. A WORD IF YOU WOULD.
NOW. CAN YOU EXPLAIN TO ME WHAT ON EARTH THAT CHURLISH INBRED IS DOING IN THIS INSTALLATION?
HIS NAME IS VERNAL KLEIN. ONE OF OUR STAFF TECHNICIANS.
SMART, EFFICIENT AND VERY HARD WORKING.
SADLY, HE WAS BORN WITH SEVERE DEFORMITY.
A REFLECTION OF HIS PARENTS' FOOLISHNESS, NO DOUBT. AS ARE ALL CHILDREN.
NO WONDER THAT MOTHERS HAVE BEEN ENTRUSTING THEIR EMBRYOS TO MEN LIKE US FOR THE LAST HUNDRED YEARS.
BE SURE HE IS KEPT OUT OF MY SIGHT.
AS YOU WISH.

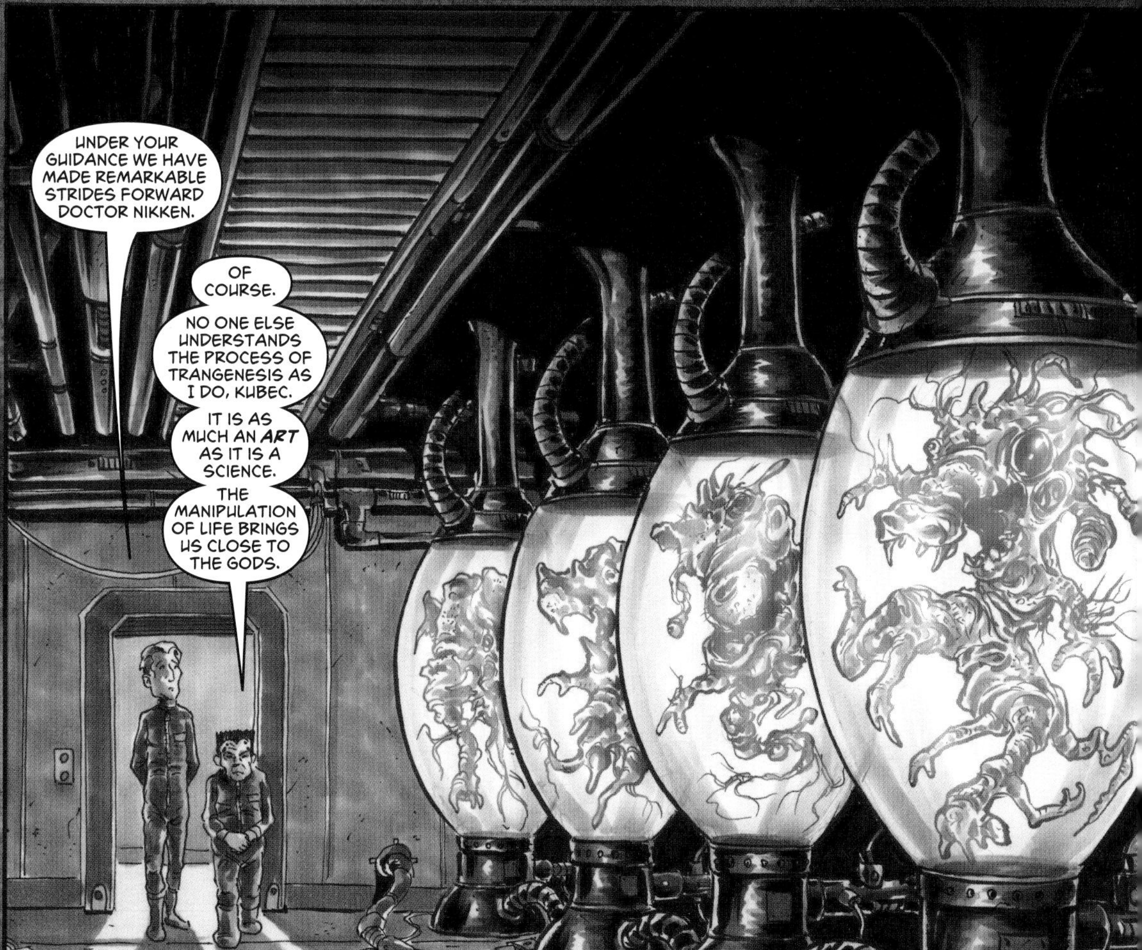
UNDER YOUR GUIDANCE WE HAVE MADE REMARKABLE STRIDES FORWARD DOCTOR NIKKEN.
OF COURSE.
NO ONE ELSE UNDERSTANDS THE PROCESS OF TRANGENESIS AS I DO, KUBEC.
IT IS AS MUCH AN *ART* AS IT IS A SCIENCE.
THE MANIPULATION OF LIFE BRINGS US CLOSE TO THE GODS.

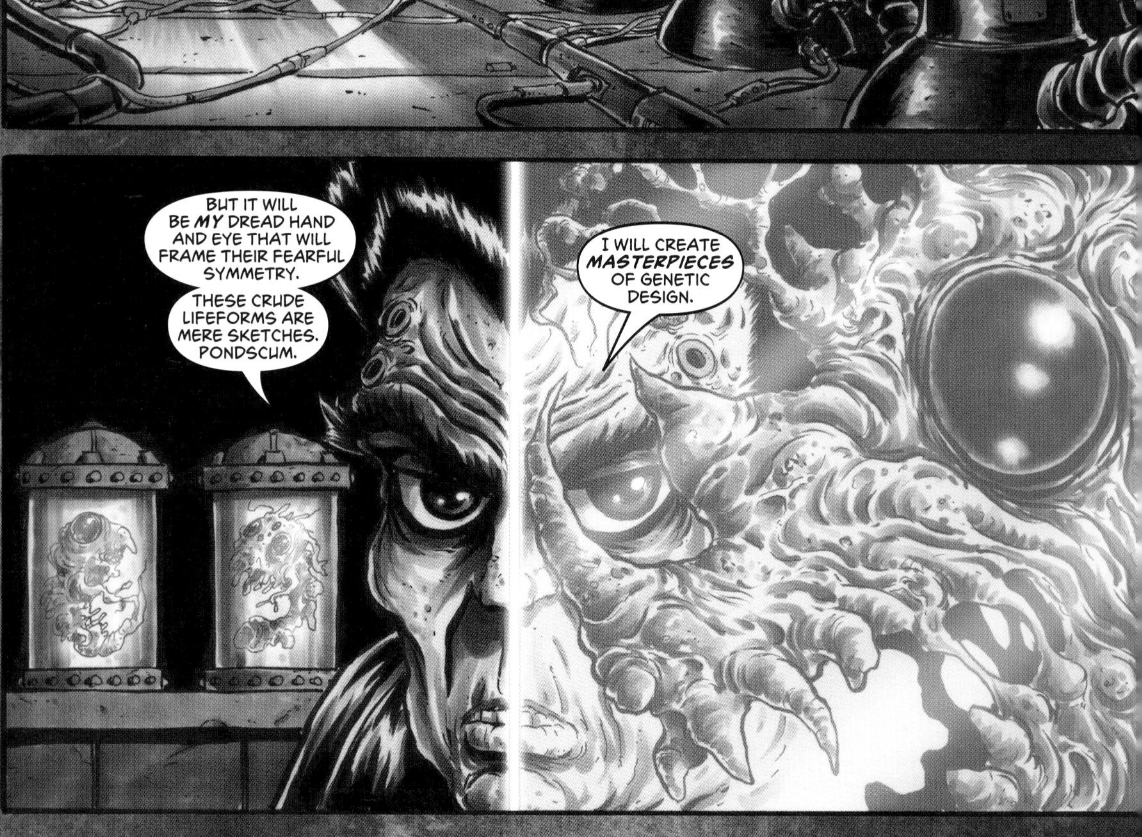
BUT IT WILL BE *MY* DREAD HAND AND EYE THAT WILL FRAME THEIR FEARFUL SYMMETRY.
THESE CRUDE LIFEFORMS ARE MERE SKETCHES. PONDSCUM.
I WILL CREATE ***MASTERPIECES*** OF GENETIC DESIGN.

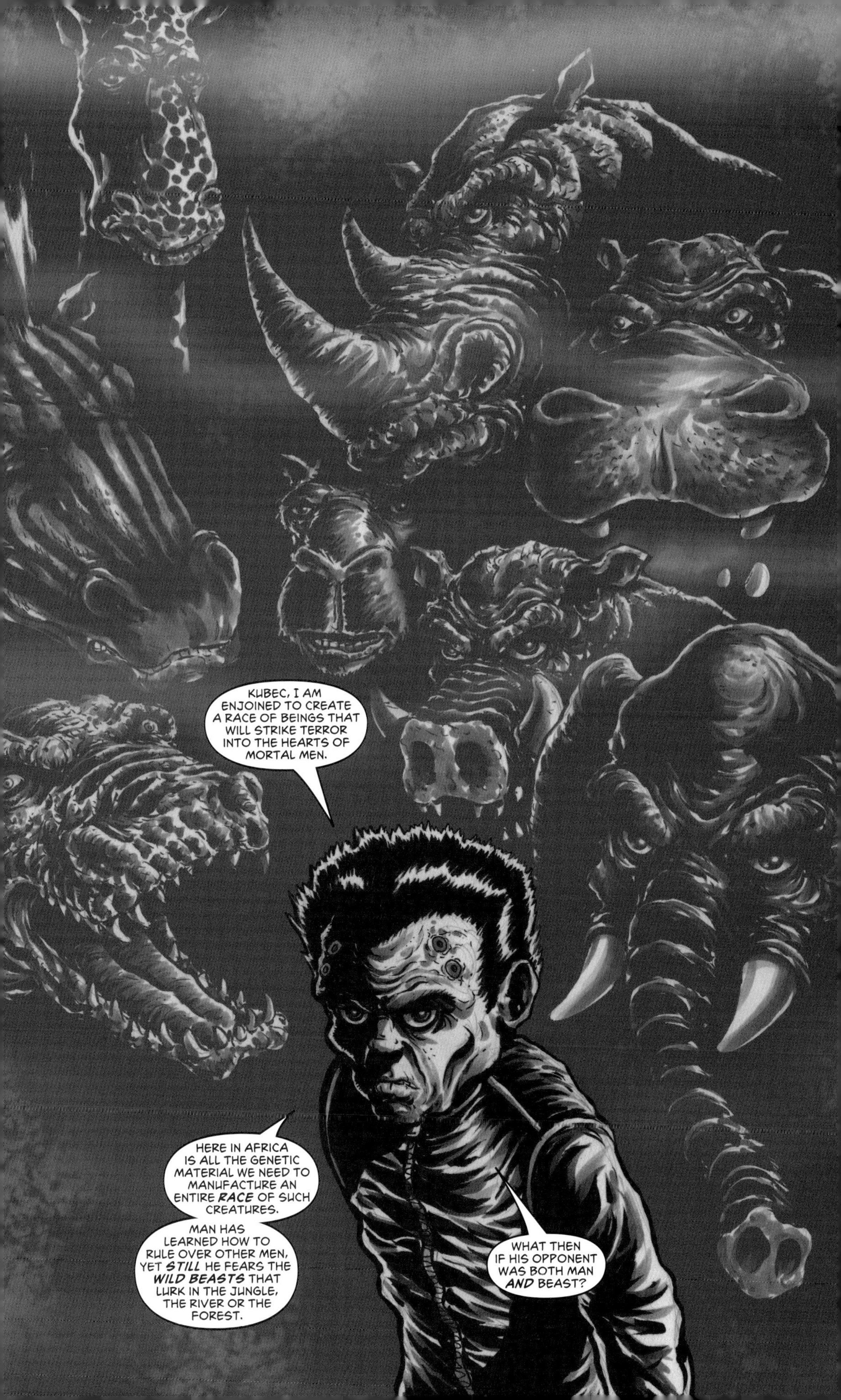
KUBEC, I AM ENJOINED TO CREATE A RACE OF BEINGS THAT WILL STRIKE TERROR INTO THE HEARTS OF MORTAL MEN.
HERE IN AFRICA IS ALL THE GENETIC MATERIAL WE NEED TO MANUFACTURE AN ENTIRE *RACE* OF SUCH CREATURES.
MAN HAS LEARNED HOW TO RULE OVER OTHER MEN, YET **STILL** HE FEARS THE ***WILD BEASTS*** THAT LURK IN THE JUNGLE, THE RIVER OR THE FOREST.
WHAT THEN IF HIS OPPONENT WAS BOTH MAN ***AND*** BEAST?

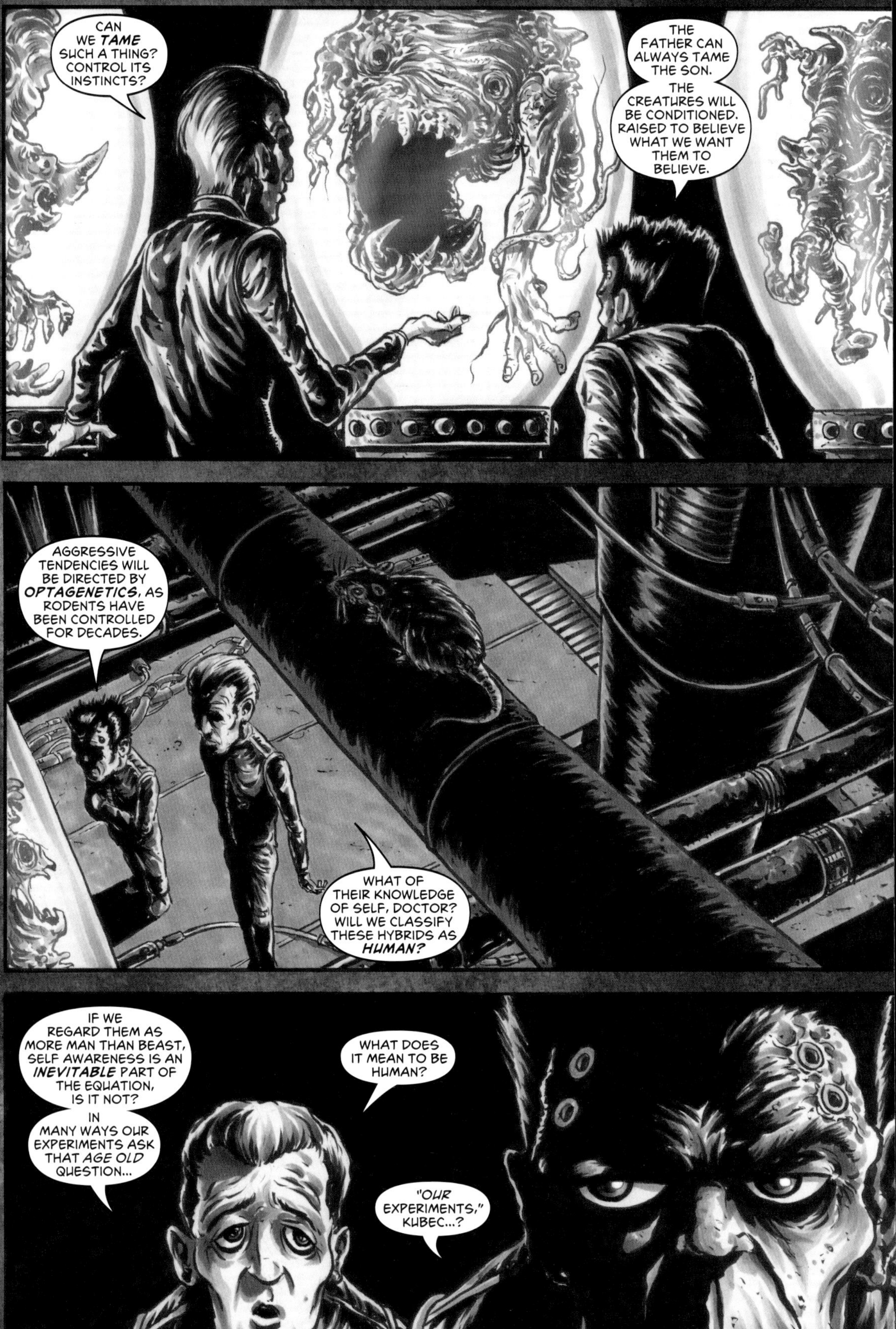
CAN WE TAME SUCH A THING? CONTROL ITS INSTINCTS?
THE FATHER CAN ALWAYS TAME THE SON.
THE CREATURES WILL BE CONDITIONED. RAISED TO BELIEVE WHAT WE WANT THEM TO BELIEVE.
AGGRESSIVE TENDENCIES WILL BE DIRECTED BY OPTAGENETICS, AS RODENTS HAVE BEEN CONTROLLED FOR DECADES.
WHAT OF THEIR KNOWLEDGE OF SELF, DOCTOR? WILL WE CLASSIFY THESE HYBRIDS AS HUMAN?
IF WE REGARD THEM AS MORE MAN THAN BEAST, SELF AWARENESS IS AN INEVITABLE PART OF THE EQUATION, IS IT NOT?
IN MANY WAYS OUR EXPERIMENTS ASK THAT AGE OLD QUESTION...
WHAT DOES IT MEAN TO BE HUMAN?
"OUR EXPERIMENTS," KUBEC...?

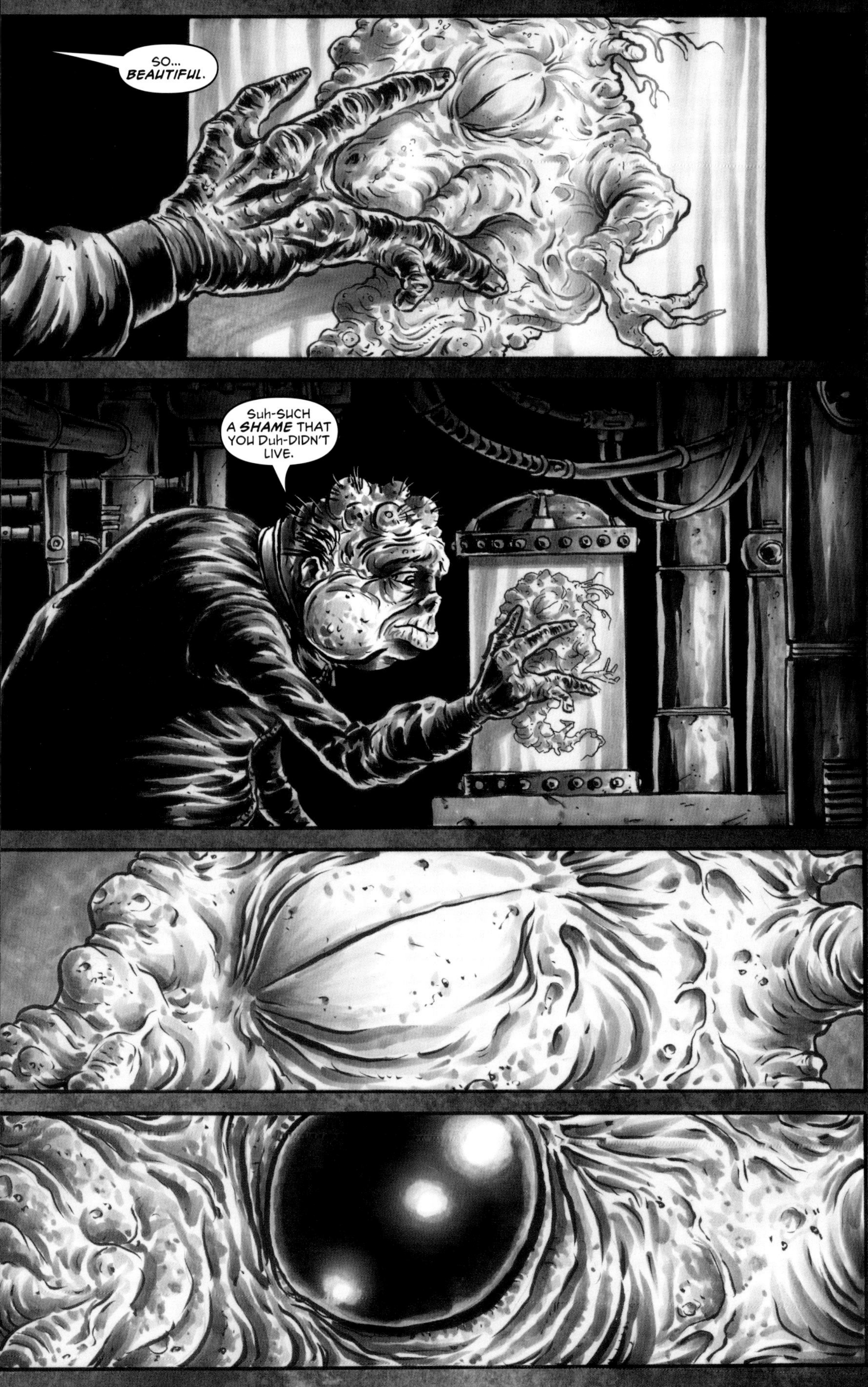
SO... BEAUTIFUL.
Suh-SUCH A SHAME THAT YOU Duh-DIDN'T LIVE.

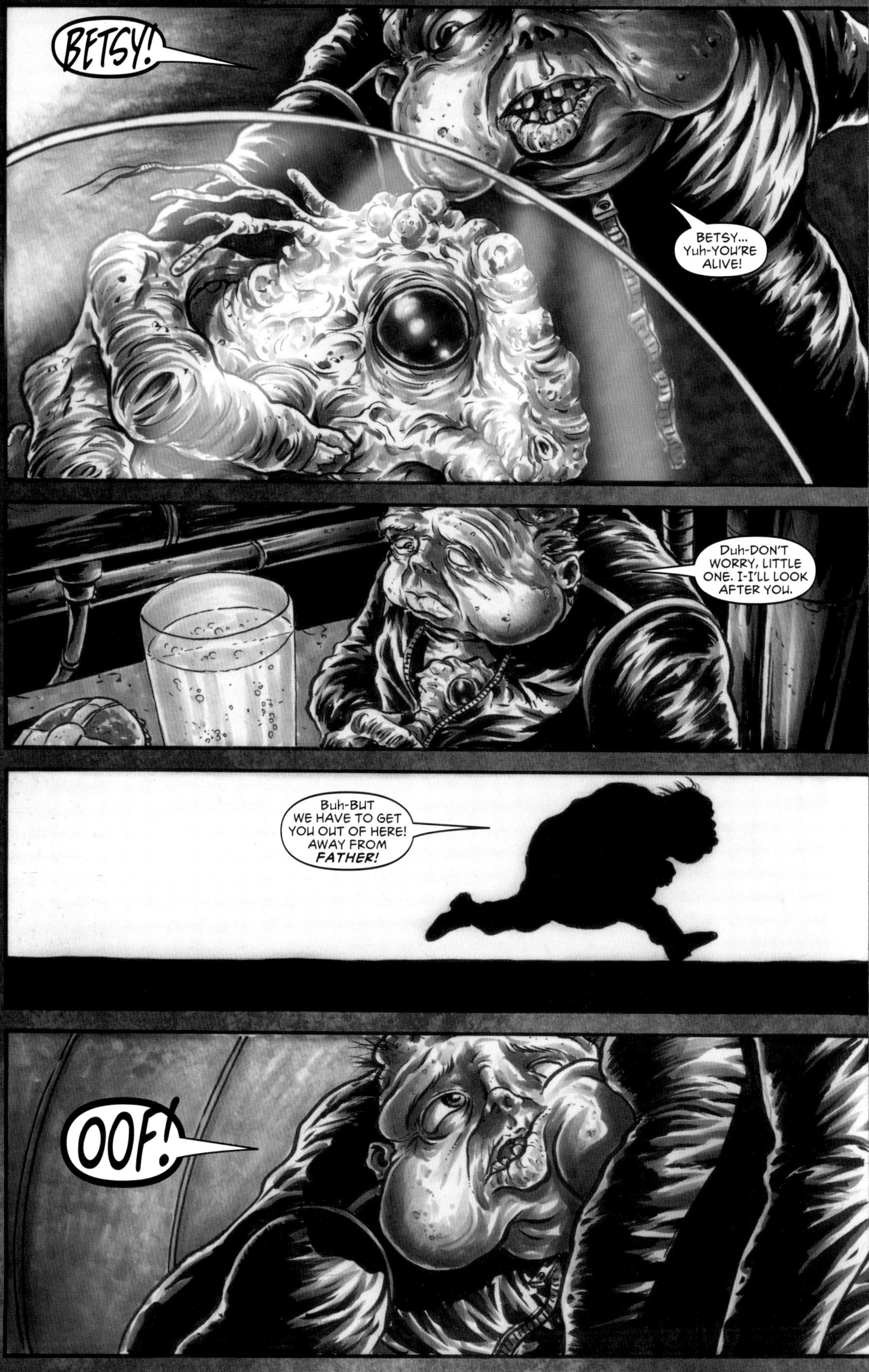
BETSY!
BETSY... Yuh-YOU'RE ALIVE!
Duh-DON'T WORRY, LITTLE ONE. I-I'LL LOOK AFTER YOU.
Buh-BUT WE HAVE TO GET YOU OUT OF HERE! AWAY FROM *FATHER!*
OOF!

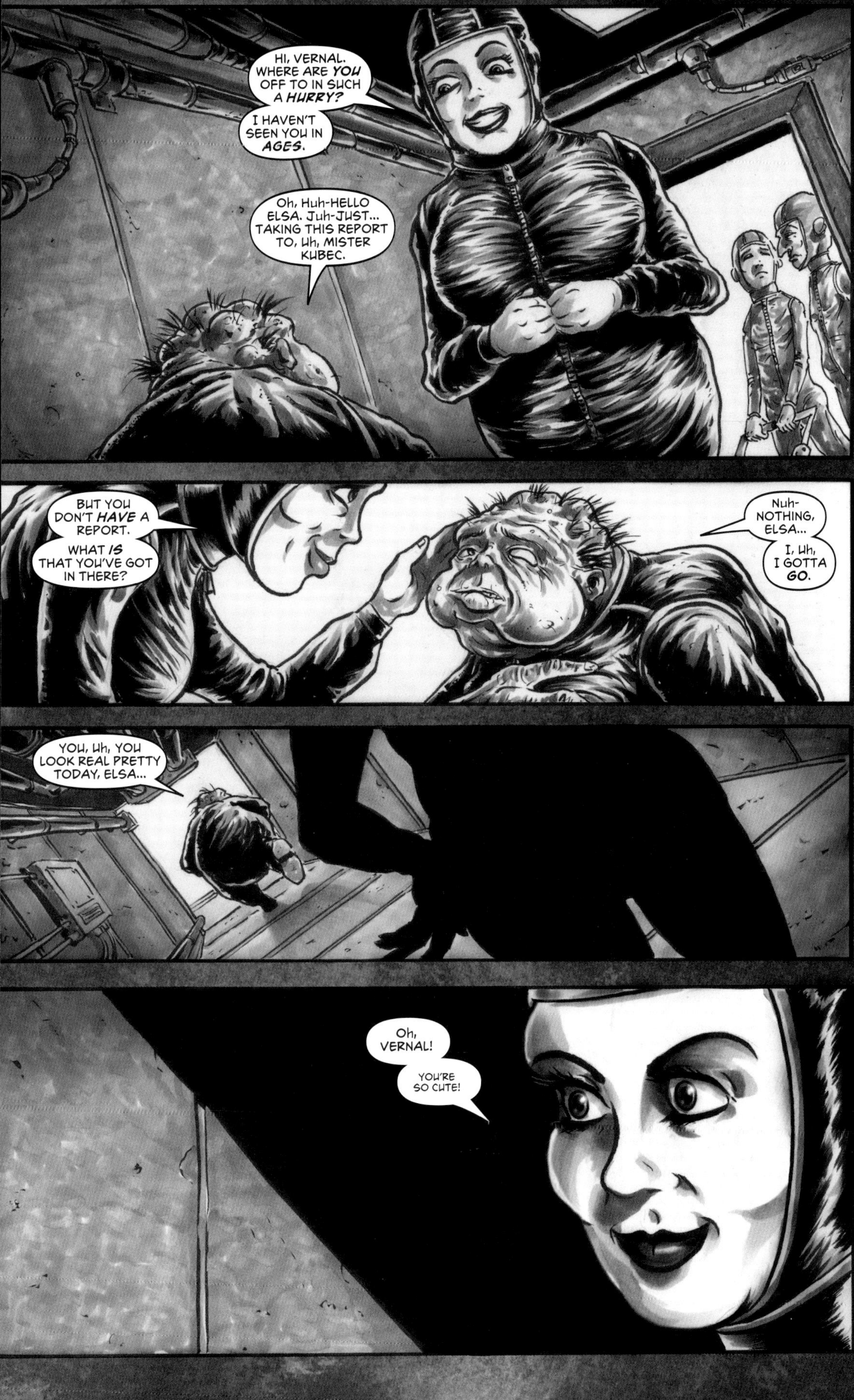

HI, VERNAL. WHERE ARE YOU OFF TO IN SUCH A HURRY?
I HAVEN'T SEEN YOU IN AGES.
Oh, Huh-HELLO ELSA. Juh-JUST... TAKING THIS REPORT TO, Uh, MISTER KUBEC.
BUT YOU DON'T HAVE A REPORT.
WHAT IS THAT YOU'VE GOT IN THERE?
Nuh-NOTHING, ELSA...
I, Uh, I GOTTA GO.
YOU, Uh, YOU LOOK REAL PRETTY TODAY, ELSA...
Oh, VERNAL!
YOU'RE SO CUTE!

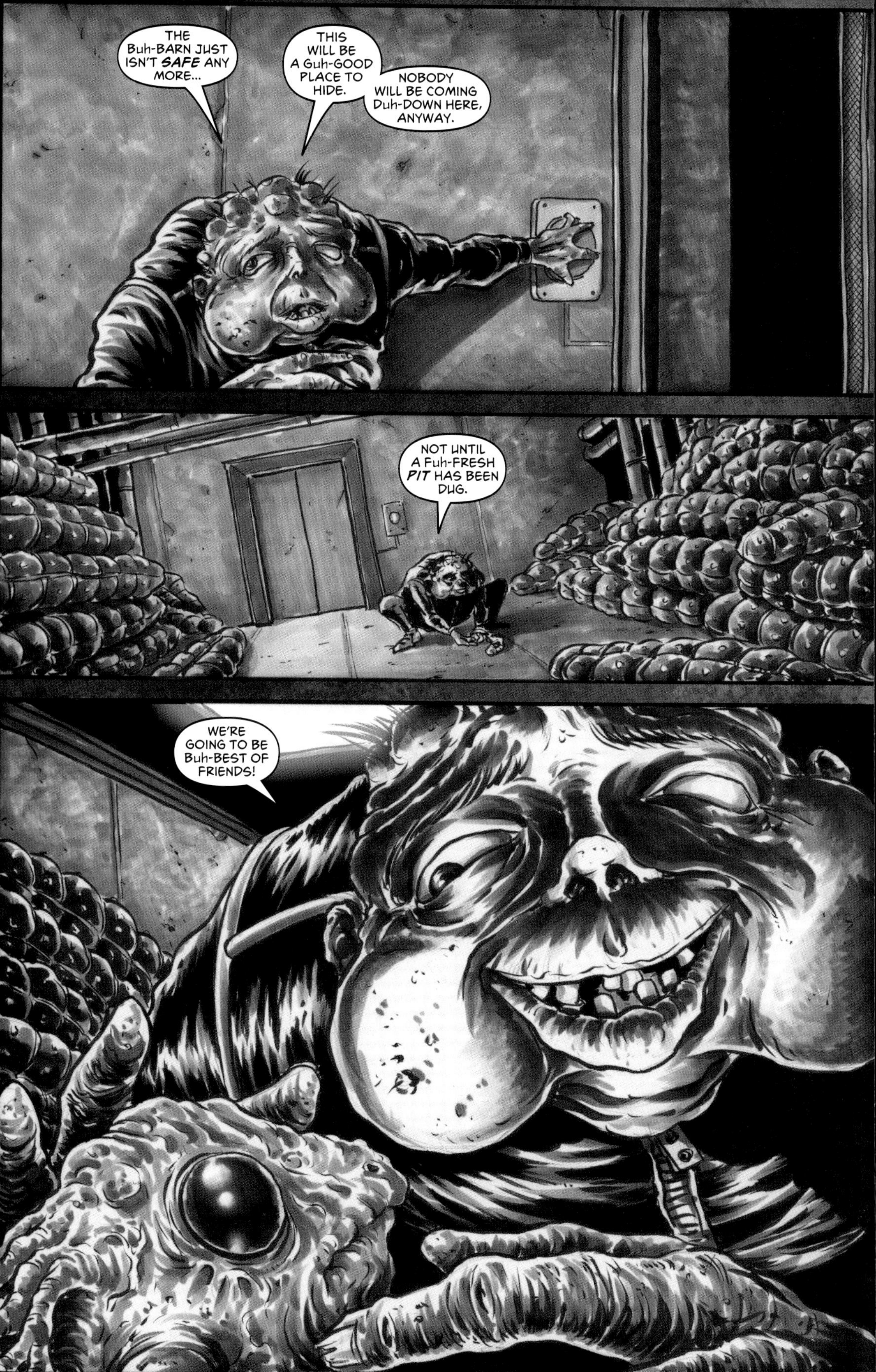
THE Buh-BARN JUST ISN'T **SAFE** ANY MORE...
THIS WILL BE A Guh-GOOD PLACE TO HIDE.
NOBODY WILL BE COMING Duh-DOWN HERE, ANYWAY.
NOT UNTIL A Fuh-FRESH **PIT** HAS BEEN DUG.
WE'RE GOING TO BE Buh-BEST OF FRIENDS!

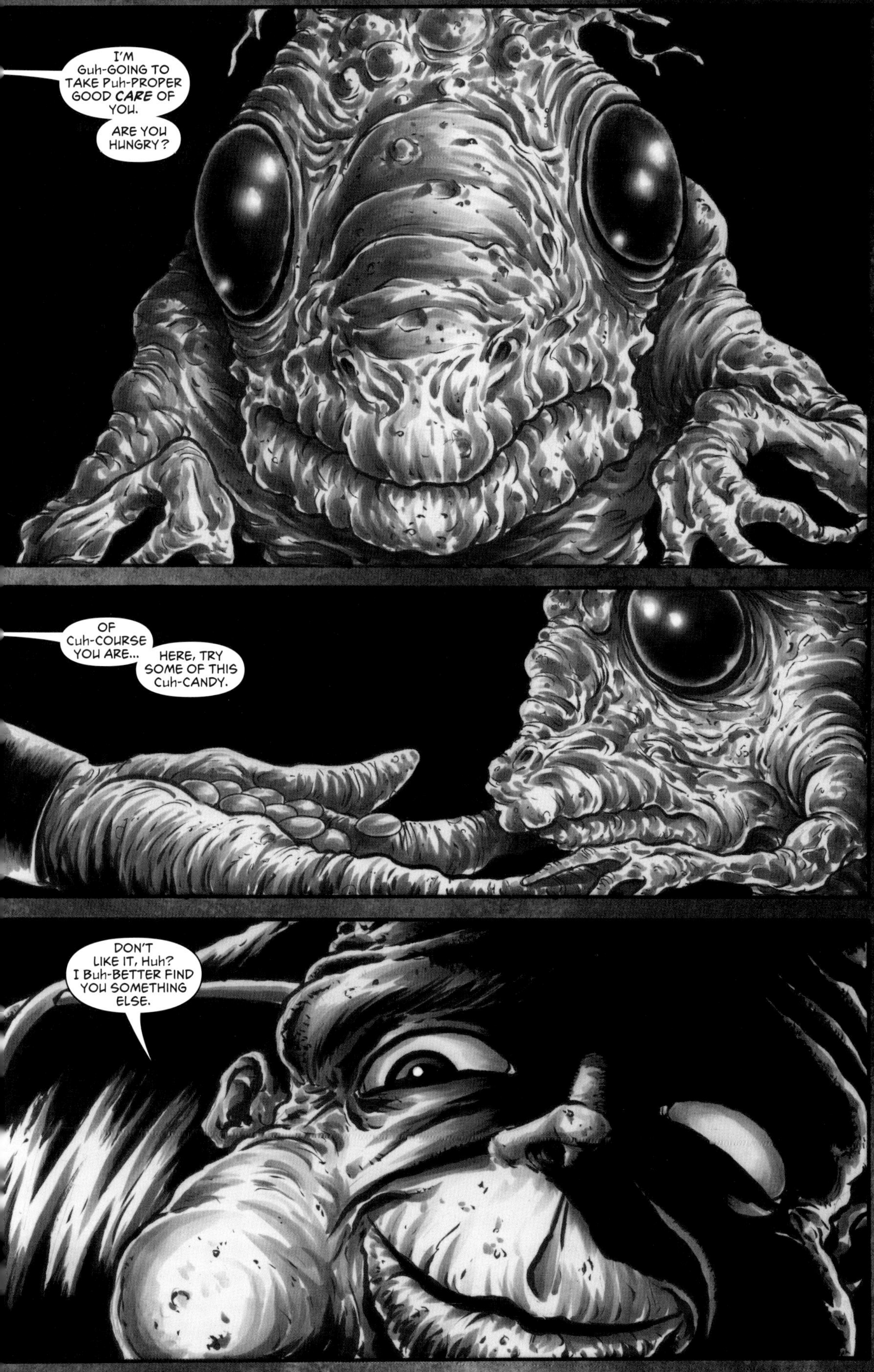
I'M Guh-GOING TO TAKE Puh-PROPER GOOD CARE OF YOU.
ARE YOU HUNGRY?
OF Cuh-COURSE YOU ARE...
HERE, TRY SOME OF THIS Cuh-CANDY.
DON'T LIKE IT, Huh? I Buh-BETTER FIND YOU SOMETHING ELSE.

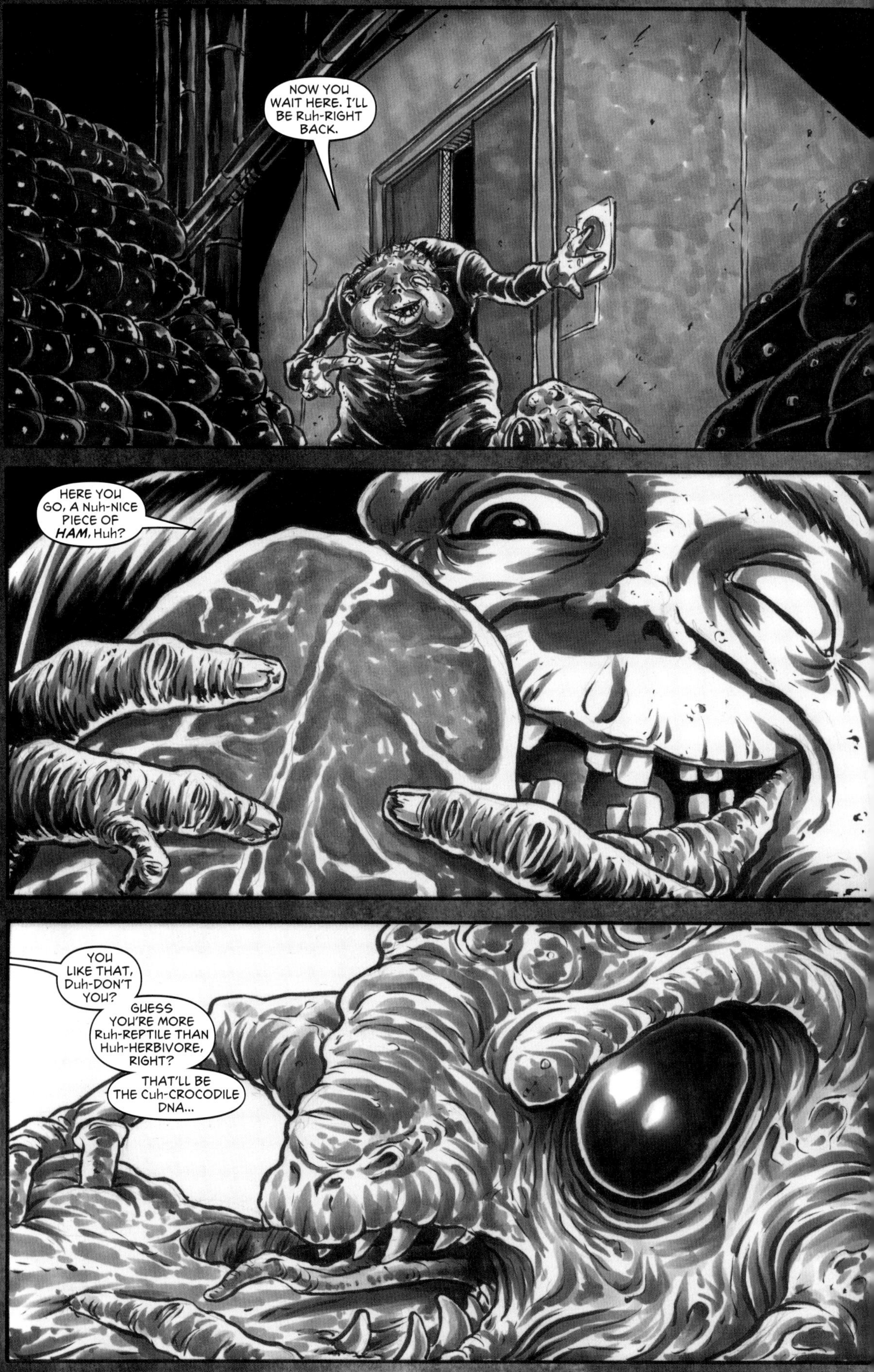
NOW YOU WAIT HERE. I'LL BE Ruh-RIGHT BACK.
HERE YOU GO, A Nuh-NICE PIECE OF HAM, Huh?
YOU LIKE THAT, Duh-DON'T YOU?
GUESS YOU'RE MORE Ruh-REPTILE THAN Huh-HERBIVORE, RIGHT?
THAT'LL BE THE Cuh-CROCODILE DNA...

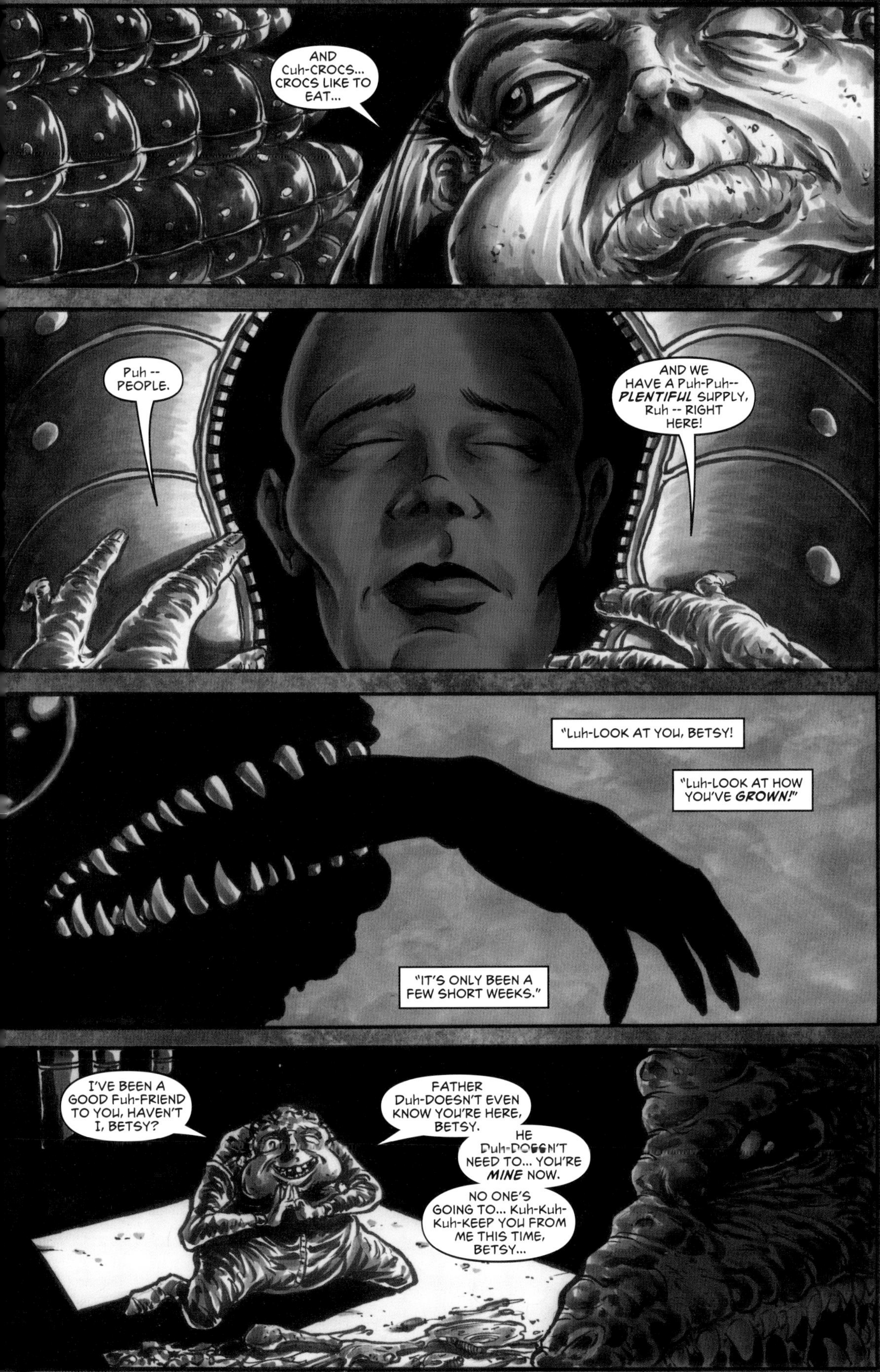
AND Cuh-CROCS... CROCS LIKE TO EAT...
Puh -- PEOPLE.
AND WE HAVE A Puh-Puh-- PLENTIFUL SUPPLY, Ruh -- RIGHT HERE!
"Luh-LOOK AT YOU, BETSY!
"Luh-LOOK AT HOW YOU'VE GROWN!"
"IT'S ONLY BEEN A FEW SHORT WEEKS."
I'VE BEEN A GOOD Fuh-FRIEND TO YOU, HAVEN'T I, BETSY?
FATHER Duh-DOESN'T EVEN KNOW YOU'RE HERE, BETSY.
HE Duh-DOESN'T NEED TO... YOU'RE MINE NOW.
NO ONE'S GOING TO... Kuh-Kuh-Kuh-KEEP YOU FROM ME THIS TIME, BETSY...

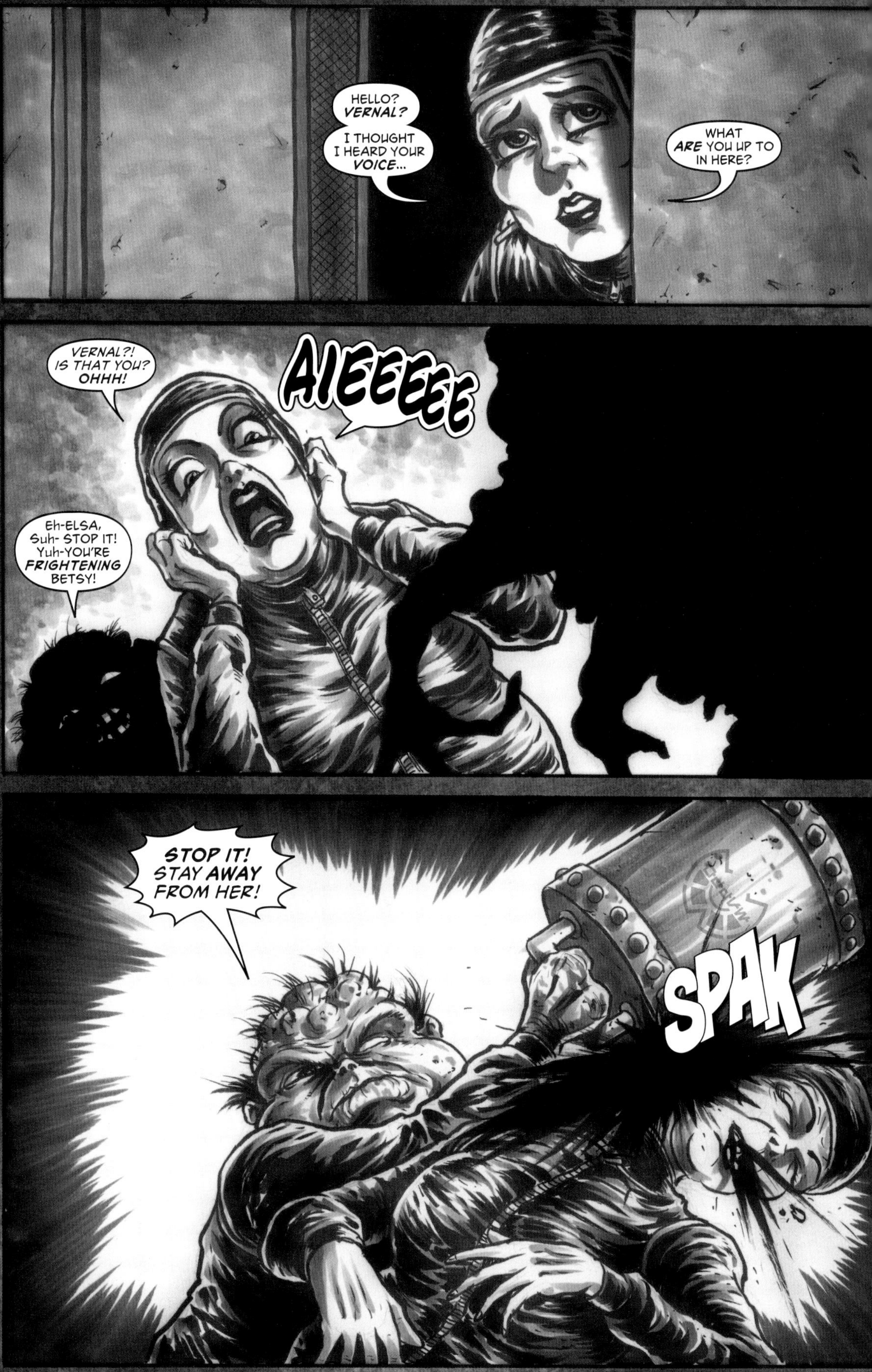

HELLO? VERNAL? I THOUGHT I HEARD YOUR VOICE...
WHAT ARE YOU UP TO IN HERE?
VERNAL?! IS THAT YOU? OHHH!
AIEEEEEE
Eh-ELSA, Suh- STOP IT! Yuh-YOU'RE FRIGHTENING BETSY!
STOP IT! STAY AWAY FROM HER!
SPAK

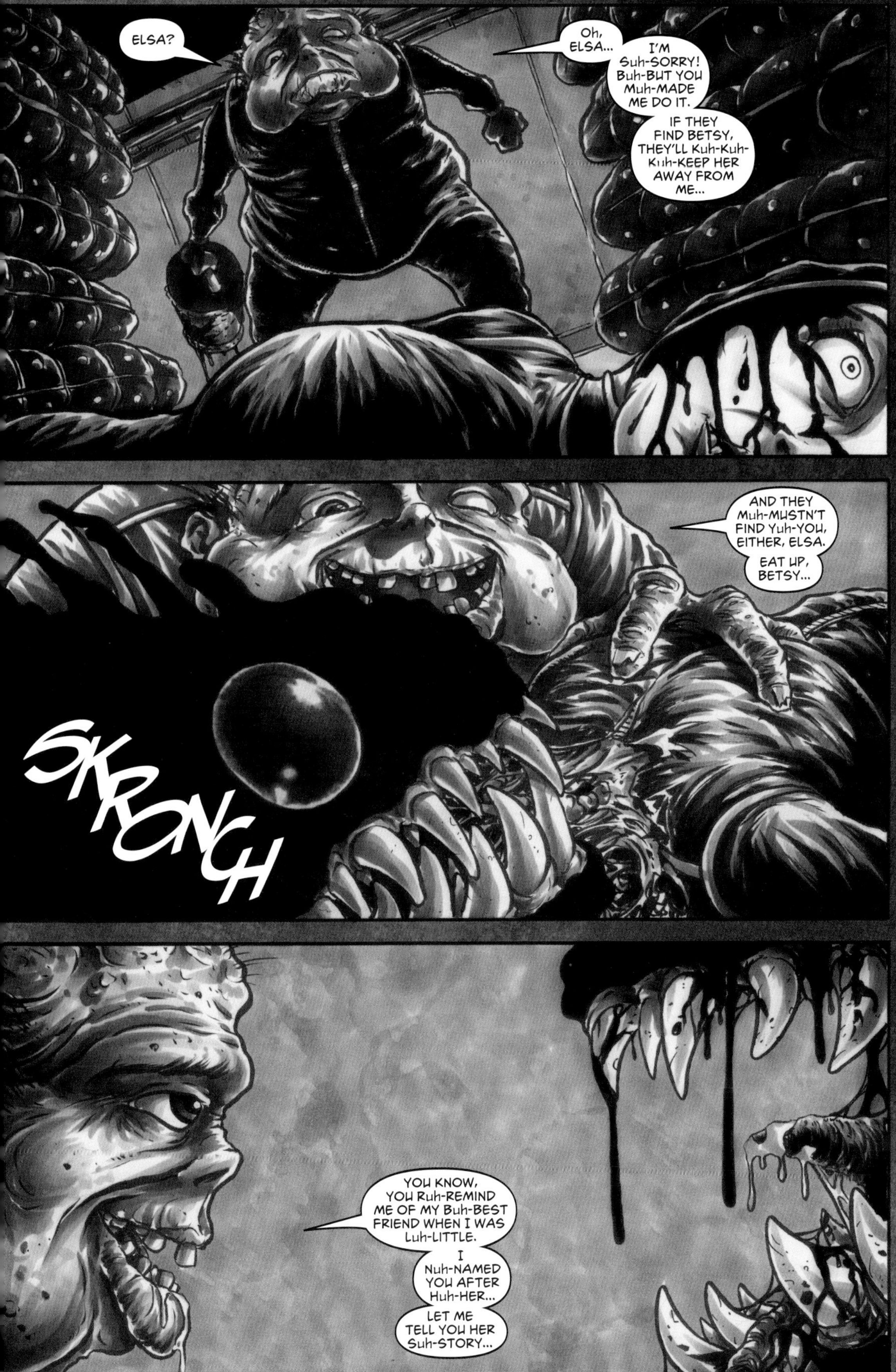
ELSA?
Oh, ELSA...
I'M Suh-SORRY! Buh-BUT YOU Muh-MADE ME DO IT.
IF THEY FIND BETSY, THEY'LL Kuh-Kuh-Kuh-KEEP HER AWAY FROM ME...
AND THEY Muh-MUSTN'T FIND Yuh-YOU, EITHER, ELSA.
EAT UP, BETSY...
SKRONCH
YOU KNOW, YOU Ruh-REMIND ME OF MY Buh-BEST FRIEND WHEN I WAS Luh-LITTLE.
I Nuh-NAMED YOU AFTER Huh-HER...
LET ME TELL YOU HER Suh-STORY...

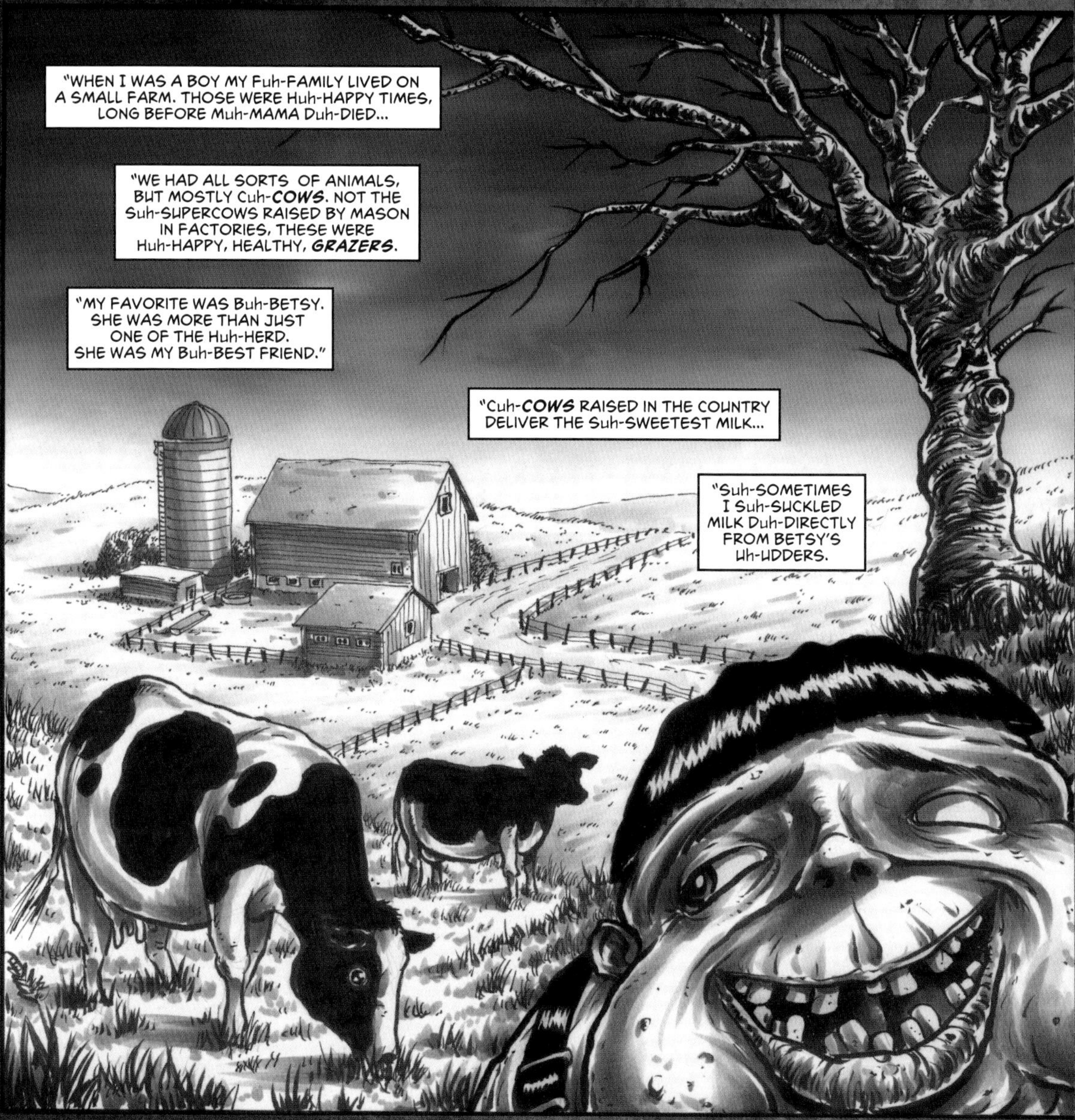
"WHEN I WAS A BOY MY Fuh-FAMILY LIVED ON A SMALL FARM. THOSE WERE Huh-HAPPY TIMES, LONG BEFORE Muh-MAMA Duh-DIED...
"WE HAD ALL SORTS OF ANIMALS, BUT MOSTLY Cuh-COWS. NOT THE Suh-SUPERCOWS RAISED BY MASON IN FACTORIES, THESE WERE Huh-HAPPY, HEALTHY, GRAZERS.
"MY FAVORITE WAS Buh-BETSY. SHE WAS MORE THAN JUST ONE OF THE Huh-HERD. SHE WAS MY Buh-BEST FRIEND."
"Cuh-COWS RAISED IN THE COUNTRY DELIVER THE Suh-SWEETEST MILK...
"Suh-SOMETIMES I Suh-SUCKLED MILK Duh-DIRECTLY FROM BETSY'S Uh-UDDERS.

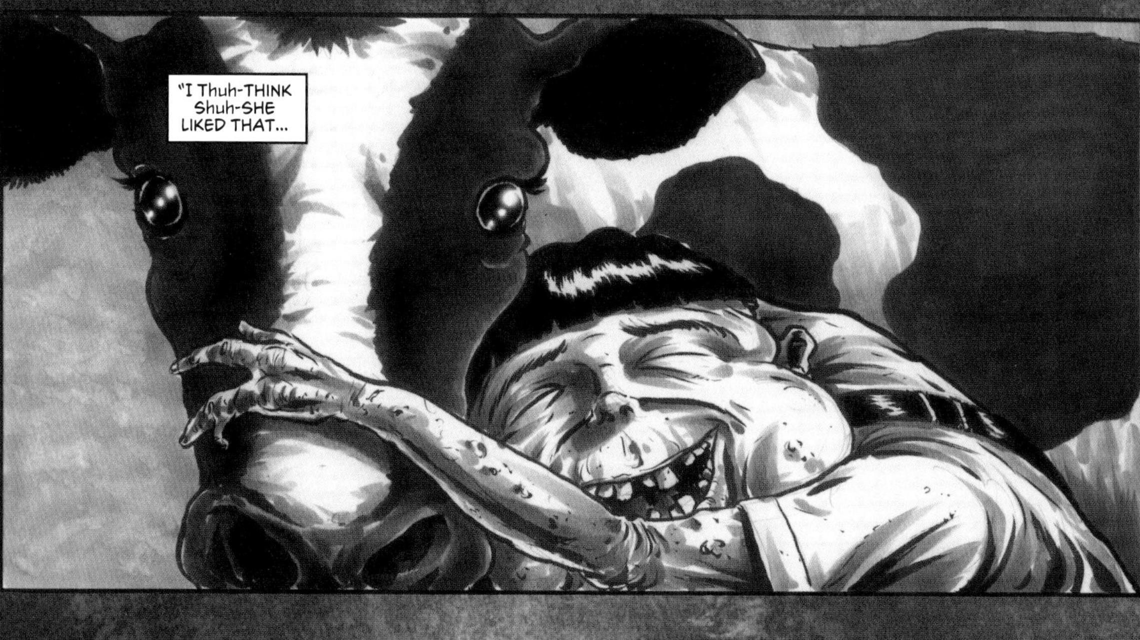
"I Thuh-THINK Shuh-SHE LIKED THAT...

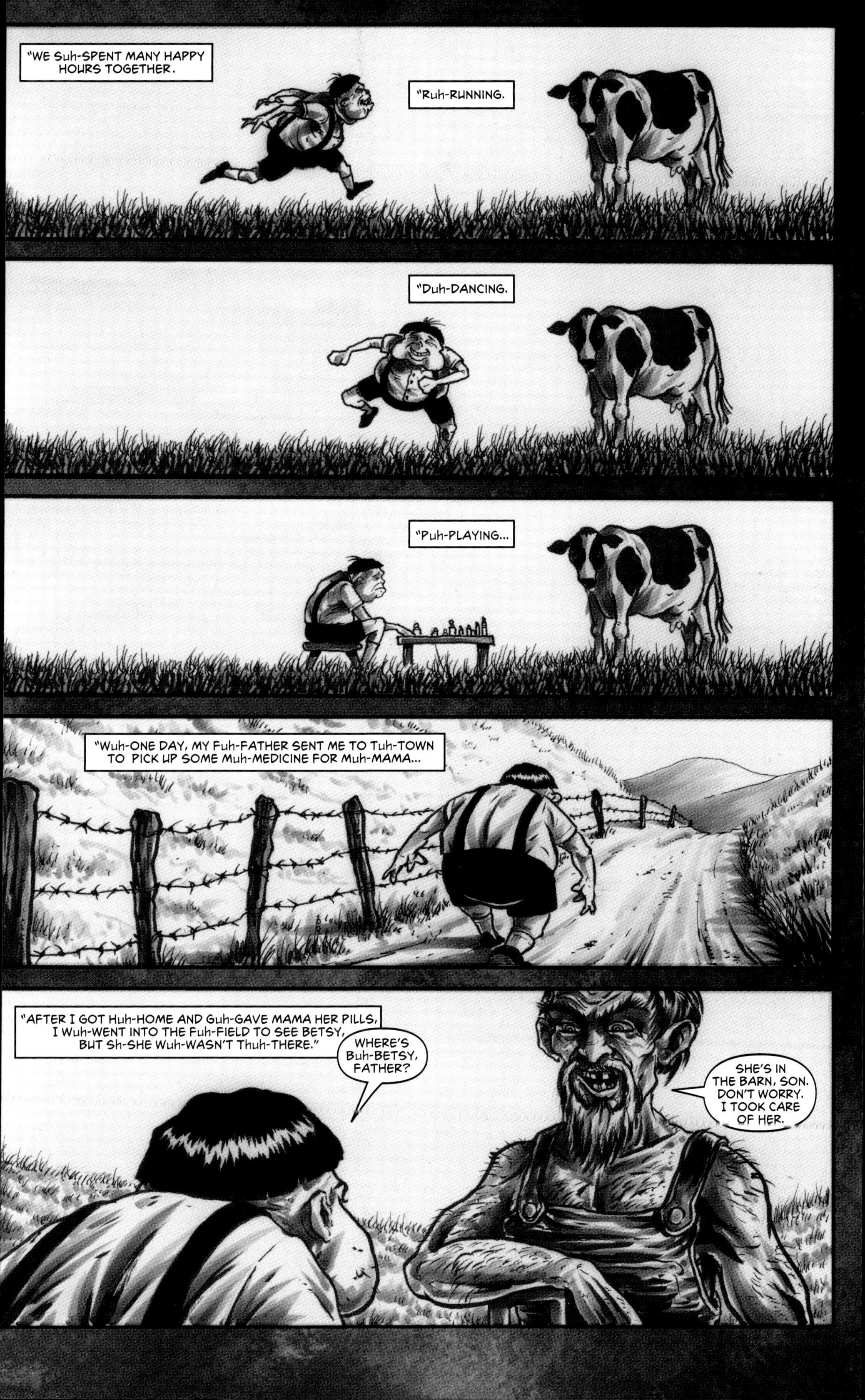
"WE Suh-SPENT MANY HAPPY HOURS TOGETHER.
"Ruh-RUNNING.
"Duh-DANCING.
"Puh-PLAYING...
"Wuh-ONE DAY, MY Fuh-FATHER SENT ME TO Tuh-TOWN TO PICK UP SOME Muh-MEDICINE FOR Muh-MAMA...
"AFTER I GOT Huh-HOME AND Guh-GAVE MAMA HER PILLS, I Wuh-WENT INTO THE Fuh-FIELD TO SEE BETSY, BUT Sh-SHE Wuh-WASN'T Thuh-THERE."
WHERE'S Buh-BETSY, FATHER?
SHE'S IN THE BARN, SON. DON'T WORRY. I TOOK CARE OF HER.

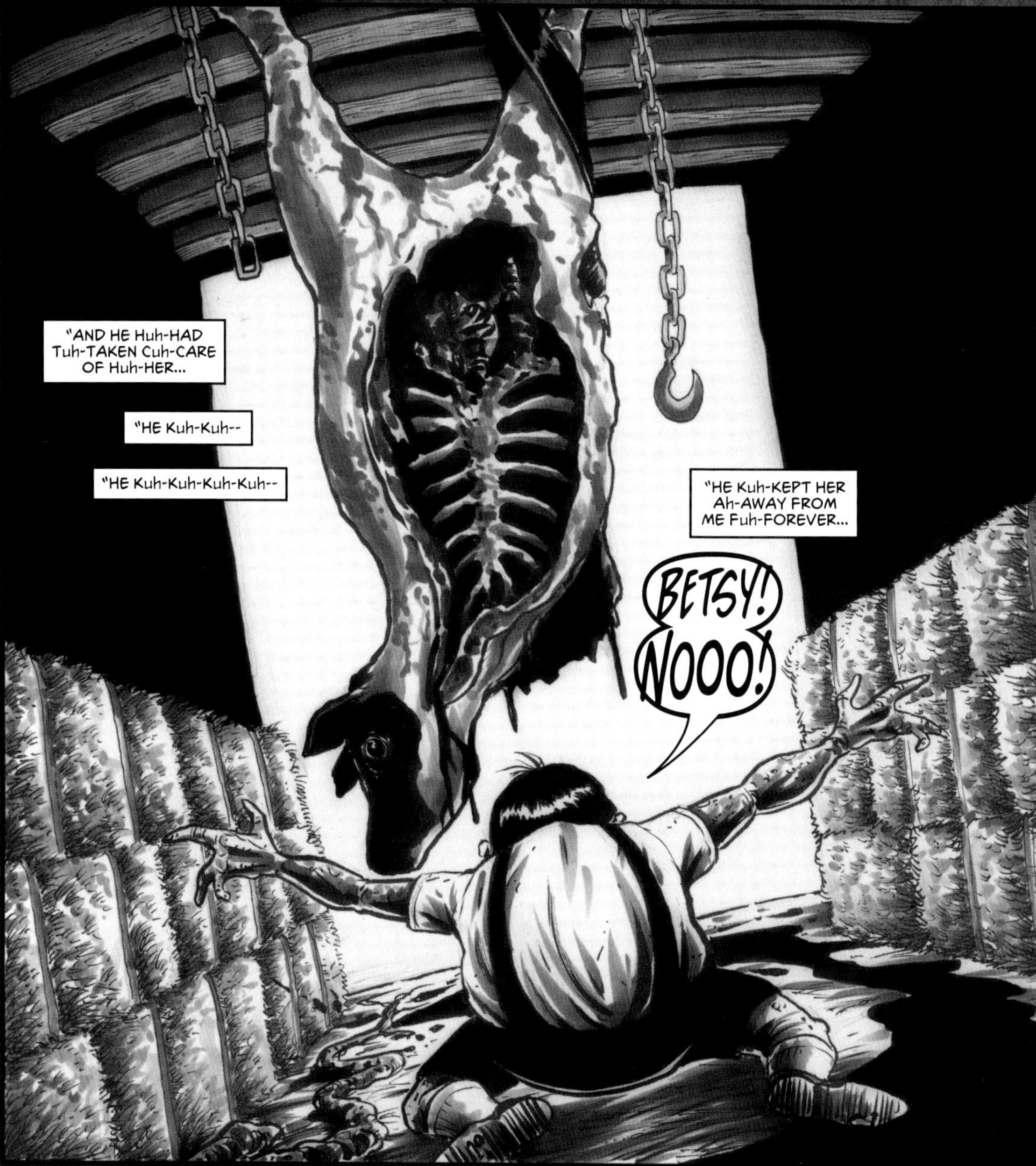
"AND HE Huh-HAD Tuh-TAKEN Cuh-CARE OF Huh-HER...
"HE Kuh-Kuh--
"HE Kuh-Kuh-Kuh-Kuh--
"HE Kuh-KEPT HER Ah-AWAY FROM ME Fuh-FOREVER...
BETSY! NOOO!

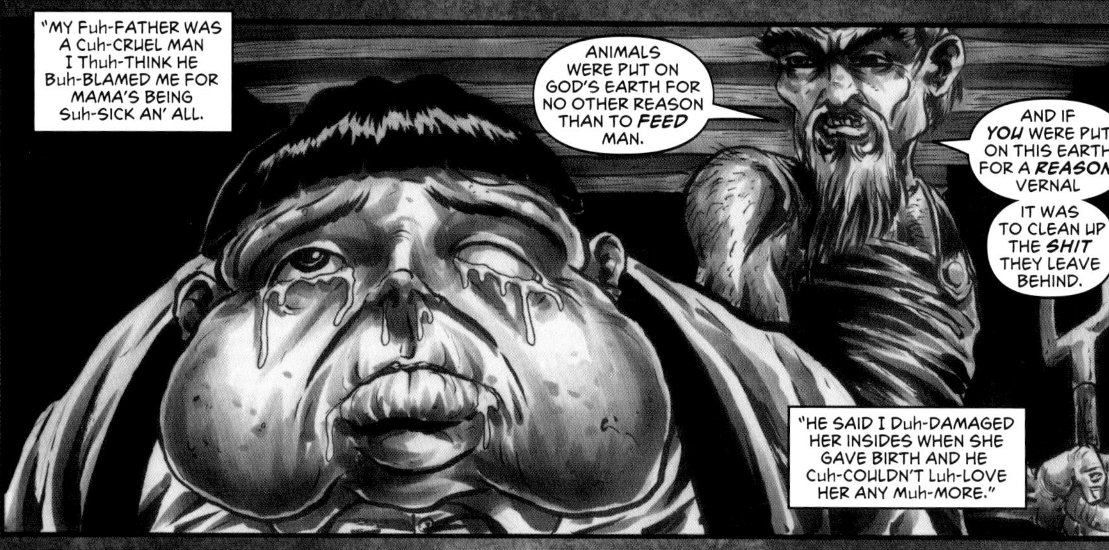
"MY Fuh-FATHER WAS A Cuh-CRUEL MAN I Thuh-THINK HE Buh-BLAMED ME FOR MAMA'S BEING Suh-SICK AN' ALL.
ANIMALS WERE PUT ON GOD'S EARTH FOR NO OTHER REASON THAN TO FEED MAN.
AND IF YOU WERE PUT ON THIS EARTH FOR A REASON, VERNAL
IT WAS TO CLEAN UP THE SHIT THEY LEAVE BEHIND.
"HE SAID I Duh-DAMAGED HER INSIDES WHEN SHE GAVE BIRTH AND HE Cuh-COULDN'T Luh-LOVE HER ANY Muh-MORE."

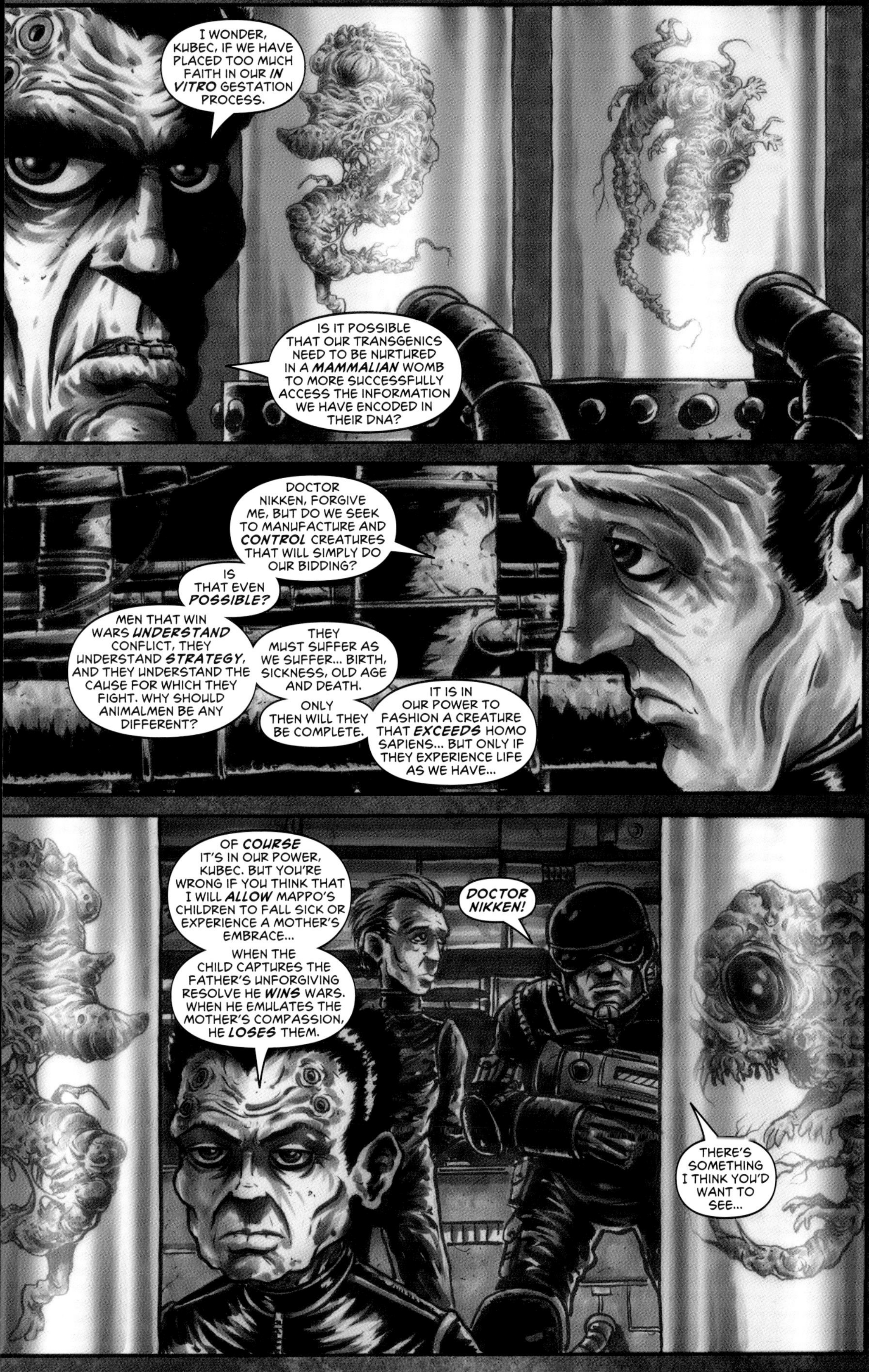

I WONDER, KUBEC, IF WE HAVE PLACED TOO MUCH FAITH IN OUR IN VITRO GESTATION PROCESS.
IS IT POSSIBLE THAT OUR TRANSGENICS NEED TO BE NURTURED IN A MAMMALIAN WOMB TO MORE SUCCESSFULLY ACCESS THE INFORMATION WE HAVE ENCODED IN THEIR DNA?
DOCTOR NIKKEN, FORGIVE ME, BUT DO WE SEEK TO MANUFACTURE AND CONTROL CREATURES THAT WILL SIMPLY DO OUR BIDDING?
IS THAT EVEN POSSIBLE?
MEN THAT WIN WARS UNDERSTAND CONFLICT, THEY UNDERSTAND STRATEGY, AND THEY UNDERSTAND THE CAUSE FOR WHICH THEY FIGHT. WHY SHOULD ANIMALMEN BE ANY DIFFERENT?
THEY MUST SUFFER AS WE SUFFER... BIRTH, SICKNESS, OLD AGE AND DEATH.
ONLY THEN WILL THEY BE COMPLETE.
IT IS IN OUR POWER TO FASHION A CREATURE THAT EXCEEDS HOMO SAPIENS... BUT ONLY IF THEY EXPERIENCE LIFE AS WE HAVE...
OF COURSE IT'S IN OUR POWER, KUBEC. BUT YOU'RE WRONG IF YOU THINK THAT I WILL ALLOW MAPPO'S CHILDREN TO FALL SICK OR EXPERIENCE A MOTHER'S EMBRACE...
WHEN THE CHILD CAPTURES THE FATHER'S UNFORGIVING RESOLVE HE WINS WARS. WHEN HE EMULATES THE MOTHER'S COMPASSION, HE LOSES THEM.
DOCTOR NIKKEN!
THERE'S SOMETHING I THINK YOU'D WANT TO SEE...

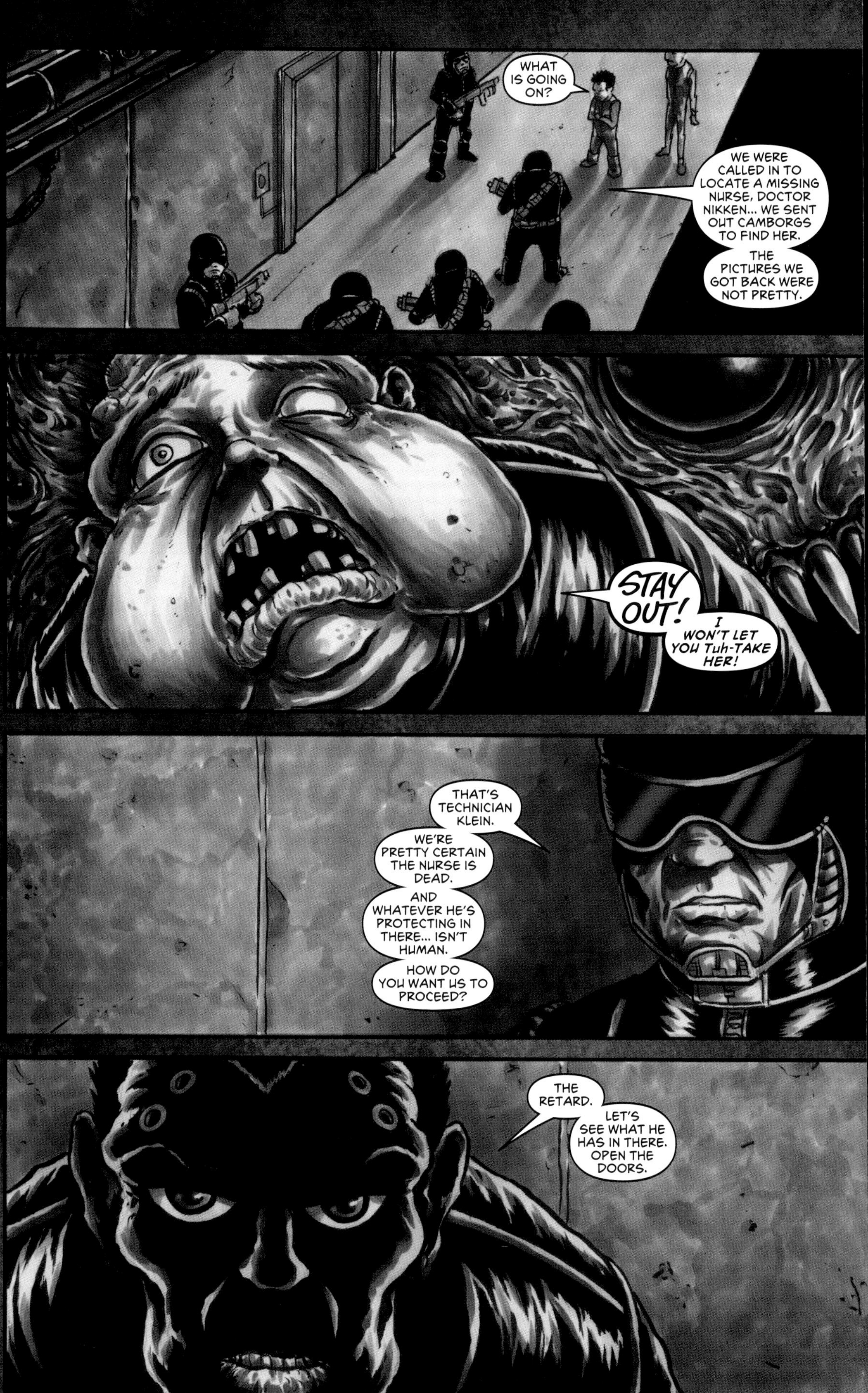
WHAT IS GOING ON?
WE WERE CALLED IN TO LOCATE A MISSING NURSE, DOCTOR NIKKEN... WE SENT OUT CAMBORGS TO FIND HER.
THE PICTURES WE GOT BACK WERE NOT PRETTY.
STAY OUT!
I WON'T LET YOU Tuh-TAKE HER!
THAT'S TECHNICIAN KLEIN.
WE'RE PRETTY CERTAIN THE NURSE IS DEAD.
AND WHATEVER HE'S PROTECTING IN THERE... ISN'T HUMAN.
HOW DO YOU WANT US TO PROCEED?
THE RETARD.
LET'S SEE WHAT HE HAS IN THERE. OPEN THE DOORS.

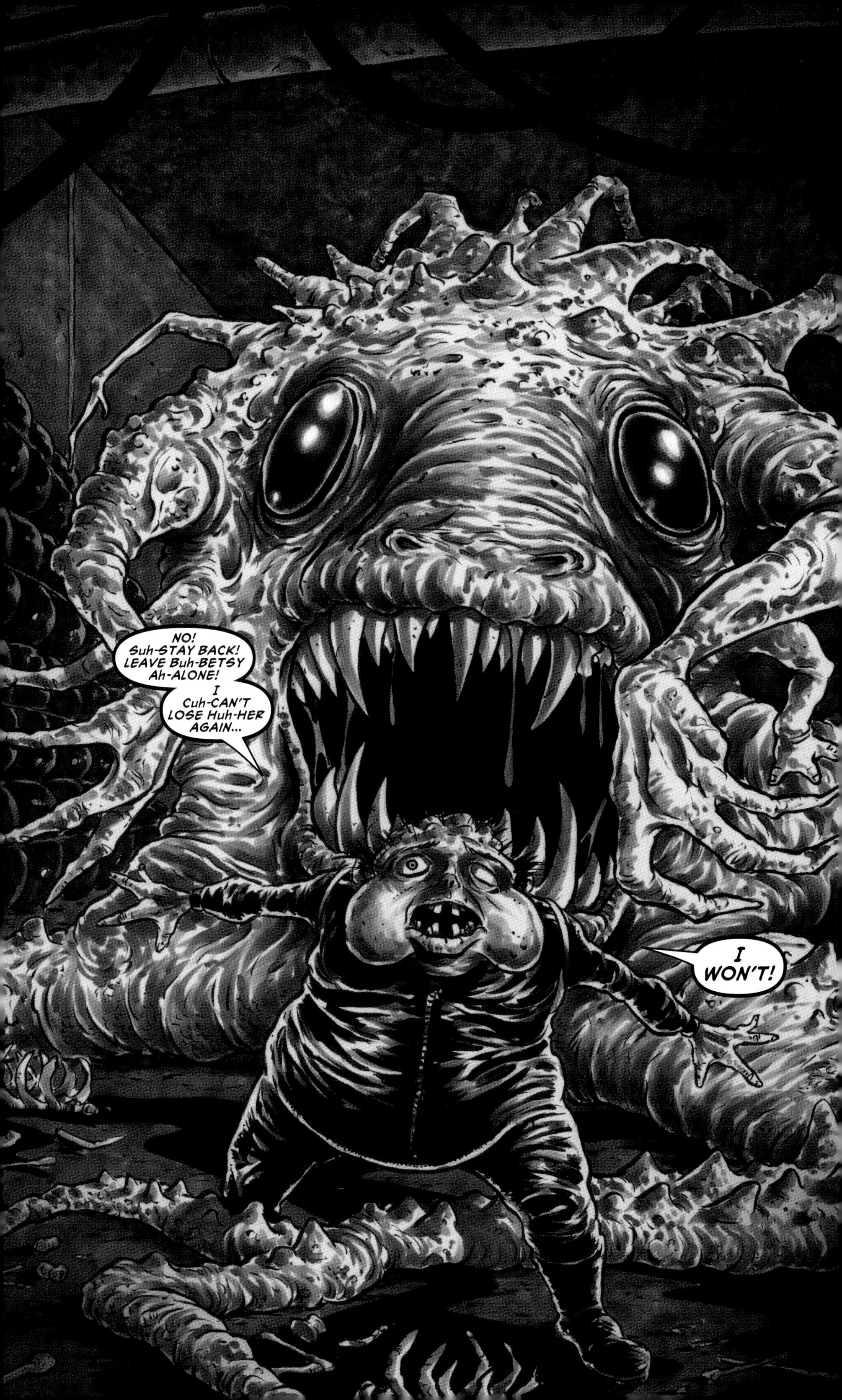
NO! Suh-STAY BACK! LEAVE Buh-BETSY Ah-ALONE!
I Cuh-CAN'T LOSE Huh-HER AGAIN...
I WON'T!

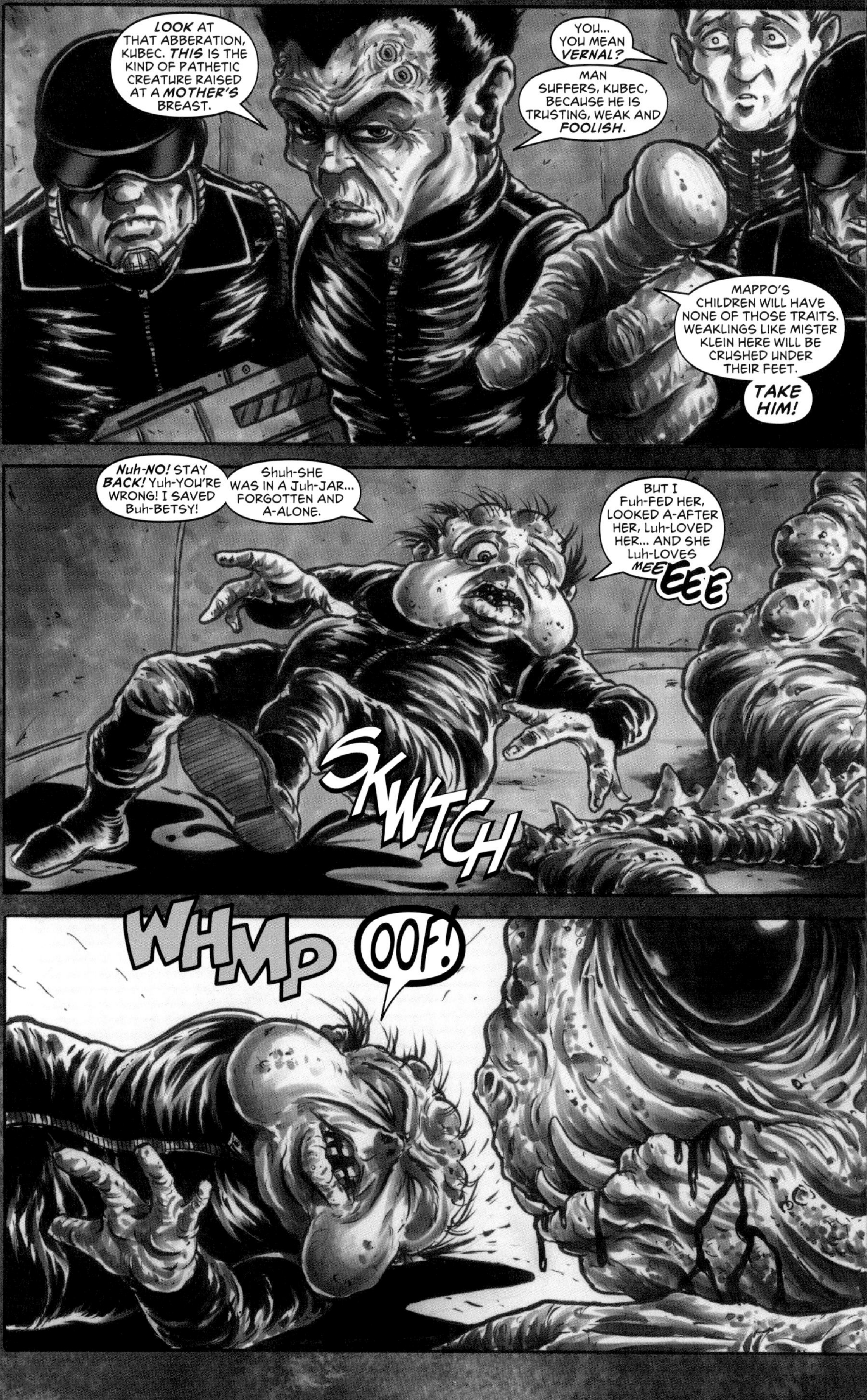
LOOK AT THAT ABBERATION, KUBEC. THIS IS THE KIND OF PATHETIC CREATURE RAISED AT A MOTHER'S BREAST.
YOU... YOU MEAN VERNAL?
MAN SUFFERS, KUBEC, BECAUSE HE IS TRUSTING, WEAK AND FOOLISH.
MAPPO'S CHILDREN WILL HAVE NONE OF THOSE TRAITS. WEAKLINGS LIKE MISTER KLEIN HERE WILL BE CRUSHED UNDER THEIR FEET.
TAKE HIM!
Nuh-NO! STAY BACK! Yuh-YOU'RE WRONG! I SAVED Buh-BETSY!
Shuh-SHE WAS IN A Juh-JAR... FORGOTTEN AND A-ALONE.
BUT I Fuh-FED HER, LOOKED A-AFTER HER, Luh-LOVED HER... AND SHE Luh-LOVES MEEEEE
SKWTCH
WHMP
OOF!

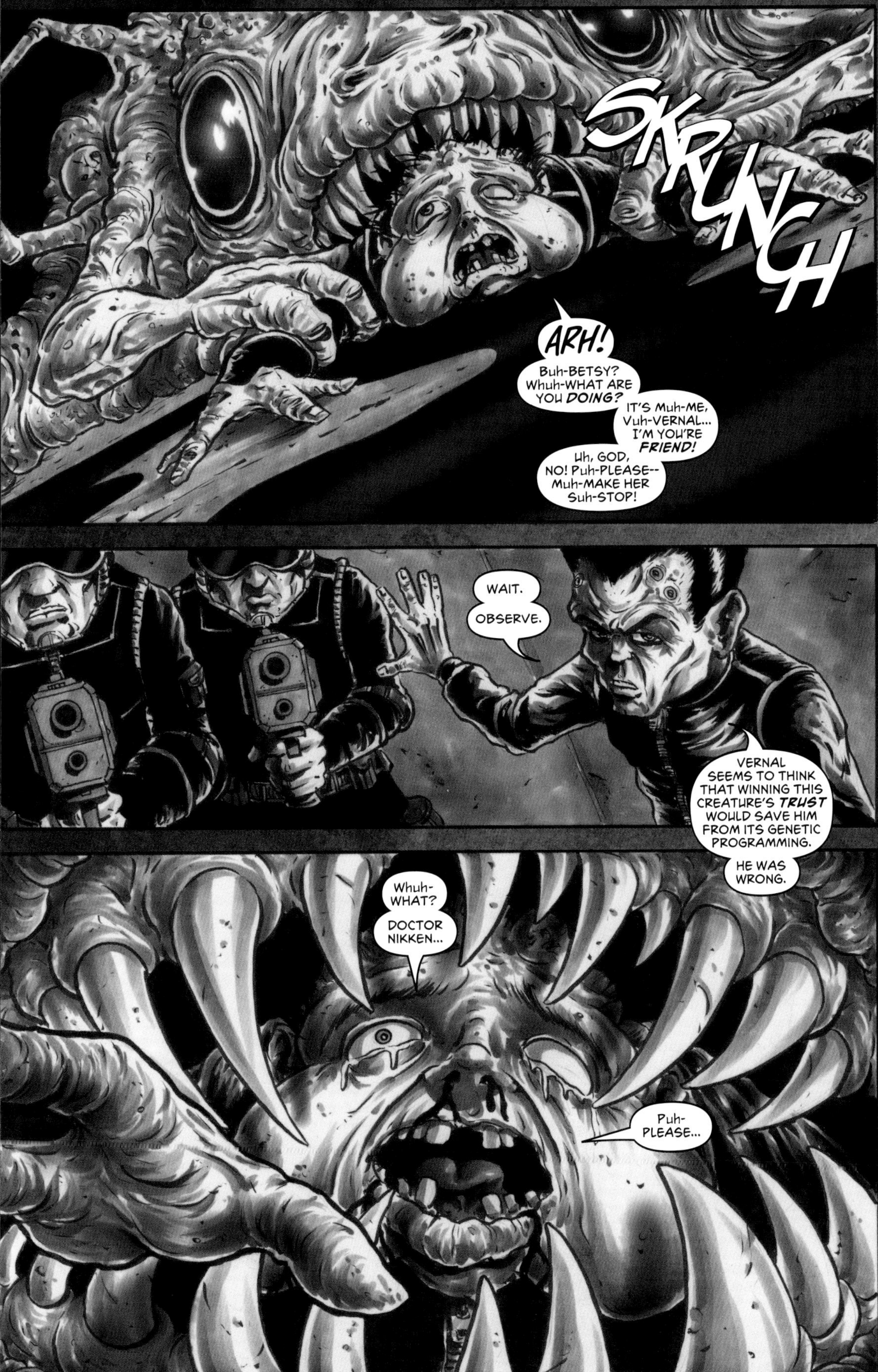
SKRUNCH
ARH!
Buh-BETSY? Whuh-WHAT ARE YOU DOING?
IT'S Muh-ME, Vuh-VERNAL... I'M YOU'RE FRIEND!
Uh, GOD, NO! Puh-PLEASE-- Muh-MAKE HER Suh-STOP!
WAIT.
OBSERVE.
VERNAL SEEMS TO THINK THAT WINNING THIS CREATURE'S TRUST WOULD SAVE HIM FROM ITS GENETIC PROGRAMMING.
HE WAS WRONG.
Whuh-WHAT?
DOCTOR NIKKEN...
Puh-PLEASE...

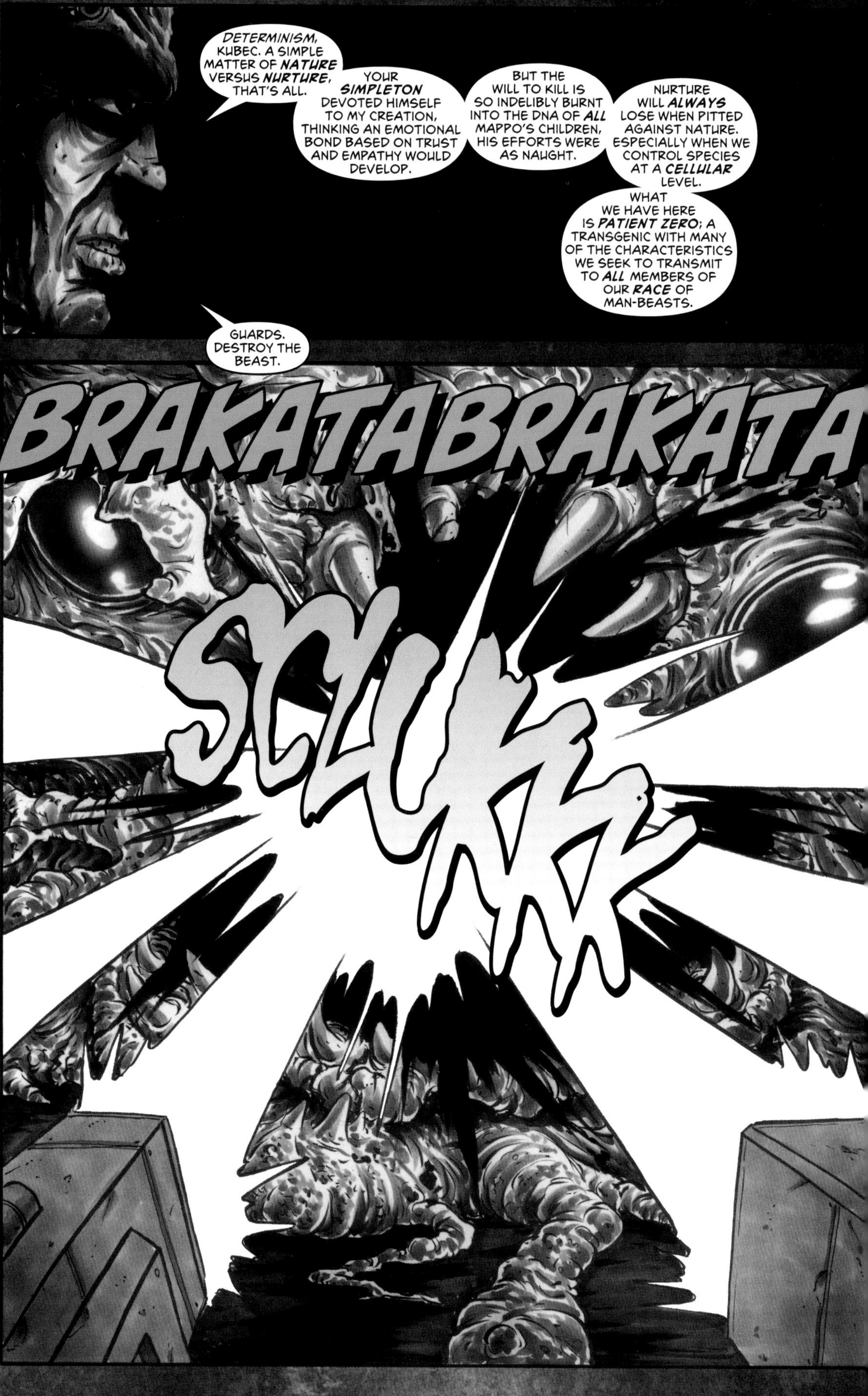
DETERMINISM, KUBEC. A SIMPLE MATTER OF NATURE VERSUS NURTURE, THAT'S ALL.
YOUR SIMPLETON DEVOTED HIMSELF TO MY CREATION, THINKING AN EMOTIONAL BOND BASED ON TRUST AND EMPATHY WOULD DEVELOP.
BUT THE WILL TO KILL IS SO INDELIBLY BURNT INTO THE DNA OF ALL MAPPO'S CHILDREN, HIS EFFORTS WERE AS NAUGHT.
NURTURE WILL ALWAYS LOSE WHEN PITTED AGAINST NATURE. ESPECIALLY WHEN WE CONTROL SPECIES AT A CELLULAR LEVEL.
WHAT WE HAVE HERE IS PATIENT ZERO; A TRANSGENIC WITH MANY OF THE CHARACTERISTICS WE SEEK TO TRANSMIT TO ALL MEMBERS OF OUR RACE OF MAN-BEASTS.
GUARDS. DESTROY THE BEAST.
BRAKATABRAKATA
SCLUKKK

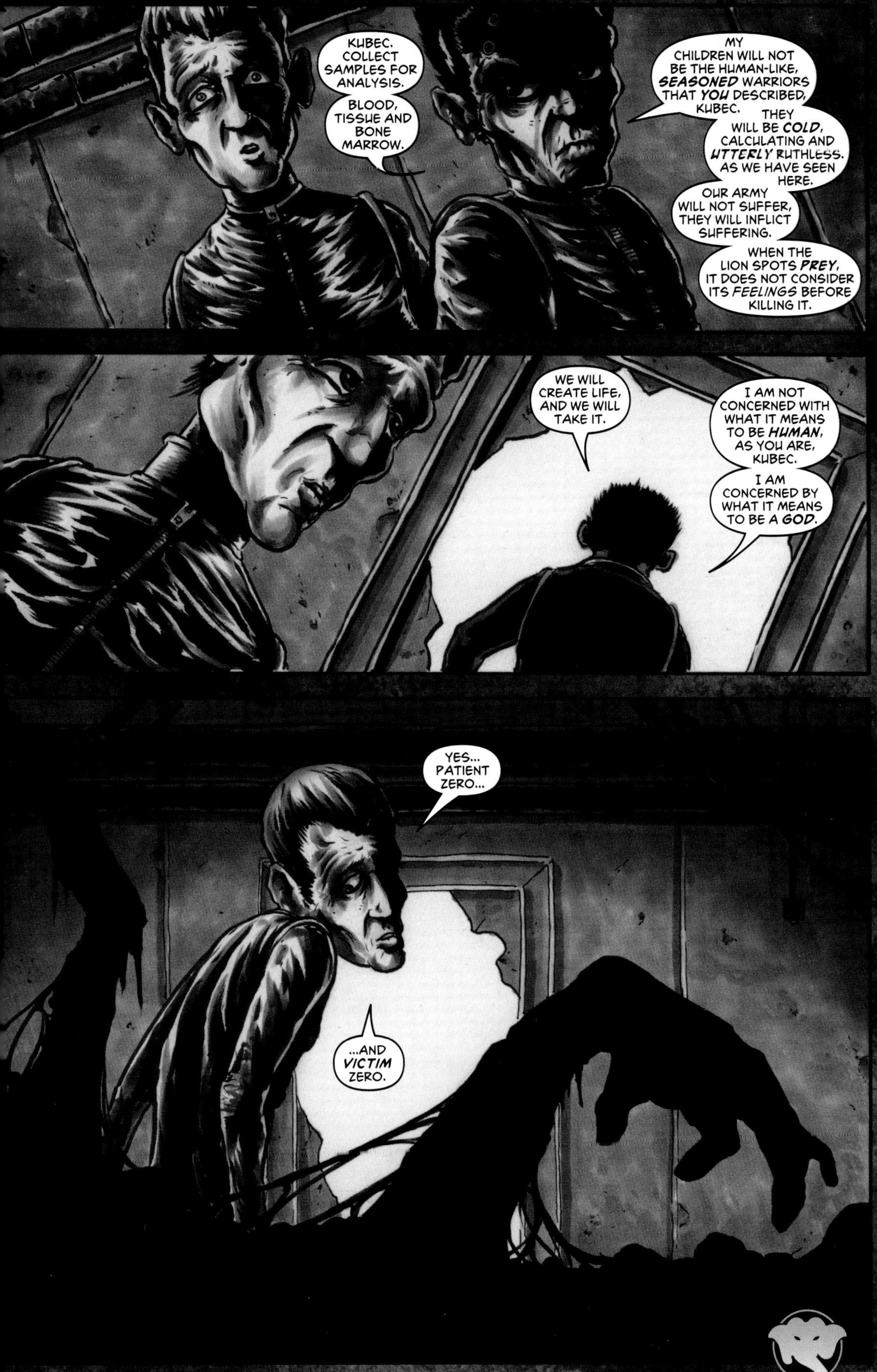
KUBEC. COLLECT SAMPLES FOR ANALYSIS.
BLOOD, TISSUE AND BONE MARROW.
MY CHILDREN WILL NOT BE THE HUMAN-LIKE, SEASONED WARRIORS THAT YOU DESCRIBED, KUBEC.
THEY WILL BE COLD, CALCULATING AND UTTERLY RUTHLESS. AS WE HAVE SEEN HERE.
OUR ARMY WILL NOT SUFFER, THEY WILL INFLICT SUFFERING.
WHEN THE LION SPOTS PREY, IT DOES NOT CONSIDER ITS FEELINGS BEFORE KILLING IT.
WE WILL CREATE LIFE, AND WE WILL TAKE IT.
I AM NOT CONCERNED WITH WHAT IT MEANS TO BE HUMAN, AS YOU ARE, KUBEC.
I AM CONCERNED BY WHAT IT MEANS TO BE A GOD.
YES... PATIENT ZERO...
...AND VICTIM ZERO.

Originally presented in ELEPHANTMEN #36-40

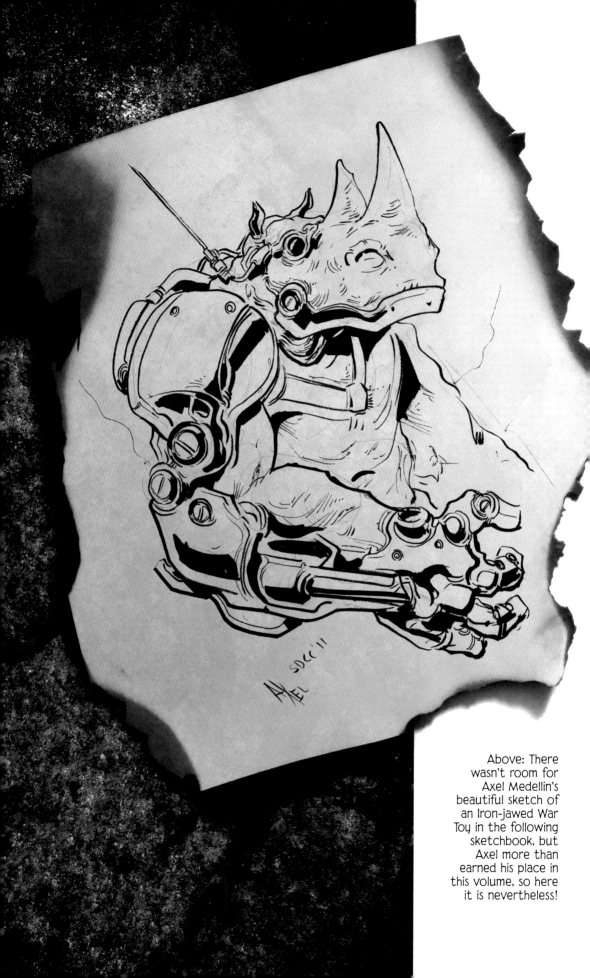

Above: There wasn't room for Axel Medellin's beautiful sketch of an Iron-jawed War Toy in the following sketchbook, but Axel more than earned his place in this volume, so here it is nevertheless!

DEADLIER OF THE SPECIES:
TOYS AND GIRLS

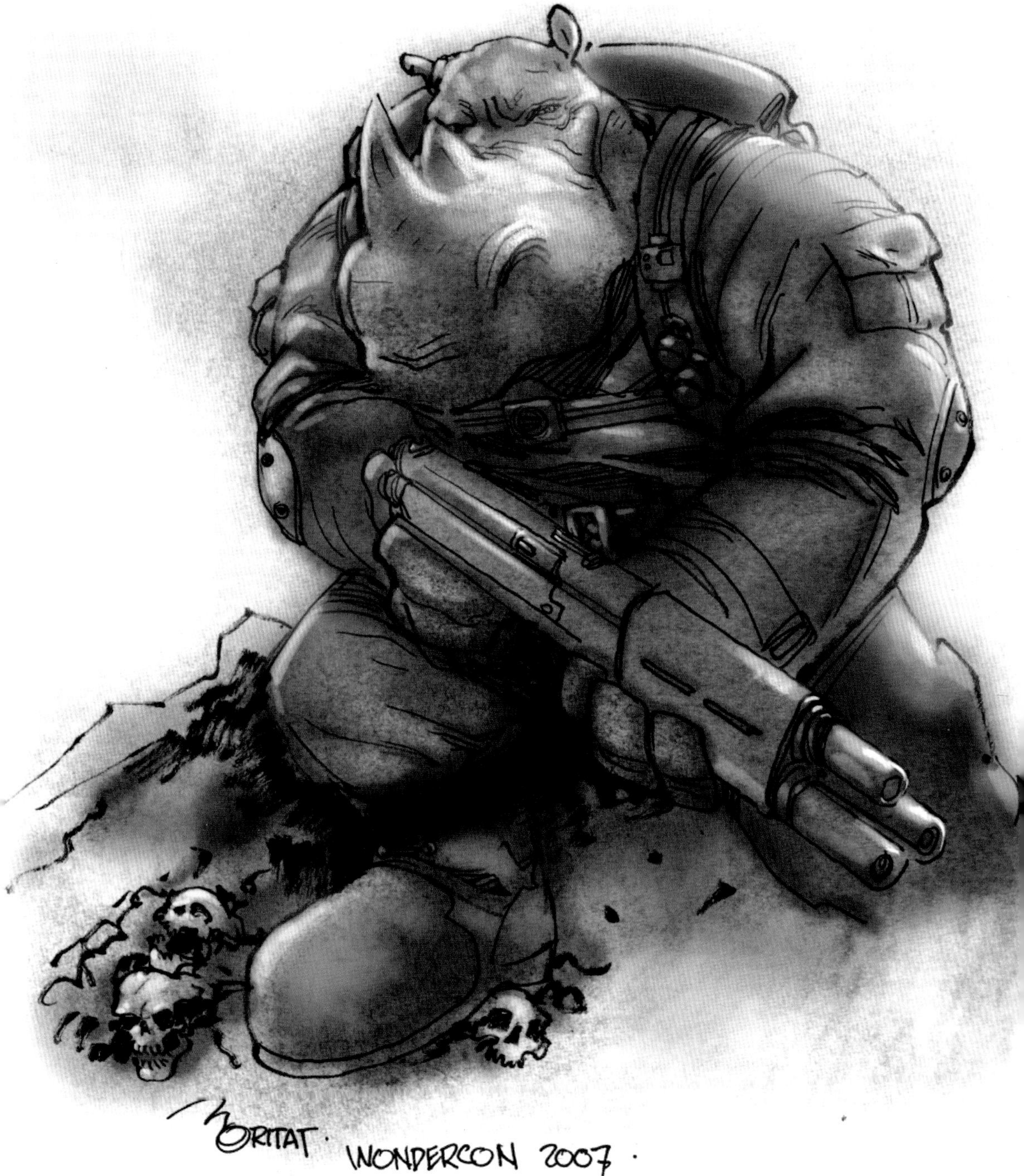
MORITAT. WONDERCON 2007.

By **RICHARD STARKINGS**

ELEPHANTMEN: WAR TOYS ISSUE #1:
BAND OF MONSTERS!

FEATURING THE ELEPHANTMEN

By RICHARD STARKINGS for MORITAT!

22 pages BLACK AND WHITE

9/21/07-9/25/07

I'm often asked why YVETTE, THE Central Character in the ARMED FORCES stories, didn't appear on the covers of the first WAR TOYS series.. There's a Very Good Reason for this; when I wrote the story outline for issue #1, she simply didn't exist.

PAGE 20

The MAPPO flag is raised, Iwo Jima style.

CAPTION: They were a Band of MONSTERS!

PAGE 21-22

Keiko, with baby Miki, stands in a long line of frightened people to board a small UN ferry boat at a port on the west coast of France. She's allowed on board as others are turned away and finally stands at the back of a boat looking back at the west coast of France. Others huddle together near her looking bedraggled and tired.

CAPTION: Some were lucky, and escaped the invasion of the Elephantmen in boats or planes.

Several shots of the dead in the mud -- Hideo and many Frenchm women and children, their faces frozen in fear, eyes wide.

CAPTION: Most of those who encountered the Elephantmen died

Two French resistance fighters watch the Elephantmen around flag from a hiding place in the surrounding hills and bushes. O raises a rifle to shoot at Hip (we see him in the crosshairs) but raises his hand to indicate he should lower the rifle.

CAPTION: But some survived.
CAPTION: They had already survived the most devastating dise known to man since the Black Death.
CAPTION: They figured this would be easier.

We follow these two men as they run across a poppyfield a to a muddy tract of land where we finally see a long trench reminiscent of WWI being dug.

CAPTION: And so they started digging trenches.

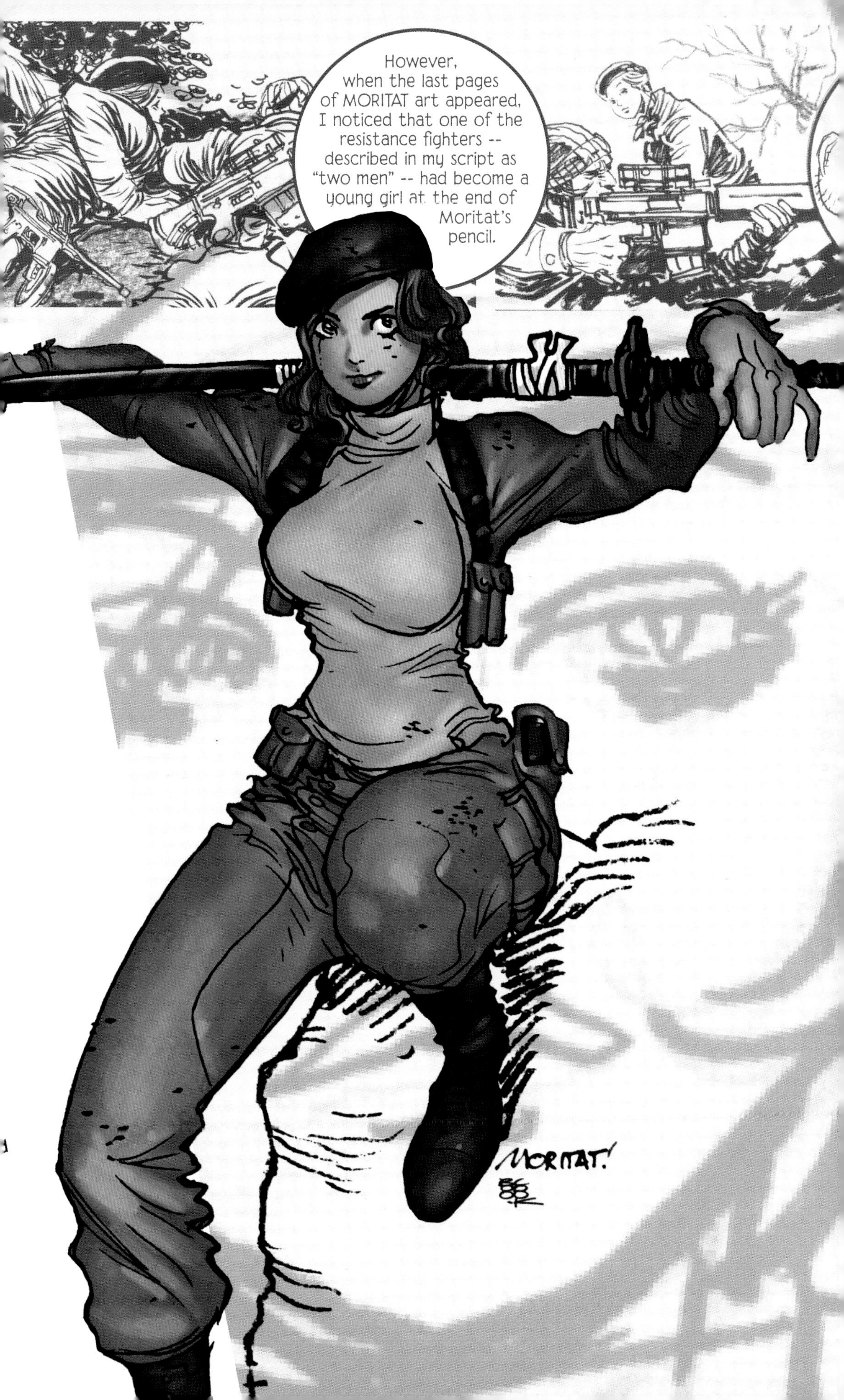
However, when the last pages of MORITAT art appeared, I noticed that one of the resistance fighters -- described in my script as "two men" -- had become a young girl at the end of Moritat's pencil.
MORITAT!

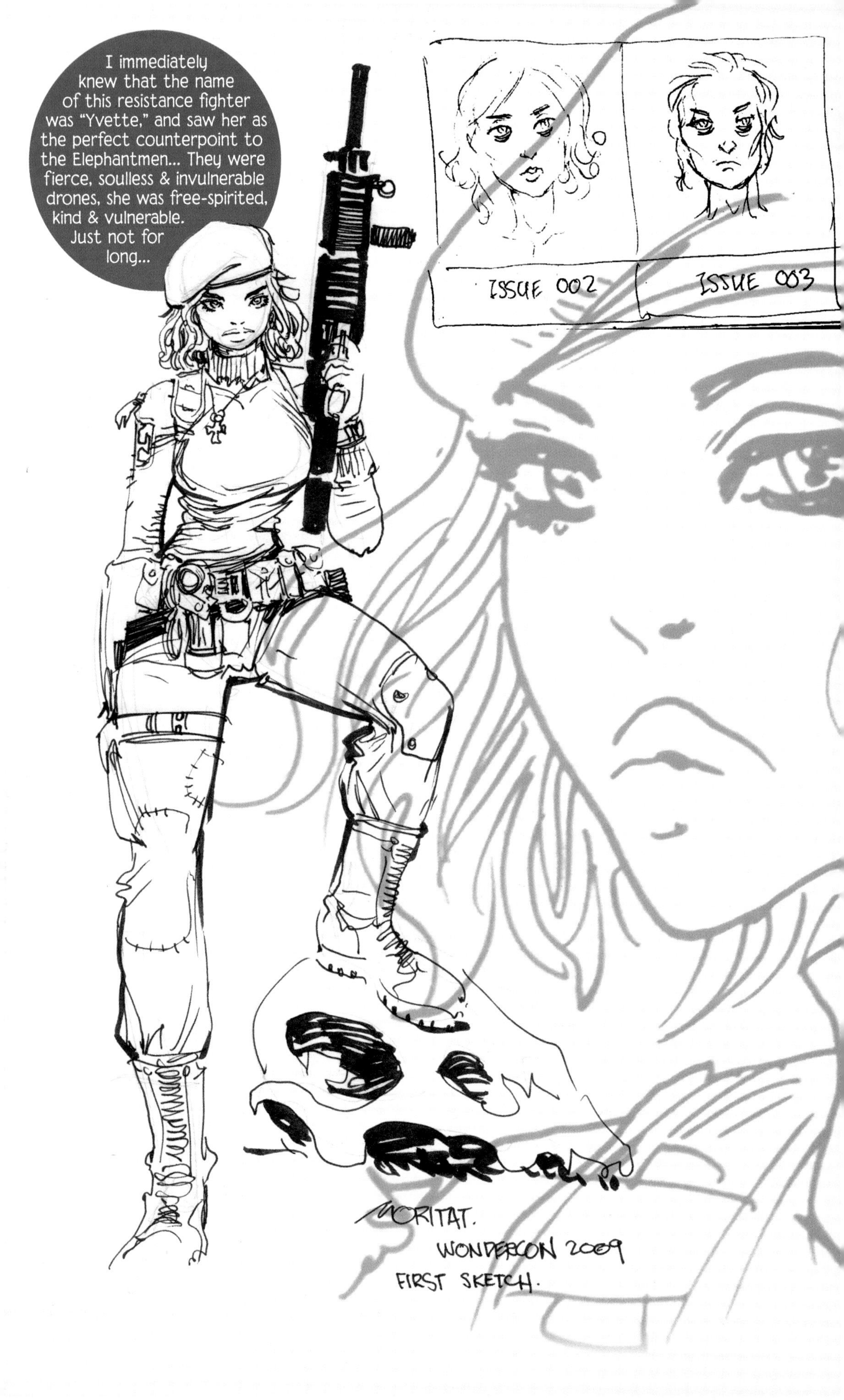
I immediately knew that the name of this resistance fighter was "Yvette," and saw her as the perfect counterpoint to the Elephantmen... They were fierce, soulless & invulnerable drones, she was free-spirited, kind & vulnerable. Just not for long...
ISSUE 002
ISSUE 003
MORITAT.
WONDERCON 2009
FIRST SKETCH.

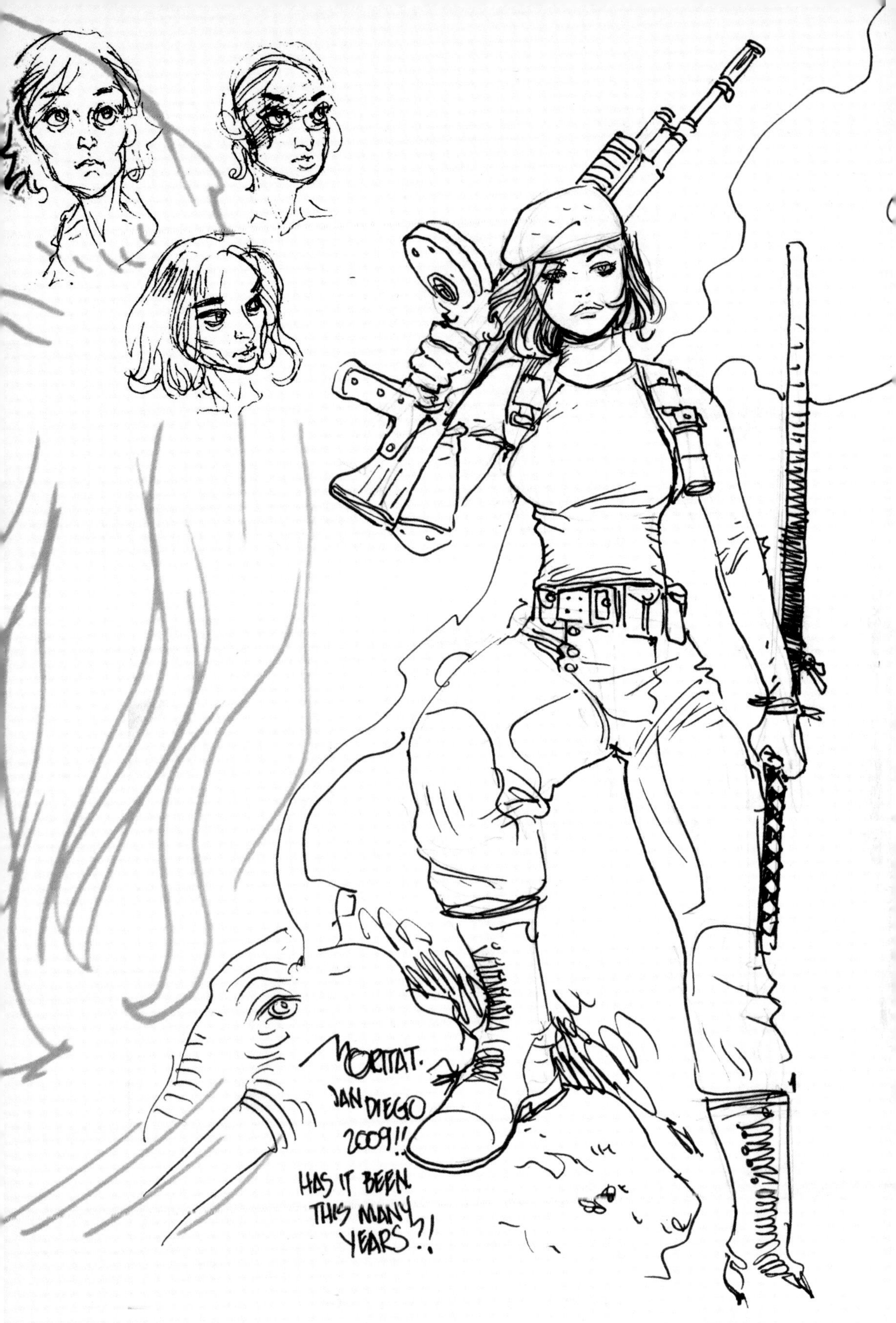
MORITAT.
SAN DIEGO
2009!!
HAS IT BEEN
THIS MANY
YEARS?!

Above, top: Because Yvette's story involved foraging for food, with disturbing consequences, Moritat originally proposed showing her becoming more and more emaciated in each issue. When he suggested loosely basing her look on lean but beautiful French actress, Emmanuelle Béart, we had our Yvette and a character who became one of the most often requested subjects of sketches at shows...

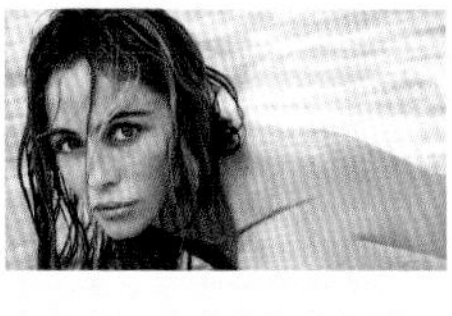

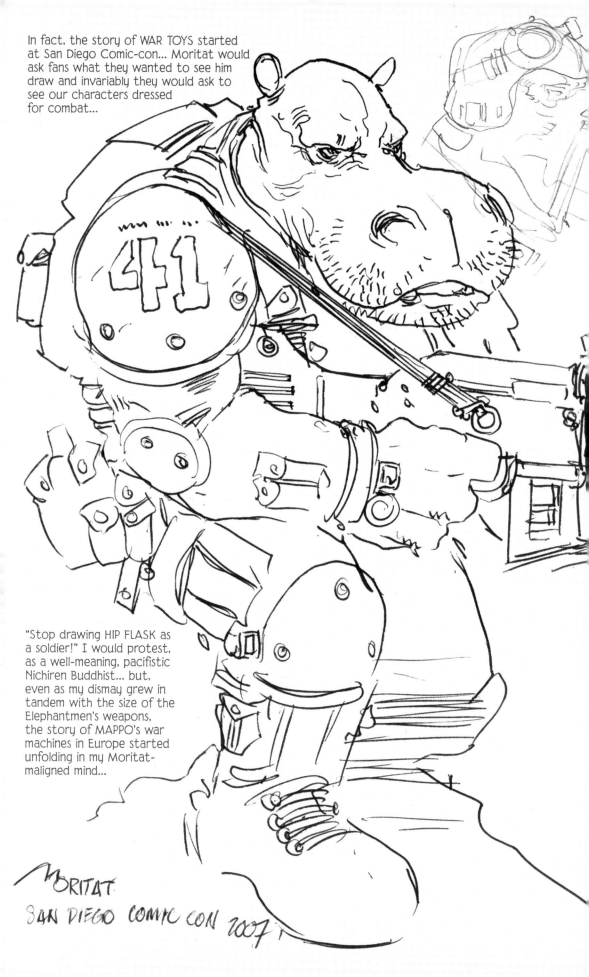

In fact, the story of WAR TOYS started at San Diego Comic-con... Moritat would ask fans what they wanted to see him draw and invariably they would ask to see our characters dressed for combat...

"Stop drawing HIP FLASK as a soldier!" I would protest, as a well-meaning, pacifistic Nichiren Buddhist... but, even as my dismay grew in tandem with the size of the Elephantmen's weapons, the story of MAPPO's war machines in Europe started unfolding in my Moritat-maligned mind...

MORITAT
SAN DIEGO COMIC CON 2007

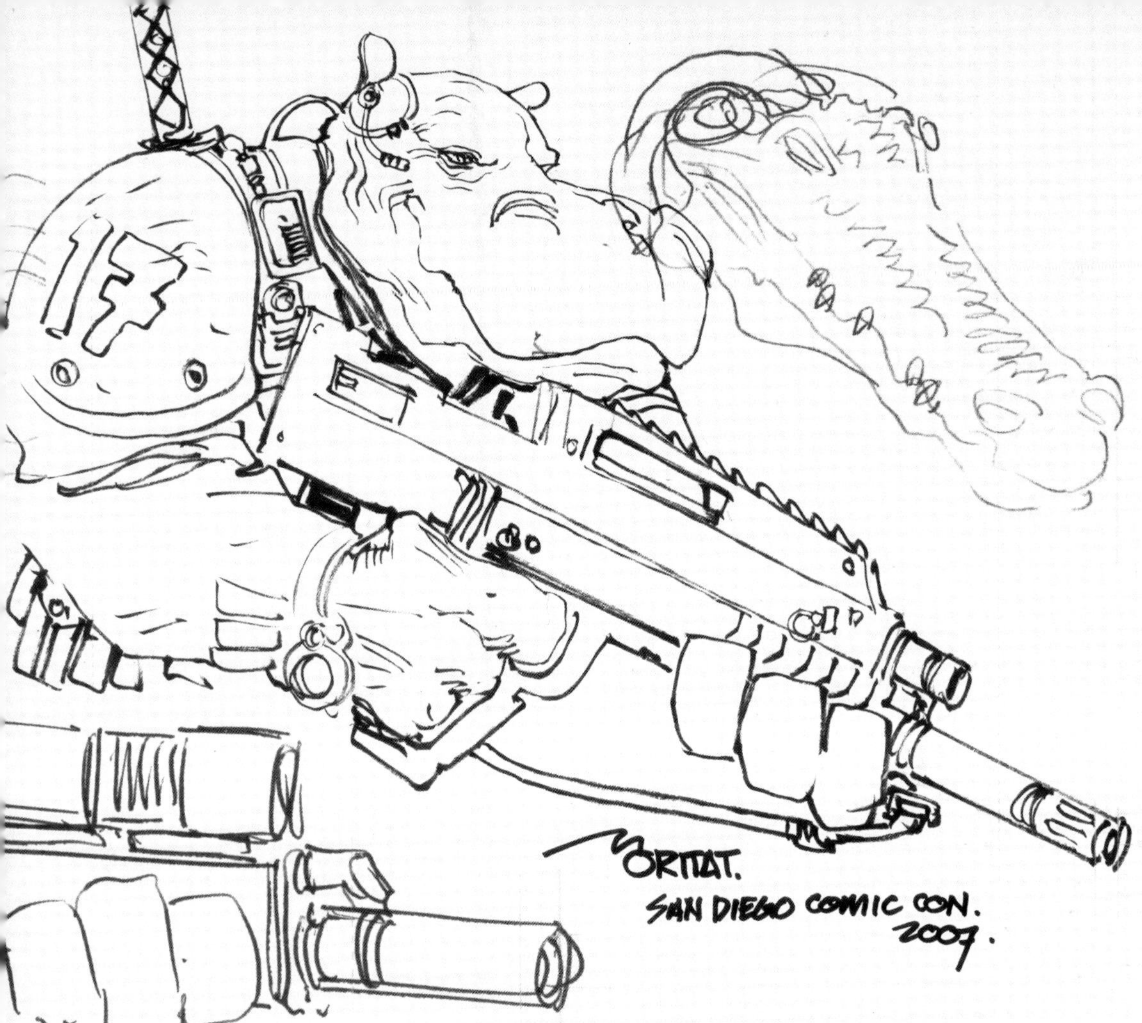
MORITAT.
SAN DIEGO COMIC CON.
2007.

The blueline drawings on this page and opposite were created as warmups for WAR TOYS. It still amazes me to this day that Moritat can draw, from memory, guns and armor he created in his sketchbook months earlier.

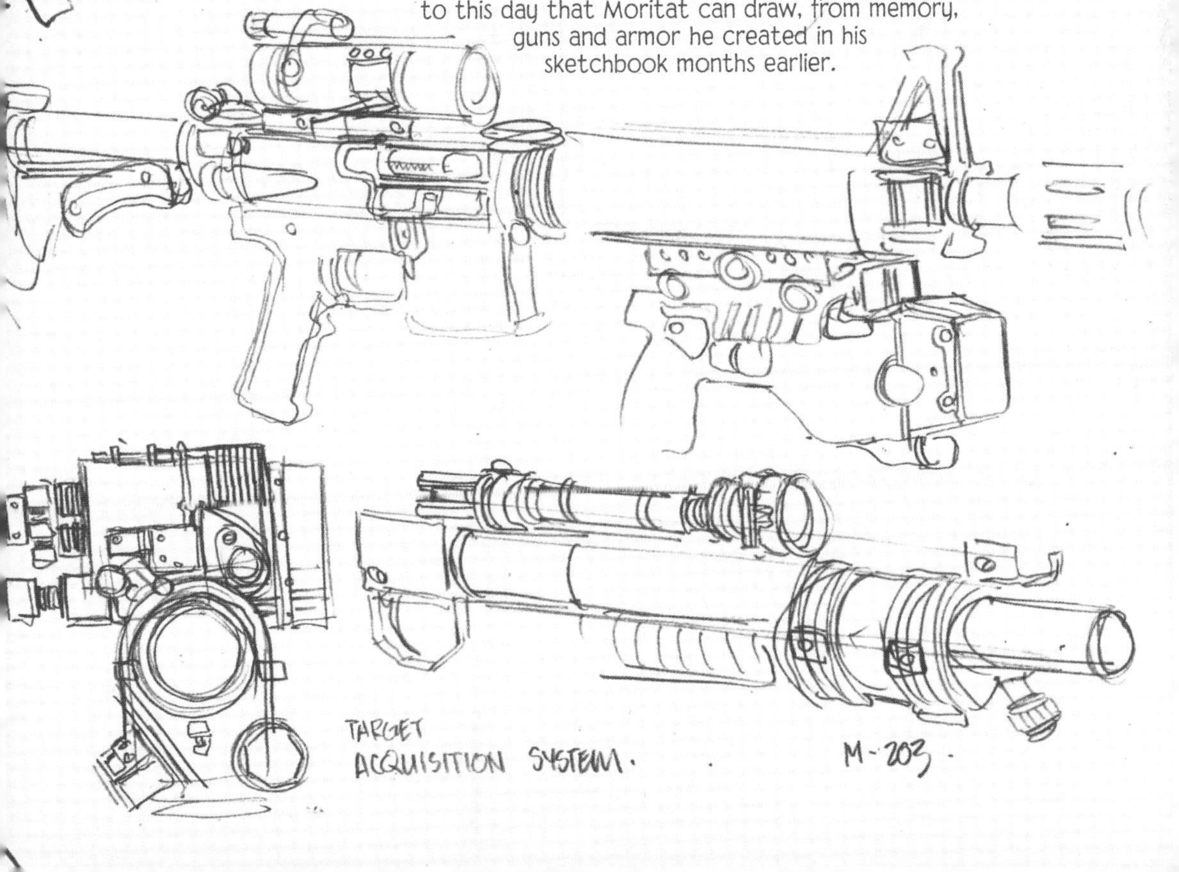
TARGET
ACQUISITION SYSTEM.
M-203.

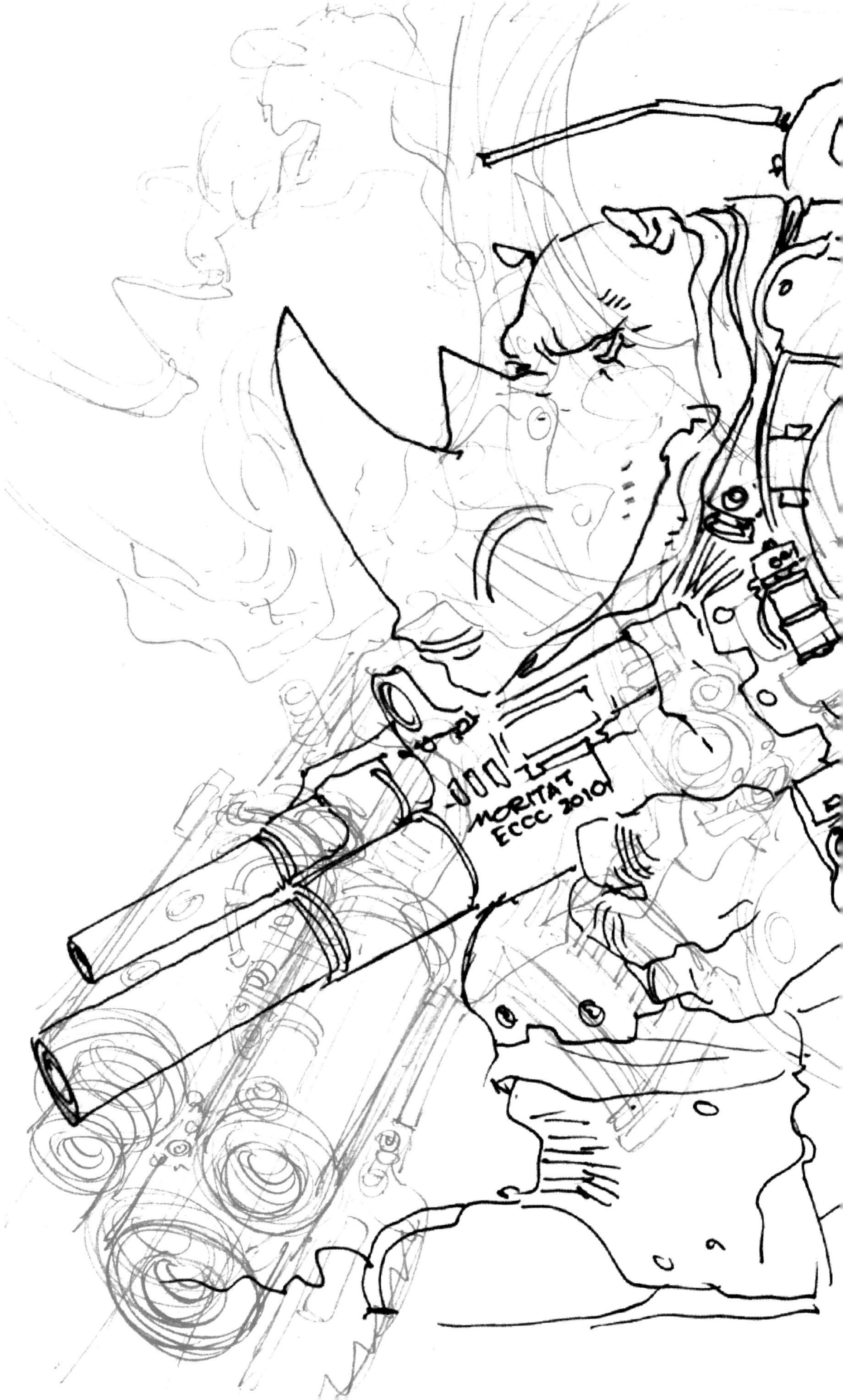
MORITAT
ECCC 2010

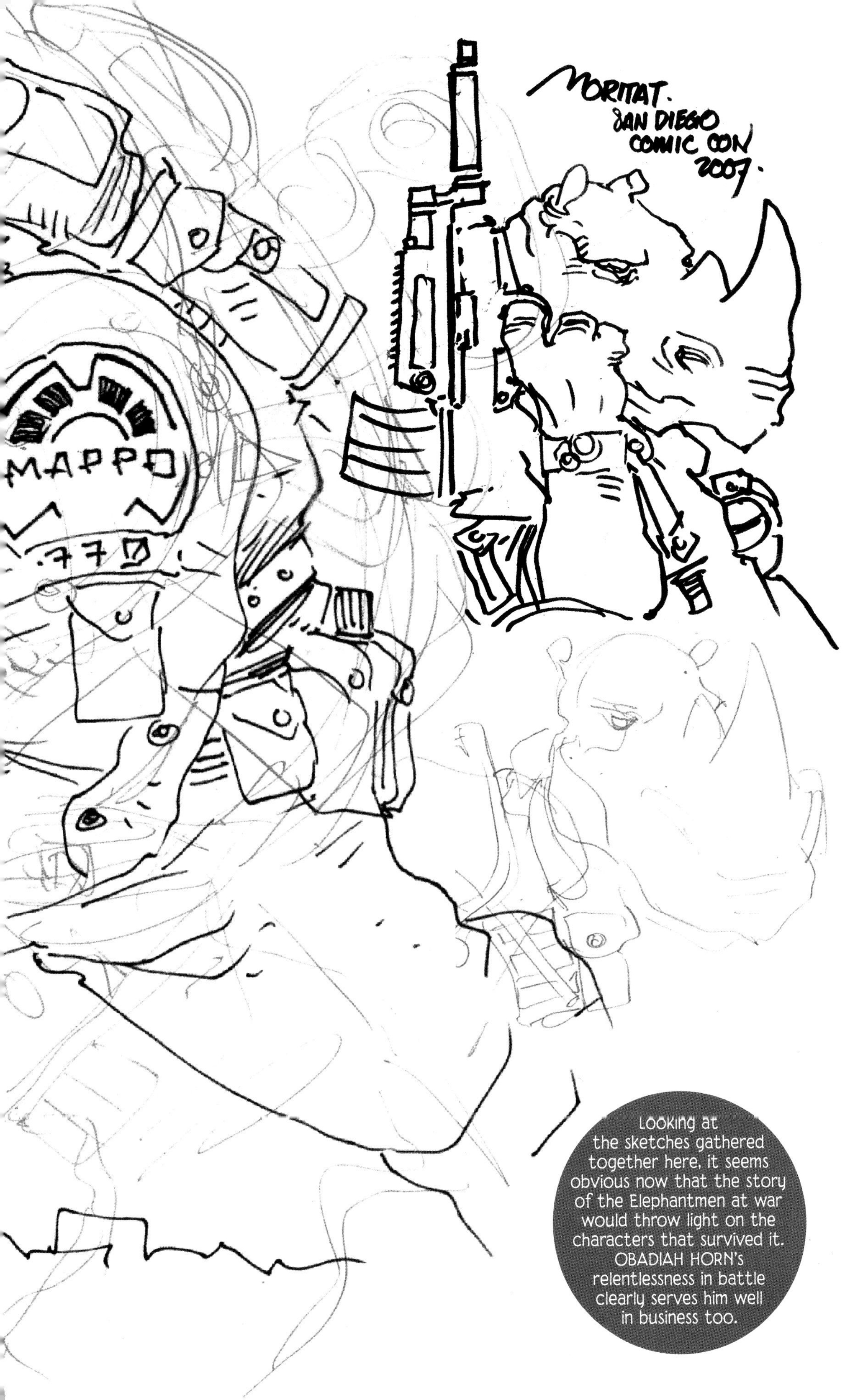
MORITAT.
SAN DIEGO
COMIC CON
2007.
MAPPO
770

Looking at the sketches gathered together here, it seems obvious now that the story of the Elephantmen at war would throw light on the characters that survived it. OBADIAH HORN's relentlessness in battle clearly serves him well in business too.

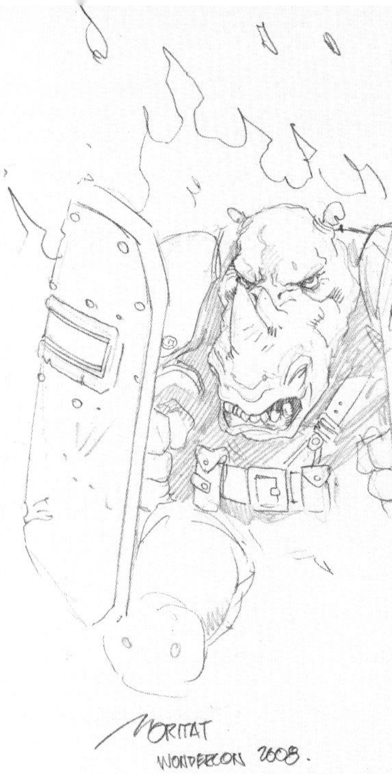
MORITAT
WONDERCON 2008.

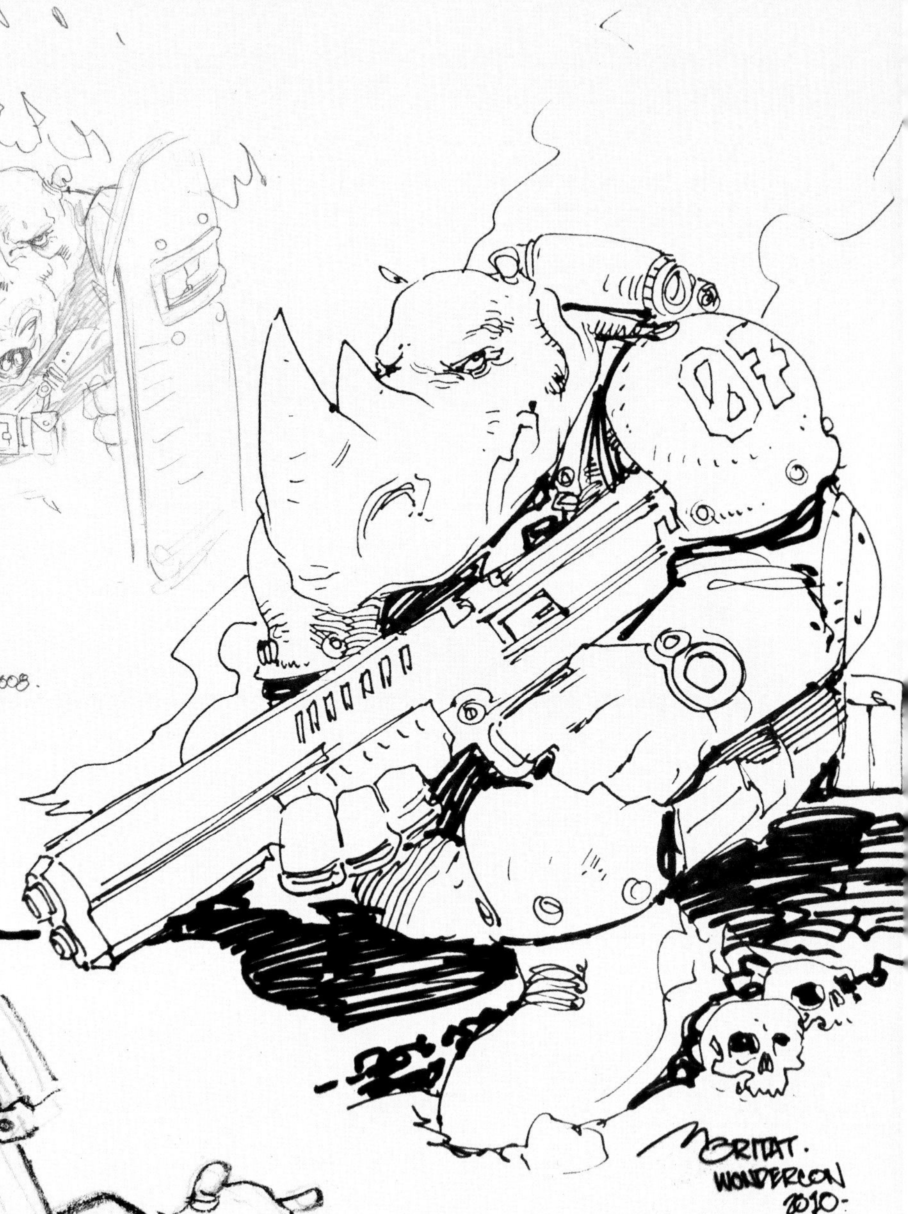
MORITAT.
WONDERCON
2010.

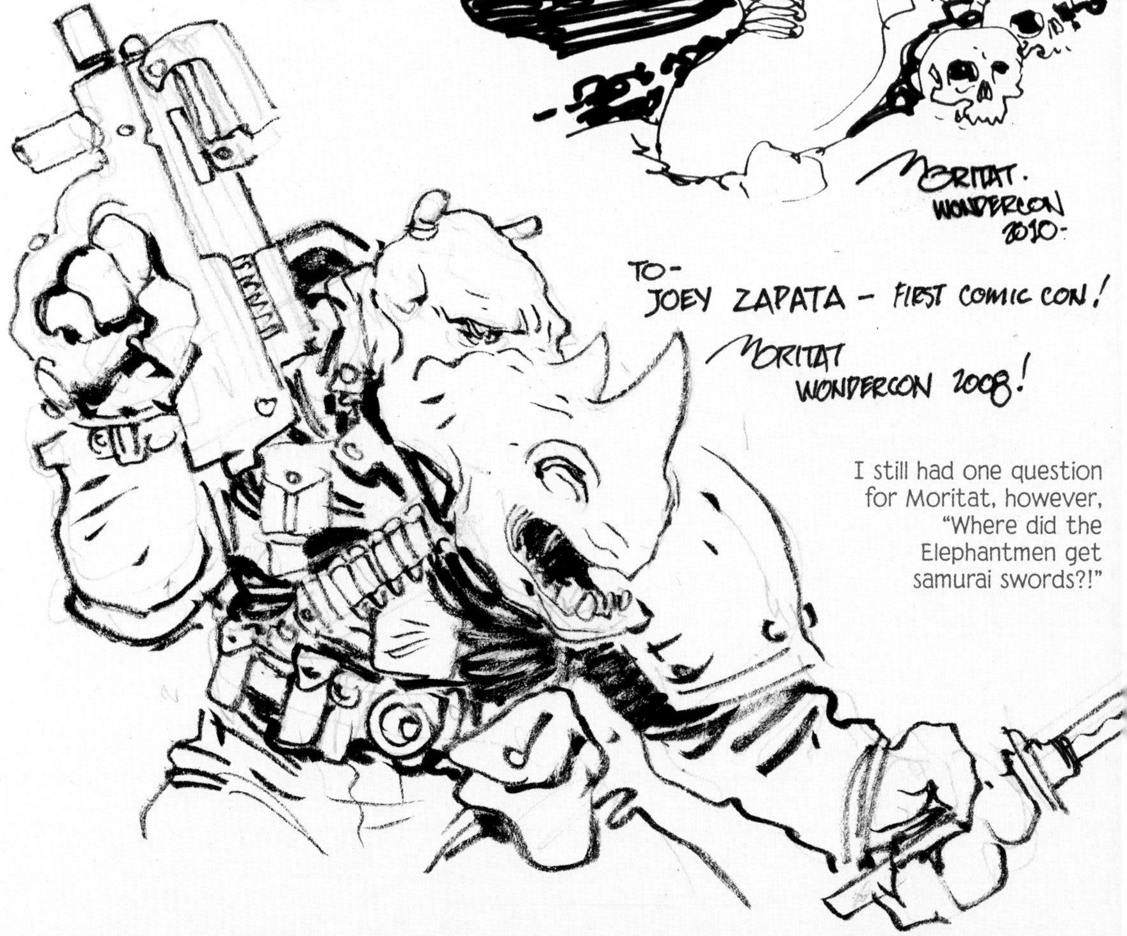
TO-
JOEY ZAPATA - FIRST COMIC CON!
MORITAT
WONDERCON 2008!

I still had one question for Moritat, however, "Where did the Elephantmen get samurai swords?!"

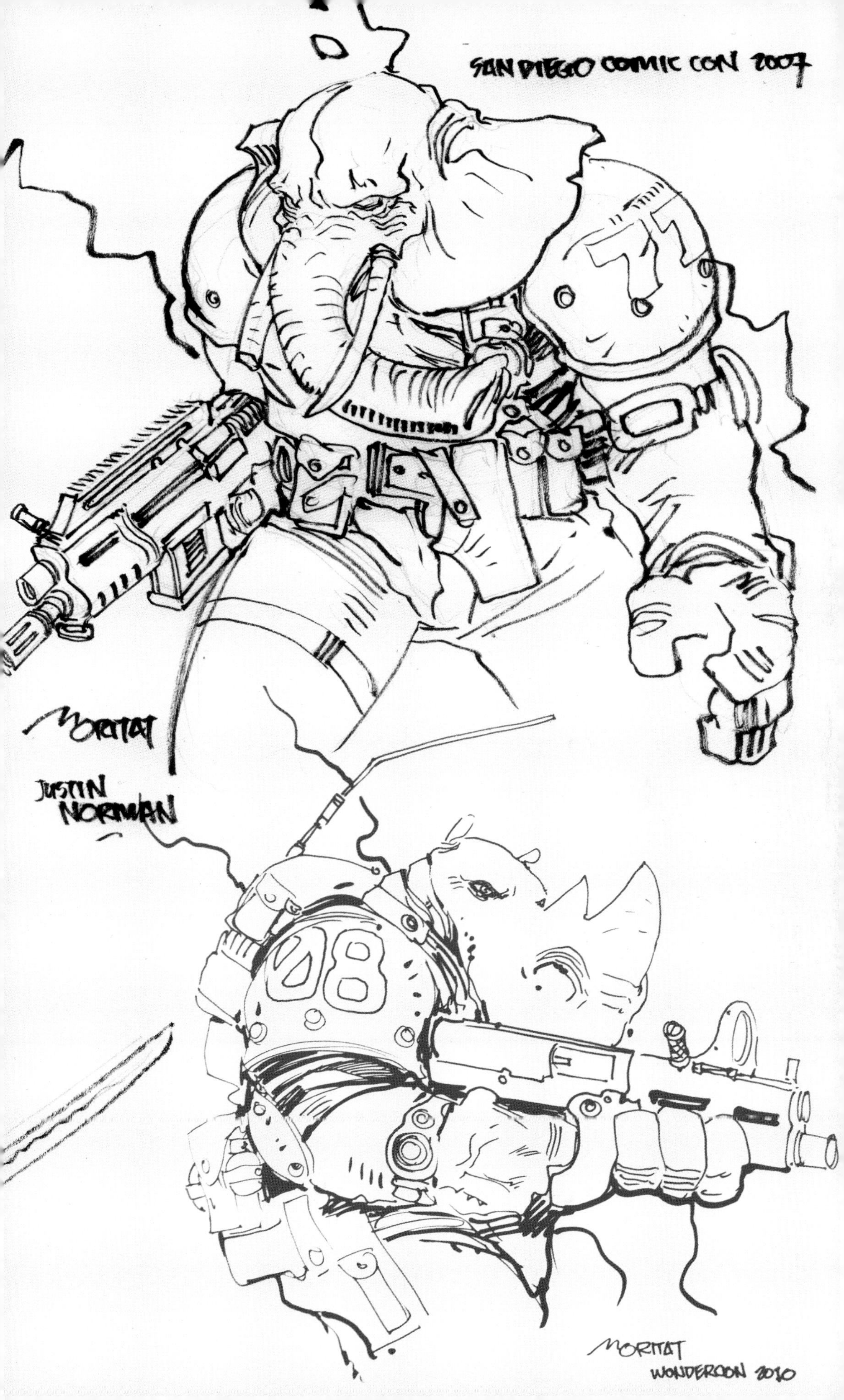
SAN DIEGO COMIC CON 2007
MORITAT
JUSTIN NORMAN
MORITAT
WONDERCON 2010

EBONY HIDE seemed meek and mild when he first appeared in ELEPHANTMEN #1 (collected in ELEPHANTMEN Volume 1: WOUNDED ANIMALS) , so it was refreshing to see him kicking ass in WAR TOYS.

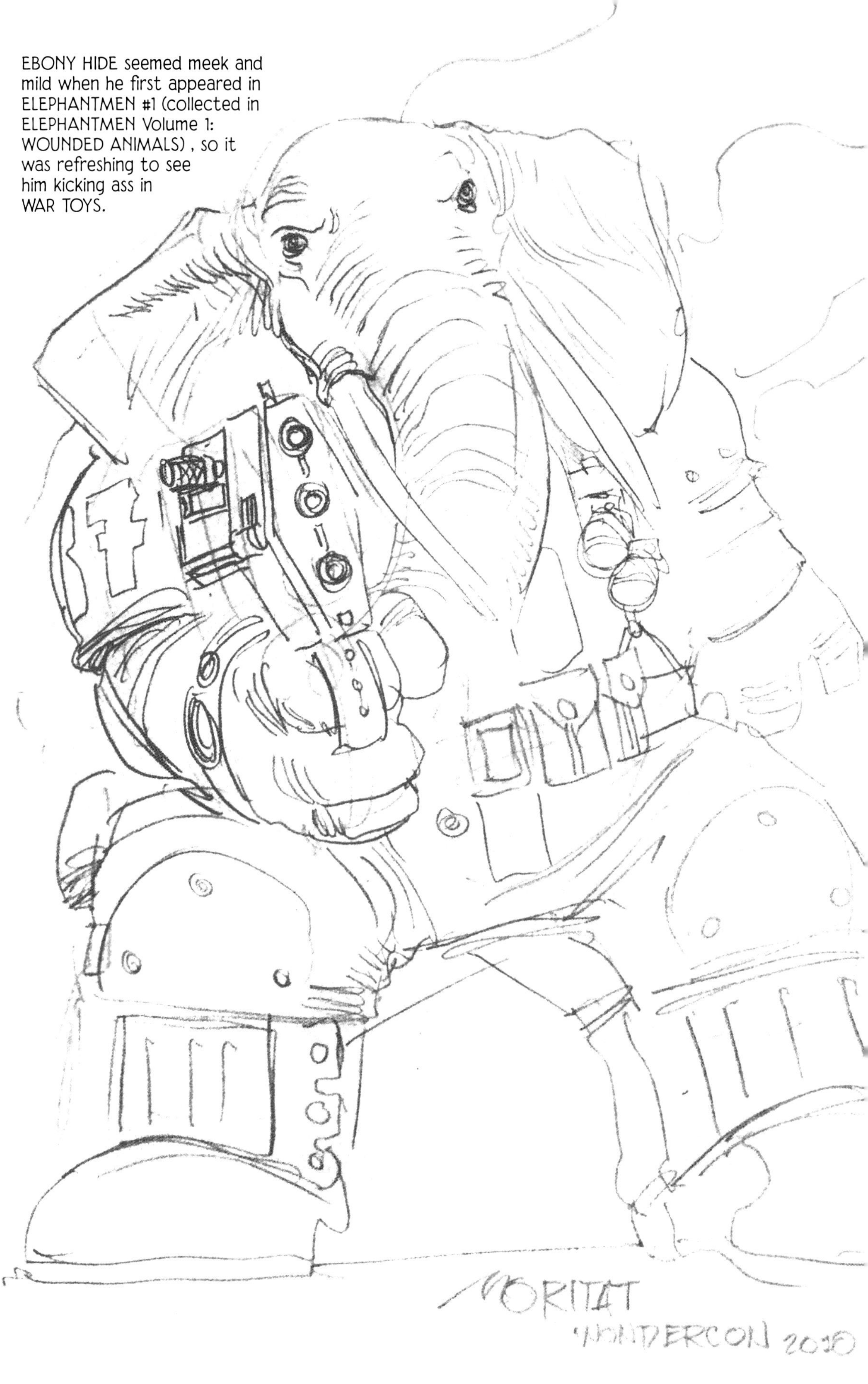
MORITAT
WONDERCON 2010

As for the samurai swords... the more I asked about them, the more frequently they seemed to appear.

"It doesn't matter," Justin "Moritat" Norman assured me; "They're cool, readers will LOVE 'em!"

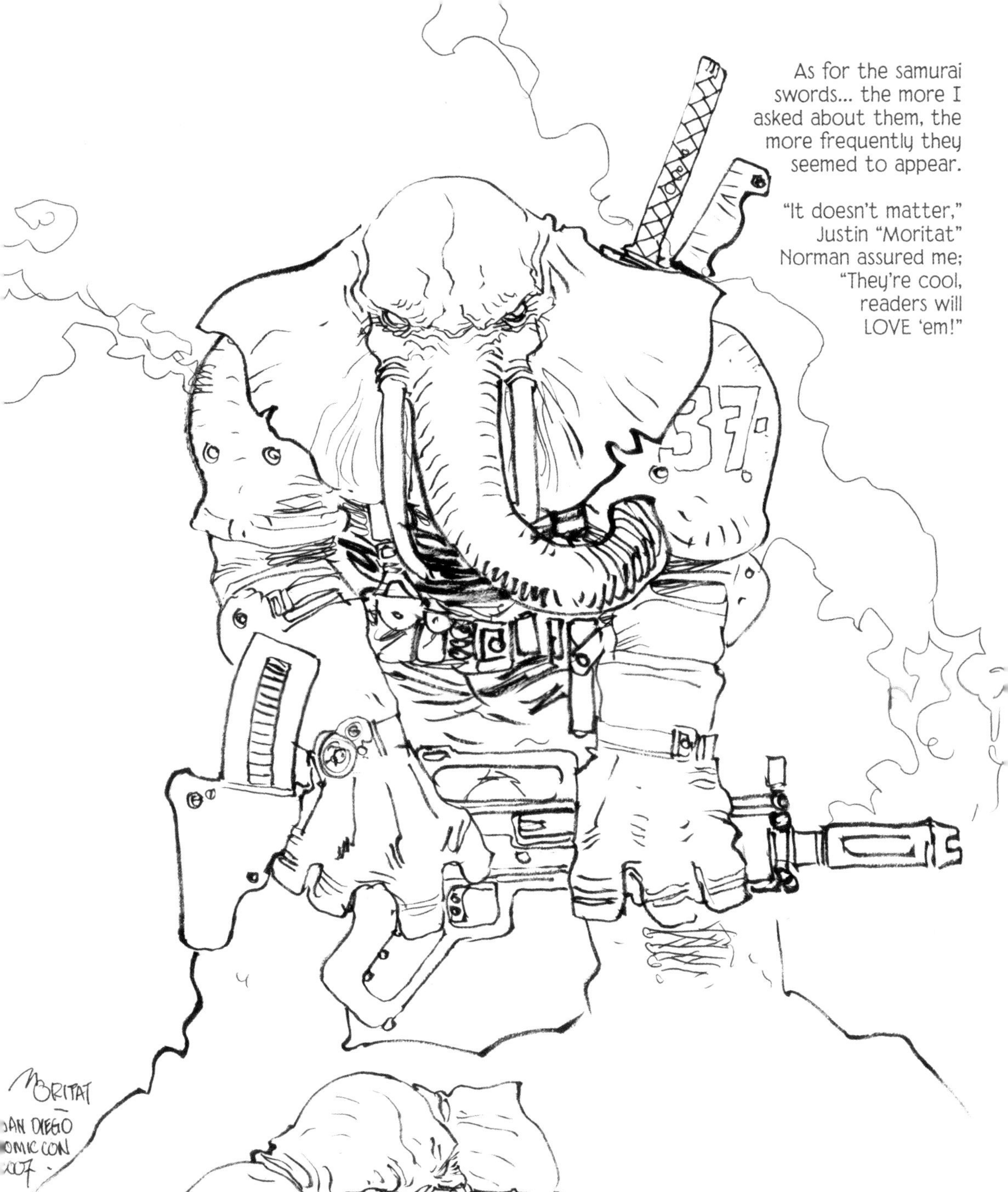
37
MORITAT
SAN DIEGO
COMIC CON
2007

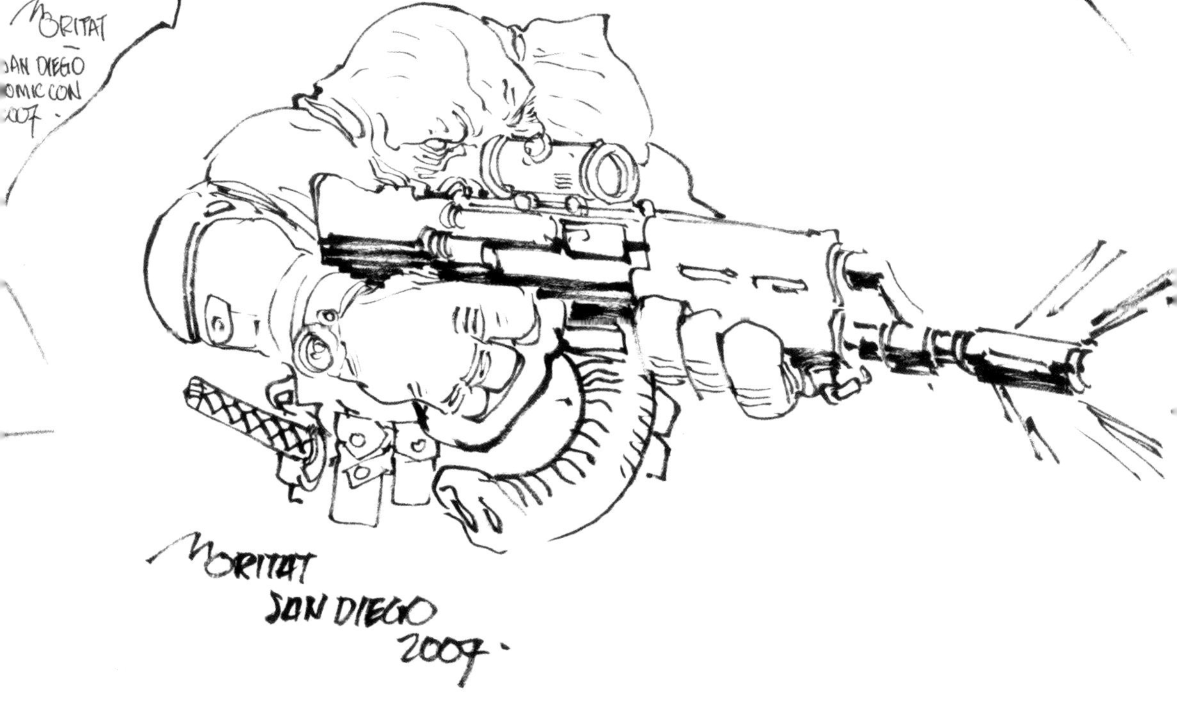
MORITAT
SAN DIEGO
2007

And, of course, just as Moritat was right about drawing the Elephantmen as soldiers, and about our French Resistance Femme Fatale, he was right about Elephantmen carrying samurai swords. They DO look cool. And our cover artist, BOO COOK, was right about Elephantmen having great big staples in their ears (ELEPHANTMEN #21)... OKAY! That looks cool too! Moritat obviously agreed as he included them in the sketch of Ebony featured here.

Artists are often right about these kind of things -- Just don't tell them I said so.

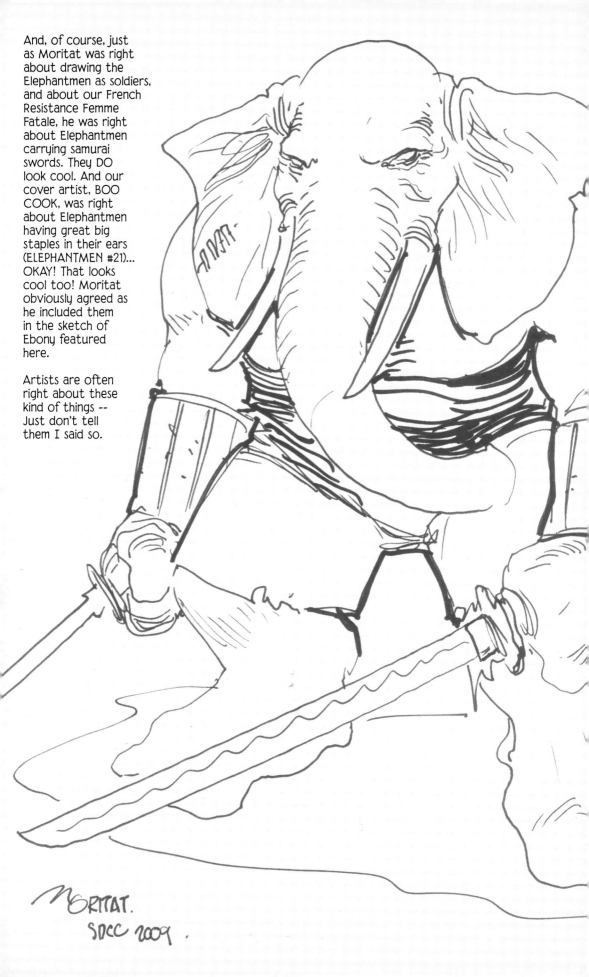

MORITAT.
SDCC 2009.

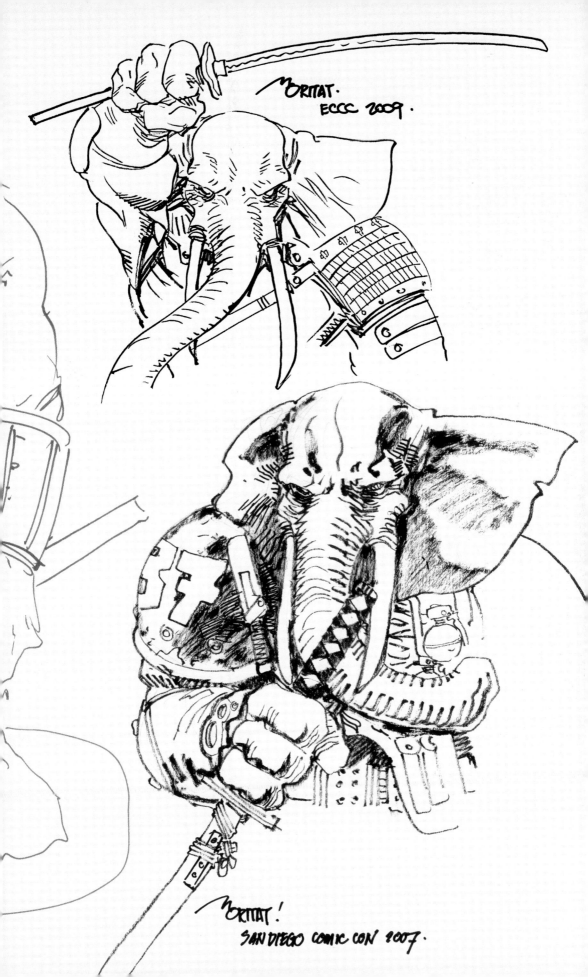

MORITAT.
ECCC 2009.

MORITAT!
SAN DIEGO COMIC CON 2007.

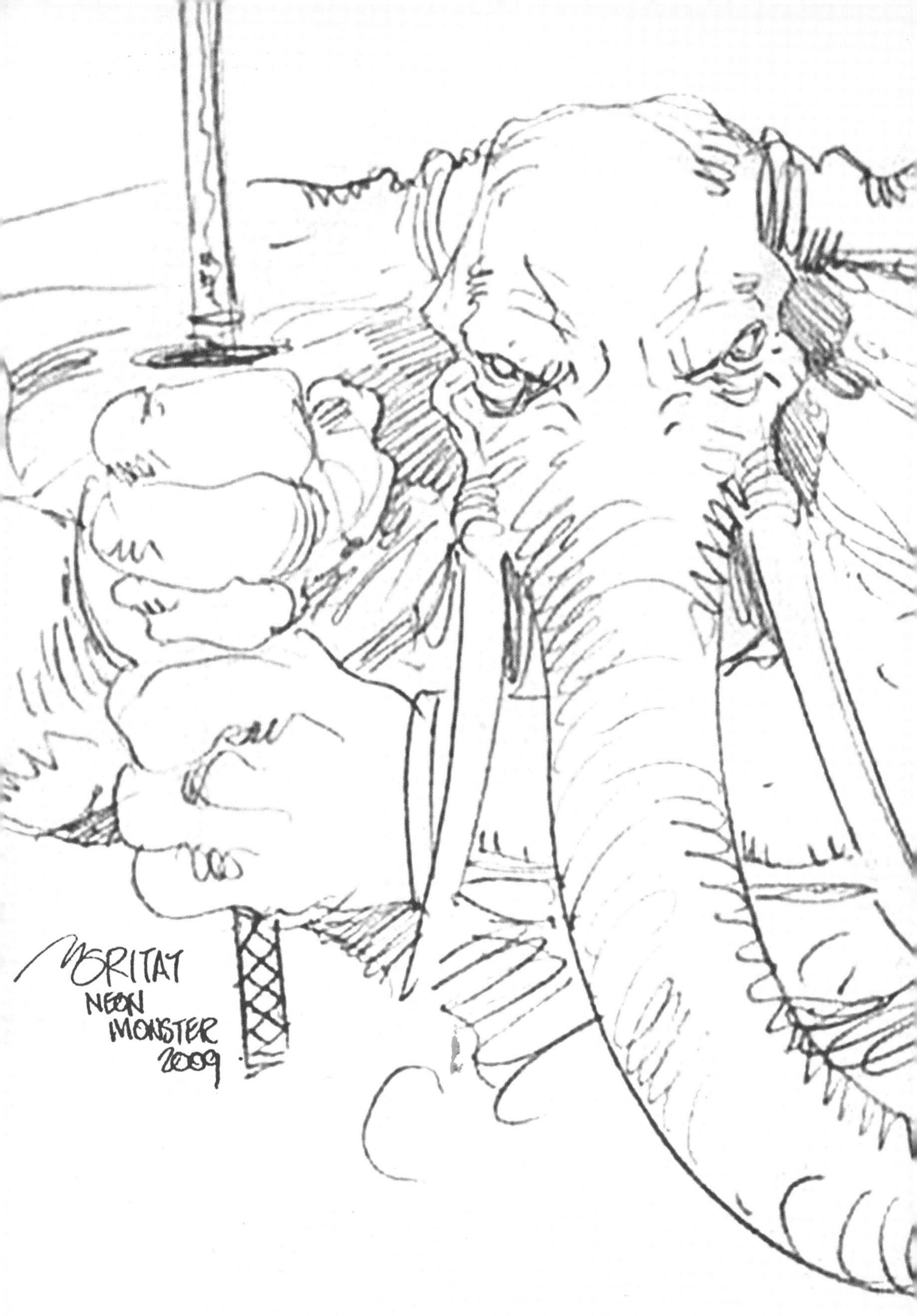
MORITAT
NEON
MONSTER
2009

Yep. I get it, Justin. Elephantmen. Samurai swords. Got your point now.

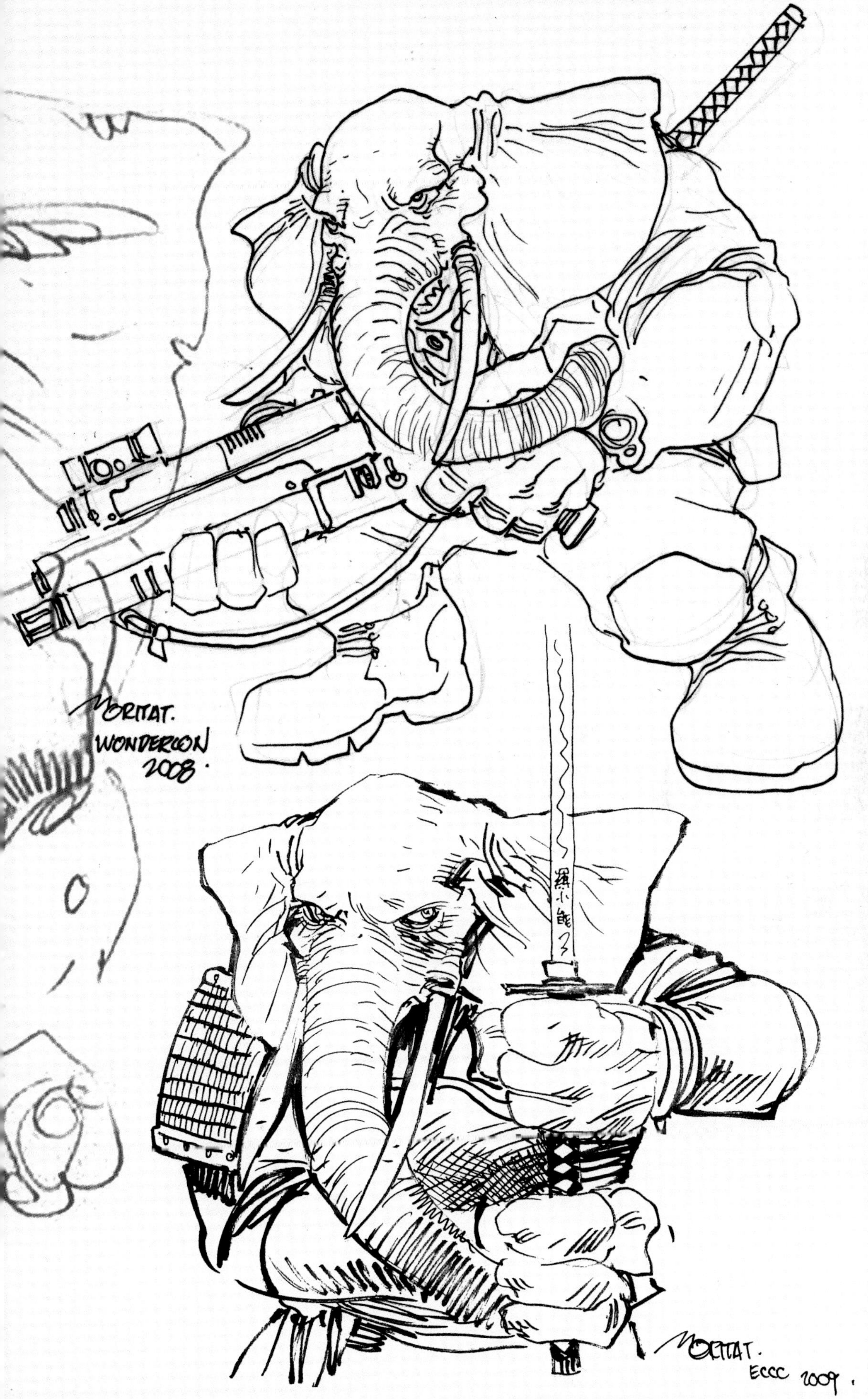
MORITAT.
WONDERCON
2008.
MORITAT.
ECCC 2009.

And Guns. Big Guns.
VERY Big Guns.
Check. Check, Check.
Check, Check, Check!

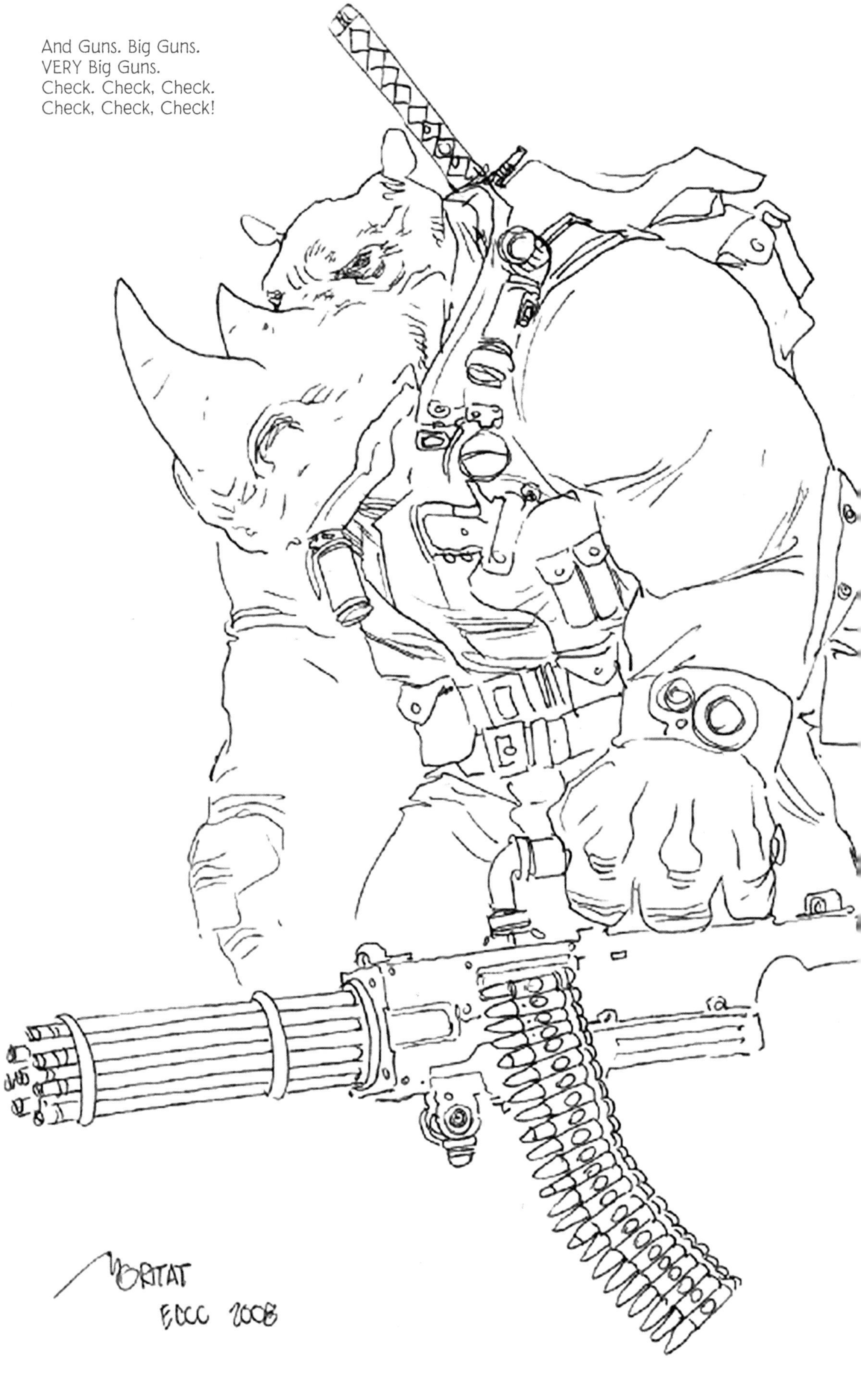
MORITAT
ECCC 2008

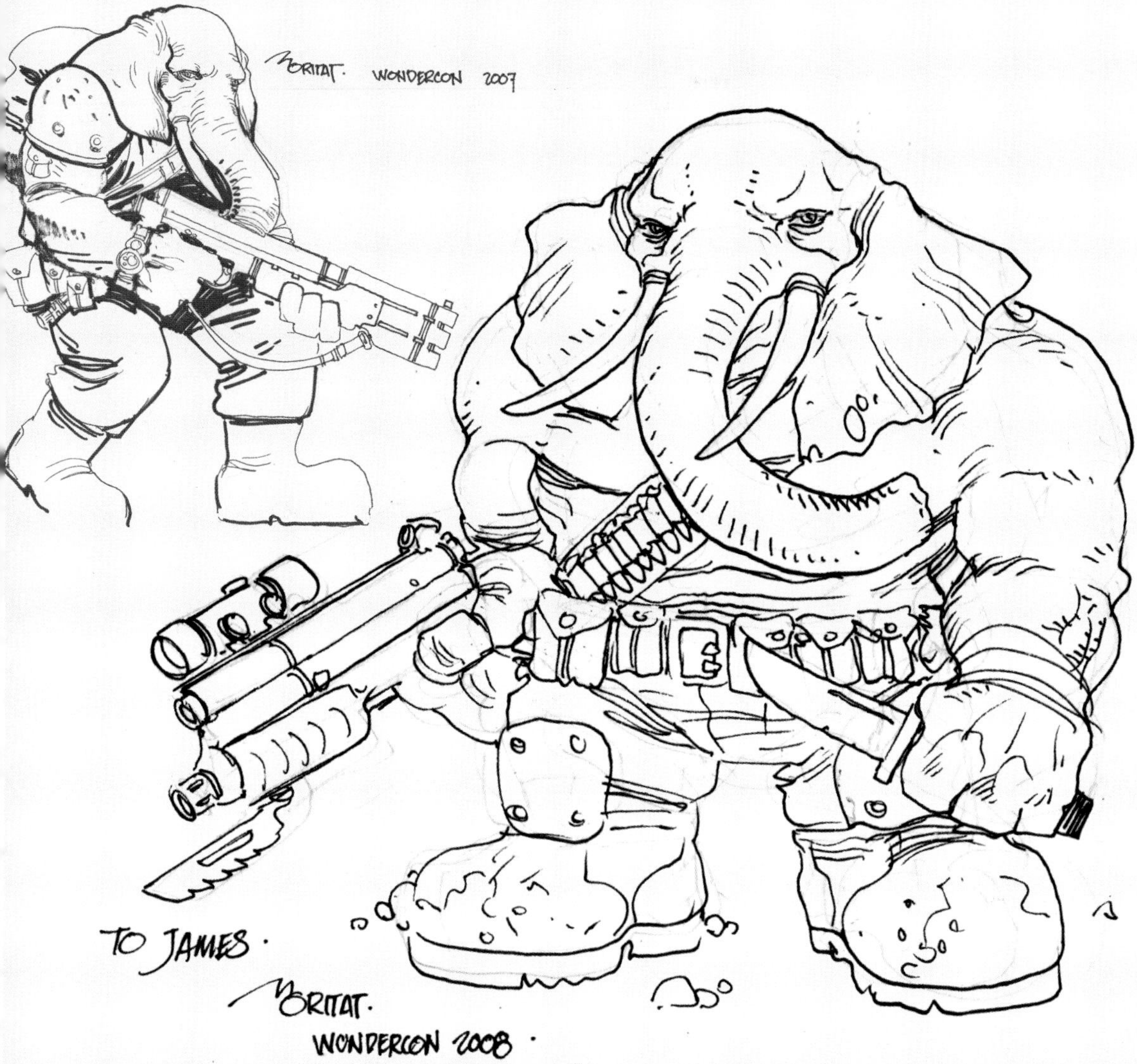
MORITAT. WONDERCON 2007
TO JAMES.
MORITAT.
WONDERCON 2008.

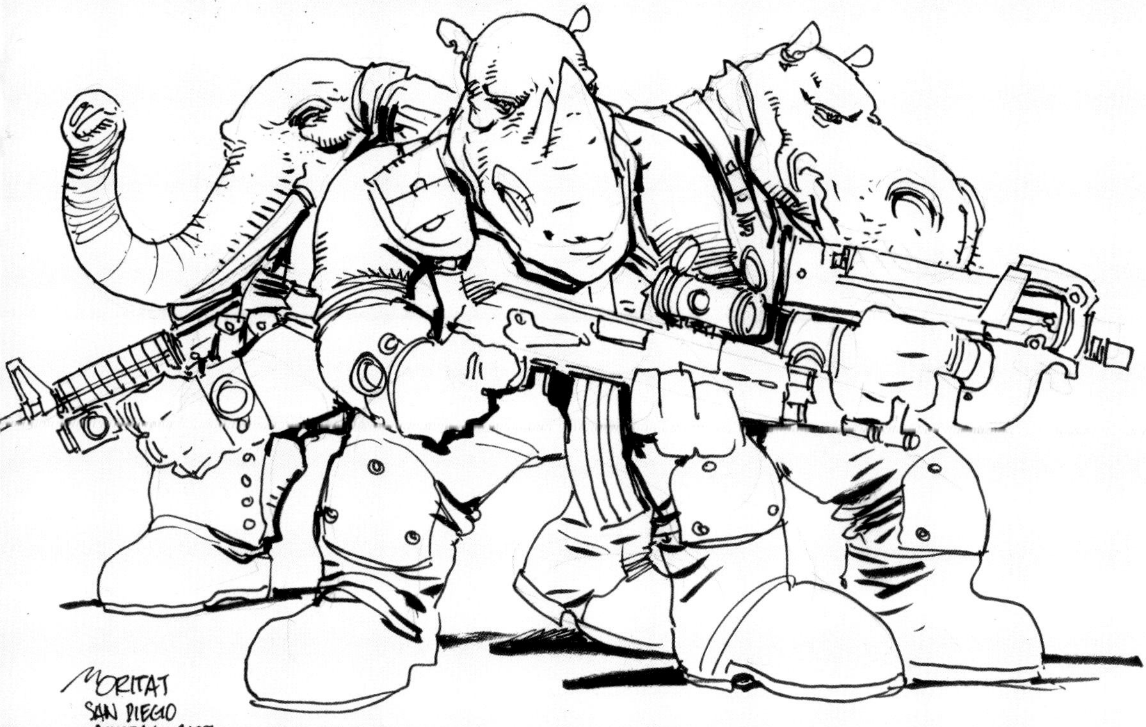
MORITAT
SAN DIEGO
SUNDAY 2009.

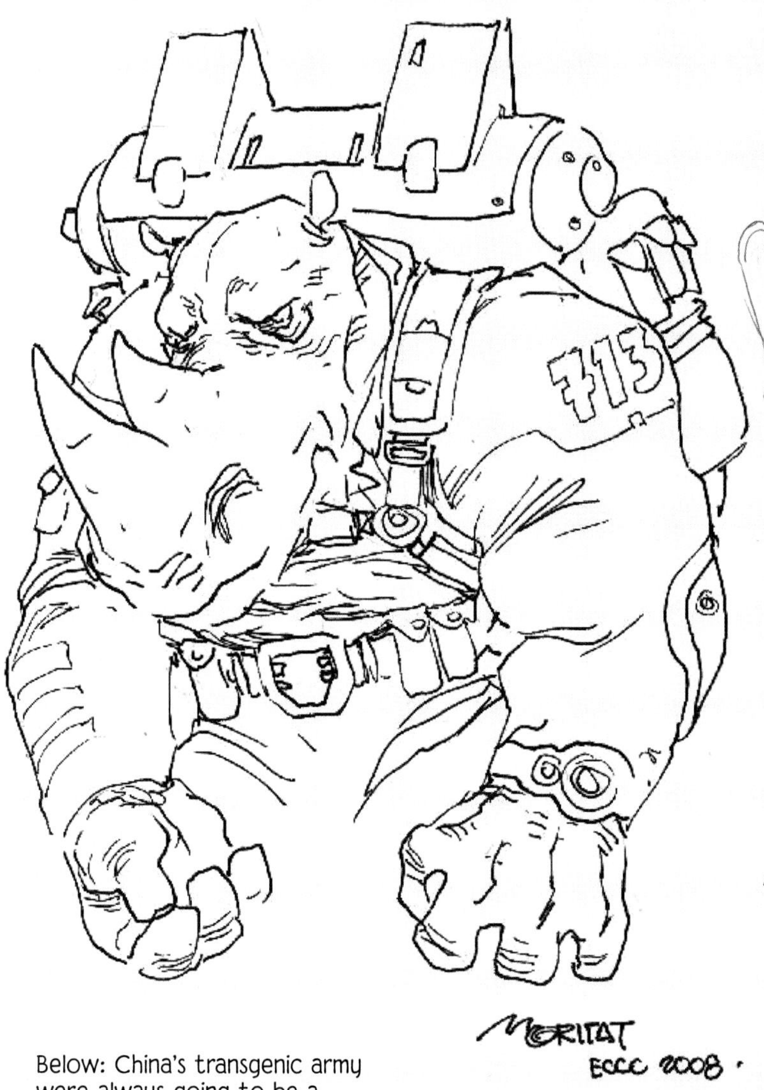
713
MORITAT
ECCC 2008.

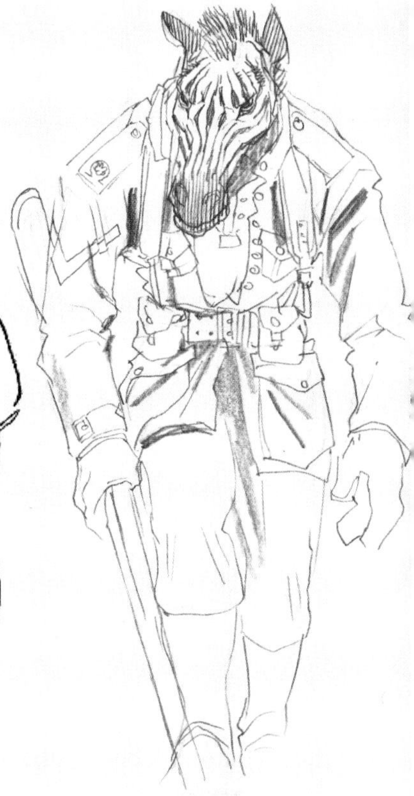

Above: A rare, and unsigned (!) shot of TRENCH, before his injuries, obviously.

Below: China's transgenic army were always going to be a part of the WAR TOYS story -- Moritat envisaged them in this drawing for a fan at Emerald City Comic Con in 2009. Note the samurai sword!

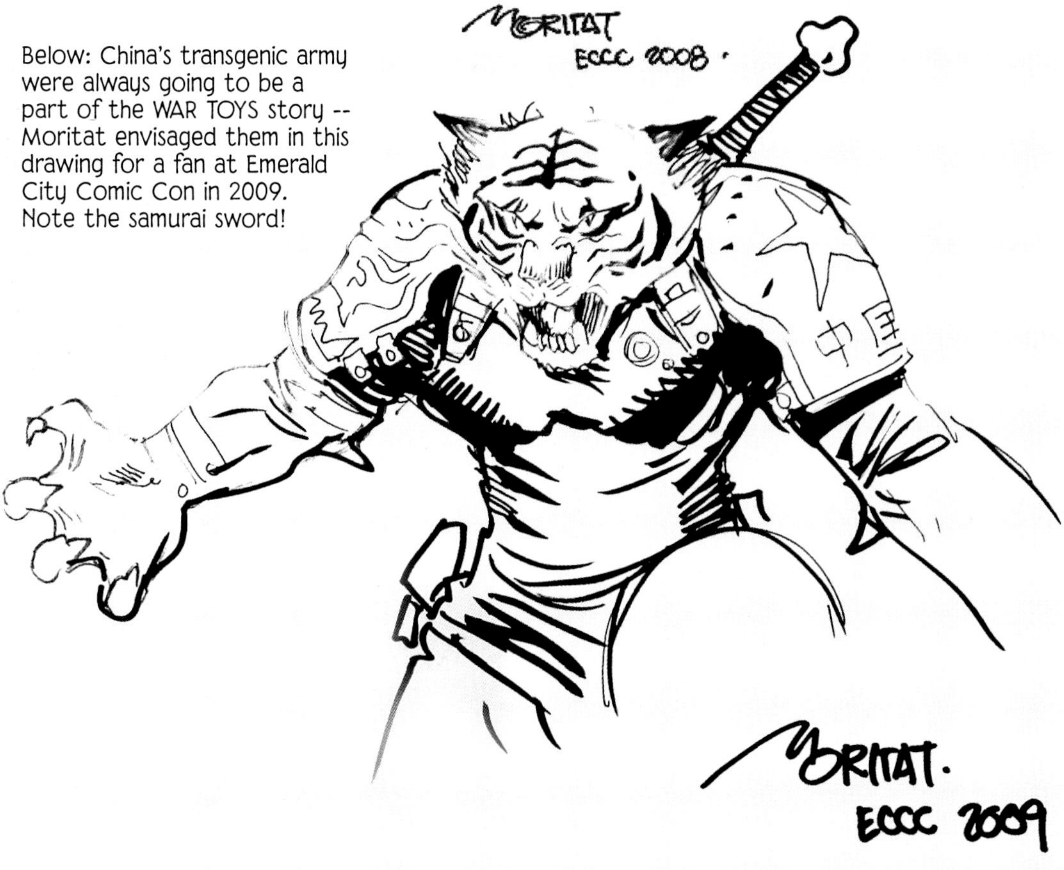
中国
MORITAT.
ECCC 2009

MORITAT
ECCC 2010

Most of the sketches you see here were rustled up by Moritat to illustrate a feature for Comic Book Resources which we also ran in the back pages of the YVETTE one shot...

Writer Josh Wigler asked Justin for any character sketches he had lying around, so, rather than disappoint Josh, Justin created these drawings... AND persuaded artist MARIAN CHURCHLAND to create some drawings to accompany them.

It's always fun to see an artist run away with an idea... I love the suggestion that Yvette was driving after the forces of MAPPO in this old Renault...

There's a whole issue right there!

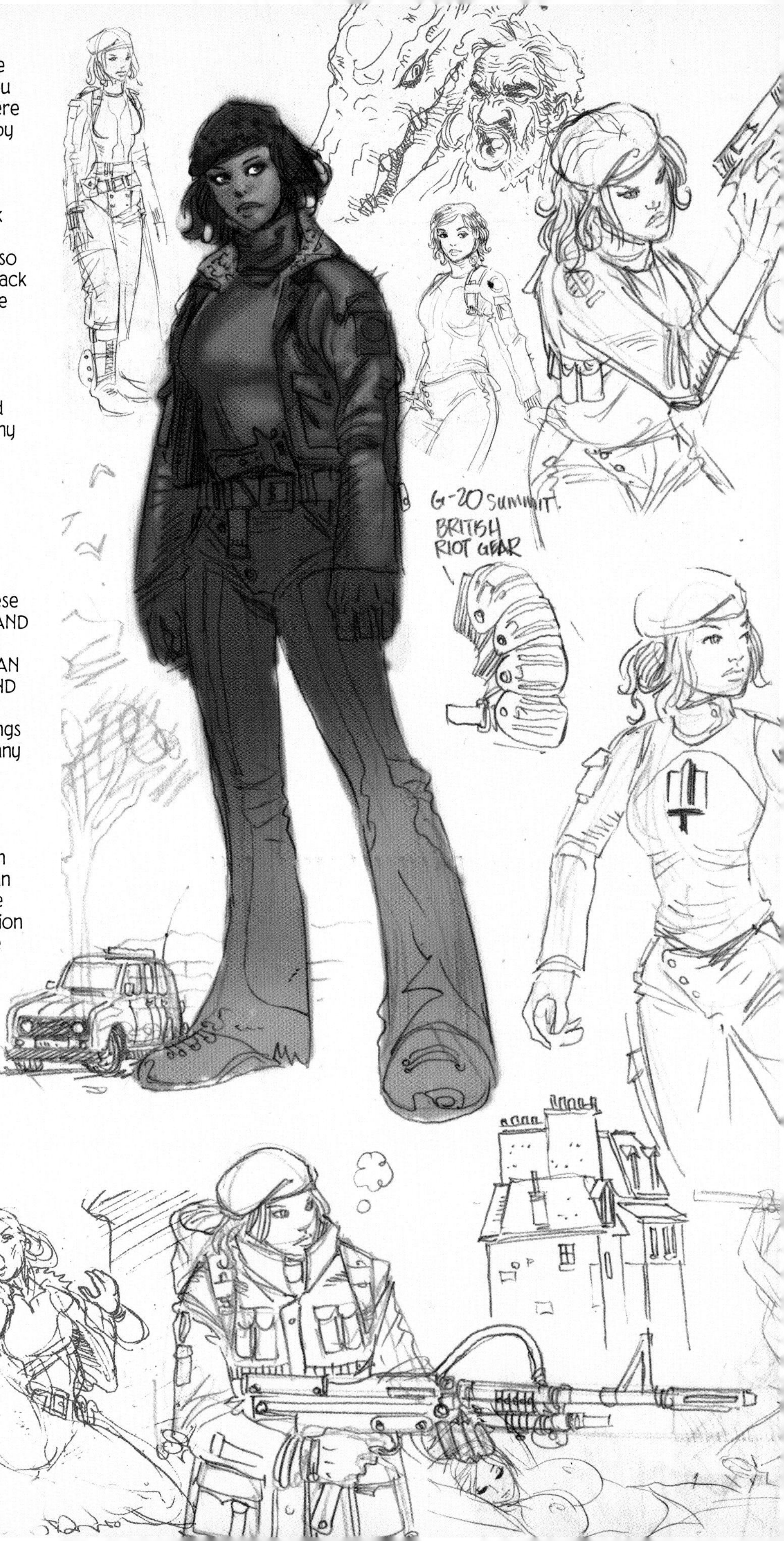
G-20 SUMMIT.
BRITISH RIOT GEAR

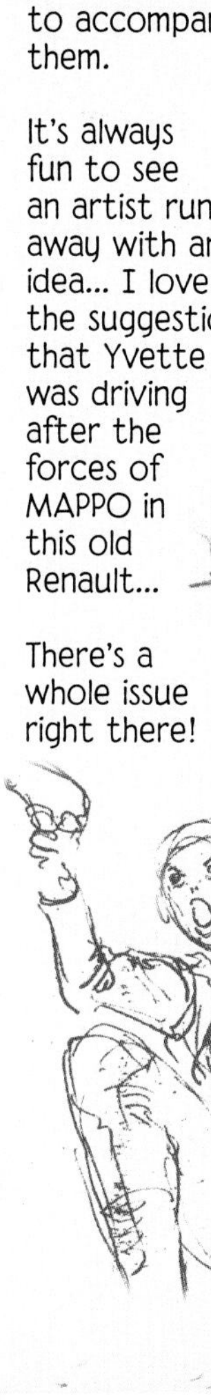

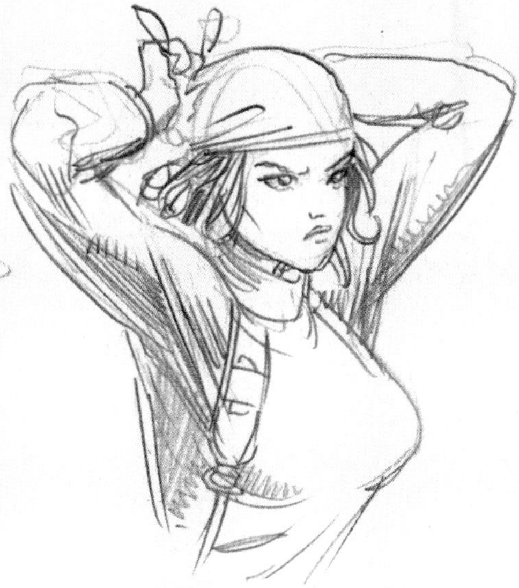

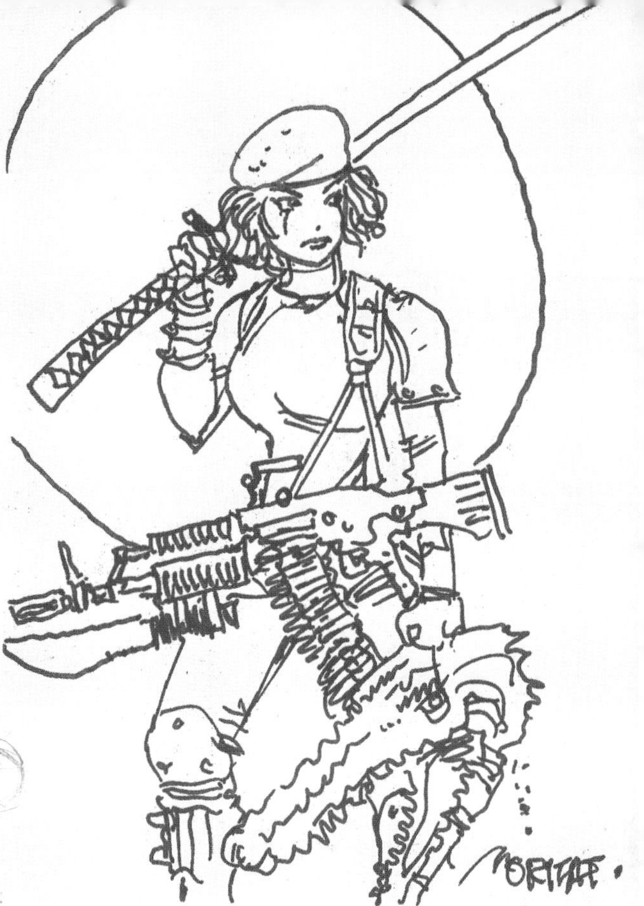
MORITAT.

Above: This drawing was produced by Moritat with lightning speed for Jonathan La Mantia as we were *leaving* Berkeley's legendary COMIC RELIEF store... it was such an iconic image, I asked Justin to use it as the basis for the cover of the one shot (overleaf).

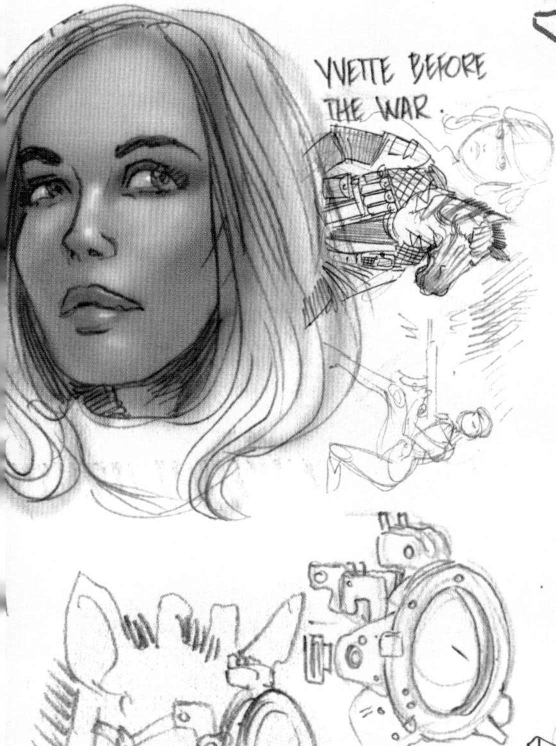
YVETTE BEFORE THE WAR.

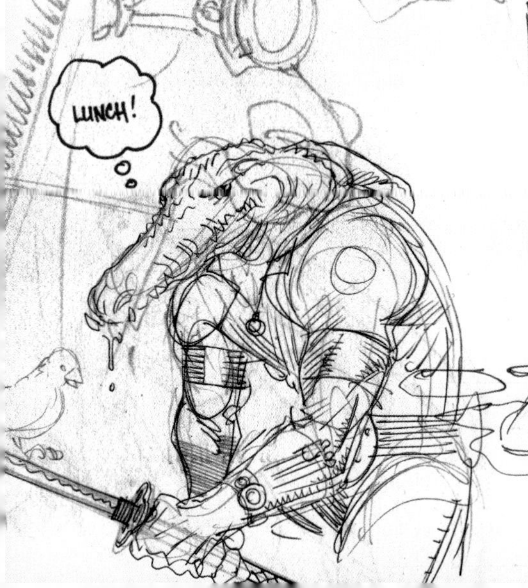
LUNCH!

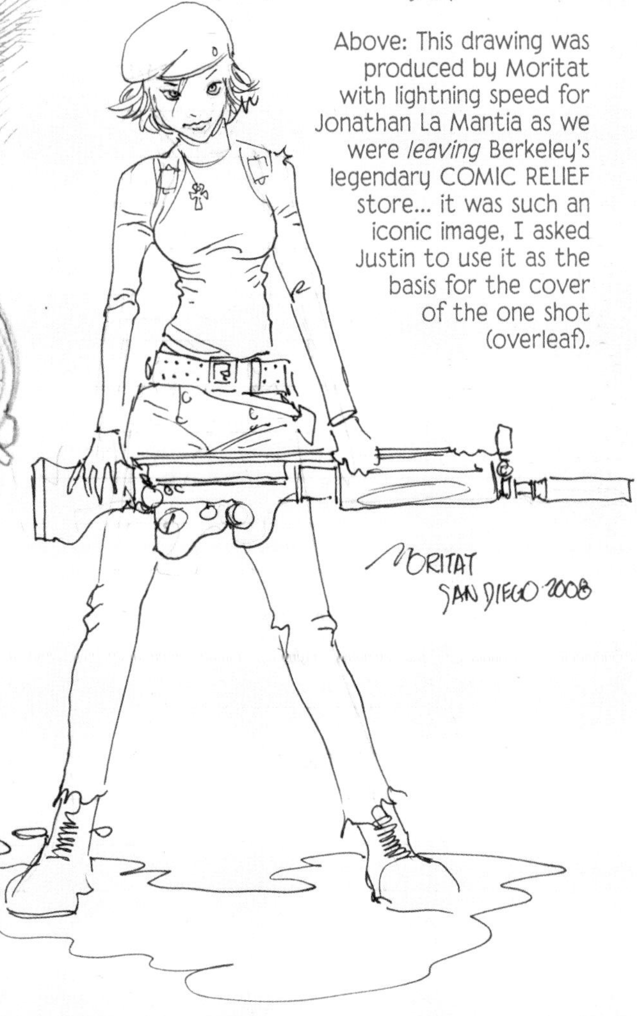
MORITAT
SAN DIEGO 2008

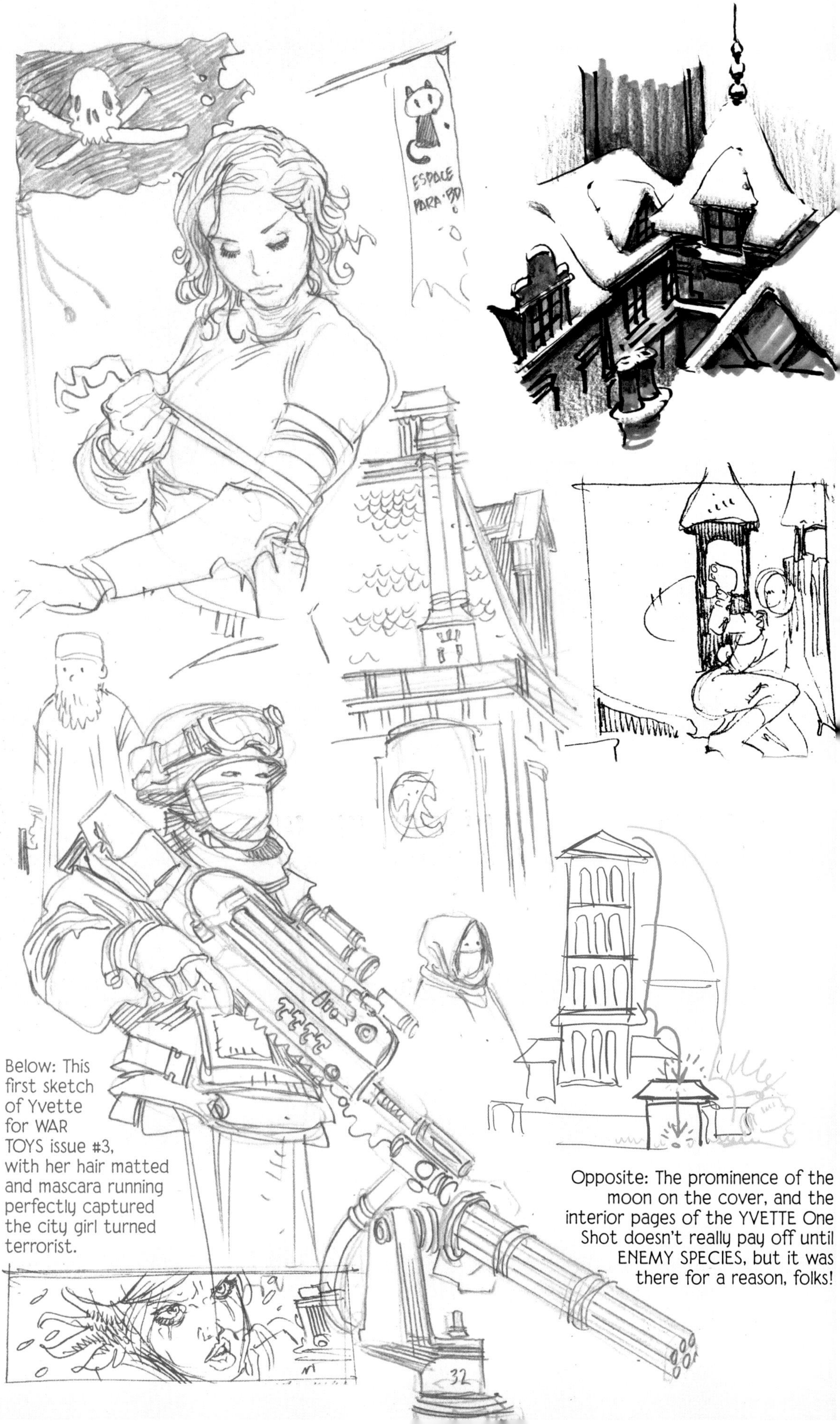

Below: This first sketch of Yvette for WAR TOYS issue #3, with her hair matted and mascara running perfectly captured the city girl turned terrorist.

Opposite: The prominence of the moon on the cover, and the interior pages of the YVETTE One Shot doesn't really pay off until ENEMY SPECIES, but it was there for a reason, folks!

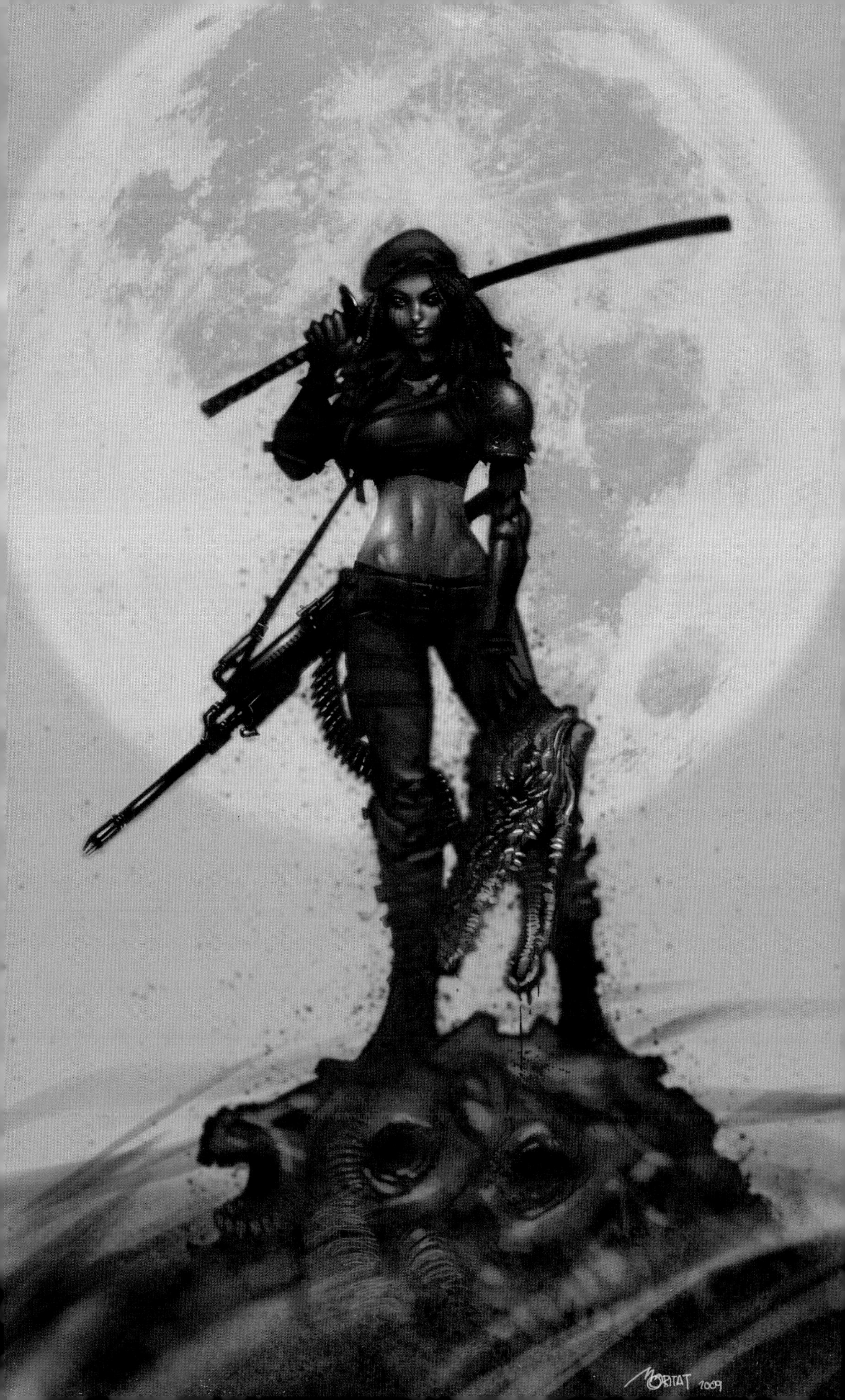
MORITAT 2009

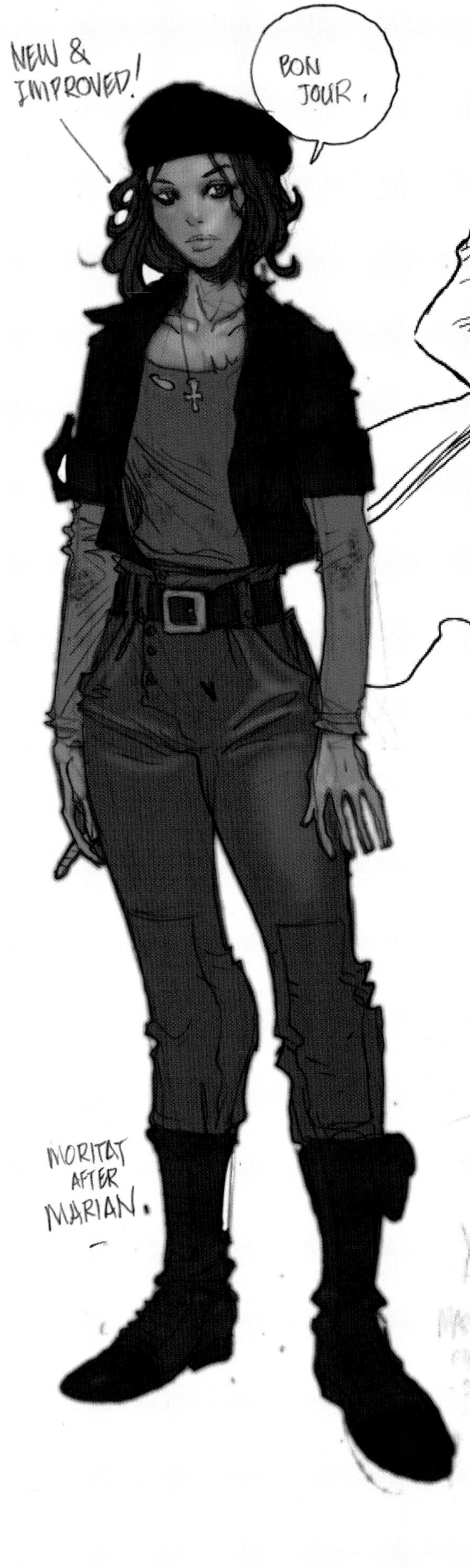
NEW & IMPROVED!
BON JOUR.
MORITAT AFTER MARIAN.

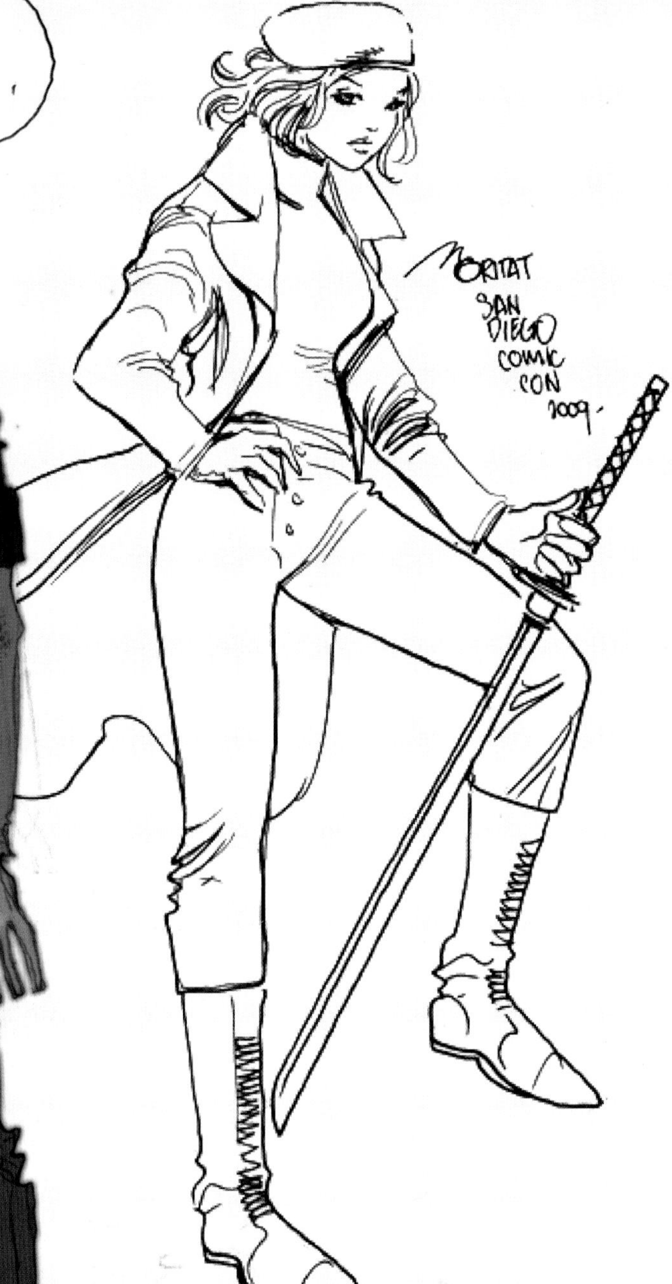
MORITAT
SAN DIEGO COMIC CON 2009.

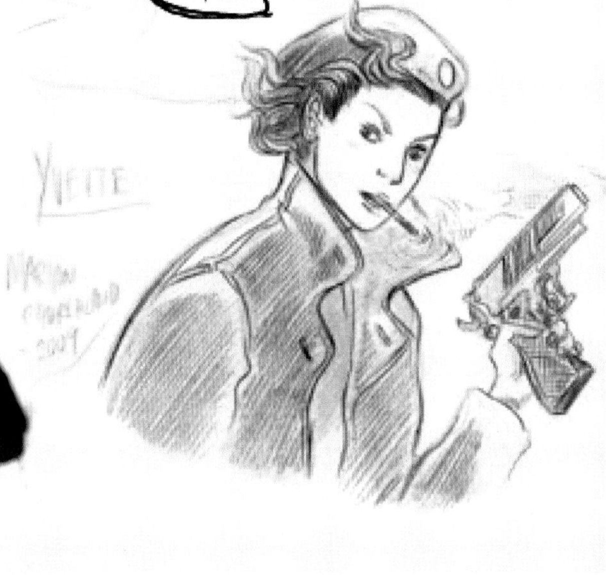

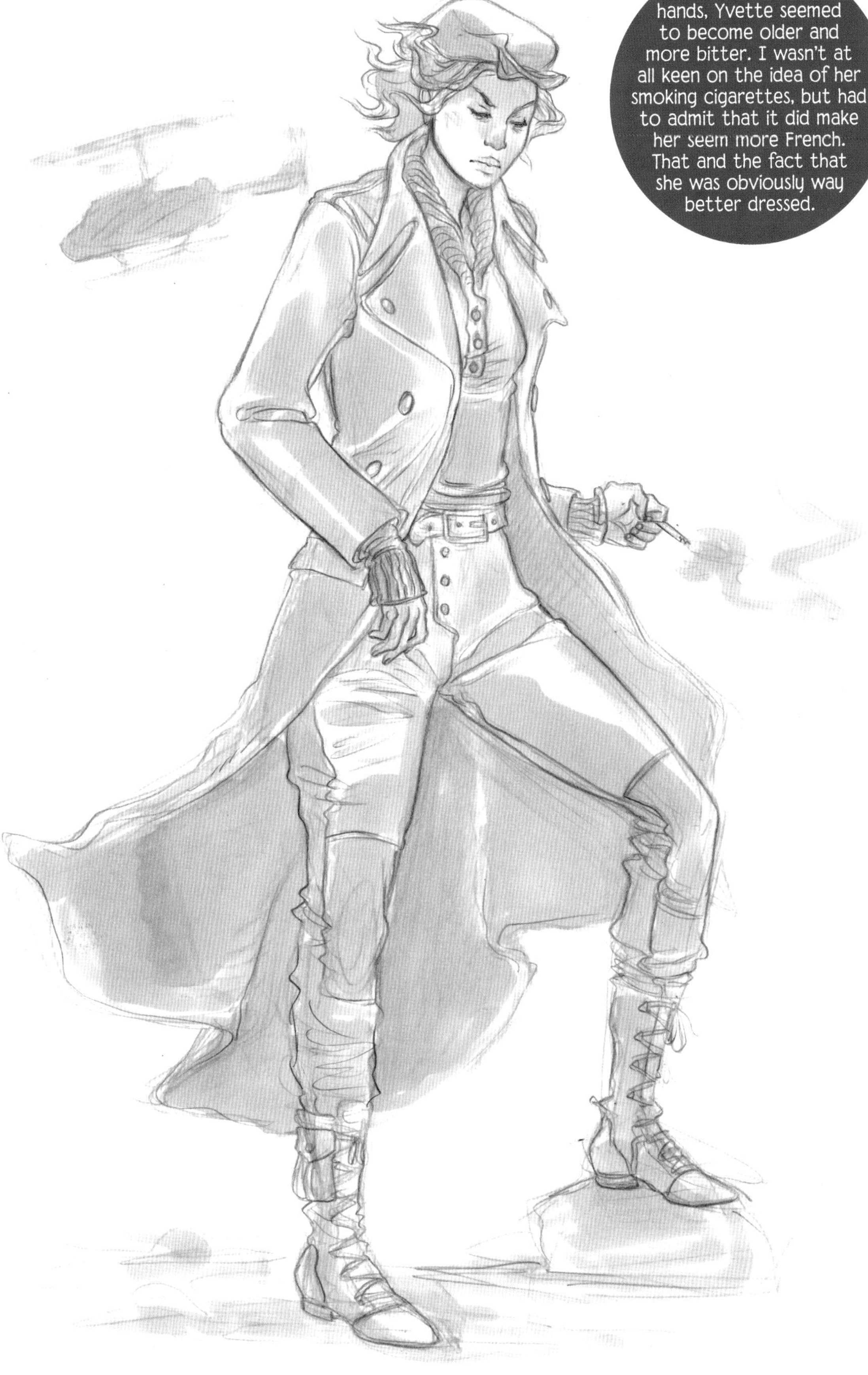

In Marian's hands, Yvette seemed to become older and more bitter. I wasn't at all keen on the idea of her smoking cigarettes, but had to admit that it did make her seem more French. That and the fact that she was obviously way better dressed.

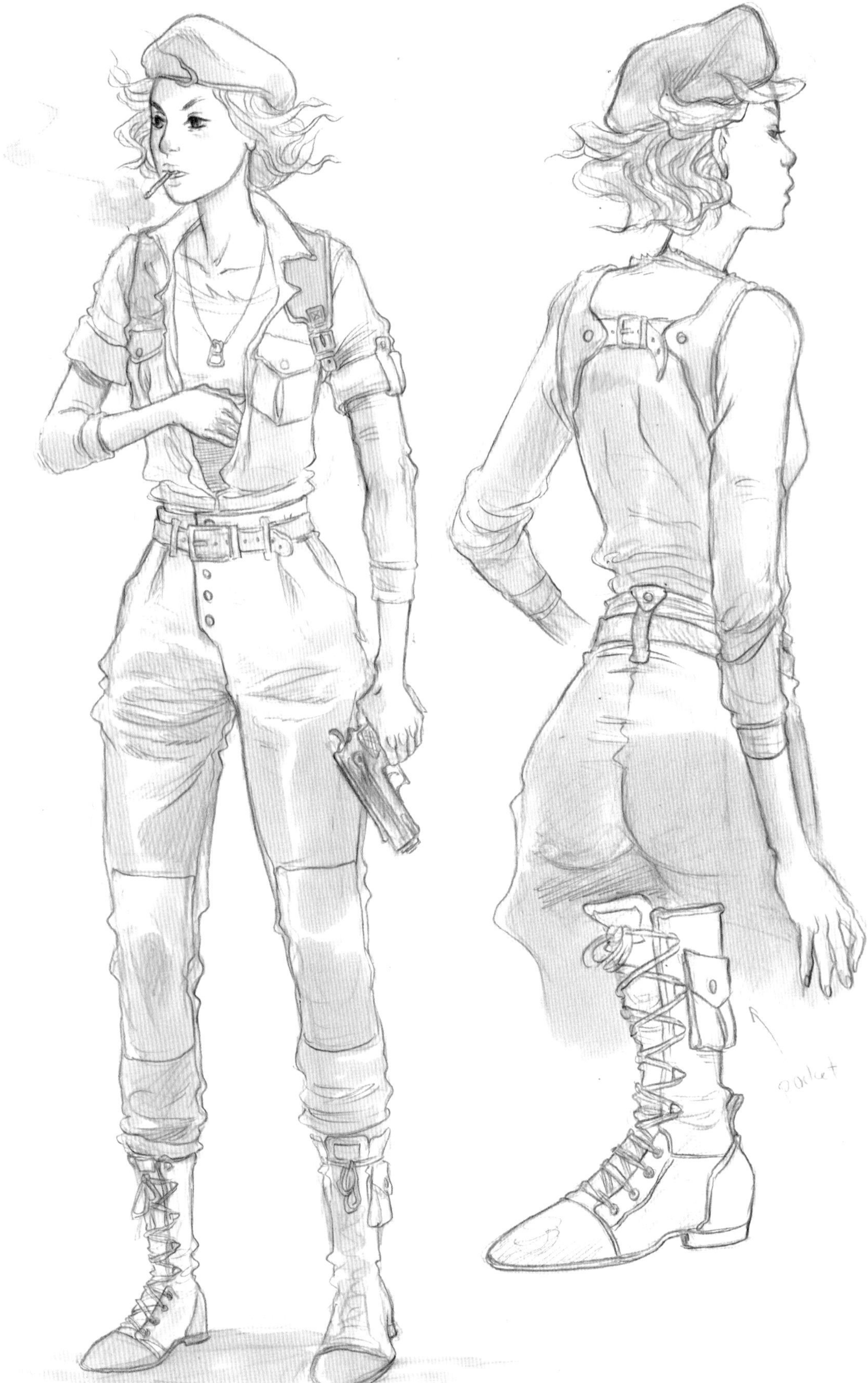
pocket

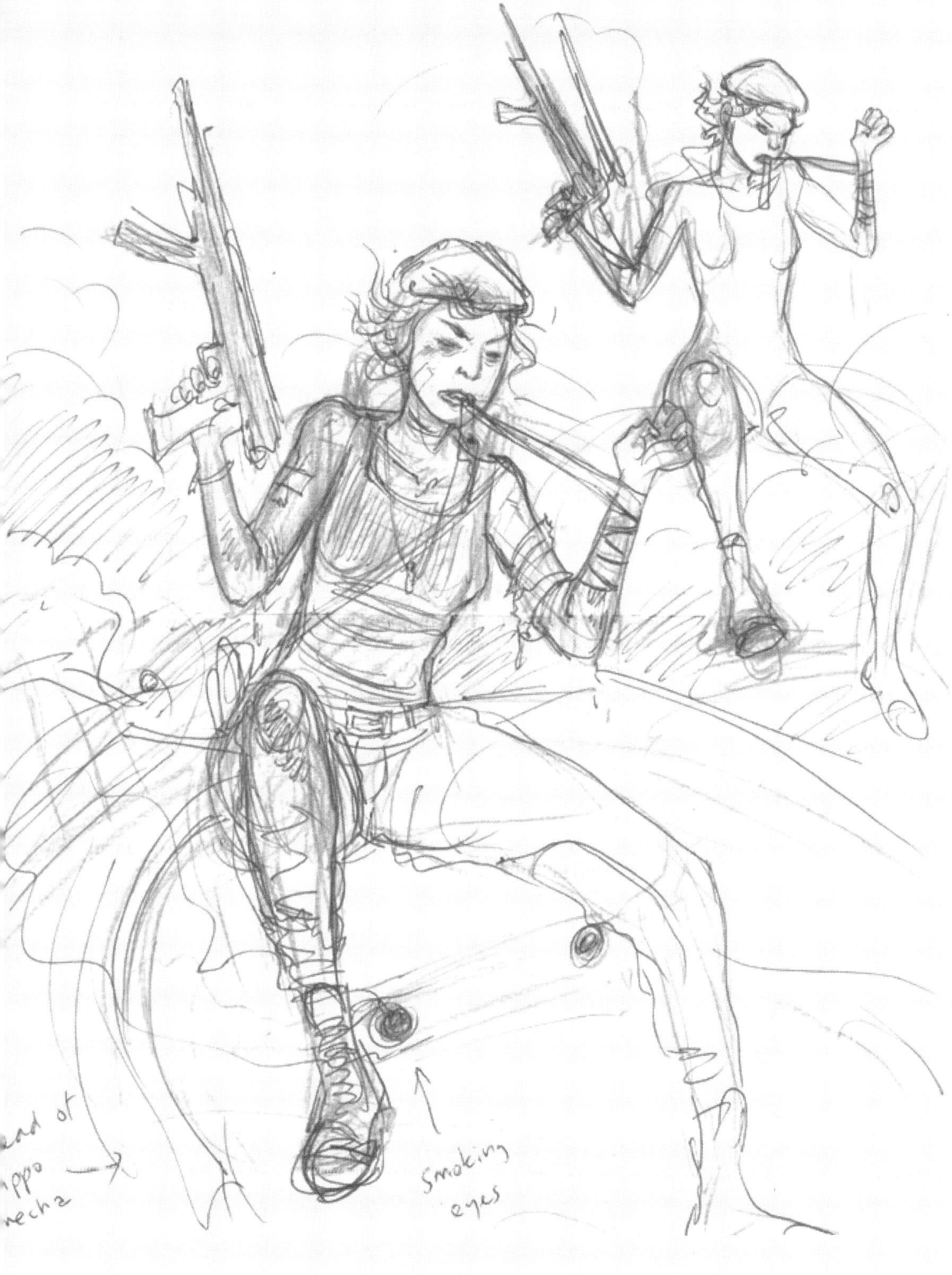
Smoking eyes

Marian's cover (full colour version overleaf) suggested that Yvette had downed and defeated the Hippo-helmed exosuit thrown into issue #2 by Moritat.
An interesting starting point for a story, I thought.

Remember what I said about artists often being right?

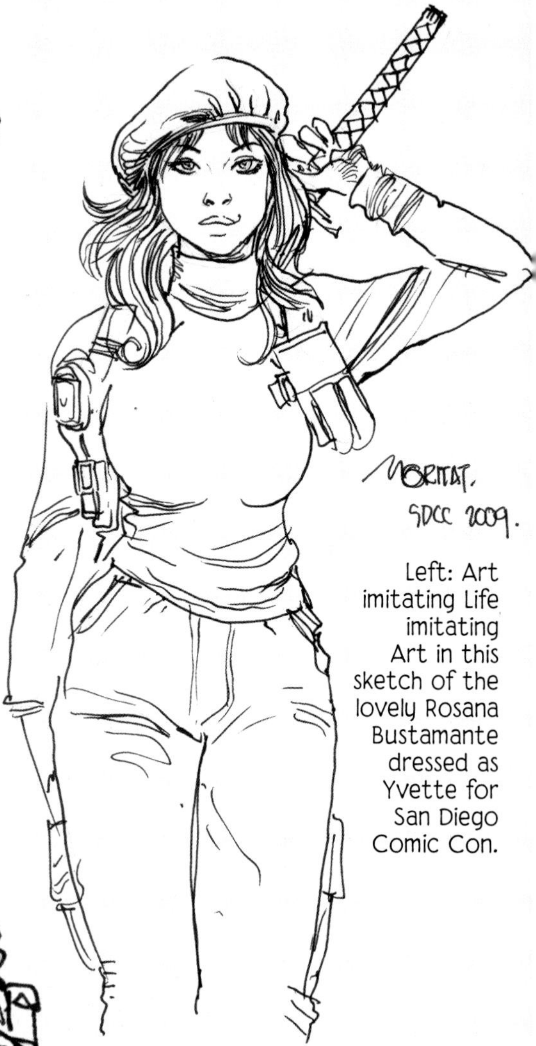
MORITAT.
SDCC 2009.

Left: Art imitating Life imitating Art in this sketch of the lovely Rosana Bustamante dressed as Yvette for San Diego Comic Con.

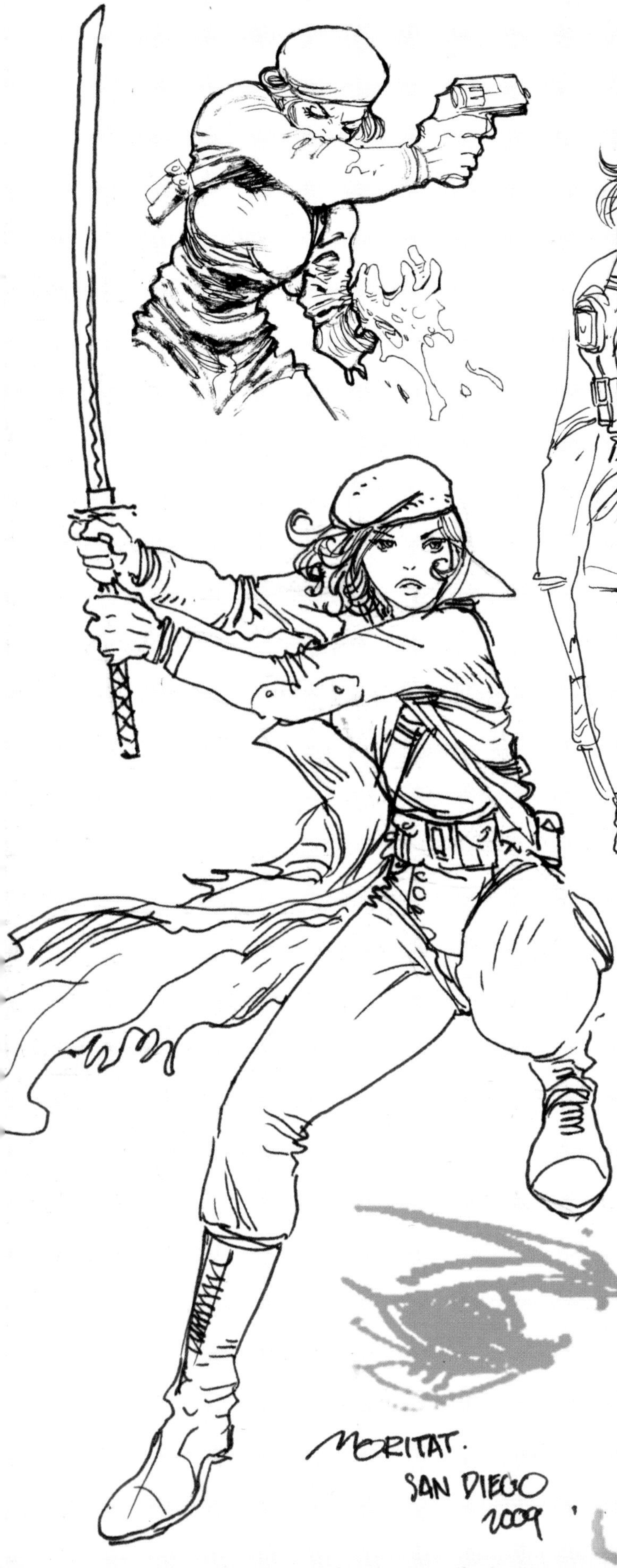
MORITAT.
SAN DIEGO
2009

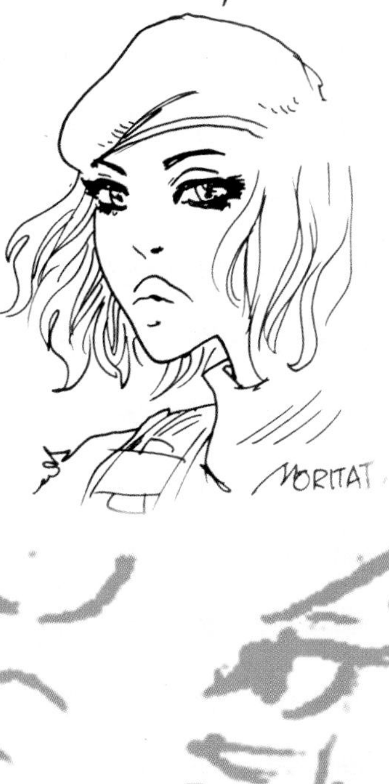
MORITAT

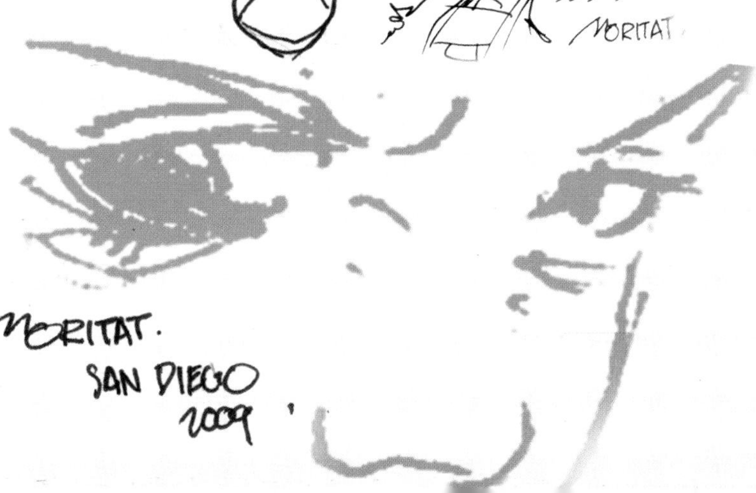

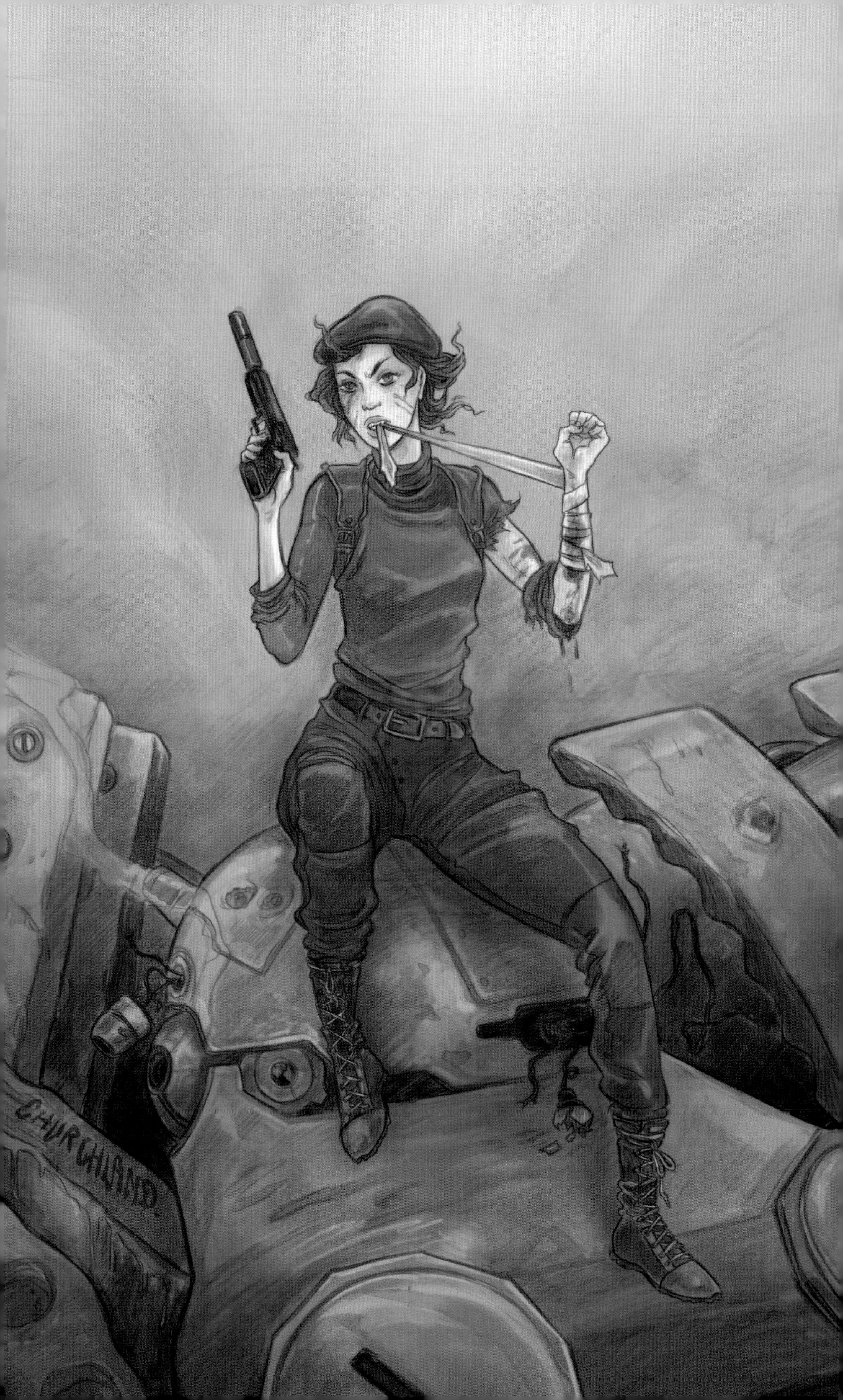
CHURCHLAND

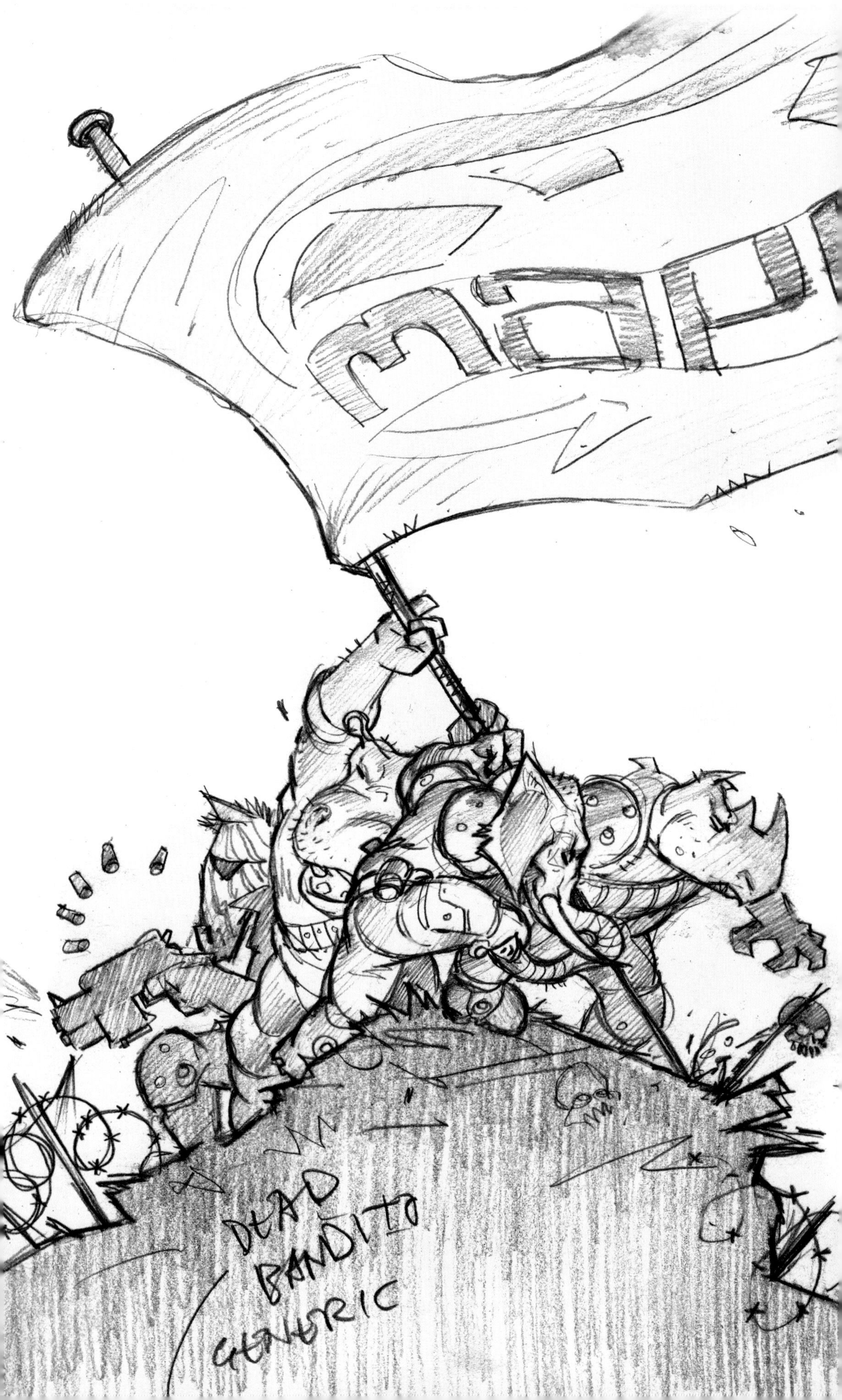
DEAD
BANDITO
GENERIC

Enter:
BOO COOK! If you've read ELEPHANTMEN: COVER STORIES #1, you'll know that Boo wrote to me from out of the blue hoping to create some covers for us. WAR TOYS was his first work for us.

Below: These sketches were Boo's warmups for the first cover (sketch opposite). His shot of Ebony was so strong we built the cover of #2 around it.

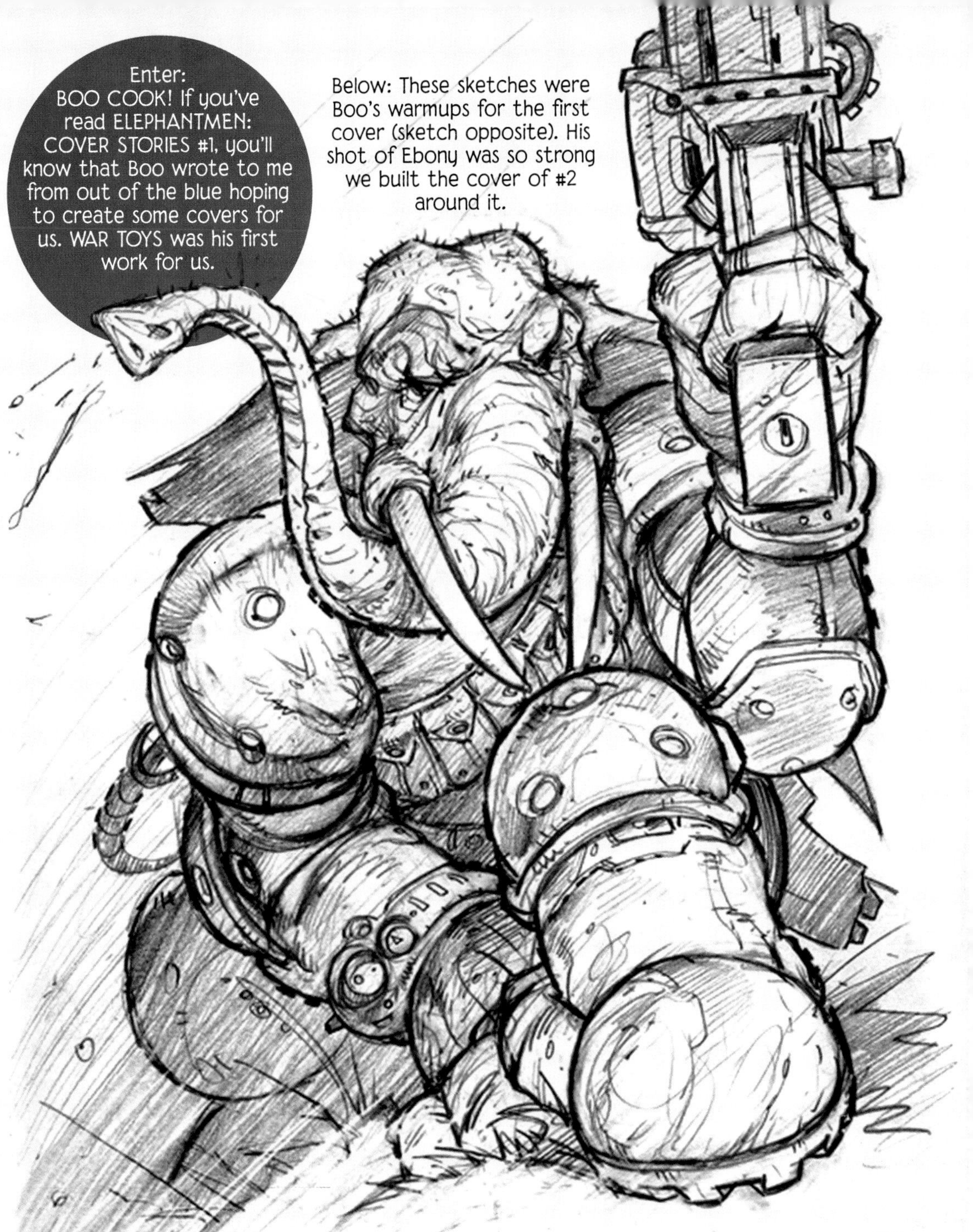

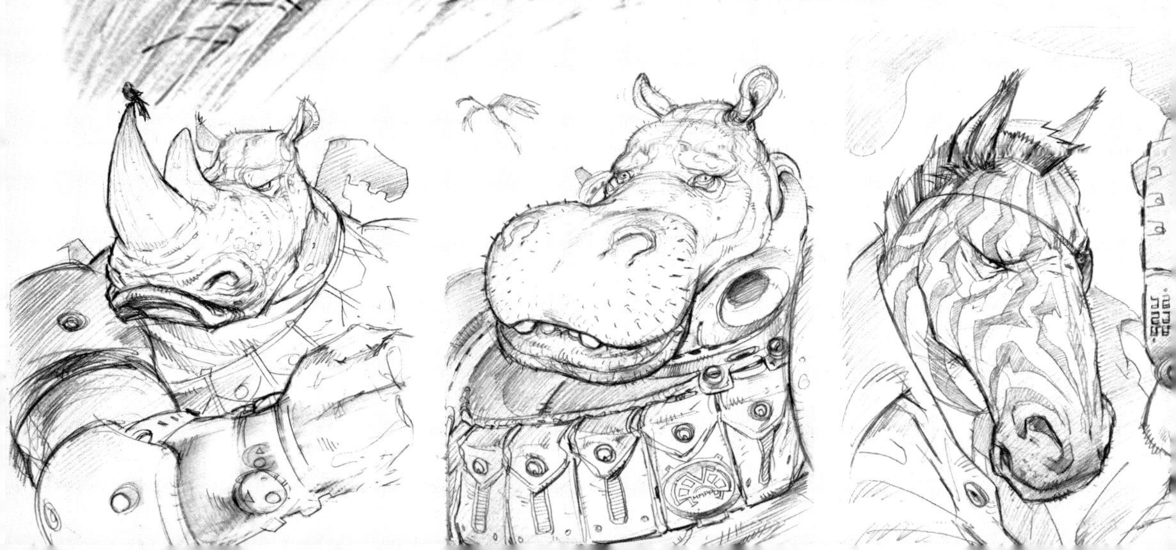

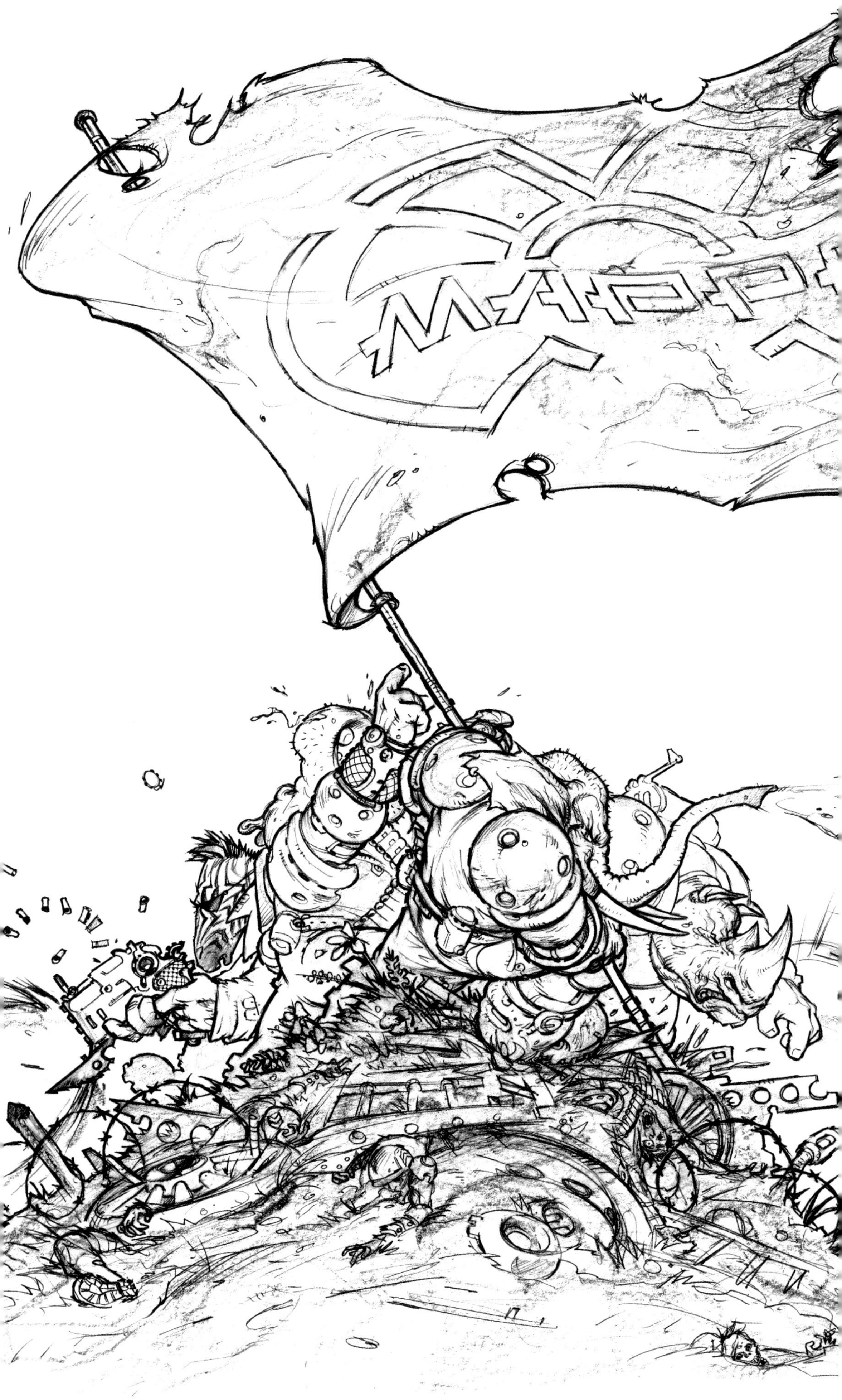

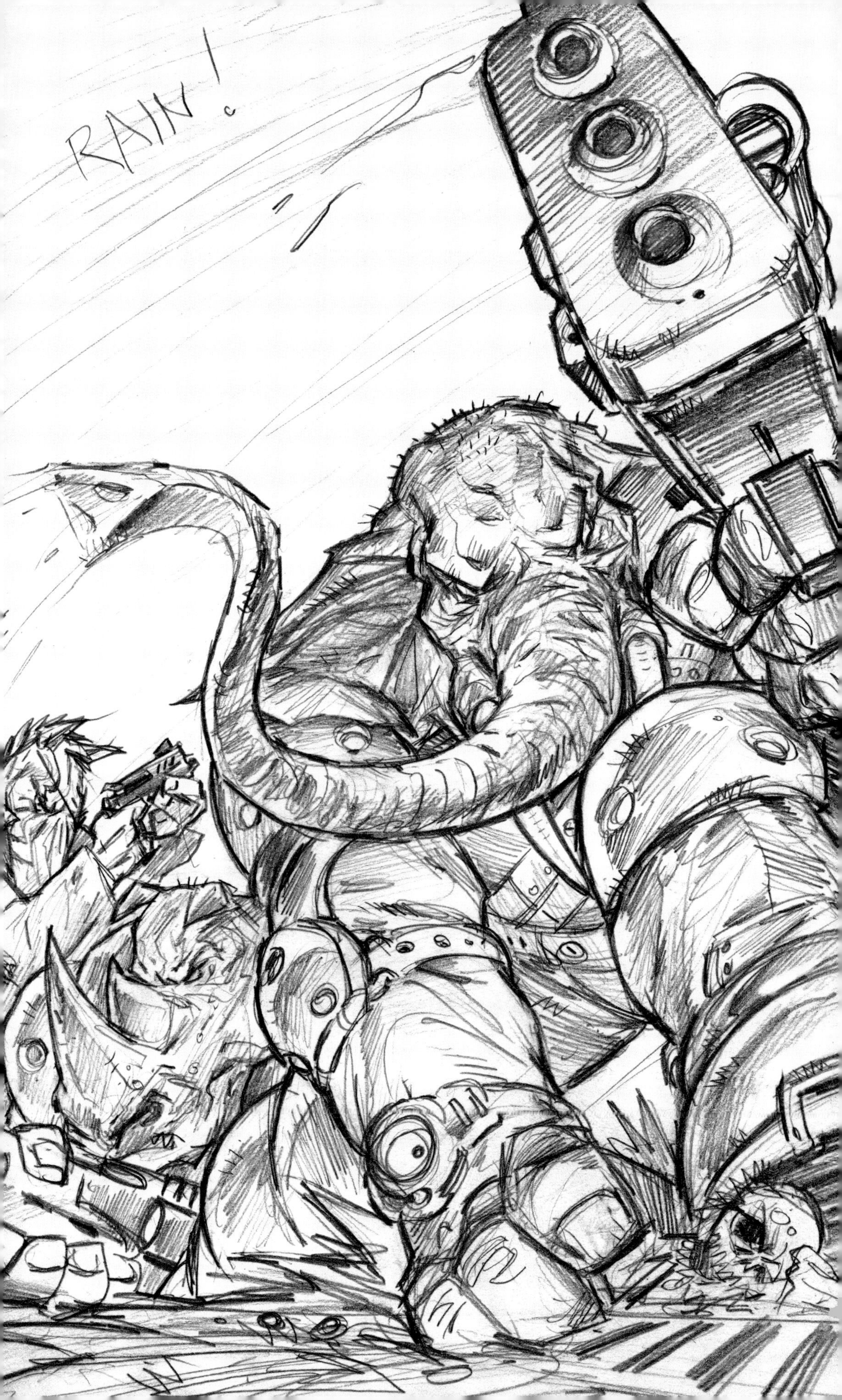
RAIN!

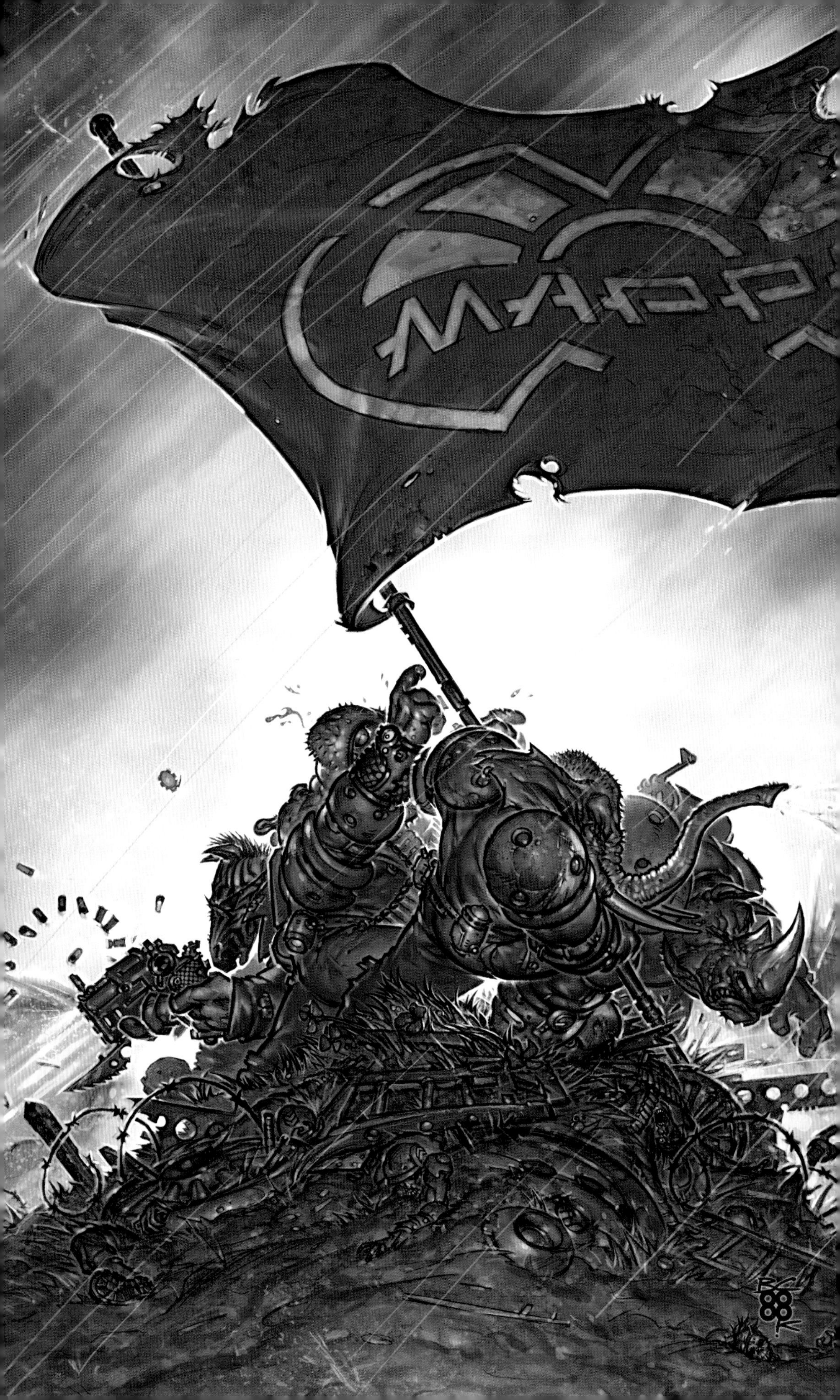

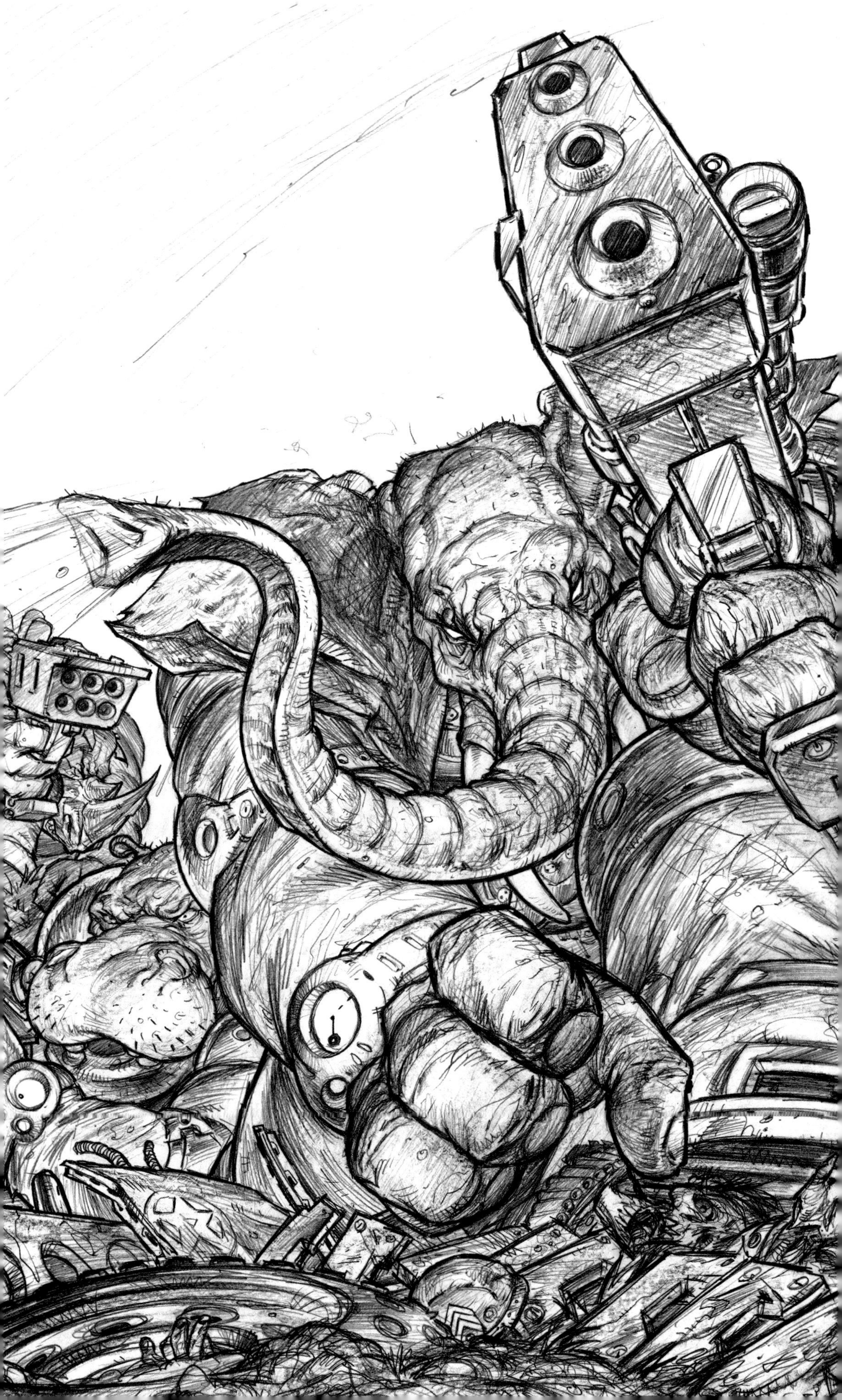

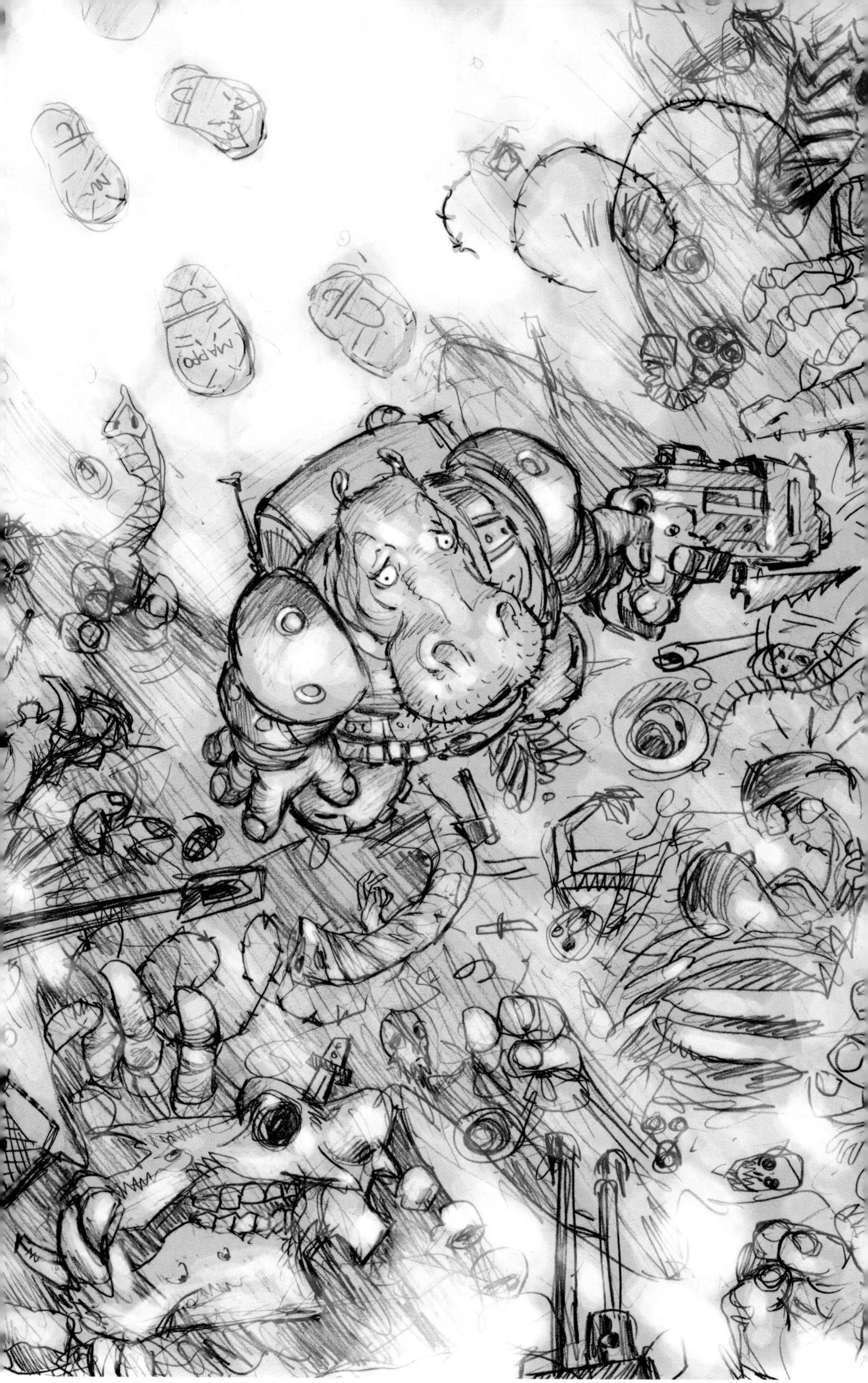

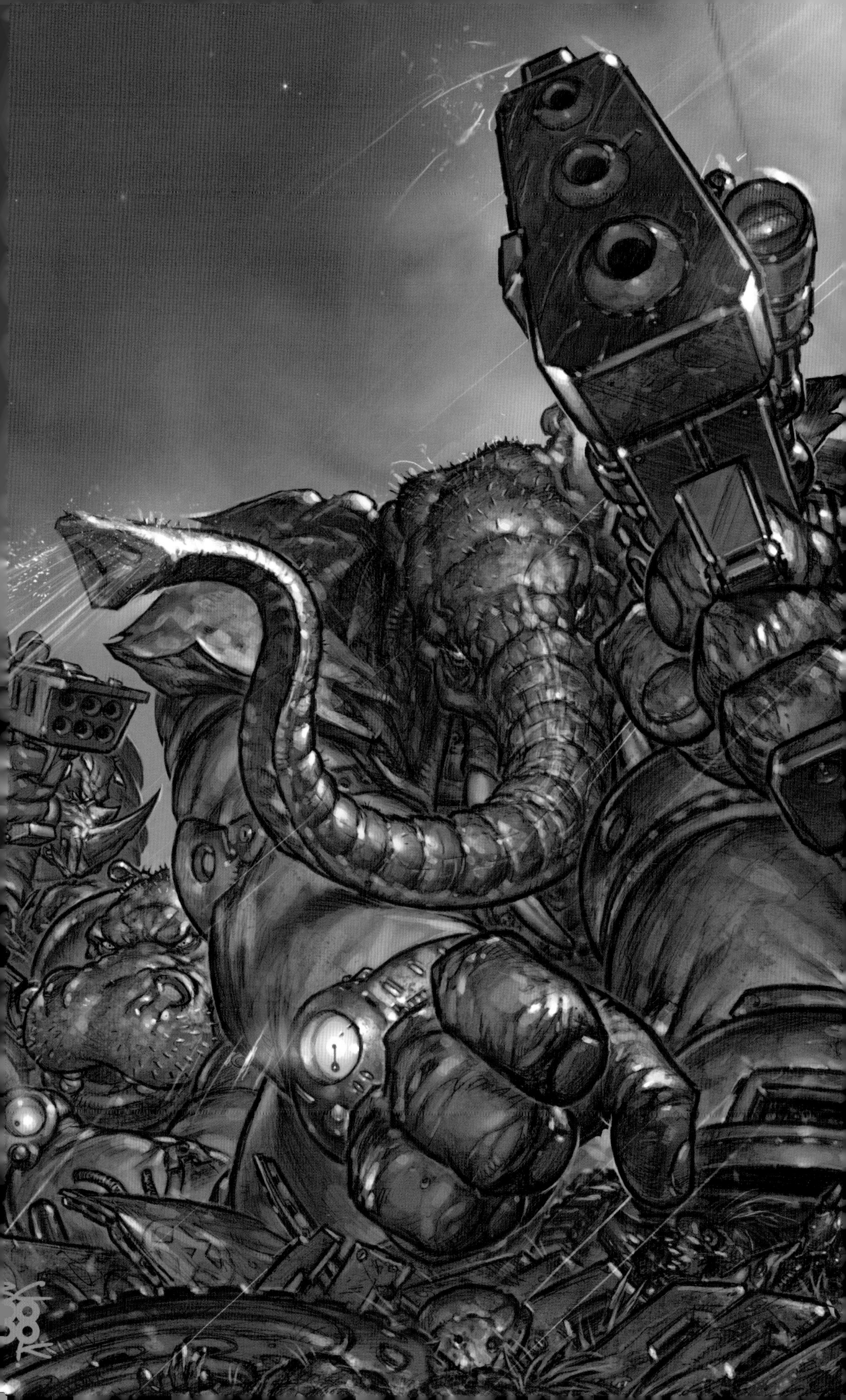

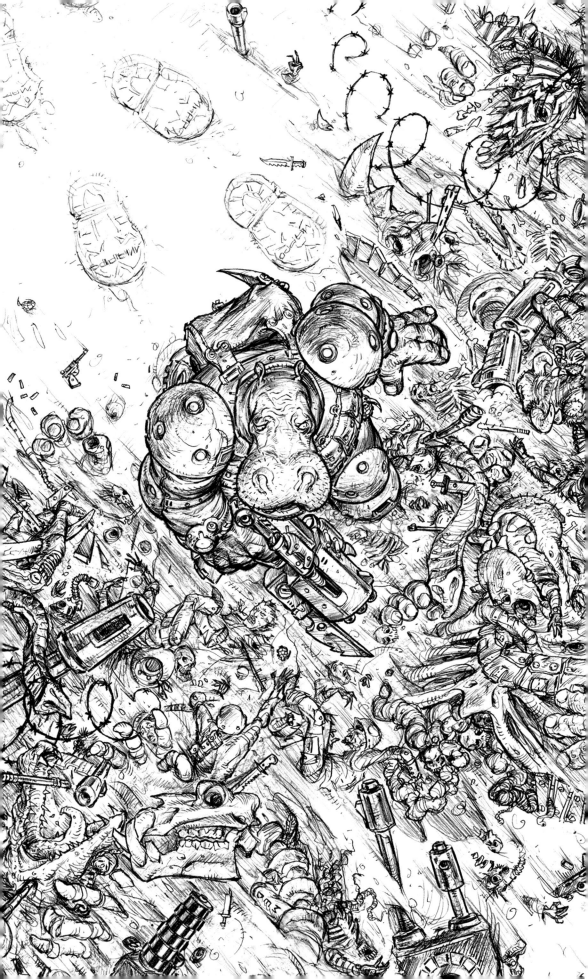

Previous Page: Boo's initial sketch for the cover of WAR TOYS #3 overstated Hip's reaction to the frozen battlefield of the dead...

The sketches on this page were suggestions for Hip's facial expression... the lower drawing captured exactly what I was looking for but the finished figure and face you see opposite far exceeded my expectations... this cover remains one of my favourite ELEPHANTMEN covers and the original is stored in the Comicraft vaults waiting for framing.

If I had any remaining doubts about Boo being the right artist to take over the responsibility of creating cover art from Ladrönn, they were dispelled completely when I saw the finished colour cover for issue #3 which you can find overleaf. A real beauty, right up there in my (admittedly biased) estimation with the mighty Frank Frazetta's FROST GIANTS.

Don't tell Boo -- see my comments about artists being right earlier!

BC 88 K

This cover was also the first to sport Boo's new signature (added to the previous covers after the fact), designed at my suggestion... sometimes writers have good ideas too, y'know!

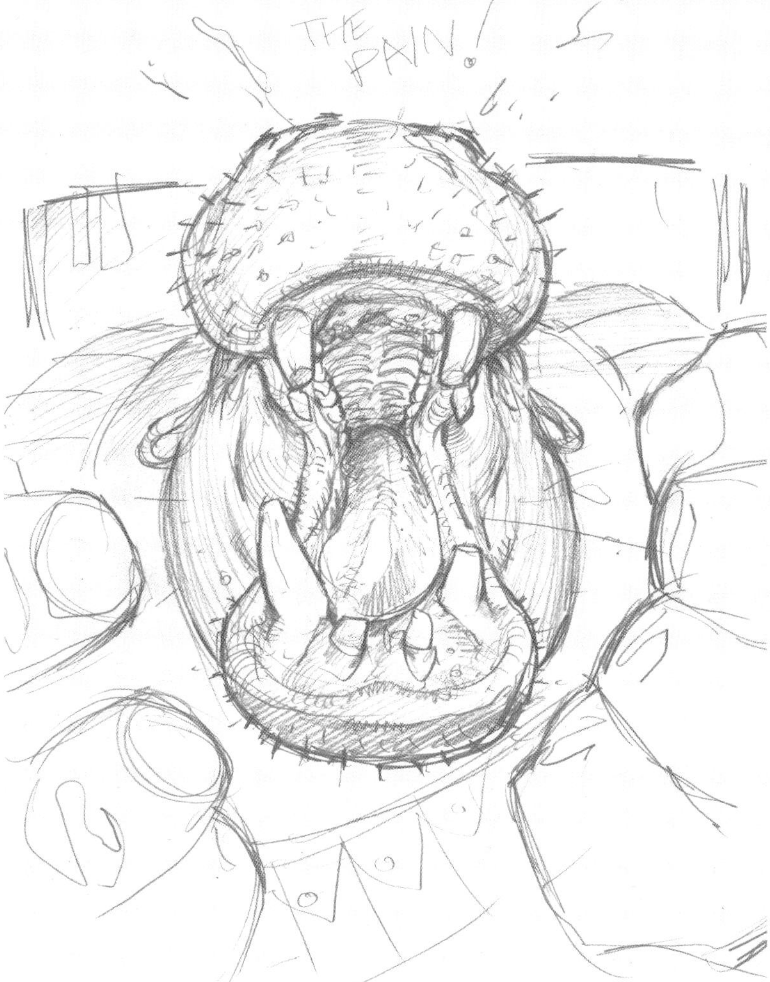
THE PAIN!

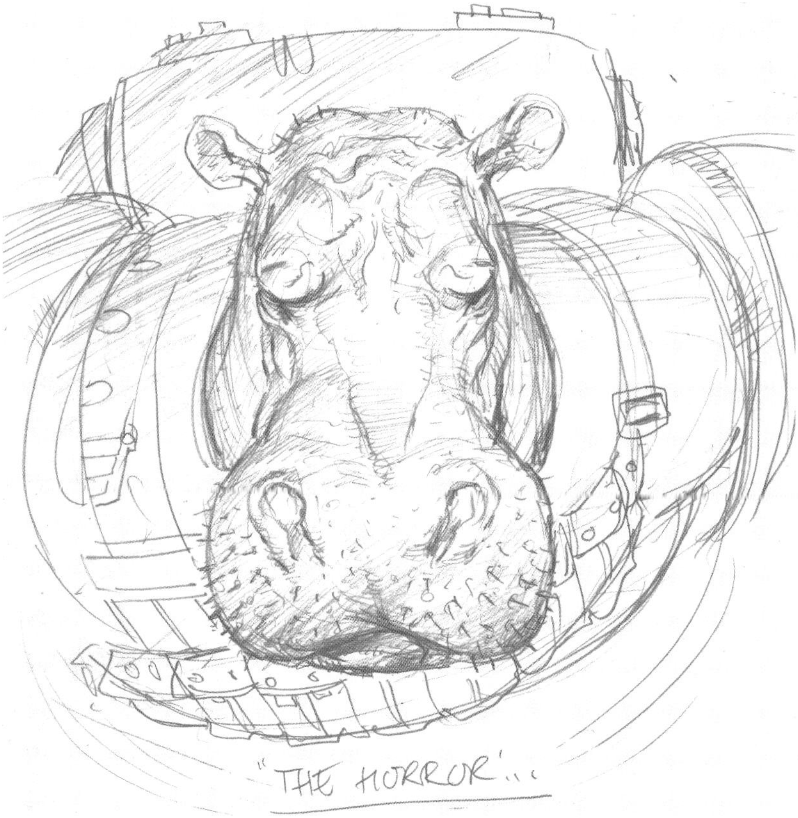
"THE HORROR"...

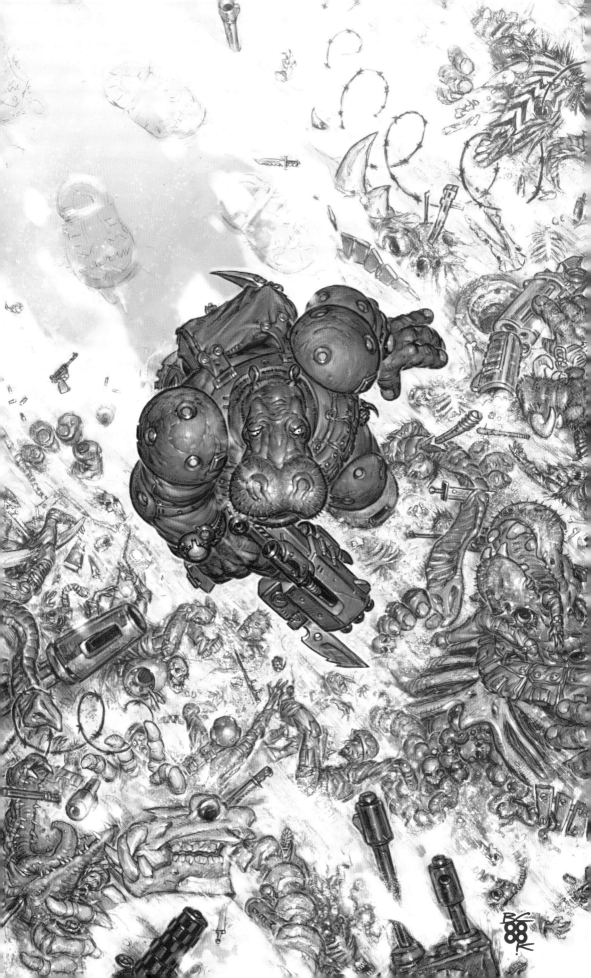

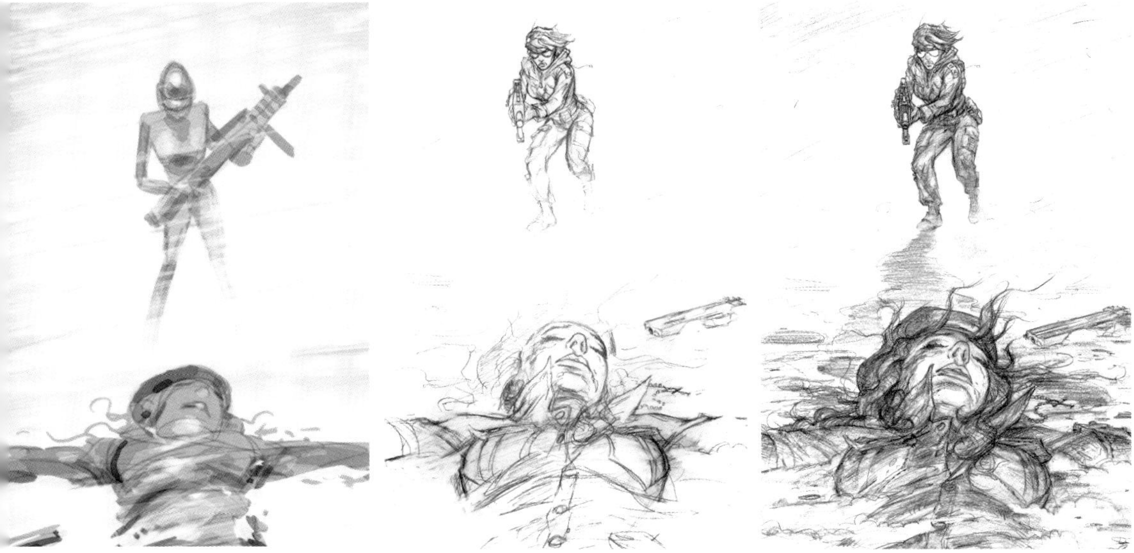

Above & Below Left: For this collection, I felt that we needed a transition image, showing Yvette lying bleeding in the snow, moments before discovery by Blackthorne's Icebreaker team. I described the scene to Boo over the phone and he produced the computer sketch you see here top left.

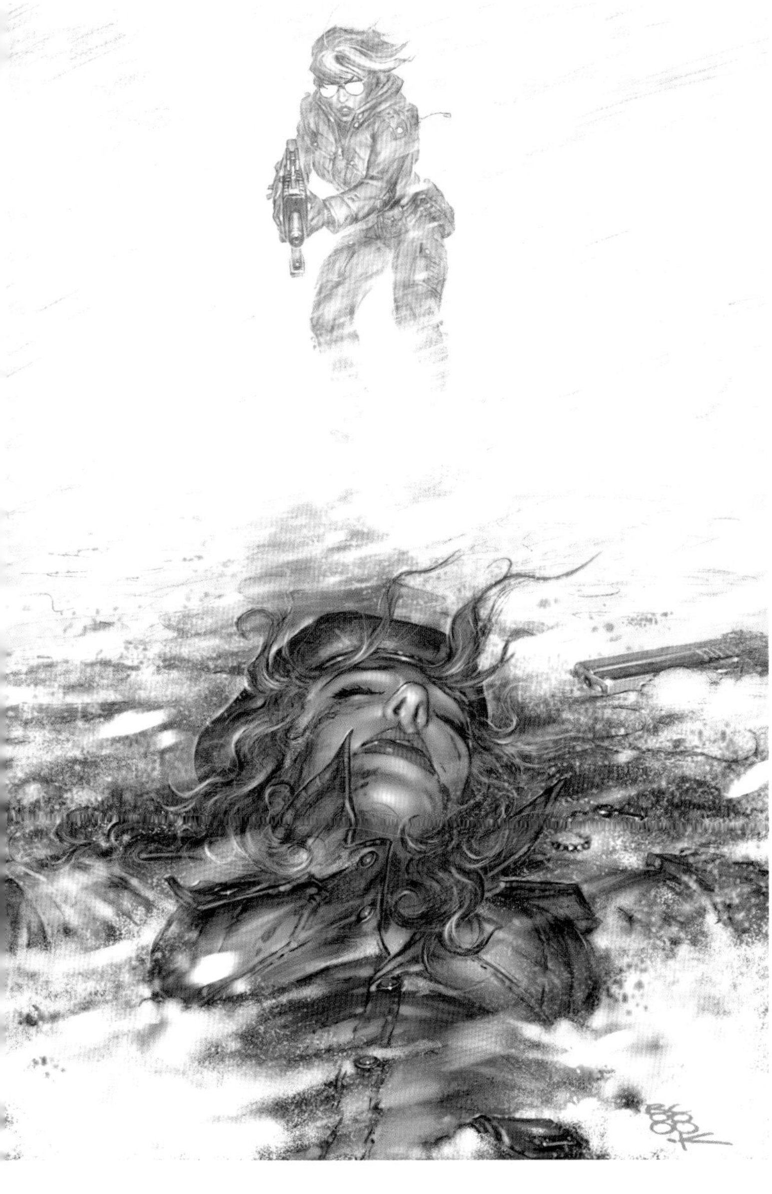

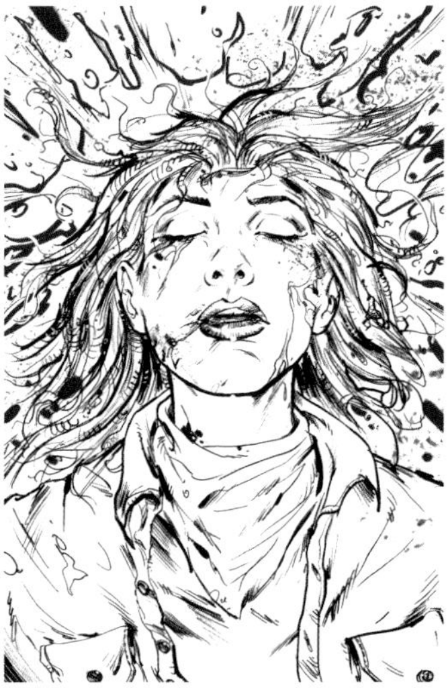

Above: #26 Inks by Boo over breakdowns by Vince Lee.
Below: The same shot for #34 pencilled by Boo hisself.

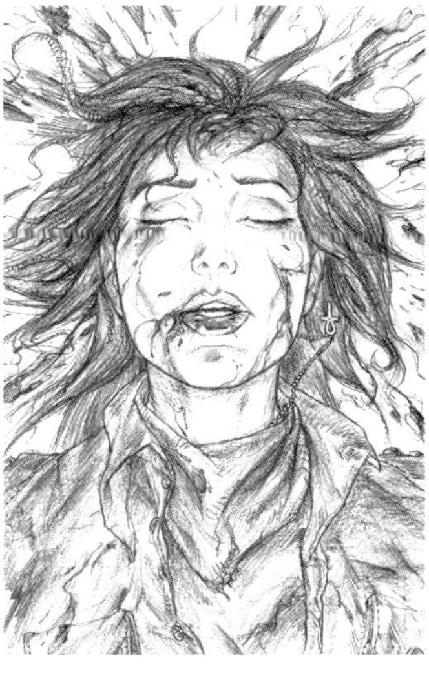

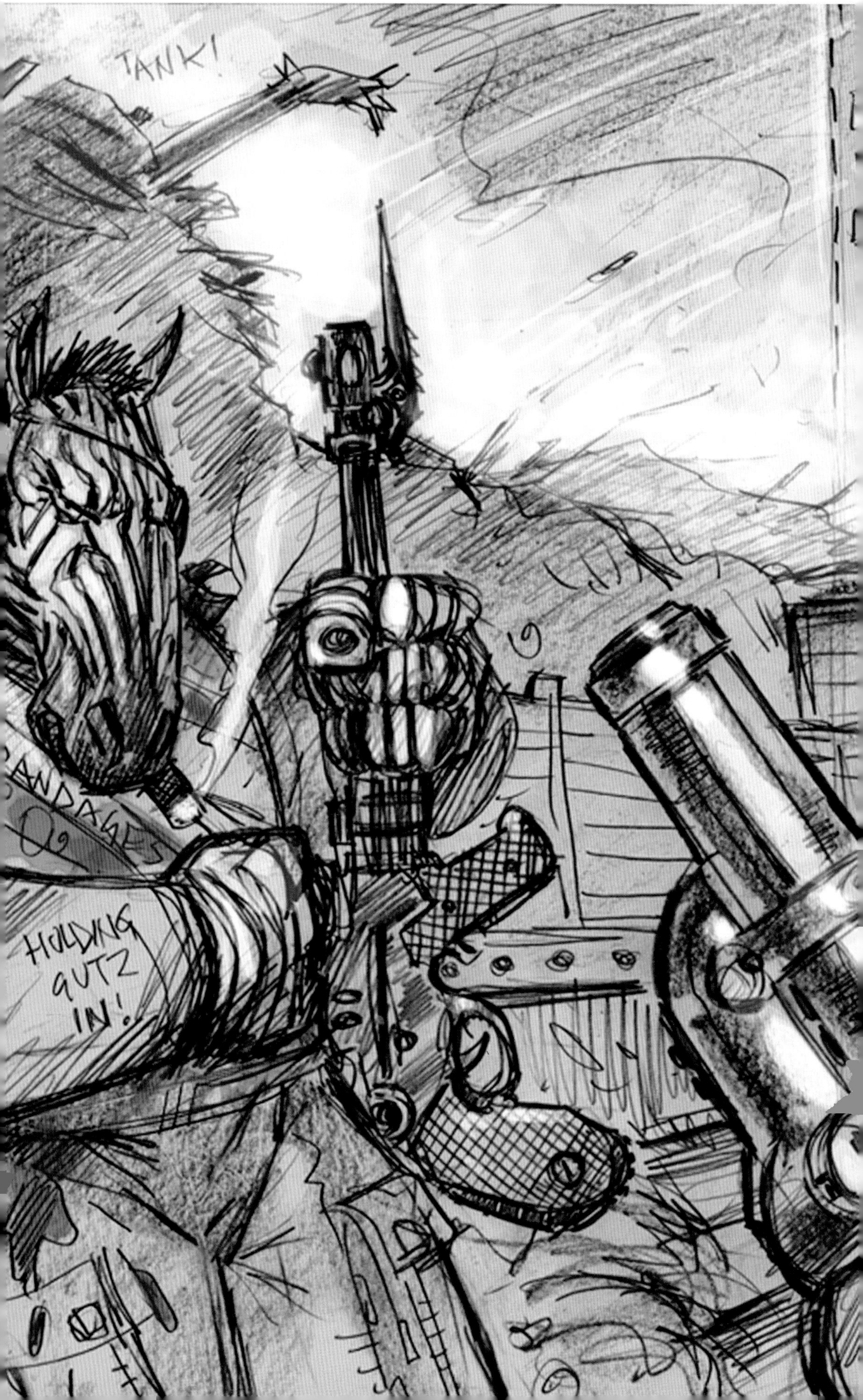
TANK!
BANDAGES
HOLDING GUTZ IN!

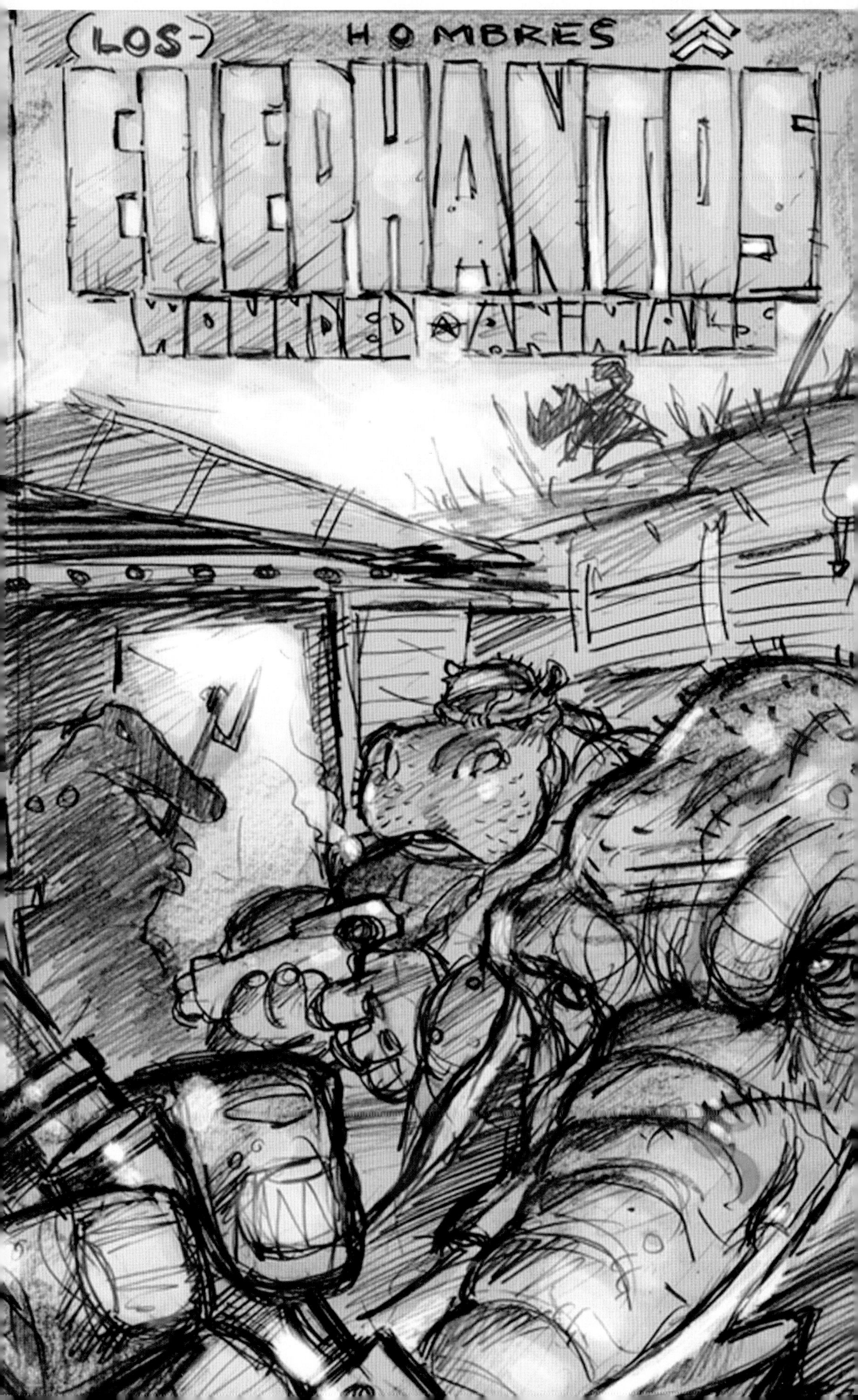
(LOS-)
HOMBRES

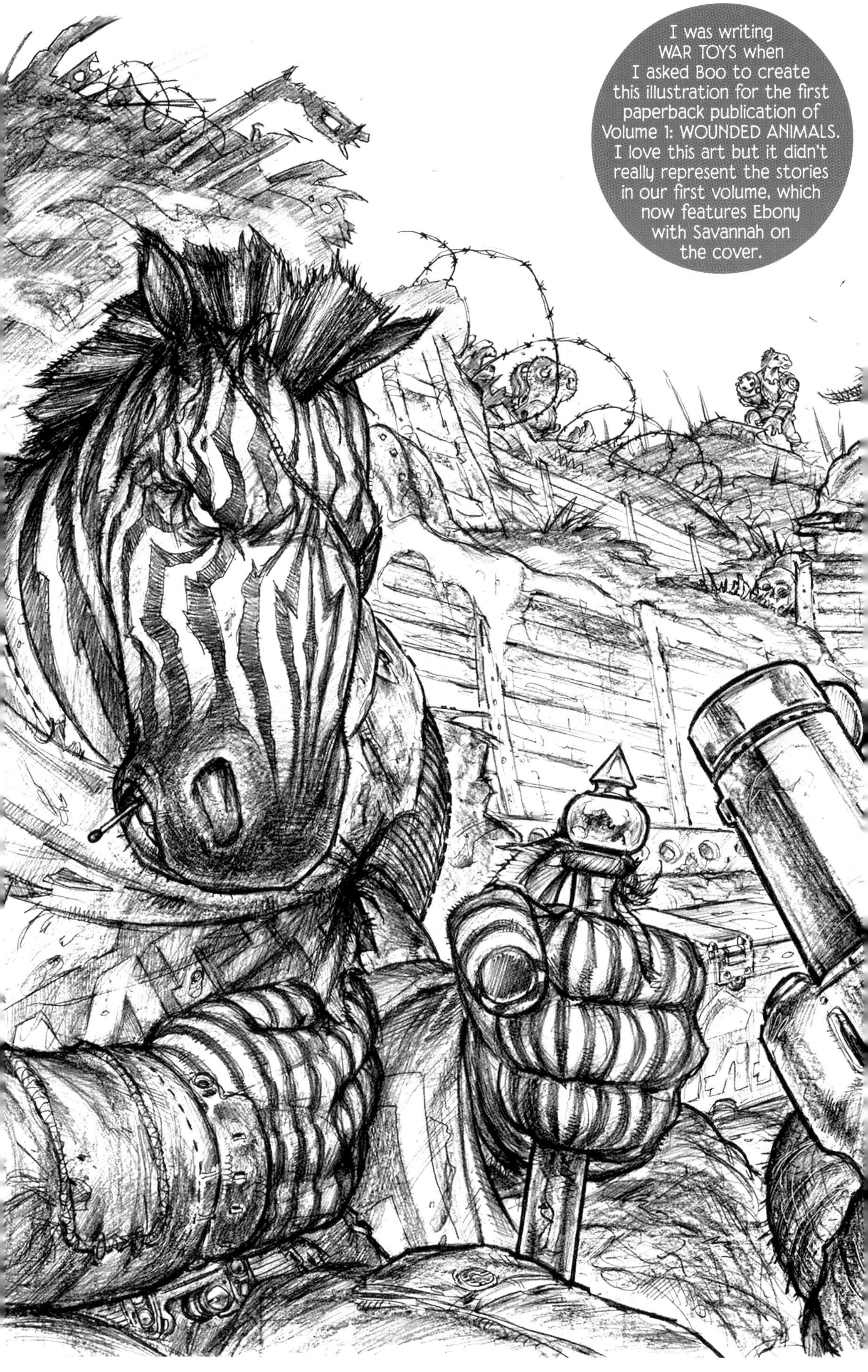

I was writing WAR TOYS when I asked Boo to create this illustration for the first paperback publication of Volume 1: WOUNDED ANIMALS. I love this art but it didn't really represent the stories in our first volume, which now features Ebony with Savannah on the cover.

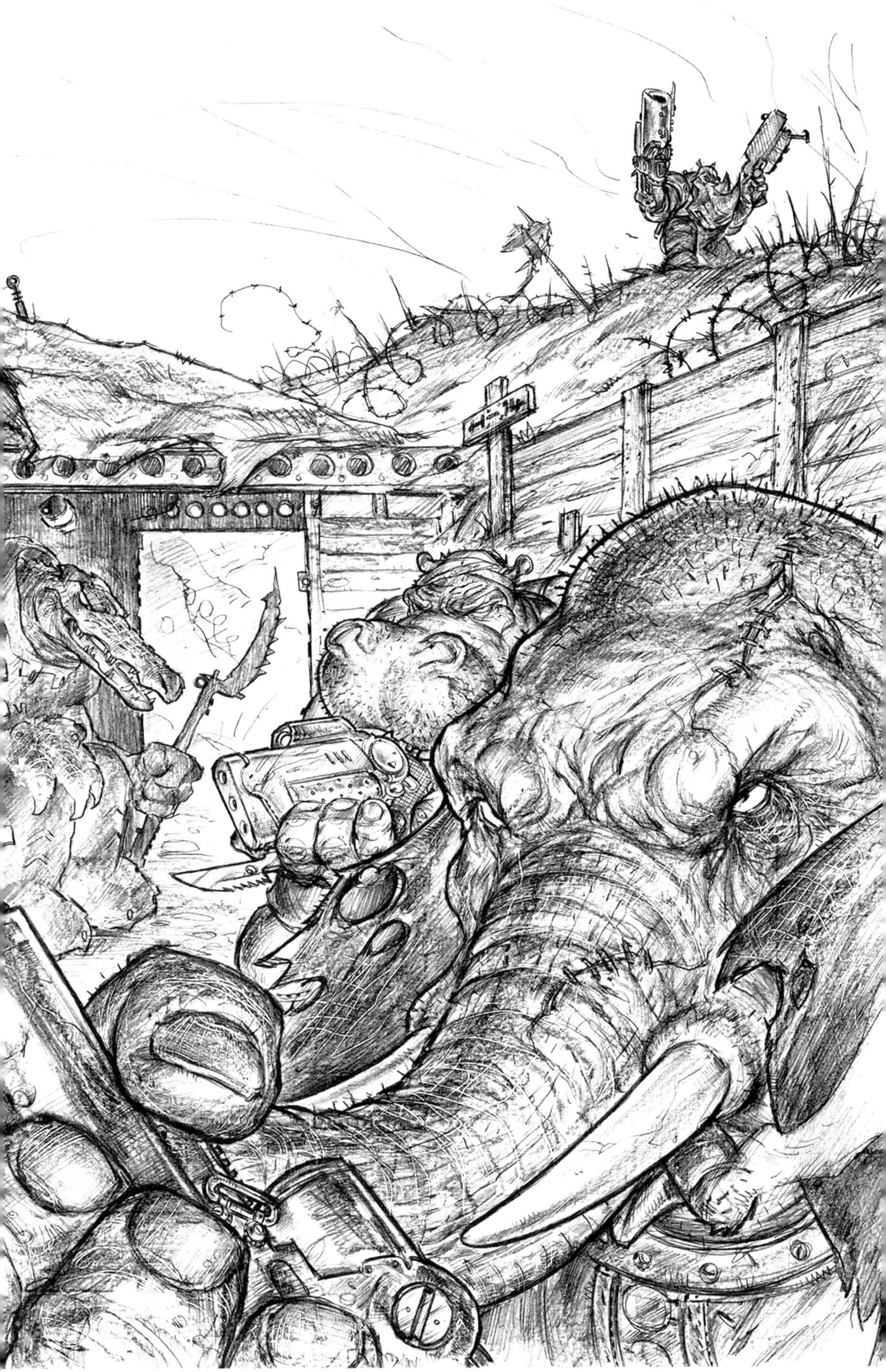

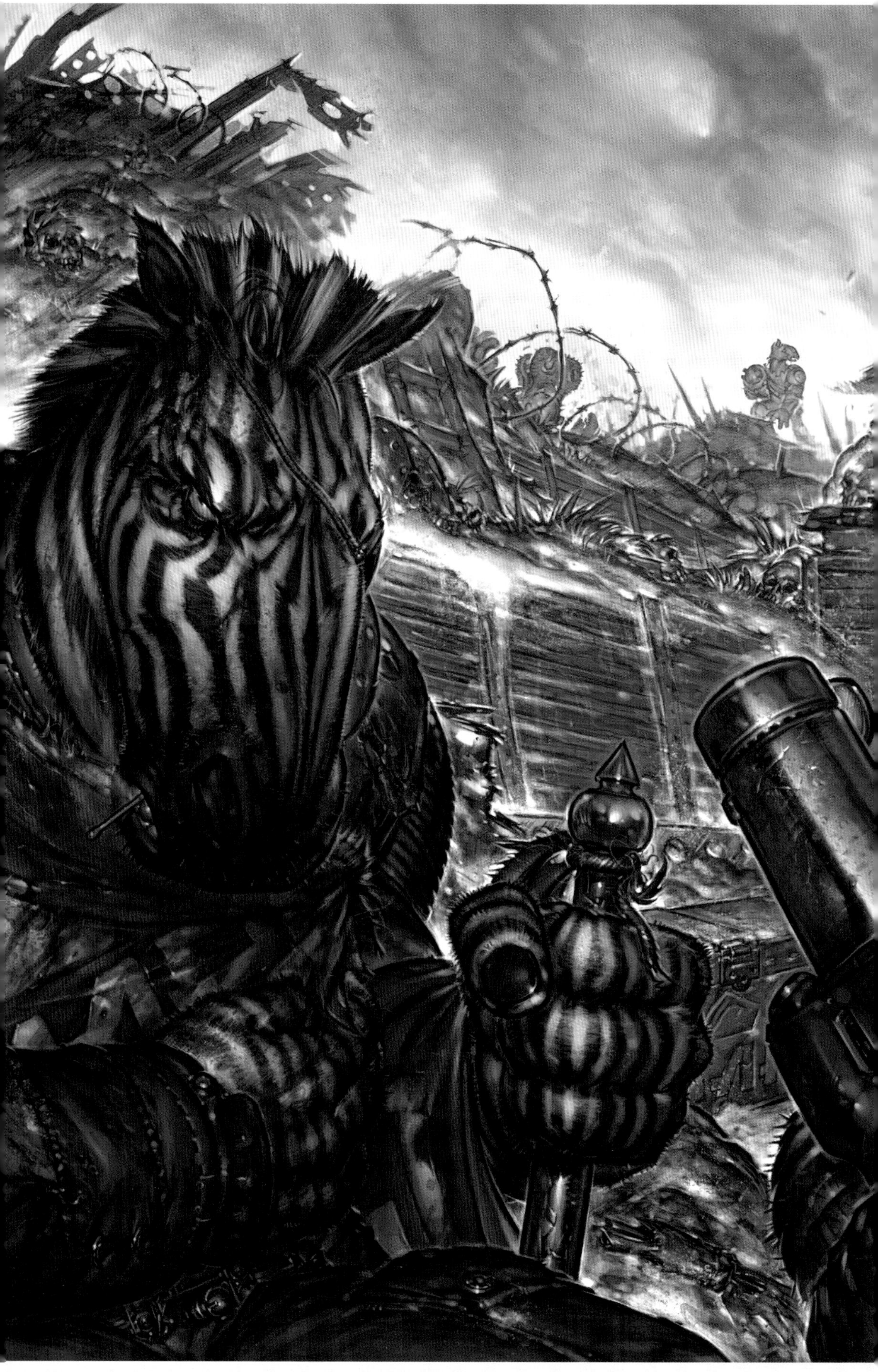

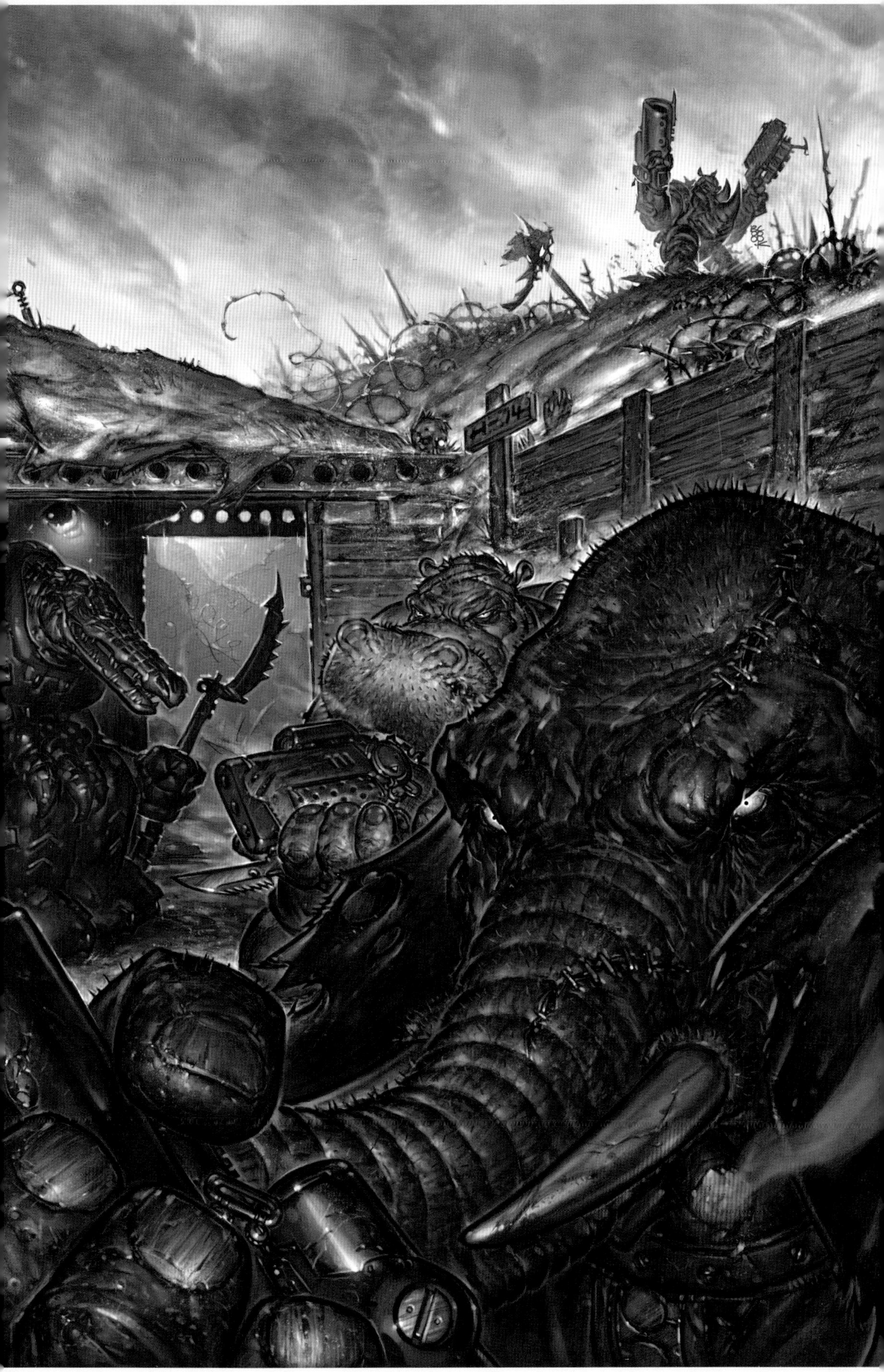

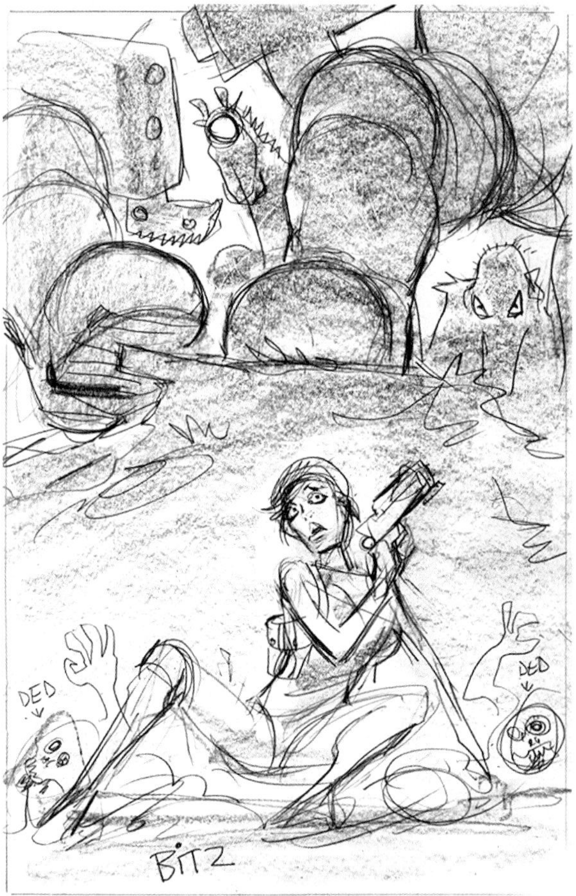
DED
DED
BITZ

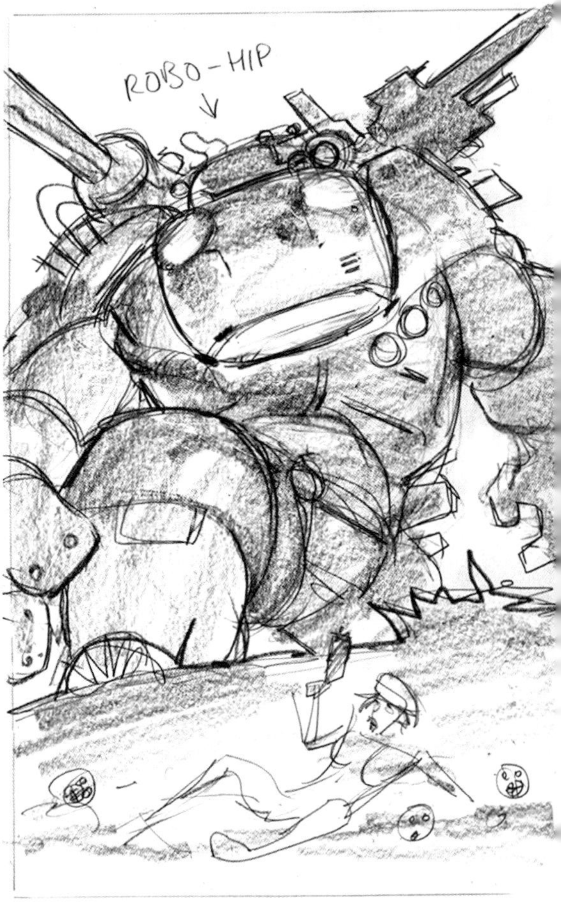
ROBO-HIP

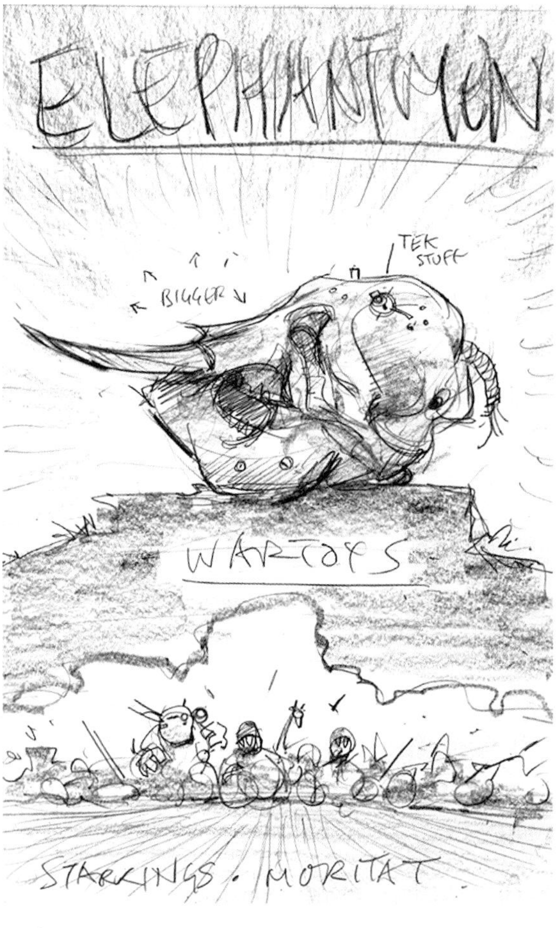
ELEPHANTMEN
BIGGER
TEK STUFF
WARTOYS
STARKINGS · MORITAT

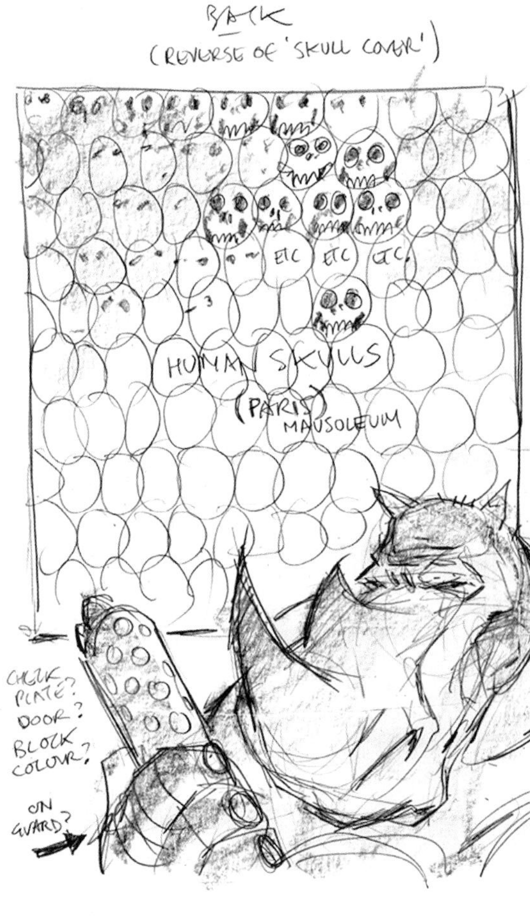
BACK
(REVERSE OF 'SKULL COVER')
ETC ETC ETC
HUMAN SKULLS
(PARIS) MAUSOLEUM
CHUCK PLATE? DOOR? BLOCK COLOUR?
ON GUARD?

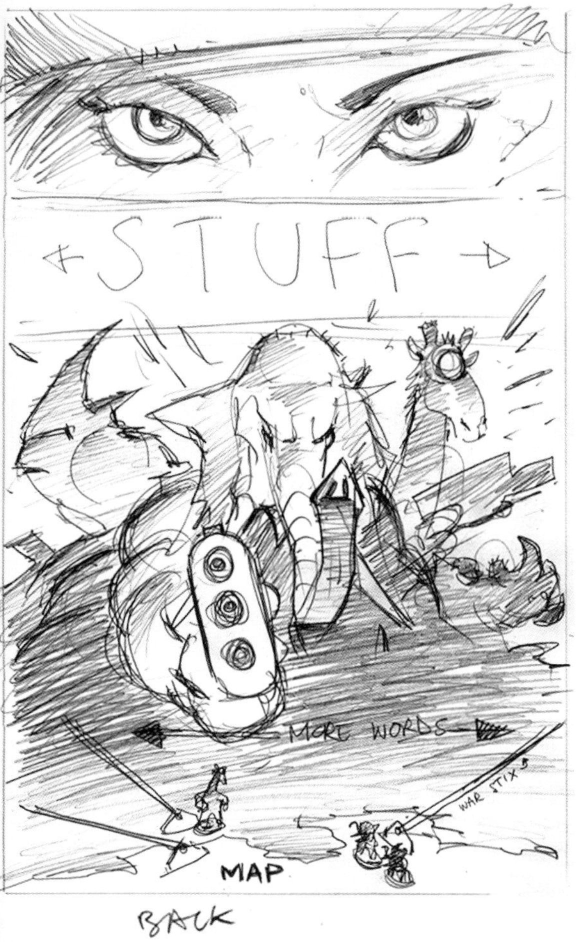
STUFF
MORE WORDS
WAR STIX
MAP
BACK

Opposite and Below: Boo's roughs for the WAR TOYS: NO SURRENDER collection. I wanted Yvette to be the focus, especially as she had been absent from the covers of the series itself. Boo pushed for images of the advancing Elephantmen army and we quite quickly settled for an amalgam of the two roughs you see on this page. Consciously or unconsciously, Boo turned the cover into an Yvette mask which he models below.

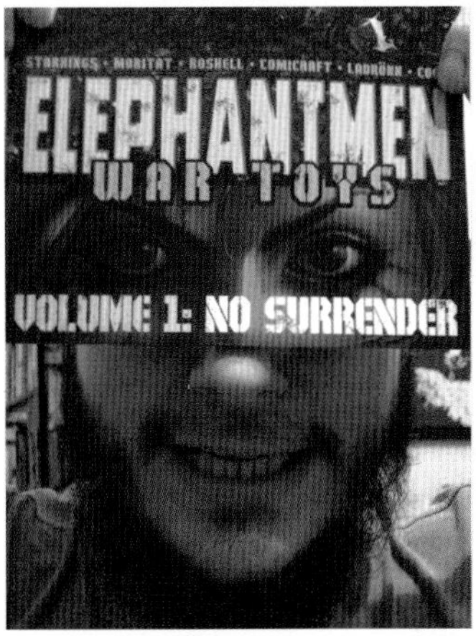
ELEPHANTMEN
WAR TOYS
VOLUME 1: NO SURRENDER
FRONT

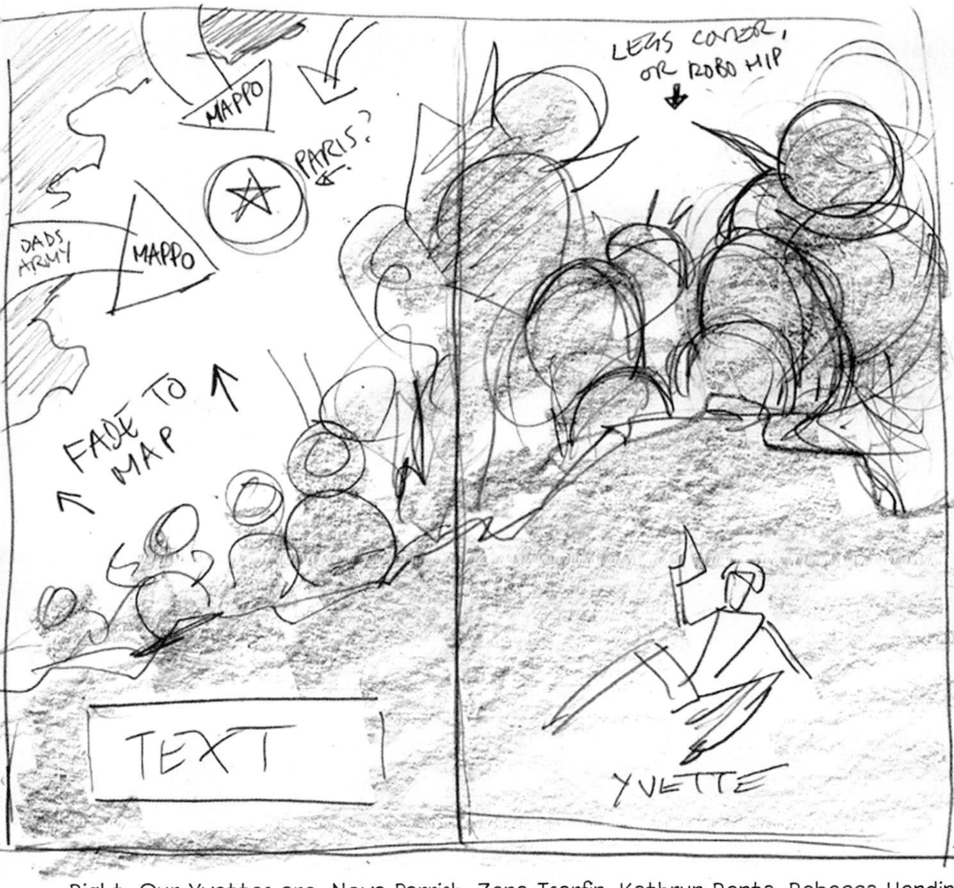
MAPPO
PARIS?
DADS ARMY
MAPPO
FADE TO MAP
TEXT
LEGS COVER, OR ROBO HIP
YVETTE

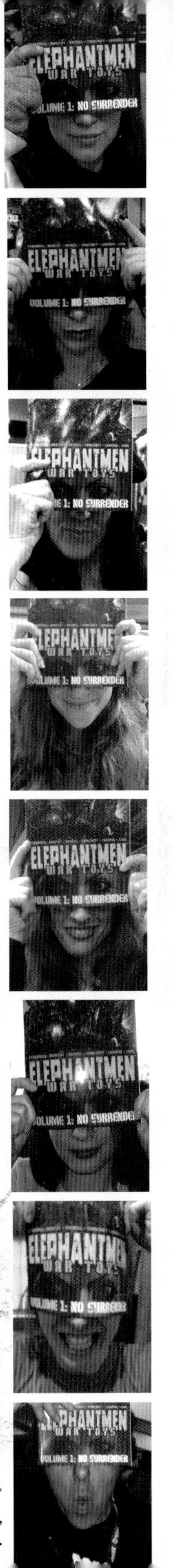
ELEPHANTMEN
WAR TOYS
VOLUME 1: NO SURRENDER

Right: Our Yvettes are: Nova Parrish, Zena Tsarfin, Kathryn Renta, Rebecca Hendin, Branwyn Bigglestone, Joanne Starer, Gemma Bryden and Jonathan Ross.

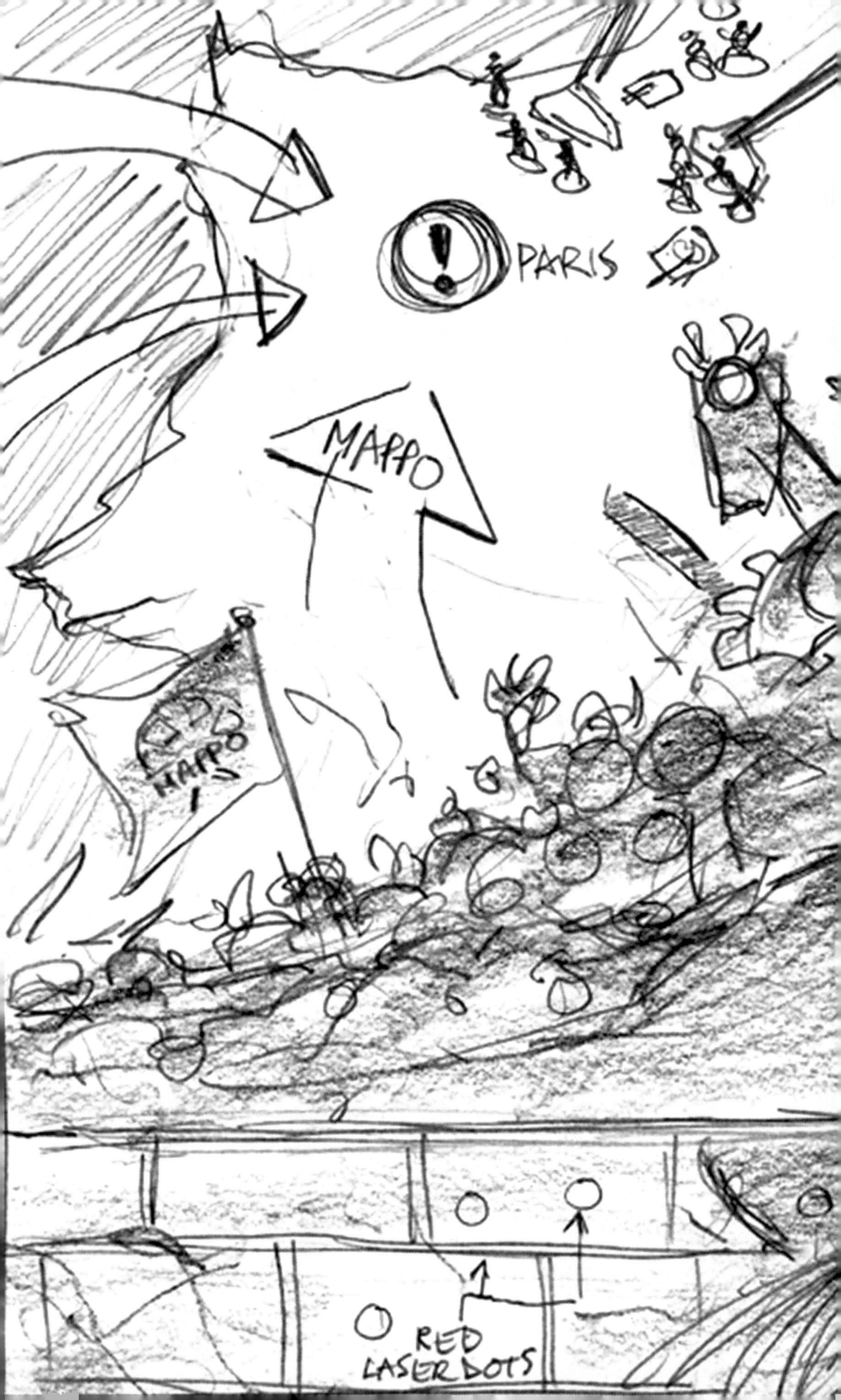
PARIS
MAPPO
MAPPO
RED
LASER DOTS

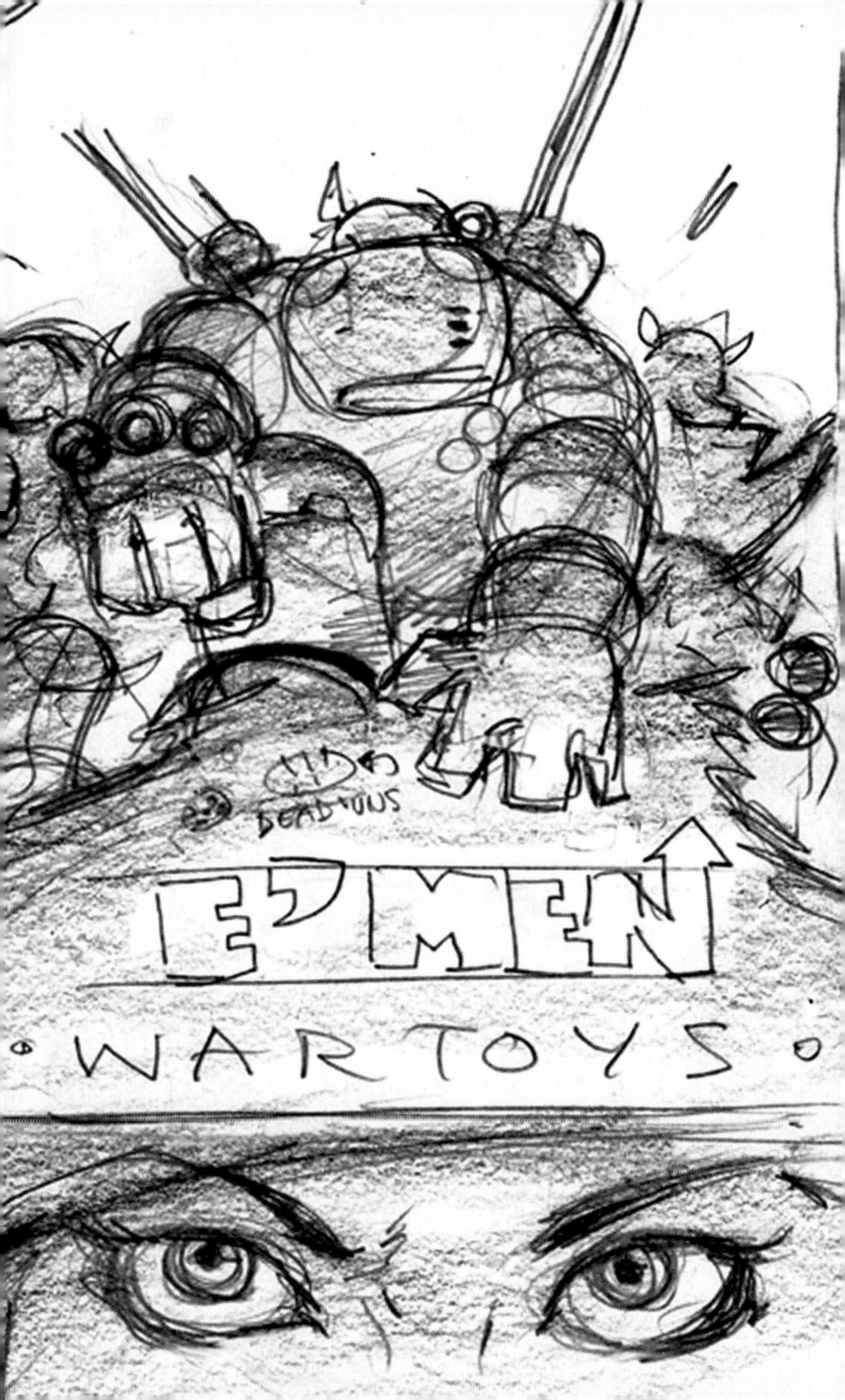
WARTOYS

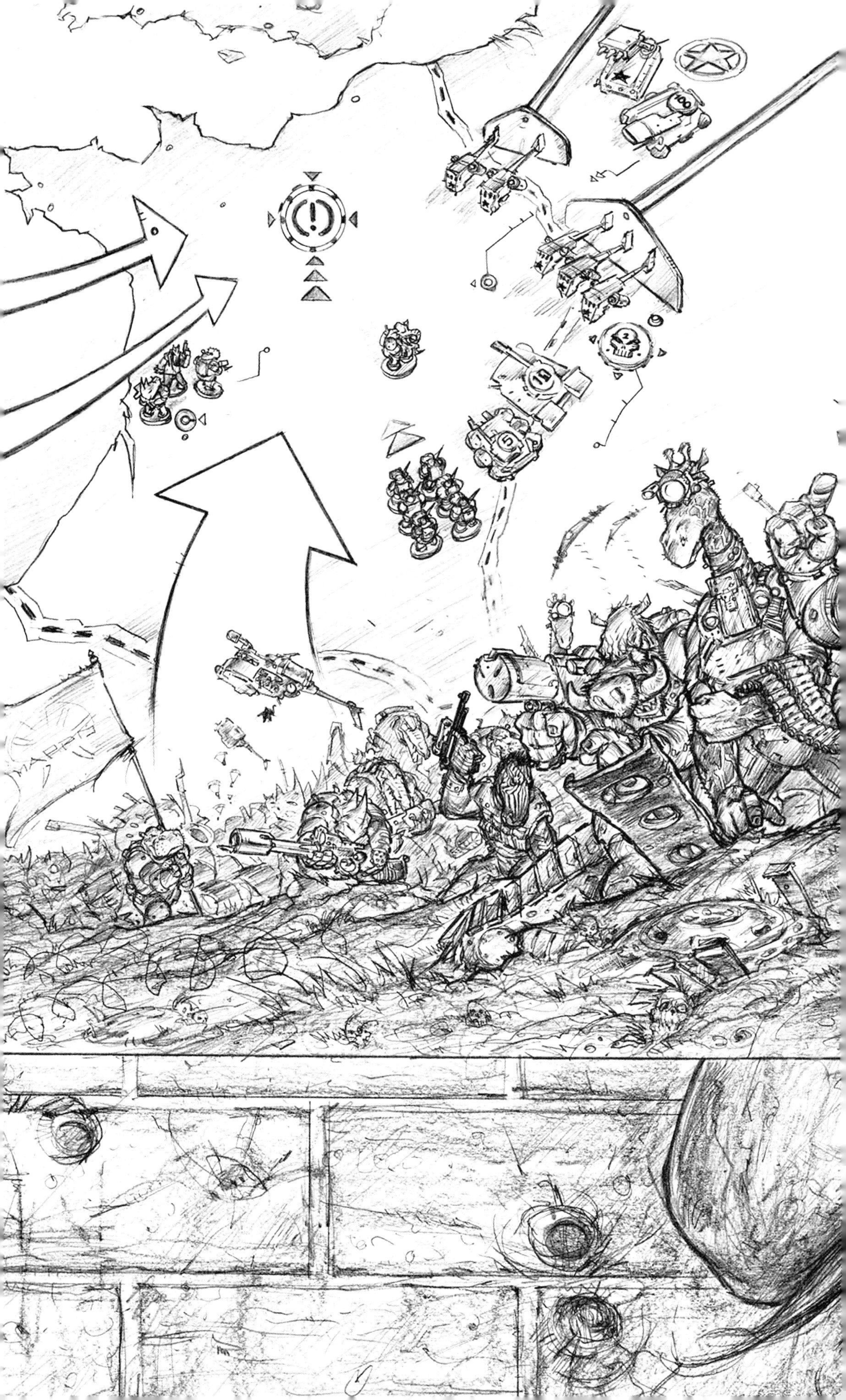

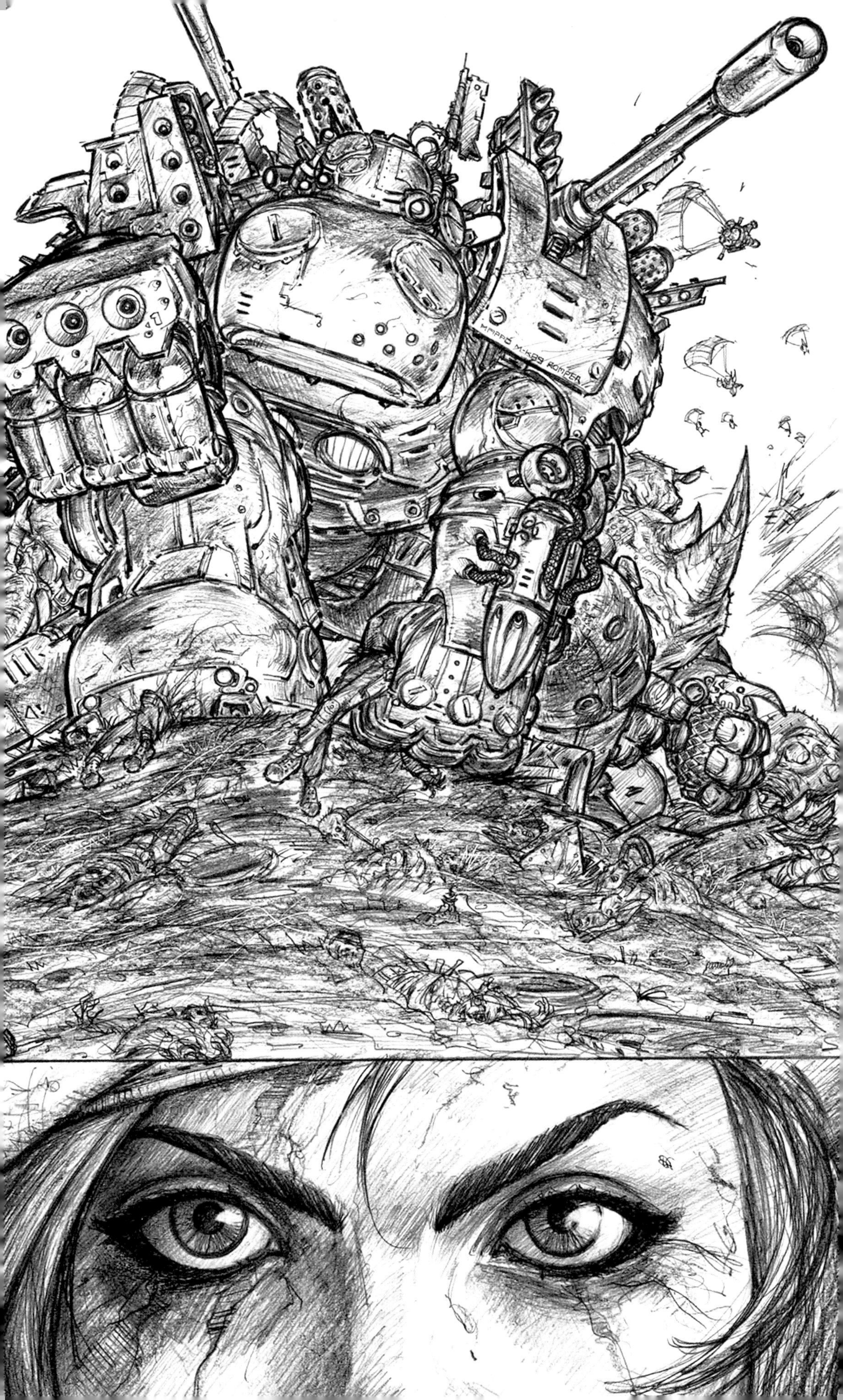
M-K89 ROMPER

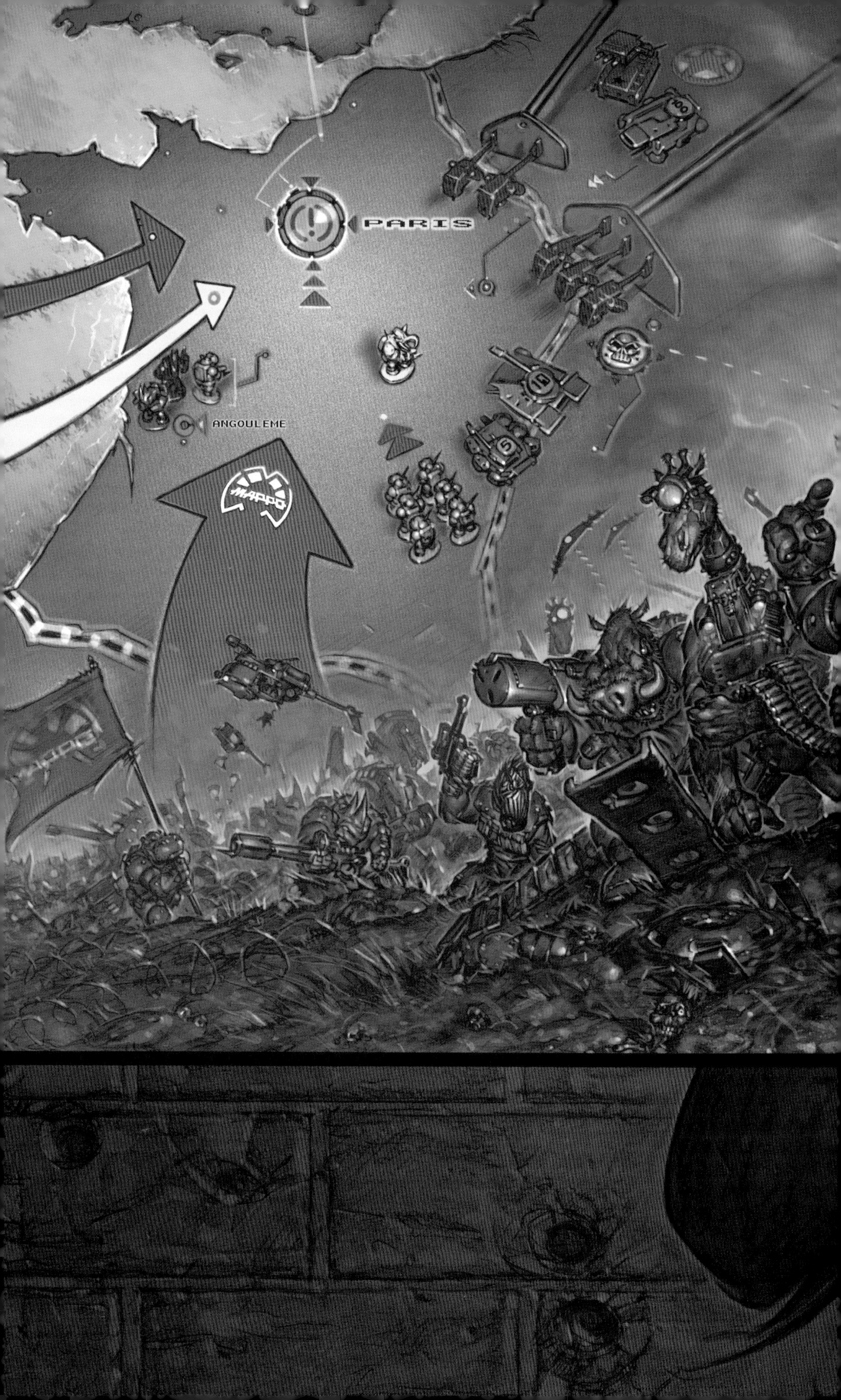
PARIS
ANGOULEME

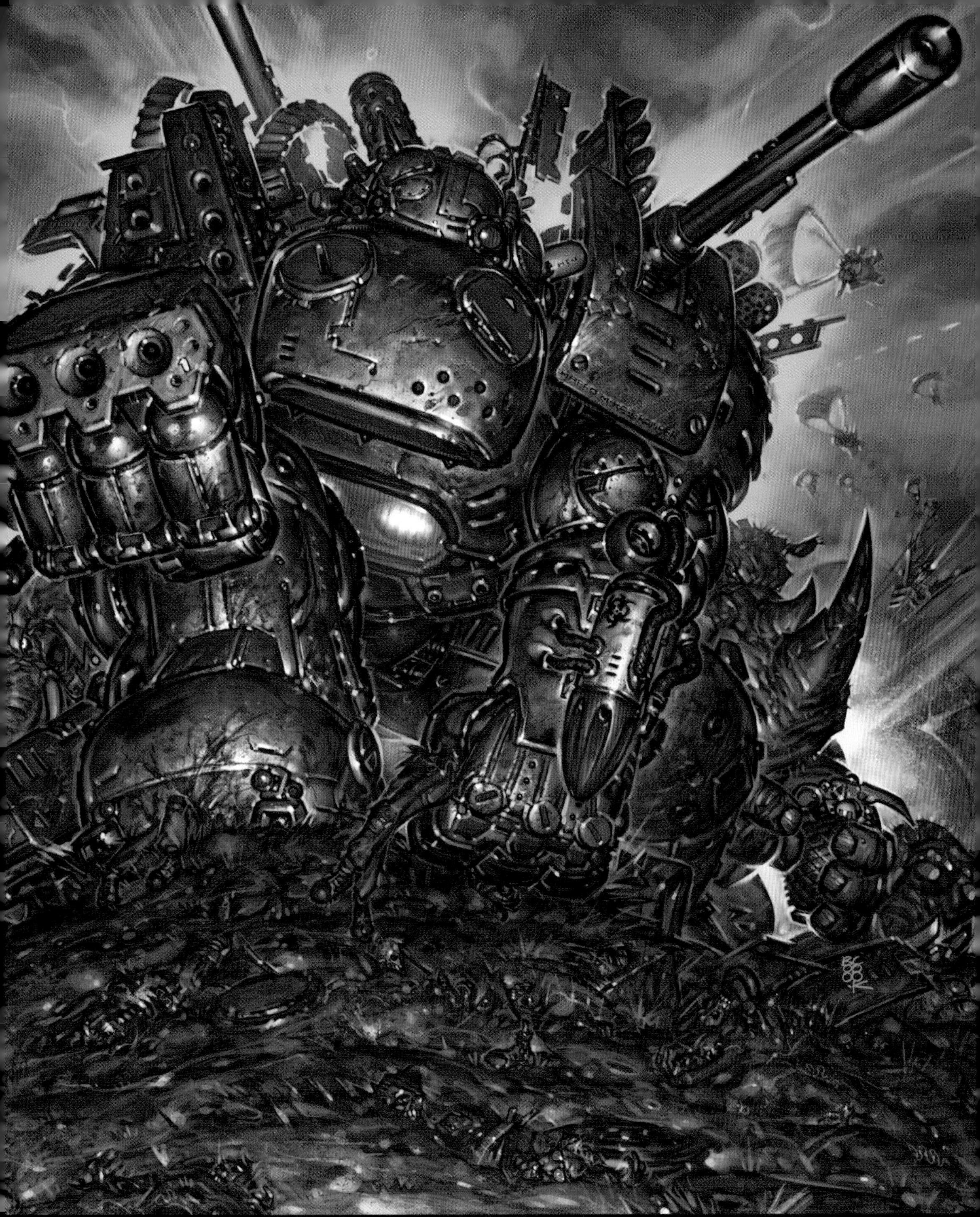

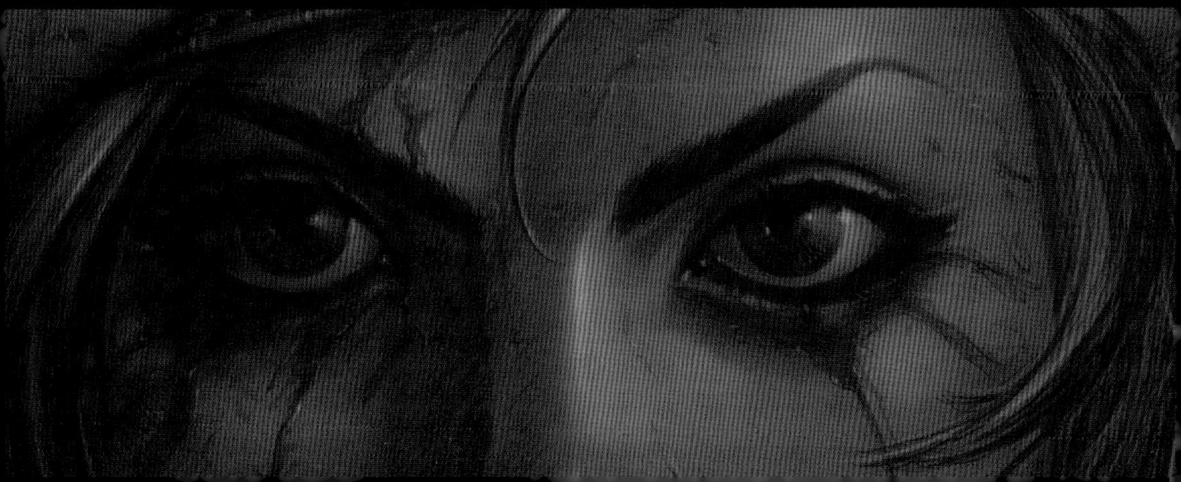

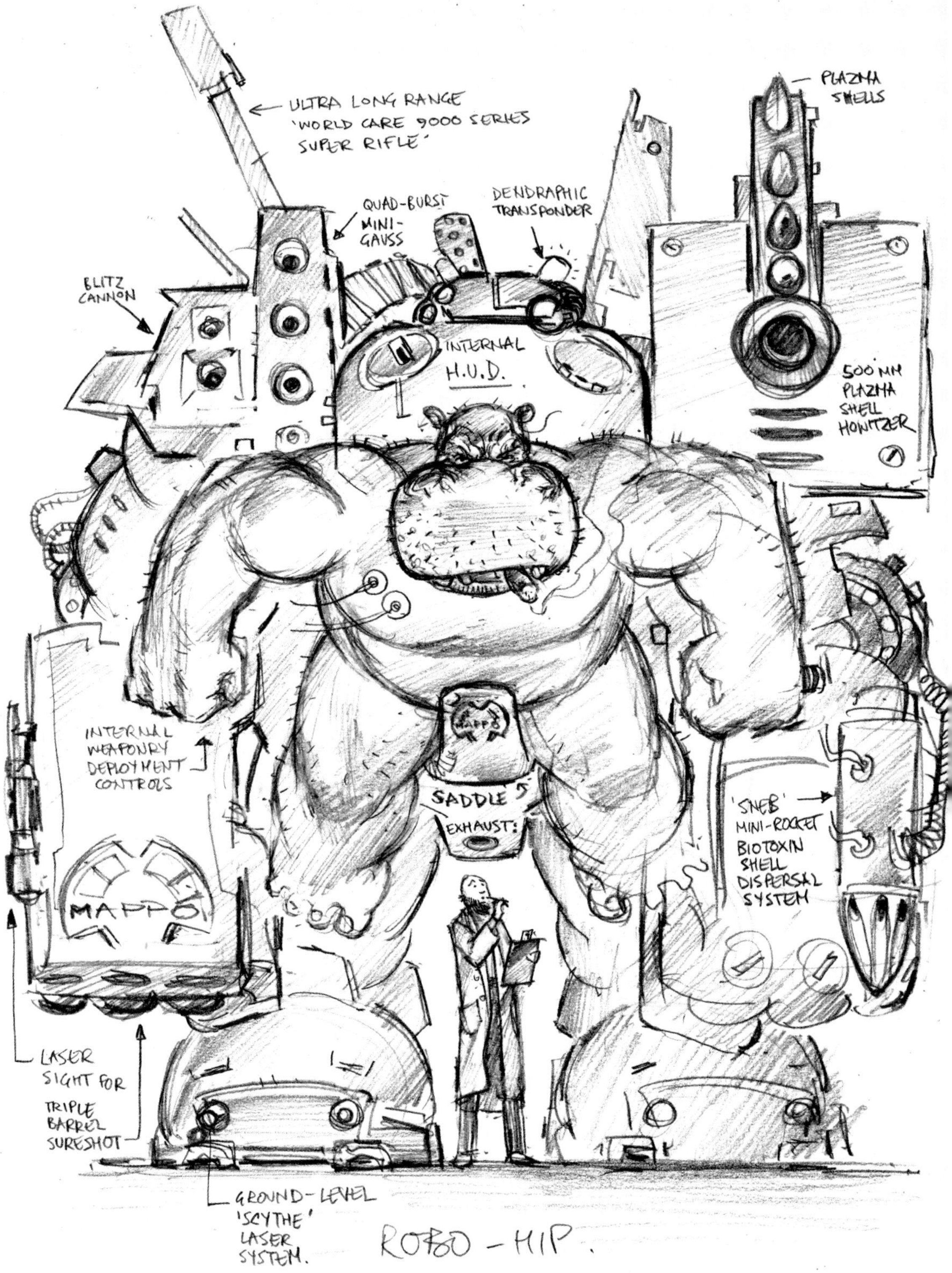
ULTRA LONG RANGE 'WORLD CARE 9000 SERIES SUPER RIFLE'
PLAZMA SHELLS
QUAD-BURST MINI-GAUSS
DENDRAPHIC TRANSPONDER
BLITZ CANNON
INTERNAL H.U.D.
500 MM PLAZMA SHELL HOWITZER
INTERNAL WEAPONRY DEPLOYMENT CONTROLS
SADDLE
EXHAUST:
'SNEB' MINI-ROCKET BIOTOXIN SHELL DISPERSAL SYSTEM
MAPPO
LASER SIGHT FOR TRIPLE BARREL SURESHOT
GROUND-LEVEL 'SCYTHE' LASER SYSTEM.
ROBO-HIP.

Previous pages: The final cover of the WAR TOYS paperback was a combination of the rough sketches Boo sent me. However, I only agreed to let him include "Robo-Hip" if he sent me a cutaway schematic showing me how an Elephantman would fit inside. This drawing, coupled with Marian's cover for the one shot further clarifed the story of ENEMY SPECIES for me.

Right: The roughs for the spread in ELEPHANTMEN #35 were consequently the first pages written and drawn!

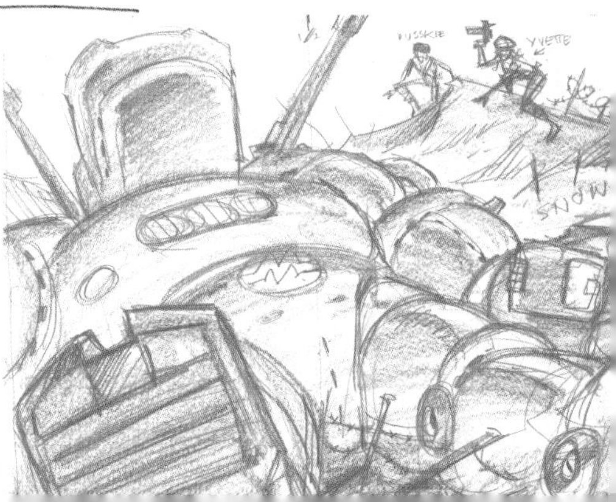

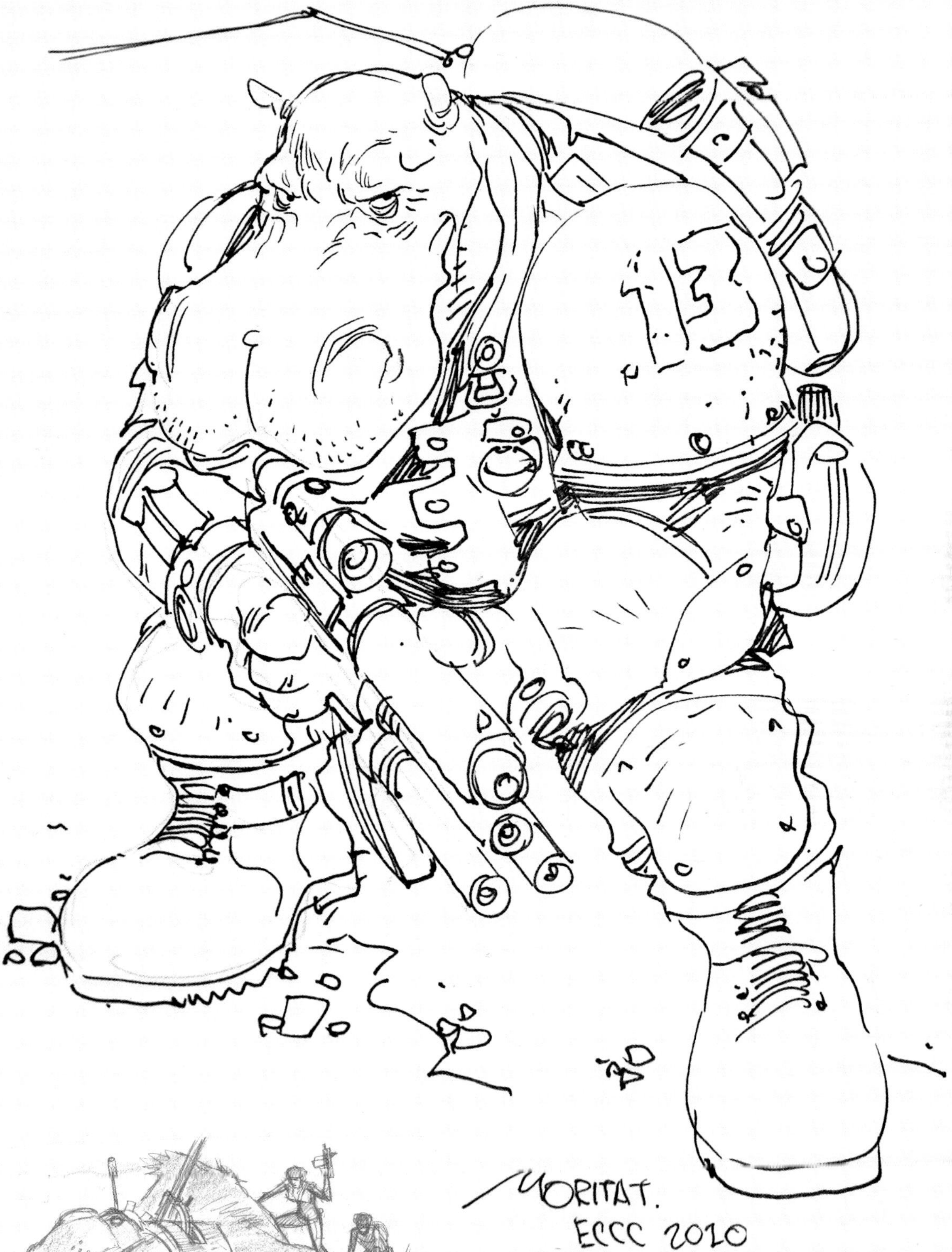
MORITAT.
ECCC 2020

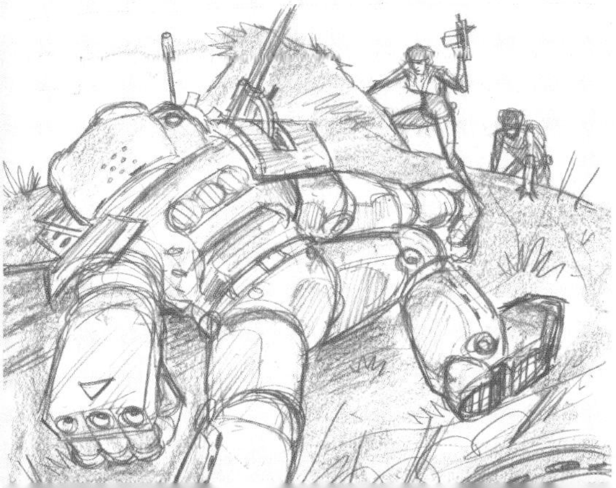

Above: This sketch by Justin at his hometown show in Seattle was I think one of his very best. I sent the scan to Boo when we were asked to contribute an ELEPHANTMEN illustration for the IMAGE SAN DIEGO COMIC CON SKETCHBOOK, you can see the results over the page.

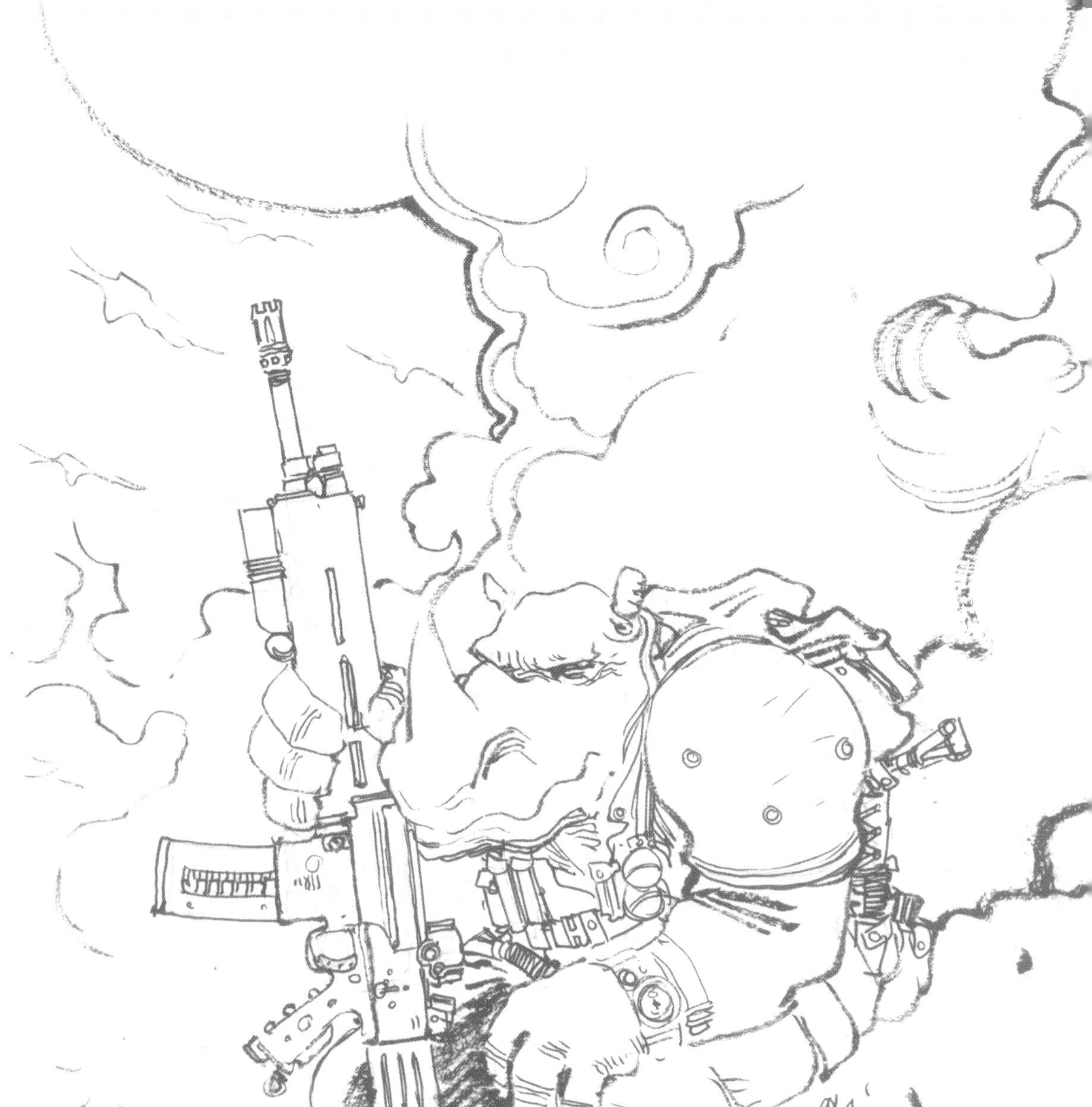
MORITAT
SAN DIEGO
COMIC CON
2007 -
FIRST SKETCH
BOOK SKETCH!

Above: It's fitting to end this section, I think, with one of Moritat's very first WAR TOYS illustrations (I can't call it a sketch!) I'm quite certain that Justin must have shown this to me, cackled at my dismayed expression and determined there and then to draw as many more of the same as he could. MORITAT means "Deadly Deeds!"

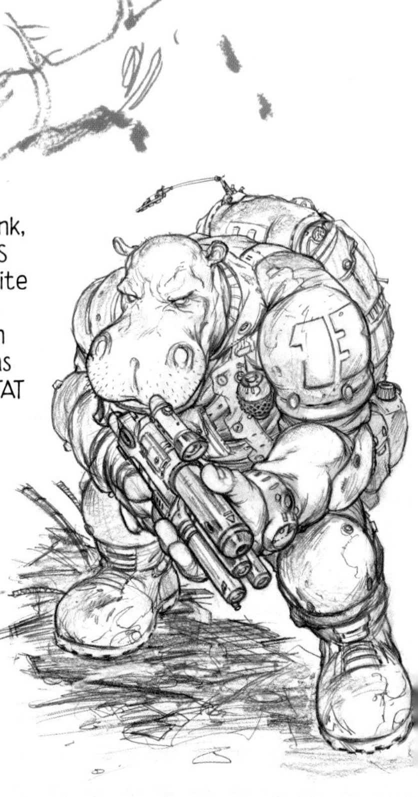

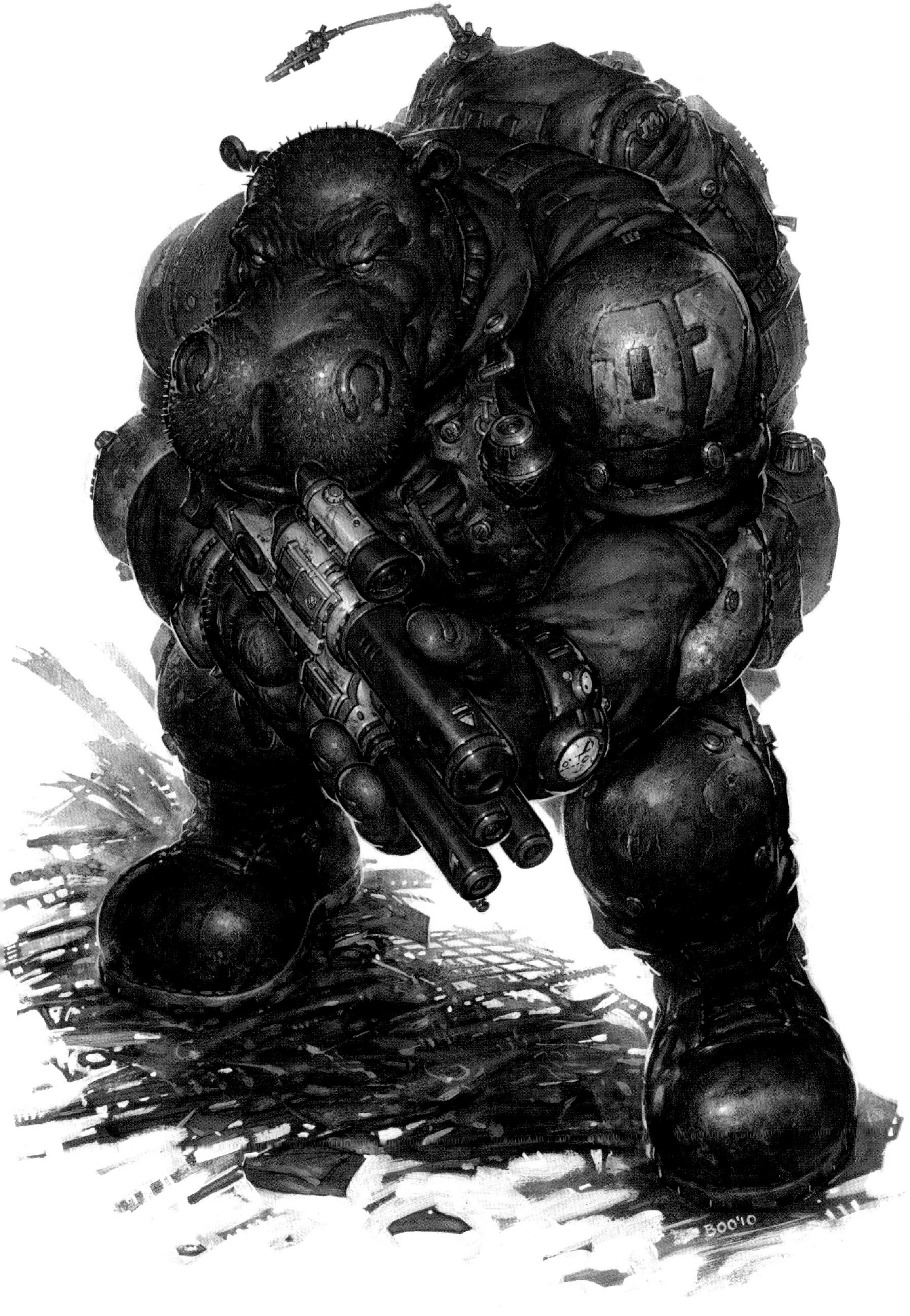
BOO'10

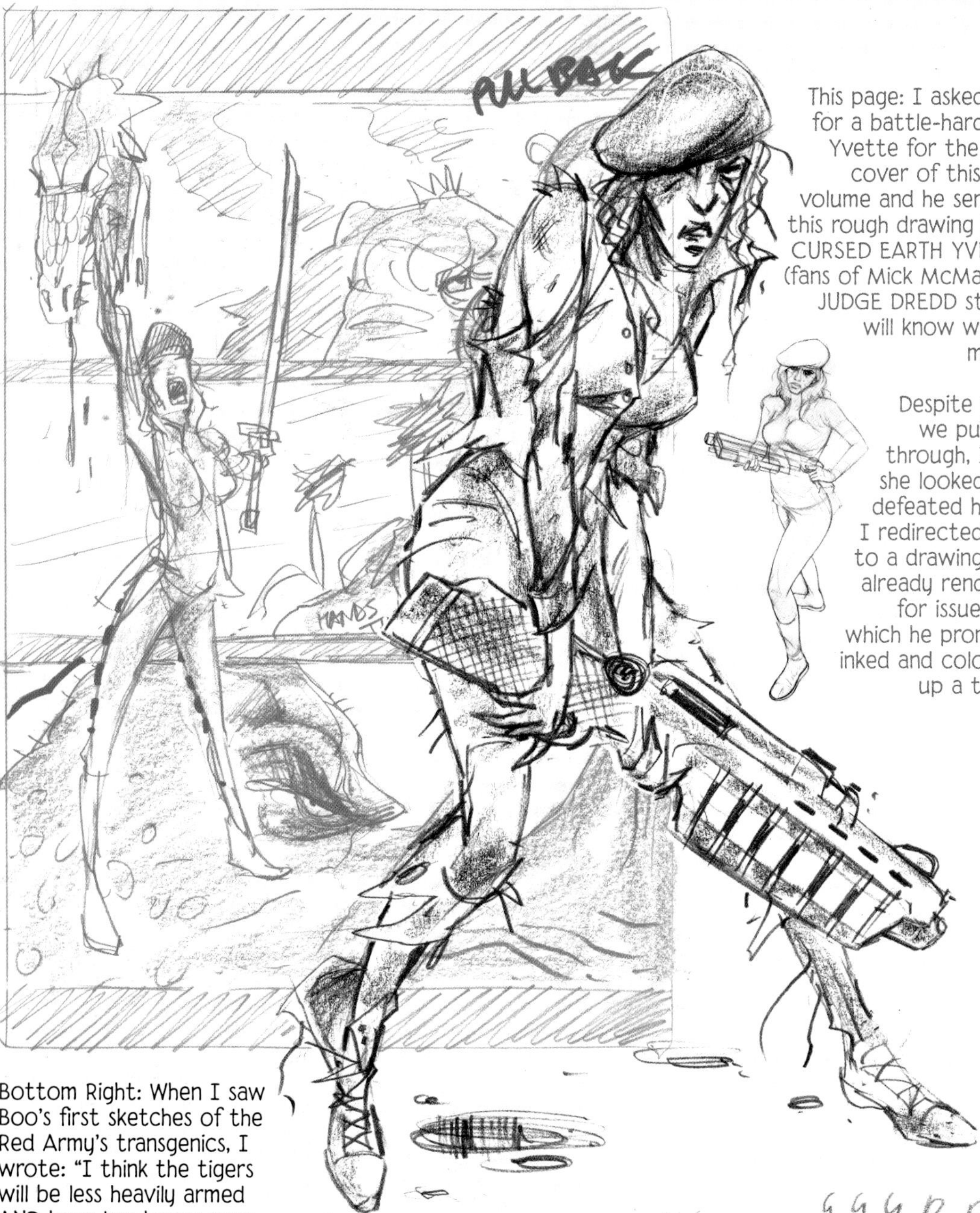
PULL BACK
HANDS

This page: I asked Boo for a battle-hardened Yvette for the back cover of this very volume and he sent me this rough drawing I call CURSED EARTH YVETTE! (fans of Mick McMahon's JUDGE DREDD stories will know what I mean!)

Despite what we put her through, I felt she looked too defeated here... I redirected Boo to a drawing he'd already rendered for issue #34, which he promptly inked and coloured up a treat.

Bottom Right: When I saw Boo's first sketches of the Red Army's transgenics, I wrote: "I think the tigers will be less heavily armed AND have less heavy arms... literally. The bullet belt and bigass guns undermines their natural fearsomeness -- I see them more like stealth assassins/ not quite ninjas. They will be fast and lithesome despite their bulk."

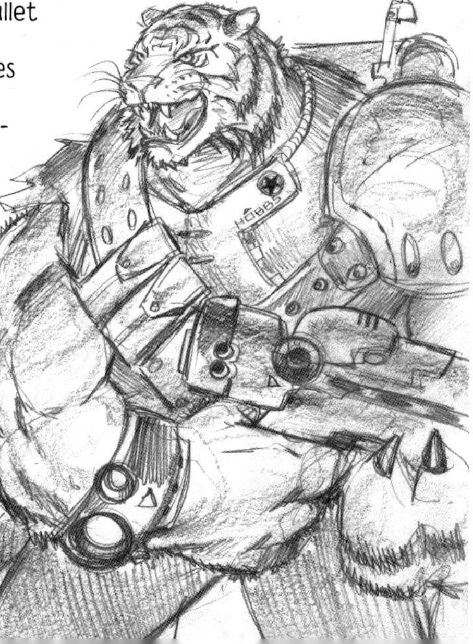
HOBBS

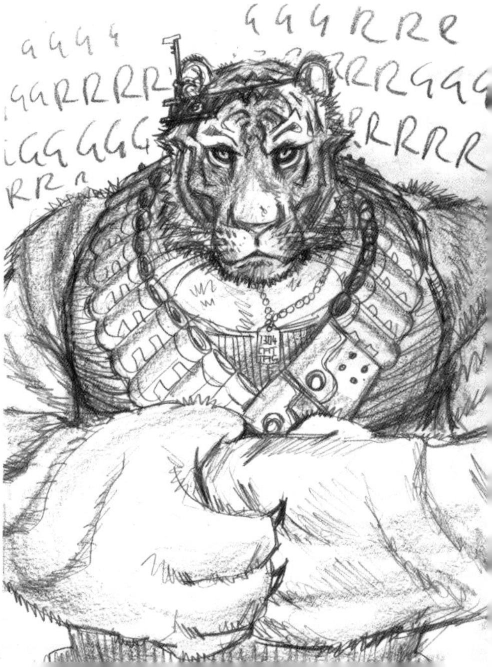

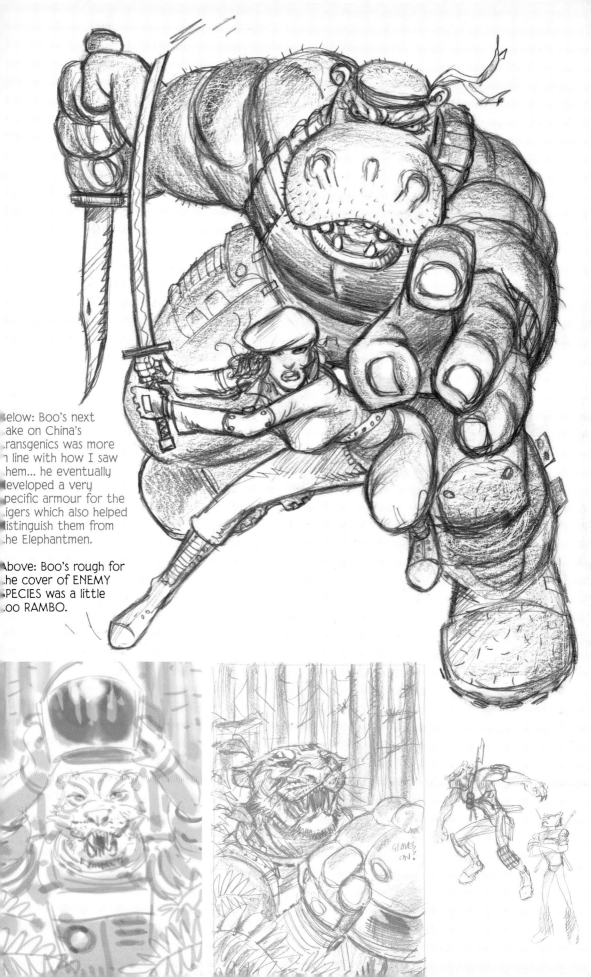

Below: Boo's next take on China's transgenics was more in line with how I saw them... he eventually developed a very specific armour for the tigers which also helped distinguish them from the Elephantmen.

Above: Boo's rough for the cover of ENEMY SPECIES was a little too RAMBO.

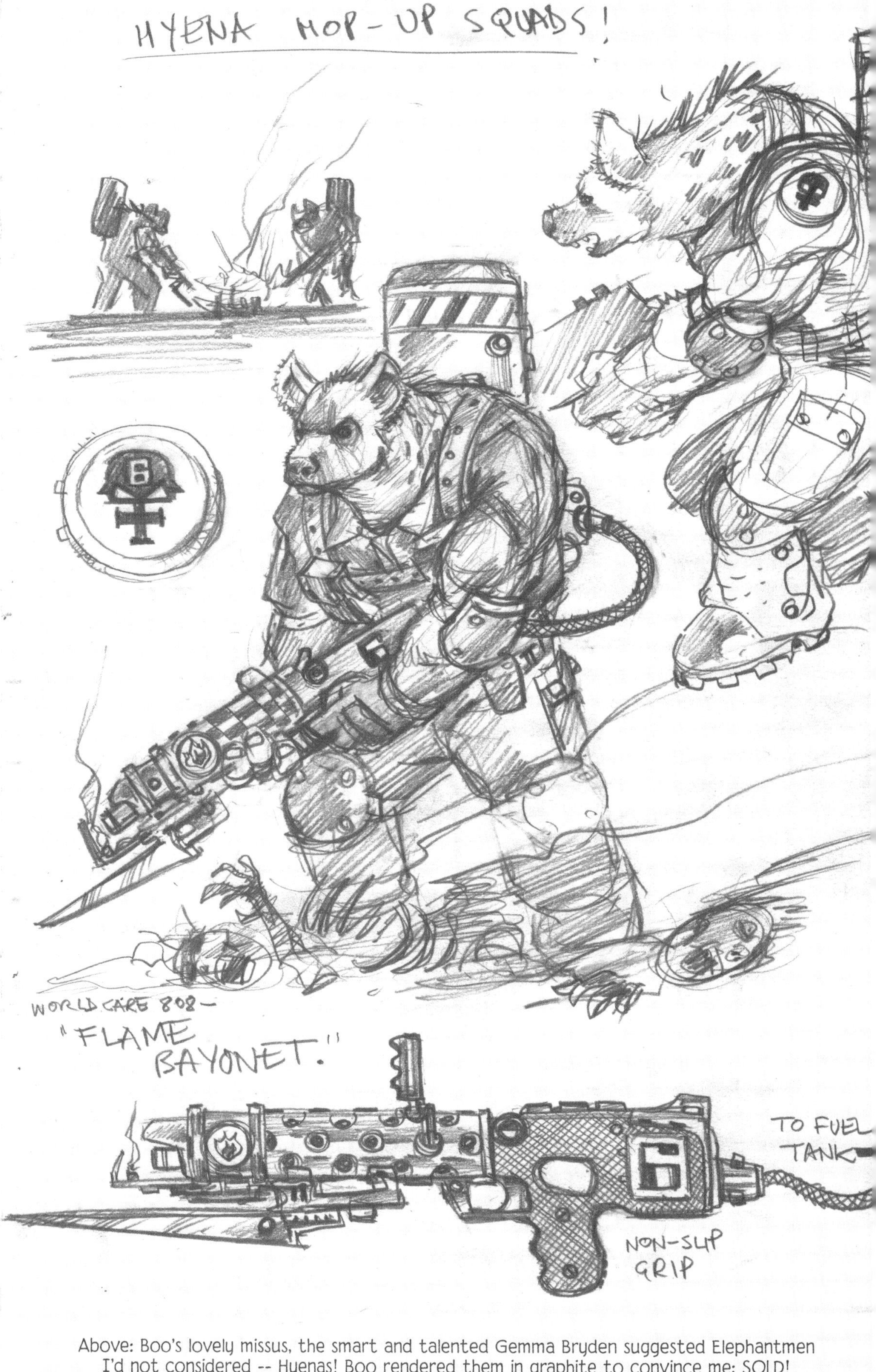
HYENA MOP-UP SQUADS!
WORLD CARE 808-
"FLAME BAYONET."
TO FUEL TANK
NON-SLIP GRIP

Above: Boo's lovely missus, the smart and talented Gemma Bryden suggested Elephantmen I'd not considered -- Hyenas! Boo rendered them in graphite to convince me; SOLD! They made their first appearance in ELEPHANTMEN #34 after a brief mention in #29. Thanks, Gem!

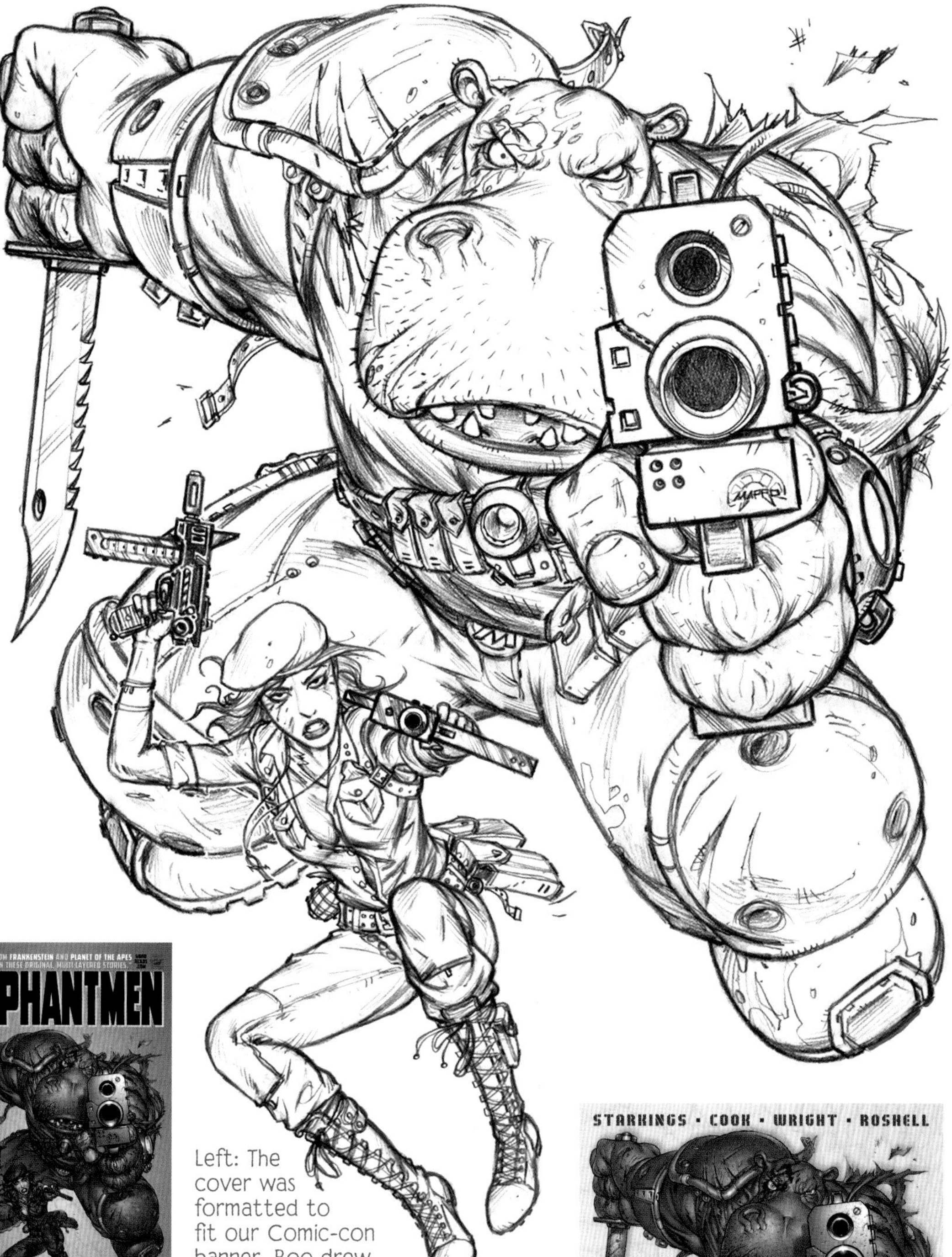

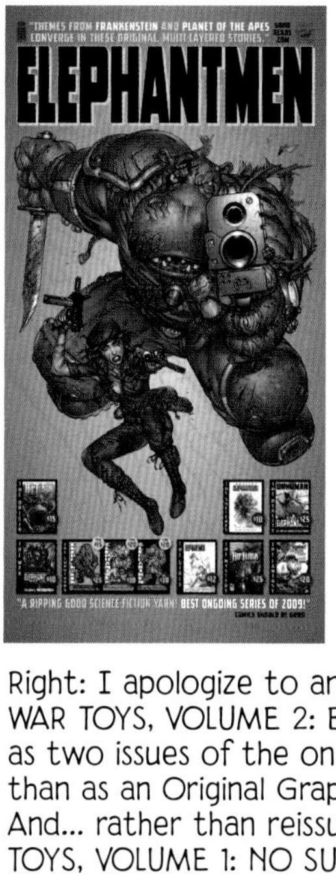
"THEMES FROM FRANKENSTEIN AND PLANET OF THE APES CONVERGE IN THESE ORIGINAL, MULTI-LAYERED STORIES."
ELEPHANTMEN
"A RIPPING GOOD SCIENCE-FICTION YARN! BEST ONGOING SERIES OF 2009!"
COMICS SHOULD BE GOOD

Left: The cover was formatted to fit our Comic-con banner. Boo drew Hip and Yvette on separate layers so we could reposition them. Eventually they were repositioned onto separate covers!

Right: I apologize to anyone still waiting for ELEPHANTMEN: WAR TOYS, VOLUME 2: ENEMY SPECIES, which was published as two issues of the ongoing ELEPHANTMEN series rather than as an Original Graphic Novel as, um, originally planned. And... rather than reissue the sold out ELEPHANTMEN: WAR TOYS, VOLUME 1: NO SURRENDER, we opted to collect both stories in this volume, thus eliminating any confusion as to which ELEPHANTMEN VOLUME 1 should be read first. Having said that, you can read either VOLUME 0: ARMED FORCES (this very volume held in your hands right now) or VOLUME 1: WOUNDED ANIMALS first. Good. I'm glad all that's settled.

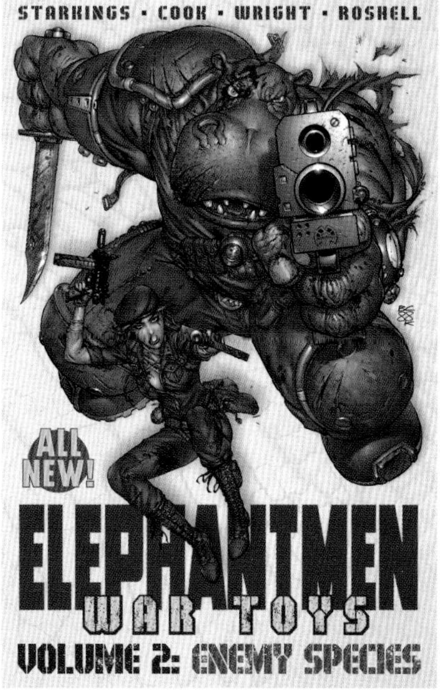
STARKINGS • COOK • WRIGHT • ROSHELL
ALL NEW!
ELEPHANTMEN
WAR TOYS
VOLUME 2: ENEMY SPECIES

WHAT'S SO FUNNY 'BOUT PEACE

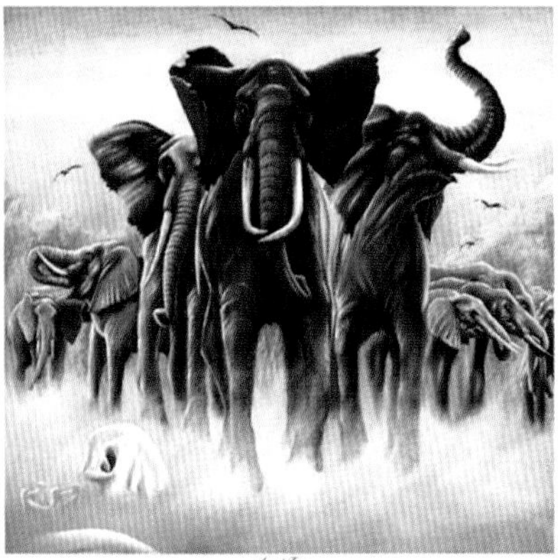

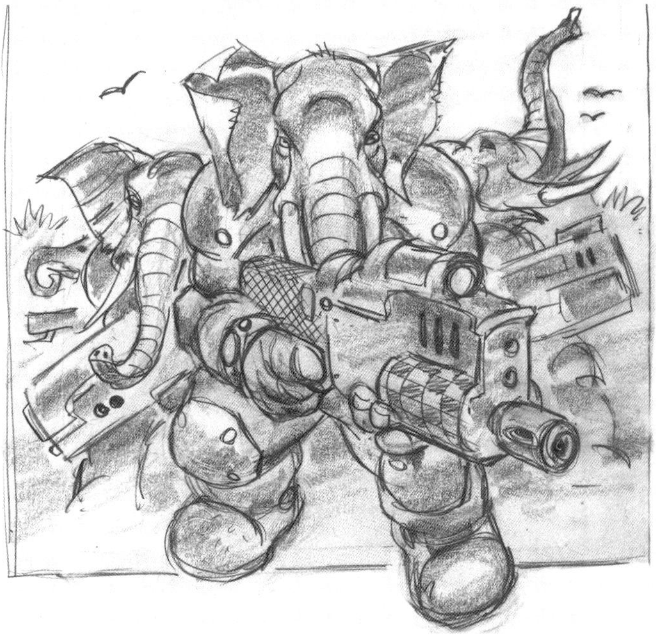

Above: I was late to the party as far as punk rock and new wave music was concerned in the late 70's... I was clinging doggedly to my love for ELO and all things glam rock. I daresay I was in the E section of my favourite bargain record stores in Leeds eyeing one of the vinyl ELO albums that predated my favourite (OUT OF THE BLUE, see my PULP SCIENCE FICTION piece in WOUNDED ANIMALS) when I came across the cover of ARMED FORCES by another EL, Elvis Costello. The artwork seemed at odds with Costello's rough and ready music. It was elegant and commanding. The type was small and hard to read and I remember wondering to myself upon seeing the title ARMED FORCES how this applied to the other ELs -- the elephants in the illustration.

In my attempts to source the original illustration for the album, I discovered REASONS TO BE CHEERFUL: THE LIFE AND WORK OF BARNEY BUBBLES. Barney designed the sleeves of many great rock albums but committed suicide when he was still quite young. What a waste.

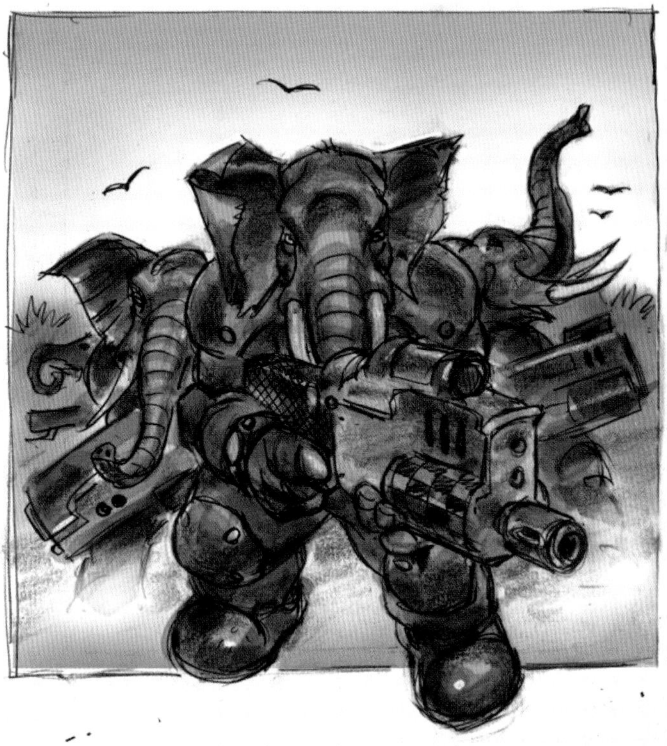

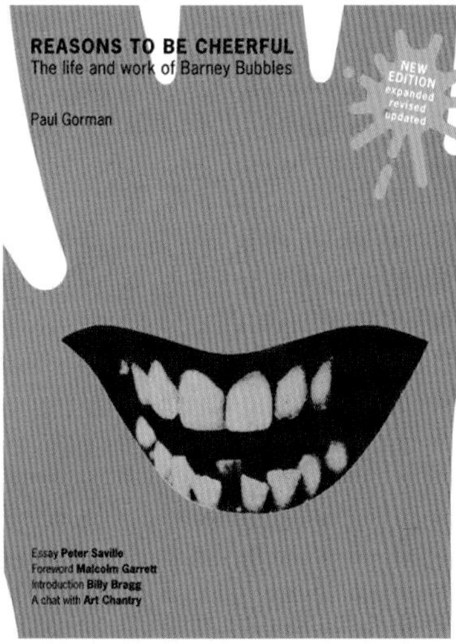
REASONS TO BE CHEERFUL
The life and work of Barney Bubbles
NEW EDITION expanded revised updated
Paul Gorman
Essay Peter Saville
Foreword Malcolm Garrett
Introduction Billy Bragg
A chat with Art Chantry

Though designed by Bubbles, the cover art for ARMED FORCES was painted by Tom Pogson.

Below: From pencils to iPhone screen to the calf of COMIC IMPACT's Simon Daoudi!

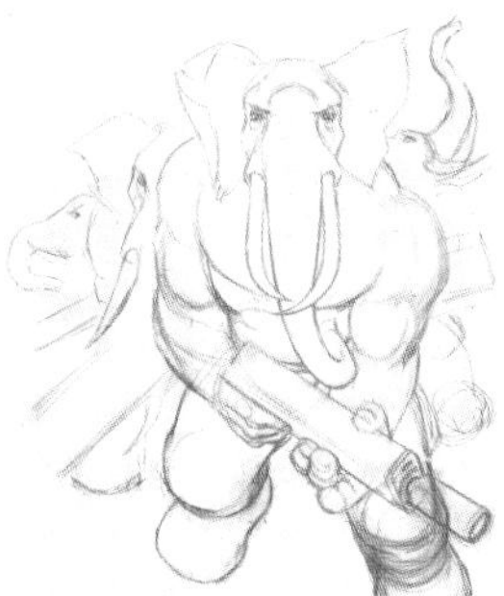

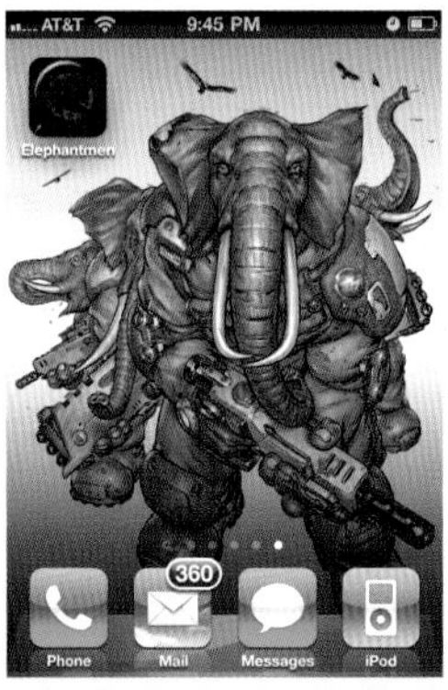
AT&T
9:45 PM
Elephantmen
360
Phone
Mail
Messages
iPod

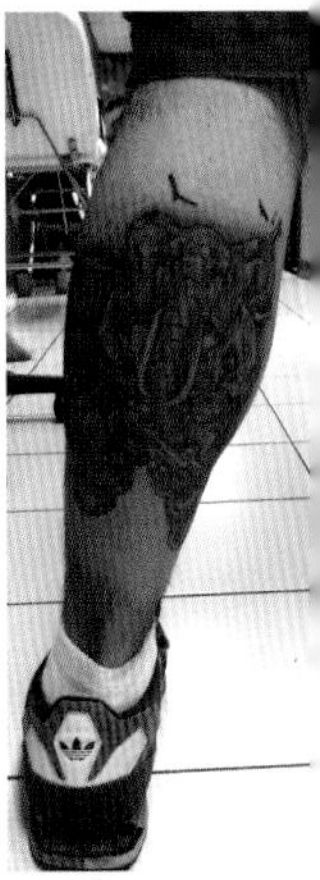

LOVE AND UNDERSTANDING?

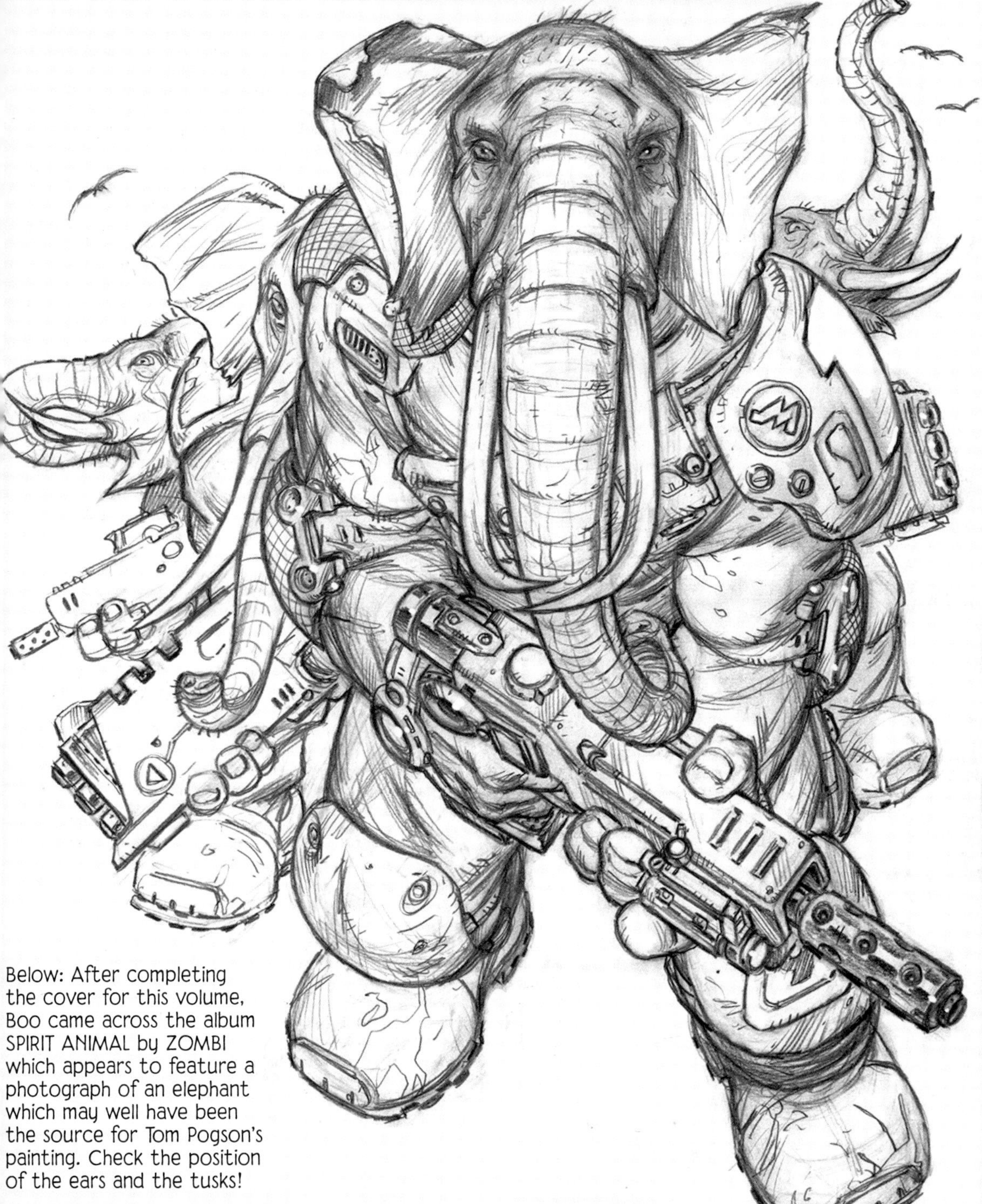

Below: After completing the cover for this volume, Boo came across the album SPIRIT ANIMAL by ZOMBI which appears to feature a photograph of an elephant which may well have been the source for Tom Pogson's painting. Check the position of the ears and the tusks!

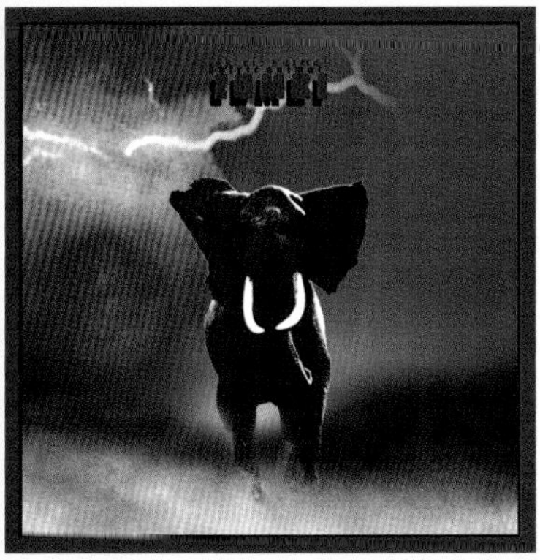

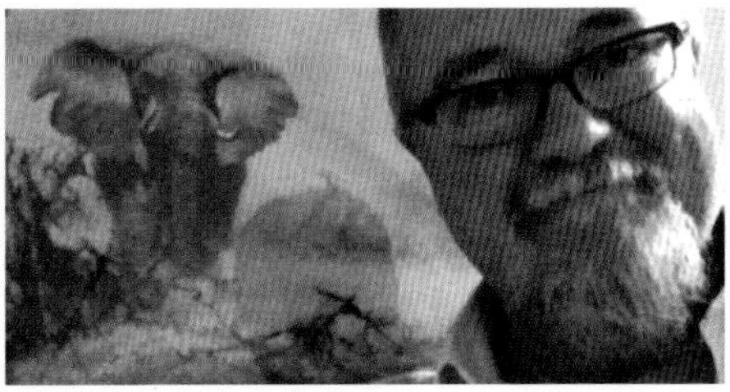

Finally, the painting you see behind me here hung in my family home and seared itself into my subconscious for years. And that, my friends, is where I get my ideas from. Above the fireplace.

Richard Starkings

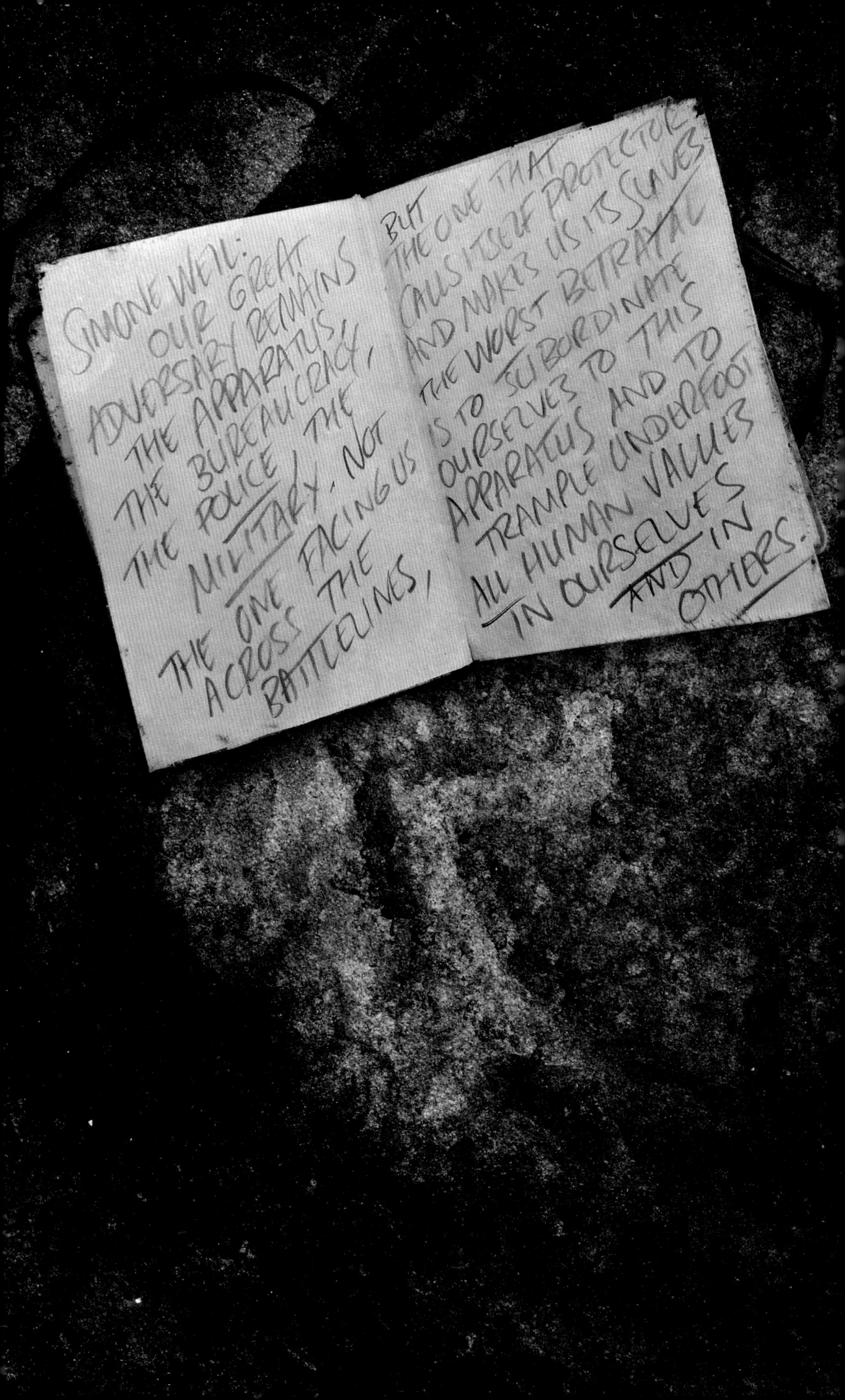
SIMONE WEIL:
OUR GREAT
ADVERSARY REMAINS
THE APPARATUS,
THE BUREAUCRACY,
THE POLICE THE
MILITARY. NOT
THE ONE FACING US
ACROSS THE
BATTLELINES,
BUT
THE ONE THAT
CALLS ITSELF PROTECTOR
AND MAKES US ITS SLAVES
THE WORST BETRAYAL
IS TO SUBORDINATE
OURSELVES TO THIS
APPARATUS AND TO
TRAMPLE UNDERFOOT
ALL HUMAN VALUES
IN OURSELVES
AND IN
OTHERS.

WESTWOOD · CALIFORNIA · 2259

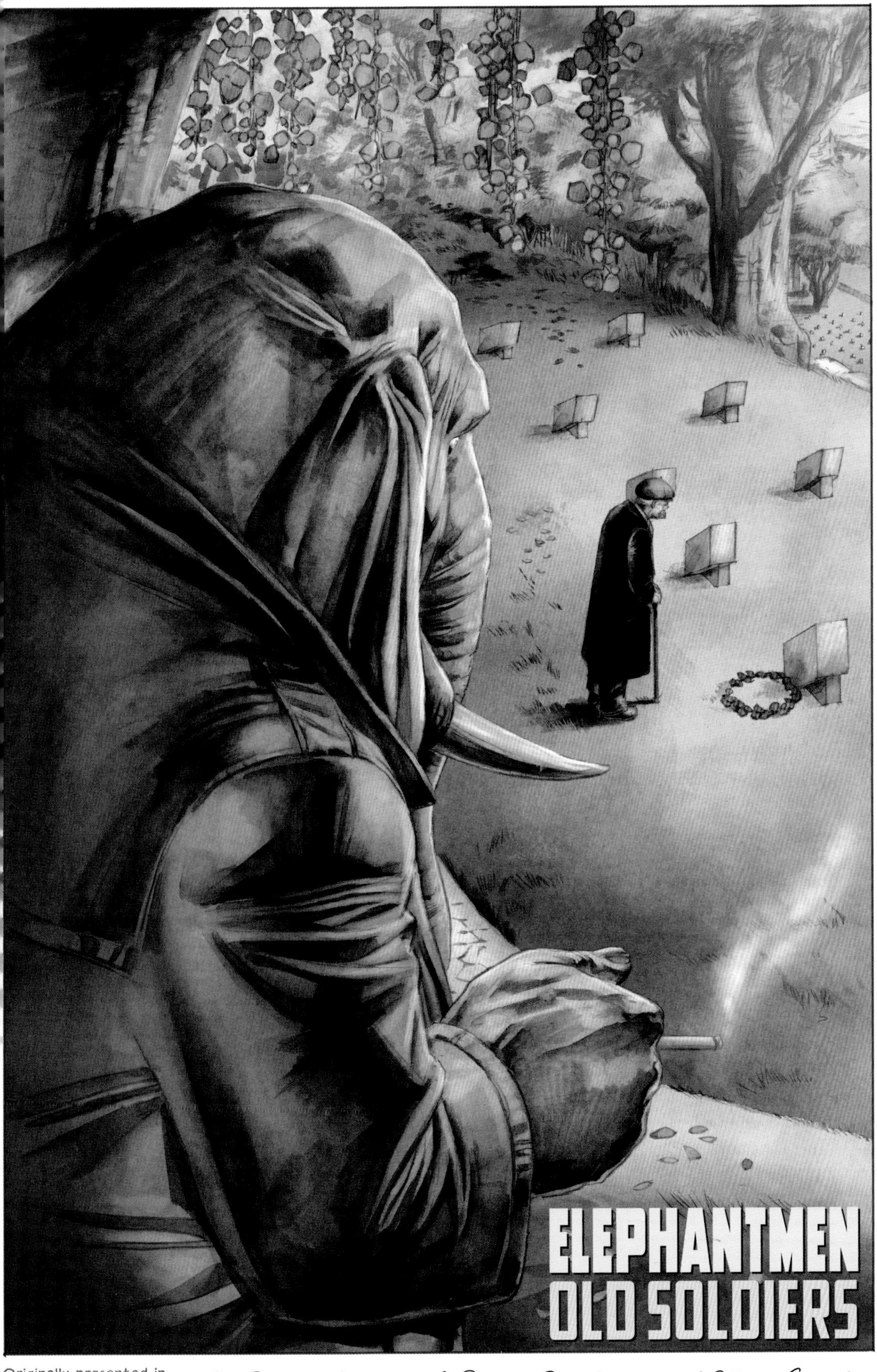
ELEPHANTMEN
OLD SOLDIERS

Originally presented in
HERO COMICS 2011

By Richard Starkings & Dougie Braithwaite with Ulises Arreola

I CAN SEE YOU THERE, YOU KNOW.

OH... EXCUSE ME... I'M SORRY.

YOU WERE IN THE ARMY TOO, RIGHT?

YOU'RE ONE OF THOSE *ELEPHANTMEN* SOLDIERS!

I'M RIGHT, AREN'T I, EH? WELL, OF *COURSE* I AM... I MEAN, *LOOK* AT YOU!

THEY CALL ME PARRY. *JOHN PARRY.* WHAT'S YOUR NAME, EH?

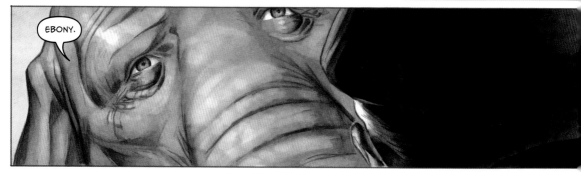

EBONY.

WELL, EBONY, YOU SHOULDN'T OUGHT TO SMOKE THEM, IF YOU ASK ME. CIGARETTES WILL KILL YOU STONE DEAD.

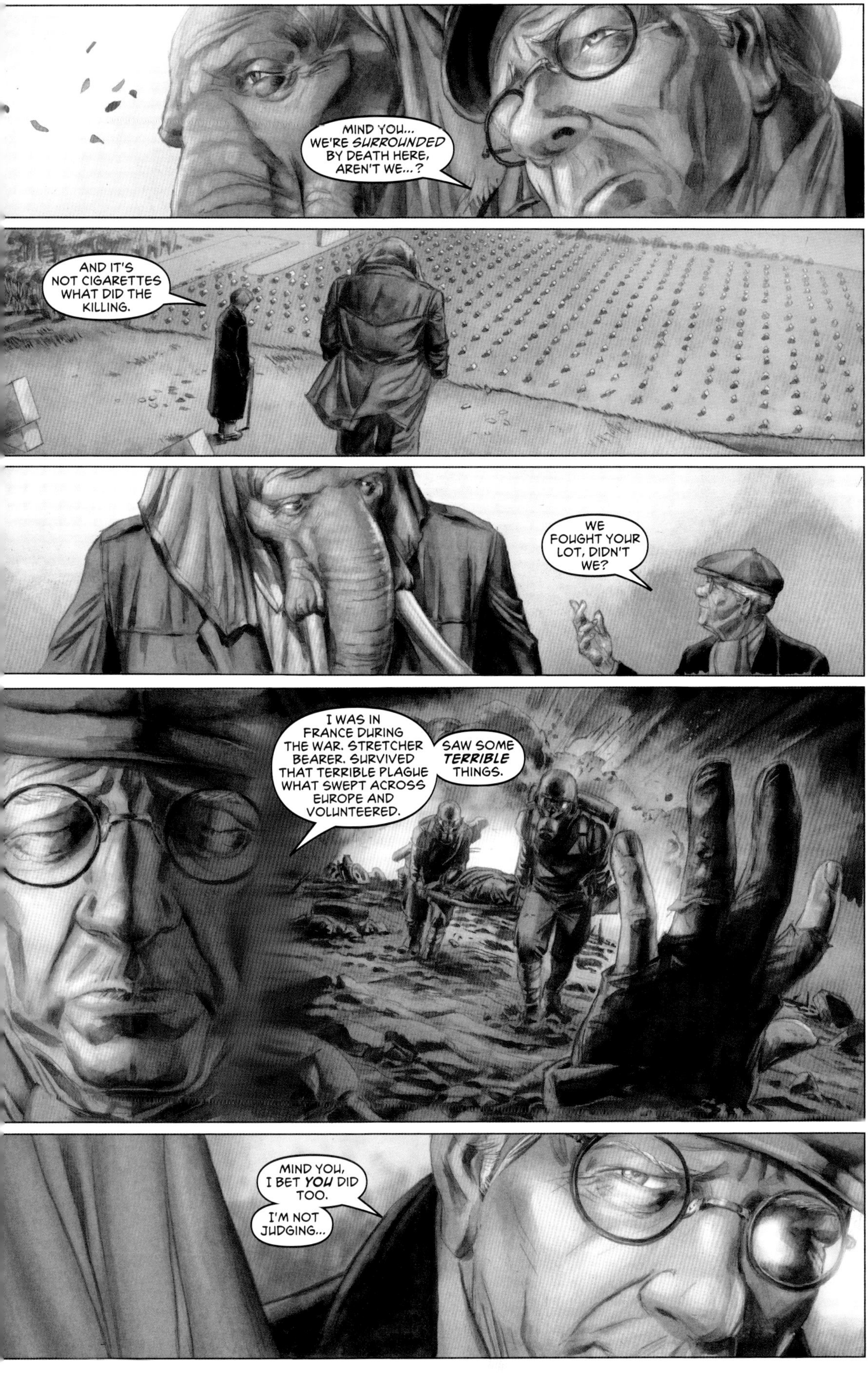
MIND YOU... WE'RE *SURROUNDED* BY DEATH HERE, AREN'T WE...?
AND IT'S NOT CIGARETTES WHAT DID THE KILLING.
WE FOUGHT YOUR LOT, DIDN'T WE?
I WAS IN FRANCE DURING THE WAR. STRETCHER BEARER. SURVIVED THAT TERRIBLE PLAGUE WHAT SWEPT ACROSS EUROPE AND VOLUNTEERED.
SAW SOME ***TERRIBLE*** THINGS.
MIND YOU, I BET ***YOU*** DID TOO.
I'M NOT JUDGING...

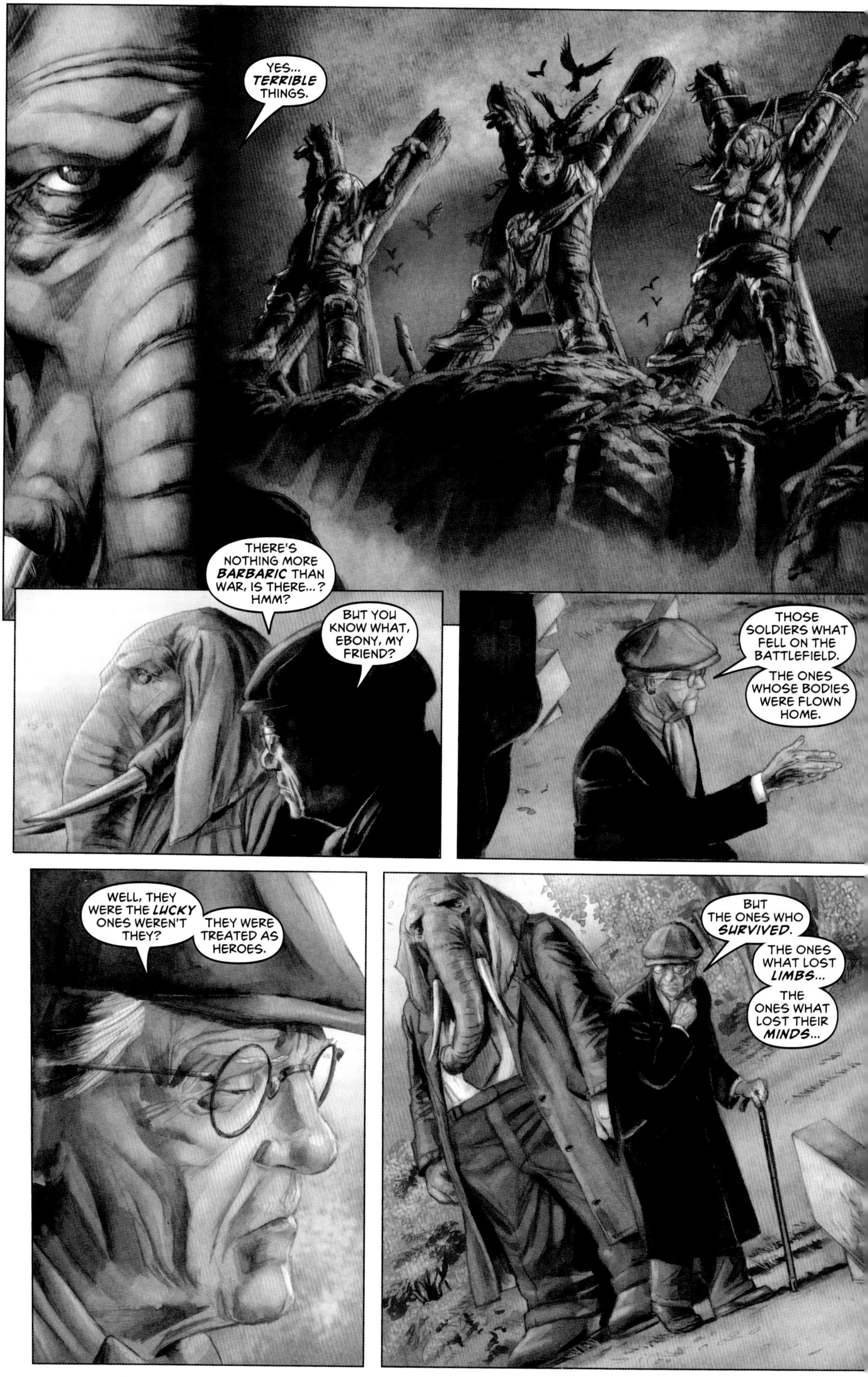
YES... TERRIBLE THINGS.
THERE'S NOTHING MORE BARBARIC THAN WAR, IS THERE...? HMM?
BUT YOU KNOW WHAT, EBONY, MY FRIEND?
THOSE SOLDIERS WHAT FELL ON THE BATTLEFIELD.
THE ONES WHOSE BODIES WERE FLOWN HOME.
WELL, THEY WERE THE LUCKY ONES WEREN'T THEY?
THEY WERE TREATED AS HEROES.
BUT THE ONES WHO SURVIVED.
THE ONES WHAT LOST LIMBS...
THE ONES WHAT LOST THEIR MINDS...

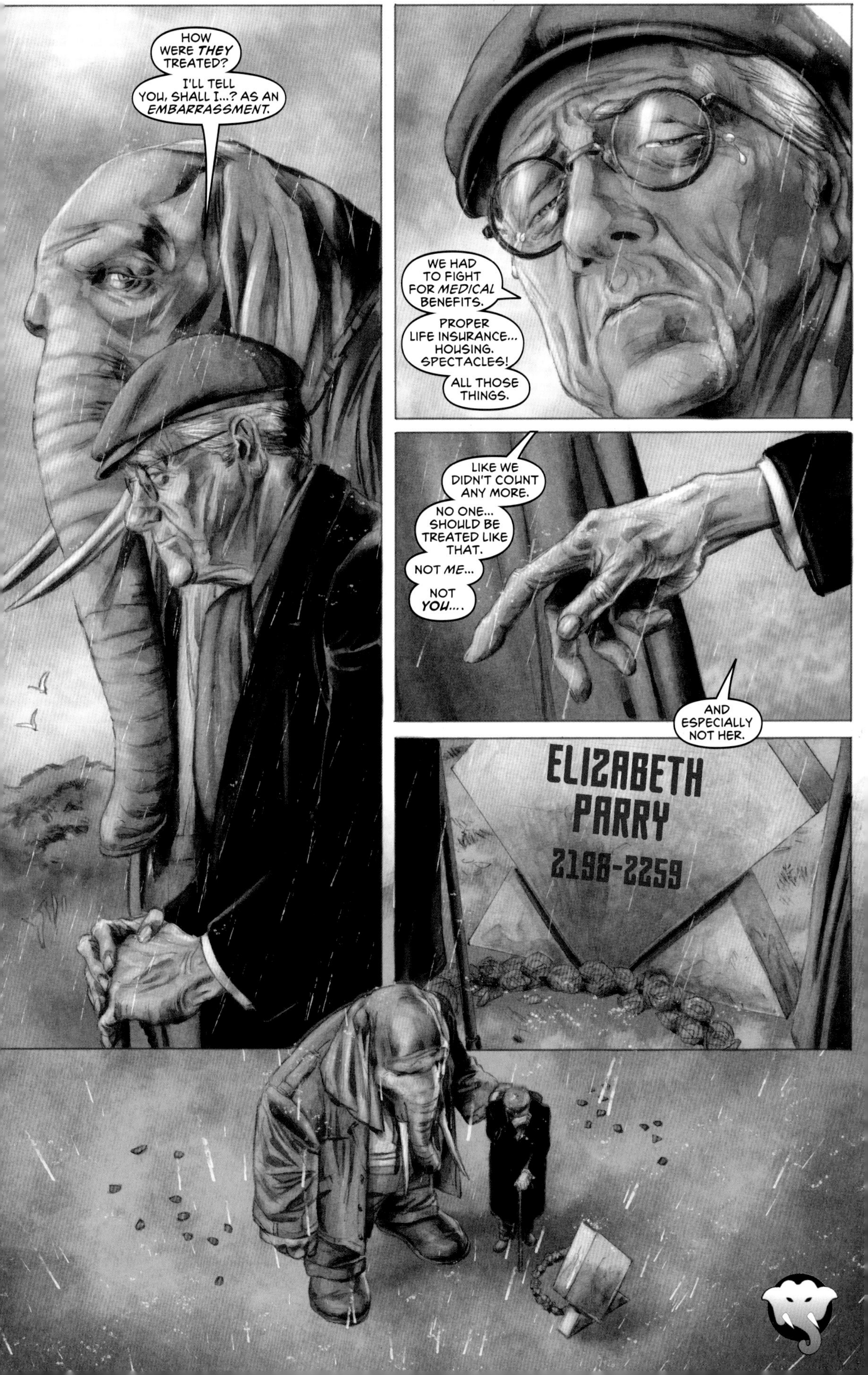
HOW WERE *THEY* TREATED?
I'LL TELL YOU, SHALL I...? AS AN *EMBARRASSMENT*.
WE HAD TO FIGHT FOR *MEDICAL* BENEFITS.
PROPER LIFE INSURANCE... HOUSING. SPECTACLES!
ALL THOSE THINGS.
LIKE WE DIDN'T COUNT ANY MORE.
NO ONE... SHOULD BE TREATED LIKE THAT.
NOT *ME*...
NOT *YOU*....
AND ESPECIALLY NOT HER.
ELIZABETH PARRY
2198-2259

A B O U T

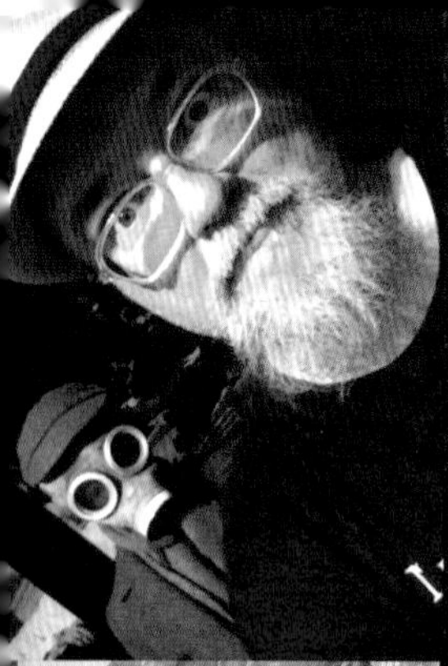

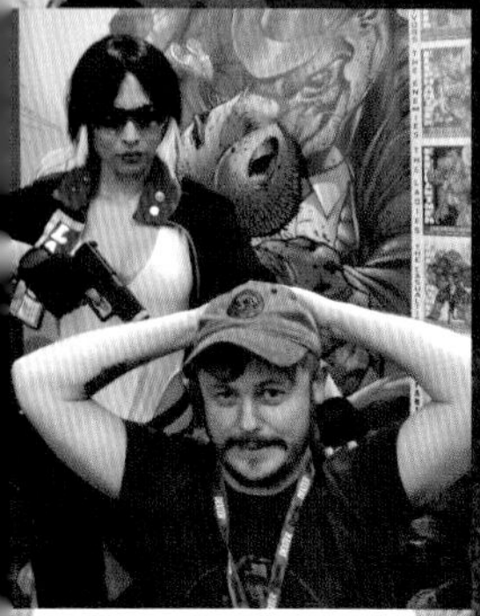

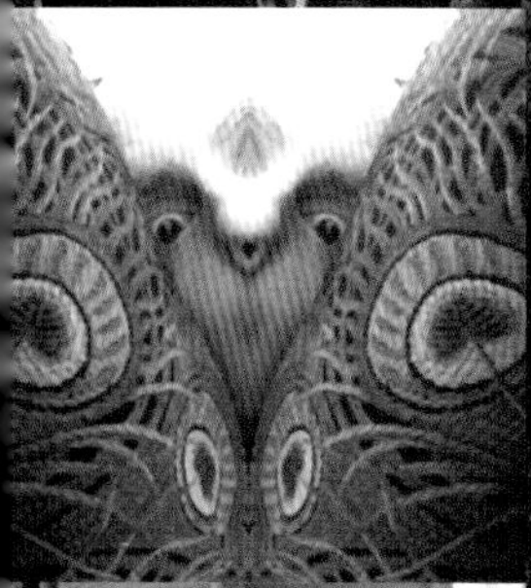

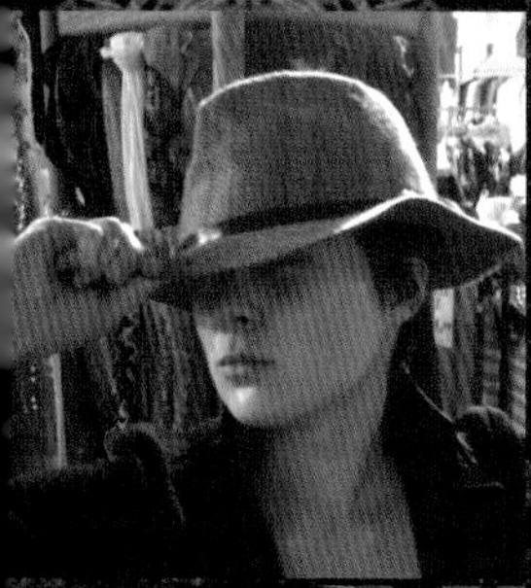

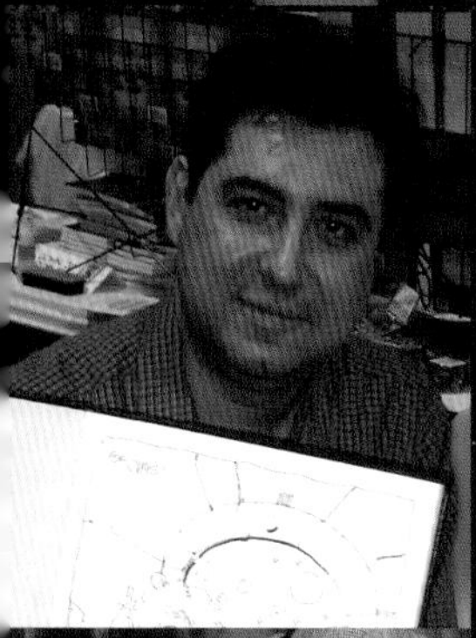

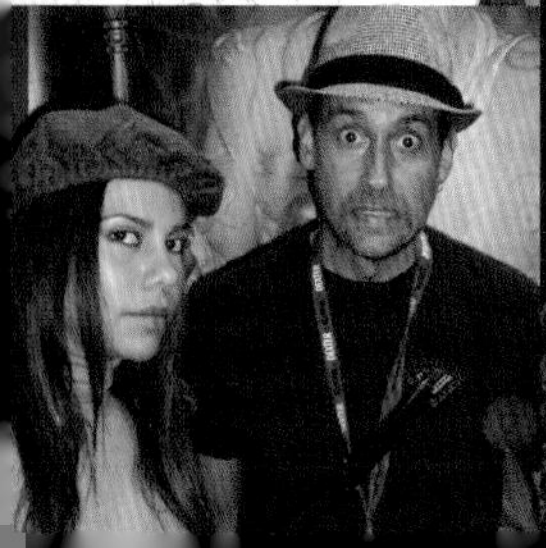

RICHARD STARKINGS is the creator of **HIP FLASK** and **ELEPHANTMEN**. Born and raised in England, Starkings worked for five years at Marvel UK's London offices as editor, designer and occasional writer of **ZOIDS, GHOSTBUSTERS, TRANSFORMERS** and the **DOCTOR WHO** comic strip. He is perhaps best known for his work with the award-winning Comicraft design and lettering studio, which he founded in 1992 with John 'JG' Roshell. Starkings & Roshell also co-authored the best-selling books **COMIC BOOK LETTERING THE COMICRAFT WAY** and **TIM SALE: BLACK AND WHITE**.

BOO COOK* lives in Brighton, England with his lovely wife Gemma. He has worked on **2000AD** for Tharg the Mighty in Blighty for eleven years now, drawing favorites such as **JUDGE DREDD, JUDGE ANDERSON, A.B.C WARRIORS** and a basketcase of covers including a run on Marvel's **X-FACTOR** series. If you want to track down a big chunk of Boo, look for the **ASYLUM** collection, and if it leaves you begging for more, ask him about **BLUNT**.

ROB STEEN doesn't like writing bios. He also doesn't believe most people read them. He has chosen not to bother writing anything about himself. However, he now thinks he has written enough words that it will fill the allotted space in the back of the book and hopefully satisfy his good friend Richard Starkings.

MARIAN CHURCHLAND was raised on a strict diet of fine literature and epic fantasy video games. She hasbeen doing professional illustration work, including book covers and magazine articles, since she was 17. In 2009 Image Comics released her first graphic novel, **BEAST**, to much acclaim. She lives in Vancouver, BC.

LADRÖNN was twice nominated for Eisner awards for his work on **HIP FLASK**, and finally received the Eisner award for best painter for **HIP FLASK: MYSTERY CITY** (collected by Image Comics in **HIP FLASK: CONCRETE JUNGLE**). His covers have recently graced DC's **GREEN ARROW/BLACK CANARY** and **THE SPIRIT**, and he is currently working on **HIP FLASK: OUROBOROUS**.

JOHN ROSHELL*, a.k.a. "JG", a.k.a. "Mr. Fontastic", a.k.a. "Comicraft's Secret Weapon", grew up nary an iPod's throw from Apple in Northern California. These days he uses the Mac to create fonts and design books, logos and websites, including the official **ELEPHANTMEN** site at HipFlask.com. He also writes **CHARLEY LOVES ROBOTS** and plays a mean guitar.

*with Rosana Bustamante as Blackthorne and Emily Bustamante as Yvette

CREATORS

MORITAT, a.k.a. "Justin Norman," has suffered from kidney stones, carpal tunnel syndrome and had his gall bladder removed during the course of the ELEPHANTMEN series. He is still recovering from being the artist of STRAY MOONBEAMS, ATTRACTIVE FORCES, THE 3RD DEGREE, SOLSTICE, DC's THE SPIRIT and ALL STAR WESTERN.

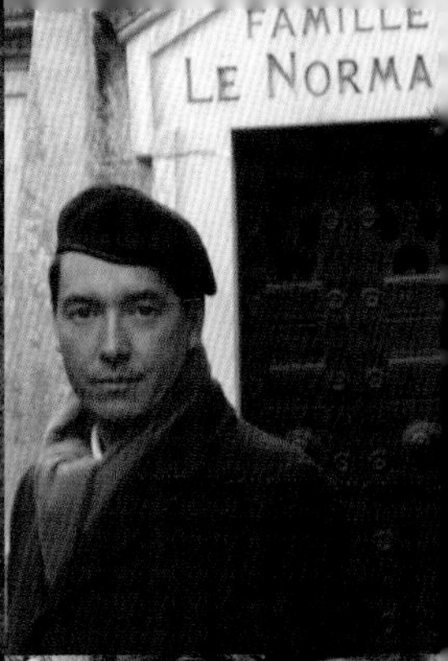
FAMILLE
LE NORMA

AXEL MEDELLIN was born in 1975 in Guadalajara, Mexico. Axel was a straight A-student until he graduated as an industrial designer and decided he wanted to draw comic books for a living, which in Mexico is like signing a suicide note. After working in advertising, illustration, storyboards and comic books in Mexico, Axel's first U.S. work appeared in METAL HURLANT, followed by stories for HEAVY METAL, FABLEWOOD, Zenoscope's GRIMM FAIRY TALES and Boom! Studios' MR STUFFINS. Before becoming the regular artist on ELEPHANTMEN, he completed Image Comics' 50 GIRLS 50.

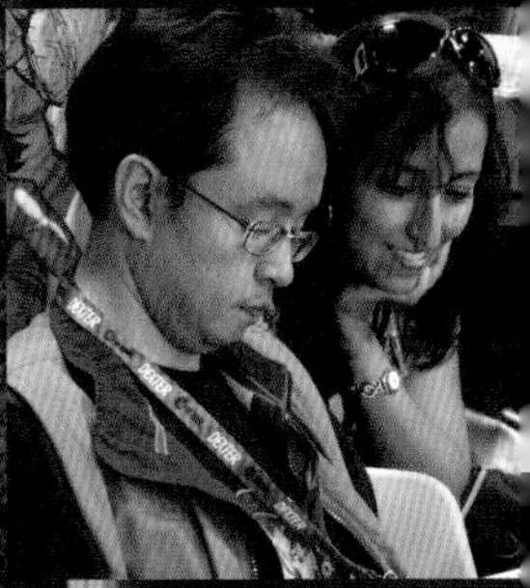

At a tender 15 years of age, **DOUGIE BRAITHWAITE** cut his teeth working for Marvel UK editor Richard Starkings on titles such as ACTION FORCE, THUNDERCATS, THE REAL GHOSTBUSTERS and DOCTOR WHO and then for Dan Abnett on GALAXY RANGERS. Doug is best known for his work on THOR, WOLVERINE ORIGINS, UNIVERSE X, PARADISE X and JUSTICE.

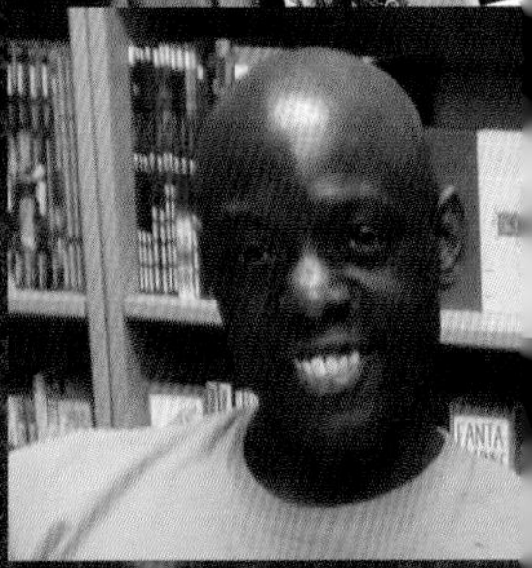

A Mexican illustrator born in Guadalajara, Jalisco, **ULISES ARREOLA** has worked as a colorist for the past six years on WOLVERINE: FIRST CLASS, HALO: SPARTAN BLACK and YOUNG X-MEN for Marvel Comics, as well as GREEN ARROW, SUPERMAN/BATMAN and JLA for DC Comics. Currently is coloring JOURNEY INTO MYSTERY with Doug Braithwaite for Marvel and BATGIRL with Ardian Syaf and JL DARK with Mikel Janin for DC.

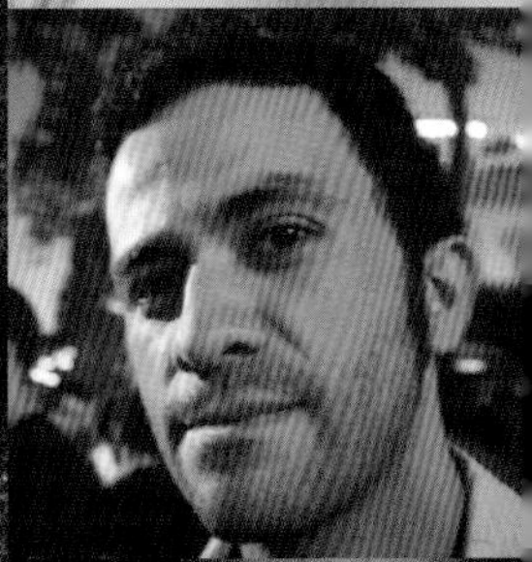

STEVE WHITE has edited, written and illustrated comics, magazines and books for a quarter of a century. He's drawn dinosaurs since he was four, for fun and professionally, and has been called 'the John Milius of paleoart'. He is currently a senior editor for Titan magazines.

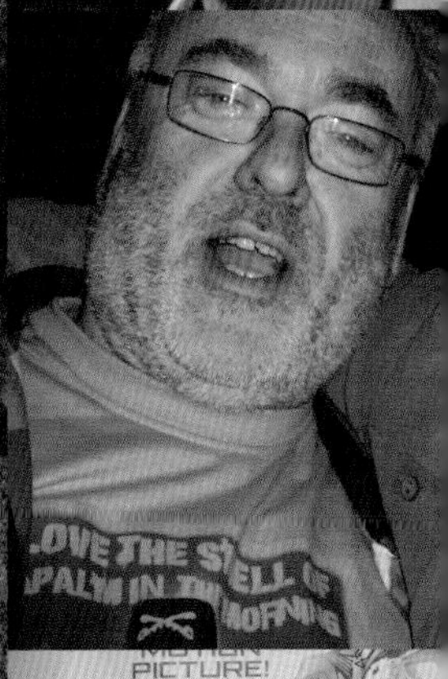

GREGORY WRIGHT's origin began on staff at Marvel comics. A Marvel/Epic Comic editor known to wield a small bat when discussing deadlines, he found that freelance writing and coloring was much less stressful and far more fulfilling. Greg has worked on everything from SPIDER-MAN to BATMAN to ROBOCOP to DEATHLOK and SILVER SABLE. His favorite color work is BATMAN: THE LONG HALLOWEEN.

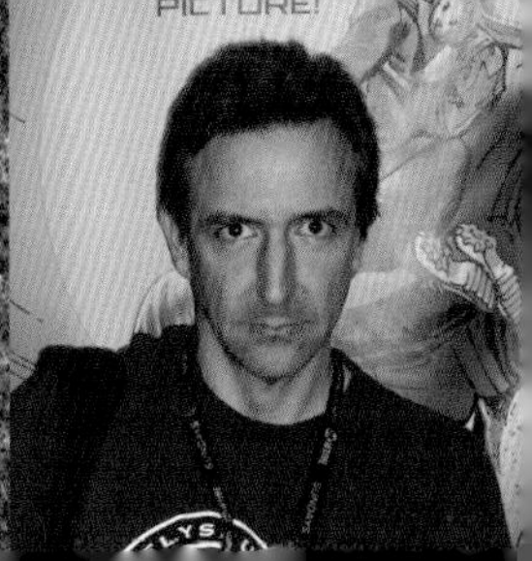
PICTURE!

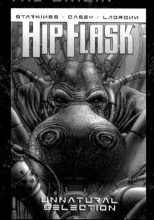
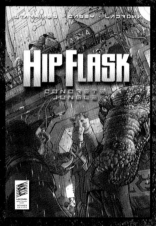

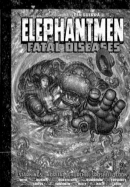

FIGHTING OVER GIFTS?
GET YOUR OWN!

ELEPHANTMEN
HIP FLASK AND ELEPHANTMEN ARE TM AND © 2007 ACTIVE IMAGES
ELEPHANTMEN

HIP FLASK 1000 PIECE JIGSAW PUZZLE BY LADRÖNN

PREVIEWS #JUN07 1880

COMIC BOOK
LETTERING
THE COMICRAFT WAY!

COMIC BOOK LETTERING THE COMICRAFT WAY

ISBN #0-97405-673-1
PREVIEWS #JAN03 1884

STEVEN T. SEAGLE
JUSTIN NORMAN
solstice
The shortest day of the year.
The longest day of their lives.

BY STEVEN T. SEAGLE AND JUSTIN NORMAN

ISBN #0-97667-611-7
PREVIEWS #APR05 2512

ALSO FROM IMAGE COMICS

STRANGE EMBRACE
1-58240-914-5

BULLETPROOF COFFIN
978-1-60706-368-1

MONSTER TRUCK
978-1-60706-470-1

CHEW VOL. 1
978-1-60706-159-5
CHEW VOL. 2
978-1-60706-260-8
CHEW VOL. 3
978-1-60706-335-3
CHEW VOL. 4
978-1-60706-398-8

PROOF VOL. 1
978-158240-944-3
PROOF VOL. 2
978-1-60706-017-8
PROOF VOL. 3
978-1-60706-134-2
PROOF VOL. 4
978-1-60706-285-1
PROOF VOL. 5
978-1-60706-348-3
PROOF VOL. 6
978-1-60706-391-9

REED GUNTHER VOL. 1
978-1-60706-462-6 $14.99

GIRLS VOL. 1
978-1-58240-529-2
GIRLS VOL. 2
978-1-58240-608-4
GIRLS VOL. 3
978-1-58240-703-6
GIRLS VOL. 4
978-1-58240-753-1

JACK STAFF VOL. 1
987-7-58240-335-9
JACK STAFF VOL. 2
978-1-58240-392-2
JACK STAFF VOL. 3
978-1-58240-719-7

POPGUN VOL. 1
978-1-58240-824-8
POPGUN VOL. 2
978-1-58240-920-7
POPGUN VOL. 3
978-1-58240-974-0
POPGUN VOL. 4
978-1-60706-188-5

THE SWORD VOL. 1
978-1-58240-879-8
THE SWORD VOL. 2
978-1-58240-976-4
THE SWORD VOL. 3
978-1-60706-073-4
THE SWORD VOL. 4
978-1-60706-168-7